G000099482

Complete Works of
Geoffrey Chaucer
in Seven Volumes

Volume VII
Chaucerian and Other Pieces,
Being A Supplement to the Complete
Works of Geoffrey Chaucer

GEOFFREY CHAUCER
EDITED BY W.W. SKEAT

COSIMOCLASSICS

NEW YORK

Why be ye wedded faster to your habits than a man is to his wyfe?
For a man may leve his wyf for a yere or two, as many men do; and if ye
leve your habit a quarter of a yere, ye shuld be holden apostatas.

—from "Jack Upland"

CONTENTS

ERRATA AND ADDENDA

P. 26, l. 45. *For* conuersion *read* conversion.

P. 32, l. 38. Mr. Bradley suggests that *maistresse* is a misprint of Thynne's for *maistres secrè,* i. e. master's secret; alluding to John of Northampton.

P. 33, l. 75. *For* may it be sayd in that thinge 'this man thou demest, *read* may it be sayd, 'in that thinge this man thou demest,

P. 50, l. 28. *For* in sacke, sowed with wolle *perhaps read* in sacke sowed, with wolle.

P. 52, ll. 107, 109. Mr. Bradley suggests that 'Caynes' and 'Cayn' are Thynne's misprints for 'Cames' and 'Cam'; where *Cam* (misread as *Cain*) means *Ham,* for which the Vulgate has *Cham.*

P. 153, l. 187. *Insert a hyphen in* gold-mastling.

P. 163, l. 520. *For* punishments *read* punishëments. (*See* note.)

P. 180, l. 1050. *For* [ful] *read* [not]. (*See* note.)

P. 186, l. 1231. End the line with a semicolon.

P. 192, l. 36. *Insert a mark of interrogation after* speketh of.

P. 206, l. 27. *For* request [the] *read* requestë. (*See* note.)

P. 213, l. 294. *For* men *perhaps read* pees. (*See* note.)

P. 215, l. 363. *For* debated *read* delated. (*See* note.)

P. 237; footnotes, l. 1. *For* 1542 *read* 1532.

P. 256, l. 371. *For* tha *read* that.

P. 458; note to l. 117. See also P. Pl. B. xiii. 277, 292.

P. 458; note to l. 53. For fuller details, see the Introduction.

P. 473; note to l. 155. Chaucer's Astrolabe was not written till 1391, after Usk's death.

P. 475; note to Ch. XI. l. 11. On the subject of Grace, see Bk. iii. ch. 8.

P. 478; note to l. 47. *For* taken from *read* compare.

INTRODUCTION

§ 1. THE following pieces are selected, as being the most important, from among the very numerous ones which have been appended to Chaucer's works in various editions.

I use the word 'appended' advisedly. It is not true that these works were all attributed to Chaucer in the black-letter editions. The Praise of Peace was marked as Gower's in Thynne's first edition of 1532. Another piece in that edition is attributed to Scogan. The Letter of Cupid is expressly dated 1402, though Chaucer died in 1400. The Flower of Curtesye contains the words 'Chaucer is dede'; and The Testament of Cresseid contains a remark which, in modern English, would run thus—'Who knows if all that Chaucer wrote is true?'

Those who, through ignorance or negligence, regard Thynne's edition of Chaucer as containing 'Works attributed to Chaucer' make a great mistake; and even if the mistake be excused on the ground that it has been very generally and very frequently made, this does not lessen its magnitude. The title of Thynne's book is very instructive, and really runs thus :—'The Workes of Geffray Chaucer newly printed, with dyuers workes which were neuer in print before, &c.' This is strictly and literally true; for it contains such works of Chaucer's as had previously been printed by Caxton, Wynkyn de Worde, and Julian Notary (see vol. i. p. 28), together with 'dyuers workes [*of various authors*] which were neuer in print before.' Which is the simple solution of the whole matter, as far as this edition is concerned. The same remarks apply to the second edition in 1542, and the third, printed about 1550. But Stowe, in 1561, altered the title so as to give it a new meaning. The title-page of his edition runs thus :—
'The Woorkes of Geffrey Chaucer, newly printed with diuers

Addicions which were neuer in printe before.' Here the authorship of Chaucer was, *for the first time*, practically claimed for the
whole of Thynne's volume. At the same time, Stowe did not
really mean what he seems to say, for it was he who first added
the words—'made by Ihon lidgate'—to the title of 'The
Flower of Curtesie,' and who first assigned a title (ascribing
the poem to *dan Ihon lidgat*) to the poem beginning 'Consider
wel'; see no. 40 (vol. i. p. 33).

§ 2. It is clear that Thynne's intention was to print a collection of poems, including all he could find of Chaucer and
anything else of a similar character that he could lay his hands
on[1]. In other words, the collection was, from the beginning,
a collection of the Works of Chaucer *and other writers*; and
this fact was in no way modified by the adoption by Stowe
and Speght of misleading titles that actually assigned to Chaucer
all the poems in the volume! See further, as to this subject,
in the discussion of The Court of Love below.

The number of pieces appended, at various times, to Chaucer's
Works are so numerous that I have been obliged to restrict
myself to giving a selection of them only.

Of the non-Chaucerian pieces printed by Thynne in 1532,
I have included all but three. The rejected pieces are those
numbered 18, 21, and 22 in the list given at p. 32 of vol. i.
They are all poor and uninteresting, but I add a few words
of description.

18. *A Praise of Women.* Noticed in vol. i. p. 37. Though
decisively rejected by Tyrwhitt, and excluded from Moxon's
reprint, it was revived (for no good reason) by Bell, and consequently appeared in the Aldine edition, which was founded
on Bell's. It enumerates the merits of womankind, and condemns the slanders of men concerning them. We ought to
worship all women out of reverence for the Queen of heaven,

---

[1] In this connection, we must not forget the curious story told in Francis
Thynne's *Animadversions* on Speght's edition of 1598, to the effect that his
father (William Thynne) had some thoughts of inserting in the volume a piece
called *The Pilgrim's Tale*, but was advised by the king to let it alone; and
this, *not* on the ground that the Tale was written after 1536, and contained
an allusion to *Perkin Warbeck*, but solely in deference to the king's remark
—'William Thynne, I doubt this will not be allowed, for I suspect the
bishops will call thee in question for it.' See F. Thynne, *Animadversions*,
&c., ed. Furnivall (Ch. Soc.), pp. 9, 89.

and we shall do well to pray to Our Lady to bring us to the heaven in which she and all good women will be found. Thynne is not the sole authority for this poem, as it occurs also (in a Scottish dress) in the Bannatyne MS., fol. 275. The whole of this MS. (written in 1568) was printed for the Hunterian Club in 1873–9; see p. 799 of that edition.

21. *The Lamentation of Mary Magdalen*. Noticed in vol. i. p. 37. This lugubrious piece was probably the wail of a nun, who had no book but a Vulgate version of the Bible, from which all her quotations are taken. It bears no resemblance to any work by Chaucer, nor to any of the pieces in the present volume. It consists of 102 seven-line stanzas. The metre resembles Lydgate's, but the final -e is hardly ever used. Bell's text is not taken from Thynne, but from some later and inferior reprint of it. For this poem, Thynne's first edition is the sole authority.

22. *The Remedy of Love*. Noticed in vol. i. p. 38. It appears that the 'remedy of love' is to be found in a consideration of the wicked ways of women. Twelve whole stanzas are taken up with a metrical translation of one of the chapters in the book of Proverbs. The author refers us to 'the fifth chapter,' but he is wrong. He means chapter vii, verses 6–27. He also quotes from Ecclesiasticus, ix. 9, and xxv. 25.

Nos. 28, 29, 30 (vol. i. p. 32) are not found in Thynne, but were first printed by Stowe. I give them below, at p. 297. The first two stanzas are Lydgate's; and probably the third is his also. It is no great matter.

No. 41 (vol. i. p. 33) was also first printed by Stowe. To save words, I have printed it below, at p. 450, from the original MS.

§ 3. I now consider the non-Chaucerian pieces in Part II. of Stowe's Edition (see vol. i. p. 33). Of these, nos. 45, 50, 56, and 59 are here reprinted.

Nos. 46, 47, 48, 49, 51, 52, 53, 54, and 55 were all taken by Stowe from MS. Trin. R. 3. 19. Perhaps they are sufficiently noticed in vol. i. p. 41, as they present few points of interest. However, I enumerate them, adding a few remarks.

No. 46. *The Craft of Lovers*. In 23 seven-line stanzas; 161 lines. Besides the copy in the Trin. MS., there are copies (almost duplicates) in MSS. Addit. 34360, fol. 73, back (p. 142), and Harl. 2251, fol. 53 (now called 52). Dated 1448 in the Trin. MS., but 1459 in the other two. The first line ought to run :—'To moralise, who list these ballets sewe'; but it is clear that some one added the words 'A similitude' in the margin, and that this remark was afterwards incorporated in the text. Hence the first line, in the latter MSS., stands :—'To moralise a similitude who list these balettis sewe'; which is more than enough for a line of five accents. After two introductory stanzas, the poem becomes a dialogue, in alternate stanzas, between a wooer, named *Cupido*, and a lass, named *Diana*[1]; the result of which is successful. This may be compared with La Belle Dame sans Merci, and with the Nut-brown Maid. The twenty-third stanza forms the author's *Conclusio*, which is followed by an Envoy in the Addit. MS. and in the Harl. MS. only. The same MSS. *seem* to superadd two more stanzas; but they really belong to another piece.

No. 47. Taken by Stowe from MS. Trin. R. 3. 19, fol. 156, back. *A Balade.* In 4 seven-line stanzas; 28 lines. Begins— 'Of their nature they greatly them delite'; i.e. Women are by nature hypocrites; they like kissing live images rather than shrines. So I advise young men to take warning : 'Beware alwaye, the blind eateth many [a] flye'; a line which is quoted from Lydgate's ballad printed at p. 295. The author then prays God to keep the fly out of his dish; and ends by congratulating himself on being anonymous, because women would else blame him.

No. 48. *The Ten Commandments of Love*; from Trin. MS., fol. 109. Also in MS. Fairfax 16. Begins :—'Certes, ferre extendeth yet my reason.' In 14 stanzas of seven-lines; the last two form the Envoy. After two introductory stanzas, the author gives the ladies their ten commandments. They are, it appears, to exhibit Faith, Entencion, Discrecion, Patience, Secretnesse, Prudence, Perseverance, Pity, Measure [Moderation], and Mercy. In the Envoy, the author says, truly enough, that he is devoid of cunning, experience, manner of enditing, reason, and eloquence; and that he is 'a man unknown.'

No. 49. *The Nine Ladies Worthy.* In 9 seven-line stanzas, one stanza for each lady. Begins : 'Profulgent in preciousnes,

---

[1] These names are given, in the margin, in MS. Addit. 34360 only.

O Sinope the quene.' Only remarkable for the curious selection made. The Nine Ladies are : (1) Sinope, daughter of Marsepia, queen of the Amazons ; see Orosius, Hist. i. 10 ; (2) Hippolyta, the Amazon, wife of Theseus ; (3) Deipyle, daughter of Adrastus, wife of Tydeus ; (4) Teuta, queen of the Illyrians ; see note to C. T., F 1453 (vol. v. p. 398) ; (5) Penthesilea the Amazon, slain by Achilles before Troy ; (6) queen Tomyris, who slew Cyrus in battle, B. C. 529 ; (7) Lampeto the Amazon, sister of Marsepia, and aunt of Sinope ; (8) Semiramis of Babylon ; (9) Menalippe or Melanippe, sister of Antiope, queen of the Amazons, taken captive by Hercules, according to Justinus, ii. 4. 23. Most of these queens are mentioned by Orosius, i. 10, ii. 1, ii. 4 ; see also Higden's Polychronicon, bk. ii. chapters 9, 21, 24, and bk. iii. c. 7. From the Trin. MS., fol. 113, back.

[No. 50. *Virelai*. Printed below, at p. 448.]

No. 51. *A Ballade*. Begins :—'In the season of Feuerere when it was full colde.' In 7 seven-line stanzas. In praise of the daisy. Very poor. From the Trin. MS., fol. 160.

No. 52. *A Ballade*. Begins—'O Mercifull and o merciable.' In 12 seven-line stanzas. The Trin. MS. has 13 stanzas ; but Stowe omitted the tenth, because it coincides with st. 19 of the Craft of Lovers. It is made up of scraps from other poems. Stanzas 1–4 form part of a poem on the fall of man, from Lydgate's *Court of Sapience* (see vol. i. p. 57). In st. 8 occurs the assonance of *hote* (hot) and *stroke* ; and in st. 9, that of *cureth* and *renueth*. From the Trin. MS., fol. 161.

No. 53. *The Judgement of Paris*. In 4 seven-line stanzas ; the first is allotted to Pallas, who tells Paris to take the apple, and give it to the fairest of the three goddesses. After this, he is addressed in succession by Juno, Venus, and Minerva (as she is now called). Then the poem ends. Trin. MS., fol. 161, back.

No. 54. *A Balade pleasaunte*. Begins—'I haue a Ladie where so she bee.' In 7 seven-line stanzas. Meant to be facetious ; e. g. 'Her skin is smothe as any oxes tong.' The author says that when he was fifteen years old, he saw the wedding of queen Jane ; and that was so long ago that there cannot be many such alive. As Joan of Navarre was married to Henry IV in 1403, he was born in 1388, and would have been sixty-two in 1450. It is an imitation of Lydgate's poem entitled A Satirical

Description of his Lady ; see Minor Poems, ed. Halliwell, p. 199. Trin. MS., fol. 205.

No. 55. *Another Balade.* Begins—'O mossie Quince, hangyng by your stalke.' In 4 seven-line stanzas, of which Stowe omits the second. A scurrilous performance. Trin. MS., fol. 205, back.

[No. 56. A Ballad by Lydgate ; printed below, at p. 295.]

No. 58 is a Balade in 9 seven-line stanzas, of no merit, on the theme of the impossibility of restoring a woman's chastity.

No. 59. *The Court of Love.* Printed below, at p. 409.

No. 60 is a genuine poem ; and no. 61 is Lydgate's Story of Thebes. And here Stowe's performance ceases.

§ 4. The subsequent additions made by Speght are discussed in vol. i. pp. 43–46. Of these, The Flower and the Leaf, Jack Upland, and Hoccleve's poem to Henry V, are here reprinted ; and Chaucer's ABC is genuine. He also reprinted the Sayings at p. 450. The pieces not reprinted here are Chaucer's Dream and Eight Goodly Questions.

Chaucer's Dream is a false title, assigned to it by Speght ; its proper name is *The Isle of Ladies.* Begins—'Whan Flora, the quene of pleasaunce.' The MS. at Longleat is said to have been written about 1550. A second MS. has been acquired by the British Museum, named MS. Addit. 10303 ; this is also in a hand of the sixteenth century, and presents frequent variations in the text. It is very accessible, in the texts by Moxon, Bell, and Morris ; but how Tyrwhitt ever came to dream that it could be genuine, must remain a mystery. I originally hoped to include this poem in the present selection, but its inordinate length compelled me to abandon my intention. In a prologue of seventy lines, the author truthfully states, at l. 60, that he is 'a slepy[1] writer.' There are many assonances, such as *undertakes, scapes* (337) ; *named, attained* (597) ; *tender, remember* (1115, 1415) ; *rome, towne* (1567). Note also such rimes as *destroied, conclude* (735) ; *queen, kneen,* pl. of *knee* (1779) ; *nine, greene* (1861) ; *vertuous, use* (1889). Some rimes exhibit the Northern dialect ; as *paines, straines,* pr. s., 909 ; *wawe, overthrawe,* pp., 1153 ; *servand, livand,* pres. pt., 1629 ; *greene, eene* (pl. of *e,* eye), 1719 ; *hand, avisand,* pres. pt., 1883 ; &c. Yet the writer is not particular ; if he wants a rime to *wroth,* he uses the Southern form

---

[1] Morris printed *sleepe,* giving no sense ; MS. 10303 has *slepye.*

goth, 785 ; but if he wants a rime to *rose*, he uses the Northern form *gose* (goes), 1287, 1523.   But before any critic can associate this poem with Chaucer, he has first to prove that it was written before 1450.   Moreover, it belongs to the cycle of metrical romances, being connected (as Tyrwhitt says) with the *Eliduc* of Marie de France ; and, perhaps, with her *Lanval*.

To the *Isle of Ladies* Speght appended two other poems, of which the former contains a single stanza of 6 lines, and the latter is a ballad in 3 seven-line tanzas.

No. 66. *Eight Goodly Questions* ; in Bell's Chaucer, iv. 421. In 9 seven-line stanzas.   First printed in 1542.   There are at least two manuscript copies ; one in the Trinity MS., marked R. 3. 15 ; and another in the Bannatyne MS., printed at p. 123 of the print of the Bannatyne MS., issued by the Hunterian Club in 1873.   In l. 19, the latter MS. corrects *tree* to *coffour*, the Scottish form of *cofre*.   It is merely expanded from the first seven lines of a poem by Ausonius, printed in Walker's *Corpus Poetarum Latinorum*, with the title Eorundem Septem Sapientum Sententiae. This English version is quite in Lydgate's style.

§ 5.   EDITIONS AND MSS. CONSULTED.

I have repeatedly explained that there were but four black-letter editions of Collected Works before Speght's ; and these I call Thynne's first edition (1532), Thynne's second edition (1542), the undated edition (about 1550, which I call 1550 for brevity), and Stowe's edition (1561) respectively.   I shall denote these editions below by the symbols 'Th.,' ed. 1542, ed. 1550, and ' S.' respectively.   Of these editions, the first is the best ; the second is derived from the first ; the third is derived from the second ; and the fourth from the third [1].   In every case it is useless to consult a later edition when an earlier one can be found.

The following is the list of the pieces which depend on the editions *only*, or for which the editions have been collated.

---

[1] The way in which the spelling was gradually altered can be seen even from the following example, in which the eighth line of the Plowman's Tale is represented :—

> Ed. 1542. And honge his harneys on a pynne ; fol. cxix.
> Ed. 1550. And honged his harnys on a pynne ; fol. xc.
> Ed. 1561. And honged his harnis on a pinne ; fol. xciii.

I always cite the earliest; that the later ones *also* contain the piece in question must, once for all, be understood.

Caxton. —XXVIII. No. VII. was also collated with a print by Caxton.

Wynkyn de Worde.—XXIII.

Wynkyn de Worde.—VIII.

Chepman and Miller (1508).—VIII.

Th.—I. IX. XI. XXII. Also collated for IV. V. VII. VIII. X. XII. XVI. XVII. XVIII. XIX. XXI. XXIII.

Thynne had access to excellent MSS., and is always worth consulting.

Ed. 1542.—II. XXVIII. Collated for VI.

An early printed edition of Jack Upland.—III.

S. (1561).—XV. Collated for XIII. XIV. XXIV. XXV. XXIX.

A printed edition of the Testament of Cresseid (1593).—XVII.

Speght (1598).—XX. Collated for III.

The following twenty MSS. have been collated or consulted.

Trentham MS.—IV. (See Introduction.)

Fairfax 16.—V. VIII. XIII. XVI. XVIII. XIX. (See vol. i. p. 51.)

Bodley 638.—V. VIII. XVIII. (See vol. i. p. 53.)

Tanner 346.—V. VIII. XVIII. XIX. (See vol. i. p. 54.)

Ashmole 59.—VII. X. XIII. (See vol. i. p. 53.)

Arch. Selden B. 24—V. VIII. XVIII. XXVI. XXVII. (See vol. i. p. 54.)

Digby 181.—V. VIII. (See vol. i. p. 54.)

Camb. Univ. Lib. Ff. 1. 6.—V. XII. XVI. XVIII. (See vol. i. p. 55.)

Pepys 2006.—VIII. (See vol. i. p. 55.)

Trin. Coll. R. 3. 19.—XIV. XVI. XXI. XXIV. XXV. XXIX. (See vol. i. p. 56.)

Trin. Coll. R. 3. 20.—V. (One of Shirley's MSS.)

Trin. Coll. O. 9. 38.—XIV.

Addit. 16165, B. M.—XIII. (See vol. i. p. 56.)

Addit. 34360, B. M.—XXI.

Harl. 372, B. M.—XVI. (See vol. i. p. 58.)

Harl. 2251, B. M.—VII. XII. XIV. (See vol. i. p. 57.)

Harl. 7578, B. M.—XIII. (See vol. i. p. 58.)

Sloane 1212, B. M.—X. (A fair copy.)

Phillipps 8151.—VI. (See Hoccleve's Poems, ed. Furnivall, p. 1.)

Ashburnham 133.—V.   (See the same, p. xxvii.)

§ 6. Conversely, I here give the authorities from which each piece is derived. For further comments on some of them, see the separate introductions to each piece below.

I. *The Testament of Love* (prose).—Th. (Thynne, 1532).

II. *The Plowmans Tale* (1380 lines).—Th. (Thynne, 1542).

III. *Jack Upland* (prose).—Early edition, Caius College library ; Speght (1598).

IV. *Praise of Peace* (385 lines).—Th. (1532) ; Trentham MS.

V. *Letter of Cupid* (476 lines).—Th. (1532) ; Fairfax, Bodley, Tanner, Selden, Ashburnham, Digby MSS.; Trin. Coll. R. 3. 20 ; Camb. Ff. 1. 6 ; also in the Bannatyne MS.

VI. *To the King's Grace* (64).—Th. (1542) ; Phillipps 8151.

VII. *A Moral Balade* (189).—Th. (1532); Caxton ; Ashmole 59, Harl. 2251. (I also find a reference to Harl. 367, fol. 85, back.)

VIII. *Complaint of the Black Knight* (681).—Th. (1532); Fairfax, Bodley, Tanner, Digby, Selden, Pepys ; Addit. 16165. Also printed, separately, by Wynkyn de Worde (n. d.) ; and at Edinburgh, by Chepman and Miller, in 1508.

IX. *The Flour of Curtesye* (270).—Th. (1532).

X. *In Commendation of our Lady* (140).—Th.; Ashmole 59 ; Sloane 1212.

XI. *To my Soverain Lady* (112).—Th.

XII. *Ballad of Good Counsel* (133).—Th. ; Camb. Ff. 1. 6 ; Harl. 2251.

XIII. *Beware of Doubleness* (104).—Stowe (1561); Fairfax 16, Ashmole 59, Harl. 7578, Addit. 16165.

XIV. *A Balade : Warning Men* (49).—Stowe (1561) ; Harl. 2251, fol. 149, back ; Trin. R. 3. 19 ; Trin. O. 9. 38.

XV. *Three Sayings* (21).—Stowe (1561).

XVI. *La Belle Dame sans Mercy* (856).—Th. ; Fairfax, Harl. 372 ; Camb. Ff. 1. 6 ; Trin. R. 3. 19, fol. 98.

XVII. *Testament of Cresseid* (616).—Th. ; Edinburgh edition (1593).

XVIII. *The Cuckoo and the Nightingale* (290).—Th.; Fairfax, Bodley, Tanner, Selden ; Camb. Ff. 1. 6.

XIX. *Envoy to Alison* (27).—Th. ; Fairfax, Tanner.

* * *
* * * *   b

---

§ 7. I. THE TESTAMENT OF LOVE; BY THOMAS USK.

Of this piece no MS. copy has been discovered. The only authority is Thynne's edition of 1532, whence all later editions have been copied more or less incorrectly. The reprints will be found to grow steadily worse, so that the first edition is the only one worth consulting.

The present edition is printed from a transcript of Thynne (1532), made by myself; the proof-sheets being carefully read with the original. In making the transcript, I have altered the symbol *u* to *v*, when used as a consonant; and (in the few places where it occurs) the consonantal *i* to *j*. I have also substituted *i* for *y* when the vowel is short, chiefly in the case of the suffix *-yng* or *-ynge*, here printed *-ing* or *-inge*. In nearly all other cases, the original spellings are given in the footnotes. Thynne's chief errors of printing occur in places where he has persistently altered the spelling of the MS. to suit the spelling in fashion in the days of Henry VIII. His chief alterations are as follows. He prints *ea* for open *ee*, written *ee* or *e* at the beginning of the fifteenth century; thus, he has *ease* for *ese*, and *please* for *plese*. He most perversely adds a useless final *e* to the words *howe*, *nowe*, and some others; and he commits the anachronism of printing *father*, *mother*, *together*, *wether*, *gather*, in place of *fader*, *moder*, *togeder*, *weder*, *gader*; whereas the termination in these words invariably appears as *-der* till shortly before 1500. Further, he prints *catche* for *cacche*, *perfection* for *perfeccion*, and the like; and in several other ways has much impaired the spelling of his original. Many of these things I have attempted to set right ; and the scholar who compares the text with the footnotes will easily see why each alteration has been made, if he happens to be at all conversant with MSS. written in the fourteenth century.

I believe that this piece is almost unparalleled as regards the shameful corruption of its text. It cannot be supposed that Thynne or any one else ever read it over with the view of seeing whether the result presented any sense. Originally written in an obscure style, every form of carelessness seems to have been employed in order to render it more obscure than before. In a great number of places, it is easy to restore the sense by the insertion of such necessary words as *of*, or *but*, or *by*. In other places, non-existent words can be replaced by real ones ; or some correction can be made that is more or less obvious. I have marked all inserted words by placing them within square brackets, as, e. g., *am* in l. 46 on p. 6. Corrections of readings are marked by the use of a dagger (†) ; thus 'I † wot wel' in l. 78 on p. 7 is my emendation of Thynne's phrase 'I wol wel,' which is duly recorded in the footnote. But some sentences remain in which the sense is not obvious ; and one is almost tempted to think that the author did not clearly know what he intended to say. That he was remarkable for a high degree of inaccuracy will appear presently.

A strange misprint occurs in Book III. ch. 4, ll. 30, 31 (p. 117), where nearly two whole lines occur twice over ; but the worst confusion is due to an extraordinary dislocation of the text in Book III. (c. iv. l. 56—c. ix. l. 46), as recently discovered by the sagacity of Mr. H. Bradley, and explained more fully below.

I have also, for the first time, revised the punctuation, which in Thynne is only denoted by frequent sloping strokes and full stops, which are not always inserted in the right places. And I have broken up the chapters into convenient paragraphs.

§ 8. A very curious point about this piece is the fact which I was the first to observe, viz. that the initial letters of the various chapters were certainly intended to form an acrostic. Unfortunately, Thynne did not perceive this design, and has certainly begun some of the chapters either with the wrong letter or at a wrong place. The sense shews that the first letter of Book I. ch. viii. should be E, not O (see the note) ; and, with this correction, the initial letters of the First Book yield the words—MARGARETE OF.

In Book II, Thynne begins Chapters XI and XII at wrong places, viz. with the word 'Certayn' (p. 86, l. 133), and the word 'Trewly' (p. 89, l. 82). He thus produces the words—VIRTW HAVE MCTRCI. It is obvious that the last word ought to be MERCI, which can be obtained by beginning Chapter XI with the word 'Every,' which suits the sense quite as well.

For the chapters of Book III, we are again dependent on Thynne. If we accept his arrangement as it stands, the letters yielded are—ON THSKNVI; and the three books combined give us the sentence :—MARGARETE OF VIRTW, HAVE MERCI ON THSKNVI. Here 'Margarete of virtw' means 'Margaret endued with divine virtue'; and the author appeals either to the Grace of God, or to the Church. The last word ought to give us the author's name; but in that case the letters require rearrangement before the riddle can be read with certainty.

After advancing so far towards the solution of the mystery, I was here landed in a difficulty which I was unable to solve. But Mr. H. Bradley, by a happy inspiration, hit upon the idea that the text might have suffered dislocation; and was soon in a position to prove that no less than six leaves of the MS. must have been out of place, to the great detriment of the sense and confusion of the argument. He very happily restored the right order, and most obligingly communicated to me the result. I at once cancelled the latter part of the treatise (from p. 113 to the end), and reprinted this portion in the right order, according to the sense. With this correction, the unmeaning THSKNVI is resolved into the two words THIN USK, i. e. 'thine Usk'; a result the more remarkable because Mr. Bradley had *previously* hit upon Usk as being the probable author. For the autobiographical details exactly coincide, in every particular, with all that is known of the career of Thomas Usk, according to Walsingham, the Rolls of Parliament, and the continuation of Higden's Polychronicon by John Malverne (ed. Lumby, vol. ix. pp. 45-6, 134, 150, 169); cf. Lingard, ed. 1874, iii. 163-7.

The date of the composition of this piece can now be determined without much error. Usk was executed on March 4, 1388, and we find him referring to past events that happened towards the end of 1384 or later. The most likely date is about 1387.

I here append an exact account of the order of the text *as it appears in Thynne*; every break in the text being denoted, in the present volume, by a dark asterisk.

Thynne's text is in a correct order from p. 1 to p. 118, l. 56:—any mouable tyme there (Th. fol. 354, col. 2, l. 11) [1].

(1) Next comes, in Thynne, the passage beginning at p. 135, l. 94:—Fole, haue I not seyd—and ending at p. 143, l. 46:—syth god is the greatest loue and the (Th. fol. 356, back, col. 1, l. 5).

(2) Next, in Thynne, the passage beginning at p. 131, l. 97:—ne ought to loke thynges with resonnyng—and ending at p. 132, l. 161, at the end of a chapter (Th. fol. 356, back, col. 2, last line).

(3) Next, in Thynne, the passage beginning at p. 124, l. 8:—Now trewly, lady—and ending at p. 128, at the end of the chapter (Th. fol. 357, last line).

(4) Next, in Thynne, the passage beginning at p. 132, new chapter :—Uery trouth (quod she)—and ending at p. 135, l. 94:—that shal bringe out frute that (Th. fol. 358, back, col. 1, l. 25).

(5) Next, in Thynne, the passage beginning at p. 118, l. 56:—is nothyng preterit ne passed—and ending at p. 124, l. 7:—euer to onbyde (Th. fol. 360, col. 1, l. 24).

(6) Next, in Thynne, the passage beginning at p. 128, new chapter :—Nowe, lady (quod I) that tree to set—and ending at p. 131, l. 97 :—vse ye (Th. fol. 360, back, col. 2, l. 9).

(7) Lastly, the text reverts to the true order, at p. 143, l. 46, with the words :—greatest wisdom (Th. fol. 360, back, col. 2, l. 9. as before). See The Athenæum, no. 3615, Feb. 6, 1897.

It is not difficult to account for this somewhat confusing dislocation. It is clear that the original MS. was written on quires of the usual size, containing 8 folios apiece. The first 10 quires, which we may call *a, b, c, d, e, f, g, h, i,* and *k,* were in the right order. The rest of the MS. occupied quire *l* (of 8 folios), and quire *m* (of only 2); the last page being blank. The seventh folio of *l* was torn up the back, so that the two leaves parted company; and the same happened to both the folios in quire *m,* leaving six leaves loose. What then happened was this :—first of all, folios l_1—l_4 were reversed and turned inside out; then

---

[1] So in Thynne. But 'tyme' really concludes a sentence; and 'there' should have a capital letter.

came the former halves of m_1 and m_2 and the latter half of l_7 ; next l_5 and l_6 (undetached), with the former half of l_7 thrust in the middle; so that the order in this extraordinary quire was as follows: l_4, l_3, l_2, l_1, all inside out, half of m_1, half of m_2, the latter half of l_7, l_5, l_6, and the former half of l_7, followed by the six undetached leaves. The last quire simply consisted of l_8 (entire), followed by the latter halves of m_2 and m_1, which were kept in the right order by the fact that the last page was blank.

It has thus become possible for us to make some progress towards the right understanding of the work, which has hitherto been much misunderstood. Warton (Hist. E. Poetry, 1840, ii. 218) dismisses it in two lines :—' It is a lover's parody of Boethius's book De Consolatione mentioned above'; whereas the author was not a lover at all, except in a spiritual sense. Even the fuller account in Morley's English Writers (1890), v. 261, is not wholly correct. The statement is there made, that 'it professes to be written, and probably was written, by a prisoner in danger of his life'; but the prison[1] may have been *at first* metaphorical, as he could hardly have written the whole work in two or three months. In Book iii. ch. 9, ll. 131, 132, he prays that 'God's hand, which has scourged him in mercy, may hereafter mercifully keep and defend him in good plight.' The whole tone of the treatise shews that he is writing to justify himself, and thinks that he has succeeded. But a stern doom was close at hand.

§ 9. The truth is that the attempts of Godwin and others to make the autobiographical statements of the author fit into the life of Chaucer, have quite led the critics out of the right track. That the author was *not* Chaucer is perfectly obvious to every one who reads the passage in the lower half of p. 140 with moderate attention ; for the author there refers to Chaucer as Love's ' noble philosophical poet in English,' who wrote a treatise of Love's servant Troilus, and who ' passeth all other makers in wit and in good reason of sentence '; praise which, however true it may be of Chaucer, the writer was certainly not entitled to claim for himself. The sole point in which the circumstances of the author agree with those of Chaucer is this—that they were both born in London ; which is, obviously, too slight a coincidence to build

---

[1] He had been imprisoned in 1384 (p. 33, l. 101) ; but at p. 49, l. 126, he is leisurely planning a *future* treatise ! At p. 60, l. 104, he is in prison *again*.

upon. Now that we know the author's name to have been Thomas Usk, the matter assumes quite another complexion. Usk was much inclined, in his early days, to a belief in Lollard opinions; but when he found that persistence in such belief was likely to lead to trouble and danger, he deemed it prudent to recant as completely as he could [1], and contemplates his consequent security with some complacency.

In just the same way, it appears that he had changed sides in politics. We first find him in the position of confidential clerk to John of Northampton, mayor of London in 1381–2 and 1382–3. In July, 1384, Usk was arrested and imprisoned in order to induce him to reveal certain secrets implicating Northampton. This he consented to do, and accused Northampton before the king at Reading, on the 18th of August. Northampton strenuously denied the charges against him, but was condemned as guilty, and sent to Corfe castle [2]. After this, Usk joined the party of Sir Nicholas Brembre, mayor of London in 1383–4, 1384–5, and 1385–6, and Collector of Customs in 1381–3, when Chaucer was Comptroller of the same. Brembre had been active in procuring the condemnation of Northampton, and was, at the close of 1386, one of the few personal adherents who remained faithful to the king. In 1387, Richard was busily devising means for the overthrow of the duke of Gloucester's regency, Brembre and Usk being on the king's side; but his attempts were unsuccessful, and, in November of the same year, the duke of Gloucester and his partisans, who were called the 'appellants,' became masters of the situation; they accused the king's councillors of treason, and imprisoned or banished their opponents. On Feb. 3, 1388, the appellants produced their charges against their victims, Brembre and Usk being among the number. Both were condemned and executed, Brembre on Feb. 20, and Usk on the 4th of March. Usk's offence was that he had been appointed sub-sheriff of Middlesex by Brembre's influence [3], with a view to the arrest of the duke of Gloucester and others of his party. His defence was that all that he had done was by the king's orders, a defence on which he doubtless relied. Unfortunately for him, it was

---

[1] See p. 128, l. 16. He did not care to be 'a stinking martyr'; p. 34, l. 115.

[2] Perhaps this is why Langland refers to 'the castel of Corf'; P. Plowman, C. iv. 140.

[3] Rolls of Parliament, iii. 234 a.

an aggravation of his crime. It was declared that he ought to have known that the king was not at the time his own master, but was acting according to the counsel of false advisers; and this sealed his fate. He was, sentenced to be drawn, hung, and beheaded, and that his head should be set up over Newgate. The sentence was barbarously carried out; he was hung but immediately cut down, and clumsily beheaded by nearly thirty strokes of a sword. 'Post triginta mucronis ictus fere decapitatus semper usque ad mortem nunquam fatebatur se deliquisse contra Johannem Northampton, sed erant omnia vera quae de eo praedicaverat coram rege in quodam consilio habito apud Radyngum anno elapso.'—Higden, App. 169. John of Malverne speaks as if he had some personal recollection of Usk, of whom he says— 'Satagebat namque astu et arte illorum amicitiam sibi attrahere quos procul dubio ante capitales hostes sibi fuisse cognovit.'— Ib. p. 45.

We can now readily understand that Usk's praise of Chaucer must have been more embarrassing than acceptable; and perhaps it was not altogether without design that the poet, in his House of Fame, took occasion to let the world know how he devoted his leisure time to other than political subjects.

§ 10. Some of the events of his life are alluded to by Usk in the present treatise. He justifies his betrayal of Northampton (p. 26, ll. 53–103, p. 28, ll. 116–201), and is grateful for the king's pardon (p. 60, ll. 120–4). He refers to his first imprisonment (p. 60, l. 104), and tells us that he offered wager of battle against all who disputed his statements (p. 60, l. 116; p. 31, l. 10); but no one accepted the wager.

He further tells us how he endeavoured to make his peace with the Church. Taking his cue from the parable of the merchantman seeking goodly pearls (p. 16, l. 84), he likens the visible Church of Christ to the pearl of great price (p. 145, l. 103; p. 94, l. 121), and piteously implores her mercy (p. 8, l. 135); and the whole tone of the piece shews his confidence that he is reasonably safe (p. 144, l. 120). He sees clearly that lollardy is unacceptable, and indulges in the usual spiteful fling against the cockle (*lolia*) which the Lollards were reproached with sowing (p. 48, l. 93). He had once been a heretic (p. 99, l. 29), and in danger of 'never returning' to the true Church (p. 99, l. 38); but he secured his safety by a full submission (p. 105, l. 133).

At the same time, there is much about the piece that is vague, shifty, and unsatisfactory. He is too full of excuses, and too plausible ; in a word, too selfish. Hence he has no real message for others, but only wishes to display his skill, which he does by help of the most barefaced and deliberate plagiarism. It was not from the Consolatio Philosophiae of Boethius, but from the English translation of that work by Chaucer, that he really drew his materials ; and he often takes occasion to lift lines or ideas from the poem of Troilus whenever he can find any that come in handy. In one place he turns a long passage from the House of Fame into very inferior prose. There are one or two passages that remind us of the Legend of Good Women (i. pr. 100, ii. 3. 38, iii. 7. 38) ; but they are remarkably few. But he keeps a copy of Chaucer's Boethius always open before him, and takes from it passage after passage, usually with many alterations, abbreviations, expansions, and other disfigurements ; but sometimes without any alteration at all. A few examples will suffice, as a large number of parallel passages are duly pointed out in the Notes.

§ 11. In Chaucer's Boethius (bk. i. pr. 3. 10), when Philosophy, the heavenly visitant, comes to comfort the writer, her first words are :—'*O my norry*, sholde I forsaken thee now?' In the Testament (p. 10, l. 37), Heavenly Love commences her consolations with the same exclamation :— ' *O my nory*, wenest thou that my maner be, to foryete my frendes or my servaunts ?' The Latin text—'An te, *alumne*, desererem ?'—does not suggest this remarkable mode of address.

This, however, is a mere beginning ; it is not till further on that plagiarisms begin to be frequent. At first, as at p. 37, the author copies the sense rather than the words ; but he gradually begins to copy words and phrases also. Thus, at p. 43, l. 38, his '*chayres* of domes' comes from Chaucer's 'heye *chayres*' in bk. i. met. 5. 27 ; and then, in the next line, we find '*vertue, shynende naturelly* . . *is hid* under cloude,' where Chaucer has '*vertu*, cler-*shyninge naturelly is hid* in derke derknesses' ; bk. i. met. 5. 28. At p. 44, l. 66, we have : ' *Whan nature brought thee forth*, come thou not *naked out of thy moders wombe*? Thou haddest no richesse '; where Chaucer has : ' *Whan* that *nature broughte thee forth out of thy moder wombe*, I receyved thee *naked*, and nedy of alle thinges '; bk. ii. pr. 2. 10. Just a few lines below (ll. 71–76) we have the sense, but not the words, of the neighbouring passage in Chaucer (ll. 23–25). Further literal imitations are pointed out in the Notes to l. 85 in the same chapter, and elsewhere. See, for example, the Notes to Book ii. ch. iv. 4, 14, 20, 61 ; ch. v. 15, 57, 65, 67, 79 ; ch. vi. 11, 30, 74, 117, 123, 129, 132, 143 ; ch. vii. 8, 14, 20, 23, 30, 39, 50, 74, 95, 98, 105, 109, 114, 117, 130, 135, 139, 148 ; &c.

Those who require conviction on this point may take such an example as this.

'O ! a noble thing and clere is power, that is not founden mighty to kepe himselfe '; (p. 70, l. 20).

'O ! a noble thing and a cleer thing is power, that is nat founden mighty to kepen it-self '; Ch. Boeth. bk. iii. pr. 5. 5–7.

The Latin text is : 'O praeclara potentia quae nec ad con-seruationem quidem sui satis efficax inuenitur.' I see no reason for supposing that the author anywhere troubled himself to consult the Latin original. Indeed, it is possible to correct errors in the text by help of Chaucer's version ; see the last note on p. 461.

§ 12. We get the clearest idea of the author's method by observing his treatment of the House of Fame, 269–359. It is worth while to quote the whole passage :—

> 'Lo ! how a woman doth amis
> *To love* him that unknown is ! ...   270
> Hit *is not* al *gold* that glareth ; ...
> Ther *may be under* goodliheed
> Kevered *many* a shrewed *vyce* ;   275
> *Therefore* be *no wight* so nyce,
> To take a love only for *chere*,
> For *speche*, or for frendly manere ;
> For this shal every woman finde
> That som *man*, of his pure kinde,   280
> Wol *shewen outward* the faireste
> *Til he have* caught that what him leste ;
> And *thanne wol* he *causes finde*,
> And swere how that she is unkinde,
> *Or fals*, or prevy, or double was ...   285
> Therfor I wol seye a proverbe,
> That " he that fully knoweth th'erbe   290
> May saufly leye hit to his yë " ...
> Allas ! is every man thus trewe,
> That every yere wolde have a newe, ...
> As thus : of *oon* he wolde *have fame*,   305
> In magnifying of his name ;

Another *for frendship*, seith he;
And yet ther shal the *thri de* be,
That shal be taken *for delyt* . . .
Allas, that ever hadde routhe   332
Any woman on any man !
Now see I wel, and telle can,
We wrecched *women conne* non art . . .   335
How sore that *ye men* conne *grone*,
Anoon, as we have yow receyved,
Certeinly we *ben deceyved* ; .. ˙   340
For through you is my name *lorn*,
And alle my actes *red and songe*
Over al this land on every tonge.   348
O wikke *Fame* ! . . .
Eek, thogh I mighte *duren ever*,
That I have doon, rekever I *never* . . .   354
And that I shal thus juged be—
" Lo, right as she hath doon, now she
Wol do eftsones, hardily." '   359

If the reader will now turn to p. 54, l. 45, and continue down to l. 81 on the next page, he will find the whole of this passage turned into prose, with numerous cunning alterations and a few insertions, yet including all such words as are printed above in italics ! That is, he will find all except the proverb in ll. 290, 291 ; but this also is not far off ; for it occurs over the leaf, on p. 56, at l. 115, and again at p. 22, ll. 44–45 ! Surely, this is nothing but book-making, and the art of it does not seem to be difficult.

§ 13. The author expressly acknowledges his admiration of Troilus (p. 140, l. 292) ; and it is easy to see his indebtedness to that poem. He copies Chaucer's curious mistake as to Styx being a pit (p. 3, l. 80, and the note). He adopts the words *let-game* (p. 18, l. 124) and *wiver* (p. 129, l. 27). He quotes a whole line from Troilus at p. 27, l. 78 (see note) ; and spoils another one at p. 34, ch. viii. l. 5, a third at p. 80, l. 116, and a fourth at p. 128, ch. vii. l. 2. We can see whence he took his allusion to 'playing raket,' and to the dock and nettle, at p. 13, ll. 166, 167 ; and the phrase to 'pype with an yvè-lefe' at p. 134, l. 50.

It is further observable that he had read a later text of Piers Plowman with some care, but he seems to quote it from memory, as at p. 18, l. 153, and p. 24, l. 118. A few other passages in which he seems to have taken ideas from this popular and remarkable poem are pointed out in the Notes. It is probable that he thence adopted the words *legistres* and *skleren* ; for which see the Glossary, and consult the Notes for the references which are there given.

§ 14. The author is frequently guilty of gross inaccuracies. He seems to confuse Cain with Ham (p. 52, ll. 107, 109), but *Cayn*, says Mr. Bradley, may be Thynne's misprint for *Cam*, i. e. Ham. He certainly confuses Perdiccas with Arrhidæus (p. 52, l. 116). He speaks of the *eighth* year, instead of the *seventh*, as being a sabbatical year, and actually declares that the ordinary week contains *seven* working-days (p. 24, ll. 102–104) ! He tells us that Sunday begins 'at the first hour after noon (!) on Saturday' (p. 82, l. 163). Hence it is not to be wondered at that some of his arguments and illustrations are quite unintelligible.

§ 15. The title of the work, viz. THE TESTAMENT OF LOVE, readily reminds us of the passage in Gower already quoted in vol. iii. p. xliii., in which the goddess Venus proposes that Chaucer should write 'his testament of love,' in order 'to sette an ende of alle his werke.' I have already explained that the real reference in this passage is to the Legend of Good Women; but I am not prepared, at present, to discuss the connection between the expression in Gower and the treatise by Usk. The fact that our author adopted the above title may have led to the notion that Chaucer wrote the treatise here discussed; but it is quite clear that he had nothing to do with it.

Professor Morley well says that 'the writer of this piece uses the word Testament in the old Scriptural sense of a witnessing, and means by Love the Divine Love, the Christian spirit encouraging and directing the wish for the grace of God, called Margaret, the pearl beyond all price.' To which, however, it is highly essential to add that Margaret is not used in the sense of 'grace' alone, but is also employed, in several passages, to signify 'the visible Church of Christ.' The author is, in fact, careful to warn us of the varying, the almost Protean sense of the word at p. 145, where he tells us that 'Margarite, a woman [i.e. properly a woman's name], betokeneth *grace, lerning*, or *wisdom of god*, or els *holy church*.' His object seems to have been to extend the meaning of the word so as to give him greater scope for ingenuity in varying his modes of reference to it. He has certainly succeeded in adding to the obscurity of his subject. That by 'holy church' he meant the visible Church of Christ of his

own time, appears from the remarkable assertion that it is 'deedly,'
i. e. mortal (p. 94, l. 121). Such an epithet is inapplicable to the
Church in its spiritual character. It may also be observed that,
however much the sense implied by Margarite may vary, it never
takes the meaning which we should most readily assign to it; i. e.
it never means a live woman, nor represents even an imaginary
object of natural human affection. The nearest approach to such
an ideal is at p. 94, l. 114, where we are told that the jewel
which he hopes to attain is as precious a pearl as a woman is
by nature.

§ 16. It hardly seems worth while to give a detailed analysis
of the whole piece. An analysis of the First Book (which is, on
the whole, the best) is given by Professor Morley; and the hints
which I have already given as to the character and situation of
the author will enable the reader to regard the treatise from
a right point of view. But it is proper to observe that the author
himself tells us how he came to divide the work into three books [1],
and what are the ideas on which each book is founded. Each of
the three books has an introductory chapter. That to the First
Book I have called a Prologue; and perhaps it would have been
strictly correct to have called the first chapters of the other books
by the same name. In the introductory chapter to the Third
Book, p. 101, he declares that the First Book is descriptive of
Error, or Deviation (which the editions print as Demacion!);
the Second, of Grace; and the Third, of Joy. In other words,
the First Book is particularly devoted to recounting the errors
of his youth, especially how he was led by others into a conspiracy
against the state and into deviation from orthodoxy. In the
Prologue, he excuses himself for writing in English, and announces
the title of the work. He then assures us that he is merely going
to gather up the crumbs that have fallen from the table, and to
glean handfuls of corn which Boethius has dropped. 'A sly
servant in his own help is often much commended'; and this
being understood, he proceeds to help himself accordingly, as has
already been explained.

§ 17. BOOK I: CH. I. In Chapter I, he describes his misery,

---

[1] Professor Morley says:—'As Boethius ... wrote three books of the Consolation of Philosophy,' &c. But Boethius wrote *five* books.

and hopes that the dice will turn, and implores the help of Margaret, here used (apparently) to typify the grace of God. He represents himself as being in prison, in imitation of Boethius; but I suspect that, *in the present passage*, the prison was metaphorical. (He had been imprisoned in 1384, and in 1387 was imprisoned again; but that is another matter.)

CH. II. Heavenly Love suddenly appears to him, as Philosophy appeared to Boethius, and is ready to console and reclaim him. She is aware of his losses, and he tries to vindicate his constancy of character.

CH. III. He describes how he once wandered through the woods at the close of autumn, and was attacked by some animals who had suddenly turned wild. To save himself, he embarks on board a ship; but the reader is disappointed to find that the adventure is wholly unreal; the ship is the ship of Travail, peopled by Sight, Lust, Thought, and Will. He is driven on an island, where he catches a glimpse of Love, and finds a Margaret, a pearl of price. He appeals to Love to comfort him.

CH. IV. Love first reproves and then consoles him. She enquires further into his complaints.

CH. V. She advises him to contemn such as have spoken against him. He complains that he has served seven years for Rachel, and prays for comfort in his eighth year. She exhorts him to perseverance.

CH. VI. He here goes into several details as to his previous conduct. The authorities threatened to keep him in prison, unless he would reveal a certain secret or plot. He was afraid that the peace of his native place, London, would suffer; and to procure its peace, he 'declared certain points.' Being charged upon oath to reveal certain secret dealings, he at once did so; for which he incurred much odium.

CH. VII. To prove that he had only spoken the truth, he offered wager of battle; and was justified by the fact that no one accepted it. He had not perjured himself, because his oath in the law-court was superior to his former oath of secrecy. He only meant truth, but was sadly slandered. It is absurd to be 'a stinking martyr' in a false cause.

CH. VIII. Love tells him he has greatly erred, and must expect much correction. Earthly fame should be despised, whilst he looks for the fame that comes after death.

Cн. IX. Love vindicates the greatness of God and the goodness of His providence.

Cн. X. The author complains of his hard fortune; he has
lost his goods and has been deprived of his office. Love explains
that adversity teaches salutary lessons, and that the true riches
may still be his own.

§ 18. Book II. In the first chapter (or Prologue) of the
Second Book, he again discusses the object of his work. In
Chapter II, Love sings him a Latin song, introducing complaints
against the clergy such as frequently occur in Piers the Plowman.
In Chapter III, we find a discourse on womankind, largely
borrowed from Chaucer's House of Fame. The next eight
chapters are chiefly devoted to a discussion of the way by which
the repentant sinner may come to 'the knot' of Heavenly bliss;
and it is here, in particular, that a large portion of Chaucer's
Boethius is freely imitated or copied. The last three chapters
recount the excellences of Margaret, which in many passages
refers rather to the visible Church than to divine Grace.

§ 19. Book III. The first chapter is again introductory,
explaining why the number of Books is three. 'The Margaret
in virtue is likened to Philosophy, with her three kinds.' It is
remarkable that this Third Book, which is dedicated to Joy, is the
dullest of the three, being largely taken up with the questions
of predestination and free will, with more borrowings from
Chaucer's Boethius. In Chapter V, Love explains how continuance in good will produces the fruit of Grace; and, in
Chapters VI and VII, shews how such grace is to be attained.
Chapter IX recurs to the subject of predestination; after which
the work comes to a formal conclusion, with excuses for its various
imperfections.

§ 20. II. The Plowmans Tale.

This piece does not appear in Thynne's first edition of 1532,
but occurs, for the first time, in the second edition of 1542, where
it is added at the end of the Canterbury Tales, after the Parson's
Tale. In the next (undated) edition, probably printed about
1550, it is placed *before* the Parson's Tale, as if it were really
Chaucer's, and the same arrangement occurs in the fourth edition,
that of 1561, by John Stowe. It is worth mentioning that some
booksellers put forward a fable as to the true date of the undated

edition being 1539, in order to enhance the value of their copies; but the pretence is obviously false, as is shewn by collation [1]; besides which, it is not likely that the Plowman's Tale would have been *at first* inserted before the Parson's Tale, *then* placed after it, and then *again* placed before it. It is best to separate the first four editions by nearly equal intervals, their dates being, respectively, 1532, 1542, about 1550, and 1561.

Comparison of the black-letter editions shews that the first is the best; and the later ones, being mere reprints, grow gradually worse. Hence, in this case, the edition of 1542 is the sole authority, and the readings of the inferior copies may be safely neglected. It is remarkable that Mr. T. Wright, in his edition of this poem printed in his Political Poems and Songs, i. 304, should have founded his text upon a reprint of Speght in 1687, when he might have taken as his authority a text more than 140 years older. The result is, naturally, that his text is much worse than was at all necessary.

According to Speght, there was once a MS. copy of this piece in Stowe's library, but no one knows what became of it. According to Todd, in his Illustrations of Gower and Chaucer, p. xxxix, there was once a black-letter edition of it, entitled 'The Plouuman's tale compylled by syr Geffray Chaucer knyght.' Todd says: 'It is of the duodecimo size, in the black letter, without date, and imprinted at London in Paules churche-yarde at the sygne of the Hyll, by Wyllyam Hyll. I have compared with the poem as printed by Urry forty or fifty lines, and I found almost as many variations between them [2]. The colophon of this book is, *Thus endeth the boke of Chaunterburye Tales.* This rarity belongs to the Rev. Mr. Conybeare, the present Professor of the Saxon language in the University of Oxford.' This edition can no longer be traced. . Hazlitt mentions a black-letter edition of this piece, printed separately by Thomas Godfray (about 1535), on twenty leaves; of which only one copy is known, viz. that at Britwell. There is also a late print of it in the Bodleian Library, dated 1606.

§ 21. It is needless to discuss the possibility that Chaucer wrote this Tale, as it is absent from all the MSS.; and it does not

---

[1] One line is enough to shew the order of the texts; see p. xv, footnote.

[2] But this proves nothing, as Urry departs from all sound texts in an erratic manner all his own.

appear that the ascription of it to him was taken seriously. It is
obvious, from the introductory Prologue (p. 147), that the author
never intended his work to be taken for Chaucer's; he purposely
chooses a different metre from any that occurs in the Canterbury
Tales, and he introduces his Ploughman as coming under the
Host's notice quite suddenly, so that the Host is constrained
to ask him—'what man art thou?' The whole manner of the
Tale is conspicuously and intentionally different from that of
Chaucer; and almost the only expression which at all resembles
Chaucer occurs in ll. 51, 52 :—

> 'I pray you that no man me reproche
> Whyl that I am my tale telling.'

Chaucer himself, before reciting his Tale of Melibeus, said
much the same thing :—

> 'And let me tellen al my tale, I preye.'

I do not know why Mr. Wright, when reprinting this piece,
omitted the Prologue. It is a pity that half of the sixth stanza is
missing.

§ 22.   At l. 1065 we meet with a most important statement :—

> 'Of freres I haye told before
> In a making of a Crede.'

It is generally agreed that the author here claims to have
previously written the well-known piece entitled Pierce the Ploughman's Crede, which I edited for the Early English Text Society
in 1867. I then took occasion to compare the language of these
two pieces (which I shall shortly call the Crede and the Tale), and
I found ample confirmation, from internal evidence, that the claim
is certainly true. There are many similarities of expression, some
of which I here lay before the reader.

FROM THE CREDE.	FROM THE TALE.
Curteis Crist (1, 140).	curteys Christ (482).
cutted cote (434).	cutted clothes (929).
y can noh3t my Crede (8).	Suche that conne nat hir Crede (413).
At marketts and myracles, we med-leth us nevere (107).	Market-beters, and medling make (871).
For we buldeth a burw3, a brod and a large (118).	And builde als brode as a citè (743).
portreid and peint (121). peynt and portred (192).	I-paynted and portred (135).
y sey coveitise catel to fongen (146).	To catche catell as covytous (385; cf. 856).

```
* * *
* * * *
```
                                                        c

FROM THE CREDE.	FROM THE TALE.
Of double worstede y-dy3t (228).	With double worsted well y-dight (1002).
Than ther lefte in Lucifer, er he were lowe fallen (374).	As lowe as Lucifer such shall fall (124).
opon the plow hongen (421).	honged at the plow (1042).
povere in gost God him-self blisseth (521).	The pore in spirit gan Christ blesse (915).
ben maysters icalled, That the gentill Jesus . . . purly defended (574).	Maysters be called defended he tho (1115).
to brenne the bodye in a bale of fijr (667).	Thou shalt be brent in balefull fyre (1234).
Thei shulden nou3t after the face . . . demen (670).	They nolde nat demen after the face (714).
Thei schulden delven and diggen and dongen the erthe,	Threshing and dyking fro town to town,
And mene mong-corn bred to her mete fongen (785).	With sory mete, and not half y-now (1043).
He mi3te no maistre ben kald, for Crist that defended (838).	Maysters be called defended he tho (1115).

The Crede is written in alliterative verse; and it will be observed that alliteration is employed in the Tale very freely. Another peculiarity in the Tale may here be noticed, viz. the use of the same rime, *fall* or *befall*, throughout Part I, with the exception of ll. 205–228. Indeed, in the first line of Part II, the author apologizes for being unable to find any more rimes for *fall*, and proceeds to rime upon *amend* throughout that Part. In Part III, he begins to rime upon *grace* in the first two stanzas, but soon abandons it for the sake of freedom; however, at l. 1276, he recurs to *grace*, and continues to rime upon it till the end. It is clear that the author possessed considerable facility of expression. We can date these pieces approximately without much error. The proceedings against Walter Brute, expressly alluded to in the Crede, l. 657, lasted from Oct. 15, 1391, to Oct. 6, 1393, when he submitted himself to the bishop of Hereford. We may well date the Crede about 1394, and the Tale (which probably soon followed it, as the author repeats some of his expressions) about 1395 [1].

Both these pieces are written in a spirited style, and are of considerable interest for the light which they throw upon many

---

[1] The expression 'the quenes heed,' at l. 158, hardly implies that there was then a queen of England. If it does, it makes the poem later than October, 1396.

of the corrupt practices of the monks, friars, and clergy. The
Crede is directed against the friars in particular, and reflects
many of the opinions of Wyclif, as will easily appear by comparing
it with Wyclif's works. See, in particular, his Fifty Heresies and
Errors of Friars (Works, ed. Arnold, iii. 366). It would have
been easy to crowd the Notes with quotations from Wyclif; but
it is sufficient to point out so obvious a source. I have not
observed any passage in which the author copies the exact
language of Langland. The dialect seems to be some form of
Midland, and is somewhat archaic; many of the verbal forms are
of some value to the philologist. Taken altogether, it is a piece
of considerable interest and merit. Ten Brink alludes to it as
'that transparent, half-prophetic allegory of the Quarrel between
the Griffin and the Pelican'; and adds—'The Griffin was the
representative of the prelates and the monks, the Pelican that
of real Christianity in Wyclif's sense. At a loss for arguments, the
Griffin calls in at last all the birds of prey in order to destroy
its rival. The Phoenix, however, comes to the help of the
Pelican, and terribly destroys the robber-brood.'

Tyrwhitt observed, with great acuteness, that Spenser's allusion,
in the Epilogue to his Shepheards Calender, to 'the Pilgrim that
the Ploughman playde awhyle,' may well refer to the author of the
Plowman's Tale rather than to Langland[1]. Cf. p. 147, l. 12. It
was natural that Spenser should mention him along with Chaucer,
because their productions were bound up together in the same
volume; a volume which was, to Spenser, a treasure-house of
archaic words.

The discussion on points of religion between the Griffin and
the Pelican clearly suggested to Dryden his discussion between
the Hind and the Panther. His choice of quadrupeds in place
of birds is certainly no improvement.

§ 23. III. Jack Upland.

Of this piece, no MS. copy is known. It is usually said to have
been first printed by Speght, in his second edition of Chaucer's
Works in 1602; but I have been so fortunate as to find a better

---

[1] The line, as it stands, is ambiguous; what Spenser meant to say was—'the
Ploughman that the Pilgrim playde awhyle'; which expresses the fact. The
subject is 'the Ploughman'; and 'that' means 'whom.'

and earlier text in the library of Caius College, Cambridge, to which my attention was drawn by a note in Hazlitt's Bibliographer's Handbook. This copy, here taken as the basis of my text, and collated with Speght, is a small book consisting of only 16 leaves. The title-page contains the following words, within a square border. ¶ Jack vp Lande | Compyled by the | famous Geoffrey | Chaucer. | Ezechielis. xiii. | ¶ Wo be vnto you that | dishonour me to me (*sic*) peo | ple for an handful of bar | lye & for a pece of bread. | Cum priuilegio | Regali.

At the end of the treatise is the colophon : ¶ Prynted for Ihon Gough. Cum Priuilegio Regali.

Hazlitt conjectures that it was printed about 1540. I think we may safely date it in 1536; for it is bound up in a volume with several other tracts, and it so happens that the tract next following it is by Myles Coverdale, and is dated 1536, being printed in just the very same type and style. We can also tell that it must have been printed after 1535, because the verse from Ezekiel xiii, as quoted on the title-page (see above), exactly corresponds with Coverdale's version of the Bible, the first edition of which appeared in that year.

The text of Jack Upland, in the Caius College copy, has the following heading, in small type :—'¶ These bē the lewed questions of Freres rytes and obseruaunces the whych they chargen more than Goddes lawe, and therfore men shulden not gyue hem what so they beggen, tyll they hadden answered and clerely assoyled these questions.'

As this copy is, on the whole, considerably superior to Speght's both as regards sense and spelling, I have not given his inferior readings and errors. In a very few places, Speght furnishes some obvious corrections; and in such instances his readings are noted.

§ 24. A very convenient reprint of Speght's text is given in Wright's edition of Political Poems and Songs (Record Series), vol. ii. p. 16. In the same volume, p. 39, is printed a reply to Jack Upland's questions by a friar who facetiously calls himself Friar Daw Topias, though it appears (from a note printed at p. 114) that his real name was John Walsingham. Nor is this all; for Friar Daw's reply is further accompanied by Jack Upland's rejoinder, printed, for convenience, below Friar Daw's text. It is most likely, as Mr. Wright concludes, that all three pieces may be dated in the same year. It was necessary that Friar Daw (who gave himself this name in order to indicate that he is a comparatively unlearned man, yet easily able to refute his audacious questioner) should produce his reply at once ; and we may be sure that Jack's rejoinder was not long delayed. Fortunately, the date can be determined with sufficient exactness ; for Jack's rejoinder contains the allusion : 'and the kyng by his juges trwe [sholde] execute his lawe, as he *did now late*, whan he hangid you traytours,' p. 86. This clearly refers to June, 1402[1], when eight Franciscan friars were hanged at Tyburn for being concerned in a plot against the life of Henry IV. We may, accordingly, safely refer all three pieces to the year 1402 ; shortly after Chaucer's death.

§ 25. It is also tolerably clear that there must have been two texts of 'Jack Upland,' an earlier and a later one. The earlier one, of which we have no copy, can easily be traced by help of Friar Daw's reply, as he quotes all that is material point by point. It only extended as far as the 54th question in the present edition (p. 199) ; after which followed two more questions which do not here reappear. The later copy also contains a few questions, not far from the beginning, which Friar Daw ignores. It is clear that we only possess a later, and, on the whole, a fuller copy. One of the omitted questions relates to transubstantiation ; and, as any discussion of it was extremely likely, at that date, to be ended by burning the disputant at the stake, it was certainly prudent to suppress it. Not perceiving this point, Mr. Wright too hastily concluded that our copy of Jack Upland is extremely corrupt, a conclusion quite unwarranted ; inasmuch as Friar Daw, in spite of his affectation of alliterative verse, quotes his adversary's questions with reasonable correctness. On this unsound theory Mr. Wright has built up another, still less warranted, viz. that the original copy of Jack Upland must have been written in alliterative verse ; for no other reason than because Friar Daw's reply is so written. It is obvious that alliteration is conspicuously absent, except in the case of the four lines (424-7), which are introduced, by way of flourish, at the end. My own belief is that our copy of Jack Upland is a second edition, i. e. an amended and extended

---

[1] Mr. Wright says 1401, and refers to Capgrave's Chronicle. But this is surely an error ; see J. H. Wylie's Hist. of Henry IV, i. 277-8 ; with a reference to the Close Rolls, 3 Hen. IV, 2. 16.

copy, which has been reasonably well preserved. It is more correct than the Plowmans Tale, and very much more correct than the Testament of Love.

§ 26. Mr. Wright further imagines that Jack Upland's rejoinder to Friar Daw's reply, which he prints from 'a contemporary MS. in the Bodleian Library at Oxford, MS. Digby 41,' was also originally in alliterative verse. This supposition is almost as gratuitous as the former; for, although there are very frequent traces of alliteration as an occasional embellishment, it is otherwise written in ordinary prose. The mere chopping up of prose into bits of not very equal length, as in Mr. Wright's print, does not produce verse of any kind. Friar Daw's verses are bad enough, as he did not understand his model (obviously the Ploughman's Crede), but he usually succeeds in making a kind of jingle, with pauses, for the most part, in the right place. But there is no verse discoverable in Jack Upland; he preferred straightforward prose, for reasons that are perfectly obvious.

For further remarks, I beg leave to refer the reader to Mr. Wright's Introduction, pp. xii–xxiv, where he will find an excellent summary of the arguments adduced on both sides. There is a slight notice of Jack Upland in Morley's English Writers, vi. 234.

§ 27. IV. John Gower: The Praise of Peace.

In Morley's English Writers, iv. 157, this poem is entitled 'De Pacis Commendatione,' on MS. authority (see p. 216). Mr. E. B. Nicholson, who has made a special study of Gower's poems, suggested 'The Praise of Peace,' which I have gladly adopted. I am much obliged to Mr. Nicholson for his assistance in various ways; and, in particular, for the generous loan of his own transcript of this poem.

§ 28. In Todd's Illustrations of Gower and Chaucer, p. 95, is a notice of a MS. 'in the present Marquis of Stafford's library at Trentham,' which had been previously described in Warton's Hist. of E. Poetry as being 'in Lord Gower's library.' Mr. Wright alludes to it as 'a contemporary MS. in the possession of his grace the duke of Sutherland.' It may be called 'the Trentham MS.' 'The Praise of Peace' was printed from it by Mr. Wright, in his Political Poems and Songs, ii. 4–15; and I have followed his text, which I denote by 'T.' At the same time, I have collated it with the text of Thynne's edition of 1532, which is a very good one. The differences are slight.

Warton describes the MS. as 'a thin oblong MS. on vellum, containing some of Gower's poems in Latin, French, and English. By an entry in the first leaf, in the handwriting and under the signature of Thomas lord Fairfax, Cromwell's general, an anti-quarian, and a lover and collector of curious manuscripts, it appears that this book was presented by the poet Gower, about 1400[1], to Henry IV; and that it was given by lord Fairfax to his friend and kinsman Sir Thomas Gower, knight and baronet, in the year 1656.' He goes on to say that Fairfax had it from Charles Gedde, Esq., of St. Andrews; and that it was at one time in the possession of King Henry VII, while earl of Richmond, who wrote in it his own name in the form 'Rychemond.'

The MS. contains (1) The Praise of Peace, *preceded by* the seven Latin lines (386–392), which I have relegated to the end of the poem, as in Thynne. The title is given in the colophon (p. 216); after which follow the twelve Latin lines (393–404), printed on the same page. (2) Some complimentary verses in Latin, also addressed to Henry IV, printed in Wright's Political Poems, ii. 1–3. (3) Fifty Balades in French, which have been printed by Stengel (Warton prints *four* of them), with the colophon —Expliciunt carmina Johīs Gower que Gallice composita *Balades* dicuntur.' (4) Two short Latin poems in elegiacs; see Warton. (5) A French poem on the Dignity or Excellence of Marriage. (6) Seventeen Latin hexameters. (7) Gower's Latin verses on his blindness, beginning—

> ' Henrici quarti primus regni fuit annus,
> Quo michi defecit visus ad acta mea,' &c.

See Todd and Warton for more minute particulars.

§ 29. The poem itself may safely be dated in the end of 1399, for reasons given in the note to l. 393. It is of some interest, as being Gower's last poem in English, and the spirit of it is excellent, though it contains no very striking lines. We have not much of Gower's work in the form of seven-line stanzas. The Confessio Amantis contains only twelve such stanzas; iii. 349-352. I draw attention to the earliest known reference (l. 295) to the game of 'tenetz'; the enumeration of the nine worthies (ll. 281–3);

---

[1] Fairfax deduced the date from the poem here printed, l. 393.

and the reference to a story about Constantine which, in the Confessio Amantis, is related at considerable length (l. 339).

We may compare with this poem the stanzas in praise of peace in Hoccleve's De Regimine Principum, quoted in Morley's English Writers (1890), vol. vi. pp. 131-2.

§ 30. V. Thomas Hoccleve: The Letter of Cupid.

This poem needs little discussion. It is known to be Hoc-cleve's; see Dr. Furnivall's edition of Hoccleve's Minor Poems, E. E. T. S., 1892, p. 72. As explained in the notes, it is rather closely imitated from the French poem entitled L'Epistre au Dieu d'Amours, written by Christine de Pisan. At the end of her poem, Christine gives the date of its composition, viz. 1399; and Hoccleve, in like manner, gives the date of his poem as 1402. The poem consists of sixty-eight stanzas, of which not more than eighteen are wholly independent of the original. The chief original passages are ll. 176–189, 316–329, and 374–434.

The poem is entirely occupied with a defence of women, such as a woman might well make. It takes the form of a reproof, addressed by Cupid to all male lovers; and is directed, in par-ticular, against the sarcasms of Jean de Meun (l. 281) in the celebrated Roman de la Rose.

Of this poem there are several MS. copies; see footnotes at p. 217. The best is probably the Ashburnham MS., but it has not yet been printed. I chiefly follow MS. Fairfax 16, which Dr. Furnivall has taken as the basis of his text.

There is also a poor and late copy in the Bannatyne MS., at fol. 269; see the print of it for the Hunterian Club, 1879; p. 783.

§ 31. VI. The same: Two Balades.

These two Balades, also by Hoccleve, were composed at the same time. The former is addressed to King Henry V, and the latter to the Knights of the Garter. They are very closely connected with a much longer poem of 512 lines, which was addressed to Sir John Oldcastle in August, 1415; and must have been written at about that date. It was natural enough that, whilst addressing his appeal to Oldcastle to renounce his heresies, the poet should briefly address the king on the same subject at the same time. I think we may safely date this piece, like the other, in August, 1415.

The remarkable likeness between the two pieces appears most in the references to Justinian and to Constantine. In fact, the reference to Justinian in l. 3 of the former of the Balades here printed would be unintelligible but for the full explanation which the companion poem affords. I have quoted, in the note to l. 3, the Latin note which is written in the margin of st. 24 of the address to Oldcastle ; and I quote here the stanza itself :—

> 'The Cristen emperour Justinian,
> As it is writen, who-so list it see,
> Made a lawe deffending every man,
> Of what condicion or what degree
> That he were of, nat sholde hardy be
> For to despute of the feith openly ;
> And ther-upon sundry peynes sette he,
> That peril sholde eschuëd be therby.'
>
> Minor Poems, ed. Furnivall, p. 14.

Compare with this the fourth stanza of Balade I.

We may regret that Hoccleve's desire to make an example of heretics was so soon fulfilled. Only three years later, in Dec. 1418, Sir John Oldcastle was captured in Wales, brought up to London, and publicly burnt.

My text follows the sole good MS. (Phillipps 8151); which I have collated with the earliest printed text, that of 1542. There is, indeed, another MS. copy of the poem in the library of Trinity College, Cambridge (R. 3. 15); but it is only a late copy made from the printed book.

§ 32. VII. Henry Scogan: A Moral Balade.

The heading to this poem is from MS. Ashmole 59; it is, unfortunately, somewhat obscure. It is, of course, not contemporaneous with the poem, but was added, by way of note, by John Shirley, when transcribing it. In fact, the third son of Henry IV was not created duke of Bedford till 1415, after the accession of Henry V ; whereas Henry V is here referred to as being still 'my lord the Prince.' Hence the poem was written in the reign of Henry IV (1399–1413); but we can easily come much nearer than this to the true date. We may note, first of all, that Chaucer is referred to as being dead (l. 65); so that the date is after 1400. Again, the poem does not appear to have been recited by the author; it was *sent*, in the author's handwriting, to the assembled guests (l. 3). Further, Scogan says that he was 'called' the 'fader,' i.e. tutor, of the young princes (l. 2); and that he sent the letter to them out of fervent regard for their welfare, in order to warn them (l. 35). He regrets that sudden age has come upon him (l. 10), and wishes to impart to them the lessons which the approach of old age suggests. All this points to a time when Scogan was getting past his regular work as tutor, though he still retained the title; which suggests a rather late date. We find, however, from the Inquisitiones post Mortem (iii. 315), that Henry Scogan died in 1407, and I have seen it noted (I forget where) that he only attained the age of forty-six. This shews that he was only relatively old, owing, probably, to infirm health; and we may safely date the poem in 1406 or 1407, the latter being the more likely. In 1407, the ages of the young princes were nineteen, eighteen, seventeen, and sixteen respectively, and it is not likely that Scogan had been their tutor for more than twelve years at most. This provisional date of 1407 sufficiently satisfies all the conditions.

The four sons of Henry IV were Henry, prince of Wales, born at Monmouth in 1388; Thomas, born in 1389, and created duke of Clarence in 1412; John, born in 1390, created duke of Bedford in 1415; and Humphrey, born in 1391, created duke of Gloucester in 1414.

§ 33. The expression *at a souper of feorthe merchande* is difficult, and I can only guess at the sense. *Feorthe* is Shirley's spelling of *ferthe*, i.e. fourth. *Merchande* is probably equivalent to O. F. *marchandie* or *marchandise*. Godefroy gives an example of the latter in the sense of 'merchant's company.' I suppose that *feorthe merchande* means 'fourth meeting of merchants,' or the fourth of the four quarterly meetings of a guild. Toulmin Smith, in his English Gilds, p. 32, says that quarterly meetings for business were common; though some guilds met only once, twice, or thrice in the course of a year.

The Vintry is described by Stow in his Survey of London (ed. Thoms, p. 90): 'Then next over against St. Martin's church, is a large house built of stone and timber, with vaults for the stowage of wines, and is called the Vintry. . . . In this house Henry Picard [lord mayor in 1356-7] feasted four kings in one day.'

I need not repeat here what I have already said about Scogan in vol. i. p. 83.

I may add to the note about Lewis John (vol. i. p. 84), that he was a person of some note. In 1423 (Feb. 8), 'Ludowicus Johan, armiger, constitutus est seneschall et receptor generalis ducatus Cornub.': see Ordinances of the Privy Council, iii. 24. He is further mentioned in the same, ii. 334, 342.

Chaucer's Balade on Gentilesse, quoted in full in ll. 105-125, is in seven-line stanzas; and is thus distinguished from the rest of the poem, which is written in eight-line stanzas. It may be noted that Scogan's rimes are extremely correct, if we compare them with Chaucer's as a standard.

Of this piece there are two early printed copies, one by Caxton, and one by Thynne (1532); and two MSS., Ashmole 59 and Harl. 2251. It is remarkable that the printed copies are better than the MSS. as regards readings.

§ 34. VIII. The Complaint of the Black Knight.

Such is the title in Thynne's edition (1532). In MS. F. (Fairfax 16), it is entitled—'Complaynte of a Loveres Lyfe'; and there is a printed edition with the title—'The Complaynte of a Louers Lyfe. Imprynted at London in the flete strete at the sygne of the Sonne, by Wynkyn de Worde'; no date, 4to. on twelve leaves. In MS. S. (Arch. Selden, B. 24), there is an erroneous colophon—'Here endith the Maying and disporte of Chaucere'; which gives the wrong title, and assigns it to the wrong author. In accordance with the last MS., it was printed, with the erroneous title—'Here begynnys the mayng or disport of chaucer'—in a volume 'Imprentit in the south gait of Edinburgh be Walter chepman and Androw myllar the fourth day of aperile the yhere of god . M.CCCCC. and viii yheris' [1508]; and this scarce copy was reprinted as piece no. 8 in The Knightly Tale of Golagrus and Gawane, &c., as reprinted by Laing in 1827.

But the fullest title is that in MS. Ad. (Addit. 16165), written out by John Shirley, who says: 'And here filowyng begynnethe a Right lusty amorous balade, made in wyse of a complaynt of a Right worshipfulle Knyght that truly euer serued his lady,

enduryng grete disese by fals envye and malebouche ; made by
Lydegate' (fol. 190, back). Some of the pages have the heading,
'The compleynte of a Knight made by Lidegate [1].'

This attribution of the poem to Lydgate, by so good a judge
as Shirley, renders the authorship certain; and the ascription
is fully confirmed by strong internal evidence. Much of it is
in Lydgate's best manner, and his imitation of Chaucer is, in
places, very close; while, at the same time, it is easy to point
out non-Chaucerian rimes, such as *whyte, brighte*, 2 ; *pitously,
malady* (Ch. *maladyë*), 137 ; *felyngly, malady*, 188 ; *mente, diligent,*
246 ; *grace, alas*, 529 ; *seyn, payn* (Ch. *peynë*), 568 ; *diurnal, fal,*
(Ch. *falle*), 590 ; *payn, agayn*, 650 ; *queen* (Ch. *quene*), *seen*, 674.
Besides which, there are two mere assonances in two consecutive
stanzas, viz. *forjuged, excused*, 274 ; and *wreke, clepe*, 284. The
occurrence of this pair of assonances is quite enough to settle the
question. If we apply a more delicate test, we may observe that,
in ll. 218–220, the word *sōre* (with long *o*) rimes with *tore*, in which
the *o* was originally short ; on this point, see vol. vi. p. xxxii.

As to this poem, Ten Brink well remarks : 'His talent was
fairly qualified for a popular form of the 'Complaint'—a sort
of long monologue, interwoven with allegory and mythology, and
introduced by a charming picture of nature. His *Complaint of
the Black Knight*, which contains reminiscences from the Romance
of the Rose, the Book of the Duchesse, and the Parlement of
Foules, was long considered a production of Chaucer's, and is still
frequently included in editions of his works—although with reser-
vations. The critic, however, will not be deceived by the
excellent descriptive passages of this poem, but will easily detect
the characteristic marks of the imitator in the management of
verse and rhyme, and especially in the diffusiveness of the story
and the monotony even of the most important parts.'

§ 35. Lydgate's reminiscences of Chaucer are often interesting.
In particular, we should observe the passages suggested by the
Roman de la Rose in ll. 36–112 ; for we are at once reminded of
Chaucer's *own version* of it, as preserved in Fragment A of the
Romaunt. After noticing that he uses *costey* (36) for the F.
costoiant, where Chaucer has *costeying* (134) ; and *attempre* (57)

---

[1] Shirley also refers to Lydgate's Temple of Glas ; see Schick's edition of
that poem ; p. lxxxii.

where Chaucer has *attempre* (131), though one French text has *atrempee*, it is startling to find him reproducing (80) Chaucer's very phrase *And softe as veluet* (R. R. 1420), where the French original has nothing corresponding either to *soft* or to *velvet!* This clearly shews that Lydgate was acquainted with Fragment A of the English version, and believed that version to be Chaucer's; for otherwise he would hardly have cared to imitate it at all.

The date of this poem is discussed in the Introduction to Schick's edition of the Temple of Glas, by the same author; pp. c, cxii. He dates it in Lydgate's early period, or about A. D. 1402.

The text is based upon Thynne's edition, which is quite as good as the MSS., though the spellings are often too late in form. The late excellent edition by E. Krausser (Halle, 1896) reached me after my text was printed. His text (from MS. F.) has much the same readings, and is accompanied by a full Introduction and eleven pages of useful notes.

§ 36. IX. The Flour of Curtesye.

This piece has no author's name prefixed to it in the first three editions; but in the fourth edition by Stowe, printed in 1561, the title is: 'The Floure of Curtesie, made by Iohn lidgate.' Probably Stowe had seen it attributed to him in some MS., and made a note of it; but I know of no MS. copy now extant.

Few poems bear Lydgate's impress more clearly; there can be no doubt as to its authorship. Schick refers it to Lydgate's early period, and dates it about 1400–1402; see his edition of the Temple of Glas, p. cxii. As it was written after Chaucer's death (see l. 236), and probably when that sad loss was still recent, we cannot be far wrong if we date it about 1401; and the Black Knight, a somewhat more ambitious effort, about 1402.

The 'Flour of Curtesye' is intended as a portrait of one whom the poet honours as the best of womankind. The character is evidently founded on that of Alcestis as described in the Prologue to the Legend of Good Women; and throughout the piece we are frequently reminded of Chaucer; especially of the Legend, the Complaint of Mars, and the Parliament of Foules.

The Envoy presents a very early example of the four-line stanza, similar to that employed in Gray's famous Elegy.

§ 37. X. A Balade in Commendation of our Lady.

This piece is attributed to 'Lidegate of Bury' in the Ashmole MS. no. 59; and the ascription is obviously correct. It abounds with evident marks of his peculiar style of metre; for which see Schick's Introduction to the Temple of Glas, p. lvi. We note in it a few reminiscences of Chaucer, as pointed out in the Notes; in particular, it was probably suggested by Chaucer's A B C, which furnished hints for ll. 27, 60, and 129. It is perhaps worth while to add that we have thus an independent testimony for the genuineness of that poem.

As an illustration of Lydgate's verse, I may notice the additional syllable after the cæsura, which too often clogs his lines. Thus in l. 8 we must group the syllables thus :—

Wherefór: now pláynly: I wól: my stýlë: dréssë. Similarly, we find *lícour* in l. 13, *pitè* (18), *líving* (24), *bémës* (25), *gínning* (31), *mércy* (33), *gárden* (36), &c., all occupying places where a monosyllable would have been more acceptable.

The poem is strongly marked by alliteration, shewing that the poet (usually in a hurry) took more than usual pains with it. In the seventh stanza (43–49) this tendency is unmistakably apparent.

It is hardly possible to assign a date to a poem of this character. I can only guess it to belong to the middle period of his career; say, the reign of Henry V. We have not yet obtained sufficient data for the arrangement of Lydgate's poems.

§ 38. Lines 121–127 are here printed for the first time. In the old editions, l. 120 is succeeded by l. 128, with the result that *Sion* (120) would not rime with *set afere* (129); but the scribe of the Ashmole MS. was equal to the emergency, for he altered l. 129 so as to make it end with *fuyrless thou sette vppon*, which is mere nonsense. Thynne has *fyrelesse fyre set on*, which is just a little better.

This addition of seven lines was due to my fortunate discovery of a new MS.; for which I was indebted to the excellent MS. 'Index of First Lines' in the British Museum. This told me that a poem (hitherto unrecognised) existed in MS. Sloane 1212, of which the first line is 'A thousand stories,' &c. On examining the MS., it turned out to be a copy, on paper, of Hoccleve's De Regimine Principum, with four leaves of vellum at the beginning, and two more at the end, covered with writing of an older character. The two vellum leaves at the end were then transposed, but have since been set right, at my suggestion. They contain a few lines of the conclusion of some other piece, followed by the unique *complete* copy of the present Balade. This copy turned out to be much the best, and restored several of the readings. Indeed, the Ashmole MS. is very imperfect, having in it a lacuna of eight stanzas (ll. 64–119). I am thus able to give quite a presentable text.

The correction that most interested me was one in l. 134, where the Ashmole MS. and Thynne have *probatyf piscyne*. On June 5, 1896, I read a paper at the Philological Society, in which (among other things) I pointed out that the right reading must certainly be *probatik*. The very next day I found the Sloane MS.; and behold, its reading was *probatyk*! It is not often that a 'conjectural emendation' is confirmed, on unimpeachable authority, within twenty-four hours.

Another remarkable correction is that of *dyamaunt* for *dyametre* in l. 87. It was all very well to compare Our Lady to a diamond; but to call her a *diameter* (as in all the editions) is a little too bad. Again, in l. 121 (now first printed) we have the remarkable expression *punical pome* for a pomegranate, which is worthy of notice; and in l. 123 we find a new word, *agnelet*, which is not to be found in the New English Dictionary.

All the printed editions print the next piece as if it *formed a part* of the present one; but they have absolutely no point in common beyond the fact of having a common authorship.

§ 39. XI. To my Soverain Lady.

In all the old editions, this piece forms part of the preceding, though it is obviously distinct from it, when attention is once drawn to the fact. Instead of being addressed, like no. X, to the Virgin, it is addressed to a lady whose name the poet wishes to commend (l. 7); and from whom he is parted (51); whereas two lovers ought to be together, if they wish to live 'well merry' (64). Her goodly fresh face is a merry mirror (73); and he has chosen her as his Valentine (111).

It is evidently a conventional complimentary poem, written to please some lady of rank or of high renown (93), one, in fact, who is 'of women chief princesse' (70). It is prettily expressed, and does Lydgate some credit, being a favourable specimen of his more playful style; I wish we had more of the same kind. L. 68—'Let him go love, and see wher [*whether*] it be game'— is excellent.

I shall here submit to the reader a pure guess, for what it is worth. My impression is that this piece, being a complimentary Valentine, was suggested by queen Katherine's visit to England; the lover whose passion is here described being no other than king Henry V, who was parted from his queen for a week. The pair arrived at Dover on Feb. 2, 1421, and Henry went on to London, arriving on Feb. 14; the queen did not arrive till Feb. 21, just in time for her coronation on Feb. 23.

This hypothesis satisfies several conditions. It explains why the lover's *English* is not good enough to praise the lady; why so many French lines are quoted; the significant allusion to the lily, i.e. the lily of France, in l. 16; the lover's consolation found in English roundels (40); the expression 'cheef princesse' in l. 70; and the very remarkable exclamation of *Salve, regina*, in l. 83, which doubtless made Thynne imagine that the poem was addressed to the Virgin Mary. The expression 'for your departing' in l. 105 does not necessarily mean 'on account of your departure from me'; it is equally in accordance with Middle-English usage to suppose that it means 'on account of your separation from me'; see *Depart* and *Departing* in the New English Dictionary.

It is well known that Lydgate provided the necessary poetry for the entry of Henry VI into London in Feb. 1432.

Some resemblances to Chaucer are pointed out in the Notes. The most interesting circumstance about this poem is that the author quotes, at the end of his third stanza, the first line of 'Merciles Beautè'; this is a strong point in favour of the attribution of that poem to his master.

This piece is distinguished from the preceding by the difference of its subject; by the difference in the character of the metre (there is here no alliteration); and, most significant of all, by its absence from MS. Ashmole 59 and MS. Sloane 1212, both of which contain the preceding piece. The two poems may have been brought together, in the MS. which Thynne followed, by the accident of being written about the same time.

§ 40. XII. Ballad of Good Counsel.

The title of this piece in Stowe's edition stands as follows:
'A balade of good counseile, translated out of Latin verses into
Englishe, by dan Iohn lidgat cleped the monke of Buri.' What
were the Latin verses here referred to, I have no means of
ascertaining.

This Ballad is eminently characteristic of Lydgate's style, and
by no means the worst of its kind. When he once gets hold of
a refrain that pleases him, he canters merrily along till he has
absolutely no more to say. I think he must have enjoyed writing
it, and that he wrote it to please himself.

He transgresses one of Chaucer's canons in ll. 79-82; where
he rimes *hardy* with *foly* and *flatery*. The two latter words are,
in Chaucer, *foly-ĕ* and *flatery-ĕ*, and never rime with a word like
hardy, which has no final *-e*.

Lydgate is very fond of what may be called *catalogues*; he
begins by enumerating every kind of possibility. You may be
rich, or strong, or prudent, &c.; or fair (22) or ugly (24); you
may have a wife (29), or you may not (36); you may be fat (43),
or you may be lean (46); or staid (57), or holy (64); your dress
may be presentable (71), or poor (72), or middling (73); you may
speak much (78) or little (80); and so on; for it is hard to come
to an end. At l. 106, he begins all over again with womankind;
and the conclusion is, that you should govern your tongue, and
never listen to slander.

Thynne's text is not very good; the MSS. are somewhat better.
He makes the odd mistake of printing *Holynesse beautie* for
Eleynes beaute (115); but Helen had not much to do with holiness.
Two of the stanzas (71-7 and 106-112) are now printed for the
first time, as they occur in the MSS. only. Indeed, MS. H.
(Harl. 2251) is the sole authority for the former of these two
stanzas.

§ 41. XIII. Beware of Doubleness.

This is a favourable example of Lydgate's better style; and
is written with unusual smoothness, owing to the shortness of the
lines. It was first printed in 1561. There is a better copy in
the Fairfax MS., which has been taken as the basis of the text.
The copy in MS. Ashmole 59 is very poor. The title—'Balade

made by Lydgate'— occurs in MS. Addit. 16165. Stowe, being
unacquainted with the phrase *ambes as* (l. 78), though it occurs
in Chaucer, turned *ambes* into *lombes*, after which he wrongly
inserted a comma; and *lombes* appears, accordingly, in all former
editions, with a comma after it. What sense readers have hitherto
made of this line, I am at a loss to conjecture.

§ 42. XIV. A Balade: Warning Men, etc.

First printed by Stowe in 1561, from the MS. in Trinity College
Library, marked R. 3. 19, which I have used in preference to the
printed edition.

There is another, and more complete copy in the same library,
marked O. 9. 38, which has contributed some excellent corrections.
Moreover, it gives a better arrangement of stanzas three and four,
which the old editions transpose. More than this, it contains
a unique stanza (36–42), which has not been printed before.

The poem also occurs in Shirley's MS. Harl. 2251, which
contains a large number of poems by Lydgate; and is there
followed by another poem of seven stanzas, attributed to Lydgate.
That the present poem is Lydgate's, cannot well be doubted; it
belongs to the same class of his poems as no. XII above. I find
it attributed to him in the reprint of 'Chaucer's Poems' by
Chalmers, in 1810.

The substitution of the contracted and idiomatic form *et* for
the later form *eteth* is a great improvement. It is due to MS.
O. 9. 38, where the scribe first wrote *ette*, but was afterwards so
weak as to 'correct' it to *etyth*. But this 'correction' just ruins
the refrain. *Et* was no doubt becoming archaic towards the
middle of the fifteenth century.

Two variations upon the last stanza occur in the Bannatyne
MS., fol. 258, back; see the print by the Hunterian Club, 1879,
pp. 754, 755.

§ 43. XV. Three Sayings.

First printed by Stowe; I know of no MS. copy. The first two
Sayings are attributed to Lydgate; so we may as well credit him
with the third. The second expresses the same statements as the
first, but varies somewhat in form; both are founded upon a Latin
line which occurs in MS. Fairfax 16 (fol. 196) and in MS. Harl.

7578 (fol. 20), and runs as follows :—'Quatuor infatuant, honor, etas, femina, uinum.'

Note that these Three Sayings constitute the *only* addition made by Stowe to Thynne in 'Part I' of Stowe's edition. See nos. 28, 29, 30 in vol. i. p. 32. Stowe introduced them *in order to fill a blank half-column* between nos. 27 and 31.

§ 44. XVI. La Belle Dame sans Mercy.

First printed in Thynne's Chaucer (1532). Tyrwhitt first pointed out that it could not possibly be his, seeing that Alan Chartier's poem with the same name, whence the English version was made, could not have been written in Chaucer's lifetime. Chartier was born in 1386, and was only fourteen years old at the time of Chaucer's death. Tyrwhitt further stated that the author's name, Sir Richard Ros, was plainly given in MS. Harl. 372, fol. 61, where the poem has this title :—'La Belle Dame Sanz Mercy. Translatid out of Frenche by Sir Richard Ros.' I have not been able to find the date of the French original, as there is no modern edition of Chartier's poems ; but it can hardly have been written before 1410, when the poet was only twenty-four years old ; and the date of the translation must be later still. But we are not wholly left to conjecture in this matter. A short notice of Sir Richard Ros appeared in Englische Studien, X. 206, written by H. Gröhler, who refers us to his dissertation 'Ueber Richard Ros' mittelenglische übersetzung des gedichtes von Alain Chartier La Belle Dame sans Mercy,' published at Breslau in 1886 ; of which Dr. Gröhler has most obligingly sent me a copy, whence several of my Notes have been derived. He tells us, in this article, that his dissertation was founded on the copy of the poem in MS. Harl. 372, which (in 1886) he believed to be unique ; whereas he had since been informed that there are three other MSS., viz. Camb. Ff. 1. 6, Trin. Coll. Camb. R. 3. 19, and Fairfax 16 ; and further, that the Trinity MS. agrees with the Harleian as to misarrangement of the subject-matter[1]. He also proposed to give a new edition of the poem in Englische Studien, but I am unable to find it ; and Dr. Kölbing courteously informs me that it never appeared.

---

[1] Which is not the case ; the text in the Trinity MS. is in the correct order.

Dr. Gröhler further tells us, that Mr. Joseph Hall, of Manchester, had sent him some account, extracted from the county history of Leicestershire by Nichols, of the family of Roos or Ros, who were lords of Hamlake and Belvoir in that county. According to Nichols, the Sir Richard Ros who was presumably the poet, was the second son of Sir Thomas Ros; and Sir Thomas was the second son of Sir W. Ros, who married Margaret, daughter of Sir John Arundel. If this be right, we gain the further information that Sir Richard was born in 1429[1], and is known to have been alive in 1450, when he was twenty-one years old.

The dates suit very well, as they suggest that the English poem was written, probably, between 1450 and 1460, or at the beginning of the second half of the fifteenth century; which sufficiently agrees with the language employed and with the probable age of the MSS. The date assigned in the New English Dictionary, s. v. *Currish*, is 1460; which cannot be far wrong. It can hardly be much later.

§ 45. The above notice also suggests that, as Sir Richard Ros was of a Leicestershire family, the dialect of the piece may, originally at least, have been North Leicestershire. Belvoir is situate in the N.E. corner of Leicestershire, not far from Grantham in Lincolnshire, and at no great distance from the birthplace of Robert of Brunne. It is well known that Robert of Brunne wrote in a variety of the Midland dialect which coincides, to a remarkable extent, with the form of the language which has become the standard literary English. Now it is easily seen that La Belle Dame has the same peculiarity, and I venture to think that, on this account, it is worth special attention. If we want to see a specimen of what the Midland literary dialect was like in the middle of the fifteenth century, it is here that we may find it. Many of the stanzas are, in fact, remarkably modern, both in grammar and expression; we have only to alter the spelling, and there is nothing left to explain. Take for example the last stanza on p. 301 (ll. 77-84):—

> 'In this great thought, sore troubled in my mind,
> Alone thus rode I all the morrow-tide,
> Till, at the last, it happèd me to find
> The place wherein I cast me to abide

---

[1] Richard Ros, born March 8, 1428-9; Nichols, Hist. of Leicestershire, vol. ii. p. 37.

When that I had no further for to ride.
And as I went my lodging to purvey,
Right soon I heard, but little me beside,
In a gardén, where minstrels gan to play.'

A large number of stanzas readily lend themselves to similar treatment; and this is quite enough to dissociate the poem from Chaucer. The great difficulty about modernising Chaucer is, as every one knows, his use of the final -e as a distinct syllable; but we may search a whole page of La Belle Dame without finding anything of the kind. When Sir Richard's words have an extra syllable, it is due to the suffix -es or the suffix -ed; and even these are not remarkably numerous; we do not arrive at *cloth-ĕs*, a plural in -es, before l. 22; and, in the course of the first four stanzas, all the words in -ed are *awak-ed*, *nak-ed*, *vex-ed*, *tourn-ed*, and *bold-ed*, none of which would be surprising to a student of Elizabethan poetry. That there was something of a Northern element in Sir Richard's language appears from the rime of *long-es* with *song-es*, in ll. 53–55; where *longes* is the third person singular of the present tense; but modern English has *belongs*, with the same suffix! Again, he constantly uses the Northern possessive pronoun *their*; but modern English does the same!

§ 46. Another remarkable point about the poem is the perfect smoothness and regularity of the metre in a large number of lines, even as judged by a modern standard. The first line—' Half in a dream, not fully well awaked '—might, from a metrical point of view, have been written yesterday. It is a pity that the poem is somewhat dull, owing to its needless prolixity; but this is not a little due to Alan Chartier. Sir Richard has only eight stanzas of his own, four at the beginning, and four at the end; and it is remarkable that these are in the seven-line stanza, while the rest of the stanzas have eight lines, like their French original, of which I here give the first stanza, from the Paris edition of 1617, p. 502. (See l. 29 of the English version.)

' N'agueres chevauchant pensoye,
Comme homme triste et douloureux,
Au dueil où il faut que ie soye
Le plus dolant des amoureux;
Puisque par son dart rigoureux
La mort me tolli ma Maistresse,
Et me laissa seul langoureux
En la conduicte de tristesse.'

I have cited in the Notes a few passages of the original text which help to explain the translation.

§ 47. The text in Thynne is a good one, and it seemed convenient to make it the basis of the edition; but it has been carefully controlled by collation with MS. Ff. 1. 6, which is, in some respects, the best MS. I am not sure that Thynne always followed his MS.; he may have collated some other one, as he professes in some cases to have done. MS. Ff. 1. 6, the Trinity MS., and Thynne's principal MS. form one group, which we may call A; whilst the Fairfax and Harleian MSS. form a second group, which we may call B: and of these, group A is the better. The MSS. in group B sadly transpose the subject-matter, and give the poem in the following order; viz. lines 1–428, 669–716, 525–572, 477–524, 621–668, 573–620, 429–476, 717–856. The cause of this dislocation is simple enough. It means that the B-group MSS. were copied from one in which three leaves, each containing six stanzas, were misarranged. The three leaves were placed one within the other, to form a sheet, and were written upon. Then the outer pair of these leaves was turned inside out, whilst the second and third pair changed places. This can easily be verified by making a little book of six leaves and numbering each page with the numbers 429–452, 453–476, 477–500, 501–524, &c. (i. e. with 24 lines on a page, ending with 716), and then misarranging the leaves in the manner indicated.

The copy in MS. Harl. 372 was printed, just as it stands, by Dr. Furnivall, in his volume entitled Political, Religious, and Love Poems, published for the E. E. T. S. in 1866; at p. 52. The text is there, accordingly, misarranged as above stated.

There is another MS. copy, as has been said above, in MS. Trin. Coll. Camb. R. 3. 19; but I have not collated it. It seems to be closely related to MS. Ff., and to present no additional information. Not only do the MSS. of the A-group contain the text in the right order, but they frequently give the better readings. Thus, in l. 47, we have the odd line—'My *pen* coud never have knowlege what it ment'; as given in MS. Ff., the Trinity MS., and Thynne. The word *pen* is altered to *eyen* in MSS. H. and F.; nevertheless, it is perfectly right, for the French original has *plume*; see the Note on the line. Other examples are given in the Notes.

In l. 174, MS. Ff. alone has the right reading, *apert*. I had
made up my mind that this was the right reading even before
consulting that MS., because the old reading —'One wyse nor
other, prevy nor *perte*'—is so extremely harsh. There is no
sense in using the clipped form of the word when the true *and
usual* form will scan so much better. See C. T., F 531, Ho.
Fame, 717. The Trinity MS. gets out of the difficulty by a
material alteration of the line, so that it there becomes—'In any
wyse, nether preuy nor perte.'

§ 48. XVII. The Testament of Cresseid.

I do not suppose this was ever supposed to be Chaucer's
even by Thynne. Line 64—'Quha wait gif all that Chaucer
wrait was trew?'—must have settled the question from the first.
No doubt Thynne added it simply as a pendant to Troilus,
and he must have had a copy before him in the Northern
dialect, which he modified as well as he could. Nevertheless,
he gives us *can* for the Southern *gan* in l. 6, *wrate* for *wrote*
in l. 64, and has many similar Northern forms.

The poem was printed at Edinburgh in 1593 with the author's
name. The title is as follows—¶ Tħe Ǯestament of CRESSEID,
Compylit be M. Robert Henrysone, Sculemai-ster in Dunfer-
meling. Imprentit at Œdin = burgh be Henrie Charteris.
MD. XCIII. The text is in 4to, ten leaves, black-letter. Only one
copy has been preserved, which is now in the British Museum;
but it was reprinted page for page in the volume presented by
Mr. Chalmers to the Bannatyne Club in 1824. The present
edition is from this reprint, with very few modifications, such
as *sh* for *sch*, and final *-y* for final *-ie* in immaterial cases. All
other modifications are accounted for in the footnotes below.
No early MS. copy is known; there was once a copy in the
Asloan MS., but the leaves containing it are lost.

Thynne's print must have been a good deal altered from the
original, to make it more intelligible. It is odd to find him
altering *quhisling* (20) to *whiskyng*, and *ringand* (144) to *tynkyng*.
I note all Thynne's variations that are of any interest. He must
have been much puzzled by *aneuch in* (which he seems to have
regarded as one word and as a past participle) before he turned
it into *enewed* (110). But in some cases Thynne gives us real
help, as I will now point out.

In l. 48, E. (the Edinburgh edition) has—'Quhill Esperus reioisit him agane'; where *Esperus* gives no good sense. But Thynne prints *esperous*, which at once suggests *esperans* (hope), as opposed to *wanhope* in the preceding line.

In l. 155, E. has *frosnit*, which Laing interprets 'frozen,' as if the pp. of *freeze* could have both a strong and weak pp. suffix at the same moment! But Thynne has *frounsed*, evidently put for *fronsit*, as used elsewhere by Henryson in The Fable of the Paddock and the Mous, l. 43:—'The Mous beheld unto her *fronsit* face.' A printer's error of *sn* for *ns* is not surprising.

In ll. 164, 178, 260, E. has *gyis* or *gyse*; but Thynne has preserved the true Chaucerian word *gyte*, which the printer evidently did not understand. It is true that in l. 164 he turned it into *gate*; but when he found it recur, he let it alone.

In l. 205, E. has *upricht* (!); which Thynne corrects.

In l. 290, Th. has *iniure* for *iniurie*, and I think he is right, though I have let *injurie* stand; *iniure* is Chaucer's form (Troil. iii. 1018), and it suits the scansion better.

In l. 382, Thynne corrects *Unto* to *To*; and in l. 386, has *Beuer* for *bawar*. In l. 441, he has *syder* for *ceder*. In l. 501, he has *plyte* for *plye*, where a letter may have dropped out in E.; but see the note (p. 525). In l. 590, his reading *tokenyng* suggests that *takning* (as in E.) should be *takining* or *takinning*; the line will then scan. The contracted form *taikning* occurs, however, in l. 232, where the word is less emphatic.

Note further, that in l. 216 the original must have had *Philogoney* (see the Note). This appears in the astonishing forms *Philologie* (E.), and *Philologee* (Th.). Laing prints *Phlegonie*, which will neither scan nor rime, without any hint that he is departing from his exemplar. All his corrections are made silently, so that one cannot tell where they occur without reference to the original.

For further information concerning Robert Henryson, schoolmaster of Dunfermline, see the preface to David Laing's edition of The Poems and Fables of Robert Henryson, Edinburgh, 1865; and Morley's English Writers, 1890, vol. vi. p. 250. He is supposed to have been born about 1425, and to have died about 1500. On Sept. 10, 1462, the Venerable Master Robert Henrysone, Licentiate in Arts and Bachelor in Decrees, was incorporated or admitted a member of the newly founded university

of Glasgow ; and he is known to have been a notary public.
Perhaps The Testament of Cresseid was written about 1460.   It
is a rather mature performance, and is his best piece.   Perhaps
it is the best piece in the present volume.

§ 49. XVIII. THE CUCKOO AND THE NIGHTINGALE.

Of this piece there are several MSS., which fall into two main
classes : (A)—Ff. (Ff. 1. 6, in the Camb. Univ. Library); T.
(Tanner 346); Th. (MS. used by Thynne, closely allied to T.) ;
and (B)—F. (Fairfax 16), and B. (Bodley 638), which are closely
allied. There is also S. (Selden, B. 24) imperfect, which has
readings of its own [1].   Of these groups, A is the better, and MS.
Ff. is, in some respects, the most important.   Nevertheless, MS.
Ff. has never been collated hitherto, so that I am able to give
a somewhat improved text.   For example, in all former editions
lines 12 and 13 are transposed.   In l. 180, the reading *haire* (as
in Bell and Morris) is somewhat comic (see the Note).   In l. 203,
MS. Ff. restores the true reading *hit*, i. e. hitteth.   Bell, by some
accident, omits the stanza in which this word occurs.   In vol. i.
p. 39, I took occasion to complain of the riming of *now* with
rescow-e in ll. 228-9, according to Bell.   The right reading, however, is not *now*, but *avow-e*, which rimes well enough.   MS. Selden
has *allowe*, which Morris follows, though it is clearly inferior and
is unsupported.   On the other hand, MS. Selden correctly, and
alone, has *leve* in l. 237 ; but the confusion between *e* and *o* is
endless, so that the false reading *loue* creates no surprise.

This poem is very interesting, and has deservedly been a
favourite one.   It is therefore a great pleasure to me to have
found the author's name.   This is given at the end of the poem
in MS. Ff. (the best MS., but hitherto neglected), where we find,
in firm distinct letters, in the same handwriting as the poem itself,
the remark—**Explicit Clanvowe**.   Remembering that the true
title of the poem is ' The Book of Cupid, God of Love [2],'
I applied to Dr. Furnivall, asking him if he had met with the
name.   He at once referred me to his preface to Hoccleve's

---

[1] There is *no* copy in MS. Harl. 7333, as said by error in vol. i. p. 39.

[2] There is no authority, except Thynne, for the title The Cuckoo and the
Nightingale.   It has been repeated in all the printed editions, but does not
appear in any MS.

Works, p. x, where Sir John Clanvowe and Thomas Hoccleve
are both mentioned in the same document (about A. D. 1385.
But Sir John Clanvowe died in 1391, and therefore could not
have imitated the title of Hoccleve's poem, which was not written
till 1402. Our poet was probably Sir Thomas Clanvowe, concerning whom several particulars are known, and who must have
been a well-known personage at the courts of Richard II and
Henry IV. We learn from Wylie's Hist. of Henry IV, vol. iii.
p. 261, that he was one of twenty-five knights who accompanied
John Beaufort (son of John of Gaunt) to Barbary in 1390. This
Sir Thomas favoured the opinions of the Lollards, but was
nevertheless a friend of 'Prince Hal,' at the time when the
prince was still friendly to freethinkers. He seems to have
accompanied the prince in the mountains of Wales; see Wylie,
as above, iii. 333. In 1401, he is mentioned as being one of
'vi Chivalers' in the list of esquires who were summoned to
a council by king Henry IV; see the Acts of the Privy Council,
ed. Nicolas, temp. Henry IV, p. 162. (It may be noted that Sir
John Clanvowe was a witness, in 1385, to the will of the widow
of the Black Prince; see Testamenta Vetusta, ed. Nicolas.)

§ 50. It now becomes easy to explain the reference to the
queen at Woodstock, which has never yet been accounted for.
The poem begins with the words—'*The God of Love!* Ah
benedicite,' quoted from Chaucer, the title of the poem being
'The Book of Cupid, *God of Love*,' as has been said; and this
title was imitated from Hoccleve's poem of 1402. But there was
no queen of England after Henry's accession till Feb. 7, 1403,
when the king married Joan of Navarre; and it was she who
held as a part of her dower the manor and park of Woodstock;
see Wylie, as above, ii. 284. Hence the following hypothesis
will suit the facts—namely, that the poem, imitating Chaucer's
manner, and having a title imitated from Hoccleve's poem of
1402, was written by Sir Thomas Clanvowe, who held Lollard
opinions[1] and was a friend (at one time) of Henry of Monmouth.
And it was addressed to Joan of Navarre, Henry's stepmother,
queen of England from 1403 to 1413, who held as a part of her

---

[1] 'In Hereford and the far West, not Oldcastle alone, but the Actons,
Cheynes, Clanvowes, Greindors, and many great gentlemen of birth, had begun
to mell of Lollardy and drink the gall of heresy.'—Wylie, Hist. of Henry IV,
vol. iii. p. 295. Sir T. Clanvowe was alive in 1404 (Test. Vetusta).

dower the manor of Woodstock. If so, we should expect it to
have been written before April, 1410, when Thomas Badby, the
Lollard, was executed in the presence of the prince of Wales.
Further, as it was probably written early rather than late in this
period, I should be inclined to date it in 1403; possibly in May,
as it relates so much to the time of spring.

I may add that the Clanvowes were a Herefordshire family,
from the neighbourhood of Wigmore. The only remarkable non-
Chaucerian word in the poem is the verb *greden*, to cry out
(A.S. *grǣdan*); a word found in many dialects, and used by
Layamon, Robert of Gloucester, Langland, and Hoccleve.

The poem is written in a light and pleasing style, which
Wordsworth has fairly reproduced. The final *-e* is suppressed in
assay-e (l. 52). The non-Chaucerian rimes are few, viz. *gren-e* and
sen-e as riming with *been* (61-5), shewing that Clanvowe cut down
those dissyllables to *green* and *seen*. And further, the forms
ron and *mon* are employed, in order to rime with *upon* (81-5);
whereas Chaucer only has the form *man*; whilst of *ran* I remember
no example at the end of a line [1].

. § 51. But there is one point about Clanvowe's verse which
renders it, for the fifteenth century, quite unique. In imitating
Chaucer's use of the final *-e*, he employs this suffix with unprece-
dented freedom, and rather avoids than seeks elision. This gives
quite a distinctive character to his versification, and is very
noticeable when attention has once been drawn to it. If, for
example, we compare it with the Parliament of Foules, which it
most resembles in general character, we find the following results.
If, in the Cuckoo and Nightingale, we observe the first 21 lines,
we shall find (even if we omit the example of *hy-e* in l. 4, and all
the examples of final *-e* at the end of a line) the following clear
examples of its use :—*low-e*, *lyk-e*, *hard-e*, *sek-e*, *hol-e* (twice),
mak-e, *hav-e*, *wys-e*, *proud-e*, *grev-e*, *trew-e*, *hert-e*, i. e. 13 examples,
besides the 5 examples of final *-en* in *mak-en*, *bind-en*, *unbind-en*,
bound-en, *destroy-en*. But in the first 21 lines of the Parliament
of Foules there are only 2 examples of the final *-e* in the middle
of a line, viz. *lust-e* (15) and *long-e* (21), whilst of the final *-en*
there is none. The difference between 18 and 2 must strike even

---

[1] The MSS. have *ran* in C. T., B 661. *Man* rimes with *can* in Parl. Foules,
479, and with *began* in the same, 563.

the most inexperienced reader, when it is once brought under his notice. However, it is an extreme case.

Yet again, if the *last* 21 lines in the Cuckoo be compared with ll. 659–679 of the Parliament (being the *last* 21 lines, if we dismiss the roundel and the stanza that follows it), we find in the former 7 examples of final *-e* and 2 of *-en*, or 9 in all, whilst in Chaucer there are 7 of final *-e*, and 1 of *-en*, or 8 in all; and this also happens to be an extreme case in the other direction, owing to the occurrence in the former poem of the words *egle*, *maple*, and *chambre*, which I have not taken into account.

This suggests that, to make sure, we must compare much longer passages. In the whole of the Cuckoo, I make about 120 such cases of final *-e*, and 23 such cases of final *-en*, or 143 in all. In 290 lines of the Parliament of Foules, I make about 68 and 19 such cases respectively; or about 87 in all. Now the difference between 143 and 87 is surely very marked.

The cause of this result is obvious, viz. that Chaucer makes a more frequent use of elision. In the first 21 lines of the Parl. of Foules, we find elisions of *men'*, *sor'*, *wak'*, *oft'* (twice), *red'* (twice), *spek'*, *fast'*, *radd'*; i.e. 10 examples; added to which, Chaucer has *joy(e)*, *love*, *knowe*, *usage*, *boke*, at the cæsura, and suppresses the *e* in *write* (written). But in ll. 1– 1, Clanvowe has (in addition to *love*, *make*, *lowe*, *make* (twice), *gladde* at the cæsura) only 3 examples of true elision, viz. *fressh'*, *tell'*, and *mak'* (15).

And further, we seldom find *two* examples of the use of the final *-e* in the *same* line in Chaucer. I do not observe any instance, in the Parl. of Foules, till we arrive at l. 94 :—'Took rest that mad-*e* me to slep-*e* faste.' But in Clanvowe they are fairly common. Examples are: Of seke-*e* folk ful hol-*e* (7); For every trew-*e* gentil hert-*e* free (21); That any hert-*e* shuld-*e* slepy be (44); I went-*e* forth alon-*e* bold-e-ly (59); They coud-*e* that servyc-*e* al by rote (71); and the like. In l. 73, we have even *three* examples in *one* line; Some song-*e* loud-*e*, as they hadd-*e* playned. From all of which it appears that the critics who have assigned the Cuckoo to Chaucer have taken no pains whatever to check their opinion by any sort of analysis. They have trusted to their own mere opinion, without looking the facts in the face.

§ 52. I will point out yet one more very striking difference. We know that Chaucer sometimes employs headless lines, such as : Twénty bókes át his béddes héed. But he does so sparingly, especially in his Minor Poems. But in the Cuckoo, they are not uncommon ; see, e. g. lines 16, 50, 72, 100, 116, 118, 146, 152, 153, 154, 155, 156, 157. 158, 161, 166, 205, 232, 242, 252, 261, 265, 268. It is true that, in Morris's edition, lines 72, 146, 153, 161, and 205 are slightly altered ; but in no case can I find that the alteration is authorised. And even then, this does not get rid of the *five consecutive* examples in ll. 154–158, which cannot be explained away. Once more, I repeat, the critics have failed to use their powers of observation.

I think the poem may still be admired, even if it be allowed that Clanvowe wrote it some three years after Chaucer's death.

§ 53. At any rate, it was admired by so good a judge of poetry as John Milton, who of course possessed a copy of it in the volume which was so pleasantly called ' The Works of Chaucer.' That his famous sonnet ' To the Nightingale ' owed something to Clanvowe, I cannot doubt. ' Thou with fresh hope the lover's heart dost fill ' is, in part, the older poet's theme ; see ll. 1–30, 149–155, 191–192. Even his first line reminds one of ll. 77, 288. If Milton writes of May, so does Clanvowe ; see ll. 20, 23, 34, 55, 70, 230, 235, 242 ; note especially l. 230. But the real point of contact is in the lines—

> ' Thy liquid notes that close the eye of day,
> First heard before the shallow cuckoo's bill,
> Portend success in love . . .
> Now timely sing, ere the rude bird of hate
> Foretell my hopeless doom in some grove nigh ;
> As thou from year to year hast sung too late
> For my relief, yet hadst no reason why :
> Whether the Muse or Love call thee his mate,
> Both them I serve, and of their train am I.'

With which compare :—

> ' That it were good to here the nightingale
> Rather than the lewde cukkow singe ': (49).
> ' A litel hast thou been to longe henne ;
> For here hath been the lew[e]de cukkow,
> And songen songes rather than hast thou ': (102).
> ' Ye, quod she, and be thou not amayed,
> Though thou have herd the cukkow er than me.
> For, if I live, it shal amended be
> The nexte May, if I be not affrayed ': (232).
> ' And I wol singe oon of my songes newe
> For love of thee, as loude as I may crye ': (247).
> ' For in this worlde is noon so good servyse
> To every wight that gentil is of kinde ': (149).

§ 54. XIX. Envoy to Alison.

This piece has always hitherto been printed *without any title*, and is made to follow The Cuckoo and the Nightingale, as if there were some sort of connection between them. This is probably because it happens to follow that poem in the Fairfax and Tanner MSS., and probably did so in the MS. used by Thynne, which has a striking resemblance to the Tanner MS. However, the poem is entirely absent from the Cambridge, Selden, and Bodley MSS., proving that there is no connection with the preceding poem, from which it differs very widely in style, in language, and in metre.

I call it an Envoy to Alison. For first, it is an Envoy [1], as it refers to the author's 'lewd book,' which it recommends to a lady. What the book is, no one can say; but it may safely be conjectured that it was of no great value. And secondly, the lady's name was Alison, as shewn by the acrostic in lines 22–27; and the author has recourse to almost ludicrous efforts, in order to secure the first four letters of the name.

Briefly, it is a very poor piece; and my chief object in reprinting it is to shew how unworthy it is of Clanvowe, not to mention Chaucer. We have no right even to assign it to Lydgate. And its date may be later than 1450.

§ 55. XX. The Flower and the Leaf.

This piece many 'critics' would assign to Chaucer, merely because they like it. This may be sentiment, but it is not criticism; and, after all, a desire to arrive at the truth should be of more weight with us than indulgence in ignorant credulity.

It is of some consequence to learn, first of all, that it is hardly possible to separate this piece from the next. The authoress of one was the authoress of the other. That The Assembly of Ladies is longer and duller, and has not held its own in popular estimation, is no sound argument to the contrary; for it is only partially true. Between the first eleven stanzas of the Assembly and the first eleven stanzas of the present poem, there is a strong general resemblance, and not much to choose. Other stanzas

---

[1] Perhaps, more strictly, a dedication, the true envoy consisting of the last six lines only. But it is no great matter.

of the Assembly that are well up to the standard of the Flower will be found in lines 456–490, 511–539. The reason of the general inferiority of the Assembly lies chiefly in the choice of the subject; it was meant to interest some medieval household, but it gave small scope for retaining the reader's attention, and must be held to be a failure.

The links connecting these poems are so numerous that I must begin by asking the reader to let me denote The Flower and the Leaf by the letter **F** (= Flower), and The Assembly of Ladies by the letter **A** (= Assembly).

The first point is that (with the sole exception of the Nutbrown Maid) no English poems exist, as far as I remember, written previously to 1500, and purporting to be written by a woman. In the case of F. and A., this is assumed throughout. When the author of F. salutes a certain fair lady, the lady replies—'*My doughter, gramercy*'; 462. And again she says, '*My fair doughter*'; 467, 500, 547. The author of A. says she was one of five ladies; 5–7, 407. Again, she was a woman; 18. The author of A. and some other ladies salute Lady Countenance, who in reply says 'fair sisters'; 370. Again, she and others salute a lady-chamberlain, who replies by calling them 'sisters'; 450; &c.

The poem A. is supposed to be an account of a dream, told by the authoress to a gentleman; with the exception of this gentleman, all the characters of the poem are *ladies*; and hence its title. The poem F. is not quite so exclusive, but it comes very near it; all the principal characters are ladies, and the chief personages are queens, viz. the queen of the Leaf and the queen of the Flower. The 'world of ladies' in l. 137 take precedence of the Nine Worthies, who were merely men. A recognition of this fact makes the whole poem much clearer.

But the most characteristic thing is the continual reference to colours, dresses, ornaments, and decorations. In F., we have descriptions of, or references to, white surcoats, velvet, seams, emeralds, purfils, colours, sleeves, trains, pearls, diamonds, a fret of gold, chaplets of leaves, chaplets of woodbine, chaplets of *agnus-castus*, a crown of gold, thundering trumpets, the treasury of Prester John, white cloaks, chaplets of oak, banners of Tartary-silk, more pearls, collars, escutcheons, kings-of-arms, cloaks of white cloth, crowns set with pearls, rubies, sapphires, and diamonds. Then there is a company all clad in one suit (or livery); heralds

and poursuivants, more chaplets and escutcheons, men in armour
with cloth of gold and horse-trappings, with bosses on their bridles
and peitrels—it is surely needless to go on, though we have only
arrived at l. 246.

In A., we have much the same sort of thing all over again,
though it does not set in before l. 83. Then we meet with
blue colours, an embroidered gown, and a purfil with a device.
After a respite, we begin again at l. 206—'Her gown was blue';
and the lady wore a French motto. Diligence tells the authoress
that she looks well in her new blue gown (259). At l. 305, there
is another blue gown, furred with gray, with a motto on the sleeve;
and there are plenty more mottoes to follow. At l. 451 we come
to a paved floor, and walls made of beryl and crystal, engraved
with stories; next, a well-apparelled chair or throne, on five stages,
wrought of 'cassidony,' with four pommels of gold, and set with
sapphires; a cloth of estate, wrought with the needle (486); cloth
of gold (521); a blue gown, with sleeves wrought tabard-wise, of
which the collar and the *vent* (slit in front of the neck) are
described as being like ermine; it was couched with great pearls,
powdered with diamonds, and had sleeves and purfils; then we
come to rubies, enamel, a great balas-ruby, and more of the same
kind. Again, it is useless to go further. Surely these descriptions
of seams, and collars, and sleeves, are due to a woman.

The likeness comes out remarkably in two parallel stanzas.
One of them is from F. 148, and the other from A. 526.

'As grete perles, round and orient,
  Diamondes fyne and rubies rede,
  And many another stoon, of which I want
  The names now; and everich on her hede
  A riche fret of gold, which, without drede,
  Was ful of statly riche stones set;
  And every lady had a chapelet,' &c.

'After a sort the coller and the vent,
  Lyk as ermyne is mad in purfeling;
  With grete perles, ful fyne and orient,
  They were couched, al after oon worching,
  With dyamonds in stede of powdering;
  The sleves and purfilles of assyse;
  They were y-mad [ful] lyke, in every wyse.'

I wonder which the reader prefers; for myself, I have really
no choice.

For I do not see how to choose between such lines as these
following :—

> And on I put my gere and myn array ; F. 26.
> That ye wold help me on with myn aray ; A. 241.
> *or,* So than I dressed me in myn aray ; A. 253.
> As grete perles, round and orient ; F. 148.
> With grete perles, ful fyne and orient ; A. 528.
> And forth they yede togider, twain and twain ; F. 295.
> See how they come togider, twain and twain ; A. 350.
> So long, alas ! and, if that it you plese
> To go with me, I shal do yow the ese ; F. 391.
> And see, what I can do you for to plese,
> I am redy, that may be to your ese ; A. 447.
> I thank you now, in my most humble wyse ; F. 567.
> We thanked her in our most humble wyse ; A. 729.

Besides these striking coincidences in whole lines, there are
a large number of phrases and endings of lines that are common
to the two poems ; such as—*the springing of the day,* F. 25,
A. 218 ; *Which, as me thought,* F. 36, A. 50 ; *wel y-wrought,*
F. 49, A. 165 ; *by mesure,* F. 58, A. 81 ; *I you ensure,* F. 60,
287, A. 52, 199 ; *in this wyse,* F. 98, A. 589 ; *I sat me doun,*
F. 118, A. 77 ; *oon and oon,* F. 144, A. 368, 543, 710 ; *by and by,*
F. 59, 146, A. 87 ; *withouten fail,* F. 369, A. 567, 646 ; *herself
aloon,* F. 458, A. 84 ; *ful demure,* F. 459, A. 82 ; *to put in wryting,*
F. 589, A. 664 ; and others that are printed out in the Notes.

Very characteristic of female authorship is the remark that the
ladies vied with each other as to which looked the best ; a remark
which occurs in *both* poems ; see F. 188, A. 384.

A construction common to both poems is the use of *very* with
an adjective, a construction used by Lydgate, but not by Chaucer ;
examples are *very rede,* F. 35 ; *very good,* F. 10, 315 ; *very round,*
A. 479.

It is tedious to enumerate how much these poems have in
common. They open in a similar way, F. with the description
of a grove, A. with the description of a garden with a maze. In
the eighth stanza of F., we come to ' a herber that benched was ' ;
and in the seventh stanza of A. we come to a similar 'herber,
mad with benches' ; both from The Legend of Good Women.

In F., the authoress has a waking vision of 'a world of ladies'
(137) ; in A. she sees in a dream the 'assembly of ladies.' In
both, she sees an abundance of dresses, and gems, and bright
colours. Both introduce several scraps of French. In both, the

e

authoress has interviews with allegorical or visionary personages, who address her either as daughter or sister. I have little doubt that the careful reader will discover more points of resemblance for himself.

§ 56. The chief appreciable difference between the two poems is that F. was probably written considerably earlier than A. This appears from the more frequent use of the final -e, which the authoress occasionally uses as an archaic embellishment, though she frequently forgets all about it for many stanzas together. In the former poem (F.) there seem to be about 50 examples, whilst in the latter (A.) there are hardly 10 [1]. In almost every case, it is correctly used, owing, no doubt, to tradition or to a perusal of older poetry. The most important cases are the abundant ones in which a final e is omitted where Chaucer would inevitably have inserted it. For example, such a line as F. 195—From the same grove, where the ladyes come out— would become, in Chaucer—From the sam-ë grov-ë wher the ladyes come out—giving at least twelve syllables in the line. The examples of the omission of final -e, where such omission makes a difference to the scansion, are not very numerous, because many such come before a vowel (where they might be elided) or at the cæsura (where they might be tolerated). Still we may note such a case as *green* in l. 109 where Chaucer would have written *gren-e*, giving *a fresh gren-ë laurer-tree*, to the ruin of the scansion. Similar offences against Chaucer's usage are *herd* for *herd-e*, 128 (cf. 191); *spek'* for *spek-e*, 140; *al* for *all-e*, plural, 165; *sight* for *sight-e*, 174; *lyf* for *lyv-e*, 182; *sam'* for *sam-e*, 195; *the tenth* for *the tenth-e*, 203; *gret* for *gret-e*, plural, 214, 225; *red* for *red-e*, 242; *the worst* for *the worst-e*, 255; *yed'* for *yed-e*, 295, 301; *fast* for *fast-e*, 304; *rejoice* for *rejoy-se*, 313; *noise* for *nois-e*, 353; *sonn'* for *son-ne*, 355, 408; *hir fresh* for *hir fres-she*, 357; *laft* for *laft-e*, pt. t., 364; *their greet* for *hir gret-e*, 377; *sick* for *sek-e*, 410; *about* for *about-e*, 411; *to soup* for *to soup-e*, 417; *without* for *without-e*, 423, 549; *the hool* for *the hol-e*, 437; *to know* for *to know-e*, 453; *past* for *pass-ede* or *past-e*, 465; *My fair* for *My fair-e*, vocative, 467, 500; *to tel* for *to tell-e*, 495; *nin'(e)* for *nyn-e*, 502; *imagin'(e)* for *imagin-en*, 525; *they last* for

---

[1] Hence F. 148, 'As gret-e perl-es, round and orient,' reappears in A. 528 without the final -e, in the form : ' With gret' perlés, *ful* fyne and orient.'

they last-e, 562 ; *thy rud(e)* for *thy rud-e*, 595.   Those who believe
that The Flower and the Leaf was written by Chaucer will have
to explain away every one of these cases ; and when they have
done so, there is more to be said.

§ 57. For it is well known that such a word as *sweetly* (96) was
trisyllabic, as *swet-e-ly*, in Chaucer ; C. T., A 221.   Similarly, our
authoress has *trewly* for *trew-e-ly*[1], 130 ; *richly* for *rich-e-ly*, 169 ;
woodbind for *wod-e-bind-e*, 485.   Similar is *ointments* for *oin-e-ments*,
409.   And, moreover, our authoress differs from Chaucer as to
other points of grammar.   Thus she has *Forshronk* as a strong
pp., 358, which ought to be *forshronk-en* or *forshronk-e*.   Still more
marked is her use of *rood* as the *plural* of the past tense, 449,
454, where Chaucer has *rid-en* ; and her use of *began* as a plural,
385, where Chaucer has *bigonn-e*.   Can these things be explained
away also ?   If so, there is more to be said.

§ 58. All the above examples have been made out, without so
much as looking at the rimes.   But the rimes are much harder
to explain away, where they differ from Chaucer's.   Here are
a few specimens.

Pas-se rimes with *was*, 27 ; so it must have been cut down to
pas !   Similarly, *hew-e* has become *hew* ; for it rimes with *grew*,
sing., 32.   *Sight-e* has become *sight*, to rime with *wight*, 37.
Brought should rather be *brought-e*, but it rimes with *wrought*, 48.
Similar difficulties occur in *peyn* (for *peyn-e*), r. w. *seyn* (62) ; *syd'*
for *syd-e*, r. w. *espy'd* for *espy-ed*, 72 ; *eet*, r. w. *sweet* for *swet-e*, 90 ;
not' for *not-e*, r. w. *sot*, 99 ; *busily*, r. w. *aspy'* for *aspy-e*, 106 ;
trewly, r. w. *armony'* for *armony-e*, 130 ; *orient* (*oriant ?*), r. w. *want*
for *want-e*, 148 ; *person* for *person-e*, r. w. *everichon*, 167.   It is
tedious to go on ; let the critic finish the list, if he knows how to
do it.   If not, let him be humble.   For there is more to come.

§ 59. Besides the grammar, there is yet the pronunciation to
be considered ; and here comes in the greatest difficulty of all.
For, in ll. 86–89, we have the unusual rime of *tree* and *be* with
pretily.   This so staggered Dr. Morris, that he was induced to
print the last word as *pretile* ; which raises the difficulty without
explaining it.   For the explanation, the reader should consult the
excellent dissertation by Dr. Curtis on The Romance of Clariodus

---

[1] The examples of *trewly* in Book Duch. 1111, 1151, are doubtful.   It is
a slippery poem to scan.   Elsewhere, we find *trew-e-ly*.

(Halle, 1894), p. 56, § 187. He remarks that a rime of this character gives evidence of the transition of M. E. long close *e* to (Italian) long *i* [as in the change from A. S. *mē* to mod. E. *me*], and adds: 'this change became general in the fifteenth century, but had begun in some dialects at an earlier date.' Its occurrence in the present poem is a strong indication that it is later than the year 1400, and effectually disposes of any supposed connection with Midland poems of the fourteenth century.

Both poems are remarkably free from classical allusions and from references to such medieval authors as are freely quoted by Chaucer. There is nothing to shew that the authoress was acquainted with Latin, though she knew French, especially the French of songs and mottoes.

The Flower and the Leaf is chiefly famous for having been versified by Dryden. The version is a free one, in a manner all his own, and is finer than the original, which can hardly be said of his 'versions' of Palamon and Arcite and The Cock and the Fox. It is doubtless from this version that many critics have formed exaggerated ideas of the poem's value; otherwise, it is difficult to understand for what reasons it was considered worthy of so great a master as Geoffrey Chaucer.

§ 60. It will be seen, from the Notes, that the authoress was well acquainted with the Prologue to The Legend of Good Women; and it can hardly be questioned that she took the main idea of the poem from that source, especially ll. 188–194 of the later text. At the same time she was well acquainted with Gower's lines on the same subject, in the Conf. Amantis, iii. 357, 358; see vol. iii. pp. xlii, 297. Gower has :—

> ' Me thoughte I sigh to-fore myn hede
> Cupide with his bowe bent,
> And like unto a parlement
> Which were ordeined for the nones,
> With him cam al the world atones [1]
> Of gentil folk, that whylom were
> Lovers; I sigh hem alle there . . .
> Her hedes kempt, and therupon
> Garlondes, nought of o colour,
> Some of the Lefe, some of the Flour, [2]
> And some of grete perles were. [3] . . .

---

[1] F. and L. 134-138.   [2] F. and L. 151-158, 333.   [3] F. and L. 148, 224.

So loude that on every syde
It thoughte as al the heven cryde [1]
In such accorde and suche a soun
Of bombard and of clarioun . . .
So glad a noise for to here.
The grene Leef is overthrowe [2] . . .
Despuiled is the somer fare,' &c. (p. 371).

§ 61. XXI. THE ASSEMBLY OF LADIES.

This has already been discussed, in some measure, in considering the preceding poem.   Both pieces were written by the same
authoress ; but the former is the more sprightly and probably
the earlier.   With the exception of the unusual rime of *tree* with
pretily (discussed above), nearly all the peculiarities of the preceding poem occur here also.   The Chaucerian final -*e* appears
now and then, as in *commaund-e* (probably plural), 203 ; *red-e*,
215 ; *countenanc-e*, 295 ; *pen-ne* [or else *seyd-e*], 307 ; *chayr-e*,
476 ; *tak-e*, 565 ; *trouth-e*, 647 ; *liv-e*, 672 ; *sem-e* (pr. s. subj.),
696.   But it is usually dropped, as in *The fresh* for *The fres-she*,
2 ; &c.   In l. 11, Thynne prints *fantasyse* for *fantasyes* ; for it
obviously rimes with *gyse* (monosyllabic) ; cf. 533-535. *Hew-e* and
new-e are cut down to *hew* and *new*, to rime with *knew*, 67. *Bold*
rimes with *told*, clipped form of *told-e*, 94 ; and so on.   So, again,
trewly appears in place of Chaucer's *trew-e-ly*, 488.   It is needless to pursue the subject.

The description of the maze and the arbour, in ll. 29–70, is
good.   Another pleasing passage is that contained in ll. 449–497 ;
and the description of a lady's dress in ll. 519–539.   As for the
lady herself—

'It was a world to loke on her visage.'

There is a most characteristic touch of a female writer in
lines 253–254 :—

'So than I dressed me in myn aray,
And asked her, *whether it were wel or no?*'

To attribute such a question as 'how will my dress do' to
a male writer is a little too dramatic for a mere narrative poem.

The two MSS. have now been collated for the first time and
afford some important corrections, of which l. 61 presents remarkable instances.   MS. Addit. 34360 is of some value.

---

[1] F. and L. 192, 193.   [2] Cf. F. and L. 358-364.

§ 62. A considerable part of The Assembly of Ladies that is now of little interest may have been much appreciated at the time, as having reference to the ordering of a large medieval household, with its chambers, parlours, bay-windows, and galleries, carefully kept in good order by the various officers and servants; such as Perseverance the usher, Countenance the porter, Discretion the chief purveyor, Acquaintance the harbinger, Largesse the steward, Bel-cheer the marshal of the hall, Remembrance the chamberlain, and the rest. The authoress must have been perfectly familiar with spectacles and pageants and all the amusements of the court; but she was too humble to aspire to wear a motto.

> ' And for my "word," I have non; this is trew.
> It is ynough that my clothing be blew
> As here-before I had commaundement;
> And so to do I am right wel content'; A. 312.

We must not forget that the period of the Wars of the Roses, especially from 1455 to 1471, was one during which the composition of these poems was hardly possible. It is obviously very difficult to assign a date to them; perhaps they may be referred to the last quarter of the fifteenth century. We must not put them too late, because The Assembly exists in MSS. that seem to be as old as that period.

§ 63. XXII. A Goodly Balade.

For this poem there is but one authority, viz. Thynne's edition of 1532. He calls it 'A goodly balade of Chaucer'; but it is manifestly Lydgate's. Moreover, it is really a triple Balade, with an Envoy, on the model of Chaucer's Fortune and Compleynt of Venus; only it has seven-line stanzas instead of stanzas of eight lines. An inspection of Thynne's volume shews that it was inserted to fill a gap, viz. a blank page at the back of the concluding lines of The Legend of Good Women, so that the translation of Boethius might commence on a new leaf.

It is obvious that the third stanza of the second Balade was missing in Thynne's MS. He did not leave it out for lack of space; for there is plenty of room on his page.

That it is not Chaucer's appears from the first Balade, where the use of the monosyllables *shal* and *smal* in ll. 8 and 10 necessitates the use of the clipped forms *al* for *al-le*, *cal* for *cal-le*, *apal* for *apal-le*, and *befal* for *befal-le*. Moreover, the whole style of it suggests Lydgate, and does not suggest Chaucer.

The sixth stanza probably began with the letter D; in which case, the initial letters of the stanzas give us M, M, M; D, D, D; J, C, Q. And, as it was evidently addressed to a lady named *Margaret* (see the Notes), we seem to see here *Margaret, Dame Jacques*. The name of *Robert Jacques* occurs in the Writs of Parliament; Bardsley's English Surnames, 2nd ed., p. 565. Of course this is a guess which it is easy to deride; but it is very difficult to account otherwise for the introduction of the letters J, C, Q in the third Balade; yet it was evidently intentional, for much force was employed to achieve the result. To make the first stanza begin with J, recourse is had to French; and the other two stanzas both begin with inverted clauses.

§ 64. XXIII. GO FORTH, KING.

I give this from Thynne's first edition; but add the Latin lines from the copy printed in Schick's edition of The Temple of Glas, at p. 68. His text is from that printed by Wynken de Worde about 1498, collated with the second and third prints from the same press at somewhat later dates, and a still later copy printed by Berthelet.

The only difference between Thynne's text and that given by Schick is that Wynken de Worde printed *ar* in the last line where Thynne has printed *be*. Schick also notes that 'the Chaucer-Prints of 1561 and 1598 omit *thou*' in l. 9; and I find that it is also omitted in the third edition (undated, about 1550). But it occurs in the edition of 1532, all the same; shewing that the later reprints cannot always be relied upon.

I have already said (vol. i. p. 40)—'Surely it must be Lydgate's.' For it exhibits his love for 'catalogues,' and presents his peculiarities of metre. Dr. Schick agrees with this ascription, and points out that its appearance in the four prints above-mentioned, in all of which it is annexed to Lydgate's Temple of Glas, tends to strengthen my supposition. I think this may be taken as removing all doubt on the subject.

§ 65. I beg leave to quote here Schick's excellent remarks upon the poem itself.

'There are similar pieces to these *Duodecim Abusiones* in earlier

English literature (see ten Brink, *Geschichte der englischen Lite-ratur*, i. 268, and note).[1] The "twelf unþēawas" existed also in Old-English; a homily on them is printed in Morris, *Old Eng. Homilies*, pp. 101-119[2]. It is based on the Latin Homily "De octo viciis et de duodecim abusivis huius saeculi," attributed to St. Cyprian or St. Patrick; see Dietrich in Niedner's *Zeitschrift für historische Theologie*, 1855, p. 518; Wanley's *Catalogus*, passim (cf. the Index *sub voce* Patrick). In the Middle-English period we meet again with more or less of these "Abusions"; see Morris, *Old Eng. Miscellany*, p. 185 (11 Abusions); Furnivall, *Early Eng. Poems*, Berlin, 1862 (Phil. Soc.), p. 161; "Five Evil Things," Wright and Halliwell, *Reliquiae Antiquae*, i. 316, and ii. 14.'

§ 66. XXIV. The Court of Love.

This piece was first printed by Stowe in 1561. Stowe happened to have access to a MS. which was really a miscellaneous collection of Middle-English pieces of various dates; and he proceeded to print them as being 'certaine workes of Geffray Chauser,' without paying any regard to their contents or style. In vol. i. pp. 33, 34, I give a list of his additions, numbered 42–60[3]. By good fortune, the very MS. in question is now in Trinity College Library, marked R. 3. 19. We can thus tell that he was indebted to it for the pieces numbered 46, 47, 48, 49, 50, 51, 53, 54, 55, 56, and 59. These eleven pieces are all alike remarkable for being non-Chaucerian; indeed, no. 56 is certainly Lydgate's. But it has so happened that no. 59, or The Court of Love, being the best of these pieces, was on that account 'attributed' to Chaucer, whilst the others were unhesitatingly rejected. And it happened on this wise.

§ 67. After Tyrwhitt had edited the Canterbury Tales afresh, it occurred to him to compile a Glossary. He rightly reasoned that the Glossary would be strengthened and made more correct if he included in it all the harder words found in the *whole* of Chaucer's Works, instead of limiting the vocabulary to words

---

[1] See the English translation in Bohn's Library, i. 214.

[2] A piece entitled 'De Duodecim Abusivis' is one of three pieces appended to Ælfric's Lives of the Saints in MS. Julius E. 7.

[3] No. 61 is The Storie of Thebes, which he of course knew to be Lydgate's; he adds it *after* the note—'Thus endeth the workes of Geffray Chaucer.'

which occur in the Canterbury Tales only.   For this purpose, he
proceeded to draw up a List of what he conceived to be Chaucer's
genuine works ; and we must remember that the only process open
to him was to consider all the old editions, and *reject* such as he
conceived to be spurious.   Hence his List is not really a list
of genuine works, but one made by striking out from all previous
lists the works which he *knew* to be spurious.   A moment's
reflection will show that this is a very different thing.

Considering that he had only his own acumen to guide him,
and had no access to linguistic or grammatical tests, still less
to tests derived from an examination of rimes or phonology,
it is wonderful how well he did his work.   In the matter of
rejection, he did not make a single mistake.   His first revision
was made by considering only the pieces numbered 1–41, in
the *first* part of Stowe's print (see vol. i. pp. 31–33) ; and he
struck out the following, on the express ground that they were
known to have been written by other authors; viz. nos. 4, 11, 13,
25, 26, 27, 28, 29, 33, and 40 [1].

Then he went over the list again, and struck out, on internal
evidence, nos. 15, 18, 21, 22, and 32 [2].

Truly, here was a noble beginning !   The only non-Chaucerian
pieces which he failed to reject explicitly, among nos. 1–41, were
the following, viz. 6 (A Goodly Balade of Chaucer), 17 (The
Complaint of the Black Knight), 20 (The Testament of Love), 31
(The Cuckoo and the Nightingale), 38 (Go forth, King), and 41
(A Balade in Praise of Chaucer).   Of course he rejected the last
of these, but it was not worth his while to say so ; and, in the
same way, he tacitly rejected or ignored nos. 6, 30, and 38.
Hence it was that nos. 6, 30, 38, and 41 did not appear in
Moxon's Chaucer, and even no. 32 was carefully excluded.
In his final list, out of nos. 1–41, Tyrwhitt actually got rid of all
but nos. 17, 20, and 31 (The Black Knight, The Testament
of Love, and The Cuckoo).

As to the remaining articles, he accepted, among the longer
pieces, nos. 59, 62, and 63, i. e. The Court of Love, Chaucer's
Dream, and The Flower and the Leaf ; to which he added nos.

---

[1] At the same time he struck out no. 56 (p. 34), as being by Lydgate.

[2] In Moxon's Chaucer, which professed to accept Tyrwhitt's canon, this piece
was omitted ; but it was revived once more by Bell.

42, 43, and 60 (as to which there is no doubt), and also the Virelai (no. 50), on the slippery ground that it *is* a virelai (which, strictly speaking, it is not).

§ 68. One result of his investigations was that an edition of Chaucer was published by Moxon (my copy is dated 1855), in which all the poems were included which Tyrwhitt accepted, followed by Tyrwhitt's Account of the Works of Chaucer.

Owing to the popularity of this edition, many scholars accepted the poems contained in it as being certainly genuine; but it is obvious that this was a very risky thing to do, in the absence of external evidence; especially when it is remembered that Tyrwhitt merely wanted to illustrate his glossary to the Canterbury Tales by adding words from other texts. The idea of drawing up a canon by the process of striking out from luxuriant lists the names of pieces that are obviously spurious, is one that should never have found acceptance.

§ 69. There is only one correct method of drawing up a canon of genuine works, viz. that adopted by Mr. Henry Bradshaw, formerly our Cambridge University Librarian. It is simple enough, viz. to take a clean sheet of paper, and enter upon it, first of all, the names of all the pieces that are admittedly genuine; and then to see if it can fairly be augmented by adding such pieces as have reasonable evidence in their favour. In making a list of this character, The Court of Love has no claim to be considered at all, as I fully proved about twenty years ago[1]; and there is an end of the matter. The MS. copy is in a hand of the sixteenth century[2], and there is no internal evidence to suggest an earlier date.

§ 70. Our task is to determine what it really is, and what can be made of it as it stands. We learn from the author that he

---

[1] See The Athenæum, Nov. 4, 1876; The Academy, June 3, 1878; Aug. 3, 1878.

[2] My remark upon the Trinity MS. in vol. i. p. 56, that 'most of the pieces are in a handwriting of a later date [than 1463], not far from 1500,' does not apply to The Court of Love. This poem, together with two poems by Lydgate, fills part of a quire of twenty-four leaves *near the end* of the MS., of which the seventeenth has been cut out and the last three are blank; and this quire is quite distinct from the rest as regards the date of the writing, which is considerably later than 1500, and exhibits a marked change. There are two *lacunæ* in the poem, one after l. 1022, and another after l. 1316; probably six stanzas are lost in each case, owing to the loss of the two corresponding leaves in the original from which the existing copy was made.

was 'a clerk of Cambridge' (913), which we may readily accept. Beyond this, there is nothing but internal evidence; but of this there is much. That our 'clerk' had read Ovid and Maximian appears from the Notes; he even seems to have imbibed something of 'the new learning,' as he makes up the names Philogenet and Philo-bone by help of a Greek adjective [1]. Dr. Schick has made it clear that he was well acquainted with Lydgate's Temple of Glas, which he imitates freely; see Schick's edition of that poem, p. cxxix. Mr. J. T. T. Brown, in his criticism on 'The Authorship of the Kingis Quair,' Glasgow, 1896, draws many parallels between The Court of Love and The Kingis Quair, and concludes that The Kingis Quair was indebted to The Court of Love; but it is tolerably certain that the indebtedness was in the other direction. For, in The Kingis Quair, some knowledge of the true use of Chaucer's final -e is still exhibited, even in a Northern poem, whilst in The Court of Love, it is almost altogether dead, though the poem is in the Midland dialect. I shall presently shew that our clerk, whilst very nearly ignoring the final -e, occasionally employs the final -en; but this he does in a way which clearly shews that he did not understand when to use it aright, a fact which is highly significant.

I am much indebted to my friend Professor Hales for pointing out another very cogent argument. He draws attention to the numerous instances in which the author of The Court of Love fails to end a stanza with a stop. There is no stop, for example, at the end of ll. 14, 567, 672, 693, 700, 763, 826, 1064, 1288; and only a slight pause at the end of ll. 28, 49, 70, 84, 189, 231, 259, 280, 371, 406, 427, &c. In Chaucer's Parlement of Foules, on the other hand, there is but one stanza without a stop at the end, viz. at l. 280; and but one with a slight pause, viz. at l. 154. The difference between these results is very marked, and would convince any mathematician. I should like to add that the same test disposes of the claims of The Flower and the Leaf to be considered as Chaucer's; it has no stop at the end of ll. 7, 70, 154, 161, 196, 231, 280, 308, 392, 476, and has mere commas at the end of ll. 28, 49, 56, 98, 119, 224, 259, 329, 336, &c. In the Assembly of Ladies this departure from Chaucer's usage has been

---

[1] I doubt if speculation as to the possible meaning of these names will really help us.

nearly abandoned, which is one reason why that piece is in a less lively style.

§ 71. The sole MS. copy of The Court of Love belongs to the sixteenth century, and there is nothing to shew that the poem itself was of earlier date. Indeed, the language of it is remarkably like that of the former half of that century. If it be compared with Sackville's famous 'Induction,' the metrical form of the stanzas is much the same; there is the same smoothness of rhythm and frequent modernness of form, quite different from the halting lines of Lydgate and Hawes. This raises a suggestion that the author may have learnt his metre from Scottish authors, such as Henryson and Dunbar; and it is surprising to find him employing such words as *celsitude* and *pulcritude*, and even riming them together, precisely as Dunbar did (ll. 611-613, and the note). One wonders where he learnt to use such words, if not from Scottish authors. Curiously enough, a single instance of the use of a Northern inflexion occurs in the phrase *me thynkes*, 874. And I admit the certainty that he consulted The Kingis Quair.

I have no space to discuss the matter at length; so shall content myself with saying that the impression produced upon me is that we have here the work of one of the heralds of the Elizabethan poetry, of the class to which belonged Nicholas Grimoald, Thomas Sackville, Lord Surrey, Lord Vaux, and Sir Francis Bryan. There must have been much fairly good poetry in the time of Henry VIII that is lost to us. Tottell's Miscellany clearly shews this, as it is a mere selection of short pieces, which very nearly perished; but for this fortunate relic, we should not have known much about Wyat and Surrey. Sackville, when at Cambridge, acquired some distinction for Latin and English verse, but we possess none of it. However, Sackville was not the author of The Court of Love, seeing that it was published in a 'Chaucer' collection in 1561, long before his death.

The fact that our clerk was well acquainted with so many pieces by Chaucer, such as The Knight's Tale, the Complaint of Pity, The Legend of Good Women, Troilus, and Anelida, besides giving us reminiscences of The Letter of Cupid, and (perhaps) of The Cuckoo and Nightingale, raises the suspicion that he had access to Thynne's edition of 1532; and it is quite possible that this very book inspired him for his effort. This suspicion becomes almost a certainty if it be true that ll. 495-496 are borrowed from Rom. Rose, 2819–20; see note at p. 545. I can find no reason for dating the poem earlier than that year.

§ 72. However this may be, the chief point to notice is that his archaisms are affectations and not natural. He frequently dispenses with them altogether for whole stanzas at a time. When they occur, they are such as he found in Chaucer abundantly; I refer to such phrases as *I-wis* or *y-wis; as blyve*; the use of *ich* for *I* (661); *besy cure* (36); *gan me dresse* (113; cf. C. T., G 1271); *by the feith I shall to god* (131; cf. Troil. iii. 1649); and many more. He rarely uses the prefix *i-* or *y-* with the pp.; we find *y-born* (976), *y-formed* (1176), *y-heried* (592), *y-sped* (977), all in Chaucer; besides these, I only note *y-fed* (975), *y-ravisshed* (153), *y-stope* (281), the last being used in the sense of Chaucer's *stope*. The most remarkable point is the almost total absence of the final *-e*; I only observe *His len-ë body* (1257); *to serv-e* (909); *to dred-e* (603); and *in thilk-ë place* (642); the last of which is a phrase (cf. R. R. 660). On the other hand, whilst thus abstaining from the use of the final *-e*, he makes large use of the longer and less usual suffix *-en*, which he employs with much skill to heighten the archaic effect. Thus we find the past participles *holden*, 62; *growen*, 182; *yoven* or *yeven*, 742; *shapen*, 816, 1354; *blowen*, 1240; the gerunds *writen*, 35; *dressen*, 179; *byden*, 321; *semen*, 607; *seken*, 838; *worshippen*, 1165, and a few others; the infinitives *maken*, 81; *byden*, 189; *quyten*, 327, &c., this being the commonest use; the present plurals *wailen*, 256; *foten*, 586; *speden*, 945, &c.; with the same form for the first person, as in *wailen*, 1113; *bleden*, 1153; and for the second person, as in *waxen*, 958; *slepen*, 999. Occasionally, this suffix is varied to *-yn* or *-in*, as in *exilyn*, v., 336; *serchyn*, v., 950; *spakyn*, pt. pl., 624; *approchyn*, pr. pl., 1212. This may be the scribe's doing, and is consistent with East Anglian spelling.

But the artificial character of these endings is startlingly revealed when we find *-en* added in an impossible position, shewing that its true grammatical use was quite dead. Yet we find such examples. A serious error (hardly the scribe's) occurs in l. 347: 'Wheder that she me *helden* lefe or loth.' *Hold* being a strong verb, the pt. t. is *held*; we could however justify the use of *held-e*, by supposing it to be the subjunctive mood, which suits the sense; but *held-en* (with *-en*) is the *plural* form, while *she* is singular; and really this use of *-e* in the subjunctive must have been long dead. In l. 684, we have a case that is even worse, viz. *I kepen in no wyse*; here the use of *-en* saves a hiatus, but the concord is false, like the Latin *ego seruamus*. In l. 928, the same thing recurs, though the scribe has altered *greven* into *growen*[1]; for this present tense is supposed to agree with *I*! A very clear case occurs in l. 725: *For if by me this mater springen out*; where the use of *-en*, again meant to save a hiatus, is excruciatingly wrong; for *mater* is singular! This cannot be the fault of the scribe. Other examples of false grammar are: *thou serven*, 290; *thou sene*, 499. But the climax is attained in l. 526, where we meet with *thay kepten ben*, where the *-en* is required for the metre. *Kepten*, as a *past participle*, is quite unique; let us drop a veil over this sad lapse, and say no more about it[2].

We may, however, fairly notice the constant use of the Northern forms *their* and *thaim* or *theim*, where Chaucer has *hir* and *hem*. The use of *their* and *them* (not *thaim*) was well established by the year 1500 in literary English, as, e.g., in Hawes and Skelton. Caxton uses all four forms, *hem* and *them*, *her* and *their*.

§ 73. I add a few notes, suggested by an examination of the rimes employed.

The final *-e* is not used at the end of a line. This is easily seen, if carefully looked into. Thus *lette* (1284) stands for *let*, for it rimes with *y-set*; *grace* and *trespace* rime with *was*, 163; *kene* rimes with *bene*, misspelling of *been*, 252; *redde*, put for *red*, rimes with *spred*, 302; *yerde*, put for *yerd*, rimes with *aferd*, 363; *ende* rimes with *frend* and *fend*, 530; and so on throughout[3]. The following assonances occur: *here*, *grene*, 253; *kepe*, *flete*, 309; and the following rimes are imperfect: *plaint*, *talent*, *consent*, 716; *frend*, *mynd*, 1056; *nonne* (for *non*), *boun*, 1149; *like* (*i* long), *stike* (*i* short), 673; and perhaps *hold*, *shuld*[4], 408; *hard*, *ferd*, 151. *Hard* is repeated, 149, 151; 1275, 1277. A curious rime

---

[1] Which looks as if the author had written *grewen* for *greven*, like a Scotchman.

[2] A very bad mistake occurs in l. 1045, viz. *thou wot* instead of *thou wost*, as if one should say in Latin *tu scio*. It rimes with *dote*, which, in Chaucer, is dissyllabic.

[3] There are many more; *fon-ne* becomes *fon*, to rime with *on*, 458; *tell-e* is cut down to *tell*, 518; *behold-e*, to *behold*, 652; *accord-e*, to *accord*, 746; &c. The reader can find out more for himself; see ll. 771, 844, 862, 896, 1032, 1334, 1389, &c. In ll. 1063-4, we have *opinion* riming with *begon*, the Chaucerian forms being *opinioun* and *bigonne* or *bigunne*!

[4] See vol. vi. p. xlv.

is that of *length* with *thynketh*, 1059 ; read *thenk'th,* and it is good enough. Noteworthy are these : *thryse* (for Chaucer's *thry-ës*), *wyse,* 537 ; *hens* (for Chaucer's *henn-ës*), *eloquence,* 935 ; *desire, here,* 961, 1301 ; *eke, like,* 561 ; *tretesse* (for Chaucer's *tretys*), *worthinesse,* 28 ; *write, aright,* 13 ; *sey* (I saw), *way,* 692. In one place, he has *discryve,* 778, to rime with *lyve*; and in another *discry* (miswritten *discryve,* 97), to rime with *high.* As in Chaucer, he sometimes has *dy,* to die, riming with *remedy,* 340, and elsewhere *dey,* to rime with *pray,* 582 ; and again *fire, fyr,* riming with *hyre,* 883, or with *desire,* 1285, and at another time the Kentish form *fere* (borrowed from Chaucer), with the same sense, r. w. *y-fere,* 622. The most curious forms are those for 'eye.' When it rimes with *degree,* 132, *see,* 768, we seem to have the Northern form *ee* or *e*; but elsewhere it rimes with *besily,* 299, *pretily,* 419, *wounderly,* 695, *dispitously,* 1139, or with *I,* 282 ; and the plural *yen* (=*y'n*) rimes with *lyne,* 135. The sounds represented by *ē* and *y* obviously afford permissible rimes ; that the sounds were not identical appears from ll. 1051–1055, which end with *me, remedy, be, dy, company* consecutively.

§ 74. Perhaps an easier way for enabling a learner to recognise the peculiarities of The Court of Love, and the difference of its language from Chaucer, is to translate some lines of it into Chaucerian English. The effect upon the metre is startling.

> So thanne I went-ë by straunge and fer-rë contrees ; 57.
> Alceste it was that kept-ë there her sojour ; 105.
> To whom obeyd-ën the ladies god-ë nynten-ë ; 108.
> And yong-ë men fel-ë cam-ë forth with lusty pace ; 110.
> O bright-ë Regina, who mad-ë thee so fair ? 141.
> And mercy ask-ë for al my gret-ë trespas ; 166.
> This eight-ë-ten-ë yeer have kept yourself at large ; 184.
> In me did never worch-ë trew-ë-ly, yit 1 ; 212.
> And ther I sey the fres-shë quene of Cartáge ; 231.
> A! new-ë com-ën folk, abyde, and woot ye why ; 271.
> Than gan I me present-ë tofor-ë the king ; 274.
> That thou be trew-ë from henn-es-forth, to thy might ; 289.
> And nam-ë-ly haw-ë-thorn brought-ën both-ë page and grom-ë ; 1433.

Very many more such examples may be given. Or take the following ; Chaucer has (L. G. W. 476) :—

> For Love ne wól nat countrepleted be.

And this is how it reappears in C. L. 429 :—

> For Love wil not be counterplęted, indede !

Here the melody of the line is completely spoilt.

In the present state of our knowledge of the history of the English language, any notion of attributing The Court of Love to Chaucer is worse than untenable; for it is wholly disgraceful. Everything points to a very late date, and tends to exclude it, not only from the fourteenth, but even from the fifteenth century.

At the same time, it will readily be granted that the poem abounds with Chaucerian words and phrases to an extent that almost surpasses even the poems of Lydgate. The versification is smooth, and the poem, as a whole, is pleasing. I have nothing to say against it, when considered on its own merits.

§ 75. Space fails me to discuss the somewhat vexed question of the Courts of Love, of which some have denied the existence. However, there seems to be good evidence to shew that they arose in Provence, and were due to the extravagances of the troubadours. They were travesties of the courts of law, with a lady of rank for a judge, and minstrels for advocates; and they discussed subtle questions relating to affairs of love, usually between troubadours and ladies. The discussions were conducted with much seriousness, and doubtless often served to give much amusement to many idle people. Not unfrequently they led to tragedies, as is easily understood when we notice that the first of one set of thirty-one Laws of Love runs as follows :—' Marriage cannot be pleaded as an excuse for refusing to love.' The reader who requires further information is referred to ' The Troubadours and Courts of Love,' by J. F. Rowbotham, M.A., London, Swan Sonnenschein and Co., 1895.

It is perhaps necessary to observe that the said Courts have very little to do with the present poem, which treats of a Court of Cupid in the Chaucerian sense (Leg. Good Women, 352). Even the statutes of the Court are largely imitated from Lydgate.

§ 76. Pieces numbered XXV–XXIX.

XXV. VIRELAY. This piece, from the Trinity MS., belongs to the end of the fifteenth century, and contains no example of the final -e as constituting a syllable. Chaucer would have used *sore* (l. 2), *more* (l. 12), *trouth* (l. 13), as dissyllables; and he would not have rimed *pleyn* and *disdayn* with *compleyn* and *absteyn*, as the two latter require a final -e. The rime of *finde* with *ende* is extraordinary.

The title 'Virelai' is given to this piece in Moxon's Chaucer, and is, strictly speaking, incorrect; in the MS. and in Stowe's edition, it has no title at all! Tyrwhitt cautiously spoke of it as being 'perhaps by Chaucer'; and says that 'it comes nearer to the description of a *Virelay*, than anything else of his that has been preserved.' This is not the case; see note to Anelida, 256; vol. i. p. 536. Tyrwhitt quotes from Cotgrave—' *Virelay*, a round, freemen's song,' and adds—' There is a particular description of a *Virlai*, in the *Jardin de plaisance*, fol. xii, where it makes the *decima sexta species Rhetorice Gallicane.*' For further remarks, see p. 554.

XXVI. PROSPERITY: BY JOHN WALTON. 'To Mr. [Mark] Liddell belongs the honour of the discovery of John Walton as the author of the little poem on fol. 119 [of MS. Arch. Seld. B. 24]. The lines occur as part of the Prologue (ll. 83–90) to Walton's translation of Boethius' *De Consolatione.'*—J. T. T. Brown, *The Authorship of the Kingis Quair*, Glasgow, 1896; p. 71. See the account of Walton in Warton's Hist. E. Poetry, sect. xx. The original date of the stanza was, accordingly, 1410; but we here find it in a late Scottish dress. The ascription of it to 'Chaucer,' in the MS., is an obvious error; it was written ten years after his death.

XXVII. LEAULTE VAULT RICHESSE. This piece, like the former, has no title in the MS.; but the words *Leaulte vault Richesse* (Loyalty deserves riches) occur at the end of it. If the original was in a Midland dialect, it must belong to the latter part of the fifteenth century. Even in these eight lines we find a contradiction to Chaucer's usage; for he always uses *lent*, pp., as a monosyllable, and *rent-e* as a dissyllable. It is further remarkable that he never uses *content* as an adjective; it first appears in Rom. Rose, 5628.

XXVIII. SAYINGS. I give these sayings as printed by Caxton; see vol. i. p. 46, where I note that Caxton did not ascribe them to Chaucer. They are not at all in his style.

In MS. Ashmole 59, fol. 78, I find a similar prophecy :—

Prophecia merlini doctoris perfecti.

Whane lordes wol leefe theire olde lawes,
And preestis been varyinge in theire sawes,
And leccherie is holden solace,
And oppressyoun for truwe purchace;

* * *
* * * *

f

And whan the moon is on dauid stall,
And the kynge passe Arthures hall,
Than[1] is [the] lande of Albyon
Nexst to his confusyoun.

It is extremely interesting to observe the ascription of these lines to *Merlin*; see King Lear, iii. 2. 95.

XXIX. BALADE. This poor stanza, with its long-drawn lines, appears in Stowe at the end of 'Chaucer's Works.' In the Trinity MS., it occurs at the end of a copy of The Parlement of Foules.

§ 77. An examination of the pieces contained in the present volume leads us to a somewhat remarkable result, viz. that we readily distinguish in them the handiwork of *at least* twelve different authors, of whom no two are much alike, whilst every one of them can be distinguished from Chaucer.

These are : (1) the author of The Testament of Love, who writes in a prose style all his own; (2) the author of The Plowmans Tale and Plowmans Crede, with his strong powers of invective and love of alliteration, whose style could never have been mistaken for Chaucer's in any age[2]; (3) the author of Jack Upland, with his direct and searching questions; (4) John Gower, with his scrupulous regularity of grammatical usages; (5) Thomas Hoccleve, who too often accents a dissyllable on the latter syllable when it should be accented on the former; (6) Henry Scogan, whose lines are lacking in interest and originality; (7) John Lydgate[3], who allows his verse too many licences, so that it cannot always be scanned at the first trial; (8) Sir Richard Ros, who writes in English of a quite modern cast, using *their* and *them* as in modern English, and wholly discarding the use of final -e as an inflexion; (9) Robert Henryson, who writes smoothly enough and with a fine vein of invention, but employs the Northern dialect; (10) Sir Thomas Clanvowe, who employs the final -e much more frequently than Chaucer or even Gower; (11) the authoress of The Flower and the Leaf and The Assembly of Ladies, to whom the final -e was an archaism, very convenient for metrical embellishment; and (12) the author of The Court of Love, who, while discarding

---

[1] The MS. has :—'Than is is lande '—by mistake.

[2] It is clear that The Plowmans Tale and Jack Upland were inserted by Thynne and Speght respectively on religious grounds.

[3] We may safely assign to Lydgate the pieces numbered XXII and XXIII, as well as those numbered VIII to XV.

the use of the final -*e*, was glad to use the final -*en* to save a hiatus or to gain a syllable, and did not hesitate to employ it where it was grammatically wrong to do so.

§ 78. If the reader were to suppose that this exhausts the list, he would be mistaken; for it is quite easy to add at least one known name, and to suggest three others. For the piece numbered XXVI, on p. 449, has been identified as the work of John Walton, who wrote a verse translation of Boethius in the year 1410; whilst it is extremely unlikely that no. XXVII, written in Lowland Scottish, was due to Henryson, the only writer in that dialect who has been mentioned above. This gives a total of *fourteen* authors already; and I believe that we require yet two more before the Virelai and the Sayings printed by Caxton (nos. XXV and XXVIII) can be satisfactorily accounted for. As for no. XIX—the Envoy to Alison—it *may* be Lydgate's, but, on the other hand, it may not. And as for no. XXIX, it is of no consequence.

Moreover, it must be remembered that I here only refer to the selected pieces printed in the present volume. If we go further afield, we soon find several more authors, all distinct from those above-mentioned, from each other, and from Chaucer. I will just instance the author of the Isle of Ladies, the authoress (presumably) of The Lamentation of Mary Magdalen, the author of The Craft of Lovers, the 'man unknown' who wrote The Ten Commandments of Love, and the author of the clumsy lines dignified by the title of The Nine Ladies Worthy. It is quite certain that *not less* than twenty authors are represented in the mass of heterogeneous material which appears under Chaucer's name in a compilation such as that which is printed in the first volume of Chalmers' British Poets; which, precisely on that very account, is useful enough in its own peculiar way.

§ 79. I believe it may be said of nearly every piece in the volume, that it now appears in an improved form. In several cases, I have collated MSS. that have not previously been examined, and have found them to be the best. The Notes are nearly all new; very few have been taken from Bell's Chaucer. Several are due to Schick's useful notes to The Temple of Glas; and some to Krausser's edition of The Black Knight, and to Gröhler's edition of La Belle Dame, both of which reached me after my own notes were all in type. I have added a Glossary of the harder words ; for others, see the Glossary already printed in vol. vi.

In extenuation of faults, I may plead that I have found it much more difficult to deal with such heterogenous material as is comprised in the present volume than with pieces all written by the same author. The style, the grammar, the mode of scansion, the dialect, and even the pronunciation are constantly shifting, instead of being reasonably consistent, as in the genuine works of Chaucer. Any one who will take the pains to observe these points, to compile a sufficient number of notes upon difficult passages, and to prepare a somewhat full glossary, may thus practically convince himself, as I have done, that not a single piece in the present volume ought ever to have been 'attributed' to Chaucer. That any of them should have been so attributed —and some of them never were —has been the result of negligence, superficiality, and incapacity, such as (it may be hoped) we have seen the last of.

I wish once more to acknowledge my obligations to Mr. E. B. Nicholson, for the loan of his transcript of The Praise of Peace ; to Mr. Bradley, for his discovery of the authorship of The Testament of Love and for other assistance as regards the same ; to Dr. E. Krausser, for his edition of The Complaint of the Black Knight ; to Dr. Gröhler, for his dissertation on La Belle Dame sans Mercy ; and to Professor Hales for his kind help as to some difficult points, and particularly with regard to The Court of Love.

THE TESTAMENT OF LOVE.

—◦—

PROLOGUE.

MANY men there ben that, with eeres openly sprad, so
moche swalowen the deliciousnesse of jestes and of ryme,
by queynt knitting coloures, that of the goodnesse or of the
badnesse of the sentence take they litel hede or els non.

Soothly, dul wit and a thoughtful soule so sore have myned 5
and graffed in my spirites, that suche craft of endyting wol not
ben of myn acqueyntaunce. And, for rude wordes and boystous
percen the herte of the herer to the in[ne]rest point, and planten
there the sentence of thinges, so that with litel helpe it is able
to springe; this book, that nothing hath of the greet flode of 10
wit ne of semelich coloures, is dolven with rude wordes and
boystous, and so drawe togider, to maken the cacchers therof
ben the more redy to hente sentence.

Some men there ben that peynten with colours riche, and
some with vers, as with red inke, and some with coles and 15
chalke; and yet is there good matere to the leude people of
thilke chalky purtreyture, as hem thinketh for the tyme; and
afterward the sight of the better colours yeven to hem more
joye for the first leudnesse. So, sothly, this leude clowdy occupacion is not to prayse but by the leude; for comunly leude 20
leudnesse commendeth. Eke it shal yeve sight, that other
precious thinges shal be the more in reverence. In Latin
and French hath many soverayne wittes had greet delyt to

---

2. delyciousnesse; (*and elsewhere*, **y** *is often replaced by* i).   4. none.
5. Sothely. wytte.   8. inrest poynte.   10. spring. boke. great floode.
12. catchers.   13. hent.   18. afterwarde.   19. leudenesse.
20. comenly.   21. leudenesse.   23. gret delyte.

* * *
* * * *
B

endyte, and have many noble thinges fulfild; but certes, there
25 ben some that speken their poysye-mater in Frenche, of whiche
speche the Frenche men have as good a fantasye as we have
in hering of Frenche mennes English.   And many termes there
ben in English, [of] whiche unneth we Englishmen connen declare
the knowleginge.   How shulde than a Frenche man born suche
30 termes conne jumpere in his mater, but as the jay chatereth
English?   Right so, trewly, the understanding of Englishmen
wol not strecche to the privy termes in Frenche, what-so-ever we
bosten of straunge langage.   Let than clerkes endyten in Latin,
for they have the propertee of science, and the knowinge in that
35 facultee; and let Frenchmen in their Frenche also endyten their
queynt termes, for it is kyndely to their mouthes; and let us
shewe our fantasyes in suche wordes as we lerneden of our dames
tonge.

And although this book be litel thank-worthy for the leudnesse
40 in travaile, yet suche wrytinges excyten men to thilke thinges that
ben necessarie; for every man therby may, as by a perpetual
mirrour, seen the vyces or vertues of other, in whiche thing
lightly may be conceyved to eschewe perils, and necessaries to
cacche, after as aventures have fallen to other people or persons.
45   Certes, [perfeccion is] the soveraynest thing of desyre, and
moste †creatures resonable have, or els shulde have, ful appetyte
to their perfeccion; unresonable beestes mowen not, sith reson
hath in hem no werking.   Than resonable that wol not is comparisoned to unresonable, and made lyke hem.   For-sothe, the
50 most soverayne and fynal perfeccion of man is in knowing of
a sothe, withouten any entent disceyvable, and in love of oon
very god that is inchaungeable; that is, to knowe and love his
creatour.

¶ Now, principally, the mene to bringe in knowleging and
55 loving his creatour is the consideracion of thinges made by the
creatour, wherthrough, by thilke thinges that ben made understonding here to our wittes, arn the unsene privitees of god
made to us sightful and knowing, in our contemplacion and
understonding.   These thinges than, forsoth, moche bringen us

---

24. fulfylde.   27. englysshe.   28. englysshe; *supply* of.   englyssh-.
29. Howe. borne.   31. englyssh. englyssh-.   32. stretche.   34. propertie.
35. facultie. lette.   39. boke. thanke worthy.   42. sene.   44. catche.
45. *I supply* perfeccion is; *to make sense.*   soueraynst.   46. creature (*sic*).
reasonable.   47, 50. perfection.   47. sythe reason.   48. reasonable.
51. one.   54. Nowe. meane.   56. be (*for* by).   57. arne.

to the ful knowleginge [of] sothe, and to the parfit love of the 60
maker of hevenly thinges. Lo, David sayth, 'thou hast delyted
me in makinge,' as who sayth, to have delyt in the tune, how god
hath lent me in consideracion of thy makinge.

Wherof Aristotle, in the boke *de Animalibus*, saith to naturel
philosophers: 'it is a greet lyking in love of knowinge their 65
creatour; and also in knowinge of causes in kyndely thinges.'
Considred, forsoth, the formes of kyndly thinges and the shap,
a greet kindely love me shulde have to the werkman that
hem made. The crafte of a werkman is shewed in the werke.
Herfore, truly, the philosophers, with a lyvely studie, many 70
noble thinges right precious and worthy to memory writen;
and by a greet swetande travayle to us leften of causes [of] the
propertees in natures of thinges. To whiche (therfore) philosophers it was more joy, more lykinge, more herty lust, in
kyndely vertues and maters of reson, the perfeccion by busy 75
study to knowe, than to have had al the tresour, al the richesse,
al the vainglory that the passed emperours, princes, or kinges
hadden. Therfore the names of hem, in the boke of perpetual
memory, in vertue and pees arn writen; and in the contrarye,
that is to sayne, in Styx, the foule pitte of helle, arn thilke pressed 80
that suche goodnesse hated. And bycause this book shal be of
love, and the pryme causes of steringe in that doinge, with passions
and diseses for wantinge of desyre, I wil that this book be cleped
THE TESTAMENT OF LOVE.

But now, thou reder, who is thilke that wil not in scorne 85
laughe, to here a dwarfe, or els halfe a man, say he wil rende
out the swerde of Hercules handes, and also he shuld sette
Hercules Gades a myle yet ferther; and over that, he had
power of strengthe to pulle up the spere, that Alisander the
noble might never wagge? And that, passing al thinge, to ben 90
mayster of Fraunce by might, there-as the noble gracious Edward
the thirde, for al his greet prowesse in victories, ne might al yet
conquere?

Certes, I wot wel, ther shal be mad more scorne and jape
of me, that I, so unworthily clothed al-togider in the cloudy cloude 95

---

60. *I supply* of. parfyte. 61. haste. 62. delyte (*this sentence is corrupt*). 64. saythe. 65. great. 66, 67. thyng*es* co*n*sydred. Forsoth (*sic*). 68. great. me (*sic*); *for* men. 72. great. *Supply* of. 73. propertyes. 75. matters of reason. perfection. 76. treasour. 79. peace. 80. stixe. 81. boke. 83. dyseases. boke. 85. nowe. 87. set. 89. pul. 92. great. 94. wote. made. 95. vnworthely.

of unconninge, wil putten me in prees to speke of love, or els
of the causes in that matter, sithen al the grettest clerkes han
had ynough to don, and (as who sayth) †gadered up clene toforn
hem, and with their sharpe sythes of conning al mowen, and
100 mad therof grete rekes and noble, ful of al plentees, to fede me
and many another. Envye, forsothe, commendeth nought his
reson that he hath in hayne, be it never so trusty. And al-though
these noble repers, as good workmen and worthy their hyre,
han al drawe and bounde up in the sheves, and mad many
105 shockes, yet have I ensample to gadere the smale crommes,
and fullen my walet of tho that fallen from the borde among
the smale houndes, notwithstandinge the travayle of the
almoigner, that hath drawe up in the cloth al the remissailes,
as trenchours, and the relief, to bere to the almesse.
110   Yet also have I leve of the noble husbande Boëce, al-though
I be a straunger of conninge, to come after his doctrine, and
these grete workmen, and glene my handfuls of the shedinge
after their handes ; and, if me faile ought of my ful, to encrese
my porcion with that I shal drawe by privitees out of the shocke.
115 A slye servaunt in his owne helpe is often moche commended ;
knowing of trouth in causes of thinges was more hardyer in the
first sechers (and so sayth Aristotle), and lighter in us that han
folowed after.   For their passing †studies han fresshed our wittes,
and our understandinge han excyted, in consideracion of trouth,
120 by sharpnesse of their resons. Utterly these thinges be no
dremes ne japes, to throwe to hogges ; it is lyflich mete for
children of trouthe ; and as they me betiden, whan I pilgrimaged
out of my kith in winter ; whan the †weder out of mesure was
boystous, and the wylde wind Boreas, as his kind asketh, with
125 dryinge coldes maked the wawes of the occian-see so to aryse
unkyndely over the commune bankes, that it was in poynte to
spille al the erthe.

**Thus endeth the Prologue ; and here-after foloweth the
first book of the Testament of Love.**

---

98. gathered. toforne.   100. made. great. plentyes.   102. reason. hayn (*sic*).
102. -thoughe.   103. hyer.   104. made.   105. gader.   106. fullyn.
amonge.   108. remyssayles.   109. relyef.   112. great.   113. encrease.
114. priuytyes.   116. knoweyng.   118. study (*sic*).   120. reasons.
121. lyfelyche meate.   122. betiden (*sic*); *past tense.*   123. wether. measure.
124. wynde Borias. kynde.   125. dryenge.   127. spyl.   (*rubric*) boke.

CHAPTER I.

ALAS! Fortune! alas! I that som-tyme in delicious houres was wont to enjoye blisful stoundes, am now drive by unhappy hevinesse to bewaile my sondry yvels in tene!

Trewly, I leve, in myn herte is writte, of perdurable letters, al the entencions of lamentacion that now ben y-nempned! For any 5 maner disese outward, in sobbing maner, sheweth sorowful yexinge from within. Thus from my comfort I ginne to spille, sith she that shulde me solace is fer fro my presence. Certes, her absence is to me an helle; my sterving deth thus in wo it myneth, that endeles care is throughout myne herte clenched; blisse of 10 my joye, that ofte me murthed, is turned in-to galle, to thinke on thing that may not, at my wil, in armes me hente! Mirth is chaunged in-to tene, whan swink is there continually that reste was wont to sojourne and have dwelling-place. Thus witless, thoughtful, sightles lokinge, I endure my penaunce in this derke prison, 15 †caitived fro frendshippe and acquaintaunce, and forsaken of al that any †word dare speke. Straunge hath by waye of intrucioun mad his home, there me shulde be, if reson were herd as he shulde. Never-the-later yet hertly, lady precious Margarit, have mynde on thy servaunt; and thinke on his disese, how lightles he 20 liveth, sithe the bemes brennende in love of thyn eyen are so bewent, that worldes and cloudes atwene us twey wol nat suffre my thoughtes of hem to be enlumined! Thinke that oon vertue of a Margarite precious is, amonges many other, the sorouful to comforte; yet †whyles that, me sorouful to comforte, is my lust 25 to have nought els at this tyme, d[r]ede ne deth ne no maner traveyle hath no power, myn herte so moche to fade, as shulde to here of a twinkling in your disese! Ah! god forbede that; but yet let me deye, let me sterve withouten any mesure of penaunce, rather than myn hertely thinking comfort in ought 30 were disesed! What may my service avayle, in absence of her that my service shulde accepte? Is this nat endeles sorowe to

---

CH. I. 2. enioy. 3. sondrye. 5. nowe. 6. disease outwarde. 7. comforte. 8. ferre. 9. hell. dethe. 10. endelesse. 12. hent. 13. swynke. 14. dwellynge-. wytlesse. 15. syghtlesse. prisone. 16. caytisned (*for* caytifued). 17. wode (!); *for* worde; *read* word. 18. made. reason. herde. 20. disease. 21. beames. 22. *For* be-went, Th. *has* be-went. 23. one. 25. wyl of; *apparently an error for* whyles (*which I adopt*). luste. 26. dede (*for* drede). 27. myne. 28. twynckelynge. disease. 29. lette (*twice*). dey. measure. 30. myne. comforte. 31. diseased. maye. aueyle. 32. endlesse.

thinke? Yes, yes, god wot; myn herte breketh nigh a-sonder.
How shulde the ground, without kyndly noriture, bringen forth
35 any frutes? How shulde a ship, withouten a sterne, in the grete see
be governed? How shulde I, withouten my blisse, my herte, my
desyre, my joye, my goodnesse, endure in this contrarious prison,
that thinke every hour in the day an hundred winter? Wel may
now Eve sayn to me, 'Adam, in sorowe fallen from welth, driven
40 art thou out of paradise, with swete thy sustenaunce to beswinke!' Depe in this pyninge pitte with wo I ligge y-stocked,
with chaynes linked of care and of tene. It is so hye from thens
I lye and the commune erth, there ne is cable in no lande maked,
that might strecche to me, to drawe me in-to blisse; ne steyers
45 to steye on is none; so that, without recover, endeles here to
endure, I wot wel, I [am] purveyed. O, where art thou now,
frendship, that som-tyme, with laughande chere, madest bothe
face and countenaunce to me-wardes? Truely, now art thou
went out of towne. But ever, me thinketh, he wereth his olde
50 clothes, and that the soule in the whiche the lyfe of frendship was
in, is drawen out from his other spirites. Now than, farewel,
frendship! and farewel, felawes! Me thinketh, ye al han taken
your leve; no force of you al at ones. But, lady of love, ye wote
what I mene; yet thinke on thy servaunt that for thy love
55 spilleth; al thinges have I forsake to folowen thyn hestes;
rewarde me with a thought, though ye do naught els. Remembraunce of love lyth so sore under my brest, that other thought
cometh not in my mynde but gladnesse, to thinke on your goodnesse
and your mery chere; †ferdnes and sorowe, to thinke on your
60 wreche and your daunger; from whiche Christ me save! My
greet joye it is to have in meditacion the bountees, the vertues,
the nobley in you printed; sorowe and helle comen at ones, to
suppose that I be †tweyved. Thus with care, sorowe, and tene
am I shapt, myn ende with dethe to make. Now, good goodly,
65 thinke on this. O wrecched foole that I am, fallen in-to so lowe,
the hete of my brenning tene hath me al defased. How shulde
ye, lady, sette prise on so foule fylthe? My conninge is thinne,
my wit is exiled; lyke to a foole naturel am I comparisoned.

---

33. wote; myne hert breketh.   34. howe.   grownde.   forthe.   35.
howe. shippe. great.   36. Howe.   39. nowe. sayne.   40. arte.
weate.   44. stretche.   45. stey. endlesse.   46. wotte. *I supply* am.
spurveyde. arte. nowe.   47. frenshyppe (*sic*).   48. nowe arte.
49. weareth.   51. Nowe.   53. leaue.   57. lythe.   59. frendes (*sic*); *for*
ferdnes; *cf.* p. 9, l. 9.   60. Christe.   61. great. bounties.   62. hel.   63. veyned
(*sic*); *for* weyued.   64. shapte. Nowe.   65. wretched.   66. heate.   68. wytte.

Trewly, lady, but your mercy the more were, I wot wel al my
labour were in ydel; your mercy than passeth right.   God graunt 70
that proposicion to be verifyed in me; so that, by truste of good
hope, I mowe come to the haven of ese.   And sith it is impossible, the colours of your qualitees to chaunge: and forsothe I
wot wel, wem ne spot may not abyde there so noble vertue
haboundeth, so that the defasing to you is verily [un]imaginable, 75
as countenaunce of goodnesse with encresinge vertue is so in you
knit, to abyde by necessary maner: yet, if the revers mighte falle
(which is ayenst kynde), I †wot wel myn herte ne shulde therfore
naught flitte, by the leste poynt of gemetrye; so sadly is it
†souded, that away from your service in love may he not departe. 80
O love, whan shal I ben plesed?   O charitee, whan shal I ben
esed?   O good goodly, whan shal the dyce turne?   O ful of
vertue, do the chaunce of comfort upwarde to falle!   O love,
whan wolt thou thinke on thy servaunt?   I can no more but here,
out-cast of al welfare, abyde the day of my dethe, or els to see the 85
sight that might al my wellinge sorowes voyde, and of the flode
make an ebbe.   These diseses mowen wel, by duresse of sorowe,
make my lyfe to unbodye, and so for to dye; but certes ye, lady,
in a ful perfeccion of love ben so knit with my soule, that deth
may not thilke knotte unbynde ne departe; so that ye and my 90
soule togider †in endeles blisse shulde dwelle; and there shal
my soule at the ful ben esed, that he may have your presence, to
shewe th'entent of his desyres.   Ah, dere god! that shal be a
greet joye!   Now, erthely goddesse, take regarde of thy servant,
though I be feble; for thou art wont to prayse them better that 95
wolde conne serve in love, al be he ful mener than kinges or
princes that wol not have that vertue in mynde.

Now, precious Margaryte, that with thy noble vertue hast
drawen me in-to love first, me weninge therof to have blisse,
[ther]-as galle and aloes are so moche spronge, that savour of 100
swetnesse may I not ataste.   Alas! that your benigne eyen, in
whiche that mercy semeth to have al his noriture, nil by no
waye tourne the clerenesse of mercy to me-wardes!   Alas! that
your brennande vertues, shyning amonges al folk, and enlumininge

---

69. wote.   72. ease.   sythe.   73. qualyties.   74. wote.   wemme
ne spotte maye.   75. *Read* unimaginable.   77. knytte.   fal.   78. wol
wel (*for* wot wel).   80. sonded; *read* souded.   maye.   81. pleased.
charyte.   82. eased.   83. comforte.   fal.   85. out caste.   daye.   se.
86. flodde.   87. diseases.   89. perfectyon.   knytte.   dethe.   91. togyther is
endelesse in blysse (!).   dwel.   92. eased.   93. thentent.   94. great.   Nowe.
95. arte wonte.   98. Nowe.   haste.   100. *I supply* ther.   104. folke.

105 al other people by habundaunce of encresing, sheweth to me
but smoke and no light! These thinges to thinke in myn herte
maketh every day weping in myn eyen to renne. These liggen
on my backe so sore, that importable burthen me semeth on my
backe to be charged; it maketh me backwarde to meve, whan
110 my steppes by comune course even-forth pretende. These
thinges also, on right syde and lift, have me so envolved with
care, that wanhope of helpe is throughout me ronne; trewly,
†I leve, that graceles is my fortune, whiche that ever sheweth it
me-wardes by a cloudy disese, al redy to make stormes of tene;
115 and the blisful syde halt stil awayward, and wol it not suffre to
me-wardes to turne; no force, yet wol I not ben conquered.

O, alas! that your nobley, so moche among al other creatures
commended by †flowinge streme †of al maner vertues, but
ther ben wonderful, I not whiche that let the flood to come
120 in-to my soule; wherefore, purely mated with sorowe thorough-
sought, my-selfe I crye on your goodnesse to have pitè on this
caytif, that in the in[ne]rest degree of sorowe and disese is left,
and, without your goodly wil, from any helpe and recovery.
These sorowes may I not sustene, but-if my sorowe shulde be
125 told and to you-wardes shewed; although moche space is bitwene
us twayne, yet me thinketh that by suche †joleyvinge wordes my
disese ginneth ebbe. Trewly, me thinketh that the sowne of my
lamentacious weping is right now flowe in-to your presence, and
there cryeth after mercy and grace, to which thing (me semeth)
130 thee list non answere to yeve, but with a deynous chere ye
commaunden it to avoide; but god forbid that any word shuld of
you springe, to have so litel routh! Pardè, pitè and mercy in
every Margarite is closed by kynde amonges many other vertues,
by qualitees of comfort; but comfort is to me right naught worth,
135 withouten mercy and pitè of you alone; whiche thinges hastely
god me graunt for his mercy!

---

105. encreasing.   110. forthe.   112, 113. trewly and leue ; *read* trewly
I leve.   113. gracelesse.   114. disease.   115. halte.   117. (*The sentence beginning* O, alas *seems hopelessly corrupt*; *there are pause-marks after* vertues
and wonderful.)   118. folowynge; *read* flowinge. by; *read* of.   119.
flode.   122. caytife. inrest. disease. lefte.   124. maye.   125. tolde.
126. ioleynynge (*sic*).   127. disease.   128. nowe.   130. the lyst
none.   131. worde.   134. qualites of comforte. worthe.

CHAPTER II.

REHERSINGE these thinges and many other, without tyme
or moment of rest, me semed, for anguisshe of disese, that
al-togider I was ravisshed, I can not telle how; but hoolly all my
passions and felinges weren lost, as it semed, for the tyme; and
sodainly a maner of drede lighte in me al at ones; nought suche 5
fere as folk have of an enemy, that were mighty and wolde hem
greve or don hem disese. For, I trowe, this is wel knowe to many
persones, that otherwhyle, if a man be in his soveraignes presence,
a maner of ferdnesse crepeth in his herte, not for harme, but of
goodly subjeccion; namely, as men reden that aungels ben aferde 10
of our saviour in heven. And pardè, there ne is, ne may no
passion of disese be; but it is to mene, that angels ben adradde,
not by †ferdnes of drede, sithen they ben perfitly blissed, [but]
as [by] affeccion of wonderfulnesse and by service of obedience.
Suche ferde also han these lovers in presence of their loves, and 15
subjectes aforn their soveraynes. Right so with ferdnesse myn
herte was caught. And I sodainly astonied, there entred in-to
the place there I was logged a lady, the semeliest and most
goodly to my sight that ever to-forn apered to any creature; and
trewly, in the blustringe of her looke, she yave gladnesse and 20
comfort sodaynly to al my wittes; and right so she doth to
every wight that cometh in her presence. And for she was so
goodly, as me thought, myn herte began somdele to be enbolded,
and wexte a litel hardy to speke; but yet, with a quakinge
voyce, as I durste, I salued her, and enquired what she was; 25
and why she, so worthy to sight, dayned to entre in-to so foule
a dongeon, and namely a prison, without leve of my kepers.
For certes, al-though the vertue of dedes of mercy strecchen to
visiten the poore prisoners, and hem, after that facultees ben had,
to comforte, me semed that I was so fer fallen in-to miserye and 30
wrecched hid caytifnesse, that me shulde no precious thing
neighe; and also, that for my sorowe every wight shulde ben
hevy, and wisshe my recovery. But whan this lady had somdele

CH. II.   2. disease.   3. tel howe.   holy.   4. loste.   5. light.
6. feare. folke.   7. done.   disease.   9. ferdenesse.   10. subiection.
11. maye.   12. disease.   meane.   13. frendes; *read* ferdnes; *see* l. 16.
perfytely. *I supply* but *and* by.   14. affection.   16. aforne.   ferdenesse.
18. lodged. moste.   19. to-forne.   21. comforte sodaynely.   dothe.   23.
myne. beganne.   27. prisone.   leaue.   28. al-thoughe.   stretchen.
29. faculties.   30. ferre.   31. wretched hyd.   thynge.   33. heauy.

apperceyved, as wel by my wordes as by my chere, what thought
35 besied me within, with a good womanly countenance she sayde
these wordes :—

'O my nory, wenest thou that my maner be, to foryete my
frendes or my servauntes? Nay,' quod she, 'it is my ful entente
to visyte and comforte al my frendshippes and allyes, as wel in
40 tyme of perturbacion as of moost propertee of blisse; in me shal
unkyndnesse never be founden: and also, sithen I have so fewe
especial trewe now in these dayes. Wherefore I may wel at more
leysar come to hem that me deserven; and if my cominge may
in any thinge avayle, wete wel, I wol come often.'

45 'Now, good lady,' quod I, 'that art so fayre on to loke,
reyninge hony by thy wordes, blisse of paradys arn thy lokinges,
joye and comfort are thy movinges. What is thy name? How
is it that in you is so mokel werkinge vertues enpight, as me
semeth, and in none other creature that ever saw I with myne
50 eyen?'

'My disciple,' quod she, 'me wondreth of thy wordes and on
thee, that for a litel disese hast foryeten my name. Wost thou
not wel that I am LOVE, that first thee brought to thy service?'

'O good lady,' quod I, 'is this worship to thee or to thyn
55 excellence, for to come in-to so foule a place? Pardè, somtyme,
tho I was in prosperitè and with forayne goodes envolved, I had
mokil to done to drawe thee to myn hostel; and yet many
werninges thou madest er thou liste fully to graunte, thyn home
to make at my dwelling-place; and now thou comest goodly by
60 thyn owne vyse, to comforte me with wordes; and so there-
thorough I ginne remembre on passed gladnesse. Trewly, lady,
I ne wot whether I shal say welcome or non, sithen thy coming
wol as moche do me tene and sorowe, as gladnesse and mirthe.
See why: for that me comforteth to thinke on passed gladnesse,
65 that me anoyeth efte to be in doinge. Thus thy cominge bothe
gladdeth and teneth, and that is cause of moche sorowe. Lo, lady,
how than I am comforted by your comminge'; and with that
I gan in teeres to distille, and tenderly wepe.

'Now, certes,' quod Love, 'I see wel, and that me over-

---

37. wenyst. foryet. 38. naye. 39. frenshippes. alyes. 40. propertye. 42.
nowe. 42, 43. maye. 45. Nowe. 46. honny. paradise. 47. comforte. howe.
49. sawe. 52. the. disease haste. Woste. 53. the. 54. worshyppe.
the. thyne. 57. the. 58. graunt thyne. 59. nowe. 60. thyne.
61. thoroughe. 62. wotte. none. 64. se. 67. howe. 69. Nowe. se.

thinketh, that wit in thee fayleth, and [thou] art in pointe 70
to dote.'

'Trewly,' quod I, 'that have ye maked, and that ever wol
I rue.'

'Wottest thou not wel,' quod she, 'that every shepherde ought
by reson to seke his sperkelande sheep, that arn ronne in-to 75
wildernesse among busshes and perils, and hem to their pasture
ayen-bringe, and take on hem privy besy cure of keping? And
though the unconninge sheep scattred wolde ben lost, renning to
wildernesse, and to desertes drawe, or els wolden putte hem-selfe
to the swalowinge wolfe, yet shal the shepherde, by businesse and 80
travayle, so putte him forth, that he shal not lete hem be lost by
no waye. A good shepherde putteth rather his lyf to ben lost for
his sheep. But for thou shalt not wene me being of werse
condicion, trewly, for everich of my folke, and for al tho that to
me-ward be knit in any condicion, I wol rather dye than suffre 85
hem through errour to ben spilte. For me liste, and it me lyketh,
of al myne a shepherdesse to be cleped. Wost thou not wel,
I fayled never wight, but he me refused and wolde negligently go
with unkyndenesse? And yet, pardè, have I many such holpe
and releved, and they have ofte me begyled; but ever, at the ende, 90
it discendeth in their owne nekkes. Hast thou not rad how kinde
I was to Paris, Priamus sone of Troy? How Jason me falsed,
for al his false behest? How Cesars †swink, I lefte it for no tene
til he was troned in my blisse for his service? What!' quod she,
'most of al, maked I not a loveday bytwene god and mankynde, 95
and chees a mayde to be nompere, to putte the quarel at ende?
Lo! how I have travayled to have thank on al sydes, and yet list
me not to reste, and I might fynde on †whom I shulde werche.
But trewly, myn owne disciple, bycause I have thee founde, at al
assayes, in thy wil to be redy myn hestes to have folowed and 100
hast ben trewe to that Margarite-perle that ones I thee shewed;
and she alwaye, ayenward, hath mad but daungerous chere;
I am come, in propre person, to putte thee out of errours, and
make thee gladde by wayes of reson; so that sorow ne disese shal

70. wytte in the. *I supply* thou.   arte.   74. shepeherde.   75. shepe.
arne.   76. amonge.   78. tho.   shepe.   loste.   79. put.   80. shepeherde.
81. put.   forthe.   let.   loste.   82. shepeherde.   lyfe.   loste.   83. shepe.
shalte.   85. mewarde.   86. throughe.   91. Haste.   radde howe.
93. *For* false *read* faire.   howe Sesars sonke (*sic*); *corrupt.*   92. sonne.
95. louedaye.   96. chese.   put.   97. howe.   thanke.   98. rest.
home; *read* whom.   99. the.   101. haste.   the.   102. ayenwarde.
made.   103. put the.   104. the.   reason.   disease.

105 no more hereafter thee amaistry. Wherthrough I hope thou
shalt lightly come to the grace, that thou longe hast desyred, of
thilke jewel. Hast thou not herd many ensamples, how I have
comforted and releved the scholers of my lore? Who hath
worthyed kinges in the felde? Who hath honoured ladyes in
110 boure by a perpetuel mirrour of their tr[o]uthe in my service?
Who hath caused worthy folk to voyde vyce and shame? Who
hath holde cytees and realmes in prosperitè? If thee liste clepe
ayen thyn olde remembraunce, thou coudest every point of this
declare in especial; and say that I, thy maistresse, have be cause,
115 causing these thinges and many mo other.'

'Now, y-wis, madame,' quod I, 'al these thinges I knowe wel
my-selfe, and that thyn excellence passeth the understanding of
us beestes; and that no mannes wit erthely may comprehende thy
vertues.'

120 'Wel than,' quod she, 'for I see thee in disese and sorowe,
I wot wel thou art oon of my nories; I may not suffre thee so to
make sorowe, thyn owne selfe to shende. But I my-selfe come
to be thy fere, thyn hevy charge to make to seme the lesse. For wo
is him that is alone; and to the sorye, to ben moned by a sorouful
125 wight, it is greet gladnesse. Right so, with my sicke frendes I am
sicke; and with sorie I can not els but sorowe make, til whan
I have hem releved in suche wyse, that gladnesse, in a maner of
counterpaysing, shal restore as mokil in joye as the passed hevinesse biforn did in tene. And also,' quod she, 'whan any of my
130 servauntes ben alone in solitary place, I have yet ever besied me
to be with hem, in comfort of their hertes, and taught hem to
make songes of playnte and of blisse, and to endyten letters of
rethorike in queynt understondinges, and to bethinke hem in what
wyse they might best their ladies in good service plese; and
135 also to lerne maner in countenaunce, in wordes, and in bering,
and to ben meke and lowly to every wight, his name and fame to
encrese; and to yeve gret yeftes and large, that his renomè may
springen. But thee therof have I excused; for thy losse and thy
grete costages, wherthrough thou art nedy, arn nothing to me
140 unknowen; but I hope to god somtyme it shal ben amended, as

---

105. the.   106. shalte. haste.   107. Haste. herde. howe.   111.
folke.   112. cyties. the. cleape.   113. poynte.   116. Nowe.   118. wytte.
120. se the in diseease.   121. wote. arte one. maye. the.   123. thyne.
125. great.   129. byforne.   131. comforte.   134. please.   135.
bearyng.   137. encrease. maye.   138. the.   139. great. wherthroughe.
arte. arne no-thinge.

thus I sayd.　In norture have I taught al myne; and in curtesye made hem expert, their ladies hertes to winne; and if any wolde [b]en deynous or proude, or be envious or of wrecches acqueyntaunce, hasteliche have I suche voyded out of my scole.　For al vyces trewly I hate; vertues and worthinesse in al my power 145 I avaunce.'

'Ah! worthy creature,' quod I, 'and by juste cause the name of goddesse dignely ye mowe bere! In thee lyth the grace thorough whiche any creature in this worlde hath any goodnesse. Trewly, al maner of blisse and preciousnesse in vertue out of 150 thee springen and wellen, as brokes and rivers proceden from their springes.　And lyke as al waters by kynde drawen to the see, so al kyndely thinges thresten, by ful appetyte of desyre, to drawe after thy steppes, and to thy presence aproche as to their kyndely perfeccion.　How dare than beestes in this worlde aught forfete 155 ayenst thy devyne purveyaunce?　Also, lady, ye knowen al the privy thoughtes; in hertes no counsayl may ben hid from your knowing.　Wherfore I wot wel, lady, that ye knowe your-selfe that I in my conscience am and have ben willinge to your service, al coude I never do as I shulde; yet, forsothe, fayned I never to 160 love otherwyse than was in myn herte; and if I coude have made chere to one and y-thought another, as many other doon alday afore myn eyen, I trowe it wolde not me have vayled.'

'Certes,' quod she, 'haddest thou so don, I wolde not now have thee here visited.'　　　　　　　　　　　165

'Ye wete wel, lady, eke,' quod I, 'that I have not played raket, "nettil in, docke out," and with the wethercocke waved; and trewly, there ye me sette, by acorde of my conscience I wolde not flye, til ye and reson, by apert strength, maden myn herte to tourne.'　　　　　　　　　　　170

'In good fayth,' quod she, 'I have knowe thee ever of tho condicions; and sithen thou woldest (in as moch as in thee was) a made me privy of thy counsayl and juge of thy conscience (though I forsook it in tho dayes til I saw better my tyme), wolde never god that I shuld now fayle; but ever I wol be redy 175 witnessing thy sothe, in what place that ever I shal, ayenst al tho that wol the contrary susteyne.　And for as moche as to me is

naught unknowen ne hid of thy privy herte, but al hast thou tho
things mad to me open at the ful, that hath caused my cominge
180 in-to this prison, to voyde the webbes of thyne eyen, to make thee
clerely to see the errours thou hast ben in.   And bycause that
men ben of dyvers condicions, some adradde to saye a sothe, and
some for a sothe anon redy to fighte, and also that I may not my-
selfe ben in place to withsaye thilke men that of thee speken
185 otherwyse than the sothe, I wol and I charge thee, in vertue of
obedience that thou to me owest, to wryten my wordes and sette
hem in wrytinges, that they mowe, as my witnessinge, ben
noted among the people.   For bookes written neyther dreden ne
shamen, ne stryve conne; but only shewen the entente of the
190 wryter, and yeve remembraunce to the herer; and if any wol in
thy presence saye any-thing to tho wryters, loke boldely ; truste on
Mars to answere at the ful.   For certes, I shal him enfourme of
al the trouthe in thy love, with thy conscience ; so that of his
helpe thou shalt not varye at thy nede.   I trowe the strongest and
195 the beste that may be founde wol not transverse thy wordes ;
wherof than woldest thou drede ? '

CHAPTER III.

GRETLY was I tho gladded of these wordes, and (as who
saith) wexen somdel light in herte ; both for the auctoritè
of witnesse, and also for sikernesse of helpe of the forsayd
beheste, and sayd : —
5   'Trewly, lady, now am I wel gladded through comfort of
your wordes.   Be it now lykinge unto your nobley to shewe
whiche folk diffame your servauntes, sithe your service ought
above al other thinges to ben commended.'
'Yet,' quod she, 'I see wel thy soule is not al out of the
10 amased cloude.   Thee were better to here thing that thee might
lighte out of thyn hevy charge and after knowing of thyn owne
helpe, than to stirre swete wordes and such resons to here ;
for in a thoughtful soule (and namely suche oon as thou art)
wol not yet suche thinges sinken.   Come of, therfore, and let

---

178. hert.   179. made.   180. the.   181. se.   183. anone. fyght. maye.
184. withsay.   the.   185. the.   188. amonge.   189. onely.
191. -thynge.   194. shalte.   195. maye.   transuers.
Ch. III.   1. gladed ; *see* l. 5.   2. somdele.   5. nowe. comforte.   6.
nowe.   7. folke.   9. se.   10. the (*twice*).   11. light.   13. one. arte.

me seen thy hevy charge, that I may the lightlier for thy comfort 15
purveye.'

'Now, certes, lady,' quod I, 'the moste comfort I might have
were utterly to wete me be sure in herte of that Margaryte I
serve; and so I thinke to don with al mightes, whyle my lyfe
dureth.'   20

'Than,' quod she, 'mayst thou therafter, in suche wyse that
misplesaunce ne entre?'

'In good fayth,' quod I, 'there shal no misplesaunce be
caused through trespace on my syde.'

'And I do thee to weten,' quod she, 'I sette never yet person 25
to serve in no place (but-if he caused the contrary in defautes
and trespaces) that he ne spedde of his service.'

'Myn owne erthly lady,' quod I tho, 'and yet remembre to
your worthinesse how long sithen, by many revolving of yeres,
in tyme whan Octobre his leve ginneth take and Novembre 30
sheweth him to sight, whan bernes ben ful of goodes as is the
nutte on every halke; and than good lond-tillers ginne shape
for the erthe with greet travayle, to bringe forth more corn to
mannes sustenaunce, ayenst the nexte yeres folowing. In suche
tyme of plentee he that hath an home and is wyse, list not to 35
wander mervayles to seche, but he be constrayned or excited.
Oft the lothe thing is doon, by excitacion of other mannes
opinion, whiche wolden fayne have myn abydinge. [Tho gan I]
take in herte of luste to travayle and see the wynding of the erthe
in that tyme of winter. By woodes that large stretes wern in, 40
by smale pathes that swyn and hogges hadden made, as lanes
with ladels their maste to seche, I walked thinkinge alone
a wonder greet whyle; and the grete beestes that the woode
haunten and adorneth al maner forestes, and heerdes gonne to
wilde. Than, er I was war, I neyghed to a see-banke; and for 45
ferde of the beestes "shipcraft" I cryde. For, lady, I trowe ye
wete wel your-selfe, nothing is werse than the beestes that
shulden ben tame, if they cacche her wildenesse, and ginne ayen
waxe ramage. Thus forsothe was I a-ferd, and to shippe me
hyed.   50

Than were there y-nowe to lacche myn handes, and drawe me

---

15. sene. comforte.   16. puruey.   17. Nowe. comforte.   21. mayste.
25. the. set.   29. howe.   30. leaue.   32. londe-.   33. great.
forthe. corne.   35. plentie. lyste.   37. doone.   38. *I supply* Tho gan I.
39. se.   40. werne.   41. swyne.   43. great. great.   44. gone; *read*
gonne.   45. ware.   46. shypcrafte.   48. catche.   49. a-ferde.   51. lache.

to shippe, of whiche many I knew wel the names. Sight was
the first, Lust was another, Thought was the thirde; and Wil eke
was there a mayster; these broughten me within-borde of this
55 shippe of Traveyle. So whan the sayl was sprad, and this ship
gan to move, the wind and water gan for to ryse, and overthwartly
to turne the welken. The wawes semeden as they kiste togider;
but often under colour of kissinge is mokel old hate prively
closed and kept. The storm so straungely and in a devouring
60 maner gan so faste us assayle, that I supposed the date of my
deth shulde have mad there his ginning. Now up, now downe,
now under the wawe and now aboven was my ship a greet
whyle. And so by mokel duresse of †weders and of stormes,
and with greet avowing [of] pilgrimages, I was driven to an yle,
65 where utterly I wende first to have be rescowed; but trewly, †at
the first ginning, it semed me so perillous the haven to cacche,
that but thorow grace I had ben comforted, of lyfe I was ful
dispayred. Trewly, lady, if ye remembre a-right of al maner
thinges, your-selfe cam hastely to sene us see-driven, and to
70 weten what we weren. But first ye were deynous of chere, after
whiche ye gonne better a-lighte; and ever, as me thought, ye
lived in greet drede of disese; it semed so by your chere.
And whan I was certifyed of your name, the lenger I loked in
you, the more I you goodly dradde; and ever myn herte on you
75 opened the more; and so in a litel tyme my ship was out of
mynde. But, lady, as ye me ladde, I was war bothe of beestes
and of fisshes, a greet nombre thronging togider; among whiche
a muskel, in a blewe shel, had enclosed a Margaryte-perle, the
moste precious and best that ever to-forn cam in my sight.
80 And ye tolden your-selfe, that ilke jewel in his kinde was so
good and so vertuous, that her better shulde I never finde, al
sought I ther-after to the worldes ende. And with that I held
my pees a greet whyle; and ever sithen I have me bethought on
the man that sought the precious Margarytes; and whan he had
85 founden oon to his lyking, he solde al his good to bye that jewel.
Y-wis, thought I, (and yet so I thinke), now have I founden the
jewel that myn herte desyreth; wherto shulde I seche further?

---

52. many; *read* meynee. knewe.   55. sayle. shyppe.   56. wynde.
58. olde.   59. kepte. storme.   61. made.   61, 62. nowe.   62. shyppe. 62,
64. great.   63. wethers; *read* weders.   64. *I supply* of.   65. as; *read* at.
66. catche.   67. thorowe.   69. came.   71. a-lyght.   72. grent. disease.
75. shyppe.   76. lad. ware.   77. great. amonge.   79. to-forne came.
82. helde.   83. peace. great.   85. one.   86. nowe.   87. myne.

Trewly, now wol I stinte, and on this Margaryte I sette me for
ever: now than also, sithen I wiste wel it was your wil that
I shulde so suche a service me take; and so to desyre that thing, 90
of whiche I never have blisse.   There liveth non but he hath
disese; your might than that brought me to suche service, that to
me is cause of sorowe and of joye.   I wonder of your worde that
ye sayn, "to bringen men in-to joye"; and, pardè, ye wete wel
that defaut ne trespace may not resonably ben put to me-wardes, 95
as fer as my conscience knoweth.

But of my disese me list now a whyle to speke, and to enforme
you in what maner of blisse ye have me thronge.   For truly
I wene, that al gladnesse, al joye, and al mirthe is beshet under
locke, and the keye throwe in suche place that it may not be 100
founde.   My brenning wo hath altred al my hewe.   Whan
I shulde slepe, I walowe and I thinke, and me disporte.   Thus
combred, I seme that al folk had me mased.   Also, lady myne,
desyre hath longe dured, some speking to have; or els at the lest
have ben enmoysed with sight; and for wantinge of these thinges 105
my mouth wolde, and he durst, pleyne right sore, sithen yvels
for my goodnesse arn manyfolde to me yolden.   I wonder, lady,
trewly, save evermore your reverence, how ye mowe, for shame,
suche thinges suffre on your servaunt to be so multiplied.
Wherfore, kneling with a lowe herte, I pray you to rue on this 110
caytif, that of nothing now may serve.   Good lady, if ye liste,
now your help to me shewe, that am of your privyest servantes
at al assayes in this tyme, and under your winges of proteccion.
No help to me-wardes is shapen; how shal than straungers in
any wyse after socour loke, whan I, that am so privy, yet of helpe 115
I do fayle?   Further may I not, but thus in this prison abyde;
what bondes and chaynes me holden, lady, ye see wel your-selfe.
A renyant forjuged hath not halfe the care.   But thus, syghing
and sobbing, I wayle here alone; and nere it for comfort of your
presence, right here wolde I sterve.   And yet a litel am I gladded, 120
that so goodly suche grace and non hap have I hent, graciously
to fynde the precious Margarite, that (al other left) men shulde
bye, if they shulde therfore selle al her substaunce.   Wo is me,

---

88. nowe.   89. Nowe.   91. none.   92. disease.   94. sayne.
95. reasonably.   96. ferre.   97. disease.   103. folke.   106. mouthe.
107. arne.   108. howe.   111. caytife.   112. nowe. helpe.   113.
protection.   114. helpe. howe.   115. socoure.   116. maye.   117. se.
119. comforte.   120. gladed.   121. none. hente.   122. lefte.   123. sel.

that so many let-games and purpose-brekers ben maked wayters,
125 suche prisoners as I am to overloke and to hinder; and, for
suche lettours, it is hard any suche jewel to winne. Is this, lady,
an honour to thy deitee? Me thinketh, by right, suche people
shulde have no maistrye, ne ben overlokers over none of thy
servauntes. Trewly, were it leful unto you, to al the goddes
130 wolde I playne, that ye rule your devyne purveyaunce amonges
your servantes nothing as ye shulde. Also, lady, my moeble is
insuffysaunt to countervayle the price of this jewel, or els to
make th'eschange. Eke no wight is worthy suche perles to were
but kinges or princes or els their peres. This jewel, for vertue,
135 wold adorne and make fayre al a realme; the nobley of vertue is
so moche, that her goodnesse overal is commended. Who is it
that wolde not wayle, but he might suche richesse have at his
wil? The vertue therof out of this prison may me deliver, and
naught els. And if I be not ther-thorow holpen, I see my-selfe
140 withouten recovery. Although I might hence voyde, yet wolde
I not; I wolde abyde the day that destenee hath me ordeyned,
whiche I suppose is without amendement; so sore is my herte
bounden, that I may thinken non other. Thus strayte, lady,
hath sir Daunger laced me in stockes, I leve it be not your wil;
145 and for I see you taken so litel hede, as me thinketh, and wol
not maken by your might the vertue in mercy of the Margaryte
on me for to strecche, so as ye mowe wel in case that you liste,
my blisse and my mirthe arn feld; sicknesse and sorowe ben
alwaye redy. The cope of tene is wounde aboute al my body,
150 that stonding is me best; unneth may I ligge for pure misesy
sorowe. And yet al this is litel ynough to be the ernest-silver in
forwarde of this bargayne; for treble-folde so mokel muste I suffer
er tyme come of myn ese. For he is worthy no welthe, that may
no wo suffer. And certes, I am hevy to thinke on these thinges;
155 but who shal yeve me water ynough to drinke, lest myn eyen
drye, for renning stremes of teres? Who shal waylen with me
myn owne happy hevinesse? Who shal counsaile me now in
my lyking tene, and in my goodly harse? I not. For ever the
more I brenne, the more I coveyte; the more that I sorow, the
160 more thrist I in gladnesse. Who shal than yeve me a contrarious

---

126. harde.   127. deytie.   133. weare.   139. ther-thorowe. se.
141. daye. destenye.   143. maye. none.   145. se.   147. stretche.
148. arne.   150. miseasy.   151. ynoughe.   153. ease. maye.   156.
teares.   157. myne. nowe.   158. harse (*sic*); *for* harme?

drink, to stanche the thurste of my blisful bitternesse? Lo, thus
I brenne and I drenche; I shiver and I swete. To this reversed
yvel wàs never yet ordeyned salve; forsoth al †leches ben unconning, save the Margaryte alone, any suche remedye to purveye.'

CHAPTER IV.

AND with these wordes I brast out to wepe, that every teere
of myne eyen, for greetnesse semed they boren out the bal of
my sight, and that al the water had ben out-ronne. Than thought
me that Love gan a litel to hevye for miscomfort of my chere;
and gan soberly and in esy maner speke, wel avysinge what 5
she sayd. Comenly the wyse speken esily and softe for many
skilles. Oon is, their wordes are the better bileved; and also, in
esy spekinge, avysement men may cacche, what to putte forth
and what to holden in. And also, the auctoritè of esy wordes is
the more; and eke, they yeven the more understandinge to other 10
intencion of the mater. Right so this lady esely and in a softe
maner gan say these wordes.

¶ 'Mervayle,' quod she, 'greet it is, that by no maner of semblaunt, as fer as I can espye, thou list not to have any recour;
but ever thou playnest and sorowest, and wayes of remedye, for 15
folisshe wilfulnesse, thee list not to seche. But enquyre of thy
next frendes, that is, thyne inwit and me that have ben thy
maystresse, and the recour and fyne of thy disese; [f]or of disese is
gladnessè and joy, with a ful †vessel so helded, that it quencheth
the felinge of the firste tenes. But thou that were wont not only 20
these thinges remembre in thyne herte, but also fooles therof to
enfourmen, in adnullinge of their errours and distroying of their
derke opinions, and in comfort of their sere thoughtes; now canst
thou not ben comfort of thyn owne soule, in thinking of these
thinges. O where hast thou be so longe commensal, that hast so 25
mikel eeten of the potages of foryetfulnesse, and dronken so of
ignorance, that the olde souking[es] whiche thou haddest of me
arn amaystred and lorn fro al maner of knowing? O, this is

---

161. drinke.   162. sweate.   163. lyches (for leches).   164. puruey.
CH. IV.   2. great-.   4. heauy.   5. easy.   6. easyly.   7. One.
8. easy speakynge.   catche.   put forthe.   9. easy.   11. ladye easely.
13. great.   14. ferre.   16. the lyste.   17. inwytte.   18. disease (*twice*).
19. nessel; *misprint for* uessel.   20. wonte.   onely.   22. distroyeng.
23. comforte.   seare.   24. comforte.   25. haste.   27. soukyng.   28. arne.

a worthy person to helpe other, that can not counsayle him-selfe!'
30 And with these wordes, for pure and stronge shame, I wox al
reed.

And she than, seing me so astonyed by dyvers stoundes,
sodainly (which thing kynde hateth) gan deliciously me comforte
with sugred wordes, putting me in ful hope that I shulde the
35 Margarite getten, if I folowed her hestes; and gan with a fayre
clothe to wypen the teres that hingen on my chekes; and than
sayd I in this wyse.

'Now, wel of wysdom and of al welthe, withouten thee may
nothing ben lerned; thou berest the keyes of al privy thinges.
40 In vayne travayle men to cacche any stedship, but-if ye, lady,
first the locke unshet. Ye, lady, lerne us the wayes and the
by-pathes to heven. Ye, lady, maken al the hevenly bodyes
goodly and benignely to don her cours, that governen us beestes
here on erthe. Ye armen your servauntes ayenst al debates with
45 imperciable harneys; ye setten in her hertes insuperable blood of
hardinesse; ye leden hem to the parfit good. Yet al thing
desyreth ye werne no man of helpe, that †wol don your
lore. Graunt me now a litel of your grace, al my sorowes
to cese.'

50 'Myne owne servaunt,' quod she, 'trewly thou sittest nye
myne herte; and thy badde chere gan sorily me greve. But
amonge thy playning wordes, me thought, thou allegest thinges to
be letting of thyne helpinge and thy grace to hinder; wherthrough,
me thinketh, that wanhope is crope thorough thyn hert. God
55 forbid that nyse unthrifty thought shulde come in thy mynde,
thy wittes to trouble; sithen every thing in coming is contingent.
Wherfore make no more thy proposicion by an impossible.
But now, I praye thee reherse me ayen tho thinges that
thy mistrust causen; and thilke thinges I thinke by reson to
60 distroyen, and putte ful hope in thyn herte. What understondest
thou there,' quod she, 'by that thou saydest, "many let-games
are thyn overlokers?" And also by "that thy moeble is insuffysaunt"? I not what thou therof menest.'

'Trewly,' quod I, 'by the first I say, that janglers evermore
65 arn spekinge rather of yvel than of good; for every age of man

---

30. woxe.   33. thynge.   36. teares.   38. Nowe. wysedom. the.
39. bearest.   40. catche.   43. done her course.   45. blode.   46.
leaden.   parfyte.   thynge.   47. wern.   wele; *read* wol.   done.   48.
nowe.   49. cease.   53. wherthroughe.   58. nowe. the.   59. reason.
60. put.   61. lette-games.   63. meanest.   65. arne.

rather enclyneth to wickednesse, than any goodnesse to avaunce.
Also false wordes springen so wyde, by the stering of false lying
tonges, that fame als swiftely flyeth to her eres and sayth many
wicked tales ; and as soone shal falsenesse ben leved as tr[o]uthe,
for al his gret sothnesse.   70

Now by that other,' quod I, 'me thinketh thilke jewel so
precious, that to no suche wrecche as I am wolde vertue therof
extende ; and also I am to feble in worldly joyes, any suche
jewel to countrevayle. For suche people that worldly joyes han
at her wil ben sette at the highest degree, and most in reverence 75
ben accepted. For false wening maketh felicitè therin to be
supposed ; but suche caytives as I am evermore ben hindred.'

'Certes,' quod she, 'take good hede, and I shal by reson to
thee shewen, that al these thinges mowe nat lette thy purpos
by the leest point that any wight coude pricke.   80

CHAPTER V.

REMEMBREST nat,' quod she, 'ensample is oon of the
strongest maner[es], as for to preve a mannes purpos ?
Than if I now, by ensample, enduce thee to any proposicion, is
it nat preved by strength ? '

'Yes, forsothe,' quod I.   5

'Wel,' quod she, 'raddest thou never how Paris of Troye and
Heleyne loved togider, and yet had they not entrecomuned of
speche? Also Acrisius shette Dane his doughter in a tour, for
suertee that no wight shulde of her have no maistry in my
service ; and yet Jupiter by signes, without any speche, had 10
al his purpose ayenst her fathers wil. And many suche mo have
ben knitte in trouthe, and yet spake they never togider ; for
that is a thing enclosed under secretnesse of privytè, why twey
persons entremellen hertes after a sight. The power in knowing,
of such thinges †to preven, shal nat al utterly be yeven to you 15
beestes ; for many thinges, in suche precious maters, ben
reserved to jugement of devyne purveyaunce ; for among lyving
people, by mannes consideracion, moun they nat be determined.

---

67. steeryng. lyeng.   68. eares.   72. wretche.   78. reason.   79.
the. let. purpose.
CH. V. 1. one.   2. maner ; *read* maneres. purpose.   3. nowe. the.
4. proued.   6. howe.   9. suertie.   15. so ; *read* to.   17. lyueng.

Wherfore I saye, al the envy, al the janglinge, that wel ny [al]
20 people upon my servauntes maken †ofte, is rather cause of esployte
than of any hindringe.'

'Why, than,' quod I, ' suffre ye such wrong ; and moun, whan
ye list, lightly al such yvels abate ? Me semeth, to you it is
a greet unworship.'

25 'O,' quod she, 'hold now thy pees. I have founden to many
that han ben to me unkynde, that trewly I wol suffre every wight
in that wyse to have disese ; and who that continueth to the ende
wel and trewly, hem wol I helpen, and as for oon of myne in-to
blisse [don] to wende. As [in] marcial doing in Grece, who
30 was y-crowned ? By god, nat the strongest ; but he that rathest
com and lengest abood and continued in the journey, and spared
nat to traveyle as long as the play leste. But thilke person, that
profred him now to my service, [and] therin is a while, and anon
voideth and [is] redy to another ; and so now oon he thinketh
35 and now another ; and in-to water entreth and anon respireth :
such oon list me nat in-to perfit blisse of my service bringe.
A tree ofte set in dyvers places wol nat by kynde endure to bringe
forth frutes. Loke now, I pray thee, how myne olde servauntes
of tyme passed continued in her service, and folowe thou after
40 their steppes ; and than might thou not fayle, in case thou worche
in this wyse.'

'Certes,' quod I, 'it is nothing lich, this world, to tyme
passed ; eke this countrè hath oon maner, and another countrè
hath another. And so may nat a man alway putte to his eye the
45 salve that he heled with his hele. For this is sothe : betwixe
two thinges liche, ofte dyversitè is required.'

'Now,' quod she, ' that is sothe ; dyversitè of nation, dyversitè of
lawe, as was maked by many resons ; for that dyversitè cometh in
by the contrarious malice of wicked people, that han envyous hertes
50 ayenst other. But trewly, my lawe to my servauntes ever hath
ben in general, whiche may nat fayle. For right as mannes †lawe
that is ordained by many determinacions, may nat be knowe for
good or badde, til assay of the people han proved it and [founden]
to what ende it draweth ; and than it sheweth the necessitè

---

19. *I supply* al.   20. efte ; *read* ofte.   24. great.   25. holde nowe
thy peace.   27. disease.   29. one. *I supply* don. *I supply* in.
31. come. abode.   32. lest.   33. nowe. *I supply* and.   34. *I supply* is.
nowe one.   35. nowe.   36. one. *per*fyte.   38. nowe. the howe.   42.
worlde.   43. one.   44. alwaye put.   45. healed.   47. Nowe.   48.
reasons.   51. lawes ; *read* lawe.   52. determinatiõs.   53. *I supply* founden.

therof, or els the impossibilitè : right so the lawe of my servauntes 55
so wel hath ben proved in general, that hitherto hath it not fayled.

Wiste thou not wel that al the lawe of kynde is my lawe, and
by god ordayned and stablisshed to dure by kynde resoun ?
Wherfore al lawe by mannes witte purveyed ought to be underput
to lawe of kynde, whiche yet hath be commune to every kyndely 60
creature ; that my statutes and my lawe that ben kyndely arn
general to al peoples. Olde doinges and by many turninges of
yeres used, and with the peoples maner proved, mowen nat so
lightly ben defased ; but newe doinges, contrariauntes suche olde,
ofte causen diseses and breken many purposes. Yet saye I nat 65
therfore that ayen newe mischeef men shulde nat ordaynen
a newe remedye ; but alwaye looke it contrary not the olde no
ferther than the malice streccheth. Than foloweth it, the olde
doinges in love han ben universal, as for most exployte[s] forth
used ; wherfore I wol not yet that of my lawes nothing be adnulled. 70
But thanne to thy purpos : suche jangelers and lokers, and
wayters of games, if thee thinke in aught they mowe dere, yet
love wel alwaye, and sette hem at naught ; and let thy port ben
lowe in every wightes presence, and redy in thyne herte to
maynteyne that thou hast begonne ; and a litel thee fayne with 75
mekenesse in wordes ; and thus with sleyght shalt thou surmount
and dequace the yvel in their hertes. And wysdom yet is to seme
flye otherwhyle, there a man wol fighte. Thus with suche thinges
the tonges of yvel shal ben stilled ; els fully to graunte thy ful
meninge, for-sothe ever was and ever it shal be, that myn enemyes 80
ben aferde to truste to any fightinge. And therfore have thou no
cowardes herte in my service, no more than somtyme thou
haddest in the contrarye. For if thou drede suche jangleres, thy
viage to make, understand wel, that he that dredeth any rayn, to
sowe his cornes, he shal have than [bare] bernes. Also he that 85
is aferd of his clothes, let him daunce naked ! Who nothing
undertaketh, and namely in my service, nothing acheveth. After
grete stormes the †weder is often mery and smothe. After
moche clatering, there is mokil rowning. Thus, after jangling
wordes, cometh " huissht ! pees ! and be stille ! " ' 90

' O good lady ! ' quod I than, ' see now how, seven yere passed ·

---

58. reasoun.   59. purueyde.   vnderputte.   61. arne.   65. diseases.
breaken.   66. mischefe.   68. stretcheth.   69. exployte forthe.   70.
nothynge.   71. purpose.   72. the.   73. lette.   porte.   75. the.
77. wysdome.   78. fyght.   79. graunt.   80. meanynge.   84. vnderstande. rayne.   85. *I supply* bare.   86. aferde.   88. great.   wether ;
read weder.   90. huysshte.   peace.   styl.   91. se nowe howe.

and more, have I graffed and †grobbed a vyne; and with al the
wayes that I coude I sought to a fed me of the grape; but frute
have I non founde. Also I have this seven yere served Laban, to
95 a wedded Rachel his doughter; but blere-eyed Lya is brought to
my bedde, which alway engendreth my tene, and is ful of children
in tribulacion and in care. And although the clippinges and
kissinges of Rachel shulde seme to me swete, yet is she so
barayne that gladnesse ne joye by no way wol springe; so that
100 I may wepe with Rachel. I may not ben counsayled with solace,
sithen issue of myn hertely desyre is fayled. Now than I pray that
to me [come] sone fredom and grace in this eight[eth] yere; this
eighteth mowe to me bothe be kinrest and masseday, after the
seven werkedays of travayle, to folowe the Christen lawe; and,
105 what ever ye do els, that thilke Margaryte be holden so, lady, in
your privy chambre, that she in this case to none other person be
committed.'

'Loke than,' quod she, 'thou persever in my service, in whiche
I have thee grounded; that thilke scorn in thyn enemyes mowe
110 this on thy person be not sothed: "lo! this man began to edefye,
but, for his foundement is bad, to the ende may he it not bringe."
For mekenesse in countenaunce, with a manly hert in dedes and
in longe continuaunce, is the conisance of my livery to al my
retinue delivered. What wenest thou, that me list avaunce suche
115 persons as loven the first sittinges at feestes, the highest stoles in
churches and in hal, loutinges of peoples in markettes and fayres;
unstedfaste to byde in one place any whyle togider; wening his
owne wit more excellent than other; scorning al maner devyse
but his own? Nay, nay, god wot, these shul nothing parten of
120 my blisse. Truly, my maner here-toforn hath ben [to] worship[pe]
with my blisse lyons in the felde and lambes in chambre;
egles at assaute and maydens in halle; foxes in counsayle, stil[le]
in their dedes; and their proteccioun is graunted, redy to ben
a bridge; and their baner is arered, like wolves in the felde.
125 Thus, by these wayes, shul men ben avaunced; ensample of
David, that from keping of shepe was drawen up in-to the order
of kingly governaunce; and Jupiter, from a bole, to ben Europes
fere; and Julius Cesar, from the lowest degrè in Rome, to be
mayster of al erthly princes; and Eneas from hel, to be king of

---

92. gronbed.   94. none.   101. Nowe.   102. *I supply* come.
103. kynrest (*sic*).   109. skorne.   110. this; *read* thus?   120. toforne.
121. worship; *read* worshippe (*verb*).   122. styl.   123. protection.

the countrè there Rome is now stonding. And so to thee I say ; 130
thy grace, by bering ther-after, may sette thee in suche plight,
that no jangling may greve the leest tucke of thy hemmes ; that
[suche] are their †jangles, is nought to counte at a cresse in thy
disavauntage.

CHAPTER VI.

EVER,' quod she, 'hath the people in this worlde desyred
to have had greet name in worthinesse, and hated foule
to bere any [en]fame ; and that is oon of the objeccions thou
alegest to be ayen thyne hertely desyre.'

'Ye, forsothe,' quod I ; 'and that, so comenly, the people wol 5
lye, and bringe aboute suche enfame.'

'Now,' quod she, 'if men with lesinges putte on thee enfame,
wenest thy-selfe therby ben enpeyred? That wening is wrong ;
see why ; for as moche as they lyen, thy meryte encreseth, and
make[th] thee ben more worthy, to hem that knowen of the soth ; 10
by what thing thou art apeyred, that in so mokil thou art encresed
of thy beloved frendes. And sothly, a wounde of thy frende [is]
to thee lasse harm, ye, sir, and better than a fals kissing in disceyvable glosing of thyne enemy ; above that than, to be wel with thy
frende maketh [voyd] suche enfame. *Ergo*, thou art encresed 15
and not apeyred.'

'Lady,' quod I, 'somtyme yet, if a man be in disese, th'estimacion of the envyous people ne loketh nothing to desertes of men,
ne to the merytes of their doinges, but only to the aventure of
fortune ; and therafter they yeven their sentence. And some 20
loken the voluntary wil in his herte, and therafter telleth his
jugement ; not taking hede to reson ne to the qualitè of the
doing ; as thus. If a man be riche and fulfild with worldly
welfulnesse, some commenden it, and sayn it is so lent by juste
cause ; and he that hath adversitè, they sayn he is weked ; and 25
hath deserved thilke anoy. The contrarye of these thinges some

---

130. nowe. the.   131. set the.   132. lest.   133. ianghes ; *read* jangles.
Ch. VI.   2. great.   beare.   3. *read* enfame ; *see l.* 6.   one.   obiections.
7. Nowe.   leasynges put on the.   8. wronge.   9. se.   encreaseth.
10. the.   11. arte encreased.   12. *I supply* is.   13. the.   harme.   false.
15. *I supply* voyd.   arte.   17. disease.   22. reason.   23. fulfylde.
24. sayne.   lente.   25. sayne.   weaked ; *read* wikked?   26. anoye.

men holden also; and sayn that to the riche prosperitè is pur-
vayed in-to his confusion; and upon this mater many autoritès
of many and greet-witted clerkes they alegen.   And some men
30 sayn, though al good estimacion forsake folk that han adversitè,
yet is it meryte and encrees of his blisse; so that these purposes
arn so wonderful in understanding, that trewly, for myn adversitè
now, I not how the sentence of the indifferent people wil jugen
my fame.'

35   'Therfore,' quod she, 'if any wight shulde yeve a trewe sentence on suche maters, the cause of the disese maist thou see
wel.   Understand ther-upon after what ende it draweth, that is to
sayne, good or badde; so ought it to have his fame †by goodnesse
or enfame by badnesse.   For [of] every resonable person, and
40 namely of a wyse man, his wit ought not, without reson to-forn
herd, sodainly in a mater to juge.   After the sawes of the wyse,
"thou shalt not juge ne deme toforn thou knowe."'

'Lady,' quod I, 'ye remembre wel, that in moste laude and
praysing of certayne seyntes in holy churche, is to rehersen their
45 conuersion from badde in-to good; and that is so rehersed, as
by a perpetual mirrour of remembraunce, in worshippinge of
tho sayntes, and good ensample to other misdoers in amendement.   How turned the Romayne Zedeoreys fro the Romaynes,
to be with Hanibal ayenst his kynde nacion; and afterwardes,
50 him seming the Romayns to be at the next degrè of confusion,
turned to his olde alyes; by whose witte after was Hanibal discomfited.   Wherfore, to enfourme you, lady, the maner-why
I mene, see now.   In my youth I was drawe to ben assentaunt
and (in my mightes) helping to certain conjuracions and other
55 grete maters of ruling of citizins; and thilke thinges ben my
drawers in; and ex[c]itours to tho maters wern so paynted and
coloured that (at the prime face) me semed them noble and
glorious to al the people.   I than, wening mikel meryte have
deserved in furthering and mayntenaunce of tho thinges, besyed
60 and laboured, with al my diligence, in werkinge of thilke maters
to the ende.   And trewly, lady, to telle you the sothe, me rought
litel of any hate of the mighty senatours in thilke citè, ne of

---

27. sayne.   29. great.   30. forsaken; *read* forsake.   31.
encrease.   32. arne.   33. nowe. howe.   36. disease. se.   37.
vnderstande.   38. fame or by goodnesse enfame; *read* fame by goodnesse
or enfame.   39. *Supply* of. reasonable.   40. wytte. reason to-forne.
41. herde.   42. toforne.   45. conuercion.   48. Howe. zedeoreys *or*
ʒedeoreys.   53. meane se nowe.   55. great.   56. exitours. werne.
61. tel.

comunes malice; for two skilles.   Oon was, I had comfort to ben
in suche plyte, that bothe profit were to me and to my frendes.
Another was, for commen profit in cominaltee is not but pees and 65
tranquilitè, with just governaunce, proceden from thilke profit;
sithen, by counsayle of myne inwitte, me thought the firste painted
thinges malice and yvel meninge, withouten any good avayling to
any people, and of tyrannye purposed.   And so, for pure sorowe,
and of my medlinge and badde infame that I was in ronne, tho 70
[the] teres [that] lasshed out of myne eyen were thus awaye
wasshe, than the under-hidde malice and the rancour of purposing
envye, forncast and imagined in distruccion of mokil people,
shewed so openly, that, had I ben blind, with myne hondes al the
circumstaunce I might wel have feled.   75

Now than tho persones that suche thinges have cast to redresse,
for wrathe of my first medlinge, shopen me to dwelle in this pynande prison, til Lachases my threed no lenger wolde twyne.   And
ever I was sought, if me liste to have grace of my lyfe and
frenesse of that prison, I shulde openly confesse how pees might 80
ben enduced to enden al the firste rancours.   It was fully
supposed my knowing to be ful in tho maters.   Than, lady,
I thought that every man that, by any waye of right, rightfully
don, may helpe any comune †wele to ben saved; whiche thing to
kepe above al thinges I am holde to mayntayne, and namely in 85
distroying of a wrong; al shulde I therthrough enpeche myn
owne fere, if he were gilty and to do misdeed assentaunt.   And
mayster ne frend may nought avayle to the soule of him that
in falsnesse deyeth; and also that I nere desyred wrathe of the
people ne indignacion of the worthy, for nothinge that ever I 90
wrought or did, in any doing my-selfe els, but in the mayntenaunce
of these foresayd errours and in hydinge of the privitees therof.
And that al the peoples hertes, holdinge on the errours syde,
weren blinde and of elde so forferth begyled, that debat and
stryf they maynteyned, and in distruccion on that other syde; 95
by whiche cause the pees, that moste in comunaltee shulde be
desyred, was in poynte to be broken and adnulled.   Also the citee
of London, that is to me so dere and swete, in whiche I was forth

---

63. One.   comforte.   64. profyte.   65. profyte.   comynaltie.   peace.
66. profyte.   68. meanynge.   71. *I supply* the *and* that.   72. rancoure.
73. forncaste.   distruction.   74. blynde.   76. Nowe.   caste.   77. dwel.
78. threde.   80. howe peace.   81. endused.   84. done.   maye.   helpe
(*repeated after* comen); *read* wele.   thynge.   86. distroyeng.   87. misdede.
88. frende maye.   94. -forthe.   debate.   95. stryfe.   distruction.   96.
peace.   comunaltie.   97. cytie.   98. forthe.

growen; (and more kyndely love have I to that place than to any
100 other in erthe, as every kyndely creature hath ful appetyte to that
place of his kyndly engendrure, and to wilne reste and pees
in that stede to abyde); thilke pees shulde thus there have ben
broken, and of al wyse it is commended and desyred. For knowe
thing it is, al men that desyren to comen to the perfit pees ever-
105 lasting must the pees by god commended bothe mayntayne and
kepe. This pees by angels voyce was confirmed, our god entringe
in this worlde. This, as for his Testament, he lefte to al his
frendes, whanne he retourned to the place from whence he cam;
this his apostel amonesteth to holden, without whiche man perfitly
110 may have non insight. Also this god, by his coming, made not
pees alone betwene hevenly and erthly bodyes, but also amonge
us on erthe so he pees confirmed, that in one heed of love oon
body we shulde perfourme. Also I remembre me wel how the
name of Athenes was rather after the god of pees than of batayle,
115 shewinge that pees moste is necessarie to comunaltees and citees.
I than, so styred by al these wayes toforn nempned, declared
certayne poyntes in this wyse. Firste, that thilke persones
that hadden me drawen to their purposes, and me not weting the
privy entent of their meninge, drawen also the feeble-witted
120 people, that have non insight of gubernatif prudence, to clamure
and to crye on maters that they styred; and under poyntes for
comune avauntage they enbolded the passif to take in the
actives doinge; and also styred innocentes of conning to crye
after thinges, whiche (quod they) may not stande but we ben
125 executours of tho maters, and auctorité of execucion by comen
eleccion to us be delivered. And that muste entre by strength of
your mayntenaunce. For we out of suche degree put, oppression
of these olde hindrers shal agayn surmounten, and putten you in
such subjeccion, that in endelesse wo ye shul complayne.
130   The governementes (quod they) of your cité, lefte in the handes
of torcencious citezins, shal bringe in pestilence and distruccion
to you, good men; and therfore let us have the comune administracion to abate suche yvels. Also (quod they) it is worthy
the good to commende, and the gilty desertes to chastice. There
135 ben citezens many, for-ferde of execucion that shal be doon; for

---

101-6. peace (*five times*). 104. thynge. perfyte. 107. left. 108. came.
109. perfytely. 110. none. 111-2. peace (*twice*). 112. one (*twice*).
113. howe. 114-5. peace (*twice*). 115. comunalties and cytes. 116.
toforne. 119. meanynge. feoble. 120. none. gubernatyfe. 122.
passyfe. 126. election. 128. agayne. 129. subiection. 131. distruction. 135. doone.

extorcions by hem committed ben evermore ayenst these purposes and al other good mevinges. Never-the-latter, lady, trewly the meninge under these wordes was, fully to have apeched the mighty senatoures, whiche hadden hevy herte for the misgovernaunce that they seen. And so, lady, whan it fel that free eleccion [was mad], by greet clamour of moche people, [that] for greet disese of misgovernaunce so fervently stoden in her eleccion that they hem submitted to every maner †fate rather than have suffred the maner and the rule of the hated governours; notwithstandinge that in the contrary helden moche comune meyny, that have no consideracion but only to voluntary lustes withouten reson. But than thilke governour so forsaken, fayninge to-forn his undoinge for misrule in his tyme, shoop to have letted thilke eleccion, and have made a newe, him-selfe to have ben chosen; and under that, mokil rore [to] have arered. These thinges, lady, knowen among the princes, and made open to the people, draweth in amendement, that every degree shal ben ordayned to stande there-as he shulde; and that of errours coming herafter men may lightly to-forn-hand purvaye remedye; in this wyse pees and rest to be furthered and holde. Of the whiche thinges, lady, thilke persones broughten in answere to-forn their moste soverayne juge, not coarted by payninge dures, openly knowlegeden, and asked therof grace; so that apertly it preveth my wordes ben sothe, without forginge of lesinges.

But now it greveth me to remembre these dyvers sentences, in janglinge of these shepy people; certes, me thinketh, they oughten to maken joye that a sothe may be knowe. For my trouthe and my conscience ben witnesse to me bothe, that this (knowinge sothe) have I sayd, for no harme ne malice of tho persones, but only for trouthe of my sacrament in my ligeaunce, by whiche I was charged on my kinges behalfe. But see ye not now, lady, how the felonous thoughtes of this people and covins of wicked men conspyren ayen my sothfast trouth! See ye not every wight that to these erroneous opinions were assentaunt, and helpes to the noyse, and knewen al these thinges better than I my-selven, apparaylen to fynden newe frendes, and clepen me fals, and

---

138. meanynge.   139. heauy.   141. election. *Supply* was mad. great (*twice*). *Supply* that.   142. disease. election.   143. face; *read* fate. 146. onely.   147. reason. to-forne.   148. shope.   149. electyon. 151. amonge.   154. to forne hande. peace.   156. to forne.   158. apertly. 159. leasynges.   160. nowe.   162. maye.   164. sayde.   165. onely. leigeaunce.   166. se. nowe.   168. Se.   171. cleapen. false.

studyen how they mowen in her mouthes werse plyte nempne?
O god, what may this be, that thilke folk whiche that in tyme of
my mayntenaunce, and whan my might avayled to strecche to
175 the forsayd maters, tho me commended, and yave me name of
trouth, in so manyfolde maners that it was nyghe in every
wightes eere, there-as any of thilke people weren; and on the
other syde, thilke company somtyme passed, yevinge me name
of badde loos: now bothe tho peoples turned the good in-to
180 badde, and badde in-to good? Whiche thing is wonder, that
they knowing me saying but sothe, arn now tempted to reply her
olde praysinges; and knowen me wel in al doinges to ben trewe,
and sayn openly that I false have sayd many thinges! And they
aleged nothing me to ben false or untrewe, save thilke mater
185 knowleged by the parties hem-selfe; and god wot, other mater
is non. Ye also, lady, knowe these thinges for trewe; I avaunte
not in praysing of my-selfe; therby shulde I lese the precious
secrè of my conscience. But ye see wel that false opinion of the
people for my trouthe, in telling out of false conspyred maters;
190 and after the jugement of these clerkes, I shulde not hyde the
sothe of no maner person, mayster ne other. Wherfore I wolde
not drede, were it put in the consideracion of trewe and of wyse.
And for comers hereafter shullen fully, out of denwere, al the
sothe knowe of these thinges in acte, but as they wern, I have
195 put it in scripture, in perpetuel remembraunce of true meninge.
For trewly, lady, me semeth that I ought to bere the name of
trouthe, that for the love of rightwysnesse have thus me †sub-
mitted. But now than the false fame, which that (clerkes sayn)
flyeth as faste as doth the fame of trouthe, shal so wyde sprede
200 til it be brought to the jewel that I of mene; and so shal I ben
hindred, withouten any mesure of trouthe.'

---

172. howe.   173. maye. folke.   174. stretch.   179. Nowe.
181. knowyuge (*sic*). sayng. arne nowe.   183. sayne.   184. nothynge.
185. wote.   186. none.   188. se.   194. werne.   195. meanynge.
196. beare.   197. submytten (!).   198. nowe. sayne.   199. dothe.
200. meane.   201. measure.

CHAPTER VII.

THAN gan Love sadly me beholde, and sayd in a changed voyce, lower than she had spoken in any tyme: 'Fayn wolde I,' quod she, 'that thou were holpen; but hast thou sayd any-thing whiche thou might not proven?'

'Pardè,' quod I, 'the persones, every thing as I have sayd, han knowleged hem-selfe.'

'Ye,' quod she, 'but what if they hadden nayed? How woldest thou have maynteyned it?'

'Sothely,' quod I, 'it is wel wist, bothe amonges the greetest and other of the realme, that I profered my body so largely in-to provinge of tho thinges, that Mars shulde have juged the ende; but, for sothnesse of my wordes, they durste not to thilke juge truste.'

'Now, certes,' quod she, 'above al fames in this worlde, the name of marcial doinges most plesen to ladyes of my lore; but sithen thou were redy, and thyne adversaryes in thy presence refused thilke doing; thy fame ought to be so born as if in dede it had take to the ende. And therfore every wight that any droppe of reson hath, and hereth of thee infame for these thinges, hath this answere to saye: "trewly thou saydest; for thyne adversaryes thy wordes affirmed." And if thou haddest lyed, yet are they discomfited, the prise leved on thy syde; so that fame shal holde down infame; he shal bringe [it in] upon none halfe. What greveth thee thyne enemye[s] to sayn their owne shame, as thus: "we arn discomfited, and yet our quarel is trewe?" Shal not the loos of thy frendes ayenward dequace thilke enfame, and saye they graunted a sothe without a stroke or fight-ing? Many men in batayle ben discomfited and overcome in a rightful quarel, that is goddes privy jugement in heven; but yet, although the party be yolden, he may with wordes saye his quarel is trewe, and to yelde him, in the contrarye, for drede of dethe he is compelled; and he that graunteth and no stroke hath feled, he may not crepe away in this wyse by none excusacion.

Ch. VII. 2. Fayne. 3. haste. 4. -thynge. 7. Yea. Howe. 9. wyste. amongest. greatest. 14. Nowe. 15. moste pleasen. 17. borne. 19. reason. the. 22. leaued. 23. *Supply* it in. 24. the. enemye (*sic*). sayne. 25. arne. 30. partie. 33. maye.

Indifferent folk wil say : " ye, who is trewe, who is fals, him-selfe
35 knowlegeth tho thinges." Thus in every syde fame sheweth to
thee good and no badde.'

'But yet,' quod I, 'some wil say, I ne shulde, for no dethe,
have discovered my maistresse ; and so by unkyndnesse they
wol knette infame, to pursue me aboute. Thus enemyes of wil,
40 in manyfolde maner, wol seche privy serpentynes queintyses, to
quenche and distroye, by venim of many besinesses, the light of
tr[o]uthe ; to make hertes to murmure ayenst my persone, to have
me in hayne withouten any cause.'

'Now,' quod she, 'here me a fewe wordes, and thou shalt fully
45 ben answered, I trowe. Me thinketh (quod she) right now, by
thy wordes, that sacrament of swering, that is to say, charging by
othe, was oon of the causes to make thee discover the malicious
imaginacions tofore nempned. Every ooth, by knittinge of copu-
lacion, muste have these lawes, that is, trewe jugement and right-
50 wysenesse ; in whiche thing if any of these lacke, the ooth is
y-tourned in-to the name of perjury. Than to make a trewe
serment, most nedes these thinges folowe. For ofte tymes, a man
to saye sothe, but jugement and justice folowe, he is forsworn ;
ensample of Herodes, for holdinge of his serment was [he]
55 dampned.

Also, to saye tr[o]uthe rightfulliche (but in jugement) otherwhile is forboden, by that al sothes be nat to sayne. Therfore in
jugement, in tr[o]uthe, and rightwisenesse, is every creature
bounden, up payne of perjury, ful knowing to make, tho[ugh] it
60 were of his owne persone, for drede of sinne ; after that worde,
"better is it to dey than live false." And, al wolde perverted people
fals report make in unkyndnesse, in that entent thy [en]fame to
reyse, whan light of tr[o]uthe in these maters is forth sprongen
and openly publisshed among commens, than shal nat suche
65 derke enfame dare appere, for pure shame of his falsnesse. As some
men ther ben that their owne enfame can none otherwyse voide
or els excuse, but †by hindringe of other mennes fame ; which
that by non other cause clepen other men false, but for [that]
with their owne falsnesse mowen they nat ben avaunsed ; or els
70 by false sklaund[r]inge wordes other men shenden, their owne

---

34. folke.   false.   36. the.   44. Nowe.   shalte.   45. answerde.
nowe.   46. swearyng.   47. one.   the.   48. othe.   copulation.   50. othe.
53. forsworne.   54. *Supply* he.   61. false.   62. reporte.   63. forthe.
67. be ; *for* by.   68. cleapen.   *Supply* that.   70. sklaundynge.   shendyn.

trewe sklaunder to make seme the lasse.   For if such men wolden
their eyen of their conscience revolven, [they] shulden seen the
same sentence they legen on other springe out of their sydes, with
so many braunches, it were impossible to nombre.   To whiche
therefore may it be sayd in that thinge, "this man thou demest, 75
therein thy-selfe thou condempnest."

But (quod she) understand nat by these wordes, that thou
wene me saye thee to be worthy sclaunder, for any mater tofore
written; truely I wolde witnesse the contrary; but I saye that
the bemes of sclaundring wordes may not be don awaye til the 80
daye of dome.   For how shulde it nat yet, amonges so greet
plentee of people, ben many shrewes, sithen when no mo but
eight persons in Noes shippe were closed, yet oon was a shrewe
and skorned his father?   These thinges (quod she) I trowe, shewen
that fals fame is nat to drede, ne of wyse persons to accepte, and 85
namely nat of thy Margarite, whose wysdom here-after I thinke to
declare; wherfore I wot wel suche thing shal nat her asterte;
than of unkyndnesse thyn ooth hath thee excused at the fulle.
But now, if thou woldest nat greve, me list a fewe thinges to
shewe.'   90

'Say on,' quod I, 'what ye wol; I trowe ye mene but trouthe
and my profit in tyme cominge.'

'Trewly,' quod she, 'that is sothe, so thou con wel kepe these
wordes, and in the in[ne]rest secrè chambre of thyne herte so
faste hem close that they never flitte; than shalt thou fynde hem 95
avayling.   Loke now what people hast thou served; whiche of
hem al in tyme of thyne exile ever thee refresshed, by the valewe
of the leste coyned plate that walketh in money?   Who was sory,
or made any rewth for thy disese?   If they hadden getten their
purpose, of thy misaventure sette they nat an hawe.   Lo, whan 100
thou were emprisonned, how faste they hyed in helpe of thy
deliveraunce!   I wene of thy dethe they yeve but lyte.   They
loked after no-thing but after their owne lustes.   And if thou liste
say the sothe, al that meyny that in this †brige thee broughten,
lokeden rather after thyne helpes than thee to have releved.   105

Owen nat yet some of hem money for his commens?   Paydest

72. *I supply* they. sene.   73. legen [*for* aleggen].   75. maye.   77. vnderstande.   78. the.   80. beames. done.   81. howe. great.   82. plentie.
83. one.   85. false.   86. wysedom.   87. wotte. thynge.   88. thyne
othe. the.   89. nowe.   91. meane.   92. profyte.   94. inrest.
95. shalte.   96. nowe. haste.   97. the.   98. sorye.   99. disease.
101. howe.   103. -thynge.   104. brigge; *read* brige.   104, 105. the.
* * * *
* * * *   D

nat thou for some of her dispences, til they were tourned out of
Selande? Who yave thee ever ought for any rydinge thou madest?
Yet, pardè, some of hem token money for thy chambre, and
110 putte tho pens in his purse, unwetinge of the renter.

Lo for which a company thou medlest, that neither thee ne
them-selfe mighten helpe of unkyndnesse; now they bere the
name that thou supposest of hem for to have. What might thou
more have don than thou diddest, but-if thou woldest in a fals
115 quarel have been a stinkinge martyr? I wene thou fleddest, as
longe as thou might, their privitè to counsayle; which thing thou
hele[de]st lenger than thou shuldest. And thilke that ought thee
money no penny wolde paye; they wende thy returne hadde ben
an impossible. How might thou better have hem proved, but thus
120 in thy nedy diseses? Now hast thou ensaumple for whom thou
shalt meddle; trewly, this lore is worth many goodes.'

CHAPTER VIII.

† EFT gan Love to †steren me [with] these wordes: 'thinke
on my speche; for trewly here-after it wol do thee lykinge;
and how-so-ever thou see Fortune shape her wheele to tourne,
this meditacion [shal] by no waye revolve. For certes, Fortune
5 sheweth her fayrest, whan she thinketh to begyle. And as me
thought, here-toforn thou saydest, thy loos in love, for thy rightwysenesse ought to be raysed, shulde be a-lowed in tyme cominge.
Thou might in love so thee have, that loos and fame shul so ben
raysed, that to thy frendes comfort, and sorowe to thyne enemys,
10 endlesse shul endure.

But if thou were the oon sheep, amonges the hundred, were lost
in deserte and out of the way hadde erred, and now to the flocke
art restoored, the shepherd hath in thee no joye and thou ayen
to the forrest tourne. But that right as the sorowe and an-
15 guisshe was greet in tyme of thyne out-waye goinge, right so
joye and gladnesse shal be doubled to sene thee converted; and

108. the.   109. pardye.   111. the.   112. nowe. beare.   114. done.
false.   117. helest; *read* heledest. the.   119. Howe.   120. diseases.
Nowe haste.   121. shalte. worthe.
CH. VIII. 1. Ofte; *read* Eft. sterne; *read* steren. *I supply* with.
2. the.   3. howe. se.   4. meditation. *I supply* shal.   6. toforne.
8. the.   9. comforte.   11. one shepe.   12. loste. nowe.   13. arte.
shepeherd. the.   15. great.   16. the.

nat as Lothes wyf ayen-lokinge, but [in] hool counsayle with the shepe folowinge, and with them grasse and herbes gadre. Never-the-later (quod she) I saye nat these thinges for no wantrust that I have in supposinge of thee otherwyse than I shulde. For trewly, I wot wel that now thou art set in suche a purpose, out of whiche thee liste nat to parte. But I saye it for many men there been, that to knowinge of other mennes doinges setten al their cure, and lightly desyren the badde to clatter rather than the good, and have no wil their owne maner to amende. They also hate of olde rancours lightly haven; and there that suche thing abydeth, sodaynly in their mouthes procedeth the habundaunce of the herte, and wordes as stones out-throwe. Wherfore my counsayl is ever-more openly and apertly, in what place thou sitte, counterplete th'errours and meninges in as fer as thou hem wistest false, and leve for no wight to make hem be knowe in every bodyes ere; and be alway pacient and use Jacobes wordes, what-so-ever men of thee clappen: "I shal sustayne my ladyes wrathe which I have deserved, so longe as my Margarite hath rightwysed my cause." And certes (quod she) I witnesse my-selfe, if thou, thus converted, sorowest in good meninge in thyne herte, [and] wolt from al vanitè parfitly departe, in consolacioun of al good plesaunce of that Margaryte, whiche that thou desyrest after wil of thyn herte, in a maner of a †moders pitè, [she] shul fully accepte thee in-to grace. For right as thou rentest clothes in open sighte, so openly to sowe hem at his worshippe withouten reprofe [is] commended. Also, right as thou were ensample of moche-folde errour, right so thou must be ensample of manyfolde correccioun; so good savour to forgoing †of errour causeth diligent love, with many playted praisinges to folowe; and than shal al the firste errours make the folowinge worshippes to seme hugely encresed. Blacke and white, set togider, every for other more semeth; and so doth every thinges contrary in kynde. But infame, that goth alwaye tofore, and praysinge worship by any cause folowinge after, maketh to ryse the ilke honour in double of welth; and that quencheth the spotte of the first enfame. Why

---

17. wyfe. *I supply* in. hoole. 20. the. 21. wotte. nowe. arte sette. 22. the. 23. bene. 26. thynge. 28. stones *repeated in* Th. 29. counsayle. apertely. 30. therrours. meanynges. ferre. 31. wystyst. leaue. 32. eare. 33. menne. the. 36. meanynge. 37. *I supply* and. wolte. parfytely. 37. consolatyoun. 38. pleasaunce. 39. hert. mothers; *read* moders. *I supply* she. 40. the. 42. *I supply* is. 44. correctioun. al; *read* of. *After* errour *I omit* distroyeng (*gloss upon* forgoing). 47. encreased. sette. 48. dothe. 49. gothe. worshippe.

wenest, I saye, these thinges in hindringe of thy name? Nay,
nay, god wot, but for pure encresing worship, thy rightwysenesse to
commende, and thy trouthe to seme the more. Wost nat wel
55 thy-selfe, that thou in fourme of making †passest nat Adam that eet
of the apple? Thou †passest nat the stedfastnesse of Noe, that
eetinge of the grape becom dronke. Thou passest nat the
chastitè of Lothe, that lay by his doughter; eke the nobley of
Abraham, whom god reproved by his pryde; also Davides
60 mekenesse, whiche for a woman made Urye be slawe. What?
also Hector of Troye, in whom no defaute might be founde, yet
is he reproved that he ne hadde with manhode nat suffred the
warre begonne, ne Paris to have went in-to Grece, by whom gan
al the sorowe. For trewly, him lacketh no venim of privè
65 consenting, whiche that openly leveth a wrong to withsaye.

Lo eke an olde proverbe amonges many other: " He that is
stille semeth as he graunted."

Now by these ensamples thou might fully understonde, that
these thinges ben writte to your lerning, and in rightwysenesse of
70 tho persones, as thus: To every wight his defaute committed
made goodnesse afterwardes don be the more in reverence and in
open shewing; for ensample, is it nat songe in holy churche,
" Lo, how necessary was Adams synne!" David the king gat
Salomon the king of her that was Uryes wyf. Truly, for reprofe
75 is non of these thinges writte. Right so, tho I reherce thy
before-dede, I repreve thee never the more; ne for no villany of
thee are they rehersed, but for worshippe, so thou continewe wel
here-after: and for profit of thy-selfe I rede thou on hem thinke.'

Than sayde I right thus: 'Lady of unitè and accorde, envy
80 and wrathe lurken there thou comest in place; ye weten wel
your-selve, and so don many other, that whyle I administred the
office of commen doinge, as in rulinge of the stablisshmentes
amonges the people, I defouled never my conscience for no
maner dede; but ever, by witte and by counsayle of the wysest,
85 the maters weren drawen to their right endes. And thus trewly
for you, lady, I have desyred suche cure; and certes, in your
service was I nat ydel, as fer as suche doinge of my cure
streccheth.'

---

52. wenyste. Naye nay god wotte.   53. encreasyng.   55-7. passeth
(twice); passyst (third time). ete.   57. eatynge. become.   61. whome.
63. begon. ganne.   65. leaueth. wronge. withsay.   68. Nowe.
71. done.   72. song.   73. howe. gate.   74. wyfe.   75. none.
76-7. the (twice).   78. profyte.   81. done.   87. ferre.   88. stretcheth.

'That is a thing,' quod she, 'that may drawe many hertes of
noble, and voice of commune in-to glory; and fame is nat but 90
wrecched and fickle. Alas! that mankynde coveyteth in so leude
a wyse to be rewarded of any good dede, sithe glorie of fame, in
this worlde, is nat but hindringe of glorie in tyme comminge!
And certes (quod she) yet at the hardest suche fame, in-to heven,
is nat the erthe but a centre to the cercle of heven? A pricke is 95
wonder litel in respect of al the cercle; and yet, in al this pricke,
may no name be born, in maner of peersing, for many obstacles,
as waters, and wildernesse, and straunge langages. And nat only
names of men ben stilled and holden out of knowleginge by these
obstacles, but also citees and realmes of prosperitè ben letted to 100
be knowe, and their reson hindred; so that they mowe nat ben
parfitly in mennes propre understandinge. How shulde than the
name of a singuler Londenoys passe the glorious name of London,
whiche by many it is commended, and by many it is lacked, and
in many mo places in erthe nat knowen than knowen? For in 105
many countrees litel is London in knowing or in spech; and yet
among oon maner of people may nat such fame in goodnes
come; for as many as praysen, commenly as many lacken. Fy
than on such maner fame! Slepe, and suffre him that knoweth
previtè of hertes to dele suche fame in thilke place there nothing 110
ayenst a sothe shal neither speke ne dare apere, by attourney
ne by other maner. How many greet-named, and many greet
in worthinesse losed, han be tofore this tyme, that now out
of memorie are slidden, and clenely forgeten, for defaute of
wrytinges! And yet scriptures for greet elde so ben defased, that 115
no perpetualtè may in hem ben juged. But if thou wolt make
comparisoun to ever, what joye mayst thou have in erthly name?
It is a fayr lykenesse, a pees or oon grayn of whete, to a thousand shippes ful of corne charged! What nombre is betwene the
oon and th'other? And yet mowe bothe they be nombred, and 120
ende in rekening have. But trewly, al that may be nombred is
nothing to recken, as to thilke that may nat be nombred. For
†of the thinges ended is mad comparison; as, oon litel, another
greet; but in things to have an ende, and another no ende,
suche comparisoun may nat be founden. Wherfore in heven to 125

---

91. wretched.   96. respecte.   97. borne.   98. onely.   101. reason.
102. parfitely. Howe.   107. one.   108. Fye.   110. nothynge.   112. Howe.
great (*twice*).   113. nowe.   115. great.   116. maye. wolte.
118. fayre. one grayne of wheate.   thousande.   120. one. thother.
121-2. maye.   123. ofte; *read* of the. made. one.   124. great.

ben losed with god hath non ende, but endlesse endureth; and
thou canst nothing don aright, but thou desyre the rumour therof
be heled and in every wightes ere; and that dureth but a pricke
in respecte of the other. And so thou sekest reward of folkes
130 smale wordes, and of vayne praysinges. Trewly, therin thou
lesest the guerdon of vertue; and lesest the grettest valour of
conscience, and uphap thy renomè everlasting. Therfore boldely
renomè of fame of the erthe shulde be hated, and fame after deth
shulde be desyred of werkes of vertue. [Trewly, vertue] asketh
135 guerdoning, and the soule causeth al vertue. Than the soule,
delivered out of prison of erthe, is most worthy suche guerdon
among to have in the everlastinge fame; and nat the body, that
causeth al mannes yvels.

CHAPTER IX.

OF twey thinges art thou answered, as me thinketh (quod
Love); and if any thing be in doute in thy soule, shewe
it forth, thyn ignoraunce to clere, and leve it for no shame.'

'Certes,' quod I, 'there is no body in this worlde, that aught
5 coude saye by reson ayenst any of your skilles, as I leve; and by
my witte now fele I wel, that yvel-spekers or berers of enfame
may litel greve or lette my purpos, but rather by suche thinge my
quarel to be forthered.'

'Ye,' quod she, 'and it is proved also, that the ilke jewel in
10 my kepinge shal nat there-thorow be stered, of the lest moment
that might be imagined.'

'That is soth,' quod I.

'Wel,' quod she, 'than †leveth there, to declare that thy insuffisance is no maner letting, as thus: for that she is so worthy,
15 thou shuldest not clymbe so highe; for thy moebles and thyn
estate arn voyded, thou thinkest [thee] fallen in suche miserie,
that gladnesse of thy pursute wol nat on thee discende.'

'Certes,' quod I, 'that is sothe; right suche thought is in myn
herte; for commenly it is spoken, and for an olde proverbe it is

---

126. none.   127. canste nothynge done. rumoure.   128. healed;
read deled? eare.   129. rewarde.   131. valoure. consyence.   134. *Supply*
Trewly, vertue.   136. prisone. guerdone.
CH. IX. 1. arte.   2. thynge.   3. thyne. leaue.   5. reason.   6. nowe.
bearers.   7. purpose,   9. Yea.   10. -thorowe. steered.   13. leneth;
read leueth.   15. thyne.   16. arne. *I supply* thee.   17. the.   18. myne
hert.

leged: "He that heweth to hye, with chippes he may lese 20
his sight." Wherfore I have ben about, in al that ever I might,
to studye wayes of remedye by one syde or by another.'

'Now,' quod she, 'god forbede †that thou seke any other
doinges but suche as I have lerned thee in our restinge-whyles,
and suche herbes as ben planted in oure gardins. Thou shalt 25
wel understande that above man is but oon god alone.'

'How,' quod I, 'han men to-forn this tyme trusted in writtes
and chauntements, and in helpes of spirites that dwellen in the
ayre, and therby they han getten their desyres, where-as first, for
al his manly power, he daunced behynde?'   30

'O,' quod she, 'fy on suche maters! For trewly, that is
sacrilege; and that shal have no sort with any of my servauntes;
in myne eyen shal suche thing nat be loked after. How often is
it commaunded by these passed wyse, that "to one god shal men
serve, and not to goddes?" And who that liste to have myne 35
helpes, shal aske none helpe of foule spirites. Alas! is nat man
maked semblable to god? Wost thou nat wel, that al vertue of
lyvelich werkinge, by goddes purveyaunce, is underput to resonable creature in erthe? Is nat every thing, a this halfe god, mad
buxom to mannes contemplation, understandinge in heven and 40
in erthe and in helle? Hath not man beinge with stones, soule of
wexing with trees and herbes? Hath he nat soule of felinge, with
beestes, fisshes, and foules? And he hath soule of reson and
understanding with aungels; so that in him is knit al maner
of lyvinges by a resonable proporcioun. Also man is mad of 45
al the foure elementes. Al universitee is rekened in him alone;
he hath, under god, principalitè above al thinges. Now is his
soule here, now a thousand myle hence; now fer, now nygh;
now hye, now lowe; as fer in a moment as in mountenaunce of
ten winter; and al this is in mannes governaunce and disposicion. 50
Than sheweth it that men ben liche unto goddes, and children of
moost heyght. But now, sithen al thinges [arn] underput to the
wil of resonable creatures, god forbede any man to winne that lordship, and aske helpe of any-thing lower than him-selfe; and than,
namely, of foule thinges innominable. Now than, why shuldest 55

---

20. maye.   23. Nowe. are; *read* that.   24. the.   25. shalte.
26. one.   27. Howe. to forne.   31. fye.   38. vnderputte.   39. thynge.
made.   40. buxome.   41. manne.   43. reason.   44. knytte.   45. lyuenges.
reasonable. made.   47. Nowe.   48. nowe. nowe ferre nowe. thousande.
49. nowe (*twice*). ferre. momente.   50. tenne. disposytion.   52. nowe.
I supply arn. vnderputte.   53. reasonable.   54. lordshippe. thynge.

thou wene to love to highe, sithen nothing is thee above but god
alone? Trewly, I wot wel that thilke jewel is in a maner even in
lyne of degree there thou art thy-selfe, and nought above, save
thus: aungel upon angel, man upon man, and devil upon devil
60 han a maner of soveraigntee; and that shal cese at the daye
of dome. And so I say: though thou be put to serve the
ilke jewel duringe thy lyfe, yet is that no servage of under-
puttinge, but a maner of travayling plesaunce, to conquere and
gette that thou hast not. I sette now the hardest: in my service
65 now thou deydest, for sorowe of wantinge in thy desyres; trewly,
al hevenly bodyes with one voyce shul come and make melody in
thy cominge, and saye—"Welcome, our fere, and worthy to entre
into Jupiters joye! For thou with might hast overcome deth;
thou woldest never flitte out of thy service; and we al shul
70 now praye to the goddes, rowe by rowe, to make thilk Margarite,
that no routh had in this persone, but unkyndely without comfort
let thee deye, shal besette her-selfe in suche wyse, that in erthe,
for parte of vengeaunce, shal she no joye have in loves service;
and whan she is deed, than shal her soule ben brought up in-to
75 thy presence; and whider thou wilt chese, thilke soule shal ben
committed." Or els, after thy deth, anon al the foresayd hevenly
bodyes, by one accorde, shal †benimen from thilke perle al the
vertues that firste her were taken; for she hath hem forfeyted
by that on thee, my servaunt, in thy lyve, she wolde not suffre
80 to worche al vertues, withdrawen by might of the hygh bodyes.
Why than shuldest thou wene so any more? And if thee liste
to loke upon the lawe of kynde, and with order whiche to me
was ordayned, sothely, non age, non overtourninge tyme but
†hiderto had no tyme ne power to chaunge the wedding, ne
85 the knotte to unbynde of two hertes [that] thorow oon assent, in
my presence, †togider accorden to enduren til deth hem departe.
What? trowest thou, every ideot wot the meninge and the privy
entent of these thinges? They wene, forsothe, that suche accord
may not be, but the rose of maydenhede be plucked. Do way,
90 do way; they knowe nothing of this. For consent of two hertes

56. nothynge. the.   57. wote. euyn.   58. arte.   59. manne (*twice*).
60. souerayyntie. cease.   61. thoughe putte.   64. haste.   64–5. nowe.
68. haste. dethe.   70. nowe pray.   71. *For* in *read* on! comforte.
72. lette the.   75. wylte.   76. dethe anone.   77. benommen; *read*
benimen.   79. the.   81. the.   83. none (*twice*).   84. hytherto.
85. *Supply* that. thorowe one.   86. togyther. dethe.   87. ydeot wotte.
88. accorde.   89. waye (*twice*).   90. consente.

alone maketh the fasteninge of the knotte; neither lawe of kynde ne mannes lawe determineth neither the age ne the qualitè of persones, but only accord bitwene thilke twaye. And trewly, after tyme that suche accord, by their consent in hert, is enseled, and put in my tresorye amonges my privy thinges, than ginneth 95 the name of spousayle; and although they breken forward bothe, yet suche mater enseled is kept in remembrance for ever. And see now that spouses have the name anon after accord, though the rose be not take. The aungel bad Joseph take Marye his spouse, and to Egypte wende. Lo! she was cleped "spouse," 100 and yet, toforn ne after, neither of hem bothe mente no flesshly lust knowe. Wherfore the wordes of trouthe acorden that my servauntes shulden forsake bothe †fader and moder, and be ad-herand to his spouse; and they two in unitè of one flesshe shulden accorde. And this wyse, two that wern firste in a litel 105 maner discordaunt, hygher that oon and lower that other, ben mad evenliche in gree to stonde. But now to enfourme thee that ye ben liche to goddes, these clerkes sayn, and in deter-minacion shewen, that "three thinges haven [by] the names of goddes ben cleped; that is to sayn: man, divel, and images"; 110 but yet is there but oon god, of whom al goodnesse, al grace, and al vertue cometh; and he †is loving and trewe, and everlasting, and pryme cause of al being thinges. But men ben goddes lovinge and trewe, but not everlasting; and that is by adop-cioun of the everlastinge god. Divels ben goddes, stirringe by 115 a maner of lyving; but neither ben they trewe ne everlastinge; and their name of godliheed th[e]y han by usurpacion, as the prophete sayth: "Al goddes of gentyles (that is to say, paynims) are divels." But images ben goddes by nuncupacion; and they ben neither livinge ne trewe, ne everlastinge. After these wordes 120 they clepen "goddes" images wrought with mennes handes. But now [art thou a] resonable creature, that by adopcion alone art to the grete god everlastinge, and therby thou art "god" cleped: let thy †faders maners so entre thy wittes that thou might folowe, in-as-moche as longeth to thee, thy †faders worship, so 125

---

93. onely.   93–4. accorde.   94. ensealed.   96. breaken forwarde.   97. ensealed. kepte.   98. se nowe. accorde.   99. bade.   101. toforne. 102. luste.   103. father and mother; *rather*, fader and moder. adherande. 105. werne.   106. one.   107. made. nowe. the.   108. sayne. 109. thre.   *I supply* by.   110. cleaped.   111. one.   112. his; *read* is. 116. lyueng.   117. thy; *read* they.   118. saythe.   121. cleapen. 122. nowe.   *I supply* art thou a. reasonable.   123. arte (*twice*). great. 124. lette.   124–5. fathers; *read* faders.   125. the. worshyppe.

that in nothinge thy kynde from his wil declyne, ne from his
nobley perverte. In this wyse if thou werche, thou art above
al other thinges save god alone; and so say no more "thyn herte
129 to serve in to hye a place."

CHAPTER X.

FULLY have I now declared thyn estate to be good, so thou
folow therafter, and that the †objeccion first †by thee
aleged, in worthinesse of thy Margaryte, shal not thee lette, as
it shal forther thee, and encrese thee. It is now to declare, the
5 last objeccion in nothing may greve.'

'Yes, certes,' quod I, 'bothe greve and lette muste it nedes;
the contrarye may not ben proved; and see now why. Whyle
I was glorious in worldly welfulnesse, and had suche goodes in
welth as maken men riche, tho was I drawe in-to companyes
10 that loos, prise, and name yeven. Tho louteden blasours; tho
curreyden glosours; tho welcomeden flatterers; tho worshipped
thilke that now deynen nat to loke. Every wight, in such erthly
wele habundant, is holde noble, precious, benigne, and wyse to
do what he shal, in any degree that men him sette; al-be-it that
15 the sothe be in the contrarye of al tho thinges. But he that can
never so wel him behave, and hath vertue habundaunt in manyfolde
maners, and be nat welthed with suche erthly goodes, is holde
for a foole, and sayd, his wit is but sotted. Lo! how fals for
aver is holde trewe! Lo! how trewe is cleped fals for wanting
20 of goodes! Also, lady, dignitees of office maken men mikel
comended, as thus: "he is so good, were he out, his pere shulde
men not fynde." Trewly, I trowe of some suche that are so
praysed, were they out ones, another shulde make him so be
knowe, he shulde of no wyse no more ben loked after: but only
25 fooles, wel I wot, desyren suche newe thinges. Wherfore I wonder
that thilke governour, out of whom alone the causes proceden
that governen al thinges, whiche that hath ordeyned this world
in workes of the kyndely bodyes so be governed, not with

127. arte.
CH. X. 1. nowe.   2. abiection; *read* objeccion. be; *read* by. the.
3. the.   4. the. encrease the. nowe.   5. obiection.   6. let.
7. maye. se nowe.   12. nowe.   14. set.   15. can ne never; *omit* ne.
18. wytte. false.   19. auer (*sic*); *for* aueir (*avoir*). howe. cleaped. false.
24. onely.   25. wotte. new.   26. whome.   27. worlde.

unstedfast or happyous thing, but with rules of reson, whiche shewen the course of certayne thinges: why suffreth he suche 30 slydinge chaunges, that misturnen suche noble thinges as ben we men, that arn a fayr parcel of the erthe, and holden the upperest degree, under god, of benigne thinges, as ye sayden right now your-selfe; shulde never man have ben set in so worthy a place but-if his degrè were ordayned noble. Alas! thou that knittest 35 the purveyaunce of al thinges, why lokest thou not to amenden these defautes? I see shrewes that han wicked maners sitten in chayres of domes, lambes to punisshen, there wolves shulden ben punisshed. Lo! vertue, shynende naturelly, for povertee lurketh, and is hid under cloude; but the moone false, forsworn (as 40 I knowe my-selfe) for aver and yeftes, hath usurped to shyne by day-light, with peynture of other mens praysinges; and trewly, thilke forged light fouly shulde fade, were the trouth away of colours feyned. Thus is night turned in-to day, and day in-to night; winter in-to sommer, and sommer in-to winter; not in 45 dede, but in misclepinge of foliche people.'

'Now,' quod she, 'what wenest thou of these thinges? How felest thou in thyn hert, by what governaunce that this cometh aboute?'

'Certes,' quod I, 'that wot I never; but-if it be that Fortune 50 hath graunt from above, to lede the ende of man as her lyketh.'

'Ah! now I see,' quod she, 'th'entent of thy mening! Lo, bycause thy worldly goodes ben fulliche dispent, thou beraft out of dignitè of office, in whiche thou madest the †gaderinge of thilke goodes, and yet diddest in that office by counsaile of wyse [before 55 that] any thing were ended; and true were unto hem whos profit thou shuldest loke; and seest now many that in thilke hervest made of thee mokel, and now, for glosing of other, deyneth thee nought to forther, but enhaunsen false shrewes by witnessinge of trouthe! These thinges greveth thyn herte, to sene thy-selfe thus 60 abated; and than, frayltè of mankynde ne setteth but litel by the lesers of suche richesse, have he never so moche vertue; and so thou wenest of thy jewel to renne in dispyt, and not ben accepted in-to grace. Al this shal thee nothing hinder. Now (quod she) first thou wost wel, thou lostest nothing that ever mightest thou 65

---

29. reason. 32. arne a fayre parsel. 33. nowe. 37. se. 39. pouertie. 40. hydde. forsworne. 44. daye (*twice*). 46. miscleapynge. 50. wotte. 52. nowe I se. thentent. meanyng. 53. berafte. 54. gatherynge. 55. *I supply* before that. 56. whose profyte. 57. nowe. 58. the (*twice*). nowe. 63. dispyte. 64. the. Nowe. 65. woste.

chalenge for thyn owne. Whan nature brought thee forth, come
thou not naked out of thy †moders wombe? Thou haddest no
richesse; and whan thou shalt entre in-to the ende of every
flesshly body, what shalt thou have with thee than? So, every
70 richesse thou hast in tyme of thy livinge, nis but lent; thou
might therin chalenge no propertee. And see now; every thing
that is a mannes own, he may do therwith what him lyketh, to
yeve or to kepe; but richesse thou playnest from thee lost; if thy
might had strecched so ferforth, fayn thou woldest have hem kept,
75 multiplyed with mo other; and so, ayenst thy wil, ben they departed
from thee; wherfore they were never thyn. And if thou laudest
and joyest any wight, for he is stuffed with suche maner richesse,
thou art in that beleve begyled; for thou wenest thilke joye to be
selinesse or els ese; and he that hath lost suche happes to ben
80 unsely.'

'Ye, forsoth,' quod I.

'Wel,' quod she, 'than wol I prove that unsely in that wise is
to preise; and so the tother is, the contrary, to be lacked.'

'How so?' quod I.

85 'For Unsely,' quod she, 'begyleth nat, but sheweth th'entent
of her working. *Et e contra*: Selinesse begyleth. For in prosperitè
she maketh a jape in blyndnesse; that is, she wyndeth him to
make sorowe whan she withdraweth. Wolt thou nat (quod she)
preise him better that sheweth to thee his herte, tho[ugh] it be
90 with bytande wordes and dispitous, than him that gloseth and
thinketh in †his absence to do thee many harmes?'

'Certes,' quod I, 'the oon is to commende; and the other to
lacke and dispice.'

'A! ha!' quod she, 'right so Ese, while †she lasteth, gloseth
95 and flatereth; and lightly voydeth whan she most plesauntly
sheweth; and ever, in hir absence, she is aboute to do thee tene
and sorowe in herte. But Unsely, al-be-it with bytande chere,
sheweth what she is, and so doth not that other; wherfore
Unsely doth not begyle. Selinesse disceyveth; Unsely put away
100 doute. That oon maketh men blynde; that other openeth their
eyen in shewinge of wrecchidnesse. The oon is ful of drede to

---

66. the forthe.   67. mothers; *read* moders.   69. the.   70. haste.
lente.   71. propertie. se nowe.   72. owne.   73. the.   74. stretched.
fayne.   76. the.   78. arte.   79. ease. loste.   84. Howe.
85. thentent.   88. Wolte.   89. the.   91. their; *read* his. the.
92. one.   94. ease. he; *read* she.   99. dothe. awaye.   100-1. one
(*twice*).   101. wretchydnesse.

lese that is not his owne; that other is sobre, and maketh men
discharged of mokel hevinesse in burthen. The oon draweth
a man from very good; the other haleth him to vertue by the
hookes of thoughtes. And wenist thou nat that thy disese hath 105
don thee mokel more to winne than ever yet thou lostest, and
more than ever the contrary made thee winne? Is nat a greet
good, to thy thinking, for to knowe the hertes of thy sothfast
frendes? Pardè, they ben proved to the ful, and the trewe have
discevered fro the false. Trewly, at the goinge of the ilke brotel 110
joye, ther yede no more away than the ilke that was nat thyn
proper. He was never from that lightly departed; thyn owne
good therfore leveth it stille with thee. Now good (quod she);
for how moche woldest thou somtyme have bought this verry
knowing of thy frendes from the flatteringe flyes that thee glosed, 115
whan thou thought thy-selfe sely? But thou that playnest of losse
in richesse, hast founden the most dere-worthy thing; that thou
clepest unsely hath made thee moche thing to winnen. And
also, for conclusioun of al, he is frende that now leveth nat his
herte from thyne helpes. And if that Margarite denyeth now nat 120
to suffre her vertues shyne to thee-wardes with spredinge bemes,
as far or farther than if thou were sely in worldly joye, trewly,
I saye nat els but she is somdel to blame.'

'Ah! pees,' quod I, 'and speke no more of this; myn herte
breketh, now thou touchest any suche wordes!' 125

'A! wel!' quod she, 'thanne let us singen; thou herest no
more of these thinges at this tyme.'

**Thus endeth the firste book of the Testament of Love;
and herafter foloweth the seconde.**

---

103. one.   105. disease.   106. done the.   107. the. great.
109. Pardy.   111. awaye.   111–2. thyne.   113. leaueth. the. Nowe.
114. howe.   115. the.   117. thynge.   118. cleapest. the. thynge.
119. nowe leaueth.   120. hert. nowe.   121. the. spreadynge beames.
122. farre.   123. somdele.   124. peace. myne.   125. breaketh nowe.
126. lette.

BOOK II.

CHAPTER I.

VERY welth may not be founden in al this worlde; and that
is wel sene. Lo! how in my mooste comfort, as I wende
and moost supposed to have had ful answere of my contrary
thoughtes, sodaynly it was vanisshed. And al the workes of man
5 faren in the same wyse; whan folk wenen best her entent for to
have and willes to perfourme, anon chaunging of the lift syde to
the right halve tourneth it so clene in-to another kynde, that never
shal it come to the first plyte in doinge.

O this wonderful steering so soone otherwysed out of knowinge!
10 But for my purpos was at the beginninge, and so dureth yet, if god
of his grace tyme wol me graunt, I thinke to perfourme this
worke, as I have begonne, in love; after as my thinne wit, with
inspiracion of him that hildeth al grace, wol suffre. Grevously,
god wot, have I suffred a greet throwe that the Romayne
15 emperour, which in unitè of love shulde acorde, and every with
other * * * * in cause of other to avaunce; and namely, sithe
this empyre [nedeth] to be corrected of so many sectes in heresie
of faith, of service, o[f] rule in loves religion. Trewly, al were
it but to shende erroneous opinions, I may it no lenger suffre.
20 For many men there ben that sayn love to be in gravel and sande,
that with see ebbinge and flowinge woweth, as riches that sodaynly
vanissheth. And some sayn that love shulde be in windy blastes,
that stoundmele turneth as a phane, and glorie of renomè, which
after lustes of the varyaunt people is areysed or stilled.
25 Many also wenen that in the sonne and the moone and other
sterres love shulde ben founden; for among al other planettes
moste soveraynly they shynen, as dignitees in reverence of estates
rather than good han and occupyen. Ful many also there ben
that in okes and in huge postes supposen love to ben grounded,
30 as in strength and in might, whiche mowen not helpen their owne

---

CH. I. 2. howe. comforte. 3. hadde. 5. folke. 6. anone.
10. purpose. 12. wytte. 14. wotte. great. 16. (*Something seems
to be lost here*). 17. *I supply* nedeth. 18. o; *read* of. 19. erronyous.
maye. 20. menne. sayne. 26. amonge.

wrecchidnesse, whan they ginne to falle.   But [of] suche diversitè
of sectes, ayenst the rightful beleve of love, these errours ben forth
spredde, that loves servantes in trewe rule and stedfast fayth in
no place daren apere.   Thus irrecuperable joy is went, and anoy
endless is entred.   For no man aright reproveth suche errours, 35
but [men] confirmen their wordes, and sayn, that badde is noble
good, and goodnesse is badde ; to which folk the prophete biddeth
wo without ende.

  Also manye tonges of greet false techinges in gylinge maner,
principally in my tymes, not only with wordes but also with armes, 40
loves servauntes and professe in his religion of trewe rule pursewen,
to confounden and to distroyen.   And for as moche as holy †faders,
that of our Christen fayth aproved and strengthed to the Jewes, as
to men resonable and of divinitè lerned, proved thilke fayth with
resones, and with auctoritès of the olde testament and of the newe, 45
her pertinacie to distroy : but to paynims, that for beestes and
houndes were holde, to putte hem out of their errour, was †miracle
of god shewed.   These thinges were figured by cominge of th'angel
to the shepherdes, and by the sterre to paynims kinges ; as who
sayth : angel resonable to resonable creature, and sterre of miracle 50
to people bestial not lerned, wern sent to enforme.   But I, lovers
clerk, in al my conning and with al my mightes, trewly I have no
suche grace in vertue of miracles, ne for no discomfit falsheedes
suffyseth not auctoritès alone ; sithen that suche [arn] heretikes
and maintaynours of falsitès.   Wherfore I wot wel, sithen that 55
they ben men, and reson is approved in hem, the clowde of errour
hath her reson beyond probable resons, whiche that cacchende
wit rightfully may not with-sitte.   By my travaylinge studie I have
ordeyned hem, †whiche that auctoritè, misglosed by mannes
reson, to graunt shal ben enduced.   60

  Now ginneth my penne to quake, to thinken on the sentences
of the envyous people, whiche alway ben redy, both ryder and
goer, to scorne and to jape this leude book ; and me, for rancour
and hate in their hertes, they shullen so dispyse, that although
my book be leude, yet shal it ben more leude holden, and by 65
wicked wordes in many maner apayred.   Certes, me thinketh,

---

31. wretchydnesse. fal. *I supply* of.   32. forthe.   33. stedfaste faythe.
34. darne.   35. endlesse.   36. *I supply* men.   37. folke.   39. great.
40. onely.   42. fathers ; *read* faders.   44. faythe.   47. put. miracles ; *read*
miracle.   48. thangel.   50. saythe.   51. werne.   53. discomfyte.
54. *I supply* arn.   55. wotte.   56. reason. erroure.   57. reason.
bewonde (*sic*). catchende wytte.   59. with ; *read* whiche.   60. reason.
61. Nowe.   62. alwaye.   63. booke. rancoure.   64. althoughe.   65. booke.

[of] the sowne of their badde speche right now is ful bothe myne eeres. O good precious Margaryte, myne herte shulde wepe if I wiste ye token hede of suche maner speche ; but trewly, I wot
70 wel, in that your wysdom shal not asterte. For of god, maker of kynde, witnesse I took, that for none envy ne yvel have I drawe this mater togider ; but only for goodnesse to maintayn, and errours in falsetees to distroy. Wherfore (as I sayd) with reson I thinke, thilke forsayd errours to distroye and dequace.
75   These resons and suche other, if they enduce men, in loves service, trewe to beleve of parfit blisse, yet to ful faithe in credence of deserte fully mowe they nat suffyse ; sithen 'faith hath no merite of mede, whan mannes reson sheweth experience in doing.' For utterly no reson the parfit blisse of love by no waye
80 may make to be comprehended. Lo ! what is a parcel of lovers joye ? Parfit science, in good service, of their desyre to comprehende in bodily doinge the lykinge of the soule ; not as by a glasse to have contemplacion of tyme cominge, but thilke first imagined and thought after face to face in beholding. What
85 herte, what reson, what understandinge can make his heven to be feled and knowe, without assaye in doinge ? Certes, noon. Sithen thanne of love cometh suche fruite in blisse, and love in him-selfe is the most among other vertues, as clerkes sayn ; the seed of suche springinge in al places, in al countreys, in al worldes shulde
90 ben sowe.

But o ! welawaye ! thilke seed is forsake, and †mowe not ben suffred, the lond-tillers to sette a-werke, without medlinge of cockle ; badde wedes whiche somtyme stonken †than caught the name of love among idiotes and badde-meninge people. Never-
95 the-later, yet how-so-it-be that men clepe thilke †thing preciousest in kynde, with many eke-names, that other thinges that the soule yeven the ilke noble name, it sheweth wel that in a maner men have a greet lykinge in worshippinge of thilke name. Wherfore this worke have I writte ; and to thee, tytled of Loves name,
100 I have it avowed in a maner of sacrifyse ; that, where-ever it be rad, it mowe in merite, by the excellence of thilke name, the more wexe in authorità and worshippe of takinge in hede ; and to

---

67. *I supply* of. nowe.   69. wotte.   70. wysdome.   71. toke.
73. reason.   75. reasons.   76. parfyte.   78–9. reason (*twice*).   79. parfyte.
80. maye. persel.   81. parfyte.   85. reason.   86. none.   88. amonge.
sayne.   88–91. sede.   91. mowen ; *read* mowe.   92. londe-tyllers. set.
93. hath ; *read* han.   94. meanynge.   95. howe. menne cleape. kynge
(*sic*) ; *read* thing.   98. great.   99. the.   101. radde.

what entent it was ordayned, the inseëres mowen ben moved. Every thing to whom is owande occasion don as for his ende, Aristotle supposeth that the actes of every thinge ben in a maner 105 his final cause. A final cause is noblerer, or els even as noble, as thilke thing that is finally to thilke ende; wherfore accion of thinge everlasting is demed to be eternal, and not temporal; sithen it is his final cause. Right so the actes of my boke 'Love,' and love is noble; wherfore, though my book be leude, the cause 110 with which I am stered, and for whom I ought it doon, noble forsothe ben bothe. But bycause that in conninge I am yong, and can yet but crepe, this leude A. b. c. have I set in-to lerning; for I can not passen the telling of three as yet. And if god wil, in shorte tyme, I shal amende this leudnesse in joininge 115 syllables; whiche thing, for dulnesse of witte, I may not in three letters declare. For trewly I saye, the goodnesse of my Margaryte-perle wolde yeve mater in endyting to many clerkes; certes, her mercy is more to me swetter than any livinges; wherfore my lippes mowen not suffyse, in speking of her ful laude and wor- 120 shippe as they shulde. But who is that [wolde be wyse] in knowing of the orders of heven, and putteth his resones in the erthe? I forsothe may not, with blere eyen, the shyning sonne of vertue in bright whele of this Margaryte beholde; therfore as yet I may her not discryve in vertue as I wolde. In tyme cominge, 125 in another tretyse, thorow goddes grace, this sonne in clerenesse of vertue to be-knowe, and how she enlumineth al this day, I thinke to declare.

CHAPTER II.

IN this mene whyle this comfortable lady gan singe a wonder mater of endytinge in Latin; but trewly, the noble colours in rethorik wyse knitte were so craftely, that my conning wol not strecche to remembre; but the sentence, I trowe, somdel have I in mynde. Certes, they were wonder swete of sowne, and they 5 were touched al in lamentacion wyse, and by no werbles of myrthe. Lo! thus gan she singe in Latin, as I may constrewe it in our Englisshe tonge.

---

104. thynge. done. 107. thynge. 110. boke. 111. done (*sic*). 112. yonge. 113. canne. sette. 114. thre. 116. thynge. maye. thre. 121. that in knowyng (*sic*); *supply* wolde be wyse *before* in knowing. 125. maye. 126. thorowe. 127. howe. CH. II. 1. meane. ganne. 4. stretche. somdele. 7. ganne.

E

'Alas! that these hevenly bodyes their light and course shewen,
10 as nature yave hem in commaundement at the ginning of the first
age; but these thinges in free choice of reson han non understondinge.   But man that ought to passe al thing of doinge, of
right course in kynde, over-whelmed sothnesse by wrongful tytle,
and hath drawen the sterre of envye to gon by his syde, that the
15 clips of me, that shulde be his shynande sonne, so ofte is seye,
that it wened thilke errour, thorow hem come in, shulde ben myn
owne defaute.   Trewly, therfore, I have me withdrawe, and mad
my dwellinge out of lande in an yle by my-selfe, in the occian
closed; and yet sayn there many, they have me harberowed; but,
20 god wot, they faylen.   These thinges me greven to thinke, and
namely on passed gladnesse, that in this worlde was wont me
disporte of highe and lowe; and now it is fayled; they that
wolden maystries me have in thilke stoundes.   In heven on
highe, above Saturnes sphere, in sesonable tyme were they
25 lodged; but now come queynte counsailours that in no house
wol suffre me sojourne, wherof is pitè; and yet sayn some that
they me have in celler with wyne shed; in gernere, there corn is
layd covered with whete; in sacke, sowed with wolle; in purse,
with money faste knit; among pannes mouled in a †whicche;
30 in presse, among clothes layd, with riche pelure arayed; in stable,
among hors and other beestes, as hogges, sheep, and neet; and
in many other wyse.   But thou, maker of light (in winking of
thyn eye the sonne is queynt), wost right wel that I in trewe name
was never thus herberowed.

35   Somtyme, toforn the sonne in the seventh partie was smiten,
I bar both crosse and mytre, to yeve it where I wolde.   With me
the pope wente a-fote; and I tho was worshipped of al holy
church.   Kinges baden me their crownes holden.   The law was
set as it shuld; tofore the juge, as wel the poore durste shewe
40 his greef as the riche, for al his money.   I defended tho taylages,
and was redy for the poore to paye.   I made grete feestes in my
tyme, and noble songes, and maryed damoselles of gentil feture,
withouten golde or other richesse.   Poore clerkes, for witte of
schole, I sette in churches, and made suche persones to preche;

---

11. none.   12. thynge.   15. sey; *read* seye *or* seyen.   16. thorowe.
17. made.   19. sayne.   20. wote.   21. wonte.   22. nowe.   24.
seasonable.   26. sayne.   27. corne.   28. layde.   29. knytte.   amonge
(*twice*).   wyche; *read* whicche.   30. layde.   31. amonge horse.   shepe.
nete.   33. woste.   36. bare.   37. went.   40. grefe.   41. pay.
great.   44. preache.

and tho was service in holy churche honest and devout, in 45
plesaunce bothe of god and of the people.   But now the leude
for symonye is avaunced, and shendeth al holy churche.   Now is
steward, for his achates ; now †is courtiour, for his debates ; now
is eschetour, for his wronges ; now is losel, for his songes, personer ; and [hath his] provendre alone, with whiche manye 50
thrifty shulde encrese.   And yet is this shrewe behynde ; free
herte is forsake ; and losengeour is take.   Lo ! it acordeth ; for
suche there ben that voluntarie lustes haunten in courte with
ribaudye, that til midnight and more wol playe and wake, but in
the churche at matins he is behynde, for yvel disposicion of his 55
stomake ; therfore he shulde ete bene-breed (and so did his
syre) his estate ther-with to strengthen.   His auter is broke, and
lowe lyth, in poynte to gon to the erthe ; but his hors muste ben
esy and hye, to bere him over grete waters.   His chalice poore,
but he hath riche cuppes.   No towayle but a shete, there god 60
shal ben handled ; and on his mete-borde there shal ben bord-
clothes and towelles many payre.   At masse serveth but a clergion ; fyve squiers in hal.   Poore chaunsel, open holes in every
syde ; beddes of silke, with tapites going al aboute his chambre.
Poore masse-book and leud chapelayn, and broken surplice with 65
many an hole ; good houndes and many, to hunte after hart and
hare, to fede in their feestes.   Of poore men have they greet
care ; for they ever crave and nothing offren, they wolden have
hem dolven !   But among legistres there dar I not come ; my
doinge[s], they sayn, maken hem nedy.   They ne wolde for 70
nothing have me in town ; for than were tort and †force nought
worth an hawe about, and plesen no men, but thilk grevous and
torcious ben in might and in doing.   These thinges to-forn-sayd
mowe wel, if men liste, ryme ; trewly, they acorde nothing.   And
for-as-moch as al thinges by me shulden of right ben governed, 75
I am sory to see that governaunce fayleth, as thus : to sene smale
and lowe governe the hye and bodies above.   Certes, that
policye is naught ; it is forbode by them that of governaunce
treten and enformen.   And right as beestly wit shulde ben

---

45. deuoute.   46. nowe.   47. Nowe.   48. stewarde. nowe. it ;
read is. nowe.   49. eschetoure. nowe.   50. *I supply* hath his.
51. encrease.   56. eate beane-.   58. lythe. gone. horse.   59. easy.
heare. great.   61. meate-. borde-.   65. boke. leude chapelayne.
66. harte.   67. great.   68. nothynge.   69. amonge. dare.   70. sayne.
71. forthe ; *read* force.   72. worthe. pleasen.   73. to-forne-.
74. nothynge.   76. sorye. se.   78. polesye.   79. treaten. wytte.

E 2

80 subject to reson, so erthly power in it-selfe, the lower shulde ben
subject to the hygher. What is worth thy body, but it be
governed with thy soule? Right so litel or naught is worth
erthely power, but if reignatif prudence in heedes governe the
smale; to whiche heedes the smale owen to obey and suffre in
85 their governaunce. But soverainnesse ayenward shulde thinke in
this wyse: "I am servaunt of these creatures to me delivered,
not lord, but defendour; not mayster, but enfourmer; not
possessour, but in possession; and to hem liche a tree in whiche
sparowes shullen stelen, her birdes to norisshe and forth bringe,
90 under suretee ayenst al raveynous foules and beestes, and not to
be tyraunt them-selfe." And than the smale, in reste and quiete,
by the heedes wel disposed, owen for their soveraynes helth and
prosperitè to pray, and in other doinges in maintenaunce therof
performe, withouten other administracion in rule of any maner
95 governaunce. And they wit have in hem, and grace to come to
suche thinges, yet shulde they cese til their heedes them cleped,
although profit and plesaunce shulde folowe. But trewly, other
governaunce ne other medlinge ought they not to clayme, ne
the heedes on hem to putte. Trewly, amonges cosinage dar
100 I not come, but-if richesse be my mene; sothly, she and other
bodily goodes maketh nigh cosinage, ther never propinquitè ne
alyaunce in lyve was ne shulde have be, nere it for her medling
maners; wherfore kindly am I not ther leged. Povert of
kinred is behynde; richesse suffreth him to passe; truly he saith,
105 he com never of Japhetes childre. Whereof I am sory that
Japhetes children, for povert, in no linage ben rekened, and
Caynes children, for riches, be maked Japhetes heires. Alas! this
is a wonder chaunge bitwene tho two Noës children, sithen that
of Japhetes ofspring comeden knightes, and of Cayn discended
110 the lyne of servage to his brothers childre. Lo! how gentillesse
and servage, as cosins, bothe discended out of two brethern of
one body! Wherfore I saye in sothnesse, that gentilesse in
kinrede †maketh not gentil linage in succession, without desert
of a mans own selfe. Where is now the lyne of Alisaundre the
115 noble, or els of Hector of Troye? Who is discended of right
bloode of lyne fro king Artour? Pardè, sir Perdicas, whom that

---

80. subiecte.   reason.   82. worthe.   83. reignatyfe.   85. ayenwarde.
87. lorde.   88. possessoure.   89. forthe bring.   90. suretie.   96. cease.
97. profyte.   pleasaunce.   99. put.   dare.   100. meane.   109. comeden
(*sic*); *read* comen?   110. howe.   111. bretherne.   113. maken; *read*
maketh.   deserte.   114. nowe.

Alisandre made to ben his heire in Grece, was of no kinges
bloode; his dame was a tombestere. Of what kinred ben the
gentiles in our dayes?   I trow therfore, if any good be in gentilesse, it is only that it semeth a maner of necessitè be input to 120
gentilmen, that they shulden not varyen fro the vertues of their
auncestres.   Certes, al maner linage of men ben evenliche in
birth; for oon †fader, maker of al goodnes, enformed hem al,
and al mortal folk of one sede arn greyned.   Wherto avaunt men
of her linage, in cosinage or in †elde-faders? Loke now the gin- 125
ning, and to god, maker of mans person; there is no clerk ne no
worthy in gentilesse; and he that norissheth his †corage with
vyces and unresonable lustes, and leveth the kynde course, to
whiche ende him brought forth his birthe, trewly, he is ungentil,
and among †cherles may ben nempned.   And therfore, he that 130
wol ben gentil, he mot daunten his flesshe fro vyces that causen
ungentilnesse, and leve also reignes of wicked lustes, and drawe
to him vertue, that in al places gentilnesse gentilmen maketh.
And so speke I, in feminine gendre in general, of tho persones,
at the reverence of one whom every wight honoureth; for her 135
bountee and her noblesse y-made her to god so dere, that his
moder she became; and she me hath had so greet in worship,
that I nil for nothing in open declare, that in any thinge ayenst her
secte may so wene.   For al vertue and al worthinesse of plesaunce
in hem haboundeth.   And although I wolde any-thing speke, 140
trewly I can not; I may fynde in yvel of hem no maner mater.'

CHAPTER III.

RIGHT with these wordes she stinte of that lamentable
melodye; and I gan with a lyvely herte to praye, if that
it were lyking unto her noble grace, she wolde her deyne to
declare me the mater that firste was begonne, in which she lefte
and stinte to speke beforn she gan to singe.   5
    'O,' quod she, 'this is no newe thing to me, to sene you men
desyren after mater, whiche your-selfe caused to voyde.'
    'Ah, good lady,' quod I, 'in whom victorie of strength is proved
above al other thing, after the jugement of Esdram, whos lordship

---

118. tombystere.   123. one. father; *read* fader.   124. folke. arne.
125. -fathers; *read* -faders.   126. clerke.   127. corare; *read* corage.
128. leaueth.   129. forthe.   130. amonge. clerkes (!); *read* cherles.
131. mote.   132. leaue.   136. bountie.   137. great.   139. maye.
    CH. III. 2. ganne. 5. beforne. 6. thynge. menne. 9. thynge. whose.

10 al lignes: who is, that right as emperour hem commaundeth,
whether thilke ben not women, in whos lyknesse to me ye aperen?
For right as man halt the principaltè of al thing under his beinge, in the masculyne gender; and no mo genders ben there
but masculyn and femenyne; al the remenaunt ben no gendres but
15 of grace, in facultee of grammer: right so, in the femenyne, the
women holden the upperest degree of al thinges under thilke
gendre conteyned. Who bringeth forth kinges, whiche that ben
lordes of see and of erthe; and al peoples of women ben born.
They norisshe hem that graffen vynes; they maken men comfort
20 in their gladde cheres. Her sorowe is deth to mannes herte.
Without women, the being of men were impossible. They conne
with their swetnesse the crewel herte ravisshe, and make it meke,
buxom, and benigne, without violence mevinge. In beautee
of their eyen, or els of other maner fetures, is al mens desyres;
25 ye, more than in golde, precious stones, either any richesse.
And in this degree, lady, your-selfe many hertes of men have
so bounden, that parfit blisse in womankynde to ben men wenen,
and in nothinge els. Also, lady, the goodnesse, the vertue of
women, by propertè of discrecion, is so wel knowen, by litelnesse
30 of malice, that desyre to a good asker by no waye conne they
warne. And ye thanne, that wol not passe the kynde werchinge
of your sectes by general discrecion, I wot wel, ye wol so enclyne
to my prayere, that grace of my requeste shal fully ben graunted.'
'Certes,' quod she, 'thus for the more parte fareth al mankynde,
35 to praye and to crye after womans grace, and fayne many fantasyes to make hertes enclyne to your desyres. And whan these
sely women, for freeltè of their kynde, beleven your wordes, and
wenen al be gospel the promise of your behestes, than graunt[en]
they to you their hertes, and fulfillen your lustes, wherthrough
40 their libertè in maystreship that they toforn had is thralled; and
so maked soverayn and to be prayed, that first was servaunt,
and voice of prayer used. Anon as filled is your lust, many of you
be so trewe, that litel hede take ye of suche kyndnesse; but
with traysoun anon ye thinke hem begyle, and let light of that
45 thing whiche firste ye maked to you wonders dere; so what
thing to women it is to loven any wight er she him wel knowe,
and have him proved in many halfe! For every glittring thing

---

10. lignes (*sic*).   11. whose lykenesse.   12. halte.   15. facultie.
17. forthe.   18. borne.   19. comforte.   20. dethe.   23. buxome.
beautie.   27. parfyte.   32. wotte.   38. graunt.   40. toforne.

is nat gold; and under colour of fayre speche many vices may
be hid and conseled.   Therfore I rede no wight to trust on you
to rathe; mens chere and her speche right gyleful is ful ofte. 50
Wherfore without good assay, it is nat worth on many †of you
to truste.   Trewly, it is right kyndely to every man that thinketh
women betraye, and shewen outward al goodnesse, til he have
his wil performed.   Lo! the bird is begyled with the mery voice
of the foulers whistel.   Whan a woman is closed in your nette, 55
than wol ye causes fynden, and bere unkyndenesse her †ton
hande, or falsetè upon her putte, your owne malicious trayson
with suche thinge to excuse.   Lo! than han women non other
wreche in vengeaunce, but †blobere and wepe til hem list stint,
and sorily her mishap complayne; and is put in-to wening that 60
al men ben so untrewe.   How often have men chaunged her
loves in a litel whyle, or els, for fayling their wil, in their places
hem set!   For fren[d]ship shal be oon, and fame with another
him list for to have, and a thirde for delyt; or els were he lost
bothe in packe and in clothes!   Is this fair?   Nay, god wot. 65
I may nat telle, by thousande partes, the wronges in trechery
of suche false people; for make they never so good a bond,
al sette ye at a myte whan your hert tourneth.   And they that
wenen for sorowe of you deye, the pitè of your false herte is flowe
out of towne.   Alas! therfore, that ever any woman wolde take 70
any wight in her grace, til she knowe, at the ful, on whom she
might at al assayes truste!   Women con no more craft in queynt
knowinge, to understande the false disceyvable conjectementes
of mannes begylinges.   Lo! how it fareth; though ye men
gronen and cryen, certes, it is but disceyt; and that preveth wel 75
by th'endes in your werkinge.   How many women have ben
lorn, and with shame foule shent by long-lastinge tyme, whiche
thorow mennes gyle have ben disceyved?   Ever their fame shal
dure, and their dedes [ben] rad and songe in many londes; that
they han don, recoveren shal they never; but alway ben demed 80
lightly, in suche plyte a-yen shulde they falle.   Of whiche slaunders
and tenes ye false men and wicked ben the verey causes; on you
by right ought these shames and these reproves al hoolly discende.

---

48. golde.   51. worthe.   on; *read* of.   53. -warde.   54. birde.
56. beare.   vnha*n*de; *read* on hande.   58. none.   59. bloder; *read*
blobere.   61. Howe.   63. sette.   frenship (*sic*).   one.   64. lyste.   delyte.
65. faire.   66. maye.   tel.   67. bo*n*de.   69. dey.   72. trust.
crafte.   74. howe.   76. thendes.   Howe.   77. lorne.   longe-.
78. thorowe.   79. *I supply* ben.   radde.   80. done.   81. fal.   83. holy.

Thus arn ye al nighe untrewe; for al your fayre speche, your
85 herte is ful fickel. What cause han ye women to dispyse? Better
fruite than they ben, ne swetter spyces to your behove, mowe ye
not fynde, as far as worldly bodyes strecchen. Loke to their
forminge, at the making of their persones by god in joye of
paradyce! For goodnesse, of mans propre body were they
90 maked, after the sawes of the bible, rehersing goddes wordes in
this wyse: "It is good to mankynde that we make to him an
helper." Lo! in paradyse, for your helpe, was this tree graffed,
out of whiche al linage of man discendeth. If a man be noble
frute, of noble frute it is sprongen; the blisse of paradyse, to
95 mennes sory hertes, yet in this tree abydeth. O! noble helpes
ben these trees, and gentil jewel to ben worshipped of every
good creature! He that hem anoyeth doth his owne shame; it is
a comfortable perle ayenst al tenes. Every company is mirthed
by their present being. Trewly, I wiste never vertue, but a woman
100 were therof the rote. What is heven the worse though Sarazins
on it lyen? Is your fayth untrewe, though †renegates maken
theron lesinges? If the fyr doth any wight brenne, blame his
owne wit that put him-selfe so far in the hete. Is not fyr gen-
tillest and most comfortable element amonges al other? Fyr
105 is cheef werker in fortheringe sustenaunce to mankynde. Shal
fyr ben blamed for it brende a foole naturelly, by his own stulty
witte in steringe? Ah! wicked folkes! For your propre malice
and shreudnesse of your-selfe, ye blame and dispyse the precious-
[es]t thing of your kynde, and whiche thinges among other
110 moste ye desyren! Trewly, Nero and his children ben shrewes,
that dispysen so their dames. The wickednesse and gyling of
men, in disclaundring of thilke that most hath hem glad[d]ed
and plesed, were impossible to wryte or to nempne. Never-the-
later yet I say, he that knoweth a way may it lightly passe; eke
115 an herbe proved may safely to smertande sores ben layd. So
I say, in him that is proved is nothing suche yvels to gesse.
But these thinges have I rehersed, to warne you women al at
ones, that to lightly, without good assaye, ye assenten not to
mannes speche. The sonne in the day-light is to knowen from
120 the moone that shyneth in the night. Now to thee thy-selfe

---

84. arne.   87. farre.   stretchen.   97. dothe.   99. wyst.   101. faythe.
thoughe rennogates.   102. leasynges.   fyre (four times)   103. wytte.
farre.   heate.   104, 112. moste.   104. element comfortable; read
comfortable element.   105. chefe.   108. precioust.   109. amonge.
112-3. gladed and plesed.   115. layde.   120. Nowe.   the.

(quod she) as I have ofte sayd, I knowe wel thyne herte; thou
art noon of al the tofore-nempned people. For I knowe wel the
continuaunce of thy service, that never sithen I sette thee
a-werke, might thy Margaryte for plesaunce, frendship, ne fayrhede
of none other, be in poynte moved from thyne herte; wherfore 125
in-to myne housholde hastely I wol that thou entre, and al the
parfit privitè of my werking, make it be knowe in thy understonding, as oon of my privy familiers. Thou desyrest (quod she)
fayn to here of tho thinges there I lefte?'

'Ye, forsothe,' quod I, 'that were to me a greet blisse.'   130

'Now,' quod she, 'for thou shalt not wene that womans condicions for fayre speche suche thing belongeth :—

CHAPTER IV.

THOU shalt,' quod she, 'understonde first among al other
    thinges, that al the cure of my service to me in the parfit
blisse in doing is desyred in every mannes herte, be he never
so moche a wrecche; but every man travayleth by dyvers studye,
and seke[th] thilke blisse by dyvers wayes. But al the endes 5
are knit in selinesse of desyre in the parfit blisse, that is suche
joye, whan men it have gotten, there †leveth no thing more to
ben coveyted. But how that desyre of suche perfeccion in
my service be kindely set in lovers hertes, yet her erroneous
opinions misturne it by falsenesse of wening. And although 10
mannes understanding be misturned, to knowe whiche shuld ben
the way unto my person, and whither it abydeth; yet wote they
there is a love in every wight, [whiche] weneth by that thing that
he coveyteth most, he shulde come to thilke love; and that
is parfit blisse of my servauntes; but than fulle blisse may not 15
be, and there lacke any thing of that blisse in any syde. Eke it
foloweth than, that he that must have ful blisse lacke no blisse in
love on no syde.'

'Therfore, lady,' quod I tho, 'thilke blisse I have desyred,
and †soghte toforn this my-selfe, by wayes of riches, of dignitè, 20

---

122. arte none. 123. set the. 124. frendeshyp. fayrehede. 127. parfyte.
128. one. 129. fayne. 130. great. 131. Nowe.
    CH. IV. 1. shalte. amonge.   2. parfyte.   4. wretche.   5. seke;
read seketh.   6. parfyte.   7. lyueth; *read* leueth. thynge.   8. howe.
perfection.   9. erronyous.   13. *I supply* whiche.   14. moste.   15.
parfyte. maye.   16. thynge.   20. sothe; *read* soghte. toforne.

of power, and of renomè, wening me in tho †thinges had ben
thilke blisse; but ayenst the heer it turneth.   Whan I supposed
beste thilke blisse have †getten, and come to the ful purpose
of your service, sodaynly was I hindred, and thrown so fer
25 abacke, that me thinketh an inpossible to come there I lefte.'

'I †wot wel,' quod she; 'and therfore hast thou fayled; for
thou wentest not by the hye way.   A litel misgoing in the ginning
causeth mikil errour in the ende; wherfore of thilke blisse thou
fayledest, for having of richesse; ne non of the other thinges thou
30 nempnedest mowen nat make suche parfit blisse in love as I shal
shewe.   Therfore they be nat worthy to thilke blisse; and yet
somwhat must ben cause and way to thilke blisse.   *Ergo*, there is
som suche thing, and som way, but it is litel in usage and that
is nat openly y-knowe.   But what felest in thyne hert of the
35 service, in whiche by me thou art entred?   Wenest aught thy-
selfe yet be in the hye way to my blisse?   I shal so shewe it to
thee, thou shalt not conne saye the contrary.'

'Good lady,' quod I, 'altho I suppose it in my herte, yet
wolde I here thyn wordes, how ye menen in this mater.'
40 Quod she, 'that I shal, with my good wil.   Thilke blisse
desyred, som-del ye knowen, altho it be nat parfitly.   For kyndly
entencion ledeth you therto, but in three maner livinges is al suche
wayes shewed.   Every wight in this world, to have this blisse, oon
of thilke three wayes of lyves must procede; whiche, after opinions
45 of grete clerkes, are by names cleped bestiallich, resonablich, [and
manlich.   Resonablich] is vertuous.   Manlich is worldlich.   Bestialliche is lustes and delytable, nothing restrayned by bridel of reson.
Al that joyeth and yeveth gladnesse to the hert, and it be ayenst
reson, is lykened to bestial living, which thing foloweth lustes and
50 delytes; wherfore in suche thinge may nat that precious blisse,
that is maister of al vertues, abyde.   Your †faders toforn you have
cleped such lusty livinges after the flessh "passions of desyre,"
which are innominable tofore god and man both.   Than, after
determinacion of suche wyse, we accorden that suche passions of
55 desyre shul nat be nempned, but holden for absolute from al other
livinges and provinges; and so †leveth in t[w]o livinges, manlich

21. thrages (*sic*); *read* thinges.   22. heere.   23. get; *read* getten.
26. wol; *read* wot.   30. pa*r*fite.   33. some (*twice*).   37. the. shalte.
con.   39. howe ye meanen.   41. so*m*e deale.   42. entention. thre.
lyuenges.   43. one.   44. thre.   45. great. cleaped. *I supply* and
manlich. Resonablich.   47. nothynge.   47-9. reason (*twice*).   49. lyueng.
thynge.   50. maye.   51. fathers. toforne.   52. lyuenges.   54.
determination.   56. lyuenges (*twice*). lyueth; *read* leveth. to; *read* two.

and resonable, to declare the maters begonne.   But to make thee
fully have understanding in manlich livinges, whiche is holden
worldlich in these thinges, so that ignorance be mad no letter,
I wol (quod she) nempne these forsayd wayes †by names and 60
conclusions. First riches, dignitè, renomè, and power shul in
this worke be cleped bodily goodes ; for in hem hath ben, a gret
throw, mannes trust of selinesse in love : as in riches, suffisance
to have maintayned that was begonne by worldly catel ; in dignitè,
honour and reverence of hem that wern underput by maistry 65
therby to obeye.   In renomè, glorie of peoples praising, after
lustes in their hert, without hede-taking to qualitè and maner of
doing ; and in power, by trouth of lordships mayntenaunce, thing
to procede forth in doing.   In al whiche thinges a longe tyme
mannes coveytise in commune hath ben greetly grounded, to come 70
to the blisse of my service ; but trewly, they were begyled, and for
the principal muste nedes fayle, and in helping mowe nat availe.
See why.   For holdest him not poore that is nedy ? '
    ' Yes, pardè,' quod I.
    ' And him for dishonored, that moche folk deyne nat to 75
reverence ? '
    ' That is soth,' quod I.
    ' And what him, that his mightes faylen and mowe nat helpen?'
    ' Certes,' quod I, ' me semeth, of al men he shulde be holden
a wrecche.'   80
    ' And wenest nat,' quod she, ' that he that is litel in renomè,
but rather is out of the praysinges of mo men than a fewe, be nat
in shame ? '
    ' For soth,' quod I, ' it is shame and villany, to him that
coveyteth renomè, that more folk nat prayse in name than preise.' 85
    ' Soth,' quod she, ' thou sayst soth ; but al these thinges are
folowed of suche maner doinge, and wenden in riches suffisaunce,
in power might, in dignitè worship, and in renomè glorie ; wherfor
they discended in-to disceyvable wening, and in that service disceit
is folowed.   And thus, in general, thou and al suche other that so 90
worchen, faylen of my blisse that ye long han desyred.   Wherfore
truly, in lyfe of reson is the hye way to this blisse ; as I thinke
more openly to declare herafter.   Never-the-later yet, in a litel to
comforte thy herte, in shewing of what waye thou art entred thy-

---

57. the.   58. lyuenges.   59. made.   60. be ; *read* by.
62. cleaped.   64. begon.   65. werne.   66. obey.   70. greatly.
73. Se.   75. folke.   80. wretch.   89. disceite.   92. reason.   94. arte.

95 selfe, and that thy Margarite may knowe thee set in the hye way,
I wol enforme thee in this wyse. Thou hast fayled of thy first
purpos, bicause thou wentest wronge and leftest the hye way on
thy right syde, as thus : thou lokedest on worldly living, and that
thing thee begyled ; and lightly therfore, as a litel assay, thou
100 songedest ; but whan I turned thy purpos, and shewed thee
a part of the hye waye, tho thou abode therin, and no deth ne
ferdnesse of non enemy might thee out of thilk way reve ; but
ever oon in thyn herte, to come to the ilke blisse, whan thou
were arested and firste tyme enprisoned, thou were loth to
105 chaunge thy way, for in thy hert thou wendest to have ben there
thou shuldest. And for I had routhe to sene thee miscaried,
and wiste wel thyn ablenesse my service to forther and encrese,
I com my-selfe, without other mene, to visit thy person in comfort
of thy hert. And perdy, in my comming thou were greetly
110 glad[d]ed ; after whiche tyme no disese, no care, no tene, might
move me out of thy hert. And yet am I glad and greetly enpited,
how continually thou haddest me in mynde, with good avysement
of thy conscience, whan thy king and his princes by huge wordes
and grete loked after variaunce in thy speche ; and ever thou
115 were redy for my sake, in plesaunce of the Margarite-perle and
many mo other, thy body to oblige in-to Marces doing, if any
contraried thy sawes. Stedfast way maketh stedfast hert, with
good hope in the ende. Trewly, I wol that thou it wel knowe ;
for I see thee so set, and not chaunginge herte haddest in my
120 service ; and I made thou haddest grace of thy kinge, in foryevenesse of mikel misdede. To the gracious king art thou mikel
holden, of whos grace and goodnesse somtyme hereafter I thinke
thee enforme, whan I shew the ground where-as moral vertue
groweth. Who brought thee to werke? Who brought this grace
125 aboute? Who made thy hert hardy? Trewly, it was I. For
haddest thou of me fayled, than of this purpos had[dest thou]
never taken [hede] in this wyse. And therfore I say, thou might
wel truste to come to thy blisse, sithen thy ginninge hath ben hard,
but ever graciously after thy hertes desyr hath proceded. Silver
130 fyned with many hetes men knowen for trew ; and safely men

---

95–6. the (*twice*).   97–100. purpose.   98. lyueng.   99. the.   100–2.
the.   101. parte. dethe.   103. one.   106. the.   107. wyst. thyne.
encrease.   108. come. mean. *For* person *read* prison ? comforte.   109.
greatly gladed.   110. disease.   111. gladde. greatly.   112. howe.
114. great.   115. peerle.   119. se the.   121. arte.   122. whose.
123. the. grounde.   124. the.   126. purpose. had ; *read* haddest thou.
I supply hede.   128. harde.   129. desyre.   130. heates.

may trust to the alay in werkinge. This †disese hath proved what way hence-forward thou thinkest to holde.'

'Now, in good fayth, lady,' quod I tho, 'I am now in; me semeth, it is the hye way and the right.'

'Ye, forsothe,' quod she, 'and now I wol disprove thy first 135 wayes, by whiche many men wenen to gette thilke blisse. But for-as-moche as every herte that hath caught ful love, is tyed with queynt knittinges, thou shalt understande that love and thilke foresayd blisse toforn declared in this[e] provinges, shal hote the knot in the hert.' 140

'Wel,' quod I, 'this inpossession I wol wel understande.'

'Now also,' quod she, 'for the knotte in the herte muste ben from one to an-other, and I knowe thy desyr, I wol thou understande these maters to ben sayd of thy-selfe, in disproving of thy first service, and in strengthinge of thilke that thou hast undertake 145 to thy Margaryte-perle.'

'A goddes halfe,' quod I, 'right wel I fele that al this case is possible and trewe; and therfore I †admitte it altogither.'

'†Understand wel,' quod she, 'these termes, and loke no contradiccion thou graunt.' 150

'If god wol,' quod I, 'of al these thinges wol I not fayle; and if I graunt contradiccion, I shulde graunte an impossible; and that were a foul inconvenience; for whiche thinges, lady, y-wis, herafter I thinke me to kepe.'

CHAPTER V.

'WEL,' quod she, 'thou knowest that every thing is a cause, wherthrough any thing hath being that is cleped "caused." Than, if richesse †causeth knot in herte, thilke richesse †is cause of thilke precious thinge being. But after the sentence of Aristotle, every cause is more in dignitè than his thinge caused; 5 wherthrough it foloweth richesse to ben more in dignitè than thilke knot. But richesses arn kyndely naughty, badde, and nedy; and thilke knotte is thing kyndely good, most praysed and desyred. *Ergo*, thing naughty, badde, and nedy in kyndely

131. diseases (*sic*). waye. -forwarde. 133-142. Nowe (*four times*). 139. toforne. 143. desyre. 145. strenghthynge. haste. 148. admytted; *read* admytte it. 149. Vnderstanden (*sic*). 149-152. contradyction (*twice*). 153. foule. ladye.
CH. V. 1. thynge. 2. -throughe. 3. causen; *read* causeth. arne; *read* is. 7. arne. 8, 9. thynge (*twice*). moste.

10 understandinge is more worthy than thing kyndely good, most
desyred and praysed! The consequence is fals; nedes, the
antecedent mot ben of the same condicion. But that richesses
ben bad, naughty, and nedy, that wol I prove; wherfore they
mowe cause no suche thing that is so glorious and good. The
15 more richesse thou hast, the more nede hast thou of helpe hem
to kepe. *Ergo*, thou nedest in richesse, whiche nede thou
shuldest not have, if thou hem wantest. Than muste richesse
ben nedy, that in their having maken thee nedy to helpes, in
suretee thy richesse to kepen; wherthrough foloweth, richesse to
20 ben nedy. Everything causinge yvels is badde and naughty; but
richesse in one causen misese, in another they mowen not evenly
strecchen al about. Wherof cometh plee, debat, thefte, begylinges,
but richesse to winne; whiche thinges ben badde, and by richesse
arn caused. *Ergo*, thilke richesse[s] ben badde; whiche badnesse
25 and nede ben knit in-to richesse by a maner of kyndely propertee;
and every cause and caused accorden; so that it foloweth, thilke
richesse[s] to have the same accordaunce with badnesse and nede,
that their cause asketh. Also, every thing hath his being by his
cause; than, if the cause be distroyed, the being of caused is
30 vanisshed. And, so, if richesse[s] causen love, and richesse[s]
weren distroyed, the love shulde vanisshe; but thilke knotte, and
it be trewe, may not vanisshe, for no going of richesse. *Ergo*,
richesse is no cause of the knot. And many men, as I sayd,
setten the cause of the knotte in richesse; thilke knitten the
35 richesse, and nothing the yvel; thilke persons, what-ever they
ben, wenen that riches is most worthy to be had; and that make
they the cause; and so wene they thilke riches be better than the
person. Commenly, suche asken rather after the quantitè than
after the qualitè; and suche wenen, as wel by hem-selfe as by
40 other, that conjunccion of his lyfe and of his soule is no more
precious, but in as mikel as he hath of richesse. Alas! how may
he holden suche thinges precious or noble, that neither han lyf ne
soule, ne ordinaunce of werchinge limmes! Suche richesse[s]
ben more worthy whan they ben in †gadering; in departing,
45 ginneth his love of other mennes praysing. And avarice †gadering
maketh be hated, and nedy to many out-helpes; and whan leveth
the possession of such goodes, and they ginne vanissh, than

---

10. thynge. moste. 11. false. 12. mote. 15. haste. 18. the.
19. suretie. 21. misease. 22. stretchen. debate. 24. arne. richesse;
read richesses. 25. propertie. 27-30. richesse; *read* richesses (*thrice*).
35. nothynge. 40. coniunction. 41. howe maye. 42. lyfe. 43.
richesse; *read* richesses. 44-5. gatheryng.

entreth sorowe and tene in their hertes. O! badde and strayte
ben thilke, that at their departinge maketh men teneful and sory,
and in the †gadering of hem make men nedy! Moche folk at 50
ones mowen not togider moche therof have. A good gest gladdeth
his hoste and al his meyny; but he is a badde gest that maketh
his hoste nedy and to be aferd of his gestes going.'

'Certes,' quod I, 'me wondreth therfore that the comune
opinion is thus: "He is worth no more than that he hath in 55
catel."'

'O!' quod she, 'loke thou be not of that opinion; for if gold or
money, or other maner of riches shynen in thy sight, whos is that?
Nat thyn. And tho[ugh] they have a litel beautee, they be nothing
in comparison of our kynde; and therfore, ye shulde nat sette 60
your worthinesse in thing lower than your-selfe. For the riches,
the fairnesse, the worthinesse of thilke goodes, if ther be any
suche preciousnesse in hem, are nat thyne; thou madest hem
so never; from other they come to thee, and to other they shul
from thee. Wherfore enbracest thou other wightes good, as 65
tho[ugh] they were thyn? Kynde hath drawe hem by hem-selfe.
It is sothe, the goodes of the erth ben ordayned in your fode
and norisshinge; but if thou wolt holde thee apayd with that
suffyseth to thy kynde, thou shalt nat be in daunger of no suche
riches; to kynde suffyseth litel thing, who that taketh hede. 70
And if thou wolt algates with superfluitè of riches be a-throted,
thou shalt hastelich be anoyed, or els yvel at ese. And fairnesse
of feldes ne of habitacions, ne multitude of meynè, may nat be
rekened as riches that are thyn owne. For if they be badde, it is
greet sclaunder and villany to the occupyer; and if they be good 75
or faire, the mater of the workman that hem made is to prayse.
How shulde other-wyse bountee be compted for thyne? Thilke
goodnesse and fairnesse be proper to tho thinges hem-selfe; than,
if they be nat thyne, sorow nat whan they wende, ne glad thee
nat in pompe and in pride whan thou hem hast. For their 80
bountee and their beautees cometh out of their owne kynde, and
nat of thyne owne person. As faire ben they in their not having
as whan thou hast hem. They be nat faire for thou hast hem;
but thou hast geten hem for the fairnesse of them-selfe. And
there the vaylance of men is demed in richesse outforth, wenen 85

50. gatheryng. folke. 53. aferde. 55. worthe. 57. golde. 58.
whose. 59. beautie. 60. set. 64-5. the (twice). 68. wolte. the
apayde. 72. ease. 73. maye. 75. great. 76. workeman. 77.
Howe. bountie. 79. the. 81. bountie. beautes. 83-4. haste (thrice).

me[n] to have no proper good in them-selfe, but seche it in
straunge thinges.   Trewly, the condicion of good wening is to
thee mistourned, to wene, your noblesse be not in your-selfe, but
in the goodes and beautee of other thinges.   Pardy, the beestes
90 that han but feling soules, have suffisaunce in their owne selfe;
and ye, that ben lyke to god, seken encrese of suffisaunce from so
excellent a kynde of so lowe thinges; ye do greet wrong to him
that you made lordes over al erthly thinges; and ye putte your
worthinesse under the nombre of the fete of lower thinges and
95 foule.   Whan ye juge thilke riches to be your worthinesse, than
putte ye your-selfe, by estimacion, under thilke foule thinges;
and than leve ye the knowing of your-selfe; so be ye viler than
any dombe beest; that cometh of shrewde vice.   Right so thilke
persons that loven non yvel for dereworthinesse of the persone,
100 but for straunge goodes, and saith, the adornement in the knot
lyth in such thing; his errour is perilous and shrewd, and he
wryeth moche venim with moche welth; and that knot may
nat be good whan he hath it getten.
     Certes, thus hath riches with flickering sight anoyed many;
105 and often, whan there is a throw-out shrewe, he coyneth al the
gold, al the precious stones that mowen be founden, to have in
his bandon; he weneth no wight be worthy to have suche thinges
but he alone.   How many hast thou knowe, now in late tyme,
that in their richesse supposed suffisance have folowed, and now
110 it is al fayled!'
     'Ye, lady,' quod I, 'that is for mis medling; and otherwyse
governed [they] thilke richesse than they shulde.'
     'Ye,' quod she tho, 'had not the flood greetly areysed, and
throwe to-hemward both gravel and sand, he had mad no med-
115 linge.   And right as see yeveth flood, so draweth see ebbe, and
pulleth ayen under wawe al the firste out-throwe, but-if good pyles
of noble governaunce in love, in wel-meninge maner, ben sadly
grounded; †the whiche holde thilke gravel as for a tyme, that
ayen lightly mowe not it turne; and if the pyles ben trewe, the
120 gravel and sand wol abyde.   And certes, ful warning in love shalt
thou never thorow hem get ne cover, that lightly with an ebbe, er

---

86. me; *read* men.   87. condytion.   88. the.   89. beautie.
91. encrease.   92. great.   93-6. put (*twice*).   101. shreude.   102. maye.
105. throwe out.   106. golde.   108. Howe. haste.   108-9. nowe.
111. misse medlyng.   112. *Supply* they.   113. floode greatly.   114.
hemwarde. sande. made.   115. floode.   116. out throw.   117.
meanynge.   118. to; *read* the.   120. sande.   121. shalte. thorowe.

thou be ware, it [ne] wol ayen meve. In richesse many men have had tenes and diseses, whiche they shulde not have had, if therof they had fayled. Thorow whiche, now declared, partly it is shewed, that for richesse shulde the knotte in herte neither ben 125 caused in one ne in other; trewly, knotte may ben knit, and I trowe more stedfast, in love, though richesse fayled; and els, in richesse is the knotte, and not in herte. And than suche a knotte is fals; whan the see ebbeth and withdraweth the gravel, that such richesse voydeth, thilke knotte wol unknitte. 130 Wherfore no trust, no way, no cause, no parfit being is in richesse, of no suche knotte. Therfore another way muste we have.

CHAPTER VI.

HONOUR in dignitè is wened to yeven a ful knot.' 'Ye, certes,' quod I, 'and of that opinion ben many; for they sayn, dignitè, with honour and reverence, causen hertes to encheynen, and so abled to be knit togither, for the excellence in soverayntè of such degrees.'   5

'Now,' quod she, 'if dignitè, honour, and reverence causen thilke knotte in herte, this knot is good and profitable. For every cause of a cause is cause of thing caused. Than thus: good thinges and profitable ben by dignitè, honour, and rever- ence caused. *Ergo*, they accorden; and dignites ben good with 10 reverences and honour. But contraries mowen not accorden. Wherfore, by reson, there shulde no dignitee, no reverence, non honour acorde with shrewes. But that is fals; they have ben cause to shrewes in many shreudnes; for with hem they accorden. *Ergo*, from beginning to argue ayenward til it come to the laste 15 conclusion, they are not cause of the knot. Lo, al day at eye arn shrewes not in reverence, in honour, and in dignitè? Yes, for- sothe, rather than the good. Than foloweth it that shrewes rather than good shul ben cause of this knot. But of this [the] contrarie of al lovers is bileved, and for a sothe openly de- 20 termined to holde.'

'Now,' quod I, 'fayn wolde I here, how suche dignitees acorden
with shrewes.'

'O,' quod she, 'that wol I shewe in manifolde wyse. Ye wene
25 (quod she) that dignites of office here in your citè is as the
sonne; it shyneth bright withouten any cloude; [of] whiche thing,
whan they comen in the handes of malicious tirauntes, there
cometh moche harm, and more grevaunce therof than of the
wilde fyre, though it brende al a strete. Certes, in dignitè of
30 office, the werkes of the occupyer shewen the malice and the
badnesse in the person; with shrewes they maken manyfolde
harmes, and moche péople shamen. How often han rancours,
for malice of the governour, shulde ben mainteyned? Hath not
than suche dignitees caused debat, rumours, and yvels? Yes,
35 god wot, by suche thinges have ben trusted to make mens understanding enclyne to many queynte thinges. Thou wottest wel
what I mene.'

'Ye,' quod I, 'therfore, as dignitè suche thing in tene y-wrought,
so ayenward, the substaunce in dignitè chaunged, relyed to bring
40 ayen good plyte in doing.'

'Do way, do way,' quod she; 'if it so betyde, but that is
selde, that suche dignitè is betake in a good mannes governaunce,
what thing is to recken in the dignitees goodnesse? Pardè, the
bountee and goodnesse is hers that usen it in good governaunce;
45 and therfore cometh it that honour and reverence shulde ben
don to dignitè bycause of · encresinge vertue in the occupyer,
and not to the ruler bycause of soverayntee in dignitè. Sithen
dignitè may no vertue cause, who is worthy worship for suche
goodnesse? Not dignitè, but person, that maketh goodnesse in
50 dignitè to shyne.'

'This is wonder thing,' quod I; 'for me thinketh, as the person
in dignitè is worthy honour for goodnesse, so, tho[ugh] a person
for badnesse ma[u]gree hath deserved, yet the dignitè leneth to
be commended.'

55 'Let be,' quod she, 'thou errest right foule; dignitè with
badnesse is helper to performe the felonous doing. Pardy, were
it kyndly good, or any propertè of kyndly vertue [that men]
hadden in hem-selfe, shrewes shulde hem never have; with hem
shulde they never accorde. Water and fyr, that ben contrarious,

---

22. Nowe. fayne. howe.   26. *I supply* of. thynge.   28. harme.
32. Howe.   34. debate.   35. wote.   37. meane.   39. ayenwarde.
44. bountie.   45. honoure.   46. done. encreasynge.   47. soverayntie.
53. magre.   57. *Supply* that.   men *and* it.   59. fire.

mowen nat togider ben assembled; kynde wol nat suffre suche 60
contraries to joyne. And sithen at eye, by experience in doing,
we seen that shrewes have hem more often than good men, siker
mayst thou be, that kyndly good in suche thing is nat appropred.
Pardy, were they kyndly good, as wel oon as other shulden
evenlich in vertue of governaunce ben worthe; but oon fayleth in 65
goodnesse, another doth the contrary; and so it sheweth, kyndly
goodnesse in dignitè nat be grounded. And this same reson
(quod she) may be mad, in general, on al the bodily goodes;
for they comen ofte to throw-out shrewes. After this, he is
strong that hath might to have grete burthens, and he is light 70
and swifte, that hath soveraintè in ronning to passe other; right
so he is a shrewe, on whom shreude thinges and badde han most
werchinge. And right as philosophy maketh philosophers, and
my service maketh lovers, right so, if dignites weren good or
vertuous, they shulde maken shrewes good, and turne her malice, 75
and make hem be vertuous. But that they do nat, as it is
proved, but causen rancour and debat. *Ergo*, they be nat good,
but utterly badde. Had Nero never ben Emperour, shulde
never his dame have be slayn, to maken open the privitè of his
engendrure. Herodes, for his dignitè, slew many children. The 80
dignitè of king John wolde have distroyed al England. Therfore
mokel wysdom and goodnesse both, nedeth in a person, the
malice in dignitè slyly to brydel, and with a good bitte of arest
to withdrawe, in case it wolde praunce otherwyse than it shulde.
Trewly, ye yeve to dignites wrongful names in your cleping. 85
They shulde hete, nat dignitè, but moustre of badnesse and
mayntenour of shrewes. Pardy, shyne the sonne never so bright,
and it bringe forth no hete, ne sesonably the herbes out-bringe of
the erthe, but suffre frostes and cold, and the erthe barayne to
ligge by tyme of his compas in circute about, ye wolde wonder, 90
and dispreyse that sonne! If the mone be at ful, and sheweth
no light, but derke and dimme to your sight appereth, and make
distruccion of the waters, wol ye nat suppose it be under cloude
or in clips, and that som prevy thing, unknowen to your wittes,
is cause of suche contrarious doinge? Than, if clerkes, that han 95
ful insight and knowing of suche impedimentes, enforme you of

---

61. ioyn.   62. sene.   menne.   63. mayste.   64-5. one (*twice*).
66. dothe.   68. made.   69. throwe out.   70. great burthyns.
77. debate.   80. slewe.   81. Englande.   82. wysedom.   88. bring
forthe. heate.   89. colde.   91. son.   93. distruction   94. some.

the sothe, very idiottes ye ben, but-if ye yeven credence to thilk
clerkes wordes.   And yet it doth me tene, to sene many wrecches
rejoycen in such maner planettes.   Trewly, litel con[ne] they on
100 philosophy, or els on my lore, that any desyr haven suche
lightinge planettes in that wyse any more to shewe.'

'Good lady,' quod I, 'tel me how ye mene in these thinges.'

'Lo,' quod she, 'the dignites of your citè, sonne and mone,
nothing in kynde shew their shyning as they shulde.   For the
105 sonne made no brenning hete in love, but freesed envye in
mennes hertes, for feblenesse of shyning hete ; and the moone
was about, under an olde cloude, the livinges by waters to
distroye.'

'Lady,' quod I, 'it is supposed they had shyned as they
110 shulde.'

'Ye,' quod she, 'but now it is proved at the ful, their beautè in
kyndly shyning fayled ; wherfore dignitè of him-selven hath no
beautee in fayrnesse, ne dryveth nat awaye vices, but encreseth ;
and so be they no cause of the knotte.   Now see, in good trouth ;
115 holde ye nat such sonnes worthy of no reverence, and dignites
worthy of no worship, that maketh men to do the more harmes ?'

'I not,' quod I.

'No ?' quod she ; 'and thou see a wyse good man, for his
goodnesse and wysnesse wolt thou nat do him worship ?   Therof
120 he is worthy.'

'That is good skil,' quod I ; 'it is dewe to suche, both reverence and worship to have.'

'Than,' quod she, 'a shrewe, for his shreudnesse, altho he be
put forth toforn other for ferde, yet is he worthy, for shrewdnesse,
125 to be unworshipped ; of reverence no part is he worthy to have,
[that] to contrarious doing belongeth : and that is good skil.
For, right as he besmyteth the dignites, thilke same thing ayenward him smyteth, or els shulde smyte.   And over this thou wost
wel (quod she) that fyr in every place heteth where it be, and
130 water maketh wete.   Why ?   For kyndely werking is so y-put in
hem, to do suche thinges ; for every kyndely in werking sheweth
his kynde.   But though a wight had ben mayre of your city
many winter togider, and come in a straunge place there he were

---

98. wretches.   99. con ; *read* conne.   100. desyre.   102. howe.
mean.   107. lyuenges.   111. nowe.   113. beautie. encreseth.
114. Nowe se.   118. se.   119. wysenesse wolte.   124. forthe toforne.
125. parte.   126. *I supply* that.   127. ayenwarde.   128. woste.
129. fyre. heateth.   132. cytie.

not knowen, he shulde for his dignitè have no reverence.   Than
neither worshippe ne reverence is kyndely propre in no dignitè, 135
sithen they shulden don their kynde in suche doinge, if any were.
And if reverence ne worshippe kyndely be not set in dignitees,
and they more therein ben shewed than goodnesse, for that in
dignitè is shewed, but it proveth that goodnesse kyndely in hem
is not grounded.   I-wis, neither worshippe, ne reverence, ne good- 140
nesse in dignitè don non office of kynde; for they have non
suche propertee in nature of doinge but by false opinion of the
people.   Lo! how somtyme thilke that in your city wern in
dignitè noble, if thou liste hem nempne, they ben now overturned bothe in worship, in name, and in reverence; wherfore 145
such dignites have no kyndly werching of worshippe and of
reverence.   He that hath no worthinesse on it-selfe, now it ryseth
and now it vanissheth, after the variaunt opinion in false hertes
of unstable people.   Wherfore, if thou desyre the knottè of this
jewel, or els if thou woldest suppose she shulde sette the knotte 150
on thee for suche maner dignitè, than thou wenest beautee or
goodnesse of thilke somwhat encreseth the goodnesse or vertue in
the body.   But dignite[es] of hemself ben not good, ne yeven
reverence ne worshippe by their owne kynde.   How shulde they
than yeve to any other a thing, that by no waye mowe they have 155
hem-selfe?   It is sene in dignitè of the emperour and of many
mo other, that they mowe not of hem-selve kepe their worshippe
ne their reverence; that, in a litel whyle, it is now up and now
downe, by unstedfaste hertes of the people.   What bountee mowe
they yeve that, with cloude, lightly leveth his shyninge?   Certes, 160
to the occupyer is mokel appeyred, sithen suche doinge doth
villanye to him that may it not mayntayne.   Wherfore thilke way
to the knotte is croked; and if any desyre to come to the knot,
he must leve this way on his lefte syde, or els shal he never come
there.   165

---

141. done none. none.   142. propertie.   143. howe. cytie werne.
144. nowe.   147. *For* He *read* That thing?   147-8. nowe (*twice*).
151. the. beautie.   152. encreaseth.   153. dignite; *read* dignitees.
154. howe.   155. thynge.   158. that that; *read* that. nowe (*twice*).
159. bountie.   160. leaueth.   161. dothe.   162. maye. waye.
164. leaue. waye.

CHAPTER VII.

AVAYLETH aught (quod she) power of might in mayntenaunce of [men, to maken hem] worthy to come to this
knot?'

'Pardè,' quod I, 'ye; for hertes ben ravisshed from suche
5 maner thinges.'

'Certes,' quod she, 'though a fooles herte is with thing
ravisshed, yet therfore is no general cause of the powers, ne of
a siker parfit herte to be loked after. Was not Nero the moste
shrewe oon of thilke that men rede, and yet had he power to
10 make senatours justices, and princes of many landes? Was not
that greet power?'

'Yes, certes,' quod I.

'Wel,' quod she, 'yet might he not helpe him-selfe out of
disese, whan he gan falle. How many ensamples canst thou
15 remembre of kinges grete and noble, and huge power †helden, and
yet they might not kepe hem-selve from wrecchednesse? How
wrecched was king Henry Curtmantil er he deyde? He had not
so moche as to cover with his membres; and yet was he oon
of the grettest kinges of al the Normandes ofspring, and moste
20 possession had. O! a noble thing and clere is power, that is not
founden mighty to kepe him-selfe! Now, trewly, a greet fole is
he, that for suche thing wolde sette the knotte in thyne herte!
Also power of rëalmes, is not thilke grettest power amonges the
worldly. powers reckened? And if suche powers han wrecched-
25 nesse in hem-selfe, it foloweth other powers of febler condicion to
ben wrecched; and than, that wrecchednesse shulde be cause of
suche a knotte! But every wight that hath reson wot wel that
wrecchednesse by no way may ben cause of none suche knotte;
wherfore suche power is no cause. That powers have wrecched-
30 nesse in hem-selfe, may right lightly ben preved. If power lacke on
any syde, on that syde is no power; but no power is wrecchednesse: for al-be-it so the power of emperours or kinges, or els
of their rëalmes (which is the power of the prince) strecchen

---

CH. VII.   2. *I supply* men, to maken hem.   8. parfyte.   9. one.
11. great.   14. disease. fal. Howe. canste.   15. great. holden;
read helden.   16. wretchydnesse. Howe wretched.   18. one.
19. greatest.   20. thynge.   21. Nowe. great.   23. greatest.
24. wretchydnesse (*several times*); wretched (*several times*).   27. reason
wote.   33. stretchen.

wyde and brode, yet besydes is ther mokel folk of whiche he
hath no commaundement ne lordshippe; and there-as lacketh his 35
power, his nonpower entreth, where-under springeth that maketh
hem wrecches. No power is wrecchednesse and nothing els;
but in this maner hath kinges more porcion of wrecchednesse
than of power. Trewly, suche powers ben unmighty; for ever
they ben in drede how thilke power from lesing may be keped 40
of sorow; so drede sorily prikkes ever in their hertes: litel
is that power whiche careth and ferdeth it-selfe to mayntayne.
Unmighty is that wrecchednesse whiche is entred by the ferdful
weninge of the wrecche him-selfe; and knot y-maked by wrecchednesse is betwene wrecches; and wrecches al thing bewaylen; 45
wherfore the knot shulde be bewayled; and there is no suche
parfit blisse that we supposed at the ginning! *Ergo*, power in
nothing shulde cause suche knottes. Wrecchednesse is a kyndely
propertee in suche power, as by way of drede, whiche they mowe
nat eschewe, ne by no way live in sikernesse. For thou wost wel 50
(quod she) he is nought mighty that wolde don that he may not
don ne perfourme.'

'Therfore,' quod I, 'these kinges and lordes that han suffisaunce at the ful of men and other thinges, mowen wel ben
holden mighty; their comaundementes ben don; it is nevermore 55
denyed.'

'Foole,' quod she, 'or he wot him-selfe mighty, or wot it
not; for he is nought mighty that is blynde of his might and wot
it not.'

'That is sothe,' quod I.   60

'Than if he wot it, he must nedes ben a-drad to lesen it. He
that wot of his might is in doute that he mote nedes lese; and so
ledeth him drede to ben unmighty. And if he recche not to lese,
litel is that worth that of the lesing reson reccheth nothing; and
if it were mighty in power or in strength, the lesing shulde ben 65
withset; and whan it cometh to the lesing, he may it not withsitte. *Ergo*, thilke might is leude and naughty. Such mightes
arn y-lyke to postes and pillers that upright stonden, and greet
might han to bere many charges; and if they croke on any syde,
litel thing maketh hem overthrowe.'   70

'This is a good ensample,' quod I, 'to pillers and postes that

34. folke.   40. howe.   41. prickes.   47. parfyte.   49. propertie.
50. woste.   51-5. done (*thrice*).   57-62. wotte (*four times*).   61. a dradde.
63. leadeth.   retche.   64. worthe.   reason retcheth.   68. arne.   great.
69. beare.   70. thynge.

I have seen overthrowed my-selfe; and hadden they ben under-put with any helpes, they had not so lightly falle.'

'Than holdest thou him mighty that hath many men armed
75 and many servauntes; and ever he is adrad of hem in his herte; and, for he gasteth hem, somtyme he mot the more fere have. Comenly, he that other agasteth, other in him ayenward werchen the same; and thus warnisshed mot he be, and of warnisshe the hour drede. Litel is that might and right leude, who-so taketh
80 hede.'

'Than semeth it,' quod I, 'that suche famulers aboute kinges and grete lordes shulde greet might have. Although a sypher in augrim have no might in significacion of it-selve, yet he yeveth power in significacion to other; and these clepe I the helpes to
85 a poste to kepe him from falling.'

'Certes,' quod she, 'thilke skilles ben leude. Why? But-if the shorers be wel grounded, the helpes shulden slyden and suffre the charge to falle; her might litel avayleth.'

'And so me thinketh,' quod I, 'that a poste alone, stonding
90 upright upon a basse, may lenger in greet burthen endure than croken pilers for al their helpes, and her ground be not siker.'

'That is sothe,' quod she; 'for as, [if] the blynde in bering of the lame ginne stomble, bothe shulde falle, right so suche pillers, so envyroned with helpes, in falling of the grounde fayleth †al-
95 togider. How ofte than suche famulers, in their moste pryde of prosperitè, ben sodainly overthrowen! Thou hast knowe many in a moment so ferre overthrowe, that cover might they never. Whan the hevinesse of suche fayling cometh by case of fortune, they mowe it not eschue; and might and power, if ther
100 were any, shulde of strength such thinges voyde and weyve; and so it is not. Lo, than! whiche thing is this power, that, tho men han it, they ben agast; and in no tyme of ful having be they siker! And if they wold weyve drede, as they mow not, litel is in worthines. Fye therfore on so naughty thing, any knot to
105 cause! Lo! in adversitè, thilk ben his foes that glosed and semed frendes in welth; thus arn his familiers his foes and his enemyes; and nothing is werse, ne more mighty for to anoy than is a familier enemy; and these thinges may they not weyve; so

---

72. sene.   73. fal.   75. adradde.   76. mote. feare.   77. ayenwarde.   78. mote.   82. great (*twice*). Althoughe.   88. fal.
90. graet (*sic*).   91. grounde.   92. *Supply* if. bearyng.   93. fal.
94. al togyther.   95. howe.   96. haste.   108. enemye.

trewly their might is not worth a cresse. And over al thinge, he
that may not withdrawe the brydel of his flesshly lustes and his 110
wrecched complayntes (now think on thy-selfe) trewly he is not
mighty; I can seen no way that lyth to the knotte. Thilke
people than, that setten their hertes upon suche mightes and
powers, often ben begyled. Pardè, he is not mighty that may do
any thing, that another may doon him the selve, and that men 115
have as greet power over him as he over other. A justice that
demeth men ayenward hath ben often demed. Buserus slew his
gestes, and he was slayn of Hercules his geste. Hugest betraysshed many men, and of Collo was he betrayed. He that with
swerde smyteth, with swerde shal be smitten.'   120

Than gan I to studyen a whyle on these thinges, and made
a countenaunce with my hande in maner to ben huisht.

'Now let seen,' quod she, 'me thinketh somwhat there is
within thy soule, that troubleth thy understanding; saye on what
it is '   125

Quod I tho, 'me thinketh that, although a man by power have
suche might over me, as I have over another, that disproveth no
might in my person; but yet may I have power and might never-
the-later.'

'See now,' quod she, 'thyne owne leudenesse. He is mighty 130
that may without wrecchednesse; and he is unmighty that may it
not withsitte; but than he, that might over thee, and he wol,
putte on thee wrecchednesse, thou might it not withsitte. *Ergo*,
thou seest thy-selfe what foloweth! But now (quod she) woldest
thou not skorne, and thou see a flye han power to don harm to 135
an-other flye, and thilke have no might ne ayenturning him-selfe
to defende?'

'Yes, certes,' quod I

'Who is a frayler thing,' quod she, 'than the fleshly body of
a man, over whiche have oftentyme flyes, and yet lasse thing than 140
a flye, mokel might in grevaunce and anoying, withouten any
withsittinge, for al thilke mannes mightes? And sithen thou
seest thyne flesshly body in kyndely power fayle, how shulde than
the accident of a thinge ben in more suretè of beinge than substancial? Wherfore, thilke thinges that we clepe power is but 145

---

109. worthe.   110. maye.   111. wretched. nowe thynke.   112. sene.
waye. lythe.   115. maye doone.   116. great.   117. ayenwarde. slewe.
118. slayne.   122. huyshte.   123. Nowe. sene.   130. Se nowe.
131. maye. wretchydnesse.   132. the.   133. put. the wretchydnesse.
134. nowe.   135. se. done harme.   141. anoyeng.   143. howe.

accident to the flesshly body; and so they may not have that
suretee in might, whiche wanteth in the substancial body. Why
there is no way to the knotte, [for him] that loketh aright after the
149 hye way, as he shulde.

CHAPTER VIII.

VERILY it is proved that richesse, dignitè, and power ben not
trewe way to the knotte, but as rathe by suche thinges the
knotte to be unbounde; wherfore on these thinges I rede no
wight truste to gette any good knotte. But what shul we saye of
5 renomè in the peoples mouthes? Shulde that ben any cause?
What supposest thou in thyn herte?'

'Certes,' quod I, 'yes, I trowe; for your slye resons I dare not
safely it saye.'

'Than,' quod she, 'wol I preve that shrewes as rathe shul ben
10 in the knotte as the good; and that were ayenst kynde.'

'Fayn,' quod I, 'wolde I that here; me thinketh wonder how
renomè shuld as wel knitte a shrewe as a good person; renomè
in every degree hath avaunced; yet wist I never the contrarye.
Shulde than renomè accorde with a shrewe? It may not sinke in
15 my stomake til I here more.'

'Now,' quod she, 'have I not sayd alwayes, that shrewes shul
not have the knotte?'

'What nedeth,' quod I, 'to reherse that any more? I wot wel
every wight, by kyndely reson, shrewes in knitting wol eschewe.'

20   'Than,' quod she, 'the good ought thilke knotte to have.'

'How els?' quod I.

'It were greet harm,' quod she, 'that the good were weyved
and put out of espoire of the knotte, if he it desyred.'

'O,' quod I, 'alas! On suche thing to thinke, I wene that
25 heven wepeth to see suche wronges here ben suffred on erthe; the
good ought it to have, and no wight els.'

'The goodnesse,' quod she, 'of a person may not ben knowe
outforth but by renomè of the knowers; wherfore he must be
renomed of goodnesse, to come to the knot.'

30   'So must it be,' quod I, 'or els al lost that we carpen.'

---

147. suretie.   148. waye.   *Supply* for him.   149. waye.
CH. VIII. 2. waye.   11. Fayne. howe.   14. maye.   16. Nowe.
18. wotte.   19. reason.   21. Howe.   22. great harme.   25. se.

'Sothly,' quod she, 'that were greet harm, but-if a good man might have his desyres in service of thilke knot, and a shrewe to be †weyved, and they ben not knowen in general but by lacking and praysing, and in renomè; and so by the consequence it foloweth, a shrewe to ben praysed and knit; and a good to be 35 forsake and unknit.'

'Ah,' quod I tho, 'have ye, lady, ben here abouten; yet wolde I see, by grace of our argumentes better declared, how good and bad do acorden by lacking and praysing; me thinketh it ayenst kynde.'   40

'Nay,' quod she, 'and that shalt thou see as yerne; these elementes han contrarious qualitees in kynde, by whiche they mowe not acorde no more than good and badde; and in [some] qualitees they acorde, so that contraries by qualitè acorden by qualitè. Is not erthe drye; and water, that is next and bitwene 45 th'erthe, is wete? Drye and wete ben contrarie, and mowen not acorde, and yet this discordaunce is bounde to acorde by cloudes; for bothe elementes ben colde. Right so the eyre, that is next the water, is wete; and eke it is hot. This eyre by his hete contrarieth water that is cold; but thilke contrariouste is oned †by 50 moysture; for bothe be they moyst. Also the fyr, that is next the †eyre and it encloseth al about, is drye, wherthrough it contrarieth †eyre, that is wete; and in hete they acorde; for bothe they ben hote. Thus by these acordaunces discordantes ben joyned, and in a maner of acordaunce they acorden by 55 conneccion, that is, knitting togither; of that accorde cometh a maner of melodye that is right noble. Right so good and bad arn contrarie in doinges, by lacking and praysing; good is bothe lacked and praysed of some; and badde is bothe lacked and praysed of some; wherfore their contrarioustee acorde bothe by 60 lacking and praysing. Than foloweth it, though good be never so mokel praysed, [it] oweth more to ben knit than the badde; or els bad, for the renomè that he hath, must be taken as wel as the good; and that oweth not.'

'No, forsothe,' quod I.   65

'Wel,' quod she, 'than is renomè no way to the knot. Lo, foole,' quod she, 'how clerkes wryten of suche glorie of renomè:—

---

31. great harme.   33. veyned; *read* weyued.   38. se. howe.   41. se.
42. qualyties.   43. *I supply* some.   46. therthe.   49. hotte.   50. colde.
co*n*trariousty. my; *read* by.   51. fyre.   52. erthe; *read* eyre (*twice*).
56. connection.   58. arne.   60. contraryoustie.   62. *I supply* it.
66. waye.   67. howe.

"O glorie, glorie, thou art non other thing to thousandes of folke
but a greet sweller of eeres!" Many oon hath had ful greet renomè
70 by false opinion of variaunt people. And what is fouler than
folk wrongfully to ben praysed, or by malice of the people giltlesse
lacked? Nedes shame foloweth therof to hem that with wrong
prayseth, and also to the desertes praysed; and vilanye and
reproof of him that disclaundreth.

75   Good child (quod she) what echeth suche renomè to the
conscience of a wyse man, that loketh and mesureth his goodnesse, not by slevelesse wordes of the people, but by sothfastnesse
of conscience? By god, nothing. And if it be fayr, a mans name
be eched by moche folkes praysing, and fouler thing that mo folk
8c not praysen? I sayd to thee a litel here-beforn, that no folk in
straunge countreyes nought praysen; suche renomè may not
comen to their eeres, bycause of unknowing and other obstacles,
as I sayde: wherfore more folk not praysen, and that is right foul
to him that renomè desyreth, to wete, lesse folk praisen than
85 renomè enhaunce. I trowe, the thank of a people is naught
worth in remembraunce to take; ne it procedeth of no wyse
jugement; never is it stedfast pardurable. It is veyne and fleing;
with winde wasteth and encreseth. Trewly, suche glorie ought to
be hated. If gentillesse be a cleer thing, renomè and glorie to
90 enhaunce, as in reckening of thy linage, than is gentilesse of thy
kinne; for-why it semeth that gentilesse of thy kinne is but
praysing and renomè that come of thyne auncestres desertes:
and if so be that praysing and renomè of their desertes make
their clere gentillesse, than mote they nedes ben gentil for their
95 gentil dedes, and not thou; for of thy-selfe cometh not such
maner gentilesse, praysinge of thy desertes. Than gentillesse of
thyne auncesters, that forayne is to thee, maketh thee not gentil,
but ungentil and reproved, and-if thou continuest not their
gentilesse. And therfore a wyse man ones sayde: "Better is it
100 thy kinne to ben by thee gentyled, than thou to glorifye of thy
kinnes gentilesse, and hast no desert therof thy-selfe."

How passinge is the beautee of flesshly bodyes, more flittinge
than movable floures of sommer! And if thyne eyen weren as good
as the lynx, that may seen thorow many stone walles, bothe fayre

---

68. arte none. thynge.   69. great. one. great.   71. folke.
74. reprofe.   75. chylde.   76. measureth.   78. fayre.   79. folke.
80. the. beforne. folke.   83. folke. foule.   84. folke.   85. thanke.
86. worthe.   88. encreaseth.   89. clere thynge.   97–100. the (*thrice*).
101. haste. deserte.   102. Howe. beautie.   104. maye sene thorowe.

and foule, in their entrayles, of no maner hewe shulde apere to 105
thy sight; that were a foule sight.   Than is fayrnesse by feblesse
of eyen, but of no kynde; wherfore thilke shulde be no way to
the knot; whan thilke is went, the knotte wendeth after.   Lo,
now, at al proves, none of al these thinges mowe parfitly ben in
understanding, to ben way to the during blisse of the knotte. 110
But now, to conclusion of these maters, herkeneth these wordes.
Very sommer is knowe from the winter: in shorter cours draweth
the dayes of Decembre than in the moneth of June; the springes
of Maye faden and †falowen in Octobre.   These thinges ben not
unbounden from their olde kynde; they have not lost her werke 115
of their propre estat.   Men, of voluntarious wil, withsitte that
hevens governeth.   Other thinges suffren thinges paciently to
werche; man, in what estat he be, yet wolde he ben chaunged.
Thus by queynt thinges blisse is desyred; and the fruit that
cometh of these springes nis but anguis and bitter; al-though it 120
be a whyle swete, it may not be with-holde; hastely they departe;
thus al-day fayleth thinges that fooles wende.   Right thus hast
thou fayled in thy first wening.   He that thinketh to sayle, and
drawe after the course of the sterre *de polo antartico,* shal he never
come northward to the contrarye sterre of *polus articus*; of whiche 125
thinges if thou take kepe, thy first out-waye-going "prison" and
"exile" may be cleped.   The ground falsed underneth, and so
hast thou fayled.   No wight, I wene, blameth him that stinteth
in misgoing, and secheth redy way of his blisse.   Now me
thinketh (quod she) that it suffyseth in my shewing; the wayes 130
by dignetè, richesse, renomè, and power, if thou loke clerely, arn
no wayes to the knotte.'

CHAPTER IX.

'EVERY argument, lady,' quod I tho, 'that ye han maked in
these fore-nempned maters, me thinketh hem in my ful
witte conceyved; shal I no more, if god wil, in the contrarye be
begyled.   But fayn wolde I, and it were your wil, blisse of the
knotte to me were declared.   I might fele the better how my 5

---

106. fayrenesse.   109-111. nowe *(twice).*   110. waye.   111. nowe.
114. folowen; *read* falowen.   115. loste.   116. estate.   119. fruite.
121. maye.   122. al-daye. haste.   125. northwarde.   127. grounde.
129. Nowe.   132. ways.
CH. IX.   4. fayne.   5. howe.

herte might assente, to pursue the ende in service, as he hath begonne.'

'O,' quod she, 'there is a melodye in heven, whiche clerkes clepen "armony"; but that is not in brekinge of voice, but it is
10 a maner swete thing of kyndely werching, that causeth joye[s] out of nombre to recken, and that is joyned by reson and by wysdome in a quantitè of proporcion of knitting. God made al thing in reson and in witte of proporcion of melody, we mowe not suffyse to shewe. It is written by grete clerkes and wyse, that,
15 in erthly thinges, lightly by studye and by travayle the knowinge may be getten; but of suche hevenly melody, mokel travayle wol bringe out in knowing right litel. Swetenesse of this paradyse hath you ravisshed; it semeth ye slepten, rested from al other diseses; so kyndely is your herte therein y-grounded.. Blisse of
20 two hertes, in ful love knitte, may not aright ben imagined; ever is their contemplacion, in ful of thoughty studye to plesaunce, mater in bringinge comfort eriche to other. And therfore, of erthly thinges, mokel mater lightly cometh in your lerning. Knowledge of understonding, that is nigh after eye, but not so
25 nigh the covetyse of knittinge in your hertes. More soverain desyr hath every wight in litel heringe of hevenly conninge than of mokel material purposes in erthe. Right so it is in propertee of my servauntes, that they ben more affiched in steringe of litel thinge in his desyr than of mokel other mater lasse in his
30 conscience. This blisse is a maner of sowne delicious in a queynte voice touched, and no dinne of notes; there is non impression of breking labour. I can it not otherwyse nempne, for wantinge of privy wordes, but paradyse terrestre ful of delicious melody, withouten travayle in sown, perpetual service in ful joye
35 coveyted to endure. Only kynde maketh hertes in understonding so to slepe, that otherwyse may it nat be nempned, ne in other maner names for lyking swetnesse can I nat it declare; al sugre and hony, al minstralsy and melody ben but soot and galle in comparison, by no maner proporcion to reken, in respect of this
40 blisful joye. This armony, this melody, this perdurable joye may nat be in doinge but betwene hevens and elementes, or twey kyndly hertes ful knit in trouth of naturel understonding, withouten weninge and disceit; as hevens and planettes, whiche thinges

---

10. ioye; *read* joyes.   11–3. reason.   14. great.   19. diseases.
hertes; *read* herte.   22. comforte.   24–5. nyghe (*twice*).   25. soueraine
desyre.   27. propertie.   29. desyre.   31. none.   32. breakynge
laboure. canne.   35. Onely.   38. soote.   39. respecte.

continually, for kyndly accordaunces, foryeteth al contrarious
mevinges, that in-to passive diseses may sowne; evermore it 45
thirsteth after more werking. These thinges in proporcion be
so wel joyned, that it undoth al thing whiche in-to badnesse by any
way may be accompted.'

'Certes,' quod I, 'this is a thing precious and noble. Alas!
that falsnesse ever, or wantrust shulde ever be maynteyned, this 50
joye to voyde. Alas! that ever any wrecche shulde, thorow wrath
or envy, janglinge dare make, to shove this melody so farre
a-backe, that openly dar it nat ben used; trewly, wrecches ben
fulfilled with envy and wrathe, and no wight els. Flebring
and tales in suche wrecches dare appere openly in every wightes 55
eere, with ful mouth so charged, [with] mokel malice moved
many innocentes to shende; god wolde their soule therwith were
strangled! Lo! trouth in this blisse is hid, and over-al under
covert him hydeth; he dar not come a-place, for waytinge of
shrewes. Commenly, badnesse goodnesse amaistreth; with my- 60
selfe and my soule this joye wolde I bye, if the goodnesse were
as moche as the nobley in melody.'

'O,' quod she, 'what goodnesse may be acompted more in
this material worlde? Truly, non; that shalt thou understonde.
Is nat every thing good that is contrariant and distroying yvel?' 65

'How els?' quod I.

'Envy, wrathe, and falsnesse ben general,' quod she; 'and
that wot every man being in his right mynde; the knotte, the
whiche we have in this blisse, is contrariaunt and distroyeth such
maner yvels. *Ergo*, it is good. What hath caused any wight 70
to don any good dede? Fynd me any good, but-if this knotte
be the cheef cause. Nedes mot it be good, that causeth so
many good dedes. Every cause is more and worthier than thing
caused; and in that mores possession al thinges lesse ben
compted. As the king is more than his people, and hath in 75
possession al his rëalme after, right so the knot is more than
al other goodes; thou might recken al thinges lasse; and that
to him longeth, oweth in-to his mores cause of worship and of
wil †to turne; it is els rebel and out of his mores defending to
voyde. Right so of every goodnesse; in-to the knotte and 80
in-to the cause of his worship [it] oweth to tourne. And trewly,

---

45. diseases.   51. wretch. thorowe.   53. dare.   53–5. wretches.
56. eare. *I supply* with.   57. innocentes; *misprint for* innocentes.
59. dare.   65. distroyeng.   66. Howe.   71. Fynde.   72. chefe.
mote.   73. thynge.   79. do; *read* to, *as in* l. 81.   81. *Supply* it.

every thing that hath being profitably is good, but nothing hath
to ben more profitably than this knot; kinges it mayntayneth,
and hem, their powers to mayntayne. It maketh misse to ben
85 amended with good governaunce in doing. It closeth hertes
so togider, that rancour is out-thresten. Who that it lengest
kepeth, lengest is glad[d]ed.'

'I trowe,' quod I, 'heretykes and misse-mening people hence-
forward wol maintayne this knotte; for therthorough shul they
90 ben maintayned, and utterly wol turne and leve their olde yvel
understanding, and knitte this goodnesse, and profer so ferre
in service, that name of servauntes might they have. Their
jangles shal cese; me thinketh hem lacketh mater now to alege.'

'Certes,' quod Love, 'if they, of good wil thus turned, as thou
95 sayst, wolen trewly perfourme, yet shul they be abled party
of this blisse to have; and they wol not, yet shul my servauntes
the werre wel susteyne in myn helpe of maintenaunce to the ende.
And they, for their good travayle, shullen in reward so ben meded,
that endelesse joye body and soule †to-gider in this shullen
100 abyden. There is ever accion of blisse withouten possible
corrupcion; there is accion perpetuel in werke without travayle;
there is everlasting passife, withouten any of labour; continuel
plyte, without cesinge coveyted to endure. No tonge may telle,
ne herte may thinke the leest point of this blisse.'
105 'God bring me thider!' quod I than.

'Continueth wel,' quod she, 'to the ende, and thou might not
fayle than; for though thou spede not here, yet shal the passion
of thy martred lyfe ben written, and rad toforn the grete Jupiter,
that god is of routhe, an high in the holownesse of heven, there
110 he sit in his trone; and ever thou shalt forward ben holden
amonge al these hevins for a knight, that mightest with no
penaunce ben discomfited. He is a very martyr that, livingly
goinge, is gnawen to the bones.'

'Certes,' quod I, 'these ben good wordes of comfort; a litel
115 myne herte is rejoyced in a mery wyse.'

'Ye,' quod she; 'and he that is in heven felith more joye,
than whan he firste herde therof speke.'

'So it is,' quod I; 'but wist I the sothe, that after disese
comfort wolde folowe with blisse, so as ye have often declared,

---

88. meanynge.   89. forwarde.   90. leaue.   93. cease. nowe.
99. togyther.   100–1. action (*twice*).   103. ceasynge. tel.   104. hert. ·
108. radde toforne. great.   110. sytte. forwarde.   114. comforte.
118. disease comforte.

I wolde wel suffre this passion with the better chere. But my 120
thoughtful sorowe is endelesse, to thinke how I am cast out
of a welfare; and yet dayneth not this yvel non herte, non hede,
to meward throwe: which thinges wolde greetly me by wayes
of comfort disporte, to weten in my-selfe a litel with other me[n]
ben y-moved; and my sorowes peysen not in her balaunce the 125
weyght of a peese. Slinges of her daunger so hevily peysen,
they drawe my causes so hye, that in her eyen they semen but
light and right litel.'

'O! for,' quod she, 'heven with skyes that foule cloudes
maken and darke †weders, with gret tempestes and huge, 130
maketh the mery dayes with softe shyning sonnes. Also the
yere with-draweth floures and beautee of herbes and of erth;
the same †yere maketh springes and jolitè in Vere so to renovel
with painted coloures, that erthe semeth as gay as heven. Sees
that blasteth and with wawes throweth shippes, of whiche the 135
living creatures for greet peril for hem dreden; right so, the
same sees maketh smothe waters and golden sayling, and comforteth hem with noble haven that firste were so ferde. Hast
thou not (quod she) lerned in thy youth, that Jupiter hath in
his warderobe bothe garmentes of joye and of sorowe? What 140
wost thou how soone he wol turne of the garment of care,
and clothe thee in blisse? Pardè, it is not ferre fro thee. Lo,
an olde proverbe aleged by many wyse :—"Whan bale is greetest,
than is bote a nye-bore." Wherof wilt thou dismaye? Hope
wel and serve wel; and that shal thee save, with thy good bileve.' 145

'Ye, ye,' quod I; 'yet see I not by reson how this blisse
is coming; I wot it is contingent; it may falle on other.'

'O,' quod she, 'I have mokel to done to clere thyne understanding, and voyde these errours out of thy mynde. I wol
prove it by reson, thy wo may not alway enduren. Every thing 150
kyndely (quod she) is governed and ruled by the hevenly bodyes,
whiche haven ful werchinge here on erthe; and after course
of these bodyes, al course of your doinges here ben governed
and ruled by kynde.

Thou wost wel, by cours of planettes al your dayes proceden; 155
and to everich of singuler houres be enterchaunged stondmele

---

121. howe.   122. none (*twice*).   123. mewarde.   greatly.
124. comforte. me; *read* men? 130. wethers; *read* weders.   132. beautie.
133. yeres; *read* yere.   136. great.   141. howe.   142. the.
143. greatest.   144. wylte.   145. the.   146. se.   reason howe.
147. wote. fal.   150. reason.
  * * *
  * * * *   G

about, by submitted worching naturally to suffre; of whiche
changes cometh these transitory tymes that maketh revolving of
your yeres thus stondmele; every hath ful might of worchinge,
160 til al seven han had her course about. Of which worchinges and
possession of houres the dayes of the weke have take her names,
after denominacion in these seven planettes. Lo, your Sonday
ginneth at the first hour after noon on the Saturday, in whiche
hour is than the Sonne in ful might of worching; of whom Son-
165 day taketh his name. Next him foloweth Venus, and after
Mercurius, and than the Moone; so than Saturnus, after whom
Jovis; and than Mars; and ayen than the Sonne; and so forth
†by .xxiiii. houres togider; in whiche hour ginning in the seconde
day stant the Moone, as maister for that tyme to rule; of whom
170 Monday taketh his name; and this course foloweth of al other
dayes generally in doing. This course of nature of these bodyes
chaunging stinten at a certain terme, limitted by their first kynde;
and of hem al governementes in this elemented worlde proceden,
as in springes, constellacions, engendrures, and al that folowen
175 kynde and reson; wherfore [in] the course that foloweth, sorowe
and joy kyndely moten entrechangen their tymes; so that
alway oon wele, as alway oon wo, may not endure. Thus seest
thou appertly, thy sorowe in-to wele mot ben chaunged; wherfore
in suche case to better syde evermore enclyne thou shuldest.
180 Trewly, next the ende of sorowe anon entreth joy; by maner
of necessitè it wol ne may non other betyde; and so thy conti[n]-
gence is disproved; if thou holde this opinion any more, thy
wit is right leude. Wherfore, in ful conclusion of al this, thilke
Margaryte thou desyrest hath ben to thee dere in thy herte, and
185 for her hast thou suffred many thoughtful diseses; herafter shal
[she] be cause of mokel mirth and joye; and loke how glad canst
thou ben, and cese al thy passed hevinesse with manifolde
joyes. And than wol I as blythly here thee speken thy mirthes
in joye, as I now have y-herd thy sorowes and thy complayntes.
190 And if I mowe in aught thy joye encrese, by my trouthe, on
my syde shal nat be leved for no maner traveyle, that I with
al my mightes right blythly wol helpe, and ever ben redy you
bothe to plese.' And than thanked I that lady with al goodly

---

162. denomination.   168. be; *for* by.   169. stante.   172. certayne.
175. *Supply* in.   177. on (*for* oon; *twice*).   178. mote.   181. conty-
gence.   184. the.   185. diseases.   186. *Supply* she.   howe. canste.
187. cense.   188. the.   189. ioy. nowe. yherde.   190. encrease.
191. leaued.

maner that I worthily coude; and trewly I was greetly rejoysed
in myne herte of her fayre behestes; and profered me to be 194
slawe, in al that she me wolde ordeyne, while my lyf lested.

CHAPTER X.

'ME thinketh,' quod I, 'that ye have right wel declared,
that way to the knot shuld not ben in none of these
disprovinge thinges; and now, order of our purpos this asketh,
that ye shulde me shewe if any way be †thider, and whiche
thilke way shulde ben; so that openly may be seye the verry 5
hye way in ful confusioun of these other thinges.'

'Thou shalt,' quod she, 'understande that [of] one of three
lyves (as I first sayd) every creature of mankynde is sprongen,
and so forth procedeth.   These lyves ben thorow names departed
in three maner of kyndes, as bestialliche, manliche, and resona- 10
bliche; of whiche two ben used by flesshely body, and the thirde
by his soule.   "Bestial" among resonables is forboden in every
lawe and every secte, bothe in Cristen and other; for every
wight dispyseth hem that liveth by lustes and delytes, as him
that is thral and bounden servaunt to thinges right foule; suche 15
ben compted werse than men; he shal nat in their degree ben
rekened, ne for suche one alowed.   Heritykes, sayn they, chosen
lyf bestial, that voluptuously liven; so that (as I first sayde to
thee) in manly and resonable livinges our mater was to declare;
but [by] "manly" lyfe, in living after flesshe, or els flesshly wayes 20
to chese, may nat blisse in this knotte be conquered, as by reson
it is proved.   Wherfore by "resonable" lyfe he must nedes it
have, sithe a way is to this knotte, but nat by the firste tway lyves;
wherfore nedes mot it ben to the thirde; and for to live in flesshe,
but nat after flessh, is more resonablich than manliche rekened 25
by clerkes.   Therfore how this way cometh in, I wol it blythely
declare.

See now (quod she) that these bodily goodes of manliche
livinges yelden †sorowfulle stoundes and smertande houres. Who-
so †wol remembre him to their endes, in their worchinges they 30

<hr>

194. worthely. greatly.   195. hert.   196. lyfe.
Ch. X.   3. nowe. purpose.   4. thyther.   5. maye be sey.   6. waye.
7. *I supply* of.   7–10. thre (*twice*).   9. thorowe.   13. christen.   17. sayne.
18. lyfe.   19. the. lyueng*es*.   20. *Supply* by. lyueng.   21. reason.
24. mote.   26. howe. waye.   28. Se nowe.   29. lyuenges.
soroufully; *read* sorowfulle.   30. wele; *read* wol.

ben thoughtful and sorie. Right as a bee that hath had his hony, anon at his flight beginneth to stinge; so thilke bodily goodes at the laste mote awaye, and than stinge they at her goinge, wherthrough entreth and clene voydeth al blisse of this knot.'

35 'Forsothe,' quod I, 'me thinketh I am wel served, in shewing of these wordes. Although I hadde litel in respect among other grete and worthy, yet had I a fair parcel, as me thought, for the tyme, in fortheringe of my sustenaunce; whiche while it dured, I thought me havinge mokel hony to myne estat. I had richesse

40 suffisauntly to weyve nede; I had dignitè to be reverenced in worship. Power me thought that I had to kepe fro myne enemyes, and me semed to shyne in glorie of renomè as manhood asketh in mene; for no wight in myne administracion coude non yvels ne trechery by sothe cause on me putte. Lady, your-selve

45 weten wel, that of tho confederacies maked by my soverains I nas but a servaunt, and yet mokel mene folk wol fully ayenst reson thilke maters maynteyne, in whiche mayntenaunce [they] glorien them-selfe; and, as often ye haven sayd, therof ought nothing in yvel to be layd to me-wardes, sithen as repentaunt

50 I am tourned, and no more I thinke, neither tho thinges ne none suche other to sustene, but utterly distroye, without medlinge maner, in al my mightes. How am I now cast out of al swetnesse of blisse, and mischevously [is] stongen my passed joy! Soroufully muste I bewayle, and live as a wrecche.

55 Every of tho joyes is tourned in-to his contrary. For richesse, now have I povertè; for dignitè, now am I emprisoned; in stede of power, wrecchednesse I suffre; and for glorie of renomè, I am now dispysed and foulich hated. Thus hath farn Fortune, that sodaynly am I overthrowen, and out of al welth dispoyled.

60 Trewly, me thinketh this way in entree is right hard; god graunt me better grace er it be al passed; the other way, lady, me thought right swete.'

'Now, certes,' quod Love, 'me list for to chyde. What ayleth thy darke dulnesse? Wol it nat in clerenesse ben sharped?

65 Have I nat by many resons to thee shewed, suche bodily goodes faylen to yeve blisse, their might so forforth wol nat strecche?

---

31. hadde.   32. anone.   36. respecte amonge.   37. great. faire.
39. estate,   42. manhode.   43. meane. -tion.   46. meane folke.
47. reason.   *I supply* they.   48. sayde.   49. nothynge. layde.
52. Howe. nowe caste.   53. *Supply* is.   54. wretche.   56. nowe
(*thrice*).   57. wretchednesse.   58. nowe.   60. entre. harde.
61. ladye.   63. Nowe.   65. reasons. the.   66. forforthe. stretche.

Shame (quod she) it is to say, thou lyest in thy wordes.   Thou
ne hast wist but right fewe that these bodily goodes had al atones;
commenly they dwellen nat togider.   He that plentè hath in riches,
of his kinne is ashamed; another of linage right noble and wel 70
knowe, but povert him handleth; he were lever unknowe.
Another hath these, but renomè of peoples praysing may he nat
have; overal he is hated and defamed of thinges right foule.
Another is fair and semely, but dignitè him fayleth; and he that
hath dignitè is croked or lame, or els misshapen and foully dis- 75
pysed.   Thus partable these goodes dwellen commenly; in one
houshold ben they but silde.   Lo! how wrecched is your truste
on thing that wol nat accorde!   Me thinketh, thou clepest thilke
plyte thou were in "selinesse of fortune"; and thou sayest, for
that the selinesse is departed, thou art a wrecch.   Than foloweth 80
this upon thy wordes; every soule resonable of man may nat dye;
and if deth endeth selinesse and maketh wrecches, as nedes of
fortune maketh it an ende.   Than soules, after deth of the body,
in wrecchednesse shulde liven.   But we knowe many that han
geten the blisse of heven after their deth.   How than may this 85
lyf maken men blisful, that whan it passeth it yeveth no wrecchednesse, and many tymes blisse, if in this lyfe he con live as he
shulde?   And wolt thou acompt with Fortune, that now at [t]he
first she hath don thee tene and sorowe?   If thou loke to the
maner of al glad thinges and sorouful, thou mayst nat nay it, that 90
yet, and namely now, thou standest in noble plyte in a good
ginning, with good forth-going herafter.   And if thou wene to be
a wrecch, for such welth is passed, why than art thou nat wel
fortunate, for badde thinges and anguis wrecchednesse ben passed?
Art thou now come first in-to the hostry of this lyfe, or els the 95
both of this worlde?   Art thou now a sodayn gest in-to this
wrecched exile?   Wenest there be any thing in this erthe stable?
Is nat thy first arest passed, that brought thee in mortal sorowe?
Ben these nat mortal thinges agon with ignorance of beestial wit,
and hast receyved reson in knowing of vertue?   What comfort is 100
in thy herte, the knowinge sikerly in my service [to] be grounded?
And wost thou nat wel, as I said, that deth maketh ende of al

---

74. faire.   75. fouly.   77. sylde. howe reetched (!).   80. arte a
wretch.   82. dethe. wretches.   83. dethe.   84–6. wretchednesse.
85. dethe. Howe.   86. lyfe.   88. wolte. now. he; *read* the.
89. done the.   91. nowe.   93. wretch.   94. wretchednesse.
95–6. nowe (*twice*).   96. sodayne.   97. wretched. thynge.   98. the
(*sic*).   100. reason. comforte.   101. hert. *I supply* to.   102. woste.

fortune? What than? Standest thou in noble plyte, litel hede
or recking to take, if thou let fortune passe dy[i]ng, or els that
105 she fly whan her list, now by thy lyve? Pardy, a man hath
nothing so leef as his lyf; and for to holde that, he doth al his
cure and diligent traveyle. Than, say I, thou art blisful and
fortunat sely, if thou knowe thy goodes that thou hast yet
†beleved, whiche nothing may doute that they ne ben more worthy
110 than thy lyf?'

'What is that?' quod I.

'Good contemplacion,' quod she, 'of wel-doing in vertue in tyme
coming, bothe in plesaunce of me and of thy Margarit-peerle.
Hastely thyn hert in ful blisse with her shal be esed. Therfore dis-
115 may thee nat; Fortune, in hate grevously ayenst thy bodily person,
ne yet to gret tempest hath she nat sent to thee, sithen the holding
cables and ankers of thy lyfe holden by knitting so faste, that
thou discomforte thee nought of tyme that is now, ne dispayre
thee not of tyme to come, but yeven thee comfort in hope of
120 weldoing, and of getting agayn the double of thy lesing, with
encresing love of thy Margarite-perle therto! For this, hiderto,
thou hast had al her ful daunger; and so thou might amende al
that is misse and al defautes that somtyme thou diddest; and
that now, in al thy tyme, to that ilke Margaryte in ful service of
125 my lore thyne herte hath continued; wherfor she ought moche
the rather enclyne fro her daungerous sete. These thinges ben
yet knit by the holding anker in thy lyve, and holden mote they;
to god I pray, al these thinges at ful ben perfourmed. For whyle
this anker holdeth, I hope thou shalt safely escape; and [in a]
130 whyle thy trewe-mening service aboute bringe, in dispyte of al
false meners that thee of-newe haten; for [in] this trewe service
thou art now entred.'

'Certayn,' quod I, 'among thinges I asked a question, whiche
was the way to the knot. Trewly, lady, how-so it be I tempt you
135 with questions and answers, in speking of my first service, I am
now in ful purpos in the pricke of the herte, that thilke service
was an enprisonment, and alway bad and naughty, in no maner
to be desyred; ne that, in getting of the knot, may it nothing
aveyle. A wyse gentil herte loketh after vertue, and none other

---

104. rcekyng.   dyng (*sic*). 106. lefe.   lyfe.   109. beloued; *read* beleued.
nothynge.   112. conte*m*plation.   114. eased.   115-9. the (*five times*).
119. comforte.   120. agayne.   encreasynge.   129. shalte. *Supply* in a.
'30. meanyng.   131. meaners.   the. *Supply* in.   132. arte nowe.
133. Certayn *begins with a large capital* C, *on fol.* 306, *verso.* amonge.
134. howe.   136. nowe.   purpose.   136-9. hert.

bodily joyes alone. And bycause toforn this in tho wayes I was 140
set, I wot wel my-selfe I have erred, and of the blisse fayled ; and
so out of my way hugely have I ronne.'

'Certes,' quod she, 'that is sothe ; and there thou hast miswent, eschewe the path from hens-forward, I rede. Wonder
I trewly why the mortal folk of this worlde seche these ways out- 145
forth ; and it is preved in your-selfe. Lo, how ye ben confounded
with errour and folly ! The knowing of very cause and way is
goodnesse and vertue. Is there any thing to thee more precious
than thy-selfe ? Thou shalt have in thy power that thou woldest
never lese, and that in no way may be taken fro thee ; and thilke 150
thing is that is cause of this knot. And if deth mowe it nat reve
more than an erthly creature, thilke thing than abydeth with thy-
selfe soule. And so, our conclusion to make, suche a knot, thus
getten, abydeth with this thinge and with the soule, as long as
they laste. A soule dyeth never ; vertu and goodnesse evermore 155
with the soule endureth ; and this knot is parfit blisse. Than
this soule in this blisse endlesse shal enduren. Thus shul hertes
of a trewe knot ben esed : thus shul their soules ben plesed : thus
perpetually in joye shul they singe.'

'In good trouth,' quod I, 'here is a good beginning ; yeve us 160
more of this way.'

Quod she, 'I said to thee nat longe sithen, that resonable lyf
was oon of three thinges ; and it was proved to the soule.

CHAPTER XI.

EVERY soule of reson hath two thinges of stering lyf, oon in
vertue, and another in the bodily workinge ; and whan the
soule is the maister over the body, than is a man maister of him-
selfe. And a man, to be a maister over him-selfe, liveth in vertu and
in goodnesse, and as reson of vertue techeth. So the soule and the 5
body, worching vertue togider, liven resonable lyf, whiche clerkes
clepen "felicitè in living " ; and therein is the hye way to this knot.
These olde philosophers, that hadden no knowing of divine grace,
of kyndly reson alone, wenden that of pure nature, withouten any

---

140. toforne.   141. sette.   wote.   142. ron.   144. pathe. -forwarde.
145. folke.   146. howe.   148. thynge. the.   150. the.   151. dethe.
152. thynge.   155. last.   156. parfite.   158. eased. pleased.
162. the. lyfe.   163. one. thre.
    Ch. XI.   1. euery (*with small* e). reason. lyfe. one. 6. lyfe. 7. lyueng.
9. reason.

10 helpe of grace, me might have y-shoned th'other livinges.
Resonably have I lived; and for I thinke herafter, if god wol,
and I have space, thilke grace after my leude knowing declare,
I leve it as at this tyme.   But, as I said, he that out-forth loketh
after the wayes of this knot, [his] conning with whiche he shulde
15 knowe the way in-forth, slepeth for the tyme.   Wherfore he that
wol this way knowe, must leve the loking after false wayes outforth, and open the eyen of his conscience, and unclose his herte.
Seest nat, he that hath trust in the bodily lyfe is so besy bodily
woundes to anointe, in keping from smert (for al-out may they nat
20 be heled), that of woundes in his true understanding he taketh no
hede; the knowing evenforth slepeth so harde : but anon, as in
knowing awake, than ginneth the prevy medicynes, for heling of
his trewe intent, inwardes lightly †helen conscience, if it be wel
handled.   Than must nedes these wayes come out of the soule
25 by stering lyfe of the body; and els may no man come to parfit
blisse of this knotte.   And thus, by this waye, he shal come to the
knotte, and to the parfit selinesse that he wende have had in
bodily goodes outforth.'
    'Ye,' quod I, 'shal he have both knot, riches, power, dignitè,
30 and renomè in this maner way?'
    'Ye,' quod she, 'that shal I shewe thee.   Is he nat riche that
hath suffisaunce, and hath the power that no man may amaistrien?
Is nat greet dignitè to have worship and reverence?   And hath
he nat glorie of renomè, whos name perpetual is during, and out
35 of nombre in comparacion?'
    'These be thinges that men wenen to getten outforth,' quod I.
    'Ye,' quod she; 'they that loken after a thing that nought is
therof, in al ne in partie, longe mowe they gapen after!'
    'That is sothe,' quod I.
40   'Therfore,' quod she, 'they that sechen gold in grene trees, and
wene to gader precious stones among vynes, and layn her nettes
in mountains to fisshe, and thinken to hunte in depe sees after
hart and hynd, and sechen in erth thilke thinges that surmounteth
heven, what may I of hem say, but folisshe ignoraunce misledeth
45 wandring wrecches by uncouth wayes that shulden be forleten,
and maketh hem blynde fro the right pathe of trewe way that

---

10. thother lyuenges.   13. leaue.   14. *I supply* his.   16. leaue.
19. anoynt.   20. healed.   22. healyng.   23. healeth; *read* helen.
25. maye. pa*r*fite.   27. pa*r*fyte.   30. waye.   31. the.   33. great.
34. whose.   35. co*m*paration.   37. thynge.   40. golde.   41. amonge.
layne.   42. hunt.   43. hynde.   45. wretches.

shulde ben used? Therfore, in general, errour in mankynde
departeth thilke goodes by mis-seching, whiche he shulde have
hole, and he sought by reson. Thus goth he begyled of that he
sought; in his hode men have blowe a jape.'   50

'Now,' quod I, 'if a man be vertuous, and al in vertue liveth,
how hath he al these thinges?'

'That shal I proven,' quod she. 'What power hath any man
to lette another of living in vertue? For prisonment, or any
other disese, [if] he take it paciently, discomfiteth he nat; the 55
tyrant over his soule no power may have. Than hath that man,
so tourmented, suche power, that he nil be discomfit; ne overcome may he nat ben, sithen pacience in his soule overcometh,
and †is nat overcomen. Suche thing that may nat be a-maistred,
he hath nede to nothing; for he hath suffisaunce y-now, to helpe 60
him-selfe. And thilke thing that thus hath power and suffisance,
and no tyrant may it reve, and hath dignitè to sette at nought al
thinges, here it is a greet dignitè, that deth may a-maistry. Wherfore thilke power [with] suffisaunce, so enclosed with dignitè, by
al reson renomè must have. This is thilke riches with suffisaunce 65
ye sholde loke after; this is thilke worshipful dignitè ye shulde
coveyte; this is thilke power of might, in whiche ye shulde truste;
this is the ilke renomè of glorie that endlesse endureth; and al
nis but substaunce in vertuous lyving.'

'Certes,' quod I, 'al this is sothe; and so I see wel that vertue 70
with ful gripe encloseth al these thinges. Wherfore in sothe
I may saye, by my trouth, vertue of my Margarite brought me
first in-to your service, to have knitting with that jewel, nat sodain
longinges ne folkes smale wordes, but only our conversacion
togider; and than I, seinge th'entent of her trewe mening with 75
florisshing vertue of pacience, that she used nothing in yvel, to
quyte the wicked lesinges that false tonges ofte in her have laid,
I have seye it my-selfe, goodly foryevenesse hath spronge out of
her herte. Unitè and accord, above al other thinges, she
desyreth in a good meke maner; and suffereth many wicked 80
tales.

Trewly, lady, to you it were a gret worship, that suche thinges
by due chastisment were amended.'

---

48. mysse.   49. reason.   51. Nowe.   52. howe.   54. let. lyueng.
55. *I supply* if.   56. maye.   59. as; *read* is.   60. ynowe.   63. great.
64. *I supply* with.   67. coueyt.   69. lyueng.   70. se.   74. onely.
con*v*ersation.   75. thentent.   76. nothynge.   77. leasynges. layde.
78. sey.   79. hert. accorde.   82. Trewly (*with large capital* T).

'Ye,' quod she, 'I have thee excused; al suche thinges as yet
85 mowe nat be redressed; thy Margarites vertue I commende wel
the more, that paciently suche anoyes suffreth. David king was
meke, and suffred mokel hate and many yvel speches; no despyt
ne shame that his enemys him deden might nat move pacience
out of his herte, but ever in one plyte mercy he used. Wherfore
90 god him-selfe took reward to the thinges; and theron suche
punisshment let falle. Trewly, by reson, it ought be ensample of
drede to al maner peoples mirth. A man vengeable in wrath no
governance in punisshment ought to have. Plato had a cause his
servant to †scourge, and yet cleped he his neibour to performe the
95 doinge; him-selfe wolde nat, lest wrath had him a-maistred; and
so might he have layd on to moche: evermore grounded vertue
sheweth th' entent fro within. And trewly, I wot wel, for her goodnesse and vertue, thou hast desyred my service to her plesance
wel the more; and thy-selfe therto fully hast profered.'
100   'Good lady,' quod I, 'is vertue the hye way to this knot that
long we have y-handled?'
'Ye, forsoth,' quod she, 'and without vertue, goodly this knot
may nat be goten.'
'Ah! now I see,' quod I, 'how vertu in me fayleth; and I, as
105 a seer tree, without burjoning or frute, alwaye welke; and
so I stonde in dispeyre of this noble knot; for vertue in me
hath no maner workinge. A! wyde-where aboute have I
traveyled!'
'Pees,' quod she, 'of thy first way; thy traveyle is in ydel;
110 and, as touchinge the seconde way, I see wel thy meninge. Thou
woldest conclude me, if thou coudest, bycause I brought thee
to service; and every of my servantes I helpe to come to this
blisse, as I sayd here-beforn. And thou saydest thy-selfe, thou
mightest nat be holpen as thou wenest, bycause that vertue in
115 thee fayleth; and this blisse parfitly without vertue may nat be
goten; thou wenest of these wordes contradiccion to folowe.
Pardè, at the hardest, I have no servant but he be vertuous in
dede and thought. I brought thee in my service, yet art thou
nat my servant; but I say, thou might so werche in vertue her-
120 after, that than shalt thou be my servant, and as for my servant

84. the.   87. dispite.   89. Werfore.   90. toke rewarde.   91. fal.
reason.   94. scoure (!); read scourge.   96. layde.   97. thentent. wotte.
99. haste.   100. waye.   104. nowe I se. howe.   105. tre.   109. Peace.
110. se. meanyng.   111. the.   112. one.   113. beforne.   114. wenyst.
115. the. maye.   116. contradiction.   118. the. arte.

acompted. For habit maketh no monk; ne weringe of gilte spurres maketh no knight. Never-the-later, in confort of thyne herte, yet wol I otherwyse answere.'

'Certes, lady,' quod I tho, 'so ye muste nedes; or els I had nigh caught suche a †cardiacle for sorowe, I wot it wel, I shulde 125 it never have recovered. And therfore now I praye [thee] to enforme me in this; or els I holde me without recovery. I may nat long endure til this lesson be lerned, and of this mischeef the remedy knowen.'

'Now,' quod she, 'be nat wroth; for there is no man on-lyve 130 that may come to a precious thing longe coveited, but he somtyme suffre teneful diseses: and wenest thy-selfe to ben unliche to al other? That may nat ben. And with the more sorowe that a thing is getten, the more he hath joye the ilke thing afterwardes to kepe; as it fareth by children in scole, that for lerninge arn 135 beten, whan their lesson they foryetten. Commenly, after a good disciplyning with a yerde, they kepe right wel doctrine of their scole.'

CHAPTER XII.

RIGHT with these wordes, on this lady I threw up myne eyen, to see her countenaunce and her chere; and she, aperceyving this fantasye in myne herte, gan her semblaunt goodly on me caste, and sayde in this wyse.

'It is wel knowe, bothe to reson and experience in doinge, 5 every active worcheth on his passive; and whan they ben togider, "active" and "passive" ben y-cleped by these philosophers. If fyr be in place chafinge thing able to be chafed or hete[d], and thilke thinges ben set in suche a distaunce that the oon may werche, the other shal suffre. Thilke Margarite thou desyrest is 10 ful of vertue, and able to be active in goodnesse: but every herbe sheweth his vertue outforth from within. The sonne yeveth light, that thinges may be seye. Every fyr heteth thilke thing that it †neigheth, and it be able to be hete[d]. Vertue of this Margarite

---

121. habyte. monke. wearynge. 122. conforte. 125. nyghe. cordiacle; *read* cardiacle. wotte. 126. nowe. *I supply* thee. 127. recouerye. 128. mischefe. 130. Nowe. wrothe. 131. maye. 132. discases. wenyst. 133. maye. 134. thynge. 135. schole. arne. 136. beaten. 138. schole.
CH. XII. 1. threwe. 2. se. 5. Reason. 7. ycleaped. 8. fyre. thynge. hete; *read* heted. 9. sette. one. 11. outforthe. 13. sey. fyre. 14. neighed; *read* neigheth. hete; *read* heted.

15 outforth †wercheth; and nothing is more able to suffre worching,
or worke cacche of the actife, but passife of the same actife; and
no passife, to vertues of this Margaryte, but thee, in al my Donet
can I fynde! So that her vertue muste nedes on thee werche;
in what place ever thou be, within distaunce of her worthinesse,
20 as her very passife thou art closed. But vertue may thee nothing
profyte, but thy desyr be perfourmed, and al thy sorowes cesed.
Ergo, through werchinge of her vertue thou shalt esely ben
holpen, and driven out of al care, and welcome to this longe by
thee desyred!'

25 'Lady,' quod I, 'this is a good lesson in ginning of my joye;
but wete ye wel forsothe, though I suppose she have moche
vertue, I wolde my spousaile were proved, and than may I live
out of doute, and rejoice me greetly, in thinking of tho vertues
so shewed.'

30 'I herde thee saye,' quod she, 'at my beginning, whan I receyved
thee firste for to serve, that thy jewel, thilke Margaryte thou
desyrest, was closed in a muskle with a blewe shel.'

'Ye, forsothe,' quod I; 'so I sayd; and so it is.'

'Wel,' quod she, 'every-thing kyndly sheweth it-selfe; this
35 jewel, closed in a blewe shel, [by] excellence of coloures sheweth
vertue from within; and so every wight shulde rather loke to the
propre vertue of thinges than to his forayne goodes. If a thing
be engendred of good mater, comenly and for the more part, it
foloweth, after the congelement, vertue of the first mater (and
40 it be not corrupt with vyces) to procede with encrees of good
vertues; eke right so it fareth of badde. Trewly, greet excellence
in vertue of linage, for the more part, discendeth by kynde to
the succession in vertues to folowe. Wherfore I saye, the †colour
of every Margarit sheweth from within the fynesse in vertue.
45 Kyndely heven, whan mery †weder is a-lofte, apereth in mannes
eye of coloure in blewe, stedfastnesse in pees betokening within
and without. Margaryte is engendred by hevenly dewe, and
sheweth in it-selfe, by fynenesse of colour, whether the engendrure
were maked on morowe or on eve; thus sayth kynde of this
50 perle. This precious Margaryte that thou servest, sheweth it-selfe
discended, by nobley of vertue, from this hevenlich dewe, norisshed

---

15. wrethe (!); *read* wercheth. nothynge.   16. catche.   17-8. the
(*twice*).   20. arte. the.   21. desyre. ceased.   22. shalte easely.
24. the.   26. thoughe.   27. maye.   28. greatly.   30. the say.
31. the.   35. *Supply* by.   38. parte.   40. encrease.   41. great.
42. parte.   43. colours; *read* colour.   45. wether; *read* weder.
46. peace.   48. coloure.

and congeled in mekenesse, that †moder is of al vertues; and, by
werkes that men seen withouten, the significacion of the coloures
ben shewed, mercy and pitee in the herte, with pees to al other;
and al this is y-closed in a muskle, who-so redily these vertues loken. 55
Al thing that hath soule is reduced in-to good by mene thinges,
as thus: In-to god man is reduced by soules resonable; and so
forth beestes, or bodyes that mowe not moven, after place ben
reduced in-to manne by beestes †mene that moven from place to
place. So that thilke bodyes that han felinge soules, and move 60
not from places, holden the lowest degree of soulinge thinges in
felinge; and suche ben reduced in-to man by menes. So it
foloweth, the muskle, as †moder of al vertues, halt the place of
mekenesse, to his lowest degree discendeth downe of heven, and
there, by a maner of virgine engendrure, arn these Margarytes 65
engendred, and afterward congeled. Made not mekenesse so
lowe the hye heven, to enclose and cacche out therof so noble
a dewe, that after congelement, a Margaryte, with endelesse vertue
and everlasting joy, was with ful vessel of grace yeven to every
creature, that goodly wolde it receyve?'   70

'Certes,' quod I, 'these thinges ben right noble; I have er this
herd these same sawes.'

'Than,' quod she, 'thou wost wel these thinges ben sothe?'

'Ye, forsothe,' quod I, 'at the ful.'

'Now,' quod she, 'that this Margaryte is ful of vertue, it is wel 75
proved; wherfore som grace, som mercy, among other vertues,
I wot right wel, on thee shal discende?'

'Ye,' quod I; 'yet wolde I have better declared, vertues in this
Margarite kyndely to ben grounded.'

'That shal I shew thee,' quod she, 'and thou woldest it lerne.' 80

'Lerne?' quod I, 'what nedeth suche wordes? Wete ye nat
wel, lady, your-selfe, that al my cure, al my diligence, and al my
might, have turned by your counsayle, in plesaunce of that perle?
Al my thought and al my studye, with your helpe, desyreth, in
worshippe [of] thilke jewel, to encrese al my travayle and al my 85
besinesse in your service, this Margaryte to gladde in some halve.
Me were lever her honour, her plesaunce, and her good chere

thorow me for to be mayntayned and kept, and I of suche thinge
in her lykinge to be cause, than al the welthe of bodily goodes ye
90 coude recken. And wolde never god but I putte my-selfe in
greet jeopardy of al that I †welde, (that is now no more but
my lyf alone), rather than I shulde suffre thilke jewel in any
pointe ben blemisshed; as ferre as I may suffre, and with my
mightes strecche.'

95 'Suche thing,' quod she, 'may mokel further thy grace, and
thee in my service avaunce. But now (quod Love) wilt thou
graunte me thilke Margaryte to ben good?'

'O! good †god,' quod I, 'why tempte ye me and tene with
suche maner speche? I wolde graunt that, though I shulde anon
100 dye; and, by my trouthe, fighte in the quarel, if any wight wolde
countreplede.'

'It is so moche the lighter,' quod Love, 'to prove our entent.'

'Ye,' quod I; 'but yet wolde I here how ye wolde prove that
she were good by resonable skil, that it mowe not ben denyed.
105 For although I knowe, and so doth many other, manifold goodnesse and vertue in this Margaryte ben printed, yet some men
there ben that no goodnesse speken; and, wher-ever your wordes
ben herd and your resons ben shewed, suche yvel spekers, lady,
by auctoritè of your excellence, shullen be stopped and ashamed!
110 And more, they that han non aquayntaunce in her persone, yet
mowe they knowe her vertues, and ben the more enfourmed in
what wyse they mowe sette their hertes, whan hem liste in-to your
service any entree make. For trewly al this to beginne, I wot
wel my-selfe that thilke jewel is so precious perle, as a womanly
115 woman in her kynde; in whom of goodnesse, of vertue, and also
of answeringe shappe of limmes, and fetures so wel in al pointes
acording, nothing fayleth. I leve that kynde her made with greet
studye; for kynde in her person nothing hath foryet[en], and that
is wel sene. In every good wightes herte she hath grace of
120 commending and of vertuous praysing. Alas! that ever kynde
made her deedly! Save only in that, I wot wel, that Nature,
in fourminge of her, in no-thinge hath erred.'

---

88. thorowe. kepte.   90. put.   91. great ieoperdye. wolde; *read*
welde. nowe. lyfe.   94. stretche.   95. maye.   96. the. nowe. wylte.
98. good good; *read* good god.   99. thoughe. anone.   100. fyght.
103. howe.   104. reasonable.   105. dothe.   108. herde. reasons.
110. none.   113. entre. wote.   115. whome.   117. nothynge. great.
118. foryet.   121. onely.

CHAPTER XIII.

'CERTES,' quod Love, 'thou hast wel begonne; and I aske
thee this question: Is not, in general, every-thing good?'

'I not,' quod I.

'No?' quod she; ' †saw not god everything that he made, and
weren right good?'   5

'Than is wonder,' quod I, 'how yvel thinges comen a-place,
sithen that al thinges weren right good.'

'Thus,' quod she, 'I wol declare. Everiche qualitè and every
accion, and every thing that hath any maner of beinge, it is of
god; and god it made, of whom is al goodnesse and al being. 10
Of him is no badnesse. Badde to be, is naught; good to be,
is somwhat; and therfore good and being is oon in understanding.'

'How may this be?' quod I. 'For often han shrewes. me
assailed, and mokel badnesse therin have I founden; and so me 15
semeth bad to be somwhat in kynde.'

'Thou shalt,' quod she, 'understande that suche maner badnesse,
whiche is used to purifye wrong-doers, is somwhat; and god it
made, and being [it] hath; and that is good. Other badnesse no
being hath utterly; it is in the negative of somwhat, and that is 20
naught and nothing being. The parties essential of being arn
sayd in double wyse, as that it is; and these parties ben founde
in every creature. For al thing, a this halfe the first being, is
being through participacion, taking partie of being; so that [in]
every creature is difference bitwene being of him through whom 25
it is, and his own being. Right as every good is a maner of
being, so is it good thorow being; for it is naught other to be.
And every thing, though it be good, is not of him-selfe good;
but it is good by that it is ordinable to the greet goodnesse.
This dualitè, after clerkes †determinison, is founden in every 30
creature, be it never so single of onhed.'

'Ye,' quod I; 'but there-as it is y-sayd that god †saw everything of his making, and [they] were right good (as your-selfe
sayd to me not longe tyme sithen), I aske whether every creature

---

Cʜ. XIII. 1. haste.   2, 4. thynge.   4. saue; *read* saw.   5. werne.
6. howe.   9. action.   12. one.   14. Howe.   18. wronge.   19. *I
supply* it.   21. arne.   24. *I supply* in.· and of; *I omit* and.   27. thorowe.
29. great. determission (!); *read* determinison.   32. ysayde. saue; *read* saw.
33. *I supply* they.

35 is y-sayd "good" through goodnesse unfourmed eyther els fourmed;
and afterward, if it be accept utterly good?'

'I shal say thee,' quod she. 'These grete passed clerkes han
devyded good in-to good being alone, and that is nothing but
†god, for nothing is good in that wyse but god: also, in good by
40 participacion, and that is y-cleped "good" for far fet and representative of †godly goodnesse. And after this maner manyfold
good is sayd, that is to saye, good in kynde, and good in gendre,
and good of grace, and good of joy. Of good in kynde Austen
sayth, "al that ben, ben good." But peraunter thou woldest
45 wete, whether of hem-selfe it be good, or els of anothers goodnesse:
for naturel goodnesse of every substaunce is nothing els than his
substancial being, which is y-cleped "goodnesse" after comparison
that he hath to his first goodnesse, so as it is inductatife by menes
in-to the first goodnesse. Boece sheweth this thing at the ful, that
50 this name "good" is, in general, name in kynde, as it is comparisoned generally to his principal ende, which is god, knotte of
al goodnesse. Every creature cryeth "god us made"; and so
they han ful apeted to thilke god by affeccion such as to hem
longeth; and in this wyse al thinges ben good of the gret god,
55 which is good alone.'

'This wonder thing,' quod I, 'how ye have by many resons
proved my first way to be errour and misgoing, and cause[d] of
badnesse and feble meninge in the grounde ye aleged to be roted.
Whence is it that suche badnesse hath springes, sithen al thinges
60 thus in general ben good, and badnesse hath no being, as ye have
declared? I wene, if al things ben good, I might than with the
first way in that good have ended, and so by goodnesse have comen
to blisse in your service desyred.'

'Al thing,' quod she, 'is good by being in participacion out of
65 the firste goodnesse, whiche goodnesse is corrupt by badnesse
and badde-mening maners. God hath [ordeyned] in good thinges,
that they ben good by being, and not in yvel; for there is absence
of rightful love. For badnesse is nothing but only yvel wil of the
user, and through giltes of the doer; wherfore, at the ginninge of
70 the worlde, every thing by him-selfe was good; and in universal
they weren right good. An eye or a hand is fayrer and betterer

---

. 35. ysayde.   36. afterwarde. accepte.   37. the. great.   39. good; *read*
god.   40. farre fette.   41. goodly; *read* godly. manyfolde.   44. saythe.
47. ycleaped.   48. meanes.   53. affection.   56. howe. reasons.
57. waye. cause; *read* caused.   59. baddesse (!).   65. corrupte.
66. meanynge. *I supply* ordeyned.   68. nothynge. onely.   71. werne. hande.

in a body set, in his kyndely place, than from the body dissevered. Every thing in his kyndly place, being kyndly, good doth werche; and, out of that place voyded, it dissolveth and is defouled him-selve. Our noble god, in gliterande wyse, by armony this world 75 ordeyned, as in purtreytures storied with colours medled, in whiche blacke and other derke colours commenden the golden and the asured paynture; every put in kyndely place, oon, besyde another, more for other glitereth. Right so litel fayr maketh right fayr more glorious; and right so, of goodnesse, and of other 80 thinges in vertue. Wherfore other badde and not so good perles as this Margaryte that we han of this matier, yeven by the ayre litel goodnesse and litel vertue, [maken] right mokel goodnesse and vertue in thy Margaryte to ben proved, in shyning wyse to be founde and shewed. How shulde ever goodnesse of pees have 85 ben knowe, but-if unpees somtyme reigne, and mokel yvel †wrathe? How shulde mercy ben proved, and no trespas were, by due justificacion, to be punisshed? Therfore grace and goodnesse of a wight is founde; the sorouful hertes in good meninge to endure, ben comforted; unitè and acord bitwene hertes knit in joye to 90 abyde. What? wenest thou I rejoyce or els accompte him among my servauntes that pleseth Pallas in undoinge of Mercurye, al-be-it that to Pallas he be knit by tytle of lawe, not according to resonable conscience, and Mercurie in doinge have grace to ben suffered; or els him that †tweyveth the moone for fayrenesse of 95 the eve-sterre? Lo! otherwhyle by nightes, light of the moone greetly comforteth in derke thoughtes and blynde. Understanding of love yeveth greet gladnesse. Who-so list not byleve, whan a sothe tale is shewed, a dewe and a deblys his name is entred. Wyse folk and worthy in gentillesse, bothe of vertue and of 100 livinge, yeven ful credence in sothnesse of love with a good herte, there-as good evidence or experience in doinge sheweth not the contrarie. Thus mightest thou have ful preef in thy Margarytes goodnesse, by commendement of other jewels badnesse and yvelnesse in doing. Stoundemele diseses yeveth several houres 105 in joye.'

'Now, by my trouthe,' quod I, 'this is wel declared, that my

---

72. sette. disceuered.   73. dothe.   75. worlde   78. putte. **one.**
79. lytle fayre.   80. fayre.   83. *Supply* maken.   **85 Howe.**
peace.   86. vnpeace.   wrothe; *read* wrathe.   87. Howe. trespeace (!).
89. meanynge.   90. acorde. knytte.   91. amonge.   92. pleaseth.
93. knytte.   94. reasonable.   95. weneth; *read* weyveth.   97. greatly.
98. great. lyste.   99. adewe.   100. folke.   101. hert.   103. prefe.
105. diseases.   107. Nowe.

Margaryte is good; for sithen other ben good, and she passeth manye other in goodnesse and vertue; wherthrough, by maner
110 necessarie, she muste be good. And goodnesse of this Margaryte is nothing els but vertue; wherfore she is vertuous; and if there fayled any vertue in any syde, there were lacke of vertue. Badde nothing els is, ne may be, but lacke and want of good and good-nesse; and so shulde she have that same lacke, that is to saye,
115 badde; and that may not be. For she is good; and that is good, me thinketh, al good; and so, by consequence, me semeth, vertuous, and no lacke of vertue to have. But the sonne is not knowe but he shyne; ne vertuous herbes, but they have her kynde werchinge; ne vertue, but it strecche in goodnesse or profyt to another, is no
120 vertue. Than, by al wayes of reson, sithen mercy and pitee ben moste commended among other vertues, and they might never ben shewed, [unto] refresshement of helpe and of comfort, but now at my moste nede; and that is the kynde werkinge of these vertues; trewly, I wene, I shal not varye from these helpes. Fyr,
125 and-if he yeve non hete, for fyre is not demed. The sonne, but he shyne, for sonne is not accompted. Water, but it wete, the name shal ben chaunged. Vertue, but it werche, of goodnesse doth it fayle; and in-to his contrarie the name shal ben reversed. And these ben impossible; wherfore the contradictorie, that is
130 necessarye, nedes muste I leve.'

'Certes,' quod she, 'in thy person and out of thy mouthe these wordes lyen wel to ben said, and in thyne understanding to be leved, as in entent of this Margaryte alone. And here now my speche in conclusion of these wordes.

CHAPTER XIV.

IN these thinges,' quod she, 'that me list now to shewe openly, shal be founde the mater of thy sicknesse, and what shal ben the medicyn that may be thy sorowes lisse and comfort, as wel thee as al other that amisse have erred and out of
5 the way walked, so that any drope of good wil in amendement [may] ben dwelled in their hertes. Proverbes of Salomon openly techeth, how somtyme an innocent walkid by the way in blynd-

---

109. wherthroughe.   111. no thynge.   113. wante.   115. maye.
119. stretche. profyte.   120. reasoñ. pytie.   121. amonge.   122. *Supply* unto. comforte. nowe.   124. Fyre.   125. none heate.   128. dothe.
133. nowe.
CH. XIV. 1. nowe.   4. the.   6. *Supply* may.   7. teacheth. howe.

nesse of a derke night; whom mette a woman (if it be leefly to saye) as a strumpet arayed, redily purveyed in turninge of thoughtes with veyne janglinges, and of rest inpacient, by dis- 10 simulacion of my termes, saying in this wyse: "Com, and be we dronken of our swete pappes; use we coveitous collinges." And thus drawen was this innocent, as an oxe to the larder.'

'Lady,' quod I, 'to me this is a queynte thing to understande; I praye you, of this parable declare me the entent.' 15

'This innocent,' quod she, 'is a scoler leringe of my lore, in seching of my blisse, in whiche thinge the day of his thought turning enclyneth in-to eve; and the sonne, of very light faylinge, maketh derke night in his conninge. Thus in derknesse of many doutes he walketh, and for blyndenesse of understandinge, he ne 20 wot in what waye he is in; forsothe, suche oon may lightly ben begyled. To whom cam love fayned, not clothed of my livery, but [of] unlefful lusty habit, with softe speche and mery; and with fayre honyed wordes heretykes and mis-meninge people skleren and wimplen their errours. Austen witnesseth of an 25 heretyk, that in his first beginninge he was a man right expert in resons and swete in his wordes; and the werkes miscorden. Thus fareth fayned love in her firste werchinges. Thou knowest these thinges for trewe; thou hast hem proved by experience somtyme, in doing to thyne owne person; in whiche thing thou hast 30 founde mater of mokel disese. Was not fayned love redily purveyed, thy wittes to cacche and tourne thy good thoughtes? Trewly, she hath wounded the conscience of many with florissh-inge of mokel jangling wordes; and good worthe thanked I it for no glose. I am glad of my prudence thou hast so manly her 35 †tweyved. To me art thou moche holden, that in thy kynde course of good mening I returne thy mynde. I trowe, ne had I shewed thee thy Margaryte, thou haddest never returned. Of first in good parfit joye was ever fayned love impacient, as the water of Siloë, whiche evermore floweth with stilnesse and privy 40 noyse til it come nighe the brinke, and than ginneth it so out of mesure to bolne, with novelleries of chaunginge stormes, that in course of every renning it is in pointe to spille al his circuit of †tbankes. Thus fayned love prively, at the fullest of his flowinge,

---

8. lefely.   11. sayeng. Come.   14. thynge.   16. scholer. 17. daye.   21. wote. one.   22. whome came.   23. *Supply* of. unleful lustye habyte.   24. misse.   26. heretyke. experte.   27. resones. 29. haste.   32. catche.   35. gladde.   36. veyned; *read* weyved. arte. 37. meanyng.   38. the.   39. parfyte.   42. measure.   43. spyl. 44. cankes (l); *read* bankes.

45 [ginneth] newe stormes [of] debat to arayse. And al-be-it that
Mercurius [servants] often with hole understandinge knowen
suche perillous maters, yet Veneriens so lusty ben and so leude
in their wittes, that in suche thinges right litel or naught don
they fele; and wryten and cryen to their felawes: "here is blisse,
50 here is joye"; and thus in-to one same errour mokel folk they
drawen. "Come," they sayen, "and be we dronken of our
pappes"; that ben fallas and lying glose, of whiche mowe they not
souke milke of helthe, but deedly venim and poyson, corrupcion
of sorowe. Milke of fallas is venim of disceyt; milke of lying glose
55 is venim of corrupcion. Lo! what thing cometh out of these
pappes! "Use we coveited collinges"; desyre we and meddle we
false wordes with sote, and sote with false! Trewly, this is the sori-
nesse of fayned love; nedes, of these surfettes sicknesse muste
folowe. Thus, as an oxe, to thy langoring deth were thou drawen;
60 the sote of the smoke hath thee al defased. Ever the deper thou
somtyme wadest, the soner thou it founde; if it had thee killed,
it had be litel wonder. But on that other syde, my trewe
servaunt[s] not faynen ne disceyve conne; sothly, their doinge
is open; my foundement endureth, be the burthen never so
65 greet; ever in one it lasteth. It yeveth lyf and blisful goodnesse
in the laste endes, though the ginninges ben sharpe. Thus of
two contraries, contrarye ben the effectes. And so thilke
Margaryte thou servest shal seen thee, by her service out of
perillous tribulacion delivered, bycause of her service in-to newe
70 disese fallen, by hope of amendement in the laste ende, with joye
to be gladded. Wherfore, of kynde pure, her mercy with grace
of good helpe shal she graunte; and els I shal her so strayne,
that with pitè shal she ben amaystred. Remembre in thyne
herte how horribly somtyme to thyne Margaryte thou trespasest,
75 and in a grete wyse ayenst her thou forfeytest! Clepe ayen thy
mynde, and know thyne owne giltes. What goodnesse, what
bountee, with mokel folowing pitè founde thou in that tyme?
Were thou not goodly accepted in-to grace? By my pluckinge
was she to foryevenesse enclyned. And after, I her styred to
80 drawe thee to house; and yet wendest thou utterly for ever
have ben refused. But wel thou wost, sithen that I in suche

45. *I supply* ginneth *and* of. debate. 46. *I supply* servants. 51. sayne.
52–4. lyeng. 54. disceyte. 55. thynge. 58. must. 60. the.
61. the. 63. seruaunt. 65. great. lyfe. 68. sene the. 70, 82.
disease. 72. graunt. 74. howe. 75. great. 76. knowe. 77.
bountie. 80. the.

sharpe disese might so greetly avayle, what thinkest in thy wit?
How fer may my wit strecche? And thou lache not on thy syde,
I wol make the knotte. Certes, in thy good bering I wol acorde
with the psauter : " I have founde David in my service true, and 85
with holy oyle of pees and of rest, longe by him desyred, utterly
he shal be anoynted." Truste wel to me, and I wol thee not
fayle. The †leving of the first way with good herte of continuance
that I see in thee grounded, this purpose to parfourme, draweth
me by maner of constrayning, that nedes muste I ben thyne helper. 90
Although mirthe a whyle be taried, it shal come at suche seson,
that thy thought shal ben joyed. And wolde never god, sithen
thyne herte to my resons arn assented, and openly hast confessed
thyne amisse-going, and now cryest after mercy, but-if mercy
folowed ; thy blisse shal ben redy, y-wis ; thou ne wost how sone. 95
Now be a good child, I rede. The kynde of vertues, in thy
Margaryte rehersed, by strength of me in thy person shul werche.
Comfort thee in this ; for thou mayst not miscary.' And these
wordes sayd, she streyght her on length, and rested a whyle.

¶ Thus endeth the seconde book, and here after foloweth
the thirde book.

BOOK III.

CHAPTER I.

OF nombre, sayn these clerkes, that it is naturel somme of
discrete thinges, as in tellinge oon, two, three, and so forth ;
but among al nombres, three is determined for moste certayn.
Wherfore in nombre certayn this werk of my besy leudenesse
I thinke to ende and parfourme. Ensample by this worlde, in 5
three tymes is devyded ; of whiche the first is cleped †Deviacion,
that is to say, going out of trewe way ; and al that tho dyeden, in
helle were they punisshed for a man[ne]s sinne, til grace and mercy
fette hem thence, and there ended the firste tyme. The seconde
tyme lasteth from the comming of merciable grace until the ende 10
of transitorie tyme, in whiche is shewed the true way in fordoinge
of the badde ; and that is y-cleped tyme of Grace. And that

---

82. greatly.   83. howe ferre maye my wytte stretche.   86. peace.
87. the.   88. leanyng (!)   89. se. the.   93. reasones arne. haste.   94.
nowe.   96. chylde.   98. Comforte the.   99. sayde. COLOPHON. booke.
boke.
BOOK. III : CH. I.   1. sayne.   2. one. thre.   3. amonge. thre.
3, 4. certayne.   4. werke.   6. thre. Demacion ; *read* Deuiacion.   8. hel.

thing is not yeven by desert of yeldinge oon benefyt for another,
but only through goodnesse of the yever of grace in thilke tyme.
15 Who-so can wel understande is shapen to be saved in souled
blisse. The thirde tyme shal ginne whan transitorie thinges of
worldes han mad their ende ; and that shal ben in Ioye, glorie, and
rest, both body and soule, that wel han deserved in the tyme of
Grace. And thus in that heven †togider shul they dwelle per-
20 petuelly, without any imaginatyfe yvel in any halve. These
tymes are figured by tho three dayes that our god was closed
in erthe ; and in the thirde aroos, shewing our resurreccion to
ioye and blisse of tho that it deserven, by his merciable grace.
So this leude book, in three maters, accordaunt to tho tymes,
25 lightly by a good inseër may ben understonde ; as in the firste,
Errour of misse-goinge is shewed, with sorowful pyne punisshed,
†that cryed after mercy. In the seconde, is Grace in good waye
proved, whiche is faylinge without desert, thilke first misse
amendinge, in correccion of tho erroures, and even way to bringe,
30 with comfort of welfare in-to amendement wexinge. And in the
thirde, Ioye and blisse graunted to him that wel can deserve it,
and hath savour of understandinge in the tyme of grace. Thus
in Ioye, of my thirde boke, shal the mater be til it ende.
  But special cause I have in my herte to make this proces
35 of a Margarit-perle, that is so precious a gemme †whyt, clere and
litel, of whiche stones or iewel[les] the tonges of us Englissh
people tourneth the right names, and clepeth hem ' Margery-
perles ' ; thus varieth our speche from many other langages. For
trewly Latin, Frenche, and many mo other langages clepeth hem,
40 Margery-perles, [by] the name ' Margarites,' or ' Margarite-perles ' ;
wherfor in that denominacion I wol me acorde to other mens
tonges, in that name-cleping. These clerkes that treten of kyndes,
and studien out the propertee there of thinges, sayn : the Margarite is a litel whyt perle, throughout holowe and rounde and
45 vertuous ; and on the see-sydes, in the more Britayne, in muskle-
shelles, of the hevenly dewe, the best ben engendred ; in whiche
by experience ben founde three fayre vertues. Oon is, it yeveth
comfort to the feling spirites in bodily persones of reson. Another

---

13. thynge. deserte. one benefyte.   14. onely.   16. gyn.   17. made.
19. togyther. dwel.   21. thre.   22. arose. resurrection.   24. boke.
thre.   25. maye.   26. erroure.   27. is (!) ; *read* that.   28. deserte.
29. correction. waye.   30. comforte.   31. canne.   34. hert. processe.
35. peerle. with ; *read* whyt (*see* l. 44).   36. iewel ; *read* iewelles.   39.
cleapeth.   40. *Supply* by.   42. treaten.   43. propertie. sayne.
44. whyte.   47. One.   48. comforte. reason.

is good; it is profitable helthe ayenst passions of sorie mens hertes.
And the thirde, it is nedeful and noble in staunching of bloode, 50
there els to moche wolde out renne. To whiche perle and vertues
me list to lyken at this tyme Philosophie, with her three speces,
that is, natural, and moral, and resonable; of whiche thinges
hereth what sayn these grete clerkes. Philosophie is knowing of
devynly and manly thinges joyned with studie of good living; 55
and this stant in two thinges, that is, conninge and opinion. Conninge is whan a thing by certayn reson is conceyved. But
wrecches and fooles and leude men, many wil conceyve a thing
and mayntayne it as for sothe, though reson be in the contrarye;
wherfore conninge is a straunger. Opinion is whyl a thing is in 60
non-certayn, and hid from mens very knowleging and by no parfit
reson fully declared, as thus: if the sonne be so mokel as men
wenen, or els if it be more than the erthe. For in sothnesse the
certayn quantitè of that planet is unknowen to erthly dwellers; and
yet by opinion of some men it is holden for more than midle-erth. 65

The first spece of philosophie is naturel; whiche in kyndely
thinges †treteth, and sheweth causes of heven, and strength of
kyndely course; as by arsmetrike, geometry, musike, and by
astronomye techeth wayes and cours of hevens, of planetes, and
of sterres aboute heven and erthe, and other elementes. 70

The seconde spece is moral, whiche, in order, of living maners
techeth; and by reson proveth vertues of soule moste worthy in
our living; whiche ben prudence, justice, temperaunce, and
strength. Prudence is goodly wisdom in knowing of thinges.
Strength voideth al adversitees aliche even. Temperaunce dis- 75
troyeth beestial living with esy bering. And Justice rightfully
jugeth; and juging departeth to every wight that is his owne.

The thirde spece turneth in-to reson of understanding; al
thinges to be sayd soth and discussed; and that in two thinges is
devyded. Oon is art, another is rethorike; in whiche two al 80
lawes of mans reson ben grounded or els maintayned.

And for this book is of Love, and therafter bereth his name,
and philosophie and lawe muste here-to acorden by their clergial
discripcions, as: philosophie for love of wisdom is declared, lawe
for mainteynaunce of pees is holden: and these with love must 85
nedes acorden; therfore of hem in this place have I touched.

---

51. ren.   52. thre.   54. sayn. great.   56. stante.   57. certayne.
58. wretches.   60. whyle.   61. -certayne. hydde.   62. parfyte reason.
64. certayne.   67. treten; *read* treteth.   69. course.   73. lyueng.
74. wysdome.   76. lyueng. easy bearyng.   78. reason.   80. one.
arte.   81. reason.   82. booke. beareth.   84. wisdome.   85. peace.

Ordre of homly thinges and honest maner of livinge in vertue, with rightful jugement in causes and profitable administracion in comminaltees of realmes and citees, by evenhed profitably to 90 raigne, nat by singuler avauntage ne by privè envy, ne by soleyn purpos in covetise of worship or of goodes, ben disposed in open rule shewed, by love, philosophy, and lawe, and yet love, toforn al other. Wherfore as sustern in unitè they accorden, and oon ende, that is, pees and rest, they causen norisshinge; and in the 95 joye maynteynen to endure.

Now than, as I have declared : my book acordeth with discripcion of three thinges; and the Margarit in vertue is lykened to Philosophy, with her three speces. In whiche maters ever twey ben acordaunt with bodily reson, and the thirde with the 100 soule. But in conclusion of my boke and of this Margarite-perle in knittinge togider, Lawe by three sondrye maners shal be lykened; that is to saye, lawe, right, and custome, whiche I wol declare. Al that is lawe cometh of goddes ordinaunce, by kyndly worching ; and thilke thinges ordayned by mannes wittes arn y-cleped right, 105 which is ordayned by many maners and in constitucion written. But custome is a thing that is accepted for right or for lawe, there-as lawe and right faylen ; and there is no difference, whether it come of scripture or of reson. Wherfore it sheweth, that lawe is kyndly governaunce; right cometh out of mannes probable 110 reson ; and custome is of commen usage by length of tyme used ; and custome nat writte is usage; and if it be writte, constitucion it is y-written and y-cleped. But lawe of kynde is commen to every nation, as conjunccion of man and woman in love, succession of children in heritance, restitucion of thing 115 by strength taken or lent; and this lawe among al other halt the soveraynest gree in worship; whiche lawe began at the beginning of resonable creature ; it varied yet never for no chaunging of tyme. Cause, forsothe, in ordayning of lawe was to constrayne mens hardinesse in-to pees, and withdrawing his yvel 120 wil, and turning malice in-to goodnesse; and that innocence sikerly, withouten teneful anoye, among shrewes safely might inhabite by proteccion of safe-conducte, so that the shrewes, harm

---

88. administration.   89. commynalties. cytes.   91. purpose.   93. susterne. one.   94. peace.   96. Nowe. boke. discription.   97–8. thre.   99. reason.   100. peerle.   101. thre.   105. constitution. 110. reason.   112. constitutyon.   113. coniunction.   114. restitution. 115. halte.   117. reasonable.   119. peace.   121. amonge   122. harme for harme.

for harme, by brydle of ferdnesse shulden restrayne. But forsothe, in kyndely lawe, nothing is commended but such as goddes
wil hath confirmed, ne nothing denyed but contrarioustee of 125
goddes wil in heven. Eke than al lawes, or custome, or els
constitucion by usage or wryting, that contraryen lawe of kynde,
utterly ben repugnaunt and adversarie to our goddes wil of heven.
Trewly, lawe of kynde for goddes own lusty wil is verily to
mayntayne; under whiche lawe (and unworthy) bothe professe 130
and reguler arn obediencer and bounden to this Margarite-perle
as by knotte of loves statutes and stablisshment in kynde, whiche
that goodly may not be withsetten. Lo! under this bonde am
I constrayned to abyde; and man, under living lawe ruled, by that
lawe oweth, after desertes, to ben rewarded by payne or by mede, 135
but-if mercy weyve the payne. So than †by part resonfully may
be seye, that mercy bothe right and lawe passeth. Th' entent
of al these maters is the lest clere understanding, to weten, at
th'ende of this thirde boke; ful knowing, thorow goddes grace,
I thinke to make neverthelater. Yet if these thinges han a good 140
and a †sleigh inseër, whiche that can souke hony of the harde
stone, oyle of the drye rocke, [he] may lightly fele nobley of mater
in my leude imaginacion closed. But for my book shal be of
joye (as I sayd, and I [am] so fer set fro thilke place frọ whens
gladnesse shulde come; my corde is to short to lete my boket 145
ought cacche of that water; and fewe men be abouten my corde
to eche, and many in ful purpos ben redy it shorter to make, and
to enclose th' entrè, that my boket of joye nothing shulde cacche,
but empty returne, my careful sorowes to encrese: (and if I dye
for payne, that were gladnesse at their hertes): good lord, send 150
me water in-to the cop of these mountayns, and I shal drinke
therof, my thurstes to stanche, and sey, these be comfortable
welles; in-to helth of goodnesse of my saviour am I holpen. And
yet I saye more, the house of joye to me is nat opened. How
dare my sorouful goost than in any mater of gladnesse thinken to 155
trete? For ever sobbinges and complayntes be redy refrete in
his meditacions, as werbles in manifolde stoundes comming about
I not than. And therfore, what maner of joye coude [I] endyte?
But yet at dore shal I knocke, if the key of David wolde the locke

---

123. ferdenesse.　124. nothynge.　125. contraryoustie.　130. law.　131.
arne.　133. maye.　134. lyueng.　135. payn.　136. be; *read* by.　parte
reasonfully.　137. sey. thentent.　139. thende. thorowe.　141. sleight;
read sleigh.　142. *I insert* he.　143. ymagination. boke.　144. *Supply*
am. ferre.　145. let.　146-8. catch.　147. purpose.　148. thentre.
150. lorde sende.　152. stanch.　157. meditatioₙs.　158. *I supply* I.

160 unshitte, and he bringe me in, whiche that childrens tonges both
openeth and closeth; whos spirit where he †wol wercheth,
departing goodly as him lyketh.

Now to goddes laude and reverence, profit of the reders,
amendement of maners of the herers, encresing of worship among
165 Loves servauntes, releving of my herte in-to grace of my jewel,
and fren[d]ship [in] plesance of this perle, I am stered in this
making, and for nothing els; and if any good thing to mennes
lyking in this scripture be founde, thanketh the maister of grace,
whiche that of that good and al other is authour and principal
170 doer.   And if any thing be insufficient or els mislyking, †twyte
that the leudnesse of myne unable conning: for body in disese
anoyeth the understanding in soule.   A disesely habitacion
letteth the wittes [in] many thinges, and namely in sorowe.   The
custome never-the-later of Love, †by long tyme of service, in
175 termes I thinke to pursue, whiche ben lyvely to yeve understanding in other thinges.   But now, to enforme thee of this
Margarites goodnesse, I may her not halfe preyse.   Wherfore, nat
she for my boke, but this book for her, is worthy to be commended,
tho my book be leude; right as thinges nat for places, but places
180 for thinges, ought to be desyred and praysed.

CHAPTER II.

'NOW,' quod Love, 'trewly thy wordes I have wel understonde.   Certes, me thinketh hem right good; and me
wondreth why thou so lightly passest in the lawe.'

'Sothly,' quod I, 'my wit is leude, and I am right blynd, and
5 that mater depe.   How shulde I than have waded?   Lightly
might I have drenched, and spilte ther my-selfe.'

'Ye,' quod she, 'I shal helpe thee to swimme.   For right as
lawe punissheth brekers of preceptes and the contrary-doers of the
written constitucions, right so ayenward lawe rewardeth and
10 yeveth mede to hem that lawe strengthen.   By one lawe this
rebel is punisshed and this innocent is meded; the shrewe is
enprisoned and this rightful is corowned.   The same lawe that
joyneth by wedlocke without forsaking, the same lawe yeveth

---

160. vnshyt.   bring.   161. whose spirite.   wel; *read* wol.   163. Nowe.
profite.   165. hert.   166. frenship.   *I supply* in.   peerle.   170. with; *read*
wyte.   172. habitation.   173. *I supply* in.   174. be; *read* by.   176. nowe.
enform the.   178–9. boke (*thrice*).
Ch. II. 1. Nowe.   4. blynde.   5. howe.   7. Yea.   the.   swym.
9. constitutions.   ayenwarde.

lybel of departicion bycause of devorse both demed and declared.' 15

'Ye, ye,' quod I, 'I fynde in no lawe to mede and rewarde in goodnes the gilty of desertes.'

'Fole,' quod she, 'gilty, converted in your lawe, mikel merit deserveth. Also Pauly[n] of Rome was crowned, that by him the maynteyners of Pompeus weren knowen and distroyed; and yet 20 toforn was this Paulyn cheef of Pompeus counsaile. This lawe in Rome hath yet his name of mesuring, in mede, the bewraying of the conspiracy, ordayned by tho senatours the deth. Julius Cesar is acompted in-to Catons rightwisnesse; for ever in trouth florissheth his name among the knowers of reson. Perdicas was 25 crowned in the heritage of Alexander the grete, for tellinge of a prevy hate that king Porrus to Alexander hadde. Wherfore every wight, by reson of lawe, after his rightwysenesse apertely his mede may chalenge; and so thou, that maynteynest lawe of kynde, and therfore disese hast suffred in the lawe, reward is 30 worthy to be rewarded and ordayned, and †apertly thy mede might thou chalenge.'

'Certes,' quod I, 'this have I wel lerned; and ever hens-forward I shal drawe me therafter, in oonhed of wil to abyde, this lawe bothe maynteyne and kepe; and so hope I best entre in-to 35 your grace, wel deservinge in-to worship of a wight, without nedeful compulsion, [that] ought medefully to be rewarded.'

'Truly,' quod Love, 'that is sothe; and tho[ugh], by consti-tucion, good service in-to profit and avantage strecche, utterly many men it demen to have more desert of mede than good wil 40 nat compelled.'

'See now,' quod I, 'how †many men holden of this the con-trary. And what is good service? Of you wolde I here this question declared.'

'I shal say thee,' quod she, 'in a fewe wordes :—resonable 45 workinges in plesaunce and profit of thy soverayne.'

'How shulde I this performe!' quod I.

'Right wel,' quod she; 'and here me now a litel. It is hardely (quod she) to understande, that right as mater by due over-chaunginges foloweth his perfeccion and his forme, right so every 50

---

17. gyltie. 18. gyltie. merite. 19. Pauly (*for* Paulyn ; *first time*). 21. toforne. chefe. 25. amonge. 25–8. reason. 26. great. 30. disease. rewarde. 31. apartly (*for* apertly). 34. onehed. 37. *I supply* that. 38. constitution. 39. profite. stretch. 42. Se. howe may. 45. the. 46. profite. 47. Howe. 48. nowe. 50. perfection.

man, by rightful werkinges, ought to folowe the lefful desyres in
his herte, and see toforn to what ende he deserveth. For many
tymes he that loketh nat after th'endes, but utterly therof is
unknowen, befalleth often many yvels to done, wherthrough, er he
55 be war, shamefully he is confounded; th'ende[s] therof neden to
be before loked. To every desirer of suche foresight in good
service, three thinges specially nedeth to be rulers in his workes.
First, that he do good; next, that he do [it] by eleccion in his
owne herte; and the thirde, that he do godly, withouten any
60 surquedry in thoughtes. That your werkes shulden be good, in
service or in any other actes, authoritès many may be aleged;
neverthelater, by reson thus may it be shewed. Al your werkes
be cleped seconde, and moven in vertue of the firste wercher,
whiche in good workes wrought you to procede; and right so
65 your werkes moven in-to vertue of the laste ende: and right in
the first workinge were nat, no man shulde in the seconde werche.
Right so, but ye feled to what ende, and seen their goodnes
closed, ye shulde no more trecche what ye wrought; but the
ginning gan with good, and there shal it cese in the laste ende, if
70 it be wel considred. Wherfore the middle, if other-wayes it drawe
than accordant to the endes, there stinteth the course of good,
and another maner course entreth; and so it is a partie by him-
selve; and every part [that] be nat accordant to his al, is foul and
ought to be eschewed. Wherfore every thing that is wrought
75 and be nat good, is nat accordant to th'endes of his al hole; it is
foul, and ought to be withdrawe. Thus the persons that neither
don good ne harm shamen foule their making. Wherfore, without
working of good actes in good service, may no man ben accepted.
Truely, the ilke that han might to do good and doon it nat, the
80 crowne of worship shal be take from hem, and with shame shul
they be anulled; and so, to make oon werke acordant with his
endes, every good servaunt, by reson of consequence, muste do
good nedes. Certes, it suffiseth nat alone to do good, but goodly
withal folowe; the thanke of goodnesse els in nought he
85 deserveth. For right as al your being come from the greetest
good, in whom al goodnesse is closed, right so your endes ben
directe to the same good. Aristotel determineth that ende and
good ben one, and convertible in understanding; and he that in

---

51. leful.   52. hert. se.   55. ware.   57. thre.   58. *I supply* it.
electyon.   59. hert.   62. reason. maye.   68. recth (*for* retch); *read*
recche.   69. cease.   73. p*arte.* *I supply* that.   73-5. foule.
77. harme.   79. done.   81. one.   82. reason.   85. greatest.

wil doth awey good, and he that loketh nat to th'ende, loketh nat
to good; but he that doth good and doth nat goodly, [and] 90
draweth away the direction of th'ende nat goodly, must nedes
be badde. Lo! badde is nothing els but absence or negative
of good, as derkenesse is absence or negative of light. Than he
that dooth [not] goodly, directeth thilke good in-to th'ende of
badde; so muste thing nat good folowe: eke badnesse to suche 95
folke ofte foloweth. Thus contrariaunt workers of th'ende
that is good ben worthy the contrary of th'ende that is good
to have.'

'How,' quod I, 'may any good dede be doon, but-if goodly it
helpe?' 100

'Yes,' quod Love, 'the devil doth many good dedes, but
goodly he leveth be-hynde; for †ever badly and in disceyvable
wyse he worketh; wherfore the contrary of th'ende him foloweth.
And do he never so many good dedes, bicause goodly is away,
his goodnes is nat rekened. Lo! than, tho[ugh] a man do good, 105
but he do goodly, th'ende in goodnesse wol nat folowe; and thus
in good service both good dede and goodly doon musten joyne
togider, and that it be doon with free choise in herte; and els
deserveth he nat the merit in goodnes: that wol I prove. For
if thou do any-thing good by chaunce or by happe, in what thing 110
art thou therof worthy to be commended? For nothing, by reson
of that, turneth in-to thy praysing ne lacking. Lo! thilke thing
doon by hap, by thy wil is nat caused; and therby shulde I
thanke or lacke deserve? And sithen that fayleth, th'ende which
that wel shulde rewarde, must ned[e]s faile. Clerkes sayn, no man 115
but willinge is blessed; a good dede that he hath doon is nat
doon of free choice willing; without whiche blissednesse may nat
folowe. *Ergo*, neither thanke of goodnesse ne service [is] in that
[that] is contrary of the good ende. So than, to good service
longeth good dede goodly don, thorow free choice in herte.' 120

'Truely,' quod I, 'this have I wel understande.'

'Wel,' quod she, 'every thing thus doon sufficiently by lawe,
that is cleped justice, [may] after-reward clayme. For lawe and
justice was ordayned in this wyse, suche desertes in goodnesse,

---

90. *I supply* and. 92. bad. negatyfe (*first time*). 94. *I supply* not.
99. done. 101. dothe. 102. even; *read* ever. 105. tho. 107–8.
done (*twice*). 108. hert. 109. merite. 111. reason. 113. done.
shulde I; *put for* shuldest thou. 115. neds (*sic*). 116-7. done (*twice*).
118. *I supply* is *and* that. 120. thorowe fre. hert. 122. done.
123. *I supply* may. rewarde claym.

125 after quantitè in doinge, by mede to rewarde; and of necessitè of
suche justice, that is to say, rightwysenesse, was free choice in
deserving of wel or of yvel graunted to resonable creatures.
Every man hath free arbitrement to chose, good or yvel to
performe.'

130   'Now,' quod I tho, 'if I by my good wil deserve this Margarit-
perle, and am nat therto compelled, and have free choice to do
what me lyketh ; she is than holden, as me thinketh, to rewarde
th'entent of my good wil.'

'Goddes forbode els,' quod Love; 'no wight meneth other-
135 wyse, I trowe ; free wil of good herte after-mede deserveth.'

'Hath every man,' quod I, 'free choice by necessary maner of
wil in every of his doinges that him lyketh, by goddes proper
purvyaunce ?   I wolde see that wel declared to my leude understanding; for "necessary" and "necessitè" ben wordes of mokel
140 entencion, closing (as to saye) so mote it be nedes, and otherwyse
may it nat betyde.'

'This shalt thou lerne,' quod she, 'so thou take hede in my
speche.   If it were nat in mannes owne libertè of free wil to do
good or bad, but to the one teyed by bonde of goddes preordi-
145 naunce, than, do he never so wel, it were by nedeful compulcion
of thilk bonde, and nat by free choice, wherby nothing he
desyreth : and do he never so yvel, it were nat man for to wyte,
but onlich to him that suche thing ordayned him to done.
Wherfore he ne ought for bad[de] be punisshed, ne for no good
150 dede be rewarded ; but of necessitè of rightwisnesse was therfore
free choice of arbitrement put in mans proper disposicion.   Truely,
if it were otherwyse, it contraried goddes charitè, that badnesse
and goodnesse rewardeth after desert of payne or of mede.'

'Me thinketh this wonder,' quod I; 'for god by necessitè
155 forwot al thinges coming, and so mote it nedes be ; and thilke
thinges that ben don †by our free choice comen nothing of necessitè but only †by wil.   How may this stonde ††togider ?   And so
me thinketh truely, that free choice fully repugneth goddes
forweting.   Trewly, lady, me semeth, they mowe nat stande
160 ††togider.'

---

130. Nowe.   134. meaneth.   135. hert.   136. fre.   138. se.
140. entention.   142. lern.   143–6. fre (twice).   148. onelych.
149. bad.   151. fre.   151. disposition.   153. payn.   155. forwote.
156. be ; for by.   fre.   157. onely be ; for by.   Howe.   157–60.
togyther ; read togider.   158. fre.

CHAPTER III.

THAN gan Love nighe me nere, and with a noble countenance of visage and limmes, dressed her nigh my sitting-
place.

'Take forth,' quod she, 'thy pen, and redily wryte these
wordes. For if god wol, I shal hem so enforme to thee, that thy 5
leudnesse which I have understande in that mater shal openly be
clered, and thy sight in ful loking therin amended. First, if thou
thinke that goddes prescience repugne libertè of arbitrement, it is
impossible that they shulde accorde in onheed of sothe to understonding.'   10

'Ye,' quod I, 'forsothe; so I it conceyve.'

'Wel,' quod she, 'if thilke impossible were away, the repugnaunce that semeth to be therin were utterly removed.'

'Shewe me the absence of that impossibilitè,' quod I.

'So,' quod she, 'I shal. Now I suppose that they mowe 15
stande togider: prescience of god, whom foloweth necessitè of
thinges comming, and libertè of arbitrement, thorow whiche thou
belevest many thinges to be without necessitè.'

'Bothe these proporcions be sothe,' quod I, 'and wel mowe
stande togider; wherfore this case as possible I admit.'   20

'Truely,' quod she, 'and this case is impossible.'

'How so?' quod I.

'For herof,' quod she, 'foloweth and wexeth another impossible.'

'Prove me that,' quod I.   25

'That I shal,' quod she; 'for somthing is comming without
necessitè, and god wot that toforn; for al thing comming he
before wot, and that he beforn wot of necessitè is comming, as
he beforn wot be the case by necessary maner; or els, thorow
necessitè, is somthing to be without necessitè; and wheder, to 30
every wight that hath good understanding, is seen these thinges
to be repugnaunt: prescience of god, whiche that foloweth necessitè, and libertè of arbitrement, fro whiche is removed necessitè?
For truely, it is necessary that god have forweting of thing withouten
any necessitè cominge.'   35

Ch. III. 1. nygh.   5. the.   6. vnderstand.   8. lyberte of arbetry
of arbitrement; *omit* arbetry of.   15. Nowe.   17. thorowe.   22. Howe.
29. beforne. maner than (*omit* than). thorowe.   30. whederto.

'Ye,' quod I; 'but yet remeve ye nat away fro myne understanding the necessitè folowing goddes be foreweting, as thus. God
beforn wot me in service of love to be bounden to this Margarite-
perle, and therfore by necessitè thus to love am I bounde ; and
40 if I had nat loved, thorow necessitè had I ben kept from al love-
dedes.'

'Certes,' quod Love, 'bicause this mater is good and necessary
to declare, I thinke here-in wel to abyde, and not lightly to passe.
Thou shalt not (quod she) say al-only, "god beforn wot me to be
45 a lover or no lover," but thus : "god beforn wot me to be a lover
without necessitè."   And so foloweth, whether thou love or not
love, every of hem is and shal be.   But now thou seest the impossibilitè of the case, and the possibilitè of thilke that thou wendest
had been impossible ; wherfore the repugnaunce is adnulled.'
50 'Ye,' quod I; 'and yet do ye not awaye the strength of necessitè, whan it is said, th[r]ough necessitè it is me in love to
abyde, or not to love without necessitè for god beforn wot it.
This maner of necessitè forsothe semeth to some men in-to co-
accion, that is to sayne, constrayning, or else prohibicion, that is,
55 defendinge ; wherfore necessitè is me to love of wil.   I understande me to be constrayned by some privy strength to the wil
of lovinge ; and if [I] no[t] love, to be defended from the wil of
lovinge : and so thorow necessitè me semeth to love, for I love ;
or els not to love, if I not love ; wherthrough neither thank ne
60 maugrè in tho thinges may I deserve.'

'Now,' quod she, 'thou shalt wel understande, that often we
sayn thing thorow necessitè to be, that by no strength to be
neither is coarted ne constrayned ; and through necessitè not
to be, that with no defendinge is removed.   For we sayn it is
65 thorow necessitè god to be immortal, nought deedliche ; and it
is necessitè, god to be rightful ; but not that any strength of
violent maner constrayneth him to be immortal, or defendeth him
to be unrightful ; for nothing may make him dedly or unrightful.
Right so, if I say, thorow necessitè is thee to be a lover or els
70 noon ; only thorow wil, as god beforn wete.   It is nat to understonde that any thing defendeth or forbit thee thy wil, whiche shal

---

38. beforne wote.   40. thorowe.   kepte.   44. shalte.   onely.   44-5.
beforne wote (*twice*).   47. nowe.   51. though ; *read* through.   52. beforne
wote.   53. coaction.   57. *Supply* I ; *for* no *read* not ; *see* l. 59.   58.
thorowe.   59. thanke.   60. maye.   61. Nowe.   shalte.   62. sayne.
thorowe.   63. throughe.   64. sayne.   65. thorowe.   67. violente.
69. thorowe.   the.   70. none.   or.ely thorowe.   beforne.   71. the.

nat be; or els constrayneth it to be, whiche shal be.　That same
thing, forsoth, god before wot, whiche he beforn seeth.　Any
thing commende of only wil, that wil neyther is constrayned
ne defended thorow any other thing.　And so thorow libertè of 75
arbitrement it is do, that is don of wil.　And trewly, my good
child, if these thinges be wel understonde, I wene that non inconvenient shalt thou fynde betwene goddes forweting and
libertè of arbitrement; wherfor I wot wel they may stande
togider.　Also farthermore, who that understanding of prescience 80
properlich considreth, thorow the same wyse that any-thing be
afore wist is said, for to be comming it is pronounced; there is
nothing toforn wist but thing comming; foreweting is but of
trouth[e]; dout[e] may nat be wist; wherfore, whan I sey that god
toforn wot any-thing, thorow necessitè is thilke thing to be com- 85
ming; al is oon if I sey, it shal be.　But this necessitè neither
constrayneth ne defendeth any-thing to be or nat to be.　Therfore
sothly, if love is put to be, it is said of necessitè to be; or els, for it
is put nat to be, it is affirmed nat to be of necessitè; nat for that
necessitè constrayneth or defendeth love to be or nat to be.　For 90
whan I say, if love shal be, of necessitè it shal be, here foloweth
necessitè the thing toforn put; it is as moch to say as if it were thus
pronounced—"that thing shal be."　Noon other thing signifyeth
this necessitè but only thus: that shal be, may nat togider be
and nat be.　Evenlich also it is soth, love was, and is, and shal 95
be, nat of necessitè; and nede is to have be al that was; and
nedeful is to be al that is; and comming, to al that shal be.
And it is nat the same to saye, love to be passed, and love
passed to be passed; or love present to be present, and love to
be present; or els love to be comminge, and love comminge to be 100
comming.　Dyversitè in setting of wordes maketh dyversitè in
understandinge; altho[ugh] in the same sentence they accorden
of significacion; right as it is nat al oon, love swete to be swete,
and love to be swete.　For moch love is bitter and sorouful, er
hertes ben esed; and yet it glad[d]eth thilke sorouful herte on 105
suche love to thinke.'
　'Forsothe,' quod I, 'outherwhile I have had mokel blisse in
herte of love that stoundmele hath me sorily anoyed.　And

　73–4. thynge.　74. commende; for comminge. onely.　75. thorowe
(twice).　76. done.　77. childe. vnderstond.　81. thorowe.　84. trouth.
dout.　85. wote. thorowe.　86. if it shal be; omit if.　92. toforne.
93. None.　94. onely.　102. altho.　103. signification. one.　105.
eased. hert.　108. hert.
　　* * *
　　* * * *　　　　　I

certes, lady, for I see my-self thus knit with this Margarite-perle
110 as by bonde of your service and of no libertè of wil, my herte wil
now nat acorde this service to love.   I can demin in my-selfe
non otherwise but thorow necessitè am I constrayned in this
service to abyde.   But alas! than, if I thorow nedeful compulsioun
maugre me be with-holde, litel thank for al my greet traveil have
115 I than deserved.'

'Now,' quod this lady, 'I saye as I sayde: me lyketh this
mater to declare at the ful, and why: for many men have had
dyvers fantasyes and resons, both on one syde therof and in the
other.   Of whiche right sone, I trowe, if thou wolt understonde,
120 thou shalt conne yeve the sentence to the partie more probable
by reson, and in soth knowing, by that I have of this mater
maked an ende.'

'Certes,' quod I, 'of these thinges longe have I had greet lust
to be lerned; for yet, I wene, goddes wil and his prescience
125 acordeth with my service in lovinge of this precious Margarite-
perle.   After whom ever, in my herte, with thursting desyre wete,
I do brenne; unwasting, I langour and fade; and the day of my
desteny in dethe or in joye I †onbyde; but yet in th'ende I am
comforted †by my supposaile, in blisse and in joye to determine
130 after my desyres.'

'That thing,' quoth Love, 'hastely to thee neigh, god graunt
of his grace and mercy!   And this shal be my prayer, til thou be
lykende in herte‾at thyne owne wil.   But now to enforme thee in
this mater (quod this lady) thou wost where I lefte; that was:
135 love to be swete, and love swete to be swete, is not al oon for to
say.   For a tree is nat alway by necessitè white.   Somtyme, er it
were white, it might have be nat white; and after tyme it is
white, it may be nat white.   But a white tree evermore nedeful
is to be white; for neither toforn ne after it was white, might it
140 be togider white and nat white.   Also love, by necessitè, is nat
present as now in thee; for er it were present, it might have be
that it shulde now nat have be; and yet it may be that it shal nat
be present; but thy love present whiche to her, Margarite, thee
hath bounde, nedeful is to be present.   Trewly, som doing of

---

109 se. peerle.   110. hert.   111. nowe.   112. thorowe.
113. thorowe.   114. thanke. great.   116. Nowe.   118. reasons.
120. shalte con.   121. reason.   123. great luste.   126. hert.
weete.   128. vnbyde (!).   129. be; *for* by.   133. nowe. the.
135. one.   138. maye.   141. nowe. the.   142. nowe. maye.
143. the.   144. some.

accion, nat by necessitè, is comminge fer toforn it be ; it may be 145
that it shal nat be comminge. Thing forsoth comming nedeful is
to be comming ; for it may nat be that comming shal nat be
comming. And right as I have sayd of present and of future
tymes, the same sentence in sothnesse is of the preterit, that is
to say, tyme passed. For thing passed must nedes be passed ; and 150
er it were, it might have nat be ; wherfor it shulde nat have
passed. Right so, whan love comming is said of love that is to
come, nedeful is to be that is said ; for thing comming never is nat
comminge. And so, ofte, the same thing we sayn of the same ; as
whan we sayn "every man is a man," or "every lover is a lover," 155
so muste it be nedes. In no waye may he be man and no man togider. And if it be nat by necessitè, that is to say nedeful, al thing
comming to be comming, than somthing comming is nat comminge, and that is impossible. Right as these termes "nedeful,"
"necessitè," and "necessary" betoken and signify thing nedes 160
to be, and it may nat otherwyse be, right [so] †this terme "impossible" signifyeth, that [a] thing is nat and by no way may it be.
Than, thorow pert necessitè, al thing comming is comming ; but
that is by necessitè foloweth, with nothing to be constrayned.
Lo ! whan that "comming" is said of thinge, nat alway thing 165
thorow necessitè is, altho[ugh] it be comming. For if I say, "to-
morowe love is comming in this Margarites herte," nat therfore
thorow necessitè shal the ilke love be ; yet it may be that it shal
nat be, altho[ugh] it were comming. Neverthelater, somtyme it
is soth that somthing be of necessitè, that is sayd "to come" ; as 170
if I say, to-morowe †be comminge the rysinge of the sonne. If
therfore with necessitè I pronounce comming of thing to come, in
this maner love to-morne comminge in thyne Margarite to thee-
ward, by necessitè is comminge ; or els the rysing of the sonne
to-morne comminge, through necessitè is comminge. Love sothely, 175
whiche may nat be of necessitè alone folowinge, thorow necessitè
comming it is mad certayn. For "futur" of future is said ; that is to
sayn, "comming" of comminge is said ; as, if to-morowe comming
is thorow necessitè, comminge it is. Arysing of the sonne, thorow
two necessitès in comming, it is to understande ; that oon is to- 180
for[e]going necessitè, whiche maketh thing to be ; therfore it shal
be, for nedeful is that it be. Another is folowing necessitè, whiche

---

145. action. ferre.   154. thynge.   155. sayne.   161. *I supply*
so.   these termes ; *read* this terme.   162. *I supply* a.   163–6. thorowe.
(*twice*).   166. altho.   167. hert.   169. altho.   171. by ; *read* be.
173. the warde.   176. thorowe.   177. made certayne.   179. thorowe.
180. one. to forgoing.

nothing constrayneth to be, and so by necessitè it is to come ; why ?
for it is to come.   Now than, whan we sayn that god beforn wot
185 thing comming, nedeful [it] is to be comming ; yet therfore make
we nat in certayn evermore, thing to be thorow necessitè comminge.   Sothly, thing comming may nat be nat comming by no
way ; for it is the same sentence of understanding as if we say
thus : if god beforn wot any-thing, nedeful is that to be comming.
190 But yet therfore foloweth nat the prescience of God, thing thorow
necessitè to be comming : for al-tho[ugh] god toforn wot al
thinges comming, yet nat therfore he beforn wot every thing
comming thorow necessitè.   Some thinges he beforn wot comming of free wil out of resonable creature.'
195   'Certes,' quod I, 'these termes "nede" and "necessitè" have
a queint maner of understanding ; they wolden dullen many
mennes wittes.'
    'Therfore,' quod she, 'I wol hem openly declare, and more
clerely than I have toforn, er I departe hen[ne]s.

CHAPTER IV.

HERE of this mater,' quod she, 'thou shalt understande
that, right as it is nat nedeful, god to wilne that he wil,
no more in many thinges is nat nedeful, a man to wilne that
he wol.   And ever, right as nedeful is to be, what that god wol,
5 right so to be it is nedeful that man wol in tho thinges, whiche
that god hath put in-to mannes subjeccion of willinge ; as, if
a man wol love, that he love ; and if he ne wol love, that he love
nat ; and of suche other thinges in mannes disposicion.   For-why,
now than that god wol may nat be, whan he wol the wil of man
10 thorow no necessitè to be constrayned or els defended for to
wilne, and he wol th'effect to folowe the wil ; than is it nedeful,
wil of man to be free, and also to be that he wol.   In this maner
it is soth, that thorow necessitè is mannes werke in loving, that
he wol do altho[ugh] he wol it nat with necessitè.'
15   Quod I than, 'how stant it in love of thilke wil, sithen men

---

184. Nowe.   185. *I supply* it.   186. certayne. thynge. thorowe.
187. maye.   190. thorowe.   191. wote.   193. thorowe.   200.
hense ; *read* hennes.
    CH. IV. 1. shalte.   6. subiection.   8. disposition.   9. nowe.
10. thorowe.   11. theffecte. folow.   12. fre.   13. thorowe.
14. altho.   15. howe stante.

loven willing of free choice in herte? Wherfore, if it be thorow
necessitè, I praye you, lady, of an answere this question to
assoyle.'

'I wol,' quod she, 'answere thee blyvely.   Right as men wil
not thorow necessitè, right so is not love of wil thorow necessitè; 20
ne thorow necessitè wrought thilke same wil.   For if he wolde
it not with good wil, it shulde nat have been wrought; although
that he doth, it is nedeful to be doon.   But if a man do sinne, it
is nothing els but to †wilne that he shulde nat; right so sinne
of wil is not to be [in] maner necessary don, no more than wil is 25
necessarye.   Never-the-later, this is sothe; if a man wol sinne,
it is necessarye him to sinne, but th[r]ough thilke necessitè nothing
is constrayned ne defended in the wil; right so thilke thing that
free-wil wol and may, and not may not wilne; and nedeful is
that to wilne he may not wilne.   But thilke to wilne nedeful is; for 30
impossible to him it is oon thing and the same to wilne and not to
wilne.   The werke, forsothe, of wil, to whom it is yeve that it be that
he hath in wil, and that he wol not, voluntarie †or spontanye it is;
for by spontanye wil it is do, that is to saye, with good wil not
constrayned: than by wil not constrayned it is constrayned to 35
be; and that is it may not †togider be.   If this necessitè maketh
libertè of wil, whiche that, aforn they weren, they might have ben
eschewed and shonned: god than, whiche that knoweth al
tr[o]uthe, and nothing but tr[o]uthe, al these thinges, as they
arn spontanye or necessarie, †seeth; and as he seeth, so they 40
ben.   And so with these thinges wel considred, it is open at the
ful, that without al maner repugnaunce god beforn wot al maner
thinges [that] ben don by free wil, whiche, aforn they weren,
[it] might have ben [that] never they shulde be.   And yet ben
they thorow a maner necessitè from free wil †discended.   45

Hereby may (quod she) lightly ben knowe that not al thinges to
be, is of necessitè, though god have hem in his prescience.   For
som thinges to be, is of libertè of wil.   And to make thee to have
ful knowinge of goddes beforn-weting, here me (quod she) what
I shal say.'   50

---

16. thorowe.   19. the.   20–1. thorowe (*thrice*).   23. dothe. doone.
24. wyl; *read* wilne; *see* l. 30.   25 *I supply* in. done.   28. thynge.
29 frewyl. maye.   30. maye.   30–1. *Some words repeated here.*   31. one.
32. whome.   33. of; *read* or.   36. togyther; *read* togider.
37. libertie. aforne.   39. truthe (*twice*).   40. arne. syght; *read* seeth.
42. beforne.   43 *I supply* that. fre. aforne.   44. *I supply* it *and* that.
45. frewyl discendeth (!).   46. maye.   48. libertie. the.   49. beforne.

'Blythly, lady,' quod I, 'me list this mater entyrely to understande.'

'Thou shalt,' quod she, 'understande that in heven is goddes
beinge; although he be over al by power, yet there is abydinge of
55 devyne persone; in whiche heven is everlastinge presence, withouten any movable tyme.   There * is nothing preterit ne passed,
there is nothing future ne comming; but al thinges togider in that
place ben present everlasting, without any meving.   Wherfore, to
god, al thing is as now; and though a thing be nat, in kyndly
60 nature of thinges, as yet, and if it shulde be herafter, yet evermore
we shul saye, god it maketh be tyme present, and now; for no
future ne preterit in him may be founde.   Wherfore his weting and
his before-weting is al oon in understanding.   Than, if weting
and before-weting of god putteth in necessitè to al thinges whiche
65 he wot or before-wot; ne thing, after eternitè or els after any
tyme, he wol or doth of libertè, but al of necessitè : whiche thing
if thou wene it be ayenst reson, [than is] nat thorow necessitè to
be or nat to be, al thing that god wot or before-wot to be or nat
to be; and yet nothing defendeth any-thing to be wist or to be
70 before-wist of him in our willes or our doinges to be don, or els
comminge to be for free arbitrement.   Whan thou hast these
declaracions wel understande, than shalt thou fynde it resonable
at prove, and that many thinges be nat thorow necessitè but
thorow libertè of wil, save necessitè of free wil, as I tofore said,
75 and, as me thinketh, al utterly declared.'

'Me thinketh, lady,' quod I, 'so I shulde you nat displese, and
evermore your reverence to kepe, that these thinges contraryen in
any understanding; for ye sayn, somtyme is thorow libertè of
wil, and also thorow necessitè.   Of this have I yet no savour,
80 without better declaracion.'

'What wonder,' quod she, 'is there in these thinges, sithen al
day thou shalt see at thyne eye, in many thinges receyven in hem-
selfe revers, thorow dyvers resons, as thus :—I pray thee (quod
she) which thinges ben more revers than "comen" and "gon"?
85 For if I bidde thee "come to me," and thou come, after, whan
I bidde thee "go," and thou go, thou reversest fro thy first
comming.'

---

53. shalte.   * A break here in Th.   59. nowe.   thynge.   61. nowe.
63. one.   66. dothe.   67. reason. I supply than is. thorowe.   69. thynge.
70. done.   71. haste.   72. declarations.   73-4. thorowe (twice).
76. displease.   78. sayne.   78-9. thorowe.   80. declaration.   82.
shalte se.   83. reasons. the.   84. gone.   85-6. thee (twice).

'That is soth,' quod I.

'And yet,' quod she, 'in thy first alone, by dyvers reson, was
ful reversinge to understande.'   90

'As how?' quod I.

'That shal I shewe thee,' quod she, 'by ensample of thinges
that have kyndly moving. Is there any-thing that meveth more
kyndly than doth the hevens eye, whiche I clepe the sonne?'

'Sothly,' quod I, 'me semeth it is most kyndly to move.'   95

'Thou sayest soth,' quod she. 'Than, if thou loke to the
sonne, in what parte he be under heven, evermore he †hyeth him
in moving fro thilke place, and †hyeth meving toward the ilke
same place; to thilke place from whiche he goth he †hyeth
comminge; and without any ceesinge to that place he neigheth 100
from whiche he is chaunged and withdrawe. But now in these
thinges, after dyversitè of reson, revers in one thinge may be seye
without repugnaunce. Wherfore in the same wyse, without any
repugnaunce, by my resons tofore maked, al is oon to believe,
somthing to be thorow necessitè comminge for it is comming, and 105
yet with no necessitè constrayned to be comming, but with
necessitè that cometh out of free wil, as I have sayd.'

Tho liste me a litel to speke, and gan stinte my penne of my
wryting, and sayde in this wyse.

'Trewly, lady, as me thinketh, I can allege authoritees grete, 110
that contrarien your sayinges. Job saith of mannes person,
"thou hast put his terme, whiche thou might not passe." Than
saye I that no man may shorte ne lengthe the day ordayned of
his †dying, altho[ugh] somtyme to us it semeth som man to do
a thing of free wil, wherthorow his deeth he henteth.'   115

'Nay, forsothe,' quod she, 'it is nothing ayenst my saying; for
god is not begyled, ne he seeth nothing wheder it shal come of
libertè or els of necessitè; yet it is said to be ordayned at god
immovable, whiche at man, or it be don, may be chaunged.
Suche thing is also that Poule the apostel saith of hem that tofore 120
wern purposed to be sayntes, as thus: "whiche that god before
wiste and hath predestined conformes of images of his †sone, that
he shulde ben the firste begeten, that is to saye, here amonges

89. reasone.   91. howe.   92. the.   97. heigheth; *read* hyeth.
98. higheth; *read* hyeth. towarde.   99. gothe. heigheth; *read* hyeth.
100. ceasynge.   101. nowe.   102. reason. sey.   104. reasons. one.
105. thorowe.   108. list. stynt.   109. sayd.   110. gret.   111. sayenges.
112. putte.   113. length.   114. doyng; *read* dying. some.   115. thynge.
-thorowe. dethe.   116. Naye. sayeng.   119. done.   120. saithe.
toforne werne.   122. wyst. sonne; *read* sone.

many brethren ; and whom he hath predestined, hem he hath
125 cleped ; and whom he hath cleped, hem he hath justifyed ; and
whom he hath justifyed, hem he hath magnifyed." This purpos,
after whiche they ben cleped sayntes or holy in the everlasting
present, wher is neither tyme passed ne tyme comminge, but ever
it is only present, and now as mokel a moment as sevin thousand
130 winter ; and so ayenward withouten any meving is nothing lich
temporel presence for thinge that there is ever present. Yet
amonges you men, er it be in your presence, it is movable thorow
libertè of arbitrement.   And right as in the everlasting present
no maner thing was ne shal be, but only *is*; and now here, in
135 your temporel tyme, somthing was, and is, and shal be, but
movinge stoundes ; and in this is no maner repugnaunce : right
so, in the everlasting presence, nothing may be chaunged ; and,
in your temporel tyme, otherwhyle it is proved movable by libertè
of wil or it be do, withouten any inconvenience therof to folowe.
140 In your temporel tyme is no suche presence as in the tother ; for
your present is don whan passed and to come ginnen entre ;
whiche tymes here amonges you everich esily foloweth other.
But the presence everlasting dureth in oonhed, withouten any
imaginable chaunging, and ever is present and now.   Trewly, the
145 course of the planettes and overwhelminges of the sonne in dayes
and nightes, with a newe ginning of his circute after it is ended,
that is to sayn, oon yeer to folowe another : these maken your
transitory tymes with chaunginge of lyves and mutacion of people,
but right as your temporel presence coveiteth every place, and al
150 thinges in every of your tymes be contayned, and as now both
seye and wist to goddes very knowinge.'
    ' Than,' quod I, ' me wondreth why Poule spak these wordes
by voice of significacion in tyme passed, that god his sayntes
before-wist hath predestined, hath cleped, hath justifyed, and
155 hath magnifyed.   Me thinketh, he shulde have sayd tho wordes
in tyme present ; and that had ben more accordaunt to the
everlasting present than to have spoke in preterit voice of passed
understanding.'
    ' O,' quod Love, ' by these wordes I see wel thou hast litel
160 understanding of the everlasting presence, or els of my before

---

124. brethern.   126. purpose.   129. onely.   nowe.   thousande.
130. ayenwarde.   132. thorowe.   134. onely.   nowe.   141. done.
142. easely.   143. onehed.   144. nowe   147. one yere.   148. mutation.
150. nowe.   151. sey.   152. spake.   153. signification.   155. sayde.
159. se.

spoken wordes; for never a thing of tho thou hast nempned was
tofore other or after other; but al at ones evenlich at the god
ben, and al togider in the everlasting present be now to understanding. This eternal presence, as I sayd, hath inclose togider
in one al tymes, in which close and one al thinges that ben in 165
dyvers tymes and in dyvers places temporel, [and] without poste-
riorità or priorità ben closed ther in perpetual now, and maked
to dwelle in present sight.   But there thou sayest that Poule shulde
have spoke thilke forsaid sentence †by tyme present, and that
most shulde have ben acordaunt to the everlasting presence, 170
why gabbest thou †in thy wordes? Sothly, I say, Poule moved
the wordes by significacion of tyme passed, to shewe fully that
thilk wordes were nat put for temporel significacion; for al [at] thilk
tyme [of] thilke sentence were nat temporallich born, whiche that
Poule pronounced god have tofore knowe, and have cleped, than 175
magnifyed.   Wherthorow it may wel be knowe that Poule used tho
wordes of passed significacion, for nede and lacke of a worde
in mannes bodily speche betokeninge the everlasting presence.
And therfore, [in] worde moste semeliche in lykenesse to everlasting presence, he took his sentence; for things that here- 180
beforn ben passed utterly be immovable, y-lyke to the everlasting
presence.   As thilke that ben there never mowe not ben present,
so thinges of tyme passed ne mowe in no wyse not ben passed;
but al thinges in your temporal presence, that passen in a litel
while, shullen ben not present.   So than in that, it is more 185
similitude to the everlasting presence, significacion of tyme passed
than of tyme temporal present, and so more in accordaunce.   In
this maner what thing, of these that ben don thorow free arbitrement, or els as necessary, holy writ pronounceth, after eternità he
speketh; in whiche presence is everlasting sothe and nothing but 190
sothe immovable; nat after tyme, in whiche naught alway ben
your willes and your actes.   And right as, while they be nat, it is
nat nedeful hem to be, so ofte it is nat nedeful that somtyme
they shulde be.'

'As how?' quod I; 'for yet I must be lerned by some 195
ensample.'

'Of love,' quod she, 'wol I now ensample make, sithen I knowe

163, 167. nowe.   166. *I supply* and.   167. therin; *read* ther in.   168.
dwel.   169. be; *read* by.   171. to; *read* in.   172–3. signification (*twice*).
173. *I supply* at.   174. were nat thilke sentence; *transpose, and insert* of.
borne.   176. Wherthorowe.   know.   177. signification.   178. spech.
179. *I supply* in; *and omit* is *after* worde.   180. toke.   181. beforne.   186.
signification.   188. thynge.   done thorowe fre.   189. writte.   197. nowe.

the heed-knotte in that yelke. Lo! somtyme thou wrytest no
art, ne art than in no wil to wryte. And right as while thou
200 wrytest nat or els wolt nat wryte, it is nat nedeful thee to wryte
or els wilne to wryte. And for to make thee knowe utterly that
thinges ben otherwise in the everlastinge presence than in
temporal tyme, see now, my good child : for somthing is in the
everlastinge presence, than in temporal tyme it was nat; in
205 †eterne tyme, in eterne presence shal it nat be. Than no reson
defendeth, that somthing ne may be in tyme temporal moving,
that in eterne is immovable. Forsothe, it is no more contrary
ne revers for to be movable in tyme temporel, and [im]movable
in eternitè, than nat to be in any tyme and to be alway in
210 eternitè; and to have be or els to come in tyme temporel, and
nat have be ne nought comming to be in eternitè. Yet never-
the-later, I say nat somthing to be never in tyme temporel, that
ever is [in] eternitè; but al-only in som tyme nat to be. For
I saye nat thy love to-morne in no tyme to be, but to-day alone
215 I deny it to be; and yet, never-the-later, it is alway in eternitè.'

'A! so,' quod I, 'it semeth to me, that comming thing or els
passed here in your temporal tyme to be, in eternitè ever now
and present oweth nat to be demed; and yet foloweth nat thilke
thing, that was or els shal be, in no maner ther to ben passed
220 or els comming; than utterly shul we deny for there without
ceesing it is, in his present maner.'

'O,' quod she, 'myne owne disciple, now ginnest thou [be]
able to have the name of my servaunt! Thy wit is clered; away
is now errour of cloude in unconning; away is blyndnesse of
225 love; away is thoughtful study of medling maners. Hastely
shalt thou entre in-to the joye of me, that am thyn owne
maistres! Thou hast (quod she), in a fewe wordes, wel and
clerely concluded mokel of my mater. And right as there is
no revers ne contrarioustee in tho thinges, right so, withouten
230 any repugnaunce, it is sayd somthing to be movable in tyme
temporel, †afore it be, that in eternité dwelleth immovable, nat
afore it be or after that it is, but without cessing; for right
naught is there after tyme; that same is there everlastinge that

---

199. arte (*twice*).   200. the.   201. the.   203. se nowe.   childe.
somthynge.   205. eternite; *read* eterne.   reason.   208. movable (!).
210. and have to be.   213. *I supply* in.   al onely.   somtyme.   215. deny
ne it; *omit* ne.   alwaye.   217. nowe.   219. thynge.   thereto; *read*
ther to.   221. ceasyng.   222. nowe.   *I supply* be.   223. witte.
224. nowe.   awaye.   226. shalte.   227. haste.   229. contrarioustie.
231. and for; *read* afore.

temporalliche somtyme nis; and toforn it be, it may not be, as
I have sayd.'   235

'Now sothly,' quod I, 'this have I wel understande; so that
now me thinketh, that prescience of god and free arbitrement
withouten any repugnaunce acorden; and that maketh the
strength of eternitè, whiche encloseth by presence during al
tymes, and al thinges that ben, han ben, and shul ben in any   240
tyme. I wolde now (quod I) a litel understande, sithen that
[god] al thing thus beforn wot, whether thilke wetinge be of tho
thinges, or els thilke thinges ben to ben of goddes weting, and so
of god nothing is; and if every thing be thorow goddes weting, and
therof take his being, than shulde god be maker and auctour   245
of badde werkes, and so he shulde not rightfully punisshe yvel
doinges of mankynde.'

Quod Love, 'I shal telle thee, this lesson to lerne. Myne
owne trewe servaunt, the noble philosophical poete in Englissh,
whiche evermore him besieth and travayleth right sore my name   250
to encrese (wherfore al that willen me good owe to do him
worship and reverence bothe; trewly, his better ne his pere in
scole of my rules coude I never fynde)—he (quod she), in a tretis
that he made of my servant Troilus, hath this mater touched, and
at the ful this question assoyled. Certaynly, his noble sayinges 255
can I not amende; in goodnes of gentil manliche speche, without
any maner of nycetè of †storiers imaginacion, in witte and in
good reson of sentence he passeth al other makers. In the boke
of Troilus, the answere to thy question mayst thou lerne. Never-
the-later, yet may lightly thyne understandinge somdel ben lerned, 260
if thou have knowing of these to-fornsaid thinges; with that thou
have understanding of two the laste chapiters of this seconde
boke, that is to say, good to be somthing, and bad to wante al
maner being. For badde is nothing els but absence of good;
and [as] that god in good maketh that good dedes ben good,   265
in yvel he maketh that they ben but naught, that they ben bad;
for to nothing is badnesse to be [lykned].'

'I have,' quod I tho, 'ynough knowing therin; me nedeth of
other thinges to here, that is to saye, how I shal come to my
blisse so long desyred.'   270

234. toforne. maye.   236. Nowe.   237. nowe. fre.   241. nowe.
242. *I supply* god. beforne.   244. nothynge. thorowe.   248. tel the.
251. encrease.   253. schole. treatise.   255. sayenges.   256. gentyl
manlyche.   257. nycite. starieres (!).   258. reason.   259. mayste.
260. somdele.   263. want.   265. *I supply* as.   267. *I supply* lykned.
269. howe.

CHAPTER V.

'IN this mater toforn declared,' quod Love, 'I have wel shewed, that every man hath free arbitrement of thinges in his power, to do or undo what him lyketh.   Out of this grounde muste come the spire, that by processe of tyme shal in greetnesse
5 sprede, to have braunches and blosmes of waxing frute in grace, of whiche the taste and the savour is endelesse blisse, in joye ever to onbyde.' *

'Now, trewly, lady, I have my grounde wel understonde; but what thing is thilke spire that in-to a tree shulde wexe?
10 Expowne me that thing, what ye therof mene.'

'That shal I,' quod she, 'blithly, and take good hede to the wordes, I thee rede.   Continuaunce in thy good service, by longe processe of tyme in ful hope abyding, without any chaunge to wilne in thyne herte, this is the spire.   Whiche, if it be wel kept
15 and governed, shal so hugely springe, til the fruit of grace is plentuously out-sprongen.   For although thy wil be good, yet may not therfore thilk blisse desyred hastely on thee discenden; it must abyde his sesonable tyme.   And so, by processe of growing, with thy good traveyle, it shal in-to more and more wexe,
20 til it be found so mighty, that windes of yvel speche, ne scornes of envy, make nat the traveyle overthrowe; ne frostes of mistrust, ne hayles of jelousy right litel might have, in harming of suche springes.   Every yonge setling lightly with smale stormes is apeyred; but whan it is woxen somdel in gretnesse, than han
25 grete blastes and †weders but litel might, any disadvantage to them for to werche.'

'Myne owne soverayne lady,' quod I, 'and welth of myne herte, and it were lyking un-to your noble grace therthrough nat to be displesed, I suppose ye erren, now ye maken jelousy, envy,
30 and distourbour to hem that ben your servauntes.   I have lerned ofte, to-forn this tyme, that in every lovers herte greet plentee of jelousyes greves ben sowe, wherfore (me thinketh) ye ne ought in no maner accompte thilke thing among these other welked wivers and venomous serpentes, as envy, mistrust, and yvel
35 speche.'

CH. V.   2. fre.   4. greatnesse.   6. ioy.   * A break here in Th.
8. Nowe.   10. meane.   12. the.   15. fruite.   16. al thoughe.   17. the.
24. somdele.   25. great. wethers; read weders.   28. hert.   29.
displeased. nowe.   31. to-forne. hert great plentie.   33. thynge.

'O fole,' quod she, 'mistrust with foly, with yvel wil medled,
engendreth that welked padde! Truely, if they were distroyed,
jelousy undon were for ever; and yet some maner of jelousy,
I wot wel, is ever redy in al the hertes of my trewe servauntes, as
thus: to be jelous over him-selfe, lest he be cause of his own 40
disese. This jelousy in ful thought ever shulde be kept, for
ferdnesse to lese his love by miskeping, thorow his owne doing in
leudnesse, or els thus: lest she, that thou servest so fervently, is
beset there her better lyketh, that of al thy good service she
compteth nat a cresse. These jelousies in herte for acceptable 45
qualitees ben demed; these oughten every trewe lover, by kyndly
[maner], evermore haven in his mynde, til fully the grace and
blisse of my service be on him discended at wil. And he that
than jelousy caccheth, or els by wening of his owne folisshe
wilfulnesse mistrusteth, truely with fantasy of venim he is foule 50
begyled. Yvel wil hath grounded thilke mater of sorowe in his
leude soule, and yet nat-for-than to every wight shulde me nat
truste, ne every wight fully misbeleve; the mene of these thinges
†oweth to be used. Sothly, withouten causeful evidence mistrust
in jelousy shulde nat be wened in no wyse person commenly; 55
suche leude wickednesse shulde me nat fynde. He that is wyse
and with yvel wil nat be acomered, can abyde wel his tyme, til
grace and blisse of his service folowing have him so mokel esed,
as his abydinge toforehande hath him disesed.'

'Certes, lady,' quod I tho, 'of nothing me wondreth, sithen 60
thilke blisse so precious is and kyndly good, and wel is and worthy
in kynde whan it is medled with love and reson, as ye toforn
have declared. Why, anon as hye oon is sprenge, why springeth
nat the tother? And anon as the oon cometh, why receyveth nat
the other? For every thing that is out of his kyndly place, by ful 65
appetyt ever cometh thiderward kyndely to drawe; and his kyndly
being ther-to him constrayneth. And the kyndly stede of this
blisse is in suche wil medled to †onbyde, and nedes in that it
shulde have his kyndly being. Wherfore me thinketh, anon as that
wil to be shewed and kid him profreth, thilke blisse shulde him 70
hye, thilk wil to receyve; or els kynde[s] of goodnesse worchen
nat in hem as they shulde. Lo, be the sonne never so fer, ever

38. vndone.   41. disease.   42. thorowe.   47. *I supply* maner.
49. catcheth.   50. venyme.   53. trust. meane.   54. owen; *read*
oweth.   58. eased.   59. diseased.   62. reason.   63. one. sprong.
64. anone. one.   66. appetite. thiderwarde.   68. vnbyde; *read* onbyde.
70. kydde.   71. kynde; *read* kyndes.   72. ferre.

it hath his kynde werching in erthe. Greet weight on hye on-
lofte caried stinteth never til it come to †this resting-place. Waters
75 to the see-ward ever ben they drawing.. Thing that is light
blythly wil nat sinke, but ever ascendeth and upward draweth.
Thus kynde in every thing his kyndly cours and his beinge-place
sheweth. Wherfore †by kynde, on this good wil, anon as it were
spronge, this blisse shulde thereon discende ; her kynde[s] wolde,
80 they dwelleden togider ; and so have ye sayd your-selfe.'

'Certes,' quod she, 'thyne herte sitteth wonder sore, this blisse
for to have ; thyne herte is sore agreved that it tarieth so longe ;
and if thou durstest, as me thinketh by thyne wordes, this blisse
woldest thou blame. But yet I saye, thilke blisse is kyndly good,
85 and his kyndely place [is] in that wil to †onbyde. Never-the-later,
their comming togider, after kyndes ordinaunce, nat sodaynly
may betyde ; it muste abyde tyme, as kynde yeveth him leve.
For if a man, as this wil medled gonne him shewe, and thilke
blisse in haste folowed, so lightly comminge shulde lightly cause
90 going. Longe tyme of thursting causeth drink to be the more
delicious whan it is atasted.'

'How is it,' quod I than, 'that so many blisses see I al day at
myne eye, in the firste moment of a sight, with suche wil accorde ?
Ye, and yet other-whyle with wil assenteth, singulerly by him-selfe ;
95 there reson fayleth, traveyle was non ; service had no tyme. This
is a queynt maner thing, how suche doing cometh aboute.'

'O,' quod she, 'that is thus. The erthe kyndely, after sesons
and tymes of the yere, bringeth forth innumerable herbes and
trees, bothe profitable and other ; but suche as men might leve
100 (though they nought in norisshinge to mannes kynde serven, or
els suche as tournen sone unto mennes confusion, in case that
therof they ataste), comen forth out of the erthe by their owne
kynde, withouten any mannes cure or any businesse in traveyle.
And the ilke herbes that to mennes lyvelode necessarily serven,
105 without whiche goodly in this lyfe creatures mowen nat enduren,
and most ben †norisshinge to mankynde, without greet traveyle,
greet tilthe, and longe abydinge-tyme, comen nat out of the erthe,
and [y]it with sede toforn ordayned, suche herbes to make springe

---

73. great.   74. this ; *read* his.   75. see warde.   77. course.   78. be ;
read by.   79. kynde ; *read* kyndes.   80. sayde.   81-2. hert.   85.
I supply is.   vnbyde ; *read* onbyde.   87. maye. leaue.   90. drinke.   92.
Howe: se. daye.   95. reason. none.   96. thynge howe.   97. seasons.
98. forthe.   99. leaue.   100. they were nought ; *omit* were.   101. soone.
102. forthe.   106. norisshen ; *read* norisshinge.   106-7. great (*twice*).
108. it ; *read* yit ; *see* l. 111. seede toforne. spring.

and forth growe. Right so the parfit blisse, that we have in meninge of during-tyme to abyde, may nat come so lightly, but with greet 110 traveyle and right besy tilth; and yet good seed to be sowe; for ofte the croppe fayleth of badde seede, be it never so wel traveyled. And thilke blisse thou spoke of so lightly in comming, trewly, is nat necessary ne abydinge; and but it the better be stamped, and the venomous jeuse out-wrongen, it is lykely to enpoysonen 115 al tho that therof tasten. Certes, right bitter ben the herbes that shewen first [in] the yere of her own kynde. Wel the more is the harvest that yeldeth many graynes, tho longe and sore it hath ben traveyled. What woldest thou demen if a man wold yeve three quarters of nobles of golde? That were a precious gift?' 120

'Ye, certes,' quod I.

'And what,' quod she, 'three quarters ful of perles?'

'Certes,' quod I, 'that were a riche gift.'

'And what,' quod she, 'of as mokel azure?'

Quod I, 'a precious gift at ful.' 125

'Were not,' quod she, 'a noble gift of al these atones?'

'In good faith,' quod I, 'for wanting of Englissh naming of so noble a worde, I can not, for preciousnesse, yeve it a name.'

'Rightfully,' quod she, 'hast thou demed; and yet love, knit in vertue, passeth al the gold in this erthe. Good wil, accordant 130 to reson, with no maner propertè may be countrevayled. Al the azure in the worlde is nat to accompte in respect of reson. Love that with good wil and reson accordeth, with non erthly riches may nat ben amended. This yeft hast thou yeven, I know it my-selfe, and thy Margarite thilke gift hath receyved; in whiche 135 thinge to rewarde she hath her-selfe bounde. But thy gift, as I said, by no maner riches may be amended; wherfore, with thinge that may nat be amended, thou shalt of thy Margarites rightwisenesse be rewarded. Right suffred yet never but every good dede somtyme to be yolde. Al wolde thy Margarite with 140 no rewarde thee quyte, right, that never-more dyeth, thy mede in merit wol purvey. Certes, such sodayn blisse as thou first nempnest, right wil hem rewarde as thee wel is worthy; and though at thyn eye it semeth, the reward the desert to passe, right can after sende suche bitternesse, evenly it to rewarde. So 145

---

109. forthe. parfyte. meanynge. 110. great. 111. seede. 117. *I supply* in. 119–122. thre (*twice*). 122. peerles. 123–6. gifte (*thrice*). 129. haste. knytte. 130. golde. 131. reason. 132. respecte. 132–3. reason (*twice*). 136. gifte. 141. the. 142. sodayne. 143. the. 144. rewarde.

that sodayn blisse, by al wayes of reson, in gret goodnesse may not ben acompted; but blisse long, both long it abydeth, and endlesse it wol laste. See why thy wil is endelesse. For if thou lovedest ever, thy wil is ever ther t'abyde and neveremore to
150 chaunge; evenhed of rewarde must ben don by right; than muste nedes thy grace and this blisse [ben] endelesse in joye to tonbyde. Evenliche disese asketh evenliche joye, whiche hastely thou shalt have.'

'A!' quod I, 'it suffyseth not than alone good wil, be it never
155 so wel with reson medled, but-if it be in good service longe travayled. And so through service shul men come to the joye; and this, me thinketh, shulde be the wexing tree, of which ye first meved. *

CHAPTER VI.

NOW, lady,' quod I, 'that tree to sette, fayn wolde I lerne.'
'So thou shalt,' quod she, 'er thou depart hence. The first thing, thou muste sette thy werke on grounde siker and good, accordaunt to thy springes. For if thou desyre grapes, thou
5 goest not to the hasel; ne, for to fecchen roses, thou sekest not on okes; and if thou shalt have hony-soukels, thou levest the frute of the soure docke. Wherfore, if thou desyre this blisse in parfit joye, thou must sette thy purpos there vertue foloweth, and not to loke after the bodily goodes; as I sayd whan thou were
10 wryting in thy seconde boke. And for thou hast set thy-selfe in so noble a place, and utterly lowed in thyn herte the misgoing of thy first purpos, this tsetling is the esier to springe, and the more lighter thy soule in grace to be lissed. And trewly thy desyr, that is to say, thy wil algates mot ben stedfast in this mater with-
15 out any chaunginge; for if it be stedfast, no man may it voyde.'

'Yes, pardè,' quod I, 'my wil may ben turned by frendes, and disese of manace and thretning in lesinge of my lyfe and of my limmes, and in many other wyse that now cometh not to mynde. And also it mot ofte ben out of thought; for no remembraunce
20 may holde oon thing continuelly in herte, be it never so lusty desyred.'

---

146. sodayne. reason.   148. last. Se.   149. tabyde.   151. *I supply* ben. ioy. vnbyde (!).   152. ioy.   157. tre.   * *A break here in* Th. CH. VI.   1. Nowe. set fayne.   3. set.   5. fetchen.   6. leauest. 8. parfite ioy. set. purpose.   10. booke. haste.   12. purpose. setteles; *read* setling.   13. desyre.   14. mote.   15–16. maye (*twice*).   17. disease. 18. nowe.   19. mote.   20. one.

'Now see,' quod she, 'thou thy wil shal folowe, thy free wil to
be grounded continuelly to abyde.   It is thy free wil, that thou
lovest and hast loved, and yet shal loven this Margaryte-perle;
and in thy wil thou thinkest to holde it.   Than is thy wil knit 25
in love, not to chaunge for no newe lust besyde; this wil techeth
thyn herte from al maner varying.   But than, although thou be
thretened in dethe or els in otherwyse, yet is it in thyn arbitrement to chose, thy love to voyde or els to holde; and thilke
arbitrement is in a maner a jugement bytwene desyr and thy 30
herte.   And if thou deme to love thy good wil fayleth, than art
thou worthy no blisse that good wil shulde deserve; and if thou
chose continuaunce in thy good service, than thy good wil
abydeth; nedes, blisse folowing of thy good wil must come by
strength of thilke jugement; for thy first wil, that taught thyn 35
herte to abyde, and halt it from th'eschaunge, with thy reson
is accorded.   Trewly, this maner of wil thus shal abyde; impossible it were to turne, if thy herte be trewe; and if every
man diligently the meninges of his wil consider, he shal wel
understande that good wil, knit with reson, but in a false herte 40
never is voyded; for power and might of keping this good wil is
thorow libertè of arbitrement in herte, but good wil to kepe
may not fayle.   Eke than if it fayle, it sheweth it-selfe that good
wil in keping is not there.   And thus false wil, that putteth out
the good, anon constrayneth the herte to accorde in lovinge of 45
thy good wil; and this accordaunce bitwene false wil and thyn
herte, in falsitè ben lykened †togider.   Yet a litel wol I say
thee in good wil, thy good willes to rayse and strengthe.   Tak
hede to me (quod she) how thy willes thou shalt understande.
Right as ye han in your body dyvers membres, and fyve sondrye 50
wittes, everiche apart to his owne doing, whiche thinges as
instrumentes ye usen; as, your handes apart to handle; feet,
to go; tonge, to speke; eye, to see: right so the soule hath
in him certayne steringes and strengthes, whiche he useth as
instrumentes to his certayne doinges.   Reson is in the soule, 55
which he useth, thinges to knowe and to prove; and wil, whiche
he useth to wilne; and yet is neyther wil ne reson al the soule;
but everich of hem is a thing by him-selfe in the soule.   And

---

22. Nowe se.   22, 23. frewyl (*twice*).   24. haste.   26. teacheth.
27. varyeng.   30. desyre.   31. arte.   36. halte.   38. hert.   40.
reason.   42. thorowe. hert.   45. anone.   47. togyther.   48. the.
strength. Take.   49. howe.   51-2. aparte (*twice*).   52. fete.   53. se.
55. Reason.   57. reason.

* * *
* * * *   K

right as everich hath thus singuler instrumentes by hemselfe,
60 they han as wel dyvers aptes and dyvers maner usinges ; and
thilke aptes mowen in wil ben cleped affeccions. Affeccion is
an instrument of willinge in his apetytes. Wherfore mokel folk
sayn, if a resonable creatures soule any thing fervently wilneth,
affectuously he wilneth ; and thus may wil, by terme of equivocas,
65 in three wayes ben understande. Oon is instrument of willing ;
another is affection of this instrument ; and the third is use, that
setteth it a-werke. Instrument of willing is thilke strength of the
soule, which that constrayneth to wilne, right as reson is instrument of resons, which ye usen whan ye loken. Affeccion of this
70 instrument is a thing, by whiche ye be drawe desyrously any-
thing to wilne in coveitous maner, al be it for the tyme out
of your mynde ; as, if it come in your thought thilke thing to
remembre, anon ye ben willing thilke to done or els to have.
And thus is instrument wil ; and affeccion is wil also, to wilne
75 thing as I said ; as, for to wilne helth, whan wil nothing theron
thinketh ; for anon as it cometh to memorie, it is in wil. And so
is affeccion to wilne slepe, whan it is out of mynde ; but anon
as it is remembred, wil wilneth slepe, whan his tyme cometh of
the doinge. For affeccion of wil never accordeth to sicknesse,
80 ne alway to wake. Right so. in a true lovers affeccion of willing,
instrument is to wilne tr[o]uthe in his service ; and this affeccion
alway abydeth, although he be sleping or thretned, or els not
theron thinking ; but anon as it cometh to mynde, anon he is
stedfast in that wil to abyde. Use of this instrument forsothe
85 is another thing by himselfe ; and that have ye not but whan
ye be doing in willed thing, by affect or instrument of wil
purposed or desyred ; and this maner of usage in my service
wysely nedeth to be ruled from wayters with envy closed, from
spekers ful of jangeling wordes, from proude folk and hautayn,
90 that lambes and innocentes bothe scornen and dispysen. Thus
in doing varieth the actes of willinge everich from other, and yet
ben they cleped "wil," and the name of wil utterly owen they to
have ; as instrument of wil is wil, when ye turne in-to purpos of
any thing to don, be it to sitte or to stande, or any such thing
95 els. This instrument may ben had, although affect and usage be
left out of doing ; right as ye have sight and reson, and yet alway

---

61. affections. Affection.   62. folke.   65. thre. One.   68. reason.
69. Affection.   74. affection.   75. thynge.   77–81. affection (*four
times*).   86. affecte.   93. purpose.   94. syt.

use ye✻ †nat to loke, [ne] thinges with resonning to prove; and so
is instrument of wil, wil; and yet varyeth he from effect and
using bothe. Affeccion of wil also for wil is cleped, but it varyeth
from instrument in this maner wyse, by that nameliche, whan it 100
cometh in-to mynde, anon-right it is in willinge desyred, and the
negatif therof with willing nil not acorde; this is closed in herte,
though usage and instrument slepe. This slepeth whan instrument and us[e] waken; and of suche maner affeccion, trewly,
some man hath more and some man lesse. Certes, trewe lovers 105
wenen ever therof to litel to have. False lovers in litel wenen
have right mokel. Lo, instrument of wil in false and trewe
bothe, evenliche is proporcioned; but affeccion is more in some
places than in some, bycause of the goodnesse that foloweth, and
that I thinke hereafter to declare. Use of this instrument is wil, 110
but it taketh his name whan wilned thing is in doing; but utterly
grace to cacche in thy blisse †desyreth to ben rewarded. Thou
most have than affeccion of wil at the ful, and use whan his
tyme asketh wysely to ben governed. Sothly, my disciple,
without fervent affeccion of wil may no man ben saved. This 115
affeccion of good service in good love may not ben grounded,
without fervent desyr to the thing in wil coveited. But he that
never reccheth to have or not to have, affeccion of wil in that
hath no resting-place. Why? For whan thing cometh to mynde,
and it be not taken in hede to comin or not come, therfore in 120
that place affeccion fayleth; and, for thilke affeccion is so litel,
thorow whiche in goodnesse he shulde come to his grace, the
litelnesse wil it not suffre to avayle by no way in-to his helpes.
Certes, grace and reson thilke affeccion foloweth. This affeccion,
with reson knit, dureth in everiche trewe herte, and evermore 125
is encresing; no ferdnesse, no strength may it remove, whyle
tr[o]uthe in herte abydeth. Sothly, whan falsheed ginneth entre,
tr[o]uthe draweth away grace and joye bothe; but than thilke
falsheed, that trouth[e] hath thus voyded, hath unknit the bond
of understanding reson bytwene wil and the herte. And who-so 130
that bond undoth, and unknitteth wil to be in other purpose
than to the first accorde, knitteth him with contrarye of reson;

---

97. ✻ *A break here in* Th. ne ought; *read* nat. *I supply* ne.　98. effecte.
99. Affection.　100. name lyche.　102. negatyfe.　103. thoughe.　104. vs.
104–8. affection (*twice*).　112. catche. desyred; *read* desyreth.　113. muste.
affection (*often*).　117. desyre.　118. retcheth.　120. comyn.　124–5.
reason (*twice*).　125. knytte.　126. encreasyng. maye.　128. ioy.
both.　129. bonde.　130–2. reason.　131. bonde vndothe.

and that is unreson. Lo, than, wil and unreson bringeth a man
from the blisse of grace; whiche thing, of pure kynde, every man
135 ought to shonne and to eschewe, and to the knot of wil and reson
confirme.

Me thinketh,' quod she, 'by thy studient lokes, thou wenest in
these wordes me to contrarien from other sayinges here-toforn
in other place, as whan thou were somtyme in affeccion of wil to
140 thinges that now han brought thee in disese, which I have thee
consayled to voyde, and thyn herte discover; and there I made
thy wil to ben chaunged, whiche now thou wenest I argue to
with[h]olde and to kepe! Shortly I say, the revers in these
wordes may not ben founde; for though dronkennesse be for-
145 boden, men shul not alway ben drinklesse. I trowe right, for
thou thy wil out of reson shulde not tourne, thy wil in one reson
shulde not †onbyde. I say, thy wil in thy first purpos with
unreson was closed; constrewe forth of the remenant what thee
good lyketh. Trewly, that wil and reson shulde be knit togider,
150 was free wil of reson; after tyme thyne herte is assentaunt to them
bothe, thou might not chaunge. But if thou from rule of reson
varye, in whiche variaunce to come to thilke blisse desyred, con-.
trariously thou werchest; and nothing may knowe wil and reson
but love alone. Than if thou voide love, than †weyvest [thou]
155 the bond that knitteth; and so nedes, or els right lightly, that
other gon a-sondre; wherfore thou seest apertly that love holdeth
this knot, and amaystreth hem to be bounde. These thinges, as
a ring in circuit of wrethe, ben knit in thy soule without departing.'

'A! let be! let be!' quod I; 'it nedeth not of this no
160 rehersayle to make; my soule is yet in parfit blisse, in thinking of
that knotte!' *

CHAPTER VII.

'VERY trouth,' quod she, 'hast thou now conceyved of these
thinges in thyne herte; hastely shalt thou be able very
joye and parfit blisse to receyve; and now, I wot wel, thou
desyrest to knowe the maner of braunches that out of the tree
5 shulde springe.'

---

133. unreason (*twice*).   135. reason.   138. sayenges. toforne.   139.
affection.   140. nowe. the. disease. the.   146. reason (*twice*).
147. vnbyde; *read* onbyde. purpose.   148. unreason. remenante. the.
150. fre.   149–151. reason (*thrice*).   154. wenest; *read* weyvest thou.
155. bonde.   156. gone.   158. ringe.   160. parfyte.   * *A break here in* Th.
    CH. VII.   1. nowe.   2. hert.   3. parfyte. nowe.   5. spring.

'Therof, lady,' quod I, 'hertely I you pray; for than leve
I †wel, that right sone after I shal ataste of the frute that I so
long have desyred.'

'Thou hast herd,' quod she, 'in what wyse this tree toforn this
have I declared, as in grounde and in stocke of wexing. First, 10
the ground shulde be thy free wil, ful in thyne herte; and the
stocke (as I sayde) shulde be continuaunce in good service by
long tyme in traveyle, til it were in greetnesse right wel woxen.
And whan this tree suche greetnesse hath caught as I have
rehersed, the braunches than, that the frute shulde forth-bringe, 15
speche must they be nedes, in voice of prayer in complayning
wyse used.'

'Out! alas!' quod I tho, 'he is soroufully wounded that
hydeth his speche, and spareth his complayntes to make! What
shal I speke the care? But payne, even lyk to helle, sore hath 20
me assayled, and so ferforth in payne me thronge, that I leve my
tree is seer, and never shal it frute forth bringe! Certes, he is
greetly esed, that dare his prevy mone discover to a true felowe,
that conning hath and might, wherthrough his pleint in any thinge
may ben amended. And mokel more is he joyed, that with herte 25
of hardinesse dare complayne to his lady what cares that he
suffreth, by hope of mercy with grace to be avaunced. Truely
I saye for me, sithe I cam this Margarit to serve, durst I never me
discover of no maner disese; and wel the later hath myn herte
hardyed suche thinges to done, for the grete bountees and worthy 30
refresshmentes that she of her grace goodly, without any desert on
my halve, ofte hath me rekened. And nere her goodnesse the
more with grace and with mercy medled, which passen al desertes,
traveyls, and servinges that I in any degre might endite, I wolde
wene I shulde be without recover, in getting of this blisse for 35
ever! Thus have I stilled my disese; thus have I covered my
care; that I brenne in sorouful anoy, as gledes and coles wasten
a fyr under deed asshen. Wel the hoter is the fyr that with
asshen it is overleyn. Right longe this wo have I suffred.'

'Lo,' quod Love, 'how thou farest! Me thinketh, the palasy- 40
yvel hath acomered thy wittes; as faste as thou hyest forward,
anon sodaynly backward thou movest! Shal nat yet al thy
leudnesse out of thy braynes? Dul ben thy skilful understandinges;

---

7. wol; *read* wel. soone. atast.   9. herde. tre.   11. grounde.
frewyl. hert.   13. greatnesse.   14. gretnesse.   20. lyke. hel.
22. tre. bring.   23. greatly eased.   28. came.   29. disease.
30. great bounties.   36. disease.   37. bren.   38. fyre (*twice*).
40. howe.   41. forwarde.   42. backwarde.

thy wil hath thy wit so amaistred.   Wost thou nat wel (quod she)
45 but every tree, in his sesonable tyme of burjoninge, shewe his
blomes fro within, in signe of what frute shulde out of him
springe, els the frute for that yere men halt delivered, be the
ground never so good?   And though the stocke be mighty at
the ful, and the braunches seer, and no burjons shewe, farwel the
50 gardiner!   He may pype with an yvè-lefe; his frute is fayled.
Wherfore thy braunches must burjonen in presence of thy lady, if
thou desyre any frute of thy ladies grace.   But beware of thy lyfe,
that thou no wode lay use, as in asking of thinges that strecchen
in-to shame!   For than might thou nat spede, by no maner way
55 that I can espy.   Vertue wol nat suffre villany out of him-selfe to
springe.   Thy wordes may nat be queynt, ne of subtel maner
understandinge.   Freel-witted people supposen in suche poesies
to be begyled; in open understandinge must every word be used.
"Voice without clere understanding of sentence," saith Aristotel,
60 "right nought printeth in herte."   Thy wordes than to abyde in
herte, and clene in ful sentence of trewe mening, platly must
thou shewe; and ever be obedient, her hestes and her wils to
performe; and be thou set in suche a wit, to wete by a loke
ever-more what she meneth.   And he that list nat to speke, but
65 stilly his disese suffer, what wonder is it, tho[ugh] he come never
to his blisse?   Who that traveyleth unwist, and coveyteth thing
unknowe, unweting he shal be quyted, and with unknowe thing
rewarded.'

'Good lady,' quod I than, 'it hath ofte be sene, that †weders
70 and stormes so hugely have falle in burjoning-tyme, and by perte
duresse han beten of the springes so clene, wherthrough the frute
of thilke yere hath fayled.   It is a greet grace, whan burjons han
good †weders, their frutes forth to bringe.   Alas! than, after
suche stormes, how hard is it to avoyde, til efte wedring and
75 yeres han maked her circute cours al about, er any frute be able
to be tasted!   He is shent for shame, that foule is rebuked of his
speche.   He that is in fyre brenning sore smarteth for disese;
him thinketh ful long er the water come, that shulde the fyr
quenche.   While men gon after a leche, the body is buryed.
80 Lo! how semely this frute wexeth!   Me thinketh, that of tho

---

47. spring. halte.　　48. grounde.　　53. wodelay. stretchen.　　56.
spring.　　58. worde.　　60–1. hert (*twice*).　　64. meaneth.　　65. disease.
69. wethers; *read* weders.　　70. fal.　　71. beaten.　　72. great.　　73.
wethers; *read* weders. forthe.　　74. howe harde.　　77. disease.　　78.
fyre.　　79. gone.　　80. howe.

frutes may no man ataste, for pure bitternesse in savour.   In this
wyse bothe frute and the tree wasten away togider, though mokel
besy occupacion have be spent, to bringe it so ferforth that it
was able to springe.   A lyte speche hath maked that al this labour
is in ydel.'   85

'I not,' quod she, 'wherof it serveth, thy question to assoyle.
Me thinketh thee now duller in wittes than whan I with thee first
mette.   Although a man be leude, commenly for a fole he is nat
demed but-if he no good wol lerne.   Sottes and foles lete lightly
out of mynde the good that men techeth hem.   I sayd therfore,   90
thy stocke must be stronge, and in greetnesse wel herted: the
tree is ful feble that at the firste dent falleth.   And although frute
fayleth oon yere or two, yet shal suche a seson come oon tyme or
other, that shal bringe out frute that [is parfit].   *Fole, have I not
seyd toforn this, as tyme hurteth, right so ayenward tyme heleth   95
and rewardeth; and a tree oft fayled is holde more in deyntee
whan it frute forth bringeth.   A marchaunt that for ones lesinge
in the see no more to aventure thinketh, he shal never with
aventure come to richesse.   So ofte must men on the oke smyte,
til the happy dent have entred, whiche with the okes owne swaye   100
maketh it to come al at ones.   So ofte falleth the lethy water on
the harde rocke, til it have thorow persed it.   The even draught
of the wyr-drawer maketh the wyr to ben even and supple-
werchinge; and if he stinted in his draught, the wyr breketh
a-sonder.   Every tree wel springeth, whan it is wel grounded and   105
not often removed.'

'What shal this frute be,' quod I, 'now it ginneth rype?'

'Grace,' quod she, 'in parfit joy to endure; and therwith thou
begon[ne].'

'Grace?' quod I; 'me thinketh, I shulde have a reward for my   110
longe travayle?'

'I shal telle thee,' quod she; 'retribucion of thy good willes
to have of thy Margarite-perle, it bereth not the name of mede,
but only of good grace; and that cometh not of thy desert, but
of thy Margarytes goodnesse and vertue alone.'   115

Quod I, 'shulde al my longe travayle have no reward but thorow

81. maye. sauoure.   83. occupation. spente. ferforthe.   84. spring.
87. the nowe.   89. fooles lette.   90. teacheth.   91. greatnesse.   93.
one (*twice*). season.   94. *I supply* is parfit.   *A break here in* Th.   95.
healeth.   96. deyntie.   97. forthe.   102. thorowe.   103-4. wyre
(*thrice*).   104. breaketh.   105. tre.   107. nowe.   108. parfyte.
109. begon; *read* begonne.   110. rewarde.   112. tel the.   113.
beareth.   114. onely. deserte.   116. rewarde. thorowe.

grace? And som-tyme your-selven sayd, rightwisnesse evenliche rewardeth, to quyte oon benefit for another.'

'That is sothe,' quod Love, 'ever as I sayde, as to him that
120 doth good, which to done he were neyther holden ne yet constrayned.'

'That is sothe,' quod I.

'Trewly,' quod she, 'al that ever thou doest to thyne Margaryteperle, of wil, of love, and of reson thou owest to done it; it is
125 nothing els but yelding of thy dette in quytinge of thy grace, which she thee lente whan ye first mette.'

'I wene,' quod I, 'right litel grace to me she delivered. Certes, it was harde grace; it hath nyghe me astrangled.'

'That it was good grace, I wot wel thou wilt it graunte, er
130 thou departe hence. If any man yeve to another wight, to whom that he ought not, and whiche that of him-selfe nothing may have, a garnement or a cote, though he were the cote or els thilke clothing, it is not to putte to him that was naked the cause of his clothinge, but only to him that was yever of the garnement.
135 Wherfore I saye, thou that were naked of love, and of thy-selfe non have mightest, it is not to putte to thyne owne persone, sithen thy love cam thorow thy Margaryte-perle. *Ergo*, she was yever of the love, although thou it use; and there lente she thee grace, thy service to beginne. She is worthy the thank of this
140 grace, for she was the yever. Al the thoughtes, besy doinges, and plesaunce in thy might and in thy wordes that thou canst devyse, ben but right litel in quytinge of thy dette; had she not ben, suche thing hadde not ben studyed. So al these maters kyndly drawen hom-ward to this Margaryte-perle, for from thence
145 were they borowed; al is hoolly her to wyte, the love that thou havest; and thus quytest thou thy dette, in that thou stedfastly servest. And kepe wel that love, I thee rede, that of her thou hast borowed, and use it in her service thy dette to quyte; and than art thou able right sone to have grace; wherfore after mede
150 in none halve mayst thou loke. Thus thy ginning and ending is but grace aloon; and in thy good deserving thy dette thou aquytest; without grace is nothing worth, what-so-ever thou

---

118. one benefyte.   120. dothe.   124. *catchword* it is; *misprinted* yet
is *on the next page.*   126. the lent.   127. lytle.   129. graunt.   131.
nothynge maye.   132. weare.   133. put; *read* putte.   134. onely.
136. put.   137. came thorowe.   138. althoughe. lent. the.   139.
thanke.   141. canste.   144. homewarde.   145. holy.   147.
the.   149. arte.   151. alone.   152. worthe.

werche. Thanke thy Margaryte of her grete grace that †hiderto thee hath gyded, and praye her of continuaunce forth in thy werkes herafter; and that, for no mishappe, thy grace over- 155 thwartly tourne. Grace, glorie, and joye is coming thorow good folkes desertes; and by getting of grace, therin shullen ende. And what is more glorie or more joye than wysdom and love in parfit charitè, whiche god hath graunted to al tho that wel †conne deserve?' And with that this lady al at ones sterte in-to 160 my herte: 'here wol I onbyde,' quod she, 'for ever, and never wol I gon hence; and I wol kepe thee from medlinge while me liste here onbyde; thyne entermeting maners in-to stedfastnesse shullen be chaunged.'

CHAPTER VIII.

SOBERLICHE tho threw I up myn eyen, and hugely tho was I astonyed of this sodayne adventure; and fayn wolde I have lerned, how vertues shulden ben knowen; in whiche thinges, I hope to god, here-after she shal me enfourmen; and namely, sithen her restinge-place is now so nygh at my wil; and anon al 5 these thinges that this lady said, I remembred me by my-selfe, and revolved the †lynes of myne understondinge wittes. Tho found I fully al these maters parfitly there written, how mis-rule by fayned love bothe realmes and citees hath governed a greet throwe; how lightly me might the fautes espye; how rules in love 10 shulde ben used; how somtyme with fayned love foule I was begyled; how I shulde love have knowe; and how I shal in love with my service procede. Also furthermore I found, of perdurable letters wonderly there graven, these maters whiche I shal nempne. Certes, non age ne other thing in erthe may the leest sillable of 15 this in no poynte deface, but clerely as the sonne in myne under-standinge soule they shynen. This may never out of my mynde, how I may not my love kepe, but thorow willinge in herte; wilne to love may I not, but I lovinge have. Love have I non, but thorow grace of this Margarite-perle. It is no maner doute, that 20 wil wol not love but for it is lovinge, as wil wol not rightfully but

---

153. great. hytherto; *read* hiderto. 154. the. forthe. 156. thorowe. 158. wysdome. 159. parfyte. 160. canne; *read* conne. 161. hert.
CH. VIII. 1. threwe. 2. fayne. 3. howe. 5. nowe. nyghe. 7. lyues (!). founde. 8. parfytely. howe. mysse-. 9. cyties. great. 10–12. howe (*five times*). 13. founde. 15. none. thynge. maye. 17. maye. 18. howe. maye. thorowe. 19. maye. none. 20. thorowe.

for it is rightful it-selve. Also wil is not lovinge for he wol love ;
but he wol love for he is lovinge ; it is al oon to †wilne to be
lovinge, and lovinges in possession to have. Right so wil wol not
25 love, for of love hath he no partie. And yet I denye not lovinge
wil [may] wilne more love to have, whiche that he hath not whan
he wolde more than he hath ; but I saye, he may no love wilne
if he no love have, through which thilke love he shuld wilne. But
to have this loving wil may no man of him-selfe, but only through
30 grace toforn-going ; right so may no man it kepe, but by grace
folowinge. Consider now every man aright, and let seen if that
any wight of him-selfe mowe this loving wel gete, and he therof
first nothing have ; for if it shulde of him-selfe springe, either it
muste be willing or not willing. Willing by him-selfe may he it not
35 have, sithen him fayleth the mater that shulde it forth bringe.
The mater him fayleth ; why ? He may therof have no knowing
til whan grace put it in his herte. Thus willing by him-selfe may
he it not have ; and not willing, may he it not have. Pardè,
every conseyt of every resonable creature otherwyse wil [wol] not
40 graunte ; wil in affirmatif with not willing by no way mowe acorde.
And although this loving wol come in myn herte by freenesse of
arbitrement, as in this booke fully is shewed, yet owe I not therfore
as moche alowe my free wil as grace of that Margaryte to me
lened. For neyther might I, without grace to-forn going and
45 afterward folowing, thilke grace gete ne kepe ; and lese shal I it
never but-if free wil it make, as in willinge otherwyse than grace
hath me graunted. For right as whan any person taketh willing
to be sobre, and throweth that away, willing to be dronke ; or els
taketh wil of drinking out of mesure ; whiche thing, anon as it is
50 don, maketh (thorow his owne gilte by free wil) that [he] leseth
his grace. In whiche thing therfore upon the nobley of grace
I mote trusten, and my besy cure sette thilke grace to kepe, that
my free wil, otherwyse than by reson it shulde werche, cause not
my grace to voyde : for thus must I bothe loke to free wil and to
55 grace. For right as naturel usage in engendring of children may
not ben without †fader, ne also but with the †moder, for neyther
†fader ne †moder in begetting may it lacke ; right so grace and

23. one. wil; *read* wilne.   26. *I supply* may.   27. maye.   29. onely.
30. toforne. maye.   31. nowe. sene.   32. get.   33. nothynge.
spring.   35. forthe bring.   36. maye.   39. reasonable. *I supply*
wol.   40. graunt. affyrmatife.   41. hert. frenesse.   43. frewyl
(*throughout*).   44. leaned.   45. afterwarde. get ; *read* gete.   50.
done. thorowe. *I supply* he.   52. set.   53. reason.   55. maye.
56-7. father (*twice*) ; *read* fader. mother (*twice*) ; *read* moder.

free wil accorden, and withoute hem bothe may not lovinge wil in
no partie ben getten.   But yet is not free wil in gettinge of that
thing so mokel thank-worthy as is grace, ne in the kepinge therof 60
so moche thank deserveth; and yet in gettinge and keping bothe
don they accorde.   Trewly, often-tyme grace free wil helpeth, in
fordoinge of contrarye thinges, that to willinge love not accorden,
and †strengtheth wil adversitees to withsitte; wherfore †al-togider
to grace oweth to ben accepted, that my willing deserveth.   Free 65
wil to lovinge in this wyse is accorded.   I remembre me wel how
al this book (who-so hede taketh) considereth [how] al things to
werchinges of mankynde evenly accordeth, as in turning of this
worde 'love' in-to trouthe or els rightwisnesse, whether that it
lyke.   For what thing that falleth to man in helping of free 70
arbitrement, thilke rightwisnesse to take or els to kepe, thorow
whiche a man shal be saved (of whiche thing al this book mencion
hath maked), in every poynte therof grace oweth to be thanked.
Wherfore I saye, every wight havinge this rightwisnesse rightful
is;   and yet therfore I fele not in my conscience, that to al 75
rightful is behoten the blisse everlastinge, but to hem that ben rightful withouten any unrightfulnesse.   Some man after some degree
may rightfully ben accompted as chaste men in living, and yet ben
they janglers and ful of envy pressed; to hem shal this blisse
never ben delivered.   For right as very blisse is without al maner 80
nede, right so to no man shal it be yeven but to the rightful, voyde
from al maner unrightfulnesse founde; so no man to her blisse
shal ben folowed, but he be rightful, and with unrightfulnesse not
bounde, and in that degree fully be knowe.   This rightfulnesse,
in as moche as in him-selfe is, of none yvel is it cause; and of al 85
maner goodnesse, trewly, it is †moder.   This helpeth the spirit
to withsitte the leude lustes of flesshly lykinge.   This strengtheth
and maintayneth the lawe of kynde; and if that otherwhyle me
weneth harm of this precious thing to folowe, therthorough is [it]
nothing the cause; of somwhat els cometh it aboute, who-so 90
taketh hede.   By rightfulnesse forsothe wern many holy sayntes
good savour in swetenesse to god almighty; but that to some
folkes they weren savour of dethe, in-to deedly ende, that com
not of the sayntes rightwisnesse, but of other wicked mennes

57-8. maye.   60. thankeworthy.   61. thanke.   62. done.   64.
strength; *read* strengtheth; *see* l. 87.   al togyther.   66. howe.   67. booke.
Supply how.   71. thorowe.   72. booke.   78. maye.   86. mother;
read moder.   89. harme.   *Supply* it.   90. nothynge.   91. werne.
93. com; *read* come.

95 badnesse hath proceded. Trewly, the ilke wil, whiche that the
Lady of Love me lerned 'affeccion of wil' to nempne, which is
in willing of profitable thinges, yvel is it not, but whan to flesshly
lustes it consenteth ayenst reson of soule. But that this thing
more clerely be understande, it is for to knowe, whence and how
100 thilke wil is so vicious, and so redy yvel dedes to perfourme.
Grace at the ginninge ordeyned thilke wil in goodnesse ever to
have endured, and never to badnesse have assented. Men shulde
not byleve, that god thilke wil maked to be vicious [in] our firste
†faders, as Adam and Eve ; for vicious appetytes, and vicious wil
105 to suche appetytes consentinge, ben not on thing in kynde ; other
thing is don for the other. And how this wil first in-to man first
assented, I holde it profitable to shewe ; but if the first condicion
of resonable creature wol be considred and apertly loked, lightly
the cause of suche wil may be shewed. Intencion of god was,
110 that rightfully and blissed shulde resonable nature ben maked,
himselfe for to kepe ; but neyther blisful ne rightful might it not
be, withouten wil in them bothe. Wil of rightfulnesse is thilke
same rightfulnesse, as here-to-forn is shewed ; but wil of blisse
is not thilke blisse, for every man hath not thilke blisse, in whom
115 the wil therof is abydinge. In this blisse, after every understandinge, is suffisaunce of covenable comoditees without any
maner nede, whether it be blisse of aungels or els thilke that
grace first in paradise suffred Adam to have. For al-though
angels blisse be more than Adams was in paradyse, yet may it not
120 be †denyed, that Adam in paradyse ne had suffisaunce of blisse ;
for right as greet herte is without al maner of coldenesse, and yet
may another herte more hete have ; right so nothing defended
Adam in paradyse to ben blessed, without al maner nede.
Al-though aungels blisse be moche more, forsothe, it foloweth
125 not [that], lasse than another to have, therfore him nedeth ; but
for to wante a thing whiche that behoveth to ben had, that may
'nede' ben cleped ; and that was not in Adam at the first
ginning. God and the Margaryte weten what I mene. Forsothe,
where-as is nede, there is wrecchednesse. †God without cause
130 to-forngoing made not resonable creature wrecched ; for him to

---

96. affectyon.   98. reason. thynge.   99. vnderstand. howe.   100.
redye.   103. vycious. *I insert* in ; Our (*sic*).   104. father ; *read* faders.
106. done. howe.   108–110. reasonable (*twice*).   113. -forne.   119, 122.
maye.   120. denyded (!).   121. great.   122. heate. nothynge.   124.
thoughe.   125. *I supply* that.   126. thynge. maye.   128. meane.
129. wretchydnesse. good ; *read* God.   130. reasonable. wretched.

understande and love had he firste maked.   God made therfore
man blissed without al maner indigence; †togider and at ones
took resonable creature blisse, and wil of blissednesse, and wil
of rightfulnesse, whiche is rightfulnesse it-selve, and libertee of
arbitrement, that is, free wil, with whiche thilke rightfulnesse may 135
he kepe and lese.   So and in that wyse [god] ordayned thilke
two, that wil (whiche that "instrument" is cleped, as here-toforn
mencion is maked) shulde use thilke rightfulnesse, by teching of
his soule to good maner of governaunce, in thought and in wordes;
and that it shulde use the blisse in obedient maner, withouten 140
any incommoditè.   Blisse, forsothe, in-to mannes profit, and
rightwisnesse in-to his worship god delivered at ones; but rightfulnesse so was yeven that man might it lese, whiche if he not lost
had, but continuelly [might] have it kept, he shulde have deserved
the avauncement in-to the felowshippe of angels, in whiche thing 145
if he that loste, never by him-selfe forward shulde he it mowe
ayenward recovere; and as wel the blisse that he was in, as
aungels blisse that to-him-wardes was coming, shulde be nome at
ones, and he deprived of hem bothe.   And thus fil man un-to
lykenesse of unresonable bestes; and with hem to corrupcion and 150
unlusty apetytes was he under-throwen.   But yet wil of blisse
dwelleth, that by indigence of goodes, whiche that he loste
through greet wrecchednesse, by right shulde he ben punisshed.
And thus, for he weyved rightfulnesse, lost hath he his blisse; but
fayle of his desyr in his owne comoditè may he not; and †where 155
comodites to his resonable nature whiche he hath lost may he not
have, to false lustes, whiche ben bestial appetytes, he is turned.
Folye of unconning hath him begyled, in wening that thilke ben
the comoditees that owen to ben desyred.   This affeccion of wil
by libertè of arbitrement is enduced to wilne thus thing that 160
he shulde not; and so is wil not maked yvel but unrightful, by
absence of rightfulnesse, whiche thing by reson ever shulde he
have.   And freenesse of arbitrement may he not wilne, whan he it
not haveth; for while he it had, thilke halp it not to kepe; so
that without grace may it not ben recovered.   Wil of commoditè, 165
in-as-moche as unrightful it is maked by willinge of yvel lustes, willing

---

132. togyther.   133. toke reasonable.   134. lybertie.   135. fre.
136. *I supply* god.   137. cleaped. toforne.   138. teachyng.   141.
profyte.   143. not loste had not; *I omit second* not.   144. *I supply*
might. kepte.   146. forwarde.   147. ayenwarde.   150. vnreasonable.
153. great wretchydnesse.   154. loste.   155. desyre. were; *read*
where.   156. reasonable. loste.   159. affection.   162. reason.
163. frenesse.   164. halpe.

of goodnesse may he not wilne; for wil of instrument to affeccion of wil is thralled, sithen that other thing may it not wilne;
for wil of instrument to affeccion desyreth, and yet ben bothe they
170 'wil' cleped. For that instrument wol, through affeccion it wilneth;
and affeccion desyreth thilke thing wherto instrument him ledeth.
And so free wil to unlusty affeccion ful servaunt is maked, for
unrightfulnesse may he not releve; and without rightfulnesse ful
fredom may it never have. For kyndly libertee of arbitrement
175 without it, veyne and ydel is, forsothe. Wherfore yet I say, (as
often have I sayd the same), whan instrument of wil lost hath
rightfulnesse, in no maner but by grace may he ayen retourne
rightfulnesse to wilne. For sithen nothing but rightfulnesse alone
shulde he wilne, what that ever he wilneth without rightfulnesse,
180 unrightfully he it wilneth. These than unrightful appetytes and
unthrifty lustes whiche the †flesh desyreth, in as mokel as they ben
in kynde, ben they nat bad; but they ben unrightful and badde for
they ben in resonable creature, where-as they being, in no waye
shulde ben suffred. In unresonable beestes neyther ben they yvel
185 ne unrightful; for there is their kynde being.

CHAPTER IX.

KNOWEN may it wel ben now of these thinges toforn
declared, that man hath not alway thilke rightfulnesse
which by dutè of right evermore haven he shulde, and by no way
by him-selfe may he it gete ne kepe; and after he it hath, if he it
5 lese, recover shal he it never without especial grace. Wherfore
the comune sentence of the people in opinion, that every thing
after destenee is ruled, false and wicked is to beleve. For though
predestinacion be as wel of good as of badde, sithen that it is
sayd, god Ɪhath destenees made, whiche he never ne wrought; but,
10 for he suffreth hem to be maked, as that he hardeth, whan he
naught missayth, or †let in-to temptacion, whan he not delivereth:
wherfore it is non inconvenient if in that maner be sayd, god toforn have destenyed bothe badde and her badde werkes, whan
hem ne their yvel dedes [he] neyther amendeth ne therto hem
15 grace †leneth. But specialliche, predestinacion of goodnesse

alone is sayd by these grete clerkes ; for in him god doth that they ben, and that in goodnesse they werchen. But the negatif herof in badnesse is holden, as the Lady of Love hath me lerned, who-so aright in this booke loketh. And utterly it is to weten, that predestinacion properly in god may not ben demed, no more 20 than beforn-weting. For in the chapitre of goddes beforn-weting, as Love me rehersed, al these maters apertly may ben founden. Al thinges to god ben now †togider and in presence duringe. Trewly, presence and predestinacion ·in nothing disacorden ; wherfore, as I was lerned how goddes before-weting and free 25 choice of wil mowe stonden †togider, me thinketh the same reson me ledeth, that destenye and free wil accorden, so that neyther of hem bothe to other in nothing contrarieth. And resonabliche may it not ben demed, as often as any thing falleth [thorow] free wil werching (as if a man another man wrongfully anoyeth, wher- 30 fore he him sleeth), that it be constrayned to that ende, as mokel folk cryeth and sayth : ' Lo, as it was destenyed of god toforn knowe, so it is thorow necessitè falle, and otherwyse might it not betyde.' Trewly, neyther he that the wrong wrought, ne he that him-selfe venged, none of thilke thinges thorow necessitè wrought ; 35 for if that [oon] with free wil there had it not willed, neyther had [he]wrought that he perfourmed ; and so utterly grace, that free wil in goodnesse bringeth and kepeth, and fro badnesse it tourn-eth, in al thinge moste thank deserveth. This grace maketh sentence in vertue to abyde, wherfore in body and in soule, in ful 40 plentee of conninge, after their good deserving in the everlastinge joye, after the day of dome shul they endelesse dwelle ; and they shul ben lerned in that kingdom with so mokel affect of love and of grace, that the leste joye shal of the gretest in glorie rejoice and ben gladded, as if he the same joye had. What wonder, 45 sith god is the gretest love and the * gretest wisdom ? In hem shal he be, and they in god. Now than, whan al false folk be ashamed, which wenen al bestialtè and erthly thing be sweter and better to the body than hevenly is to the soule ; this is the grace and the frute that I long have desyred ; it doth me good the 50 savour to smelle.

---

16. sayde. great. dothe.   17. negatyfe.   21. beforne (*twice*). 22. apertely maye.   23. nowe to-gyther.   24. nothynge   25. howe. 26. togyther. reason.   27. leadeth. frewyl.   28. reasonablyche.   29. demyd. *I supply* thorow. frewyl.   32. folke. toforne know.   33. thorowe. fal.   34. wronge.   35. thorowe.   36-7. *I supply* oon *and* he.   39. thanke. 41. plentie.   42. ioy. dwel.   43. kyngdome. affecte.   44-6. greatest (*twice*). * *A break here in* Th.   47. folke.   48. swetter.   50. dothe.   51. smel.

Crist, now to thee I crye of mercy and of grace; and graunt, of thy goodnes, to every maner reder ful understanding in this leude pamflet to have; and let no man wene other cause in
55 this werke than is verily the soth.   For envy is ever redy, al innocentes to shende; wherfore I wolde that good speche envy evermore hinder.

But no man wene this werke be sufficiently maked; for goddes werke passeth man[ne]s; no man[ne]s wit to parfit werke may by no
60 way purvay th'ende.   How shuld I than, so leude, aught wene of perfeccion any ende to gete?   Never-the-later, grace, glorie, and laude I yelde and putte with worshipful reverences to the sothfast god, in three with unitè closed, whiche that the hevy langour of my sicknesse hath turned in-to mirthe of helth to recover.   For
65 right as I was sorowed thorow the gloton cloud of manifolde sickly sorow, so mirth [of] ayencoming helth hath me glad[d]ed and gretly comforted.   I beseche and pray therfore, and I crye on goddes gret pitè and on his mokel mercy, that this[e] present scorges of my flessh mow maken medecyne and lechecraft of
70 my inner man[ne]s helth; so that my passed trespas and tenes through weping of myn eyen ben wasshe, and I, voyded from al maner disese, and no more to wepe herafter, y-now be kept thorow goddes grace; so that goddes hand, whiche that merciably me hath scorged, herafter in good plite from thence merciably me
75 kepe and defende.

In this boke be many privy thinges wimpled and folde; unneth shul leude men the plites unwinde.   Wherfore I pray to the holy gost, he lene of his oyntmentes, mennes wittes to clere; and, for goddes love, no man wonder why or how this question come to
80 my mynde.   For my greet lusty desyr was of this lady to ben enfourmed, my leudenesse to amende.   Certes, I knowe not other mennes wittes, what I shulde aske, or in answere what I shulde saye; I am so leude my-selfe, that mokel more lerninge yet me behoveth.   I have mad therfore as I coude, but not
85 sufficiently as I wolde, and as mater yave me sentence; for my dul wit is hindred by †stepmoder of foryeting and with cloude of unconning, that stoppeth the light of my Margarite-perle, wherfore it may not shyne on me as it shulde.   I desyre not

52. Christ. the.   59. mans; *read* mannes (*twice*).   61. get.   62. put.
63. thre.   66. *I supply* of.   68. this; *read* thise.   69. medecyn.
lechcraft.   70. mans.   72. I now; *for* y-now.   73. thorowe. hande.
80. great. desyre.   84. made.   86. wytte. -mother; *read* moder.

only a good reder, but also I coveite and pray a good book-
amender, in correccion of wordes and of sentence; and only this 90
mede I coveite for my travayle, that every inseër and herer of
this leude fantasye devoute horisons and prayers to god the greet
juge yelden; and prayen for me in that wyse, that in his dome
my sinnes mowe ben relesed and foryeven. He that prayeth for
other for him-selfe travayleth. 95

Also I praye, that every man parfitly mowe knowe thorow what
intencion of herte this tretys have I drawe. How was it, that
sightful manna in deserte to children of Israel was spirituel
mete? Bodily also it was, for mennes bodies it †norisshed;
and yet, never-the-later, Crist it signifyed. Right so a jewel 100
betokeneth a gemme, and that is a stoon vertuous or els a perle.
Margarite, a woman, betokeneth grace, lerning, or wisdom of
god, or els holy church. If breed, thorow vertue, is mad holy
flesshe, what is that our god sayth? 'It is the spirit that
yeveth lyf; the flesshe, of nothing it profiteth.' Flesshe is flesshly 105
understandinge; flessh without grace and love naught is worth.
'The letter sleeth; the spirit yeveth lyfelich understanding.'
Charitè is love; and love is charitè.

God graunt us al[le] therin to be frended!
And thus THE TESTAMENT OF LOVE is ended. 110

---

89. onely. booke.   90. correction.   onely.   92. great.   94. released.
96. thorowe.   97. treatyse.   Howe.   99. meate.   norissheth; *read*
norisshed.   100. Christ.   101. stone.   103. thorowe.   made.   104.
saythe.   spyrite.   105. lyfe.   109. al; *read* allë.

L

II. THE PLOWMANS TALE.

—·—

Here beginneth the Plowmans Prologue.

THE Plowman plucked up his plow,
   Whan midsommer mone was comen in,
And sayd, 'his beestes shuld ete y-now,
And lig in the grasse, up to the chin;
They ben feble, both oxe and cow,   5
Of hem nis left but boon and skin.'
He shook of share, and cultre of-drow,
And hong his harneys on a pin.

He took his tabard and his staf eke,
And on his, heed he set his hat;   10
And sayde, he wolde saynt Thomas seke,
On pilgrimage he goth forth plat.
In scrippe he bar both breed and lekes,
He was forswonke and all forswat;
Men might have seen through both his chekes, 15
And every wang-toth and where it sat.

Our hoste beheld wel all about,
And saw this man was sunne y-brent;
He knew well by his senged snout,
And by his clothes that were to-rent,   20
He was a man wont to walke about,
He nas nat alway in cloystre y-pent;
He coud not religiousliche lout,
And therfore was he fully shent.

From Thynne (ed. 1542). *I give rejected spellings.*
1. Ploweman; plowe.   3. eate ynowe.   4. lyge; chynne.   5. cowe.
6. bone; skynne.   7. shoke; -drowe.   8. honge; pynne.   9. toke;
tabarde; staffe.   12. pylgremage; platte.   13. bare.   14. forswatte.
15. sene.   17. behelde wele.   18. sawe.   19. knewe; snoute.
23. coulde; loute.

Our host him axed, 'what man art thou?'   25
'Sir,' quod he, 'I am an hyne;
For I am wont to go to the plow,
And erne my mete yer that I dyne.
To swete and swinke I màke avow,
My wyf and children therwith to fynd,   30
And servë god, and I wist how;
But we lewd men ben full[y] blynd.

For clerkes saye, we shullen be fayn
For hir lyvelod [to] swete and swinke,
And they right nought us give agayn,   35
Neyther to ete ne yet to drinke.
They mowe by lawë, as they sayn,
Us curse and dampne to hell[e] brinke;
Thus they putten us to payn,
With candles queynt and belles clinke.   40

They make us thralles at hir lust,
And sayn, we mowe nat els be saved;
They have the corn and we the dust,
Who speketh ther-agayn, they say he raved.'

'What, man,' quod our host, 'canst thou preche?   45
Come neer, and tell us some holy thing.'
'Sir,' quod he, 'I herde ones teche
A prest in pulpit a good preching.'
'Say on,' quod our host, 'I thee beseche.'
'Sir, I am redy at your bidding.   50
I pray you that no man me reproche
Whyl that I am my tale telling.

**Thus endeth the prologue, and here foloweth the first
part of the tale.**

---

27. plowe.   28. meate.   29. auowe.   30. wyfe; fynde.
31. howe.   32. leude; bene; full (*read* fully; *see* l. 24); blynde.   33.
fayne.   34. her; *supply* to; swet.   35. agayne.   36. eate.   37. The
(*for* They; 1550, They); sayne.   38. hell.   39. payne.   41. her.
42. sayne.   43. corne.   44. speaketh.   45. preache.   46. nere;
thynge.   47. ons (1550, ones); teache.   48. preachynge.   49. Saye;
the.   51. praye; noman.   52. Whyle; tellynge.   COLOPHON: fyrst
parte.

PART I.

A STERNË stryf is stered newe
  In many stedes in a stounde,
-Of sondry sedes that ben sewe;   55
It semeth that som ben unsounde.
For some be gretë growen †on grounde,
Some ben souple, simple and small;
Whether of hem is falser founde,
The falser, foul mote him befall!   60

That oon syde is, that I of tell,
Popes, cardinals, and prelates,
Parsons, monkes, and freres fell,
Priours, abbottes of grete estates;
Of heven and hell they kepe the yates,   65
And Peters successours they ben all;
This is demed by oldë dates;
But falshed, foul mote it befall!

The other syde ben poore and pale,
And people put [al] out of prees;   70
And semë caytifs sore a-cale,
And ever in oon without encrees,
† I-cleped lollers and londlees;
Who toteth on hem, they been untall.
They ben arayed all for the pees;   75
But falshed, foul mote it befall!

Many a countrey have I sought,
To know the falser of these two;
But ever my travail was for nought,
All so fer as I have go.   80
But as I wandred in a wro,
In a wode besyde a wall,
Two foules saw I sitte tho;
The falser, foul mote him befall!

---

53. stryfe.   55. bene.   57. great; vngrounde (!).   58. souble (*error for* souple).   60. foule.   61. one.   63. freers.   64. great.
65. heuyn.   68. foule mought.   70. *Supply* al; prease.   71. caytyffes.
72. one; encrease.   73. I-clepeth (!); londlese.   74. bene.   75. peace.
76. foule.   78. knowe.   79. trauayle.   80. ferre.   82. woddc.
83. sawe.

That oon did plede on the Popes syde,   85
A Griffon of a grim stature.
A Pellicane withouten pryde
To these lollers layde his lure;
He mused his matter in mesure,
To counsayl Christ ever gan he call.   90
The Griffon shewed as sharp as fyre,
But falshed, foul mote it befall!

The Pellican began to preche
Both of mercy and of mekeness;
And sayd, that "Christ so gan us teche,   95
And meke and merciable gan bless.
The Evangely bereth witness
A lamb, he lykneth Christ over-all,
In tokening that he mekest was,
Sith pryde was out of heven fall.   100

And so shulde every Christned be;
Preestes, Peters successours,
Beth lowlich and of low degree,
And usen none erthly honours,
Neyther crown, ne curious cove[r]tours,   105
Ne †pelure, ne other proudë pall;
Ne nought to cofren up greet tresours;
For falshed, foul mote it befall!

Preest[e]s shuld for no cattel plede,
But chasten hem in charitè;   110
Ne to no batail shuld men lede
For inhaunsing of hir own degree;
Nat wilnë sittings in hy see,
Ne soverayntè in hous ne hall;
All worldly worship defye and flee;   115
For who willeth highnes, foul shal fall!

85. one.   86. grymme.   89. measure.   90. counsayle.   91. sharpe.
92. foule.   93. preache.   94. mekenesse.   95. teache.   96. blesse.
97. beareth wytnesse.   98. lambe; lykeneth.   99. tokenynge.   103. low-
lyche; lowe.   105. crowne; couetours (*read* covertours).   106. pylloure
(*for* pelure).   107. great treasours.   108. foule.   109. Preests shulde.
111. bateyle shulde.   112. her owne.   113. syttynges; hye.   114. souer-
ayntie; house.   115. worshippe.   116. Who so (*omit* so); foule shall.

Alas! who may such sayntes call
That wilneth welde erthly honour?
As lowe as Lucifer such shal fall,
In baleful blacknesse y-builde hir bour;   120
That eggeth the people to errour,
And maketh hem to hem [be] thrall;
To Christ I hold suche oon traytour,
As lowe as Lucifer such shal fall.

That willeth to be kinges peres,   125
And hygher than the emperour;
Some that were but pore freres
Now wollen waxe a warryour.
God is nat hir governour,
That holdeth no man his †peragall;   130
Whyl covetyse is hir counsaylour,
All such falshed mot nedë fall.

That hye on horse willeth ryde
In glitterand golde of grete aray,
I-paynted and portred all in pryde;   135
No commun knight may go so gay.
Chaunge of clothing every day,
With golden girdles grete and small;
As boystous as is bere at bay;
All such falshed mot nedë fall.   140

With prydë †punysheth the pore,
And somë they sustayn with sale;
Of holy churche maketh an hore,
And filleth hir wombe with wyne and ale;
With money filleth many a male,   145
And chaffren churches when they fall,
And telleth the people a lewed tale;
Such falsë faytours, foul hem fall!

---

117. suche.   118. erthlye.   119. suche shall.   120. y-buylden her
boure.   122. them to hem; *supply* be.   123. holde; one.   124. suche
one shall (*om.* one).   125. peeres.   127. poore freers.   128. Nowe.
129. her.   130. noman; permagall.   131. Whyle; her.   132. suche; mote.
134. glytterande; great araye.   136. commen; maye; gaye.   137. daye.
138. great.   139. baye.   140. suche; mote.   141. punyshed (!);
see l. 143.   142. sustayne.   144. her.   147. leude.   148. Suche;
foule them befall (*see* ll. 156, 164).

With chaunge of many maner metes,
With song and solace sitting long,   150
And filleth hir wombë, and fast fretes,
And from the metë to the gong;
And after mete with harp and song,
And ech man mot hem lordes call;
And hotë spyces ever among;   155
Such falsë faytours, foul hem fall!

And myters mo than oon or two,
I-perled as the quenes heed;
A staf of golde, and †perrey, lo!
As hevy as it were mad of leed;   160
With cloth of gold both newe and reed,
With glitterand †gown as grene as gall,
By dome will dampnë men to deed;
All suche faytours, foul hem fall!

And Christes people proudly curse   165
With brode bokes, and braying bell;
To putte pennyes in hir purse
They woll sell both heven and hell;
And in hir sentence, and thou wilt dwell,
They willen gesse in hir gay hall;   170
And though the soth thou of hem tell,
In greet cursinge shalt thou fall.

That is blessed, that they blesse,
And cursed, that they cursë woll;
And thus the people they oppresse,   175
And have their lordshippes at full;
And many be marchauntes of woll,
And to purse penyes woll come thrall;
The porë people they all to-pull,
Such falsë faytours, foul hem fall!   180

---

149. meates.   150. songe; syttynge longe.   151. her.   152. meate;
gonge.   153. meate; harpe; songe.   154. eche; mote.   155. amonge.
156. Suche; foule.   157. one.   159. staffe; pyrrey; *read* perrey.
160. made; lead.   161. golde; redde.   162. glytterande; golde (*repeated
from* l. 161; *read* gown).   164. foule.   167. her.   168. hel.   169. her.
170. her gaye.   172. great.   179. poore.   180. Suche; foule.

Lordes motë to hem loute,
Obeysaunt to hir brode blessing;
They ryden with hir royall route
On a courser, as it were a king;
With saddle of golde glitt[e]ring   185
With curious harneys quayntly crallit,
Styroppes gaye of gold-mastling;
All suche falshed, foul befall it!

Christes ministers †cleped they been,
And rulen all in robberye;   190
But Antichrist they serven clene,
Attyred all in tyrannye;
Witnesse of Johns prophecye,
That Antichrist is hir admirall,
Tiffelers attyred in trecherye;   195
All suche faytours, foul hem fall!

Who sayth, that some of hem may sinne,
He shal be †demed to be deed;
Some of hem woll gladly winne
All ayenst that which god forbed;   200
"All-holyest" they clepen hir heed,
That of hir rulë is regall;
Alas! that ever they eten breed;
For all such falshed woll foul fall.

Hir heed loveth all honour,   205
And to be worshipped in worde and dede;
Kinges mot to hem knele and coure;
To the apostles, that Christ forbede;
To popes hestes such taketh more hede
Than to kepe Christes commaundëment;   210
Of gold and silver mot ben hir wede,
They holdeth him hole omnipotent.

182, 3. her.   184. kynge.   185. glyttryng (1550, glytteryng).
187. golde.   188. foule.   189. clepen (!); bene.   194. Antichriste; her.
196. foule.   198. done (*but* 1550, dome; *read* demed).   200. whiche.
201, 202. her.   204. suche; foule.   205. Her.   207. mote.   208.
forbede (=forbēd).   209. suche.   211. mote; her.

He ordayneth by his ordinaunce
To parish-preestes a powére;
To another a greter avaunce,   215
A greter poynt to his mystere;
But for he is hyghest in erth here,
To him reserveth he many a poynt;
But to Christ, that hath no pere,
Reserveth he neither opin ne joynt.   220

So semeth he above[n] all,
And Christ aboven him nothing;
Whan he sitteth in his stall,
Dampneth and saveth as him think.
Such pryde tofore god doth stink;   225
An angell bad John to him nat knele,
But only to god do his bowing;
Such willers of worship must evil fele.

They ne clepen Christ but *sanctus deus*,
And clepen her heed *Sanctissimus;*   230
They that such a sect[ë] sewis,
I trowe, they taken hem amisse.
In erth[ë] here they have hir blisse,
Hir hye master is Belial;
†Christ his people from hem wisse!   235
For all such falsë will foul fall!

They mowë both[ë] binde and lose,
And all is for hir holy lyf;
To save or dampne they mowë chose,
Betwene hem now [ther] is gret stryf.   240
Many a man is killed with knyf,
To wete which of hem have lordship shall;
For such, Christ suffred woundes fyve;
For all such falshed will foul fall.

215, 216. greater.   224. thynke.   225. Suche; stynke.   227. bowynge.
228. must nede euyll; *I omit* nede.   231. suche; sect sewys.   233. her.
234. Her.   235. Chrystes (!); *read* Christ his.   236. suche; foule.
238. her; lyfe.   240. *Supply* ther; great stryfe.   241. a knyfe (*om.* a).
243. suche.   244. suche; foule.

Christ sayd : *Qui gladio percutit*   245
With swerdë shall [he surely] dye ;
He bad his preestes pees and grith,
And bad hem not drede for to dye ;
And bad them be both simple and slye,
And carkë not for no cattall,   250
And †truste on god that sitteth on hye ;
For all [such] falsë shull foul fall.

These wollen makë men to swere
Ayenst Christes commaundëment ;
And Christes membres all to-tere   255
On rode as he wer newe y-rent.
Suche lawes they make by commun assent,
Ech on it choweth as a ball ;
Thus the pore be fully shent,
But ever falshed foule it †fall !   260

They usen [never] no symonye,
But sellen churches and prioryes ;
Ne [yet] they usen no envye,
But cursen all hem contraryes ;
And hyreth men by dayes and yeres   265
With strength to holde hem in hir stall ;
And culleth all hir adversaryes ;
Therefor, falshed ! foul thou fall !

With purse they purchase personage,
With purse they paynen hem to plede ;   270
And men of warrë they woll wage,
To bringe hir enemyes to the dede.
And lordes lyves they woll lede,
And moche take, and give but small ;
But he it so get, from it shall shede,   275
And make such falsë right foul fal !

---

246. *Supply* he surely.   247. peace.   248. bade.   251. trusteth (!).
252. *Supply* such; foule.   256. roode.   257. co*m*men.   258. Echeon.
259. poore.   260. befall ; *read* fall.   261. *Supply* never.   263. *Supply* yet.
266. her.   267. her.   268. foule; falle.   272. her.   276. suche; foule.

They halowe nothing but for hyre,
Churchë, font, ne vestëment;
And make[n] orders in every shyre,
But preestes paye for the parchement;   280
Of ryatours they taken rent,
Therwith they smere the shepes skall;
For many churches ben oft suspent;
All such falshed, yet foul it fall!

Some liveth nat in lecherye,   285
But haunten wenches, widdowes, and wyves,
And punisheth the pore for putrye;
Them-selfe it useth all their lyves.
And but a man to them [him] shryves,
To heven comë never he shall;   290
He shal be cursed as be captyves,
To hell they sayn that he shall fall.

There was more mercy in Maximien,
And in Nero, that never was good,
Than [there] is now in some of them   295
Whan he hath on his furred hood.
They folowe Christ that shedde his blood
To heven, as bucket in-to the wall;
Suche wreches ben worse than wood;
And all such faytours, foule hem fall!   300

They give hir almesse to the riche,
To maynteynours, and to men of lawe;
For to lordes they woll be liche,
An harlottes sone nat worth an hawe!
Sothfastnessë suche han slawe,   305
They kembe hir crokets with cristall;
And drede of god they have down drawe;
All suche faytours, foul hem fall!

---

282. shyppes (!); 1550, shepes.   283. ofte.   284. suche; foule.
287. poore.   289. *Supply* him.   292. sayne.   295. *Supply* there;
nowe; them.   296. hoode.   297. blode.   298. buckette; (wall = well).
299. wode.   300. suche.   301. her.   302. *Omit* to ?   304. sonne;
worthe.   306. her crokettes; christall.   307. downe.   308. foule.

They maken parsons for the penny,
And canons of hir cardinals;   310
Unnethes amongest hem all any
That he ne hath glosed the gospell fals!
For Christ made never no cathedrals,
Ne with him was no cardinall
Wyth a reed hatte as usen mynstrals;   315
But falshed, foul mote it befall!

†Hir tything, and hir offring both,
They cle[y]meth it by possessio[u]n;
Thérof nill they none forgo,
But robben men as [by] raunsoun.   320
The tything of *Turpe lucrum*
With these maisters is meynall;
Tything of bribry and larson
Will makë falshed full foul fall!

They taken to fermë hir sompnours   325
To harme the people what they may;
To pardoners and false faytours
Sell hir seles, I dar well say;
And all to holden greet array,
To multiply hem more metall,   330
They drede full litell domes day
Whan all such [falsë] shall foul fall.

Suche harlottes shull men disclaunder
For they shullen make hir gree,
And ben as proude as Alexaunder,   335
And sayn to the pore, "wo be ye!"
By yere ech preest shall paye his fee
To encrese his lemmans call;
Suche herdes shull well yvell thee,
And all such falsë shull foul fall!   340

---

310. her.   315. Redde; vsyn.   316. falsshed foule.   317. Their
(*read* Hir); her.   318. clemeth; *see* l. 525.   320. *Supply* by;
raunsome.   324, 332, 340. foule.   324. to fall (*omit* to).   325. her.
328. her seales; dare.   329. great.   332. suche; *supply* false.
334. her.   336. sayne; poore.   337. eche preeste.   338. encrease.
339. heerdes; the.   340. suche.

And if a man be falsly famed,
And woldë make purgacioun,
Than woll the officers be agramed,
And assigne him fro town to town;
So nede he must[e] paye raunsoun   345
Though he be clene as is cristall,
And than have an absolutioun;
But all such falsë shull foul fall!

Though he be gilty of the dede,
And that he [yet] may money pay,   350
All the whyle his purse woll blede
He may use it fro day to day!
These bishoppes officers goon full gay,
And this game they usen over-all;
The pore to pill is all †thir pray;   355
All such falsë shull foul fall!

Alas! god ordayned never such lawe,
Ne no such craft of covetyse;
He forbad it, by his sawe,
Such governours mowen of god agryse;   360
For all his rules †ben rightwyse.
These newe poyntes ben pure papall,
And goddes lawë they dispyse;
And all such faytours shul foul fall!

They sayn that Peter had the key   365
Of hevin and hell, to have and hold;
I trowe Peter took no money
For no sinnes that he sold!
Such successours ben to bold,
In winning all their wit they wrall;   370
Hir conscience is waxen cold;
And all such faytours, foule hem fall!

---

341. falsely.   344. towne (*twice*).   345. raunsome.   346. christall.
348. suche.   348, 356, 364. foule.   349. gyltie.   350. *Supply* yet; maye.
352. maye.   353. gone.   355. poore; theyr (*read* hir).   356. suche.
357. suche.   358. suche crafte.   359. forbade.   360. Suche.
361. is (*read* ben).   363. dispyce.   364. suche.   365. sayne.
366. heuyn; holde.   367. toke.   368. solde.   369. Suche; bolde.
370. wytte.   371. colde.   372. suche.

Peter was never so great a fole
To leve his key with such a lorell,
Or to take such cursed such a tole   375
He was advysed nothing well.
I trowe, they have the key of hell;
†Hir maister is of that place marshall;
For there they dressen hem to dwell,
And with fals Lucifer there to fall.   380

They ben as proude as Lucifer,
As angry, and as envious;
From good fayth they ben full fer,
In covetyse they ben curious;
To catche catell as covytous   385
As hound, that for hunger woll yall;
Ungoodly, and ungracious;
And nedely, such falshed shal foul fall!

The pope, and he were Peters heyr,
Me think, he erreth in this cas,   390
Whan choyse of bishoppes is in dispeyr,
To chosen hem in dyvers place;
A lord shall write to him for grace,
For his clerke †pray anon he shall;
So shall he spede[n] his purchas;   395
And all such falsë, foule hem fall!

Though he †conne no more good,
A lordes prayer shal be sped;
Though he be wild of will or wood,
Nat understanding what men han red,   400
A boster, and (that god forbede!)
As good a bishop †as my hors Ball,
Suche a pope is foule be-sted,
And at [the] lastë woll foul fall!

---

374. leaue.   375. suche (*twice*).   378. Theyr (*for* Hir).
380. false Lucifere.   381. Lucifarie.   383. faythe; farre.
386. hounde; hungre.   387. vngratious.   388. suche.   388, 396,
404. foule.   389. heyre.   390. thynke; case.   391. dispeyre.
393. lorde.   394. anone pray.   395. purchase.   396. suche.
397. can (*read* conne).   398. spedde.   399. wylde.   400. redde.
401. leude boster (*om.* leude).   402. byshoppe; is (*read* as); borse.
403. be stedde.   404. *Supply* the; last.

He maketh bishops for erthly thank,   405
And nothing for Christes sake;
Such that ben ful fatte and rank,
To soulë hele non hede they take.
Al is well don what ever they make,
For they shal answere at †ones for all;   410
For worldes thank, such worch and wake,
And all such falsë shall foul fall!

Suche that †connë nat hir Crede
With prayer shull be mad prelates;
Nother †conne the gospell rede,   415
Such shull now welde hye estates.
The hye goodes frendship hem makes,
They toteth on hir somme totall;
Such bere the keyes of hell-yates,
And all such falsë shall foul fall.   420

They forsake, for Christes love,
Traveyl, hunger, thurst, and cold;
For they ben ordred ever all above
Out of youthe til they ben old.
By the dore they go nat in-to the fold,   425
To helpe †thir sheep they nought travall;
Hyred men all suche I holde,
And all such falsë, foule hem fall!

For Christ hir king they woll forsake,
And knowe him nought for his povert;   430
For Christes lovë they woll wake,
And drink pyment [and] ale apart.
Of god they seme nothing a-ferd;
As lusty liveth, as Lamuall,
And dryve hir sheep into desert;   435
All such faytours shull foul fall!

---

405. byshoppes.   407. Suche; ranke.   408. heale none.   409. done.
410. one fors (!); *misprint.*   411. thanke suche.   412. suche.
412, 420, 436. foule.   413. canne; *read* conne; her.   414. made.
415. canne.   416. Suche; nowe.   418. her.   419. Suche.
420. suche.   422. Traueyle hungre; colde.   424. olde.   425. folde.
426. theyr (*for* hir); shepe.   428. suche.   429. her.   430. pouerte.
432. drynke; pyément; *supply* and; aparte.   433. a ferde.   434. as dyd
(*om.* dyd).   435. dryuen her shepe; deserte.   436. suche.

Christ hath twelve apostels here ;
Now say they, ther may be but oon,
That may nat erre in no manere ;
Who leveth nat this, ben lost echoon!   440
Peter erred, so dide nat John ;
Why is he cleped the principall?
Christ cleped him Peter, but himself the stoon ;
All falsë faytours, foule hem fall !

Why cursen they the croysery,   445
Christes Christen crëatures?
For bytwene hem is now envy
To be enhaunsed in honours.
And Christen livers, with hir labours,
For they leve on no man mortall,   450
†Ben do to dethe with dishonours ;
And all such falsë, foule hem fall !

What knoweth a tillour at the plow
The popes name, and what he hat?
His crede suffyseth him y-now,   455
And knoweth a cardinall by his hat.
Rough is the pore, unrightly lat,
That knoweth Christ his god royall ;
Such maters be nat worth a gnat ;
But such false faytours, foule hem fall !   460

A king shall knele and kisse his sho ;
Christ suffred a sinfull kisse his feet.
Me thinketh, he holdeth him hye y-now,
So Lucifer did, that hye †seet.
Such oon, me thinketh, him-self foryet,   465
Either to the trouth he was nat call ;
Christ, that suffred woundes wet,
Shall makë such falshed foul fall !

---

437. xij.   438. Nowe; there; one.   440. echone.   443. stone.
447. nowe.   449. her.   450. leuyn.   451. But (*read* Ben).
452. suche.   453. plowe.   454. hate (!).   455. to hym (*om.* to) ;
ynowe.   456. hatte.   457. poore ; latte.   459. Suche ; gnatte.
460. suche.   461. showe.   462. to kysse (*om.* to) ; fete.   463. ynowe.
464. sette ; *read* seet (=sat).   465. Suche one ; hym selfe foryete.
466. *For* call *read* tall (?) ; *cf. l.* 74.   467. wete.   468. suche ; foule.
      * * * *
* * * *   M

They layeth out hir largë nettes
For to take silver and gold,   470
Fillen coffers, and sackes fettes,
There-as they soules cacche shold.
Hir servaunts be to them unhold,
But they can doublin thir rentall
To bigge hem castels, and bigge hem hold;   475
And all such falsë, foule hem fall!

Here endeth the first part of this tale, and herafter
foloweth the seconde part.

PART II.

To accorde with this wordë "fal"
     No more English can I find;
Shewe another now I shall,
For I have moche to say behind,   480
How preestes han the people pynd,
As curteys Christ hath me [y-]kend,
And put this matter in my mind
To make this maner men amend.

Shortly to shende hem, and shewe now   485
How wrongfully they worche and walke;
O hye god, nothing they tell, ne how,
But in goddes word, ttell many a balke.
In hernes holde hem and in halke,
And prechin of tythes and offrend,   490
And untruely of the gospell talke;
For his mercy, god it amend!

---

469. her.   470. golde.   472. catche sholde.   473. Her seruauntes;
them (*read* hem); vnholde.   474. theyr (*for* hir).   475. holde.
476. suche.   478. fynde.   479. nowe.   480. saye behynde.
481. Howe; pynde.   482. kende; *see* l. 530.   483. putte; mynde.
484. amende.   485. nowe.   486. Howe.   487. howe.   488. worde;
telleth (*see* l. 487).   490. offrende.   492. amende.

What is Antichrist to say
But evin Christes adversáry?
Such hath now ben many a day   495
To Christes bidding full contráry,
That from the trouthë clenë vary;
Out of the wayë they ben wend;
And Christes people untruely cary;
God, for his pitè, it amend!   500

That liven contráry to Christes lyf,
In hye pride agaynst mekenesse;
Agaynst suffraunce they usen stryf,
And angre ayenst sobrenesse;
Agaynst wisdom, wilfulnesse;   505
To Christes tales litell tend;
Agaynst mesúre, outragiousnesse;
But whan god woll, it may amend!

Lordly lyf ayenst lowlinesse,
And demin all without mercy;   510
And covetyse ayenst largesse,
Agaynst trewth[e], trechery;
And agaynst almesse, envy;
Agaynst Christ they comprehend.
For chastitè, they maynteyn lechery; 515
God, for his gracë, this amend!

Ayenst penaunce they use delytes,
Ayenst suffraunce, strong defence;
Ayenst god they use yvel rightes,
Agaynst pitè, punishments;   520
Open yvell ayenst continence;
Hir wicked winning wors dispend;
Sobrenesse they sette in-to dispence;
But god, for his goodnesse, it amend!

---

493. saye.   495. Suche hathe nowe.   497. varry.   498. wende.
500. pytie; amende.   501. lyfe.   503. sufferaunce; stryfe.   505. wyse-
dome.   5c6. tende.   507. measure.   508. maye amende.   509. lyfe.
514. comprehende.   515. maynteyne.   516. amende.   517. delyghtes.
518. stronge.   519. vsen.   520. Agaynste pytie punishementes.
522. Her; worse dispende.   524. amende.

M 2

Why cleymen they hoolly his powére,   525
And wranglen ayenst all his hestes?
His living folowen they nothing here,
But liven wors than witles beestes.
Of fish and flesh they loven feestes,
As lordes, they ben brode y-kend;   530
Of goddes pore they haten gestes;
God, for his mercy, this amend!

With †Dives such shall have hir doom
That sayn that they be Christes frendes,
And do nothing as they shuld doon;   535
All such ben falser than ben fendes.
On the people they ley such bendes,
As god is in erthe, they han offend;
Sucour for suchë Christ now sende us,
And, for his mercy, this amend!   540

A token of Antichrist they be.
His careckes ben now wyde y-know;
Receyved to preche shall no man be
Without[ë] token of him, I trow.
Ech Christen preest to prechen ow,   545
From god abovë they ben send.
Goddes word to all folk for to show,
Sinfull man for to amend.

Christ sente the pore for to preche;
The royall riche he did nat so;   550
Now dar no pore the people teche,
For Antichrist is over-all hir fo.
Among the people he mot go;
He hath bidden, all such suspend;
Some hath he hent, and thinketh yet mo;   555
But all this god may well amend

---

525. holy.   528. worse; wytlesse.   529. fyshe; fleshe.   530. ykende.
531. poore.   532. amende.   533. Dyuers (*read* Dives); suche; her dome.
534. sayne.   535. shulde done.   536. suche.   537. suche.   538. offende.   539. nowe.   540. amende.   542. nowe; yknowe.   544. trowe.
545. Eche; owe (!).   546. sende.   547. worde; folke; showe.
548. amende.   549. poore.   551. Nowe dare; poore.   552. her foe.
553. Amonge; mote.   554. suche suspende.   555. hente.   556. amende.

All tho that han the world forsake,
And liven lo[w]ly, as god bad,
In-to hir prison shullen be take,
Betin and bounden, and forth lad.   560
Herof I rede no man be drad;
Christ sayd, his [servaunts] shulde be shend;
Ech man ought herof be glad;
For god ful well it woll amend.

They take on hem royáll powére,   565
And saye, they havë swerdes two,
Oon curse to hell, oon slee men here;
For at his taking Christ had no mo,
Yet Peter had [that] oon of tho.
But Christ to Peter. smyte gan defend,   570
And in-to the sheth bad putte it tho;
And all such mischeves god amend!

Christ bad Peter kepe his sheep,
And with his swerde forbad him smyte;
Swerd is no tole with sheep to kepe   575
But to shep[h]erdes that sheep woll byte.
Me thinketh, suche shep[h]erdes ben to wyte
Ayen hir sheep with swerd that contend;
They dryve hir sheep with greet dispyte;
But al this god may well amend.   580

So successours to Peter be they nought
Whom [that] Christ madë cheef pastour;
A swerd no shep[h]erde usen ought
But he wold slee as a bochour.
For who-so were Peters successour   585
Shuld bere his sheep till his bak bend,
And shadowe hem from every shour;
And all this god may wel amend.

---

557. worlde.   558. loly; badde.   559. her.   560. forthe ladde.
561. dradde.   562. *Supply* servaunts; shende.   563. Eche; gladde.
564, 572, 580, 588. amende.   567. One; one.   569. *Supply* that; one.
570. defende.   571. badde.   572. suche.   573. badde; shepe.
574. forbade.   575. Swerde; shepe.   576. shepe.   578. her shepe; swerde;
contende.   579. her shepe; great.   582. *Supply* that; chefe pastoure.
583. swerde.   584. bochoure.   586. Shulde; shepe; backe bende.
587. shoure.

Successours to Peter ben these
In that that Peter Christ forsook,   590
That had lever the love of god [to] lese
Than a shep[h]erde had to lese his hook.
He culleth the sheep as doth the cook;
Of hem [they] taken the woll untrend,
And falsely glose the gospell-book;   595
God, for his mercy, †them amend!

After Christ had take Peter the kay,
Christ sayd, he mustë dye for man;
That Peter to Christ gan withsay;
Christ bad him, 'go behind, Sathan!'   600
Such counsaylours many of these men han
For worldes wele, god to offend;
Peters successours they ben for-than,
But all such god may well amend.

For Sathan is to say no more   605
But he that contrary to Christ is;
In this they lernë Peters lore,
They sewen him whan he did mis;
They folowe Peter forsothe in this,
In al that Christ wolde †him reprende,   610
Nat in that that longeth to hevin blis;
God for his mercy hem amend!

Some of the apostels they sewen in cas,
Of ought that I can understonde,
Him that betrayed Christ, Judas,   615
That bar the purse in every londe;
And al that he might sette on honde,
He hidde and stal, and [gan] mispend;
His rule these traytours han in honde;
Almighty god [now] hem amend!   620

---

590. forsoke.   591. *Supply* to (*as in* l. 592).   592. hoke.   593. shepe;
dothe; coke.   594. *Supply* they; vntrende.   595. -boke.   596. them
amende.   600. badde; behynde.   601. Suche.   602. offende.
604. suche; amende.   606. *Read* contrar.   608. mysse.   610. Peter
(*read* him); reprehende.   611. But nat (*om.* But); heuyn blysse.   612.
amende.   613. case.   616. bare.   618. stale; *supply* gan; myspende.
620. *Supply* now; amende.

And at last his lord gan tray
Cursedly, through his covetyse;
So wolde these trayen him for money,
And they wisten in what wyse!
They be seker of the selfe ensyse;   625
From all sothnesse they ben frend;
And covetyse chaungen with queyntyse;
Almighty god all suche amend!

Were Christ on erthë here eft-soon,
These wolde dampnë him to dye;   630
All his hestes they han fordon,
And sayn, his sawes ben heresy;
Ayenst his †maundëments they cry,
And dampne all his to be [y-]brend;
For it lyketh nat hem, such losengery;   635
God almighty hem amend!

These han more might in England here
Than hath the king and all his lawe,
They han purchased hem such powére
To taken hem whom [they] list nat knawe;   640
And say, that heresy is hir sawe,
And so to prison woll hem send;
It was nat so by elder dawe,
God, for his mercy, it amend!

The kinges lawe wol no man deme   645
Angerliche, withouten answere;
But, if any man these misqueme,
He shal be baited as a bere;
And yet wel wors they woll him tere,
And in prisón woll hem [be] pend   650
In gyves, and in other gere;
Whan god woll, it may [a]mend.

---

622. hys false (*om.* false). 626. frende = fremd. 628. amende. 629. efte
sone.   631. fordone.   632. sayne.   633. And ayenst (*omit* And); commaundementes (*read* maundements); crye.   634. brende.   635. suche.
636. amende.   637. Englande.   638. kynge.   639. suche.   640. *Supply*
they (*or* hem); lyste.   641. her.   642. prysone; sende.   644. amende.
648. bayghted.   649. worse.   650. prysone; *supply* be; pende.
652. maye mende.

The king taxeth nat his men
But by assent of the comminaltè;
But these, ech yere, woll raunsom hem   655
Maysterfully, more than dóth he;
Hir seles, by yerë, better be
Than is the kinges in extend;
Hir officers han gretter fee;
But this mischeef [may] god amend!   660

For who-so woll prove a testament
Thát is natt all worth ten pound,
He shall paye for the parchëment
The third part of the money all round.
Thus the people is raunsound,   665
They say, such part to hem shulde apend;
There as they grypen, it goth to ground;
God, for his mercy, it amend!

A simple fornicacioun,
Twenty shillings he shall pay;   670
And than have an absolucioun,
And al the yere usen it forth he may!
Thus they letten hem go a-stray,
They recke nat though the soul be brend;
These kepin yvell Peters key,   675
And all such shep[h]erdes god amend!

Wonder is, that the parliament
And all the lordes of this lond
Here-to taken so litell entent
To helpe the people out of hir hond;   680
For they ben harder in †hir bond,
Wors bete[n] and [more] bitter brend
Than to the king is understond;
God him helpe this to amend!

---

654. assente.   655. eche.   657. Her seales.   658. extende.   660. mischefe; *supply* may; amende.   662. worthe tenne pounde.   664. thyrde
parte; rounde.   665. raunsounde.   666. saye suche parte; apende.   667.
gothe; grounde.   668. amende.   669. fornycatioun.   670. shyllynges;
paye.   671. absolution.   672. forthe; maye.   674. soule; brende.
676. suche; amende.   678. londe.   680. her honde.   681. theyr (*for*
hir); bonde.   682. Worse beate; *supply* more; brende.   683. vnderstande.
684. amende.

What bisshoppes, what religio[u]ns   685
Han in this lande as moch lay-fee,
Lordshippes, and possessio[u]ns
More than the lordes, it semeth me!
That maketh hem lese charitè,
They mowë nat to god attend;   690
In erthe they have so high degree,
God, for his mercy, it amend!

The emperour yaf the pope somtyme
So hyghe lordship him about,
That, at [the] laste, the sely kyme,   695
The proudë popë putte him out!
So of this realme is in dout,
But lordes be ware and †them defend;
For now these 'folk be wonder stout,
The king and lordes now this amend!   700

Thus endeth the seconde part of this tale, and herafter
foloweth the thirde.

PART III.

M OYSES lawe forbood it tho,
        That preestes shuld no lordshippes welde,
Christes gospel biddeth also
Thát they shuld no lordship helde;
Ne Christes apostels were never so bold   705
No such lordshippes to †them enbrace;
But smeren hir sheep and kepe hir fold;
God amende hem for his grace!

685. *Read* religiouns.   686. moche laye.   690. attende.   691. hyghe.
692. amende.   694. aboute.   695. *Supply* the.   697. doute.   698. them
defende.   699. nowe; folke; stoute.   700. kynge; nowe; amende.
701. forbode.   702. shulde.   704. shulde; lordshyppe.   705. bolde.
706. suche lordeshyppes; them (*for* hem).   707. her shepe; her folde.

For they ne ben but countrefet,
Men may knowe hem by hir fruit;   710
Hir gretnesse maketh hem god foryet,
And take his mekenesse in dispyt.
And they were pore and had but lyte,
They nolde nat demen after the face,
But norishe hir sheep, and hem nat byte;   715
God amende hem for his grace!"

Grifon.

"What canst thou preche ayenst chanons
Thát men clepen seculere?"
  Pelican. "They ben curates of many towns,
On erthë they have greet powére.   720
They han greet prebendes and dere,
Some two or three, and some [han] mo,
A personage to ben a playing-fere,
And yet they serve the king also;

And let to fermë all that fare   725
To whom that woll most give therfore;
Some woll spende, and some woll spare,
And some woll laye it up in store.
A cure of soule[s] they care nat for,
Só they mowë money take;   730
Whether hir soules be wonne or lore,
Hir profits they woll nat forsake.

They have a gedering procuratour
That can the pore people enplede,
And robben hem as a ravinour,   735
And to his lord the money lede;
And cacche of quicke and eke of dede,
And richen him and his lord eke,
And to robbe the pore can give good rede
Of olde and yonge, of hole and seke.   740

---

709. countrefete.   710. her fruite.   711. Her; foryete.   712. dispyte.
713. poore.   715. her shepe.   720-1. great.   722. thre; *supply* han.
723. playeng.   724. kynge.   725. lette.   729. soule; fore.   731. her.
732. Her profytes.   734. poore.   736. lorde.   737. catche.   738. lorde.
739. poore.   740. syke (*for* seke); *see l.* 1313.

Therwith they purchase hem lay-fee
In londë, there hem lyketh best,
And builde †als brode as a citè
Both in the est, and eke in the west.
To purchase thus they ben ful prest;   745
But on the pore they woll nought spend,
Ne no good give to goddes gest,
Ne sende him some that all hath send.

By hir service such woll live,
And trussè that other in-to tresour;   750
Though all hir parish dye unshrive,
They woll nat give a rosë-flour.
Hir lyf shuld be as a mirrour
Bothe to lered and to leude also,
And teche the people hir leel labour;   755
Such mister men ben all misgo.

Some of hem ben hardë nigges,
And some of hem ben proude and gay;
Some spende hir good upon [hir] gigges,
And finden hem of greet aray.   760
Alas! what think these men to say
That thus dispenden goddis good?
At the dredfull domes day
Such wrecches shul be worse than wood.

Some hir churc[h]es never ne sye,   765
Ne never o peny thider ne sende;
Though the pore parishens for hunger dye,
O peny on hem wil they nat spende.
Have they receivinge of the rent,
They reck never of the remënant;   770
Alas! the devill hath clene hem blent!
Suche oon is Sathanas sojournant.

---

743. also (*read* als).   746. poore; spende.   748. sende.   749. her; suche.
750. treasour.   751. her paryshe.   752. -floure.   753. Her lyfe shulde.
755. her lele.   756. Suche.   759. her; *supply* hir.   760. great.
761. thynke.   763. dredfull.   764. Suche wretches.   765. her.
767. poore; hungre.   769. rente.   770. recke.   772. one.

And usen horedom and harlotry,
Covetysë, pompe, and pride,
Slouthë, wrathe, and eke envy,   775
And sewen sinne by every syde.
Alas! where thinkë such t'abyde?
How woll they accomptes yeld?
From hy god they mow hem nat hyde,
Such willers wit is nat worth a neld.   780

They ben so roted in richesse,
That Christes povert is foryete,
Served with so many messe,
Hem thinketh that manna is no mete.
All is good that they mow get,   785
They wenë to live evermore;
But, whan god at dome is set,
Such tresour is a feble store.

Unneth mot they matins say,
For counting and for court-holding;   790
And yet he jangleth as a jay,
And understont him-self nothing.
He woll serve bothe erl and king
For his fynding and his fee,
And hyde his tything and his offring;   795
This is a feble charitè.

Other they ben proude, or coveytous,
Or they ben harde, or [els] hungry,
Or they ben liberall or lecherous,
Or els medlers with marchandry;   800
Or maynteyners of men with maistry,
Or stewardes, countours, or pledours,
And serve god in hypocrisy;
Such preestes ben Christes fals traytours!

---

773. horedome.   777. suche tabyde.   778. Howe; yelde.   779. hye; mowe.
780. Suche; wytte; nelde.   782. foryet.   785. mowe gete.   787. sette.
788. Suche treasour.   789. mote; saye.   790. holdynge.   791. iaye.
792. selfe nothynge.   793. erle; kynge.   795. tythynge; offrynge.
798. *Supply* els.   804. false.

They ben false, they ben vengeable,　　805
And begylen men in Christes name;
They ben unstedfast and unstable;
To tray hir lord, hem thinketh no shame.
To servë god they ben full lame,
Goddes theves, and falsly stele;　　810
And falsly goddes word defame;
In winning is hir worldes wele.

Antichrist these serven all;
I pray thee, who may say [me] nay?
With Antichrist such [folk] shull fall,　　815
They folowen him in dede and fay;
They servin him in riche array,
To servë Christ such falsly fayn;
Why, at the dredful domes day,
Shull they not folowe him to payn?　　820

That knowen hem-self, that they don ill
Ayenst Christes commaundëment,
And amende hem never ne will,
But serve Sathan by one assent.
Who sayth [the] sothe, he shal be shent,　　825
Or speketh ayenst hir fals living;
Who-so well liveth shal be brent,
For such ben gretter than the king!

Pope, bishoppes, and cardinals,
Chanons, persons, and vicaire,　　830
In goddes service, I trow, ben fals,
That sacramentës sellen here.
And ben as proude as Lucifere;
Ech man loke whether that I ly!
Who-so speketh ayenst hir powére,　　835
It shall be holden heresy.

---

808. her lorde.　811. falsely; worde.　812. her.　814. the; *supply* me.
815. suche; *supply* folk.　　818. suche falsely fayne.　　819. dredeful.
820. payne.　821. selfe; done.　825. *Supply* the.　　826. her false.
828. suche.　830. *Read* vikere.　831. trowe; false.　834. Eche; lye.
835. *Read* Who speke ayeinës; her.

Loke how many orders take
Only of Christ, for his servyce,
That the worldes goodes forsake?
Who-so taketh orders †on other wyse,   840
I trow, that they shall sore agryse!
For all the glose that they conne,
All sewen not this [same] assyse;
In yvell tyme they thus bigonne.

Loke how many among hem all   845
Holden not this hyë way!
With Antichrist they shullen fall,
For they wolden god betray.
God amende hem, that best may!
For many men they maken shende;   850
They weten well, the sothe I say,
Bút the divell hath foule hem blend.

Some [up]on hir churches dwell,
Apparailled porely, proude of port;
The seven sacraments they don sell,   855
In cattel-cacching is hir comfort.
Of ech mattér they wollen mell,
And don hem wrong is hir disport;
To afray the people they ben fell,
And holde hem lower then doth the lord.   860

For the tythinge of a ducke,
Or of an apple, or an ay,
They make men swere upon a boke;
Thus they foulen Christes fay.
Such beren yvell heven-kay,   865
They mowen assoyl, they mowë shryve;
With mennes wyves strongly play,
With trewë tillers sturte and stryve

---

837. howe.   838. Onely; Christe.   840. or (*read* on).   841. trowe.
843. *Supply* same.   845. howe; amonge.   846. waye.   848. betraye.
849. maye.   851. saye.   852. blende.   853. on (*read* upon); her.
854. poorely; porte.   855. sacramentes; done.   856. catchynge; her
comforte.   857. eche.   858. done; wronge; her dysporte.   859. afraye.
860. lorde.   862. aye.   863. sweare.   865. Suche bearen; heauen.
866. assoyle.   868. true (*better* trewë).

At the wrestling, and at the wake ;
And chefe chauntours at the nale ;   870
Market-beters, and medling make,
Hoppen and houten with heve and hale.
At fayrë freshe, and at wynë stale,
Dyne and drinke, and make debat ;
The seven sacraments set at sale ;   875
How kepe such the kayes of heven-gat ?

Mennes wyves they wollen holde ;
And though that they ben right sory,
To speke they shull not be so bolde
For sompning to the consistory ;   880
And make hem say [with] mouth "I ly,"
Though they it sawë with hir y ;
His lemman holden openly,
No man so hardy to axë why !

He wol have tythinge and offringe,   885
Maugrè who-so-ever it gruche ;
And twyës on the day woll singe ;
Goddes prestes nere none suche !
He mot on hunting with dogge and bic[c]he,
And blowen his horn, and cryën "hey !"   890
And sorcery usen as a wicche ;
Such kepen yvell Peters key.

Yet they mot have som stocke or stoon
Gayly paynted, and proudly dight,
To maken men [to] †leven upon,   895
And say, that it is full of might ;
About such, men sette up greet light,
Other such stockes shull stand therby
As darkë as it were midnight,
For it may makë no ma[i]stry.   900

---

869. wrestlynge.   871. Markette beaters ; medlynge.   874. debate.
875. sacramentes ; sayle (!).   876. Howe ; suche ; gate.   879. speake.
880. sompnynge.   881. saye ; *supply* with ; lye.   882. her eye.   887. twyse ;
daye he (*om.* he).   889. mote.   890. horne.   891. wytche.   892. Suchen.
893. mote ; some ; stone.   †895. *Supply* to ; lyuen.   896. saye.   897.
Aboute suche ; great.   898. suche ; stande.   900. maye.

That lewed people see it mow,
Thou, Mary, worchest wonder thinges;
About that, that men offren to now,
Hongen broches, ouches, and ringes;
The preest purchaseth the offringes,   905
But he nill offre to none image;
Wo is the soule that he for singes,
That precheth for suche a pilgrimage!

To men and women that ben pore,
That ben [in] Christes own lykenesse,   910
Men shullen offre at hir dore
That suffren honger and distresse;
And to suche imáges offre lesse,
That mow not felë thurst ne cold;
The pore in spirit gan Christ blesse,   915
Therfore offreth to feble and old.

Buckelers brode, and swerdes longe,
+Baudriks, with baselardes kene,
Such toles about hir necke they honge;
With Antichrist such preestes been;   920
Upon hir dedes it is well sene
Whom they serven, whom they hono[u]ren;
Antichristes they ben clene,
And goddes goodes fa[l]sly deuouren.

Of scarlet and grene gay[ë] gownes,   925
That mot be shapë for the newe,
To clippen and kissen counten in townes
The damoseles that to the daunce sewe;
Cutted clothes to sewe hir hewe,
With longë pykes on hir shoon;   930
Our goddes gospell is not trewe,
Eyther they serven the divell or noon!

---

901. That it leude people se mowe.   902. Mary thou (*om.* thou).
903. Aboute; nowe.   909. poore.   910. *Supply* in; owne.   911. her.
914. mowe; colde.   915. poore; sprete; Christe.   916. olde.   917.
sweardes.   918. Baudryke (*read* Baudriks).   919. Suche; her.   920.
suche; bene.   921. her.   922. Whome (*twice*).   923. bene.   925. gay.
926. mote.   929. her.   930. her shone.   932. none.

Now ben prestes pokes so wyde,
Men must enlarge the vestëment;
The holy gospell they don hyde,   935
For they contrarien in rayment.
Such preestes of Lucifer ben sent,
Lyk conquerours they ben arayd,
Proude pendaunts at hir ars y-pent,
Falsly the truthe they han betrayd.   940

Shryft-silver suchë wollen aske is,
And woll men crepë to the crouche;
None of the sacraments, save askes,
Without[ë] mede shall no man touche.
On hir bishop their warant vouche,   945
That is lawe of the decrè;
With mede and money thus they mouche,
And † this, they sayn, is charitè!

In the middes of hir masse
They nill have no man but for hyre,   950
And, full shortly, let forth passe;
Such shull men finde[n] in ech shyre
That personages for profite desyre,
To live in lykinge and in lustes;
I dar not sayn, *sans ose ieo dyre*,   955
That such ben Antichristes preestes.

Or they yef the bishops why,
Or they mot ben in his servyce,
And holden forth hir harlotry;
Such prelats ben of feble empryse.   960
Of goddes grame such men agryse,
For such mattérs that taken mede;
How they excuse hem, and in what wyse,
Me thinketh, they ought greetly drede.

---

933. Nowe.   934. That men (*om.* That).   935. done.   937. Suche.
938. Lyke.   arayde.   939. The proude (*om.* The); pendauntes; her.
940. Falsely; betrayde.   941. Shryfte-.   943. sacramentes.   945. her
byshoppe.   948. thus (*read* this); sayne.   949. her.   952. Suche;
eche.   953. profyte.   955. dare; sayne.   956. suche.   957. byshoppes.
958. mote.   959. her.   960. Suche prelates.   961 suche.   962. suche.
963. Howe.   964. greatly.

They sayn, that it to no man longeth   965
To reprove † hem, though they erre;
But falsely goddes good they fongeth,
And therwith maynteyn wo and werre.
Hir dedes shuld be as bright as sterre,
Hir living, lewed mannes light;   970
They say, the popë may not erre,
Nede must that passë mannes might.

Though a prest ly with his lemman al night,
And tellen his felowe, and he him,
He goth to massë anon-right,   975
And sayeth, he singeth out· of sinne!
His bryde abydeth him at his inne,
And dighteth his dyner the mene whyle;
He singeth his masse for he wolde winne,
And so he weneth god begyle!   980

Hem thinketh long till they be met;
And that they usen forth all the yere;
Among the folk when he is set,
He holdeth no man half his pere;
Of the bishop he hath powére   985
To soyle men, or els they ben lore;
His absolucion may make † hem skere;
And wo is the soul that he singeth for!"

The Griffon began for to threte,
And sayd, "of monkes canst thou ought?"   990
    The Pellican sayd, "they ben full grete,
And in this world moch wo hath wrought.
Saynt Benet, that hir order brought,
Ne made hem never on such manere;
I trowe, it cam never in his thought   995
That they shulde use so greet powér[e];

---

965. sayne.   966. them (*for* hem).   967. goddes goodesse (!).
968. maynteyne.   969. Her; shulde.   970. Her lyuynge leude.
971. saye; maye.   972. muste.   973. lye.   975. anone.   978. meane.
981. longe; mette.   983. Amonge; folke; sette.   984. halfe.
985. byshoppe.   987. absolution maye; them (*for* hem).   988. soule;
fore.   993. her.   994. suche.   995. came.   996. great.

That a man shulde a monk lord cal,
Ne serve on kneës, as a king.
He is as proud as prince in pall
In mete, and drink, and [in] all thing;   1000
Some weren myter and ring,
With double worsted well y-dight,
With royall mete and riche drink,
And rydeth on courser as a knight.

With hauke[s] and with houndes eke,   1005
With broches or ouches on his hode,
Some say no masse in all a weke,
Of deyntees is hir moste fode.
With lordshippes and with bondmen
This is a royall religioun;   1010
Saynt Benet made never none of hem
To have lordship of man ne town.

Now they ben queynte and curious,
With fyn cloth cladde, and served clene,
Proude, angry, and envyous,   1015
Malyce is mochë that they mene.
In cacching crafty and covetous,
Lordly liven in greet lyking;
This living is not religious
According to Benet in his living.   1020

They ben clerkes, hir courtes they oversee,
Hir pore tenaunts fully they flyte;
The hyer that a man amerced be,
The gladlyer they woll it wryte.
This is fer from Christes povertè,   1025
For all with covetyse they endyte;
On the pore they have no pitè,
Ne never hem cherish, but ever hem byte.

---

997. monke lorde.   998. kynge.   999. proude.   1000. meate;
drynke; *supply* in.   1001. wearen; rynge.   1003. meate; drynke.
1004. on a (*om.* a).   1007. saye.   1008. deynties; her; foode.   1010. religion.
1012. lordshyppe; towne.   1013. Nowe.   1014. fyne clothe.   1016. meane.
1017. catchynge.   1018. great lykynge.   1019. lyuynge.   1020. Ac-
cordynge; Benette; lyuynge.   1021. her; ouerse.   1022. Her poore
tenaunce.   1023. hyre (1550, hyer).   1025. farre.   1027. poore.
1028. cheryshe.

And comunly suche ben comen
Of pore people, and of hem begete,   1030
That this perfeccion han y-nomen;
Hir †faders ryde not but on hir fete,
And travaylen sore for that they ete,
In povert liveth, yonge and old;
Hir †faders suffreth drought and wete,   1035
Many hongry meles, thurst, and cold.

All this the monkes han forsake
For Christes love and saynt Benet;
To pryde and esë have hem take;
This religio[u]n is yvell beset.   1040
Had they ben out of religioun,
They must have honged at the plow,
Threshing and dyking fro town to town
With sory mete, and not half y-now.

Therfore they han this all forsake,   1045
And taken to riches, pryde, and ese;
Full fewe for god woll monkes hem make,
Litell is suche order for to prayse!
Saynt Benet ordayned it not so,
But bad hem be [ful] cherelich;   1050
In churlich maner live and go,
Boystous in erth, and not lordlych.

They disclaunder saynt Benet,
Therfore they have his holy curse;
Saynt Benet with hem never met   1055
But-if they thought to robbe his purse!
I can no more herof [now] tell,
But they ben lykë tho before,
And clenë serve the divell of hell,
And ben his tresour and his store.   1060

1029. commenly.   1030. poore.   1031. perfection.   1032. Her fathers
ryden; her.   1034. olde.   1035. Her fathers.   1036. colde.   1037. And
all (*om.* And).   1038. Benette.   1039. ease.   1040. besette.   1042. plowe.
1043. Threshynge; dykynge; towne; fowne.   1044. halfe ynowe.
1046. ease.   1050. badde; *supply* ful; cherelyche.   1051. churlyche.
1052. earth.   1053. Benette.   1055. mette.   1057. *Supply* now.
1060. treasoure.

And all suche other counterfaytours,
Chanons, canons, and such disgysed,
Ben goddes enemies and traytours,
His true religion han foul dispysed.
Of freres I have told before   1065
In a making of a 'Crede,'
And yet I coud tell worse and more,
But men wold werien it to rede!

As goddes goodnes no man tell might,
Wryte ne speke, ne think in thought,   1070
So, hir falshed and hir unright
May no man tell, that ever god wrought."
    The Gryffon sayd, "thou canst no good,
Thou cam never of no gentill kind;
Other, I trow, thou waxest wood,   1075
Or els thou hast [y-]lost thy mynd.

Shuld holy churchë have no heed?
Who shuld be her governayl?   ·
Who shuld her rule, who shuld her reed,
Who shuld her forthren, who shuld avayl?   1080
Ech man shall live by his travayl;
Who best doth, shall have moste mede;
With strength if men the churche assayl,
With strength men must defende her nede.

And the pope were purely pore,   1085
Nedy, and nothing ne had,
He shuld be driven from dore to dore;
The wicked of him nold not be drad.
Of such an heed men wold be sad,
And sinfully liven as hem † list;   1090
With strength, amendes † shuld be made,
With wepen, wolves from sheep be † wist.

1062. suche.   1064. foule.   1065. tolde.   1066. makynge.
1067. coulde.   1068. wolde.   1069. goodnesse.   1070. speake; thynke.
1071. her (twice).   1074. came; kynde.   1075. trowe.   1076. loste; mynde.
1077-80. shulde.   1078. gouernayle.   1080. auayle.   1081. Eche;
trauayle.   1083. assayle.   1085. poore.   1086. nothynge; hadde.
1087. shulde.   1088. nolde; dradde.   1089. wolde; sadde.   1090. lust
(read list).   1091. such (read shuld).   1092. shepe; wust (read wist).

If the pope and prelats wold
So begge and bidde, bowe, and borowe,
Holy churche shuld stand full cold,   1095
Hir servaunts sitte and soupë sorowe!
And they were noughty, foule, and horowe,
To worship god men woldë wlate;
Bothe on even and on morowe
Such harlotry men woldë hate.   1100

Therfore men of holy churche
Shuld ben honest in all thing,
Worshipfully goddes workes werche,
So semeth it, to serve Christ hir king
In honest and in clene clothing;   1105
With vessels of golde and clothes riche,
To god honestly to make offring;
To his lordship non is liche."

The Pellican caste an houge cry,
And sayd, " alas! why sayest thou so?   1110
Christ is our heed that sitteth on hy,
Heddes ne ought we have no mo.
We ben his membres both also,
And † fader he taught us to cal him als;
Maysters be called defended he tho;   1115
All other maysters ben wicked and fals,

That taketh maystry in his name,
Gostly, and for erthly good;
Kinges and lordes shuld lordship han,
And rule the people with myldë mode.   1120
Christ, for us that shedde his blood,
Bad his preestes no maystership have,
Ne carkë nat for cloth ne fode;
From every mischef he will hem save.

1093. prelates wolde.   1095. shulde stande; colde.   1096. Her seruauntes.   1098. worshyppe.   1100. Suche.   1102. Shulde; thynge.
1104. her kynge.   1105. clothynge.   1107. offrynge.   1108. lordshypppe (!)
none.   1109. crye.   1111. hye.   1114. father.   1115. to be (om. to).
1116. *Read* wikke?   1118. Gostly; earthly.   1119. shulde; hane.
1121. blode.   1122. Badde.   1124. myschefe.

Hir riche clothing shal be rightwysnesse,   1125
Hir tresour, trewë lyf shal be;
Charitè shal be hir richesse,
Hir lordship shal be unitè;
Hope in god, hir honestè;
Hir vessell, clenë conscience;   1130
Pore in spirit, and humilitè,
Shal be holy churches defence."

"What," sayd the Griffon, "may thee greve
That other folkes faren wele?
What hast thou to donë with hir † leve?   1135
Thy falsheed ech man may fele.
For thou canst no catell gete,
But livest in londe, as a lorell,
With glosing gettest thou thy mete;
So fareth the devell that wonneth in hell.   1140

He wold that ech man ther shuld dwell,
For he liveth in clene envy;
So with the tales that thou doest tell
Thou woldest other people distry,
With your glose, and your heresy,   1145
For ye can live no better lyf,
But clenë in hypocrisy,
And bringest thee in wo and stryf.

And therwith have [ye] not to done,
For ye ne have[n] here no cure;   1150
Ye serve the divell, † not god ne man,
And he shall payë you your hyre.
For ye woll farë well at feestes,
And warm [be] clothed for the colde,
Therfore ye glose goddes hestes,   1155
And begyle the people, yonge and olde.

1125–30. Her.   1125. clothynge.   1126. treasoure; lyfe.   1128. lordshyppe.   1131. Poore; spirite.   1133. the.   1135. haste; lyue (*read*
leve*).   1136. eche.   1139. glosynge.   1141. wolde; eche; there
shulde.   1142. enuye.   1146. lyfe.   1148. the; stryfe.   1149. *Supply*
ye.   1151. neyther (*read* not).   1154. warme; *supply* be.

And all the seven sacraments
Ye speke ayenst, as ye were sly,
Ayenst tythings with your entents,
And on our lordes body falsly ly.   1160
All this ye don to live in ese,
As who sayeth, ther ben non suche;
And sayn, the pope is not worth a pese,
To make the people ayen him gruche.

And this commeth in by fendes,   1165
To bringe the Christen in distaunce;
For they wold that no man were frendes;
Leve thy chattring, with mischaunce!
If thou live well, what wilt thou more?
Let other men live as hem list;   1170
Spende in good, or kepe in store;
Other mennes conscience never thou nist.

Ye han no cure to answere for;
What meddell ye, that han not to don?
Let men live as they han don yore,   1175
For thou shalt answere for no † mon."
   The Pellican sayd, " Sir, nay, [nay],
I dispysed not the pope,
Ne no sacrament, soth to say;
But speke in charitè and good hope.   1180

But I dispyse hir hyë pryde,
Hir richesse, that shuld be pore in spryt;
Hir wickednesse is knowe so wyde,
They servë god in fals habyt;
And turnen mekenesse into pryde,   1185
And lowlinesse into hy degrè,
And goddes wordes turne and hyde;
And that am I moved by charitè

To lettë men to livë so
With all my conning and al my might,   1190
And to warne men of hir wo
And to tell hem trouth and right.
The sacraments be soulë-hele
If they ben used in good use;
Ayenst that speke I never a del,   1195
For then were I nothing wyse.

But they that use hem in mis manére,
Or sette hem up to any sale,
I trow, they shall abye hem dere;
This is my reson, this is my tale.   1200
Who-so taketh hem unrightfulliche
Ayenst the ten commaundëments,
Or by glosë wrechedliche
Selleth any of the sacraments,

I trow, they do the devell homage   1205
In that they weten they do wrong;
And therto, I dar well wage,
They serven Satan for al her song.
To tythen and offren is hoolsom lyf,
So it be don in dew manére;   1210
A man to houselin and to shryve,
Wedding, and all the other in-fere,

So it be nother sold ne bought,
Ne take ne give for covetyse;
And it be so taken, it is nought;   1215
Who selleth hem so, may sore agryse.
On our Lordes body I do not ly,
I say soth, thorow trewë rede,
His flesh and blood, through his mystry,
Is there, in the forme of brede.   1220

1190. connynge.   1191. her.   1193. sacramentes.   1195. speake; dele.
1196. nothynge.   1197. vsen; mysse.   1199. trowe.   1200. reason.
1202. commaundementes.   1204. sacramentes.   1205. trowe.   1206. wronge.
1207. dare.   1208. songe.   1209. holsome lyfe.   1210. done; dewe.
1212. Weddynge.   1213. solde.   1216. maye.   1217. lye.   1218. saye;
thorowe.   1219. fleshe; blode; mystrye.

How it is there, it nedeth not stryve,
Whether it be subget or accident,
But as Christ was, when he was on-lyve,
So is he there, verament.
If pope or cardinall live good lyve,   1225
As Christ commaunded in his gospell,
†Ayenës that woll I not stryve;
But, me thinketh, they live not well.

For if the pope lived as god bede,
Pryde and hyghnesse he shuld dispyse,   1230
Richesse, covetyse, and crowne on hede,
Mekenesse and povert he shulde use."
    The Gryffon sayd, he shulde abye—
"Thou shal[t] be brent in balefull fyre;
And all thy secte I shall distrye,   1235
Ye shal be hanged by the swyre!

Ye shullen be hanged and to-drawe.
Who giveth you levë for to preche,
Or speke †agaynës goddes lawe,
And the people thus falsly teche?   1240
Thou shalt be cursed with boke and bell,
And dissevered from holy churche,
And clene y-dampned into hell,
Otherwyse but ye woll worche!"

    The Pellican sayd, "that I ne drede;   1245
Your cursinge is of litell value;
Of god I hope to have my mede,
For it is falshed that ye shewe.
For ye ben out of charitè
And wilneth vengeaunce, as did Nero;   1250
To suffren I woll redy be;
I drede not that thou canst do.

1221. Howe.   1222. subgette.   1227. Ayenst.   1230. shulde.
1232. pouerte.   1235. dystrye.   1238. leaue; preache.   1239. speake
agaynst.   1240. falsely teache.   1245. sayde.   1248. falshede.

Christ bad ones suffre for his love,
And so he taught all his servaunts;
And but thou amend for his sake above,   1255
I drede not all thy mayntenaunce.
For if I drede the worldes hate,
Me thinketh, I were litell to prayse;
I drede nothing your hye estat,
Ne I drede not your disese.   1260

Wolde ye turne and leve your pryde,
Your hyë port, and your richesse,
Your cursing shuld not go so wyde;
God bring you into rightwysnesse!
For I drede not your tyranny,   1265
For nothing that ye can doon;
To suffre I am all redy,
Siker, I recke never how soon!"

The Griffon grinned as he were wood,
And loked lovely as an owle!   1270
And swor, by cockes hertë blood,
He wolde him terë, every doule!
"Holy churche thou disclaundrest foule!
For thy resons I woll thee all to-race;
And make thy flesh to rote and moule;   1275
Losell, thou shalt have hardë grace!"

The Griffon flew forth on his way;
The Pellican did sitte and weep;
And to him-selfë he gan say,
"God wolde that any of Christes sheep   1280
Had herd, and y-takë kepe
Eche a word that here sayd was,
And wolde it wryte and well it kepe!
God wolde it were all, for his grace!"

1253. badde.   1254. seruauntes.   1255. amende.   1259. nothynge;
estate.   1260. dysease.   1261. leaue.   1262. porte.   1263. cursynge
shulde.   1264. brynge.   1266. nothynge; done.   1268. howe soone.
1269. wode.   1271. swore; bloode.   1274. reasons; the.   1275. fleshe.
1276. shalte.   1277. flewe; waye.   1278. wepe.   1279. saye.
1280. shepe.   1281. herde.   1282. worde.   1283. wrytte.

Plowman. I answerde, and sayd I wolde,   1285
If for my travayl any wold pay.

Pelican. He sayd, "yes; these that god han sold;
For they han [greet] store of money!"

Plowman. I sayd, "tell me, and thou may,
Why tellest thou mennës trespace?"   1290

Pelican. He said, "to amende hem, in good fay,
If god woll give me any grace.

For Christ him-selfe is lykned to me,
That for his people dyed on rode;
As fare I, right so fareth he,   1295
He fedeth his birdes with his blode.
But these don yvell †ayenës good,
And ben his foon under frendes face;
I tolde hem how hir living stood;
God amende hem, for his grace!"   1300

Plowman. "What ayleth the Griffon, tell [me] why,
That he holdeth on that other syde?"

Pellican. "For they two ben [of kind], lykly,
And with [lyk] kindes robben wyde.
The foul betokeneth [evill] pryde,   1305
As Lucifer, that hygh †flowe was;
And sith he did him in evell hyde,
For he agilted goddes grace.

As bird [that] flyeth up in the ayr,
And liveth by birdes that ben meke,   1310
So these be flowe up in dispayr,
And shenden sely soules eke.
The soules that ben in sinnes seke,
He culleth hem; knele therfore, alas!
For brybry goddes forbode breke,   1315
God amende it, for his grace!

1286. trauayle; any man wolde (*om.* man).   1287. solde.   1288. *Supply*
greet.   1293. lykened.   1297. done; ayenst gode.   1298. fone.
1299. howe her lyuynge stode.   1301. *Supply* me.   1303. *Supply*
Pellican (*wrongly prefixed to* l. 1305); *supply* of kind.   1304. *Supply* lyk.
1305. foule; *supply* evill.   1306. flewe (*read* flowe; *see* l. 1311).
1309. hyrde; *supply* that; ayre.   1311. into (*read* in); dyspayre.

The hinder part is a lyoun,
A robber and a ravinere,
That robbeth the people in erth a-down,
And in erth holdeth non his pere;   1320
So fareth this foul, both fer and nere;
With temporel strength they people chase,
As a lyon proud in erthë here;"
God amende hem for hys grace!"

He flew forth with his winges twayn,   1325
All drouping, dased, and dull.
But soone the Griffon cam agayn,
Of his foules the erth was full;
The Pellican he had cast to pull.
So greet a nombre never seen ther was;   1330
What maner of foules, tellen I woll,
If god woll give me of his grace.

With the Griffon comen foules fele,
Ravins, rokes, crowes, and pye,
Gray foules, agadred wele,   1335
Y-gurd, above they woldë hye.
Gledes and bosardes weren hem by;
Whyt molles and puttockes token hir place;
And lapwinges, that wel conneth ly,
This felowship han for-gerd hir grace.   1340

Longe the Pellican was out,
But at [the] laste he cometh agayn;
And brought with him the Phenix stout.
The Griffon wolde have flowe full fayn;
His foules, that flewen as thycke as rayn,   1345
The Phenix tho began hem chace;
To fly from him it was in vayn,
For he did vengeaunce and no grace.

1317. parte.   1319. earth a downe.   1320. none.   1321. foule;
ferre.   1322. And wyth (*om.* And).   1323. proude; earth.   1325. (Pellican
is written above this line); flewe; twayne.   1326. droupynge.   1327. came
agayne.   1328. earth.   1330. great; sene there.   1336. Igurde.
1338. Whyte; her.   1339. lye.   1340. for gerde her.   1342. *Supply* the.
1343. stoute.   1344. fayne.   1345. rayne.   1347. flye; vayne.

He slew hem down without mercy,
Ther astartë neyther free ne thrall ;   1350
On him they cast a rufull cry
When the Griffon down was fall.
He beet hem not, but slew hem all ;
Whither he hem drove, no man may trace ;
Under the erthe, me thought, they yall ;   1355
Alas ! they had a feble grace !

The Pellican then axed right,
"For my wryting if I have blame,
Who woll for me fight of flight?
Who shall sheldë me from shame ?   1360
    He that had a mayd to dame,
The lamb that slayn [for sinners] was,
Shall sheldë me from gostly blame ;
For erthly harm is goddes grace.

Therfore I praye every man,   1365
Of my wryting have me excused."
This wryting wryteth the Pellican,
That thus these people hath dispysed ;
For I am, fresh, fully advysed,
I nill not maynteyn his manace.   1370
For the devell is † oft disguysed,
To bringe a man to yvell grace.

Wyteth the Pellican, and not me,
For herof I nil not avowe,
In hy ne in low, ne in no degrè,   1375
But as a fable take it ye mowe.
To holy churche I will me bowe ;
Ech man to amende him, Christ send space !
And for my wryting me alowe
He that is almighty, for his grace.'   1380

Finis.

·1349. slewe; downe.   1350. There.   1352. downe.   1353. bete;
slewe.   1358. wrytynge,   1361. mayde.   1362. And the lambe
(*om.* And); *supply* for sinners.   1364. erthely harme.   1366-7. wrytynge.
1369. freshe.   · 1370. maynteyne.   1371. often (*read* oft).   1375. hye;
lowe.   1378. Eche; sende.   1379. wrytynge.

III. JACK UPLAND.

I, JACK UPLANDE, make my mone to very god and to all true belevinge in Christ, that Antichrist and his disciples, by colour of holines, walken and deceiven Christes church by many fals figures, wherethrough, by Antichrist and his, many vertues been transposed to vices.   5

But the fellest folk that ever Antichrist found been last brought into the church, and in a wonder wyse; for they been of divers sectes of Antichrist, sowen of divers countrees and kinredes. And all men knowen wel, that they ben not obedient to bishoppes, ne lege men to kinges; neither they tillen ne sowen, weden, ne repen woode, corn, ne gras, neither nothing that man shuld helpe but only hem-selves, hir lyves to sustein. And these men han all maner power of god, as they sayen, in heaven and in earth, to sell heaven and hell to whom that hem lyketh; and these wrecches wete never where to been 15 hemselves.

And therfore, frere, if thine order and rules ben grounded on goddes law, tell thou me, Jack Upland, that I aske of thee; and if thou be or thinkest to be on Christes syde, kepe thy pacience.

Saynt Paul techeth, that al our dedes shuld be don in charitè, 20 and els it is nought worth, but displesing to god and harm to oure owne soules. And for because freres chalengen to be gretest clerkes of the church, and next folowinge Christ in livinge, men shulde, for charitè, axe hem some questions, and

From C. (=printed copy in Caius Coll. library, Cambridge); _I give here rejected spellings; readings marked_ Sp. _are from_ Speght.

3. walkyn. deceauen.   5, 6, 7. bene (_for_ been; _very often_).   6. folke. founde.   9. kynreddes.   11. grasse, nether nething (_sic_).   12. onely. her lyfes.   13. had; Sp. han.   15. hym (_for_ hem). wreches.   16. -selfes. 18. the.   20. teacheth. don.   21. not; Sp. nought. dyspleasynge. harme. 22. because (Sp. that).   23. greatest.

25 pray hem to grounde their answers in reson and in holy writ ; for
els their answere wolde nought be worth, be it florished never so
faire ; and, as me think, men might skilfully axe thus of a frere.

   1. Frere, how many orders be in erthe, and which is the
perfitest order ?   Of what order art thou ?   Who made thyn
30 order ?   What is thy rule ?   Is there ony perfiter rule than Christ
himselfe made ?   If Christes rule be moost perfit, why rulest
thou thee not therafter ?   Without more, why shall a frere be
more punished if he breke the rule that his patron made, than if
he breke the hestes that god himself made ?

35 2. Approveth Christ ony more religions than oon, that saynt
James speketh of.   If he approveth no more, why hast thou left
his rule, and taken another ?   Why is a frere apostata, that leveth
his order and taketh another secte ; sith there is but oon religion
of Christ ?

40 3. Why be ye wedded faster to your habits than a man is to his
wyfe ?   For a man may leve his wyf for a yere or two, as many
men do ; and if † ye leve your habit a quarter of a yere, ye shuld
be holden apostatas.

   4. Maketh youre habit you men of religion, or no ?   If it
45 do, than, ever as it wereth, your religion wereth ; and, after that
the habit is better, is you[r] religion better.   And whan ye liggen
it besyde you, than lig ye youre religion besyde you, and ben
apostatas.   Why by ye you so precious clothes, sith no man
seketh such but for vaine glorie, as saynt Gregory saith ?

50 5. What betokeneth youre grete hood, your scaplerye, youre
knotted girdel, and youre wyde cope ?

   6. Why use ye al oon colour, more then other Christen men
do ?   What betokeneth that ye been clothed all in one maner
clothinge ?

55 7. If ye saye it betokeneth love and charitè, certes, than ye be
ofte ypocrites, whan ony of you hateth other, and in that, that ye
wollen be said holy by youre clothinge.

   8. Why may not a frere were clothing of an-other secte of
freres, sith holines stondeth not in the clothes ?

---

25. reason. write.   26. hot ; Sp. nought.   28. earthe.   29. thyne.
31. perfyte.   32. the.   33. break.   34. breake.   35. one.
36. speaketh. mor ;   Sp. more. lef ; Sp. left.   37. leaueth.   38. one.
39. Christe.   40. abytes ; Sp. habits.   41. leaue. wyfe. yeare.   42. you ;
read ye. leaue. abyte ; Sp. habit. yeare.   44. abyte ; Sp. habit.
45. weareth (twice).   46. the abbyte ; Sp. your habit.   48. apostatase ; Sp.
apostataes. by ; Sp. buy.   50. greate hoode.   51. coape.   52. one
coloure.   53. bene.   57. sayde. clotynge (!).   58. maye. weare clothynge.

9. Why holde ye silence in one howse more than in another; 60
sith men ought over-al to speke the good and leve the evell?

10. Why ete you flesh in one house more than in another,
if youre rule and youre order be perfit, and the patron that
made it?

11. Why gette ye your dispensacions, to have it more esy? 65
Certes, either it semeth that ye be unperfit; or he, that made it
so hard that ye may not holde it. And siker, if ye holde not the
rule of youre patrons, ye be not than hir freres; and so ye lye
upon youre-selves!

12. Why make ye you as dede men whan ye be professed; 70
and yet ye be not dede, but more quicke beggars than ye were
before? And it semeth evell a deed man to go aboute and
begge.

13. Why will ye not suffer youre novices here your councels in
youre chapter-house, er that they been professed; if youre coun- 75
cels been trew, and after god[d]es lawe?

14. Why make ye you so costly houses to dwell in; sith Christ
did not so, and dede men shuld have but graves, as falleth to
dede men? And yet ye have more gorgeous buildinges than
many lordes of Englonde. For ye maye wenden through the 80
realme, and ech night, wel nigh, ligge in youre owne courtes;
and so mow but right few lordes do.

15. Why hyre ye to ferme youre limitors, gevinge therfore
eche yeer a certain rente; and will not suffer oon in an-others
limitacion, right as ye were your-selves lordes of contreys? 85

16. Why be ye not under youre bisshops visitacions, and liege
men to oure kinge?

17. Why axe ye no letters of bretherhedes of other mens
prayers, as ye desyre that other men shulde aske letters of you?

18. If youre letters be good, why graunte ye them not generally 90
to al maner men, for the more charitè?

19. Mow ye make ony man more perfit brother for your
prayers, than god hath by oure beleve, by our baptyme and his
owne graunte? If ye mowe, certes, than ye be above god.

---

60. Sp. *om.* in *before* another. 61. speake. leaue. 62. eate. 65. easy.
66. ether; Sp. either. vnperfyte. 67. harde. seker; Sp. siker. 68. her.
69. selfes. 70. ye you; Sp. *om.* ye (!). 70, 71. deade (*twice*). beggers;
Sp. beggars. ye; Sp. you. 72. deade. 74. heare. 75. eare; Sp. ere.
Sp. haue ben (C. *om.* haue). 78. Sp. falleth it to. 78, 79. deade (*twice*).
79. gorgeous buyldi*n*ges; Sp. courts. 80. maye; Sp. now (*error for* mow).
81. welnygh; Sp. will (!). 83. here; Sp. heire (*read* hyre). geuynge.
84. yeare. certayne. one. 91. Sp. of men. 92. perfyte. Sp. brether (!).
93. baptyme; Sp. baptisme.

95　20. Why make ye men beleve that your golden trentall songe of you, to take therfore ten shillinges, or at the leest fyve shillinges, will bringe soules out of helle, or out of purgatorye? If this be sooth, certes, ye might bring all soules out of payne. And that wolle ye nought; and than ye be out of charitè.

100　21. Why make ye men beleve, that he that is buried in youre habit shall never come in hell; and ye wite not of youre-selfe, whether ye shall to hell, or no? And if this were sooth, ye shulde selle youre high houses, to make many habites, for to save many mens soules.

105　22. Why stele ye mens children for to make hem of youre secte; sith that theft is agaynst goddes heste; and sithe youre secte is not perfit? Ye know not whether the rule that ye binde him to, be best for him or worst!

23. Why undernime ye not your brethren, for their trespas
110 after the lawe of the gospell; sith that underneminge is the best that may be? But ye put them in prison ofte, whan they do after goddes lawe; and, by saynt Austines rule, if ony did amisse and wolde not amende him, ye should put him from you.

24. Why covete ye shrifte, and burying of other mens parishens,
115 and non other sacrament that falleth to Christen folke?

25. Why busie ye not to here shrifte of poore folke, as well as of riche lordes and ladyes; sith they mowe have more plentee of shrifte-fathers than poore folk may?

26. Why saye ye not the gospel in houses of bedred men; as
120 ye do in riche mens, that mowe go to churche and here the gospell?

27. Why covette ‡ye not to burye poore folk among you; sith that they ben moost holy, as ye sayn that ye ben for youre povertee?

125　28. Why will ye not be at hir diriges, as ye been at riche mens; sith god prayseth hem more than he doth riche men?

29. What is thy prayer worth; sith thou wilt take therefore? For of all chapmen ye nede to be moost wyse; for drede of symonye.

130　30. What cause hast thou that thou wilt not preche the

---

96. Sp. *om.* the. least. 97. oute. 98, 102. south; Sp. sooth. 101. abyte; Sp. habit. 103. abytes. 105. steale. 107. wether; Sp. whether. 109. vndermyne (*for* vndernyme); Sp. vnderneme. 111. maye. presonne; Sp. prison. 112. Sp. Augustines. dyd; Sp. doe. 114. buryenge. 115. none. 116. heare; Sp. heare to. 117. plentie. 118. folke maye. 120. heare. 122. *Both* you. folke amonge. 123. sayne. 124. pouertye. 125. her. bene. 126. Sp. other (*for* riche). 128. Sp. *om.* of. 130. wylte. preache.

gospell, as god sayeth that thou shuldest; sith it is the best lore, and also oure beleve?

31. Why be ye evell apayed that secular prestes shulde preche the gospel; sith god him-selfe hath boden hem?

32. Why hate ye the gospell to be preched; sith ye be so 135 moche holde thereto? For ye winne more by yere with *In principio*, than with all the rules that ever youre patrons made. And, in this, minstrels been better than ye. For they contraryen not to the mirthes that they maken; but ye contraryen the gospell bothe in worde and dede. 140

33. Frere, whan thou receivest a peny for to say a masse, whether sellest thou goddes body for that peny, or thy prayer, or els thy travail? If thou sayest thou wolt not travaile for to saye the masse but for the peny, †than certes, if this be soth, than thou lovest to littel mede for thy soule. And if thou sellest 145 goddes body, other thy prayer, than it is very symony; and art become a chapman worse than Judas, that solde it for thirty pens.

34. Why wrytest thou hir names in thy tables, that yeveth thee moneye; sith god knoweth all thing? For it semeth, by thy 150 wryting, that god wolde not rewarde him but thou wryte him in thy tables; god wolde els forgetten it.

35. Why berest thou god in honde, and sclaundrest him that he begged for his mete; sith he was lord over all? For than hadde he ben unwyse to have begged, and no nede therto. 155

36. Frere, after what law rulest thou thee? Wher findest thou in goddes law that thou shuldest thus begge?

37. What maner men nedeth for to begge? Of whom oweth suche men to begge? Why beggest thou so for thy brethren? 160

If thou sayest, for they have nede; than thou doest it for the more perfeccion, or els for the leest, or els for the mene. If it be the moost perfeccion of all, than shulde al thy brethren do so; and than no man neded to begge but for him-selfe, for so shuld no man begge but him neded. And if it be the leest perfeccion, why 165 lovest thou than other men more than thy-selfe? For so thou art

---

133. payed; Sp. apaid. preache. 134. gosgel (!). Sp. bodden. hym; Sp. hem. 135. preached. 136. yeare. 139. myrtes; Sp. mirths. 142. Sp. thy; C. *om.* (*before* prayer). 144. Sp. that certes (*error for* than certes); C. & certes. 149. her. the. 150. thynge. 151. Sp. writest; Sp. *om.* him. 152. Sp. forgotten (!). 153. bearest. 154. meate. 156. the. 159. C. Of; Sp. For. 162. perfection (*but* perfeccion *in l.* 163). least. meane (*often*). 165. least. 166. arte.

not well in charitè; sith thou shuldest seke the more perfeccion
after thy power, livinge thy-selfe moost after god; and thus, leving
that imperfeccion, thou shuldest not so begge for hem. And if
170 it is a good mene thus to begge as thou doest, than shuld no man
do so but they ben in this good mene; and yet such a mene,
graunted to you, may never be grounded in goddes lawe; for
than both lered and lewed that ben in mene degrè of this worlde
shuld go aboute and begge as ye do. And if all suche shuld do
175 so, certes, wel nigh al the world shuld go aboute and begge as
ye do: and so shulde there be ten beggers agaynst oon yever.

38. Why procurest thou men to yeve thee hir almes, and sayest
it is so meedful; and thou wilt not thy-selfe winne thee that
mede?

180   39. Why wilt thou not begge for poore bedred men, that ben
poorer than ony of youre secte, that liggen, and mow not go
aboute to helpe themselves; sith we be all brethren in god, and
that bretherhed passeth ony other that ye or ony man coude
make? And where moost nede were, there were moost perfeccion;
185 either els ye holde hem not youre pure brethren, or worse. But
than ye be imperfite in your begginge.

40. Why make ye you so many maisters among you; sith it
is agaynst the techinge of Christ and his apostels?

41. Whos ben all your riche courtes that ye han, and all your
190 riche jewels; sith ye sayen that ye han nought, in proper ne in
comune? If ye sayn they ben the popes, why † geder ye then, of
poore men and of lordes, so much out of the kinges honde to make
your pope riche? And sith ye sayen that it is greet perfeccion to
have nought, in proper ne in comune, why be ye so fast aboute to
195 make the pope (that is your † fader) riche, and putte on him imperfeccion? Sithen ye sayn that your goodes ben all his, and he
shulde by reson be the moost perfit man, it semeth openlich that
ye ben cursed children, so to sclaunder your † fader, and make
him imperfit. And if ye sayn that tho goodes be yours, then do
200 ye ayenst youre rule; and if it be not ayenst your rule, than might

---

167. charytye. sithe.   168. leauynge.   169. Sp. them (*for* hem).   170.
doeste.   173. learned and lewd; Sp. lerid and leaud.   174. Sp. *om.* suche.
176. one.   177. the here.   178. C. medefull; Sp. needful. the.   182.
themselfes.   183. coulde.   185. hym; Sp. them (*read* hem). C. or; Sp. but.
187. amonge.   188. teachynge.   189. Whose. rych.   190. yewels; Sp.
iewels. improper ne; Sp. ne in proper ne in.   191. cumune; Sp. common.
sayne. gether; Sp. gather.   192. Sp. *om.* of.   193. great.   194. in proper
ne comune; Sp. in proper be (!) in common.   195. father rych. put.   197.
reason. perfite.   198. father.   199. imperfyte. sayne. Sp. the (*for* tho).

ye have both plough and cart, and labour as other good men don,
and not so begge to by losengery, and ydell, as ye don.   And if ye
say that it is more perfeccion to begge than to travaill or worch
with youre hand, why preche ye not openly, and teche all men to
do so, sith it is the best and moost perfit lyf to helpe of her 205
soules, as ye make children to begge that might have been riche
heyres?

42. Why make ye not your festes to poore men, and yeveth
hem yeftes, as ye don to the riche; sith poore men han more
nede than the riche?   210

43. What betokeneth that ye go tweyne and tweyne † togeder?
If ye be out of charitè, ye accorden not in soule.

44. Why begge ye, and take salaries therto, more than other
prestes; sith he that moost taketh, most charge he hath?

45. Why holde ye not saynt Fraunces rule and his testament; 215
sith Fraunces saith, that god shewed him this living and this
rule?   And certes, if it were goddes will, the pope might not
fordo it; or els Fraunces was a lyar, that sayde on this wyse.
And but this testament that he made accorde with goddes will,
els erred he as a lyar that were out of charitè; and as the law 220
sayeth, he is accursed that letteth the rightfull last will of a deed
man lacke.   And this testament is the last will of Fraunces that
is a deed man; it seemeth therefore that all his freres ben
cursed.

46. Why wil ye not touche no coined money with the crosse, 225
ne with the kinges heed, as ye don other jewels both of golde and
silver?   Certes, if ye despyse the crosse or the kinges heed, than
ye be worthy to be despysed of god and the kinge.   And sith ye
will receyve money in your hertes and not with youre handes, it
seemeth that ye holde more holinesse in your hondes than in your 230
hertes; and than be ye false to god.

47. Why have ye exempt you fro our kinges lawes and visiting
of our bishoppes more than other Christen men that liven in this
realme, if ye be not gilty of traitory to our realme, or trespassers
to oure bishoppes?   But ye will have the kinges lawes for trespas 235
don to you; and ye wil have power of other bishops more than

---

201. carte. done.   202. lesyngery; Sp. losengery. done.   204. preach.
teach.   205. perfyte lyfe.   206. be; Sp. bin.   208. feastes.   209. done.
rych.   211. together.   212. charitie.   214. Sp. om. 2nd he.   220. C. as;
Sp. is (!) charytie.   221. Sp. accursed; C. cursede. C. om. last. dead.
222. Sp. om. lacke. least; Sp. last.   223. dead. C. om. therefore.   226.
hedde. done.   227. heade.   229. receaue.   229, 231. hartes (twice).
231. Sp. om. ye.   232. exempte.   234. gyltye. traytery. trespasers.
235. Sp. your (for oure). Sp. the trespasse (for trespas).   236. done.

other prestes ; and also have leave to prison youre brethren as
lordes in youre courtes, more than other folkes han that ben the
kinges lege men.

240   48. Why shal some secte of you freres paye eche yere a certaine
to hir generall provinciall or minister, or els to hir soverains, but-if
he stele a certain number of children, as some men sayn ?   And
certes, if this be soth, than be ye constrayned, upon certaine
payne, to do thefte, agaynst goddes commaundement, *non*
245 *furtum facies.*

49. Why be ye so hardy, to graunte, by letters of fraternitè, to
men and women, that they shall have part and merit of all your
good dedes ; and ye witen never whether god be apayed with
youre dedes because of youre sinne ?   Also ye witen never whether
250 that man or woman be in state to be saved or damned ; than shall
he have no merit in heven for his owne dedes, ne for none other
mans.   And all were it so, that he shuld have part of youre good
dedes ; yet shulde he have no more than god would geve him,
after that he were worthy ; and so much shall eche man have of
255 goddes yefte, withoute youre limitacion.   But if ye will saye that
ye ben goddes felowes, and that he may not do without youre
assent, than be ye blasphemers to god.

50. What betokeneth that ye have ordeined, that when such
oon as ye have mad youre brother or sister, and hath a letter of
260 your sele, that letter † mot be brought in youre holy chapter and
there be red ; or els ye will not praye for him ?   But and ye willen
not praye specially for all other that weren not mad youre brethren
or sistren, than were ye not in right charitè ; for that ought to be
commune, and namely in goostly thinges.

265   51. Frere, what charitè is this—to overcharge the people by
mighty begginge, under colour of prechinge or praying or masses
singing ?   Sith holy writ biddeth not thus, but even the contrary ;
for al such goostly dedes shulde be don freely, as god yeveth hem
freely.

270   52. Frere, what charitè is this—to begyle children or they
commen to discrecion, and binde hem to youre orders, that been

---

240. eche yeare ; Sp. ech a yere.   241. her (*twice*).   242. steale. certayne.
sayne.   247. merite.   248. whyther ; Sp. whether. payde ; Sp. apayed.
249. weten ; Sp. witten.   251. meryte. heauen.   252. man (*for* mans, s
having dropped out) ; Sp. mans.   253. ye (*for* he) ; Sp. he.   256. folowes :
Sp. fellowes. maye.   258. tokeneth ; Sp. betokeneth.   259. one. made.
260. seale. mought (*read* mot).   261. redde ; Sp. rad. Sp. And but.
262. Sp. *om. 1st* not. specyally ; Sp. especially. made.   264. co*m*mne (!).
goostely ; Sp. ghostly.   266. myghtie. coloure. preachynge. prayeng.
267. write.   268. done frely.   269. frely.   271. him ; Sp. hem.

not grounded in goddes lawe, against hir frendes wil? Sithen by this foly ben many apostatas, both in will and dede, and many ben apostatas in hir will during all hir lyfe, that wolde gladly be discharged if they wist how; and so, many ben apostatas that 275 shulden in other states have ben trewe men.

53. Frere, what charitè is this—to make so mony freres in every countrey, to the charge of the people? Sith persounes and vicares alone, ye, secular prestes alone, ye, monkes and chanons alone, with bishops above hem, were y-nough to the 280 church, to do prestes office. And to adde mo than y-nough is a foul errour, and greet charge to the people; and this is openly against goddes will, that ordeined all thinges to be don in weight, nomber, and mesure. And Christ himself was apayed with twelve apostles and a few disciples, to preche and do prestes office to all 285 the hole world; than was it better don than it is now at this tyme by a thousand deel. And right so as foure fingers with a thumbe in a mannes hande, helpeth a man to worche, and double nomber of fingers in one hond shuld lette him more; and the more nomber that there were, passing the mesure of goddes ordinaunce, 290 the more were a man letted to worke: right so, as it semeth, it is of these newe orders that ben added to the church, without grounde of holy writ and goddes ordinaunce.

54. Frere, what charitè is this—to lye to the people, and saye that ye folowe Christ in povertè more than other men don? 295 And yet, in curious and costly howsinge, and fyne and precious clothing, and delicious and lykinge fedinge, and in tresoure and jewels and riche ornamentes, freres passen lordes and other riche worldly men; and soonest they shuld bringe hir cause aboute, be it never so costly, though goddes lawe be put abacke. 300

55. Frere, what charitè is this—to † gader up the bokes of holy writ and putte hem in tresory, and so emprisoune hem from secular prestes and curates; and by this cautel lette hem to preche the gospell freely to the people without worldly mede; and also to defame good prestes of heresy, and lyen on hem openly, 305

---

272. her.　　273-275. apostatase; Sp. apostataes.　　278. personnes.
280. him; Sp. them.　　282. foule. greate.　　283. done.　　284. measure.
payd; Sp. apaied.　　285. preache.　　286. Sp. whole. Sp. *om. 2nd* it.
287. deal; Sp. dele.　　289. let. Sp. and so the (*om.* so).　　290. measure.
293. wryte.　　295. pouertye. done.　　297. treasoure.　　298. rych.
299. wordly; Sp. worldly. bring her.　　300. costely. abake; Sp. abacke.
301. gather (*read* gader).　　302. wryte. put. emprysonne.　　303. let.
him; Sp. hem.　　304. preache. frely. wordely; Sp. worldly.

for to lette hem to shew goddes lawe, by the holy gospell, to the
Christen people?

56. Frere, what charitè is this—to fayn so much holines in
your bodily clothing, that ye clepe your habit, that many blinde
310 foles desyren to dye therin more than in an-other? And also,
that a frere that leveth his habit (late founden of men), may not
be assoiled till he take it again, but is an apostata, as ye sayn,
and cursed of god and man both? The frere beleveth treuth and
pacience, chastitè, mekenesse, and sobrietè ; yet for the more
315 part of his lyfe he may soone be assoiled of his prior ; and if he
bringe hoom to his house much good by yere, be it never so
falsly begged and pilled of the poore and nedy people in courtes
aboute, he shal be hold[en] a noble frere! O lord, whether this
be charitè!

320   57. Frere, what charitè is this—to prese upon a riche man,
and to entyce him to be buried among you from his parish-
church, and to suche riche men geve letters of fraternitè confirmed
by youre generall sele, and therby to bere him in honde that he
shall have part of all your masses, matins, prechinges, fastinges,
325 wakinges, and all other good dedes don by your brethren of youre
order (both whyles he liveth and after that he is deed), and yet
ye witen never whether youre dedes be acceptable to god, ne
whether that man that hath that letter be able by good living to
receive ony part of youre dedes? And yet a poore man, that ye
330 wite wel or supposen in certain to have no good of, ye ne geve
no such letters, though he be a better man to god than suche
a riche man ; nevertheles, this poore man doth not recche therof.
For, as men supposen, suche letters and many other that freres
behesten to men, be full of false deceites of freres, out of reson
335 and god[d]es lawe and Christen mens faith.

58. Frere, what charitè is this—to be confessoures of lordes
and ladyes, and to other mighty men, and not amend hem in hir
living; but rather, as it semeth, to be the bolder to pille hir poore
tenauntes and to live in lechery, and there to dwelle in your office of
340 confessour, for winning of worldly goodes, and to be holden grete

---

306. let.   308. fayn.   309. bodely.   309, 311. abyte; Sp. habit.
311. leaueth.   311, 315. maye.   312. Sp. *om.* an. sayne.   315. parte.
316. home. by yeare ; Sp. by the yeare.   317. courtes & ; Sp. countries
(*perhaps better*).   318. C. Sp. hold (*for* holden).   320. *Both* prease.
323. seale. beare.   324. parte. preachynges.   325. done.   326. dead.
329. receaue.. 330. certaine.   331. no ; Sp. to (!).   332. rych. reche ;
Sp. retch.   334. behesten ; Sp. behoten. reason ; Sp. all reason.   337.
laydes (*for* ladyes). her.   338. pyl her.   339. dwel.   340. greate.

by colour of suche goostly offices ? This seemeth rather pryde
of freres than charitè of god.

59. Frere, what charitè is this—to sayn that who-so liveth
after youre order, liveth most parfitly, and next foloweth the
state of aposteles in povertè and penaunce; and yet the wysest 345
and gretest clerkes of you wende, or sende, or procure to the
court of Rome to be mad cardinales or bishoppes or the popes
chapelayns, and to be assoiled of the vowe of povertè and
obedience to your ministers ; in the which, as ye sayn, standeth
moost perfeccion and merite of youre orders? And thus ye faren 350
as Pharisees, that sayen oon, and do another to the contrarye.

60. Why name ye more the patron of youre order in youre
Confiteor, whan ye beginne masse, than other saintes, as apostels,
or marters, that holy churche holde[th] more glorious than hem,
and clepe hem youre patrons and youre avowries? 355

61. Frere, whet[h]er was saint Fraunces, in making of his rule
that he sette thyne order in, a fole and lyar, or els wyse and trew? If
ye sayn that he was not a fole but wyse ; ne a lyar, but trew ; why
shewe ye the contrary by youre doing, whan by youre suggestion to
the pope ye said that Fraunces rule was mad so hard that ye might 360
not live to holde it without declaracion and dispensacion of the
pope ? And so, by youre dede, ye lete your patron a fole, that made
a rule so hard that no man may wel kepe [it] ; and eke youre
dede proveth him a lyar, where he sayeth in his rule, that he took
and lerned it of the holy gooste. For how might ye, for shame, 365
praye the pope to undo that the holy goost biddeth, as whan ye
prayed him to dispense with the hardnesse of your order?

62. Frere, which of the foure orders of freres is best, to a man
that knoweth not which is the beste, but wolde fain enter into the
beste and none other ? If thou sayest that thyn is the best, than 370
sayest thou that noon of the other is as good as thyn ; and in this
eche frere in the three other orders wolle say that thou lyest ; for
in the selve maner eche other frere woll say that his order is
beste. And thus to eche of the foure orders ben the other three
contrary in this poynte ; in the which if ony say sooth, that is oon 375

---

341. coloure.   344. mooste perfytely.   345. wyseste.   346. greatest
clarkes.   347. made.   348. chappelaynes. povertye.   351. one.   354. hol
(*for* holy) ; Sp. holy.   holde ; Sp. hold (*read* holdeth).   them.   357. set.
358. sayne.   359. shew.   360. C. that Fraunces rule was made so harde ;
Sp. that your rule that Francis made was so hard.   C. might ; Sp. mow.   363.
harde.   maye.   *Supply* it.   364. toke.   365. learned.   366. Sp. *om.* to.
C. byddeth ; Sp. bit.   Sp. when ; C. *om.*   369. fayne.   370. thyne.
371. none.   thyne.   372, 374. thre.   373. C. selfe ; Sp. self same.
375. one.

aloon ; for there may but oon be the beste of foure. So foloweth
it, that if ech of these orders answered to this question as thou
doest, three were false and but oon trew ; and yet no man shulde
wite who that were. And thus it semeth, that the moost part of
380 freres ben or shulde be lyars in this poynt, and they shulde
answere therto. If †ye say that an-other ordre of the freres is
better than thyn or as good ; why toke ye not rather therto as to
the better, whan thou mightest have chosen at the beginning ?
And eke, why shuldest thou be an apostata, to leve thyn order
385 and take thee to that that is better ? And so, why goest thou not
from thyn order into that ?

63. Frere, is there ony perfiter rule of religion than Christ,
goddes sone, gave in his gospell to his brethren, or than that
religion that saynt James in his epistle maketh mencion of ?   If
390 †ye saye 'yes,' than puttest thou on Christ, that is wysdom of
god the † fader, uncunning, unpower, or evil will. For eyther
than he coude not make his rule so good as an-other did his,
(and so he hadde be uncunning, that he might not make his rule
so good as another man might, and so were he unmighty and not
395 god) ; or he wolde not make his rule so perfit as an-other did his
(and so had he ben evill-willed, namely to himselfe !) For if he
might, and coude, and wold[e] have mad a rule perfit without
defaute, and did not, he was not goddes sone almighty. For if
ony other rule be perfiter than Christes, than must Christes rule
400 lacke of that perfeccion by as much as the other were more
perfiter ; and so were defaute, and Christ had failed in makinge
of his rule. But to putte ony defaute or failinge in god, is
blasphemy. If thou saye that Christes rule and that religion
that saynt James maketh mencion of, is the perfitest ; why holdest
405 thou not than thilke rule without more ? And why clepest thou
thee rather of saynt Frances or saynt Dominiks rule or religion or
order, than of Christes rule or Christes order ?

64. Frere, canst thou assigne ony defaute in Christes rule of
the gospell, with the whiche he taught al men sikerly to be saved,
410 if they kepte it to hir endinge ? If thou saye it was to hard,
than sayest thou that Christ lyed ; for he saide of his rule : ' My

376. alone. one.   378. thre. one.   381. *Both* you ; *read* ye.   382. thine.
384. apostate ; Sp. apostata. leaue.   385. the.   388. sonne.   390. *Both*
you ; *read* ye. wysdome.   391. father vncunyng. Sp. *om.* eyther.   392,
397. coulde (*twice*).   393. Sp. had he.   395. perfyte.   397. made. perfyte.
398. defate ; Sp. default. sonne.   401. weren.   402. put.   404. C. that
saynt ; Sp. which saint. the perfytest ; Sp. perfectest.   405. Sp. *om.* than.
406. the (*read* thee).   408. Sp. any default or (!) assigne.   409. sekerly ;
Sp. sikerly.   410. her. harde.

yoke is softe, and my burthen light.' If thou saye Christes rule
was to light, that may be assigned for no defaute, for the better
may it be kept. If thou sayst that there is no defaute in Christes
rule of the gospell, sith Christ him-selfe saith it is light and esy : 415
what nede was it to patrons of freres to adde more therto, and so
to make an harder religion, to save freres, than was the religion
that Christes apostels and his disciples helden and weren saved
by ; but-if they wolden that her freres saten above the apostels
in heven, for the harder religion that they kepen here ? And so 420
wolde they sitten in heven above Christ himselfe for the moo and
strait observaunces ; than so shulde they be better than Christ
himselfe, with misc[h]aunce !

> Go now forth, and frayne youre clerkes,
> And grounde you in goddes lawe, and geve Jack answere. 425
> And whan ye han assoiled me that I have said, sadly in
> treuth,
> I shall soill thee of thyn order, and save thee to heven !

If freres cunne not or mow not excuse hem of these questions
asked of hem, it semeth that they be horrible gilty against god
and hir even-Christen ; for which gyltes and defautes it were 430
worthy that the order that they calle hir order were for-don. And
it is wonder that men susteyne hem or suffer hem live in suche
maner. For holy writ biddeth that thou do well to the meke,
and geve not to the wicked, but forbid to geve hem breed, lest
they be mad thereby mightier through you. Finis. 435

¶ Prynted for Jhon Gough.
Cum Priuilegio Regali.

---

415. easye. 416. mor; Sp. more. 418. that; Sp. of (!). 420, 421. heauen
(*twice*). 421. Christe. 424. frayen (*for* frayne) ; Sp. fraine. 425. C. ye in ;
Sp. ye you in (*read* you in). 426. sayde. *Read*—And whan ye han soiled
that I saide, sadly in treuthe. 427. soyll the. thyne. order; Sp. orders.
the; Sp. thee. heauen. 428. C. cunne; Sp. kun. 430. her. 431. her.
fordone. 432. hem lyue; Sp. hir live. 433. wryte. 434. bread leste.
435. made. Sp. *om.* Finis.

IV. JOHN GOWER

UNTO THE WORTHY AND NOBLE KINGE HENRY THE FOURTH.

———◆———

O NOBLE worthy king, Henry the ferthe,
    In whom the gladde fortune is befalle
The people to governe here upon erthe,
God hath thee chose, in comfort of us alle;
The worship of this land, which was doun falle,   5
Now stant upright, through grace of thy goodnesse,
Which every man is holde for to blesse.

The highe god, of his justyce alone,
The right which longeth to thy regalye
Declared hath to stande in thy persone ;   10
And more than god may no man justifye.
Thy title is knowe upon thyn auncestrye ;
The londes folk hath eek thy right affermed ;
So stant thy regne, of god and man confermed.

Ther is no man may saye in other wyse   15
That god him-self ne hath the right declared ;
Wherof the land is boun to thy servyse,
Which for defaute of helpe hath longe cared.
But now ther is no mannes herte spared
To love and serve, and worche thy plesaunce ;   20
And al this is through goddes purveyaunce.

From Th. (Thynne, ed. 1532.) ; *corrected by* T. (Trentham MS.) *I give the
rejected spellings of* Th. (Thynne), *except where they are corrected by the* MS.
   1. T. worthi noble.   3. T. *om.* here.   4. *Both* the.   T. chose; Th.
chosen.   9. T. regalie; Th. regaly.   11. T. iustifie ; Th. iustify.   12. T.
ancestrie; Th. auncestry.   17. T. boun ; Th. bounde.   20. T. wirche.

In alle thing which is of god begonne
Ther foloweth grace, if it be wel governed;
Thus tellen they whiche olde bokes conne,
Wherof, my lord, I wot wel thou art lerned.   25
Aske of thy god; so shalt thou nat be werned
Of no request [the] whiche is resonable;
For god unto the goode is favorable.

King Salomon, which hadde at his askinge
Of god, what thing him was levest to crave,   30
He chees wysdom unto the governinge
Of goddes folk, the whiche he wolde save;
And as he chees, it fil him for to have;
For through his wit, whyl that his regne laste,
He gat him pees and reste, unto the laste.   35

But Alisaundre, as telleth his historie,
Unto the god besoughte in other weye,
Of al the worlde to winne the victorie,
So that under his swerde it might[e] obeye;
In werre he hadde al that he wolde preye.   40
The mighty god behight[e] him that behest;
The world he wan, and hadde it of conquest.

But though it fil at thilke tyme so,
That Alisaundre his asking hath acheved,
This sinful world was al[le] payën tho;   45
Was noon whiche hath the highe god beleved;
No wonder was, though thilke world was greved.
Though a tyraunt his purpos mighte winne,
Al was vengeaunce, and infortune of sinne.

But now the faith of Crist is come a-place   50
Among the princes in this erthe here,
It sit hem wel to do pitè and grace,
But yet it mot be tempred in manere.
For as they fynden cause in the matere

26. T. Axe; Th. Aske. 27. T. reqwest; Th. request. (*Perhaps read*—Of no request the whiche is resonable.) 29. T. axinge; Th. askyng. 30. Th. *om.* to. 31. T. ches; Th. chase. Th. *om.* the. 33. T. ches; Th. chase. 35. T. gat; Th. gate. T. pes; Th. peace. *So* T.; Th. in-to his last. 36. T. histoire; Th. storie. 39. T. might; Th. myght. 41. *Both* behight. T. beheste. 42. Th. *om.* he. *Both* had. T. conqweste. 44. T. axinge. T. achieued; Th. atcheued. 45. *Both* al. T. paiene; Th. paynem. 46. T. belieued. 47. T. grieued. 48. T. mihte; Th. might. 50. T. feith; Th. faithe. 53. T. mot; Th. must. 54. Th. *om.* as.

Upon the poynt, what afterward betyde,   55
The lawe of right shal nat be layd a-syde.

So may a king of werre the viage
Ordayne and take, as he therto is holde,
To clayme and aske his rightful heritage
In alle places wher it is with-holde.   60
But other-wyse, if god him-selve wolde
Afferme love and pees bitween the kinges,
Pees is the beste, above alle erthly thinges.

Good is t'eschewe werre, and nathelees
A king may make werre upon his right;   65
For of bataile the fynal ende is pees;
Thus stant the lawe, that a worthy knight
Upon his trouthe may go to the fight.
But-if so were that he mighte chese,
Betre is the pees of which may no man lese.   70

To stere pees oughte every man on-lyve,
First, for to sette his liege lord in reste,
And eek these othre men, that they ne stryve;
For so this land may standen atte beste.
What king that wolde be the worthieste,   75
The more he mighte our deedly werre cese,
The more he shulde his worthinesse encrese.

Pees is the cheef of al the worldes welthe,
And to the heven it ledeth eek the way;
Pees is of soule and lyfe the mannes helthe   80
Of pestilence, and doth the werre away.
My liege lord, tak hede of that I say,
If werre may be left, tak pees on honde,
Which may nat be withoute goddes sonde.

With pees stant every crëature in reste,   85
Withoute pees ther may no lyf be glad;
Above al other good, pees is the beste;
Pees hath him-self, whan werre is al bestad;
The pees is sauf, the werre is ever adrad.

---

56. T. leid; Th. layde.   57. T. viage: Th. voyage.   59. T. axe.
61. T. silve; Th. selfe.   62, 63. T. pes; Th. peace.   70. T. Betre; Th.
Better.   71. *Both* peace. T. euery man; Th. eueriche. T. alyue.   74. Th.
lande; T. world.   76. T. cesse; Th. cease.   77. T. encresse; Th. encrease.
78. T. chief; Th. chefe.   79, 81, 82. T. weie, aweie, seie.   83. *Both* lefte.

Pees is of al[le] charitè the keye,   90
Whiche hath the lyf and soule for to weye.

My liege lord, if that thee list to seche
The sothe ensamples, what the werre hath wrought,
Thou shalt wel here, of wyse mennes speche,
That deedly werre tourneth in-to nought.   95
For if these olde bokes be wel sought,
Ther might thou see what thing the werre hath do
Bothe of conquest and conquerour also.

For vayne honóur, or for the worldes good,
They that whylom the stronge werres made,   100
Wher be they now? Bethink wel, in thy mood,
The day is goon, the night is derke and fade;
Hir crueltè, which made hem thanne glade,
They sorowen now, and yet have naught the more;
The blood is shad, which no man may restore.   105

The werre is moder of the wronges alle;
It sleeth the preest in holy chirche at masse,
Forlyth the mayde, and doth her flour to falle.
The werre maketh the grete citee lasse,
And doth the lawe his reules overpasse.   110
Ther is nothing, wherof mescheef may growe
Whiche is not caused of the werre, I trowe.

The werre bringth in póverte at his heles,
Wherof the comun people is sore greved;
The werre hath set his cart on thilke wheles   115
Wher that fortune may not be beleved.
For whan men wene best to have acheved,
Ful ofte it is al newe to beginne;
The werre hath nothing siker, thogh he winne.

For-thy, my worthy prince, in Cristes halve,   120
As for a part whos fayth thou hast to gyde,
Ley to this olde sore a newe salve,
And do the werre away, what-so betyde.
Purchace pees, and sette it by thy syde,

---

90. *Both* al.   92. *Both* the.   93. T. that; Th. what.   96. T. soght;
Th. ysought.   97. *Both* se.   98. T. conqueste.   101. T. bethenk.
102. *Both* gone. 103. *Both* Her. 108. T. *om.* doth; Th. dothe. 110. *Both*
dothe. T. reules; Th. rules.   111. T. meschef; Th. myschefe.   113. T.
bringth; Th. bringeth.   114. T. comon; Th. commen.   121. T. to; Th. be.

And suffre nat thy people be devoured;   125
So shal thy name ever after stande honóured!

If any man be now, or ever was
Ayein the pees thy prevy counsaylour,
Let god be of thy counsayl in this cas,
And put away the cruel werreyour.   130
For god, whiche is of man the creatour,
He wolde not men slowe his creature
Withoute cause of deedly forfayture.

Wher nedeth most, behoveth most to loke;
My lord, how so thy werres be withoute,   135
Of tyme passed who that hede toke,
Good were at home to see right wel aboute;
For evermore the worste is for to doute.
But, if thou mightest parfit pees attayne,
Ther shulde be no cause for to playne.   140

Aboute a king, good counsayl is to preyse
Above al othre thinges most vailable;
But yet a king within him-self shal peyse
And seen the thinges that be resonable.
And ther-upon he shal his wittes stable   145
Among the men to sette pees in evene,
For love of him whiche is the king of hevene.

A! wel is him that shedde never blood
But-if it were in cause of rightwysnesse!
For if a king the peril understood   150
What is to slee the people, thanne, I gesse,
The deedly werres and the hevinesse
Wher-of the pees distourbed is ful ofte,
Shulde at som tyme cesse and wexe softe.

O king! fulfilled of grace and of knighthode,   155
Remembre upon this poynt, for Cristes sake;
If pees be profred unto thy manhode,
Thyn honour sauf, let it nat be forsake!
Though thou the werres darst wel undertake,

129, T. Lete; Th. Lette.   130. Th. crewel warryour.   132. Th. slough.   136. T. than; Th. that.   137. *Both* se.   146. T. euene; Th. euyn.   147. T. heuene; Th. heuyn.   148. T. Ha.   153. Th. *om.* the. 155. Th. *om.* 2nd of.

* * *
* * * *

P

After resoun yet temper thy corage;   160
For lyk to pees ther is non avauntage.

My worthy lord, thenk wel, how-so befalle
Of thilke lore, as holy bokes sayn;
Crist is the heed, and we be membres alle,
As wel the subject as the soverayn.   165
So sit it wel, that charitè be playn,
Whiche unto god him-selve most accordeth,
So as the lore of Cristes word recordeth.

In th'olde lawe, or Crist him-self was bore,
Among the ten comaundëments, I rede,   170
How that manslaughter shulde be forbore;
Such was the wil, that tyme, of the godhede.
But afterward, whan Crist took his manhede,
Pees was the firste thing he leet do crye
Ayenst the worldes rancour and envye.   175

And, or Crist wente out of this erthe here,
And stigh to heven, he made his testament,
Wher he bequath to his disciples there
And yaf his pees, which is the foundement
Of charitè, withouten whos assent   180
The worldes pees may never wel be tryed,
Ne lovë kept, ne lawë justifyed.

The Jewes with the payens hadden werre,
But they among hem-self stode ever in pees;
Why shulde than our pees stonde out of herre, 185
Which Crist hath chose unto his owne encrees?
For Crist is more than was Moÿses;
And Crist hath set the parfit of the lawe,
The whiche shulde in no wyse be withdrawe.

To yeve us pees was causë why Crist dyde,   190
Withoute pees may nothing stonde avayled;
But now a man may see on every syde
How Cristes fayth is every day assayled,
With the payens distroyed, and so batayled

That, for defaute of helpe and of defence,   195
Unneth hath Crist his dewe reverence.

The righte fayth to kepe of holy chirche
The firste poynt is named of knighthode;
And every man is holde for to wirche
Upon the poynt that stant to his manhode.   200
But now, alas! the fame is spred so brode
That every man this thing [alday] complayneth;
And yet is ther no man that help ordayneth.

The worldes cause is wayted over-al;
Ther be the werres redy, to the fulle;   205
But Cristes owne cause in special,
Ther ben the swerdes and the speres dulle.
And with the sentence of the popes bulle
As for to doon the folk payën obeye,
The chirche is tourned al another weye.   210

It is wonder, above any mannes wit,
Withoute werre how Cristes fayth was wonne;
And we that been upon this erthë yit
Ne kepe it nat as it was first begonne.
To every crëature under the sonne   215
Crist bad him-self, how that we shulde preche,
And to the folke his evangely teche.

More light it is to kepe than to make;
But that we founden mad to-fore the hond
We kepe nat, but lete it lightly slake;   220
The pees of Crist hath al to-broke his bond.
We reste our-self, and suffren every lond
To slee eche other as thing undefended;
So stant the werre, and pees is nat amended.

But though the heed of holy chirche above   225
Ne do nat al his hole businesse
Among the men to sette pees and love,
These kinges oughten, of hir rightwysnesse,
Hir owne cause among hem-self redresse.

---

200. Th. that; T. which.   201. T. helas; T. sprad.   202. *I supply*
alday.   203. Th. that; T. which.   209. T. do; Th. done. T. paien;
Th. payne (*for* payen).   211. T. to wo der; Th. wonder. *For* any *read* a!
216. Th. *om* how.   217. T. euangile.   219. *Both* made. Th. *om*. the.
222. Th. selfe; T. selue.   227. T. men; Th. people.

Thogh Peters ship, as now, hath lost his stere,   230
It lyth in hem that barge for to stere.

If holy chirche after the dewetè
Of Cristes word ne be nat al avysed
To make pees, accord, and unitè
Among the kinges that be now devysed,   235
Yet, natheles, the lawë stant assysed
Of mannes wit, to be so resonable
Withoute that to stande hem-selve stable.

Of holy chirche we ben children alle,
And every child is holde for to bowe   240
Unto the moder, how that ever it falle,
Or elles he mot reson disalowe.
And, for that cause, a knight shal first avowe
The right of holy chirche to defende,
That no man shal the privilege offende.   245

Thus were it good to setten al in evene
The worldes princes and the prelats bothe,
For love of him whiche is the king of hevene ;
And if men shulde algate wexen wrothe,
The Sarazins, whiche unto Crist ben lothe,   250
Let men be armed ayenst hem to fighte,
So may the knight his dede of armes righte.

Upon three poynts stant Cristes pees oppressed ;
First, holy chirche is in her-self devyded ;
Which oughte, of reson, first to be redressed ;   255
But yet so high a cause is nat decyded.
And thus, whan humble pacience is pryded,
The remenaunt, which that they shulde reule,
No wonder is, though it stande out of reule.

Of that the heed is syk, the limmes aken ;   260
These regnes, that to Cristes pees belongen,
For worldes good, these deedly werres maken,
Which helpelees, as in balaunce, hongen.
The heed above hem hath nat underfongen

231. Th. the (*for* that).   232. Th. dewte ; T. duete.   238. T. hem-
selue ; Th. him-selfe.   242. Th. must.   246. T. *om.* good. T. euene ;
Th. euyn.   248. T. heuene ; Th. heuyn.   253. *Both* thre.   254. Th. *om.* is.
256. *Both* highe.   260. T. sick ; Th. sicke.   263. Th. helplesse ; T. heliples.

To sette pees, but every man sleeth other;   265
And in this wyse hath charitè no brother.

The two defautes bringen in the thridde
Of miscreants, that seen how we debate;
Between the two, they fallen in a-midde
Wher now al-day they fynde an open gate.   270
Lo! thus the deedly werre stant al-gate.
But ever I hopë of king Henries grace,
That he it is which shal the pees embrace.

My worthy noble prince, and king anoynt,
Whom god hath, of his grace, so preserved,   275
Behold and see the world upon this poynt,
As for thy part, that Cristes pees be served.
So shal thy highe mede be reserved
To him, whiche al shal quyten atte laste;
For this lyf herë may no whyle laste.   280

See Alisandre, Hector, and Julius,
See Machabeus, David, and Josuë,
See Charlemayne, Godfray, and Arthus
Fulfild of werre and of mortalitee!
Hir fame abit, but al is vanitee;   285
For deth, whiche hath the werres under fote,
Hath mad an ende, of which ther is no bote.

So may a man the sothe wite and knowe,
That pees is good for every king to have;
The fortune of the werre is ever unknowe,   290
But wher pees is, ther ben the marches save.
That now is up, to-morwe is under grave.
The mighty god hath alle grace in honde;
Withouten him, men may nat longe stonde.

Of the tenetz to winne or lese a chace   295
May no lyf wite, or that the bal be ronne;
Al stant in god, what thing men shal purchace:
Th'ende is in him, or that it be begonne;
Men sayn, the wolle, whan it is wel sponne,

---

269. *Both* Betwene.   274. T. enoignt.   276. *Both* Beholde; se.   278.
Th. deserved (!).   280. *Both* lyfe.   281. T. Ector.   282. T. Machabeu.
283. T. Godefroi Arthus.   287. *Both* made.   288. T. mai; Th. many !).
289. T. man (*for* king).   291. Th. is (*for* ben).   292. T. *om.* up.
295. T. tenetz; Th. tennes.   296, 298. T. er (*for* or).

Doth that the cloth is strong and profitable, 300
And elles it may never be durable.

The worldes chaunces upon aventure
Ben ever set; but thilke chaunce of pees
Is so behovely to the crëature
That it above al other is peerlees. 305
But it may nat †be gete, nathelees,
Among the men to lasten any whyle,
But wher the herte is playn, withoute gyle.

The pees is as it were a sacrament
To-fore the god, and shal with wordes playne 310
Withouten any double entendëment
Be treted; for the trouthe can nat feyne.
But if the men within hem-self be vayne,
The substaunce of the pees may nat be trewe,
But every day it chaungeth upon newe. 315

But who that is of charitè parfyte,
He voydeth alle sleightes fer aweye,
And set his word upon the same plyte
Wher that his herte hath founde a siker weye;
And thus, whan conscience is trewly weye, 320
And that the pees be handled with the wyse,
It shal abyde and stande, in alle wyse.

Th'apostel sayth, ther may no lyf be good
Whiche is nat grounded upon charitè;
For charitè ne shedde never blood. 325
So hath the werre, as ther, no propertè;
For thilke vertue which is sayd 'pitè'
With charitè so ferforth is acquaynted
That in her may no fals sembla[u]nt be paynted.

Cassodore, whos wryting is authorysed 330
Sayth: 'wher that pitè regneth, ther is grace';
Through which the pees hath al his welthe assysed,
So that of werre he dredeth no manace.
Wher pitè dwelleth, in the same place

---

305. Th. is (*for* it). Th. *om.* is. T. piereles; Th. peerles. 306. *Both* begete;
read be gete. 316. T. perfit. 318. T. plit. 321. Th. these (*for* the
pees). Th. ben. 326. T. proprite. 329. *Both* semblant. 330.
T. Cassodre. *Both* writinge. T. auctorized. 331. Th. *om.* ther.

Ther may no deedly crueltè sojourne 335
Wherof that mercy shulde his wey[e] tourne.

To see what pitè, forth with mercy, doth,
The cronique is at Rome, in thilke empyre
Of Constantyn, which is a tale soth,
Whan him was lever his owne deth desyre 340
Than do the yonge children to martyre.
Of crueltee he lefte the quarele;
Pitè he wroughte, and pitè was his hele.

For thilke mannes pitè which he dede
God was pitous, and made him hool at al; 345
Silvester cam, and in the same stede
Yaf him baptyme first in special,
Which dide away the sinne original,
And al his lepre it hath so purifyed,
That his pitè for ever is magnifyed. 350

Pitè was cause why this emperour
Was hool in body and in soule bothe;
And Rome also was set in thilke honour
Of Cristes fayth, so that the leve, of lothe
Whiche hadden be with Crist tofore wrothe, 355
Receyved werë unto Cristes lore.
Thus shal pitè be praysed evermore.

My worthy liege lord, Henry by name,
Which Engëlond hast to governe and righte,
Men oughten wel thy pitè to proclame, 360
Which openliche, in al the worldes sighte,
Is shewed, with the helpe of god almighte,
To yeve us pees, which long hath be debated,
Wherof thy prys shal never be abated.

My lord, in whom hath ever yet be founde 365
Pitè, withoute spotte of violence,
Keep thilke pees alway, withinne bounde,
Which god hath planted in thy conscience.
So shal the cronique of thy pacience
Among the saynts be take in-to memórie 370
To the loënge of perdurable glorie.

---

336. T. wei; Th. way. 337. *Both* se. 342. T. crualte; Th. creweltie. 347.
T. baptisme. 359. Th. England. 370. T. seintz; Th. sayntes. T memoire;
Th. memory. 371. T. loenge; Th. legende (!). T. gloire; Th. glory.

And to thyn erthely prys, so as I can,
Whiche every man is holde to commende,
I Gower, which am al thy liege man,
This lettre unto thyn excellence I sende,   375
As I, whiche ever unto my lyves ende
Wol praye for the stat of thy persone,
In worshipe of thy sceptre and of thy trone.

Nat only to my king of pees I wryte,
But to these othre princes Cristen alle,   380
That eche of hem his owne herte endyte
And cese the werre, or more mescheef falle.
Set eek the rightful pope upon his stalle ;
Keep charitè, and draw pitè to honde,
Maynteyne lawe ; and so the pees shal stonde.   385

**Explicit carmen de pacis commendacione, quod ad laudem
et memoriam serenissimi principis domini Regis Henrici
quarti, suus humilis orator Johannes Gower composuit.**

Electus Christi,   pie rex Henrice, fuisti,
Qui bene venisti,   cum propria regna petisti ;
Tu mala vicisti   -que bonis bona restituisti,
Et populo tristi   nova gaudia contribuisti.

Est mihi spes lata,   quod adhuc per te renovata   390
Succedent fata   veteri probitate beata ;
    Est tibi nam grata   gratia sponte data.

Henrici quarti primus regni fuit annus
    Quo mihi defecit visus ad acta mea.
Omnia tempus habent, finem natura ministrat,   395
    Quem virtute sua frangere nemo potest.
Ultra posse nihil, quamvis mihi velle remansit;
    Amplius ut scribam non mihi posse manet.
Dum potui, scripsi, sed nunc quia curua senectus
    Turbauit sensus, scripta relinquo scolis.   400
Scribat qui veniet post me discretior alter,
    Ammodo namque manus et mea penna silent.
Hoc tamen in fine verborum queso meorum,
    Prospera quod statuat regna futura deus.   404

¶ *Explicit.*

---

378. Th. *om. 2nd of. Both* throne.   382. T. sese (*for* cese) ; Th. se (!).
T. er (*for* or).   T. meschiefe ; Th. myschefe.   383. *Both* Sette.   384. T.
draugh.   385. T. Maintene ; Th. Maynteyn.   399. Th. curua ; T. torua.

V. THOMAS HOCCLEVE.

THE LETTER OF CUPID.

—— •• ——

Litéra Cupidinis, dei Amoris, directa subditis suis Amatoribus.

CUPIDO, unto whos comaundëment
　　The gentil kinrede of goddes on hy
And people infernal been obedient,
And mortel folk al serven besily,
The goddesse sonë Cithera soothly,　　　　　　　5
To alle tho that to our deitee
Ben sugets, hertly greting sende we !

In general, we wolë that ye knowe
That ladies of honour and reverence,
And other gentil women, haven sowe　　　　　　10
Such seed of compleynt in our audience
Of men that doon hem outrage and offence,
That it our eres greveth for to here ;
So pitous is th'effect of this matere.

Passing al londes, on the litel yle　　　　　　　15
That cleped is Albion they most compleyne ;
They seyn, that there is croppe and rote of gyle.
So conne tho men dissimulen and feyne
With stonding dropes in hir eyen tweyne,

From F (Fairfax); various readings from B (Bodley 638) ; T (Tanner 346) ; S (Arch. Selden B. 24) ; A (Ashburnham MS.) ; Tr. (Trin. Coll. Cam. R. 3. 20). *Also in* Th. (Thynne, ed. 1532); D (Digby 181); Ff (Camb. Univ. Library, Ff. 1. 6) ; *and in the* Bannatyne MS.　　2. F. goddis an.　　3. F. pepill. F. ben.　　4. A. folk ; F. folke. F. besely ; A. bisyly.　　5. F. Th. Of the ; S. *om.* Of.　　S. Cithera ; F. Sythera. S. sothly ; F. oonly.　　6. A. Tr. alle ; F. al.　　7. F. sugetes.　　8. A. wole ; F. wol.　　10. F. wymen. A. han I-sowe.　　11. F. Suche.　　12. A. doon ; F. do.　　13. F. oure.　　14. F. pitouse ; effecte.　　15. A. And passyng*e* alle londes on this yle.　　17. A. seyn ; F. seye.　　18. A. dissimulen ; F. dyssimule.　　19. A. Tr. S. Th. in ; F. on. F. her.

When that hir hertes feleth no distresse, 20
To blinden women with hir doublenesse.

Hir wordes spoken ben so syghingly,
With so pitousë chere and contenaunce,
That every wight that meneth trewely
Demeth that they in herte have such grevaunce; 25
They seyn so importáble is hir penaunce
That, but hir lady lust to shewe hem grace,
They right anoon †mot sterven in the place.

'A, lady myn!' they seyn, 'I yow ensure,
As doth me grace, and I shal ever be, 30
Whyl that my lyf may lasten and endure,
To yow as humble and lowe in ech degree
As possible is, and kepe al thing secree
Right as your-selven liste that I do;
And elles moot myn herte breste a-two.' 35

Ful hard it is to knowe a mannes herte;
For outward may no man the trouthe deme;
When word out of his mouthe may noon asterte
But it by reson any wight shuld queme,
So is it seyd of herte, as hit wolde seme. 40
O feythful woman, ful of innocence,
Thou art deceyved by fals apparence!

By proces women, meved of pitee,
Wening that al thing were as thise men sey,
They graunte hem grace of hir benignitee 45
For that men shulde nat for hir sake dey;
And with good herte sette hem in the wey
Of blisful lovë—kepe it if they conne;
Thus other-whylë women beth y-wonne.

20. A. herte.   20–22. F. her.   23. A. And with so pitous. S. Tr. pitouse a.   24. A. trewely; F. truly.   25. F. hert.   A. han swich.   26. A. seyn; F. sey.   F. her.   27. F. her.   Tr. list.   F. schew.   28. F. anoone.   F. *om.* mot; S. Tr. most; Th. must (*but read* mot); cf. l. 35.   29. A. seyn; F. sey.   F. yowe; Th. you.   31. F. While.   F. lyfe.   A. lasten; F. last.   33. F. Th. thing as; A. S. *om.* as.   34. F. youre.   F. self; S. seluen.   Th. lyste; F. lyst; A. lykith.   35. A. moot myn herte; F. myn hert mote.   A. breste; F. brest.   36. F. herd. Th. knowe a mannes; F. know a manys.   A. herte; F. hert.   37. F. outwarde.   38. S. word; F. worde.   F. non astert.   39. *So* S. Tr.; A. sholde any wight by reson; F. Th. by reson semed euery wight to queme.   40. F. seyde; Th. sayd.   F. hert; Th. herte.   41. F. *om.* of.   42. F. arte.   F. be; Th. by.   43. F. processe. A. Tr. S. wom*m*en meeued of; F. moveth oft woman.   44. S. that; *rest om.*   46. F. her.   47. F. hert set.   48. F. blesful.   A. S. they; F. ye.   49. F. And thus; A. S. Tr. *om.* And.

And whan this man the pot hath by the stele,   50
And fully is in his possessioun,
With that woman he kepeth not to dele,
After if he may fynden in the toun
Any woman, his blinde affeccioun
On to bestowë; evel mote he preve!   55
A man, for al his othes, is hard to leve!

And, for that every fals man hath a make,
(As un-to every wight is light to knowe),
Whan this traitour this woman hath forsake,
He faste him spedeth un-to his felowe;   60
Til he be there, his herte is on a lowe;
His fals deceyt ne may him not suffyse,
But of his treson telleth al the wyse.

Is this a fair avaunt? is this honour,
A man him-self accuse thus, and diffame?   65
Now is it good, confesse him a traitour,
And bringe a woman to a sclandrous name,
And telle how he her body hath do shame?
No worship may he thus to him conquere,
But greet esclaundre un-to him and here!   70

To herë? Nay, yet was it no repreef;
For al for vertu was it that she wroughte;
But he that brewed hath al this mischeef,
That spak so faire, and falsly inward thoughte,
His be the sclaundre, as it by reson oughte,   75
And un-to her a thank perpetuel,
That in a nede helpe can so wel!

Althogh of men, through sleyght and sotiltee,
A sely, simple, and innocent woman
Betrayed is, no wonder, sith the citee   80

---

50. A. S. pot; Th. pan; F. penne.   52. A. he keepith; F. kepeth he.
S. not; A. nat; F. no more.   53. A. fynden; F. fynde. F. tovne.
55. A. On to; F. Vnto.   56. A. hard; F. herde. A.S. leue; F. beleue.   59.
Th. traytour; F. traytoure.   60. A. faste him speedith; F. fast spedeth him.
61. Th. herte; F. hert.   62. A. S. Tr. ne; F. om.   64. F. faire avaunte.   65.
F. silfe.   66. S. A. Tr. Now; F. om.   S. A. him; F. Th. himselfe.   A. S. a; F.
om.   67. A.S. a (2); F. om.   68. F. tel; hir; hathe.   69. F. worshippe.   70.
A. greet; F. grete.   S. a sclander; T. Th. disclaunder.   71. F. hir; reprefe.
72. A. Tr. it; rest om.   F. wroght.   73. F. myschefe.   74. F. spake; thoght.
75. F. be; Th. by.   F. oght.   76. S. a thank; Tr. hye thank; F. thank.
77. D. Th. A. nede; F. rede.   78. Th. through; F. thorgh.

Of Troye—as that the storie telle can—
Betrayed was, through the disceyt of man,
And set on fyre, and al doun over-throwe,
And finally destroyed, as men knowe.

Betrayen men not citees grete, and kinges?   85
What wight is that can shape remedye
Ageynes thise falsly purpósed thinges?
Who can the craft such craftes to espye
But man, whos wit ay redy is t'aplye
To thing that souneth in-to hy falshede?   90
Women, beth ware of mennes sleight, I rede!

And furthermore han thise men in usage
That, where as they not lykly been to spede,
Suche as they been with a double visage
They prócuren, for to pursewe hir nede;   95
He prayeth him in his causé to procede,
And largely guerdoneth he his travayle;
Smal witen wommen how men hem assayle!

Another wrecche un-to his felowe seyth:
'Thou fisshest faire! She that thee hath fyred   100
Is fals and inconstaunt, and hath no feyth.
She for the rode of folke is so desyred
And, as an hors, fro day to day is hyred
That, when thou twinnest fro hir companye,
Another comth, and blered is thyn eyë!   105

'Now prikke on fastë, and ryd thy journey
Whyl thou art there; for she, behind thy bak,
So liberal is, she wol no wight with-sey,
But smertly of another take a snak;
For thus thise wommen faren, al the pak!   110
Who-so hem trusteth, hanged mote he be!
Ay they desyren chaunge and noveltee!'

---

81. A. that; *rest om.* F. tel.   82. Th. through; F. thorgh.   83. A. S. Tr.
Th. al; F. *om.* F. dovne.   84. F. fynaly.   85. A. Tr. Betrayen; B. S. T.
Betray; F. Betraied.   86. F. is yt that; S. A. Tr. *om.* yt.   87. A. Ageynes;
F. Ayens.   F. falsely.   88. F. crafte suche.   89. F. wytte; A. Tr. wil.
A. Tr. ay reedy is; S. redy ay is; F. is euer redy.   A. tapplie; Th. taply; F.
to aplye.   90. A. hy; S. Tr. hie; F. *om.*   93. T. A. Tr. as; F. *om.*   F. ben.
94. B. A. Tr. Th. they; F. *om.*   95. Th. pursewe; F. pursw.   98. A.
Smal witen; F. Lytell wote; Tr. Litel knowe.   99. F. wrechch; Th. wretche.
101. F. inconstant; feythe.   105. F. cometh.   106. F. fast (*read* faste).
F. ride (*read* ryd).   107. F. While.   Th. behynd; F. behinde.   F. bake.   109.
A. snak; F. snake; Th. smacke.   110. F. thes; pake.   111. Th. mote; F. mot.

Wher-of procedeth this but of envye ?
For he him-selve her ne winne may,
He speketh her repreef and vileinye,   115
As mannes blabbing tonge is wont alway.
Thus dyvers men ful often make assay
For to distourben folk in sondry wyse,
For they may not acheven hir empryse.

Ful many a man eek wolde, for no good,   120
(That hath in love his tyme spent and used)
Men wiste, his lady his axing withstood,
And that he were of her pleynly refused,
Or wast and veyn were al that he had mused ;
Wherfore he can no better remedye   125
But on his lady shapeth him to lye :

'Every womman,' he seyth, 'is light to gete ;
Can noon sey "nay," if she be wel y-soght.
Who-so may leyser han, with her to trete,
Of his purpós ne shal he faile noght,   130
But he on madding be so depe y-broght
That he shende al with open hoomlinesse ;
That loven wommen nat, as that I gesse !'

To sclaundre wommen thus, what may profyte
To gentils namely, that hem armen sholde,   135
And in defence of wommen hem delyte
As that the ordre of gentilesse wolde ?
If that a man list gentil to be holde,
He moot flee al that ther-to is contrarie ;
A sclaundring tonge is his grete adversarie.   140

A foul vice is of tonge to be light ;
For who-so michel clappeth, gabbeth ofte.
The tonge of man so swift is and so wight
That, whan it is areysed up-on lofte,

---

114. F. selfe hyr.   115. F. hir reprefe ; vileyny.   116. F. tong.   118.
F. folke.   120. F. eke.   124. F. wer. A. D. Th had ; F. hath.   126. F.
shapith.   129. F. han leyser ; D. T. Th. leisur haue ; A. Tr. leiser han.
130. F. purpose.   131. Th. madnesse.   132. F. homelynesse.   133. F.
wymmen.   134. F. sclaunder women.   135. F. Too.   139. A. Al moot
he flee.   140. Th. tonge ; F. tong.   141. F. foule. A. vice ; Th. vyce ;
F. thing.   143. A. Tr. Th. S. man ; F. men.

Resoun it seweth so slowly and softe,   145
That it him never over-take may:
Lord! so thise men ben trusty in assay!

Al-be-it that man fynde oo woman nyce,
Inconstant, rechelees, or variable,
Deynouse or proud, fulfilled of malyce,   150
Withouten feyth or love, and deceyvable,
Sly, queynt, and fals, in al unthrift coupable,
Wikked and feers, and ful of crueltee,
It foloweth nat that swiche al wommen be.

Whan that the high god aungels formed had,   155
Among hem alle whether ther werë noon
That founden was malicious and bad?
Yis! al men woot that ther was many oon
That, for hir pryde, fil from heven anoon.
Shul men therfore alle aungels proude name?   160
Nay! he that that susteneth is to blame.

Of twelve apostels oon a traitour was;
The remënant yit godë were and trewe.
Than, if it happe men fyndë, per cas,
Oo womman fals, swich good is for t'eschewe,   165
And deme nat that they ben alle untrewe.
I see wel mennes owne falsenesse
Hem causeth wommen for to trusten lesse.

O! every man oghte have an herte tendre
Unto womman, and deme her honurable,   170
Whether his shap be outher thikke or slendre,
Or be he bad or good; this is no fable.
Every man woot, that wit hath resonable,
That of a womman he descended is:
Than is it shame, of her to speke amis.   175

---

147. Th. ben; Tr. been; F. beth. A. at (for in). A. Th. assay; F. asay.
148. F. hyt.   F. o; Th. one.   149. F. varriable.   150. S.
and (for or).   S. proud; F. proude.   152. F. vnthrift; Th. vntrust.
154. F. swich; D. Th. suche.   155. D. god the hie.   156. A. alle;
F. al.   A. whether; F. wheither.   A. was (for were).   160. F. al.
161. F. om. 2nd that.   163. Tr. goode; F. good.   164. F. caas.   165.
Th. good is; F. is good.   166. F. al.   167. Th. owne falsenesse; F.
oone falsnesse.   169. F. oght.   171. F. wheither.   172. F. badde.
173. F. witte.   175. F. hir.

A wikked tree good fruit may noon forth bring,
For swich the fruit is, as that is the tree.
Tak hede of whom thou took thy biginning;
Lat thy moder be mirour unto thee.
Honoure her, if thou wolt honoured be!   180
Dispyse thou her nat, in no manere,
Lest that ther-by thy wikkednesse appere!

An old provérbë seyd is in English:
Men seyn, 'that brid or foul is dishonest,
What that he be, and holden ful churlish,   185
That useth to defoule his owne nest.'
Men, to sey wel of wommen it is best,
And nat for to despyse hem ne deprave,
If that they wole hir honour kepe and save.

Thise ladies eek compleynen hem on clerkes   190
That they han maad bokës of hir diffame,
In which they lakken wommen and hir werkes
And speken of hem greet repreef and shame,
And causëlees yive hem a wikked name.
Thus they despysed been on every syde,   195
And sclaundred, and bilowen on ful wyde.

The sory bokes maken mencioun
How they betrayden, in especial,
Adam, David, Sampsoun, and Salamoun,
And many oon mo; who may rehersen al   200
The treson that they havë doon, and shal?
The world hir malice may not comprehende;
As that thise clerkes seyn, it hath non ende.

Ovyde, in his boke called 'Remedye
Of Lovë,' greet repreef of wommen wryteth;   205
Wherin, I trowe, he dide greet folye,
And every wight that in such cas delyteth.

176. F. tre gode frute.   177. F. swiche; A. swich.   178. F. Take.
179. F. Merour; Th. myrronr. ˙   180. F. Honure; honured.   181. A.
nat hir.   183. F.'seyde; Th. sayd.   184. F. foule.   185. F. chirlyssh;
Th. churlysshe.   187. F. wymen: Th. women.   188. D. B. T. A. Tr.
for to despyse; F. to displesen.   189. F. wol.   191. F. made.   192.
A. they lakken; Th. they dispyse; F. dispisen they. Th. women and her; F.
wommans; A. wommenes.   193. F. grete reprefe.   194. F. yiven; D. yeve;
Th. yeue.   195. F. ben.   198. Th. D. especial; F. special.   203. F.
theys; noon.   205. F. grete reprefe.   206. F. grete.   207. F. case.

A clerkes custom is, whan he endyteth
Of wommen, be it prose, or ryme, or vers,
Sey they ben wikke, al knowe he the revers.   210

And that book scolers lerne in hir childhede,
For they of wommen be war sholde in age,
And for to love hem ever been in drede,
Sin to deceyve is set al hir corage.
They seyn, peril to caste is avantage,   215
And namely, suche as men han in be wrapped ;
For many a man by woman hath mishapped.

No charge is, what-so that thise clerkes seyn ;
Of al hir wrong wryting I do no cure ;
Al hir travayle and labour is in veyn.   220
For, betwex me and my lady Nature,
Shal nat be suffred, whyl the world may dure,
Thise clerkes, by hir cruel tyrannye,
Thus upon wommen kythen hir maistrye.

Whylom ful many of hem were in my cheyne   225
Y-tyed, and now, what for unweldy age
And for unlust, may not to love atteyne,
And seyn, that love is but verray dotage.
Thus, for that they hem-self lakken corage,
They folk excyten, by hir wikked sawes,   230
For to rebelle agayn me and my lawes.

But, maugre hem that blamen wommen most,
Suche is the force of myn impressioun,
That sodeinly I felle can hir bost
And al hir wrong imaginacioun.   235
It shal not been in hir eleccioun
The foulest slutte of al a toun refuse,
If that me list, for al that they can muse ;

---

208. F. custome.   209. F. women.   D. B. A. Th. *om.* 1*st* or.   210.
F. Seye ; Th. Say.   211. F. boke.   212. F. women.   213. F.
louen ; S. D. Tr. Th. loue.   215. A. They (*glossed* s. libri).   F. perylle ;
Th. *perel.* F. cast.   216. F. B. wrappes (!)   217. D. S. Th. women.   F. B.
myshappes (!)   218. S. Th. is ; F. *om.*   A. that ; *rest om.*   222. A. S.
T. nat ; D. Th. not ; F. noon.   F. while.   223. F. tyranie. 224. F. wy*m*men.
225. D. Th. many ; F. mony.   F. wer.   226. Th. Tyed ; A. Tyd.   228.
F. werray ; S. veray ; D. verry ; Th. very.   229. F. selfe ; D. silf.
230. F. folke.   232. F. mawgre ; Th. maugre.   233. F. *om.* the.
234. F. sodenly ; Th. sodainly.   236. F. ben ; Th. be.   F. ellecciou*n.*
237. F. tovne ; A. town.

But her in herte as brenningly desyre
As thogh she were a duchesse or a quene;   240
So can I folkes hertes sette on fyre,
And (as me list) hem sende joye or tene.
They that to wommen been y-whet so kene
My sharpe persing strokes, how they smyte,
Shul fele and knowe; and how they kerve and byte. 245

Perdee, this grete clerk, this sotil Ovyde
And many another han deceyved be
Of wommen, as it knowen is ful wyde;
Wot no man more; and that is greet deyntee,
So excellent a clerk as that was he,   250
And other mo that coude so wel preche
Betrapped were, for aught they coude teche.

And trusteth wel, that it is no mervayle;
For wommen knewen pleynly hir entente.
They wiste how sotilly they coude assayle   255
Hem, and what falshood they in herte mente;
And thise clerkes they in hir daunger hente.
With oo venym another was distroyed;
And thus thise clerkes often were anoyed.

Thise ladies ne thise gentils, nevertheles,   260
Were noon of tho that wroughten in this wyse;
But swiche filthes as were vertules
They quitten thus thise olde clerkes wyse.
To clerkes forthy lesse may suffyse
Than to deprave wommen generally;   265
For worship shul they gete noon therby.

If that thise men, that lovers hem pretende,
To wommen weren feythful, gode, and trewe,
And dredde hem to deceyven or offende,

---

239. Th. her; F. hir. Th. herte; F. hert. F. brenyngly.   241. F.
hertys set.   242. F. Ioy.   243. F. ben.   244. Th. sharpe; F. sharp.
248. F. women.   249. S. Wote; A. Wat; F. Th. What (!). F. grete; Th.
great.   252. F. aght; Th. aught.   253. Th. it; F. ys (!) F. mervaylle; Th.
meruayle.   254. F. women knywen; entent.   255. F. sotyly.   256. F.
falshode; Th. falsheed. F. hert ment; Th. herte mente.   257. F. this
clerkys. F. hent; Th. hente.   261. F. wroghten; Th. wrought. F. wysse;
Th. wyse.   262. S. fillokes (for filthes). F. weren; Th. were.   263. F.
wisse; Th. wyse.   263, 264. F. clerkis.   264. A. Th. To; F. D. The (!).
266. F. worshippe; Th. worshyp.   268. F. women. F. good.   269. F.
dreden; Th. dredde.

* * *
* * * *   Q

Wommen to love hem wolde nat eschewe.   270
But every day hath man an herte newe ;
It upon oon abyde can no whyle.
What fors is it, swich a wight to begyle ?

Men beren eek thise wommen upon honde
That lightly, and withouten any peyne,   275
They wonne been ; they can no wight withstonde
That his disese list to hem compleyne.
They been so freel, they mowe hem nat refreyne ;
But who-so lyketh may hem lightly have ;
So been hir hertes esy in to grave.   280

To maister Iohn de Meun, as I suppose,
Than it was a lewd occupacioun
In making of the Romance of the Rose ;
So many a sly imaginacioun
And perils for to rollen up and doun,   285
So long proces, so many a sly cautele
For to deceyve a sely damosele !

Nat can I seen, ne my wit comprehende
That art and peyne and sotiltee sholde fayle
For to conquére, and sone make an ende,   290
Whan man a feble place shal assayle ;
And sone also to venquisshe a batayle
Of which no wight dar maken resistence,
Ne herte hath noon to stonden at defence.

Than moot it folwen of necessitee,   295
Sin art asketh so greet engyn and peyne
A womman to disceyve, what she be,
Of constauncë they been not so bareyne
As that somme of thise sotil clerkes feyne ;
But they ben as that wommen oghten be,   300
Sad, constant, and fulfilled of pitee.

---

270. F. Women.   271. F. hert.   273. A. swich oon for to.   274. F.
eke this women.   276. F. ben.   280. F. ben ; hertys ; craue (!).   281.
F. I (!) ; *for* To. Th. Moone.   282. F. lewde.   286. F. longe processe.
F. slye ; Th. slygh.   287. F. damesele ; Th. damosel.   288. F. wytte.
289. F. peyn ; Th. payne.   T. Th. schulde ; F. holde (!).   291. F.
assaylle ; Th. assayle.   292. F. bataylle ; Th. batayle.   293. F. whiche.
294. F. hert ; Th. herte.   295. F. yt moot folowen ; A. moot it folwen.
296. F. grete.   297. F. dysceve.   298. F. constance ; ben.   299. F.
lerkys.   301. F. pite.

How frendly was Medea to Jasoun
In the conquéring of the flees of gold!
How falsly quitte he her affeccioun
By whom victórie he gat, as he hath wold!　　305
How may this man, for shame, be so bold
To falsen her, that from his dethe and shame
Him kepte, and gat him so gret prys and name?

Of Troye also the traitour Eneas,
The feythles wrecche, how hath he him forswore　　310
To Dido, that queen of Cartágë was,
That him releved of his smertes sore!
What gentilesse might she han doon more
Than she with herte unfeyned to him kidde?
And what mischeef to her ther-of betidde!　　315

In my Legende of Martres men may fynde
(Who-so that lyketh therin for to rede)
That ooth noon ne behest may no man bynde;
Of reprevable shame han they no drede.
In mannes herte trouthe hath no stede;　　320
The soil is noght, ther may no trouthe growe!
To womman namely it is nat unknowe.

Clerkes seyn also: 'ther is no malyce
Unto wommannes crabbed wikkednesse!'
O woman! How shalt thou thy-self chevyce,　　325
Sin men of thee so muchel harm witnesse?
No fors! Do forth! Takë no hevinesse!
Kepë thyn ownë, what men clappe or crake;
And somme of hem shul smerte, I undertake!

Malyce of wommen, what is it to drede?　　330
They slee no men, distroyen no citees;
They not oppressen folk ne overlede,

302. F. frendely; Th. frendly.　　303. F. flee (!); golde.　　304. F. quyt;
hir.　　305. F. gate; wolde. 306. F. bolde.　307. F. hir.　　308. F. kept;
grete.　　310. F. wrechch; Th. wretche; A. man.　　314. F. That (for
Than). F. hert; Th. herte.　315. F. mischefe; hir.　316. Th. natures (for
Martres).　　318. F. oothe in no; A. ooth noon ne; S. T. Th. othe ne.
320. A. Th. herte; F. hert.　A. In herte of man conceites trewe arn dede.
324. A. wommannes; Th. D. womans; F. a womans. Th. wicked crabbydnesse.
326. F. the; harme.　　327. F. No fors; A. Yee strab (or scrab). Th. Beth
ware women of her fykelnesse. F. take; S. and take.　　329. F. smert;
Th. smerte.　331. F. sle.　332. F. folke.
Q 2

Betraye empyres, remes, ne duchees,
Ne men bereve hir landes ne hir mees,
Empoyson folk, ne houses sette on fyre,   235
Ne false contractes maken for non hyre !

Trust, perfit love, and entere charitee,
Fervent wil, and entalented corage
To thewes gode, as it sit wel to be,
Han wommen ay, of custome and usage ;   340
And wel they can a mannes ire aswage
With softe wordes discreet and benigne ;
What they be inward, sheweth outward signe.

Wommannes herte un-to no crueltee
Enclyned is, but they ben charitable,   345
Pitous, devout, fulle of humilitee,
Shamfaste, debonaire, and amiable,
Dredful, and of hir wordes mesurable :
What womman thise hath not, peraventure,
Ne folweth nat the wey of her nature.   350

Men seyn : ‘our firste moder, natheles,
Made al man-kynde lese his libertee,
And naked it of joye, douteles ;
For goddes hestes disobeyed she,
Whan she presumed tasten of a tree,   355
Which god forbad that she nat ete of sholde ;
And, nad the devel been, namore she wolde.’

Th’ envýous swelling that the feend, our fo,
Had unto man in herte, for his welthe,
Sente a serpent, and made her for to go   360
To disceyve Eve ; and thus was mannes helthe
Beraft him by the fende, right in a stelthe,
The womman noght knowing of the deceyt ;
God wot, ful fer was it from her conceyt.

335. F. Empoysone folkys ; set.   337. F. perfyte.   338. D. B. Th.
A. entalented ; F. entenlented.   339. F. Be ; Th. Al ; *rest* To. F. sytt.
340. F. women.   342. A. softe ; F. Th. soft.   343. F. outwarde.
344. A. Wommannes ; F. Th. Womans.   346. F. Pitouse devoute ful.
348. F. *om.* and.   350. F. hir.   351. F. oure ; Th. our. A. firste ; F. Th.
first.   353. F. Ioy ; Th. ioye.   356. A. nat ; F. ne.   . 357. F. nade ; Th. ne
had ; A. nad. F. she ne wolde.   358. F. The enviouse ; Tr. Thenvyous.
F. suellyng. F. fend.   359. Th. herte ; F. D. hert.   359. F. Sent ; hir.   361.
F. deceyve ; Th. disceyue.   363. F. woman.   364. F. Gode wote ; hir.

Wherfore I sey, this godë womman **Eve**   365
Our fader Adam ne deceyved noght.
Ther may no man for a deceyt it preve
Proprely, but-if that she, in her thoght,
Had it compassed first, er it was wroght;
And, for swich was nat her impressioun,   370
Men calle it may no déceyt, by resoun.

No wight deceyveth but he it purpóse;
The feend this déceyt caste, and nothing she.
Than is it wrong to demen or suppose
That she sholde of this harm the cause be.   375
Wyteth the feend, and his be the maugree;
And for excused have her innocence,
Sauf only that she brak obedience.

And touching this, ful fewe men ther been,
Unnethes any, dar I saufly seye—   380
Fro day to day, as that men mow wel seen,
But that the hest of god they disobeye.
Have this in mynde, sires, I yow preye;
If that ye be discreet and resonable,
Ye wol her holde the more excusable.   385

And wher men seyn, 'in man is stedfastnesse,
And woman is of her corage unstable,'
Who may of Adam bere swich witnesse?
Telleth me this:—was he nat chaungeable?
They bothe weren in a caas semblable,   390
Sauf willingly the feend deceyved Eve,
And so did she nat Adam, by your leve.

Yet was this sinne happy to mankynde,
The feend deceyved was, for al his sleight;
For aught he coude him in his sleightes wynde,   395

God, to discharge mankynde of the weight
Of his trespas, cam doun from hevenes height,
And flesh and blood he took of a virgyne,
And suffred deeth, him to deliver of pyne.

And god, to whom ther may nothing hid be,   400
If he in woman knowe had such malyce
As men of hem recorde in generaltee,
Of our lady, of lyf reparatryce,
Nolde han be born ; but, for that she of vyce
Was voyde, and of al vertu (wel he wiste)   405
Endowed, of her to be bore him liste.

Her heped vertu hath swich excellence
That al to lene is mannes facultee
To déclare it, and therfor in suspence
Her duë preysing put mot nedes be.   410
But this we witen verrayly, that she,
Next god, the best frend is that to man longeth ;
The key of mercy by her girdil hongeth.

And of mercy hath every man swich nede
That, cessing that, farwel the joye of man !   415
Of her power now taketh right good hede ;
She mercy may, wol, and purchace can.
Displese her nat, honoureth that womman,
And other wommen alle, for her sake !
And, but ye do, your sorowe shal awake.   420

Thou precious gemme, O martir Margarete,
Of thy blood draddest noon effusioun !
Thy martirdom ne may I nat foryete ;
Thou, constant womman in thy passioun,
Overcoom the feendes temptacioun ;   425
And many a wight converted thy doctryne
Unto the feith of god, holy virgyne !

---

397. F. trespase ; Th. trespace.   F. the hevenes ; A. Tr. S. Th. *om.* the.
398. F. tooke.   401. F. suche.   403. F. Yf (*for* Of). F. lyfe.   405.
F. woyde ; Th. voyde.   406. F. hir.   408. F. leene ; Th. leane ; S. low ;
A. weyke.   410. Th. dewe.   F. moot.   411. A. we witen ; *rest* I sey.
F. verraly.   412. F. men (*for* man).   413. F. mercye ; hir girdille.   414.
F. mercye.   415. F. farewel ; Ioy.   417. F. mercye.   418. F.
honureth ; Th. honoureth.   419. A. Tr. alle ; F. al.   423. F. martirdome.
Th. Thou louer trewe. thou mayden mansuete.   425. F. feendis.   427.
From A ; F. B. *omit* (!).

But understondeth, I commende hir noght
By enchesoun of hir virginitee;
Trusteth right wel, it cam not in my thoght;　430
For ever I werrey ayein chastitee,
And ever shal; but this, lo! meveth me,
Her loving herte and constant to her lay
Dryve out of rémembraunce I ne may.

In any boke also wher can ye fynde,　435
That of the werkes or the dethe or lyf
Of Jesu speketh, or maketh any mynde,
That womman him forsook, for wo or stryf?
Wher was ther any wight so ententyf
Abouten him as wommen? Pardee, noon!　440
Th'apostels him forsoken, everichoon.

Womman forsook him noght; for al the feyth
Of holy chirche in womman lefte only.
This is no lees, for holy writ thus seyth;
Loke, and ye shal so fynde it, hardely.　445
And therfore it may preved be therby,
That in womman regneth stable constaunce
And in men is the chaunge and variaunce!

Now holdeth this for ferme and for no lye,
That this trewe and just commendacioun　450
Of wommen is nat told for flaterye,
Ne to cause hem pryde or elacioun,
But only, lo! for this entencioun,
To yeve hem corage of perseveraunce
In vertu, and hir honour to enhaunce.　455

The more vertu, the lasse is the pryde;
Vertu so digne is, and so noble in kynde
That vyce and she wol not in-fere abyde.

---

430. A. nat; Tr. not; *rest* neuer.　431. F. *om.* I.　433. F. hert; hir.
434. F. of my; Th. *om.* my.　435-448. *Precedes* 421-434 *in* Th.　435.
F. where.　436. F. werkis; lyfe.　438. F. wommen (*read* womman,
as in l. 442). F. stryfe.　439. F. ententyfe.　441. *So* Th.; F. B. forsoken
hym.　442. F. forsooke.　443. F. left oonly.　444. Tr. holy wryt thus;
F. thus holy wryt.　445. F. Lok.　446. *So* A.; F. B. I may wel preve
herby.　447, 448. F. constance, variance.　450. F. trew; Th. trewe.
451. A. is nat told for; F. tolde I nat for; Th. tel I for no.　453. F.
oonly loo.　455. F. honure; Th. honour. Th. auaunce.　458. A. S.
she; *rest* he.

She putteth vyce clene out of her mynde,
She fleeth from him, she leveth him behynde.   460
O womman, that of vertu art hostesse,
Greet is thyn honour and thy worthinesse!

Than wol we thus concluden and diffyne:
We yow comaunde, our ministres, echoon
That redy been to our hestes enclyne,   465
That of thise false men, our rebel foon,
Ye do punisshëment, and that anoon!·
Voide hem our court and banish hem for ever
So that ther-inne they ne come never.

Fulfilled be it, cessing al delay;   470
Look that ther be non excusacioun.
Writen in th'ayr, the lusty month of May,
In our paleys (wher many a millioun
Of loveres trewe han habitacioun)
The yere of grace joyful and jocounde   475
A thousand and foure hundred and secounde.

**Explicit litera Cupidinis, dei amoris, directa suis sub-
ditis amatoribus.**

459, 460. A. S. She ; *rest* He. S. hir; F. hi (!) ; *rest* his.   461. F. wertu.
462. F. Gret ; honor.   464. F. oure ; echon.   465. F. oure.   466.
F. D. *om.* false. F. reble ; Th. rebel.   469. A. ynne; F. in. F. more neuer ;
A. *om.* more.   471. S. Tr. that ; *rest om.*   472. F. the ayer ; A. their ; Tr.
theyre. F. moneth.   473. F. oure ; where ; milion.   474. F. louers trwe.
475. F. Iocunde.
COLOPHON. D.T. amatoribus ; F. *om.* B. *has*—The lettre of Cupide, god
of love, directed to his suggestys louers.

VI. TO THE KINGES MOST NOBLE GRACE; AND TO THE LORDES AND KNIGHTES OF THE GARTER.

———•———

Cestes Balades ensuyantes feurent faites au tres noble Roy Henry le quint (que dieu pardoint!) et au tres honourable conpaignie du Jarter.

I.

TO you, welle of honour and worthinesse,
   Our Cristen king, the heir and, successour
Un-to Justinians devout tendrenesse
In the feith of Jesu, our redemptour;
And to you, lordes of the Garter, 'flour   5
Of chevalrye,' as men you clepe and calle;
The lord of vertu and of grace auctour
Graunte the fruit of your loos never appalle!

O lige lord, that han eek the lyknesse
Of Constantyn, th'ensaumple and the mirour   10
To princes alle, in love and buxumnesse
To holy chirche, O verray sustenour
And piler of our feith, and werreyour
Ageyn the heresyës bitter galle,
Do forth, do forth, continue your socour!   15
Hold up Cristes baner; lat it nat falle!

This yle, or this, had been but hethenesse,
Nad been of your feith the force and vigour!
And yit, this day, the feendes fikilnesse
Weneth fully to cacche a tyme and hour   20
To have on us, your liges, a sharp shour,
And to his servitude us knitte and thralle.
But ay we truste in you, our prótectour;
On your constaunce we awayten alle.

Commandeth that no wight have hardinesse,   25
O worthy king, our Cristen emperour,
Of the feith to despute more or lesse
Openly among people, wher errour
Springeth al day and engendreth rumour.
Maketh swich lawe, and for aught may befalle,   30
Observe it wel; ther-to be ye dettour.
Doth so, and god in glorie shal you stalle.

II.

YE lordes eek, shyninge in noble fame,
To whiche appropred is the maintenaunce
Of Cristes cause; in honour of his name   35
Shove on, and putte his foos to the outrance!
God wolde so; so wolde eek your ligeaunce;
To tho two prikketh you your duëtee.
Who-so nat kepeth this double observaunce
Of merit and honour naked is he!   40

Your style seith that ye ben foos to shame;
Now kythe of your feith the perséveraunce,
In which an heep of us arn halte and lame.
Our Cristen king of England and of Fraunce,
And ye, my lordes, with your alliaunce,   45
And other feithful people that ther be
(Truste I to god) shul quenche al this nuisaunce
And this land sette in hy prosperitee.

---

19. P. fikilnesse; Ed. crabbydnesse.   20. P. Weeneth; Ed. Weneth.
22. P. seruiture; Ed. seruytude.   25. P. Commandith; Ed. Commaundeth.
26. Ed. O; P. Our. Ed. our; P. and.   27. Ed. dispute.   28. P. where;
Ed. Her.   29. P. Spryngith; engendrith.   30. P. Makith.   P. aght; Ed.
ought.   31. P. been; Ed. be.   32. P. Dooth.   33. P. Yee.   34.
P. approped (!).   38. Ed. duite.   39. P. keepith; Ed. kepeth.   40.
P. nakid; Ed. naked.   41. Ed. *om.* that.   P. yee been.   43. P. arn; Ed.
he.   44. P. Engeland and; Ed. England and of.   45. P. yee.   46. P.
othir.   47. P. qwenche. P. nusance; Ed. noysaunce (*read* nuisance).

Conquest of hy prowesse is for to tame
The wilde woodnesse of this mescreaunce ;   50
Right to the rote repe ye that same !
Slepe nat this, but, for goddes plesaunce
And his modres, and in signifiaunce
That ye ben of seint Georges liveree,
Doth him servyce and knightly obeisaunce ;   55
For Cristes cause is his, wel knowen ye !

Stif stande in that, and ye shul greve and grame
The fo to pees, the norice of distaunce ;
That now is ernest, torne it into game ;
Dampnáble fro feith werë variaunce !   60
Lord lige, and lordes, have in rémembraunce,
Lord of al is the blessed Trinitee,
Of whos vertu the mighty habundaunce
You herte and strengthe in feithful unitee !   Amen.

Cest tout.

---

49. P. Conqueste ; Ed. Conquest.   50. Ed. myscreaunce.   51. P. roote
rype ; Ed. rote repe.   P. yee.   52. P. Sleepe ; Ed. Slepe.   54. P. yee
been.   55. P. Dooth.   56, 57. P. yee.   57. P. shuln ; Ed. shal.
P. greene.   58. Ed. the ; P. and.   59. Ed. tourne.   60. Ed. Nowe
kythe of your beleue tho constaunce.   62. P. blissid ; Ed. blysfull.

VII. A MORAL BALADE.

BY HENRY SCOGAN, SQUYER.

———◆———

Here foloweth next a Moral Balade, to my lord the Prince, to my lord of Clarence, to my lord of Bedford, and to my lord of Gloucestre, by Henry Scogan; at a souper of feorthe merchande in the Vyntre in London, at the hous of Lowys Johan.

MY noble sones, and eek my lordes dere,
    I, your fader called, unworthily,
Sende un-to you this litel tretys here
Writen with myn owne hand full rudëly;
Although it be that I not reverently   5
Have writen to your estats, yet I you praye,
Myn unconning taketh benignëly
For goddes sake, and herken what I seye.

I complayn sore, whan I remembre me
The sodeyn age that is upon me falle;   10
More I complayn my mispent juventè
The whiche is impossible ayein to calle.

From Th. (Thynne, ed. 1542); *collated with* A. (Ashmole 59), *and* Cx. (Caxton); *readings also given from* H. (Harl. 2251).

TITLE; *from* A. (*which has* folowethe nexst); Cx. *has* Here next foloweth a tretyse, whiche John Skogan sente vnto the lordes and gentilmen of the kynges hows, exortyng them to lose no tyme in theyr yougthe, but to vse vertues; Th. *has* Scogan vnto the lordes and gentylmen of the kynges house.

1. Th. A. sonnes.   2. Th. A. vnworthely.   3. Th. lytel treatyse; A. balade folowing.   4. Th. with; A. H. of.   5. Th. H. Although; Cx. And though; A. Yitte howe.   6. Th. A. estates. A. yet; H. Th. Cx. *om.* 8. Cx. herkne (*better*).   9. Th. me sore; A. H. *om.* me.   10. A. H. falle; Th. fal.   11. Th. But more; A. H. Cx. *om.* But. Th. iuuentute.   12. Th. ayen for; A. ageine. A. H. calle; Th. cal.

But certainly, the most complaynte of alle
Is for to thinke, that I have been so nycc
That I ne wolde no virtue to me calle   15
In al my youthe, but vyces ay cheryce.

Of whiche I aske mercy of thee, lord,
That art almighty god in majestè,
Beseking thee, to make so even accord
Betwix thee and my soule, that vanitè   20
Of worldly lust, ne blynd prosperitè
Have no lordship over my flesshe so frele.
Thou lord of reste and parfit unitè,
Put fro me vyce, and keep my soules hele.

And yeve me might, whyl I have lyf and space, 25
Me to conforme fully to thy plesaunce;
Shewe upon me th'abundaunce of thy grace,
In gode werkes graunt me perséveraunce.
Of al my youthe forget the ignoraunce;
Yeve me good wil, to serve thee ay to queme; 30
Set al my lyf after thyn ordinaunce,
And able me to mercy, or thou deme!

My lordes dere, why I this complaint wryte
To you, alle whom I love entierly,
Is for to warne you, as I can endyte,   35
That tyme y-lost in youthe folily
Greveth a wight goostly and bodily,
I mene hem that to lust and vyce entende.
Wherfore, I pray you, lordes, specially,
Your youthe in vertue shapeth to dispende. 40

Planteth the rote of youthe in suche a wyse
That in vertue your growing be alway;

---

13. Th. H. certainly; A. comvnely. Th. A. moste. A. H. alle; Th. al.
14. A. H. for; Th. *om.* A. beon; Th. be.   15. A. H. no; Th. *om.* A.
vertue; Th. vertues. A. calle; Th. cal.   16. A. ay; Th. aye.   17.
A. thee; Th. the. Th. lorde.   18. Th. H. god; A. lorde.   20. Th.
Betwyxe; A. Bytwene.   21. A. H. Of; Th. Cx. *om.* Th. blynde.   22. A.
so freel; Th. H. to frele.   23. Th. lorde; perfyte.   24. A. H. Cx. soules;
Th. soule.   25. Th. whyle; lyfe.   26. A. H. confourme; Th. confyrme (!).
27. A. H. vpon; Th. to.   28. Th. And in; A. H. *om.* And.   30. A. thee;
Th. the.   31. Th. lyfe. A. H. thy governaunce.   34. A. alle whome;
Cx. whom that; Th. whom. Th. moste entyerly; Cx. A. entierly.   36. A.
eloste; Th. loste; H. Cx. lost.   37. A. H. goostely and bodely; Th. Cx. bodily
and gostly.   38. Th. meane.   39. A. I prey you lordes; Th. lordes I pray
you. A. tendrely.   41. Cx. *transposes* 41–80 *and* 81–125. A. Plantethe;
Th. Cx. Plante.

Loke ay, goodnesse be in your exercyse,
That shal you mighty make, at eche assay,
The feend for to withstonde at eche affray.   45
Passeth wysly this perilous pilgrimage,
Thinke on this word, and werke it every day;
That shal you yeve a parfit floured age.

Taketh also hede, how that these noble clerkes
Write in hir bokes of gret sapience,   50
Saying, that fayth is deed withouten werkes;
So is estat withoute intelligence
Of vertue; and therfore, with diligence,
Shapeth of vertue so to plante the rote,
That ye therof have ful experience,   55
To worship of your lyfe and soules bote.

Taketh also hede, that lordship ne estat,
Withoute vertue, may not longe endure;
Thinketh eek 'how vyce and vertue at debat
Have been, and shal, whyles the world may dure;   60
And ay the vicious, by aventure,
Is overthrowe; and thinketh evermore
That god is lord of vertue and figure
Of al goodnesse; and therfore folowe his lore.

My mayster Chaucer, god his soulë have!   65
That in his langage was so curious,
He sayde, the fader whiche is deed and grave,
Biquath nothing his vertue with his hous
Unto his sone; therfore laborious
Ought ye to be, beseching god, of grace,   70
To yeve you might for to be vertuous,
Through which ye might have part of his fayr place.

43. A. ay; Th. alway.   45. Cx. The frende (!) for to withstonde; A. For
to withstonde the feonde; Th. The fende to withstande.   46. Th. peryllous;
H. perilous.   47. H. Th. Cx. werke; A. vse.   48. Th. parfyte.   50.
Th. Writen; A. Wrote. Th. her. Th. great; H. grete; A. noble.   52.
So A.; Th. And right so is estate with negligence.   57. A. Then kepe
also that.   58. Cx. A. Withoute; Th. Without.   59. Cx. vice; A. H.
Th. vices.   60. A. whiles; Th. while. Th. worlde.   61. A. H. ay;
Th. Cx. euer.   63. Th. lorde of al; H. A. lord of.   67. Th. sayd that
the; A. saide that the; H. Cx. om. that. Th. father; A. H. fader.   68. H.
A. Beqwath; Th. Byqueth. Th. house.   69. So A. Cx.; Th. children and
therefore laborouse.   70. H. Th. Ought; A. Aught; Cx. Owe. Th. om. to.
Th. besekyng; A. beseching.   72. Th. haue; A. H. gete. Th. parte. A.
feyre; Th. H. om.

Here may ye see that vertuous noblesse
Cometh not to you by way of auncestrye,
But it cometh thorugh leefful besinesse   75
Of honest lyfe, and not by slogardrye.
Wherfore in youthe I rede you edefye
The hous of vertue in so wys manere
That in your age it may you kepe and gye
Fro the tempest of worldly wawes here.   80

Thinketh how, betwixë vertue and estat
There is a parfit blessed mariage;
Vertue is cause of pees, vyce of debat
In mannes soule; for which, with ful corage,
Cherissheth vertue, vyces to outrage: 85
Dryveth hem away; let hem have no wonning
In your soules; leseth not the heritage
Which god hath yeve to vertuous living.

Taketh hede also, how men of povre degree
Through vertue have be set in greet honour,   90
And ever have lived in greet prosperitee
Through cherisshing of vertuous labour.
Thinketh also, how many a governour
Called to estat, hath oft be set ful lowe
Through misusing of right, and for errour,   95
Therfore I counsaile you, vertue to knowe.

Thus 'by your eldres may ye nothing clayme,'
As that my mayster Chaucer sayth expresse,
'But temporel thing, that man may hurte and mayme';
Than is god stocke of vertuous noblesse;   100
And sith that he is lord of blessednesse,
And made us alle, and for us alle deyde,

---

74. A. Comþe.   75. A. thorugh; Cx. thurgh; Th. by.   A. leofful; Th.
leful; H. leeful.   77. Th. you ye; A. H. *om.* ye.   78. Th. house. A.
soo wyse; Th. H. suche a.   79. Th. *om.* it.   80. H. A. worldly; Th.
worldes.   81. Th. howe betwyxe; A. howe bytwene.   82. Th. parfyte.
84. H. A. for whiche with full; Th. the whiche be ful of.   85. Th. than
vertue; A. *om.* than.   86. A. Cx. *om.* 1*st* hem.   87. A. leese; H. lesith.
89. Th. howe. A. poure; Th. poore.   90, 91. Th. great.   92. Th.
H. Through; A. By.   94. Th. H. Called; A. Calde. A. offt; H. Th. Cx.
om.   95. A. for; Th. H. Cx. of.   96. Th. And therfore; *rest om.* And.
97. A. By auncetrye thus; Th. H. Thus by your auncestres; Cx. Thus by your
eldres.   99. Th. men (*for* man).   100. Cx. Than god is.   101. Th.
sythe; lorde. Th. blyssednesse; A. blessednesse.   102. A. That (*for* And).
A. H. alle; Th. al (1). Cx. alle; Th. al (2). *For* us alle A. *has* mankynde that.

Folowe his vertue with ful besinesse,
And of this thing herke how my mayster seyde:—

The firste stok, fader of gentilesse, 105
What man that claymeth gentil for to be
Must folowe his trace, and alle his wittes dresse
Vertu to sewe, and vyces for to flee.
For unto vertu longeth dignitee,
And noght the revers, saufly dar I deme, 110
Al were he mytre, croune, or diademe.

This firste stok was ful of rightwisnesse,
Trewe of his word, sobre, pitous, and free,
Clene of his goste, and loved besinesse
Ageinst the vyce of slouthe, in honestee; 115
And, but his heir love vertu, as dide he,
He is noght gentil, though he riche seme,
Al were he mytre, croune, or diademe.

Vyce may wel be heir to old richesse;
But ther may no man, as men may wel see, 120
Bequethe his heir his vertuous noblesse;
That is appropred unto no degree,
But to the firste fader in magestee
That maketh him his heir, that can him queme,
Al were he mytre, croune, or diademe. 125

Lo here, this noble poete of Bretayne
How hyely he, in vertuous sentence,
The losse in youthe of vertue can complayne;
Wherfore I pray you, dooth your diligence,
For your estats and goddes reverence, 130
T'enprintë vertue fully in your mynde,
That, whan ye come in your juges presence,
Ye be not set as vertules behynde.

Ye lordes have a maner now-a-dayes,
Though oon shewe you a vertuous matere, 135

103. *So* A.; Th. H. Foloweth hym in vertue. 105-125. Chaucer's poem of
Gentilesse is here quoted; see vol. i. p. 392. 127. A. Howe hyely he; Th.
Howe lightly. 128. A. lesse (!); Th. losse. A. H. in; Th. on. 129. A.
Wherfore; Th. And therefore. A. doothe; Th. with (!). 130. A. estates;
Th. profyte. 131. A. Tenprynte; Th. Tempereth (!). A. H. vertue fully; Th.
fully vertue. 132. Cx. in; A. H. in-to; Th. to. 133. A. H. sette as vertu-
lesse; Th. vertulesse than. 134. H. Cx. Ye; A. For yee; Th. Many. Th. A.
nowe. 135. Cx. H. you; Th. hem. A. Thaughe one of you here of a gode matere.

* * *
* * * *   R

Your fervent youthe is of so false alayes
That of that art ye have no joy to here.
But, as a ship that is withouten stere
Dryveth up and doun, withouten governaunce,
Wening that calm wol lastë, yeer by yere,   140
Right so fare ye, for very ignoraunce.

For very shamë, knowe ye nat, by réson
That, after an ebbe, ther cometh a flood ful rage?
In the same wyse, whan youth passeth his séson,
Cometh croked and unweldy palled age;   145
Sone after comen kalends of dotage;
And if your youth no vertue have provyded,
Al men wol saye, fy on your vassalage!
Thus hath your slouth fro worship you devyded.

Boëce the clerk, as men may rede and see,   150
Saith, in his Boke of Consolacioun,
What man desyreth †thave of vyne or tree
Plentee of fruit, in the †yping sesoun,
Must ay eschewe to doon oppressioun
Unto the rote, whyle it is yong and grene;   155
Ye may wel see, by this conclusioun,
That youthë vertulees doth mochel tene.

Seeth, there-ayenst, how vertuous noblesse
Roted in youthe, with good perséveraunce,

136. Cx. H. Your feruent; Th. Her feruent; A. Your vnsure.   137. Th.
arte. Cx. H. ye; Th. they. A. That of suche artes you liste not to.   138.
Cx. A. withouten; Th. without a.   139. A. withouten; Th. without.
140. Th. calme. A. wol laste you; Th. wolde last. Th. yere by yere.
141. Cx. A. H. ye; Th. they.   142. Cx. A. H. ye; Th. they.   143. A.
Cx. om. ful.   144. A. Right euen so whane.   145. A. Comthe.   146.
A. Soone; Th. And sone. Th. comen the; Cx. come; A. comthe.   147.
Th. if that; Cx. A. H. om. that. Cx. A. your; Th. her. A. H. no vertue haue;
Cx. no vertue hath; Th. haue no vertue.   148. Th. fye. Cx. A. your; Th. her.
149. A. H. your; Th. her. Cx. H. you; Th. hem. A. has Thus hathe youre
youthe and slouthe you al misgyded.   152. Cx. A. H. to haue; Th. om.
(read haue). 153. A. Plenty of; Cx. Plentyuous; Th. Plentous. Th. fruite.
A. H. Cx. the; Th. om. A. H. Cx. riping; Th. reapyng.   154. A. H.
Cx. ay; Th. euer. A. doon; Th. do.   156. A. H. Cx. Yee may; Th. Thus
may ye. A. H. wele see; Cx. see; Th. se wel. A. H. this; Th. that. A. Cx.
conclusioun; Th. inclusyon (!).   157. A. youthe; Th. youth. A. Th. vertulesse. Th. moche; Cx. ofte muche; A. ay michil (read mochel).   158. Th.
Nowe seeth; A. H. Cx. om. Nowe. Th. howe; A. that.   159. A. youthe;
Th. youth.

Dryveth away al vyce and wrecchednesse,   160
As slogardrye, ryote and distaunce !
Seeth eek how vertue causeth suffisaunce,
And suffisaunce exyleth coveityse !
And who hath vertue hath al abundaunce
Of wele, as fer as reson can devyse.   165

Taketh hede of Tullius Hostilius,
That cam fro povertee to hy degree ;
Through vertue redeth eek of Julius
The conquerour, how povre a man was he ;
Yet, through his vertue and humanitee,   170
Of many a countree had he governaunce.
Thus vertue bringeth unto greet degree
Eche wight that list to do him entendaunce.

Rede, here-ayenst, of Nero vertulees ;
Taketh hede also of proude Balthasar ;   175
They hated vertue, equitee, and pees.
Loke how Antiochus fil fro his char,
That he his skin and bones al to-tar !
Loke what meschauncë they had for hir vyces !
Who-so that wol not by these signes be war,   180
I dar wel say, infortunat or nyce is.

I can no more ; but here-by may ye see
How vertue causeth parfit sikernesse,
And vyces doon exyle prosperitee ;
The best is, ech to chesen, as I gesse.   185

---

160. A. Cx. vyce; H. vice; Th. vyces.   161. A. Al (*for* As). A. al
ryote; H. Cx. Th. *om.* al.   162. Th. eke howe.   163. *So* A. Cx.;
H. *om*; Th. *has* Seeth eke howe vertue voydeth al vyce (!).   164.
Th. H. Cx. whoso; A. *om.* so.   165. Th. ferre; A. far. Th. reason.
167. A. came frome pouertee; Th. fro pouert came. Th. hygh; A. hye.
168. Th. eke.   169. Th. howe poore.   170. A. H. Cx. humanite ;
Th. his humylite.   171. Th. *om.* a.   172. A. unto gret; Cx. to
hye; Th. a man to great.   173. A. Cx. list; Th. H. lust. Th. entendaunce ; *rest* attendaunce.   174. Th. nowe of; A. H. Cx. *om.* nowe.
177. Th. And loke; *rest om.* And. Th. howe; chare.   178. Th. tare.   179.
A. meschaunces.   180. Th. H. Cx. *om.* that. Th. ware.   181. A. Th.
infortunate. A. H. Cx. or; Th. and.   182. Th. no more nowe say; Cx. no
more say; H. no more; A. more (!). Th. herby; se.   183. A. Th. Howe.
A. Th. perfyte.   184. A. done exyle; Th. H. exylen al; Cx. exyles al.
185. Th. eche man to; Cx. man to; A. dethe to (dethe *is put for* eche). A.
cheesen; Th. chose.

Doth as you list, I me excuse expresse;
I wolde be sory, if that ye mischese.
God you conferme in vertuous noblesse,
So that through negligence ye nothing lese!   189

Explicit.

---

186. Th. A. Dothe.   187. A. Cx. wil (*for* wolde). Th. right sorie ; A.
H. Cx. *om.* right.   188. A. you conferme ; Th. confyrme you.   189. A.
no thing ; Cx. H. nothing ; Th. not it.   COLOPHON. Cx. Thus endeth
the traytye wiche John Skogan sent to the lordes and estates of the kynges
hous.

VIII. JOHN LYDGATE.

THE COMPLAINT OF THE BLACK KNIGHT;
OR, THE COMPLAINT OF A LOVERES
LYFE.

————◆————

I N May, whan Flora, the fresshe lusty quene,
   The soile hath clad in grene, rede, and whyte,
And Phebus gan to shede his stremes shene
Amid the Bole, with al the bemes brighte,
And Lucifer, to chace awey the night,   5
Ayen the morowe our orizont hath take
To bidde lovers out of hir sleepe awake,

And hertes hevy for to recomforte
From dreriheed of hevy nightes sorowe,
Nature bad hem ryse, and hem disporte,   10
Ayen the goodly, gladde, greye morowe;
And Hope also, with seint Johan to borowe,
Bad, in dispyt of daunger and dispeyre,
For to take the hoolsom lusty eyre:

And with a sigh I gan for to abreyde   15
Out of my slombre, and sodainly up sterte
As he, alas! that nigh for sorowe deyde,
My sekenes sat ay so nigh my herte.
But, for to finde socour of my smerte,

From Th. (Thynne, ed. 1532); *collated with* F. (Fairfax 16); B. (Bodley 638, *imperfect*); T. (Tanner 346); D. (Digby 181); S. (Arch. Selden B. 24); *I have also consulted* Ad. (Addit. 16165); *and* P. (Pepys 2006).   2. Th. reed; F. D. rede.   4. S. his (*for 2nd* the).   5. Th. away; F. awey. 6. Th. D. orizont; F. T. S. orisont.   7. Th. bidde al; MSS. *om.* al. F. T. *om.* lovers.   10. Th. bade. F. T. D. S. *om. 2nd* hem.   11. D. gladde; *rest* glad. *All* grey (*or* gray).   13. Th. Bade; MSS. Bad. *All* dispyte (dispite).   14. S. go take (*rest om.* go).   15. Th. syghe.   16. F. out stert. 18. Th. sicknesse; MSS. sekenes. F. S. sat; *rest* sate. Th. aye. Th. nye.

Or at the leste som réles of my peyne,   20
That me so sore halt in every veyne,

I roos anon, and thoghte I wolde goon
Into the wode, to here the briddes singe,
Whan that the misty vapour was agoon
And clere and faire was the morowning ;   25
The dewe also, lyk silver in shyning
Upon the leves, as any baume swete,
Til fyry Tytan, with his persaunt hete,

Had dryed up the lusty licour newe
Upon the herbes in the grene mede,   30
And that the floures, of many dyvers hewe,
Upon hir stalkes gonne for to sprede
And for to splaye[n] out hir leves on-brede
Agayn the sonne, gold-burned in his spere,
That doun to hem caste his bemes clere.   35

And by a river forth I gan costey
Of water clere as berel or cristal
Til at the laste I found a litel wey
Toward a park, enclosed with a wal
In compas rounde, and by a gate smal   40
Who-so that wolde frely mighte goon
Into this park, walled with grene stoon.

And in I wente, to here the briddes song,
Whiche on the braunches, bothe in playn and vale,
So loude songe, that al the wode rong   45
Lyke as it shulde shiver in peces smale ;
And, as me thoughte, that the nightingale

---

20. F. atte ; T. at ; *rest* at the. S. sum ; *rest* some, su*m*me. P. reles ; D.
relece ; T. relese ; F. relesse ; Th. release.   21. F. halt ; Th. halte.   22.
T. S. roos ; *rest* rose. Th. thought.   23. Th. wodde ; S. wod ; *rest* wode.
Th. byrdes.   24. Th. T. D. vapoure ; F. S. vapour. F. D. agoon ; T. Th.
agone.   25. F morownyng ; T. morownynge ; Th. moronyng.   26. Th.
lyke ; F. lykyng (!) ; *rest* like ; *read* lyk.   27. Th. leaues.   32. F. the (*for*
hir).   33. Th. D. splaye ; F. T. S. splay ; *read* splayen. F. S. on ; *rest* in.
34. Th. T. Agayne ; F. Ageyn ; D. Ayen. S. gold ; *rest* golde.   35. Th.
T. downe ; F. dovn ; D. down ; S. doun.   36. Th. forthe.   37. F. berel ;
S. beriall ; Th. byrel ; T. byrell ; D. birele.   39. D. S. Toward ; F.
Tovard ; Th. T. Towarde.   40. Th. compace ; MSS. compas.   41. T.
myghte ; S. m*ic*hty (!) ; *rest* might. Th. gone ; F. goon.   42. S. park ;
rest parke.   43. T. wente ; *rest* went. Th. byrdes ; *rest* briddes. S. song ;
rest songe.   44. Th. branches ; F. T. D. braunches. Th. and (*correctly*) ;
rest omit.   45. Th. sange ; S. sang ; P. song ; F. T. D. songe. Th. woode.
S. P. rong ; *rest* ronge.   47. T. thoughte ; Th. F. D. thought.

With so gret mighte her voys gan out-wreste
Right as her herte for love wolde breste.

The soil was playn, smothe, and wonder softe   50
Al oversprad with tapites that Nature
Had mad her-selve, celured eek alofte
With bowes grene, the floures for to cure,
That in hir beautè they may longe endure
From al assaut of Phebus fervent fere,   55
Whiche in his spere so hote shoon and clere.

The eyre attempre, and the smothe wind
Of Zepherus, among the blossomes whyte,
So hoolsom was and norisshing by kind,
That smale buddes, and rounde blomes lyte   60
In maner gonnen of her brethe delyte
To yeve us hope that hir fruit shal take,
Ayens autumpne, redy for to shake.

I saw ther Daphne, closed under rinde,
Grene laurer, and the hoolsom pyne ;   65
The myrre also, that wepeth ever of kinde ;
The cedres hye, upright as a lyne ;
The philbert eek, that lowe doth enclyne
Her bowes grene to the erthe adoun
Unto her knight, y-called Demophoun.   70

Ther saw I eek the fresshe hawëthorn
In whyte motlè, that so swote doth smelle,
Ash, firre, and ook, with many a yong acorn,

---

48. T. myghte ; *rest* might. T. D. wraste ; S. brest ; Th. F. wrest.   49.
T. breste ; D. braste ; Th. F. brest ; S. to-brest.   51. F. T. P. tapites ;
Th. D. tapettes.   52. Th. F. T. -selfe (*better* selve). F. celured ; D.
coloured ; S. silu*e*red ; Th. T. couered.   54. Th. beautie. F. T. may not
(*for* may).   55. S. assaut ; *rest* assaute.   56. Th. sphere ; hotte. Th.
F. T. D. shone (*read* shoon).   57, 59. S. wynd, kynd ; *rest* wynde, kynde.
58. S. P. among ; *rest* amonge. T. blossomes ; D. blossoms ; Th. blosomes ;
F. blosmes.   59. *All* holsom (holsum). Th. F. T. D. and so ; S. *om.* so.
60. F. T. blomes ; S. blomys ; Th. blosmes ; D. blossoms.   61. *All* gan,
can ; *see* l. 579.   62. S. that ; *rest om.* F. their ; T. theire ; Th. D. there ;
S. thai ; *read* hir.   63. F. D. Ayens ; Th. Ayenst ; T. Agayne.   64. T. S.
saw ; Th. F. D. sawe (!). F. ther ; *rest* the ; *cf.* l. 71. S. Daphin ; *rest*
Daphene ; *read* Daphne.   65. Th. holsome ; *rest* holsom (-sum).   68. F.
phibert ; Th. T. filberte ; D. filberde ; S. filbard. Th. F. dothe.   69. Th.
S. adoun ; *rest* doun.   70. F. I-called ; *rest* called.   71. Th. T. D. sawe.
P. hawethorn ; *rest* hawthorn, hawthorne, hauthorne.   72. S. motle ; F.
motele ; *rest* motley. (*Read* swoot ?). Th. dothe smel.   73. *All* Asshe ;
read Ash. *All* oke ; *read* ook. S. ʒong ; T. fressh (!) ; *rest* yonge. S.
accorne ; *rest* acorne.

And many a tree—mo than I can telle;
And, me beforn, I saw a litel welle,   75
That had his cours, as I gan beholde,
Under an hille, with quikke stremes colde.

The gravel gold, the water pure as glas,
The bankes rounde, the welle envyroning;
And softe as veluët the yonge gras   80
That therupon lustily cam springing;
The sute of trees aboute compassing
Hir shadowe caste, closing the welle rounde,
And al the herbes growing on the grounde.

The water was so hoolsom and vertuous   85
Through might of herbes growing there besyde,
Not lyk the welle, wher-as Narcisus
Y-slayn was, through vengeaunce of Cupyde,
Where so covertly he didë hyde
The grayn of cruel dethe upon ech brinke,   90
That deeth mot folowe, who that ever drinke;

Ne lyk the pittë of the Pegacè
Under Pernaso, where poetës slepte;
Nor lyk the welle of pure chastitè
Which that Dyane with her nymphes kepte,   95
Whan she naked into the water lepte,
That slow Acteon with his houndes felle
Only for he cam so nigh the welle!

Bút this welle, that I here reherce,
So hoolsom was, that it wolde aswage   100
Bollen hertes, and the venim perce
Of pensifheed, with al the cruel rage,
And evermore refresshe the visage
Of hem that were in any werinesse
Of greet labour, or fallen in distresse.   105

---

74. Th. tel.   75. S. beforn; D. before; *rest* beforne. Th. sawe; wel.
76. T. cours; S. courss; *rest* course.   77. Th. hyl; quicke streames.   78.
S. P. gold; D. colde; *rest* golde   78, 80. F. glas, gras; Th. glasse, grasse.
79. wel.   80. Ad. velowet.   81. Th. T. D. lustely (T. lustily) came (cam)
springyng; F. lustely gan syng (!); S. lustily gan spryng.   83. Th. F. wel;
T. D. welle.   85. *From this point I silently correct obvious errors in spelling
of* Th. *by collation with the* MSS. Th. holsome. S. and; *rest* and so.   86.
Th. Thorowe. S. there; *rest omit.*   87, 92, 94. *I read* lyk *for* lyke.   87.
F. T. D. Narcius (!).   89. T. dyde; *rest* dyd, did.   90. S. cruell; *rest
omit.*   95. Th. that; *rest* as. F. T. P. his; *rest* her.   101. S. perce; D.
perce; Th. peerce; F. T. perysh (!)   103. Th. ouermore (!).

And I, that had, through daunger and disdayne,
So drye a thrust, thoughte I wolde assaye
To taste a draughte of this welle, or twayne,
My bitter langour if it mighte alaye ;
And on the banke anon adoun I lay,   110
And with myn heed unto the welle I raughte,
And of the water drank I a good draughte ;

Wherof, me thought, I was refresshed wele
Of the brenning that sat so nigh my herte,
That verily anon I gan to fele   115
An huge part relesed of my smerte ;
And therwithallë anon up I sterte,
And thoughte I wolde walke, and see more
Forth in the parke, and in the holtes hore.

And through a laundë as I yede a-pace   120
And gan aboute faste to beholde,
I found anon a délitable place
That was beset with treës yonge and olde,
Whose names here for me shal not be tolde ;
Amidde of whiche stood an herber grene,   125
That benched was, with colours newe and clene.

This herber was ful of floures inde,
In-to the whiche as I beholde gan,
Betwix an hulfere and a wodëbinde,
As I was war, I saw wher lay a man   130
In blakke and whyte colour, pale and wan,
And wonder deedly also of his hewe,
Of hurtes grene and fresshe woundes newe.

And overmore distrayned with sekenesse,
Besyde al this, he was, ful grevously ;   135
For upon him he had an hoot accesse,
That day by day him shook ful pitously ;
So that, for constreynt of his malady
And hertly wo, thus lying al alone,
It was a deeth for to here him grone.   140

---

107. Th. F. thrust ; T. thurste ; P. D. thurst.   110. S. adoun ; Th.
F. P. downe ; *rest* down, doun.   113-126. S. *omits*.   122. Th. delect-
able.   127. D. ynde ; T. Iende ; F. cende (?) ; Th. gende ; S. of lnde.
138. S. constreynt ; *rest* constraynyng.

Wherof astonied, my foot I gan withdrawe,
Greetly wondring what it mighte be
That he so lay, and hadde no felawe,
Ne that I coude no wight with him see ;
Wherof I hadde routhe, and eek pitè,   145
And gan anon, so softely as I coude,
Among the busshes me prively to shroude ;

If that I mighte in any wyse espye
What was the cause of his deedly wo,
Or why that he so pitously gan crye   150
On his fortune, and on his ure also ;
With al my might I layde an ere to,
Every word to marke, what he seyde,
Out of his swough among as he abrayde.

But first, if I shulde make mencioun   155
Of his persone, and plainly him discryve,
He was in sothe, without excepcioun,
To speke of manhode, oon the best on-lyve ;
Ther may no man ayen the trouthe stryve.
For of his tyme, and of his age also   160
He proved was, ther men shulde have ado,

For oon the beste there, of brede and lengthe
So wel y-mad by good proporcioun,
If he had be in his deliver strengthe ;
But thought and seknesse were occasioun   165
That he thus lay, in lamentacioun,
Gruffe on the grounde, in place desolat,
Sole by him-self, awhaped and amat.

And, for me semeth that it is sitting
His wordes al to putte in remembraunce,   170
To me, that herdë al his complayning
And al the groundë of his woful chaunce,
If ther-withal I may you do plesaunce,
I wol to you, so as I can, anon,
Lyk as he sayde, reherce hem everichon.   175

---

147. Th. priuely me ; *rest* me priuely. (*Read* busshes prively me shroude ?).
151. Th. *om. 2nd* his.   154. *For* among *perhaps read* anon.   159. S.
the ; *rest omit.*   162. Th. therto ; *rest* there.   168. F. P. awaped.   175.
D. hem ; S. thame ; *rest om.*

But who shal helpe me now to complayne ?
Or who shal now my style gye or lede ?
O Niobè, let now thy teres rayne
In-to my penne ; and helpe eek in this nede,
Thou woful Mirre, that felest my herte blede   180
Of pitous wo, and myn hand eek quake
Whan that I wryte, for this mannes sake !

For unto wo accordeth complayning
And doleful cherë unto hevinesse ;
To sorowe also, syghing and weping,   185
And pitous mourning, unto drerinesse ;
And whoso that shal wryten of distresse
In party nedeth to knowe felingly
Cause and rote of al such malady.

But I, alas ! that am of witte but dulle,   190
And have no knowing of such matere,
For to discryve and wryten at the fulle
The woful complaynt, which that ye shal here,
But even-lyk as doth a skrivenere
That can no more what that he shal wryte,   195
But as his maister besyde doth endyte ;

Right so fare I, that of no sentement
Saye right naught, as in conclusioun,
But as I herde, whan I was present,
This man complayne with a pitous soun ;   200
For even-lyk, without addicioun
Or disencrees, either more or lesse,
For to reherce anon I wol me dresse.

And if that any now be in this place
That fele in love brenning or fervence,   205
Or hindred werë to his lady grace
With false tonges, that with pestilence
Slee trewe men that never did offence
In word nor dede, ne in hir entent—
If any suche be here now present,   210

179. Th. *om.* this.   181. *So all.*   184. F. delful ; T. delefull ; S.
dulefull ; D. doilfull.   187. S. quhoso ; *rest* who. S. writen ; *rest* write
(wryte).   191. D. no knowyng haue ; *rest* haue no knowyng.   192.
S. writen ; *rest* write (wryte).   198. F. S. as ; *rest om.*   202. Th.
disencrease ; F. disencrese ; T. disencrece ; D. disencrees.   205. S. louyng.
206. F. hindered ; S. hinderit ; *rest* hindred.

Let him of routhe lay to audience,
With doleful chere and sobre countenaunce,
To here this man, by ful high sentence,
His mortal wo and his gret perturbaunce
Cómplayning, now lying in a traunce,　　　　　　　215
With lokes upcaste, and with ruful chere,
Th' effect of whiche was as ye shal here.—

Compleynt.

THE thought oppressed with inward sighes sore,
　　The painful lyf, the body languisshing,
The woful gost, the herte rent and tore,　　　　　220
The pitous chere, pale in compleyning,
The deedly face, lyk ashes in shyning,
The salte teres that fro myn eyën falle,
Parcel declare grounde of my peynes alle:

Whos herte is grounde to blede in hevinesse;　　　225
The thought, resceyt of wo and of complaynt;
The brest is cheste of dole and drerinesse;
The body eek so feble and so faynt;
With hote and colde myn acces is so meynt,
That now I chiver for defaute of hete,　　　　　230
And, hoot as gleed, now sodainly I swete.

Now hoot as fyr, now cold as asshes dede,
Now hoot fro cold, now cold fro hete agayn;
Now cold as ys, now as coles rede
For hete I brenne; and thus, betwixe twayne,　　　235
I possed am, and al forcast in payne;
So that my hete plainly, as I fele,
Of grevous cold is causë, every-deel.

This is the cold of inward high disdayne,
Cold of dispyt, and cold of cruel hate;　　　　　240
This is the cold that doth his besy payne
Ayeines trouthe to fighte and to debate.
This is the cold that wolde the fyr abate

212. F. T. deleful; S. dulfull; D. wofull.　　214. S. grete; *rest om.*
216. S. with full; *rest omit* (*I omit* full).　　COMPLEYNT; *in* F. *only.*
225. D. grownded.　　227. F. S. dule; D. dooll.　　230. Th. T. chyuer;
F. shyuer; D. chevir; S. chill.　　233. T. D. fro; S. from; Th. F. for
(*twice*).　　234. Th. T. D. yse; F. Ise; S. Iss.　　239. S. distress.
241. *So* D. P.; S. doth his besyness; Th. euer doth his besy payne; F. *euere*
doth besy peyn; T. euur doth his bysy hate (*sic*).　　242. T. Agaynes; F. D.
Ayens; Th. Ayenst; S. Aȝeynis. S. and to; *rest om.* to.　　243. Th. *om.* wolde.

Of trewe mening ; alas ! the harde whyle !
This is the cold that wolde me begyle. 245

For ever the better that in trouthe I mente
With al my mighte faythfully to serve,
With herte and al for to be diligent,
The lesse thank, alas ! I can deserve !
Thus for my trouthe Daunger doth me sterve. 250
For oon that shulde my deeth, of mercy, lette
Hath mad despyt newe his swerd to whette

Ayeines me, and his arowes to fyle
To take vengeaunce of wilful crueltè ;
And tonges false, through hir sleightly wyle, 255
Han gonne a werre that wil not stinted be ;
And fals Envye, Wrathe, and Enmitè,
Have conspired, ayeines al right and lawe,
Of hir malyce, that Trouthe shal be slawe.

And Male-Bouche gan first the tale telle, 260
To slaundre Trouthe, of indignacioun ;
And Fals-Report so loude rong the belle,
That Misbeleve and Fals-Suspeccioun,
Have Trouthe brought to his dampnacioun,
So that, alas ! wrongfully he dyeth, 265
And Falsnes now his placë occupyeth,

And entred is in-to Trouthes lond,
And hath therof the ful possessioun.
O rightful god, that first the trouthe fond,
How may thou suffre such oppressioun, 270
That Falshood shulde have jurisdiccioun
In Trouthes right, to slee him giltëlees ?
In his fraunchyse he may not live in pees.

Falsly accused, and of his foon forjuged,
Without answere, whyl he was absent, 275
He dampned was, and may not ben excused,

245. T. wolde ; S. wold ; Th. D. wol ; F. will.   247. T. myghte ;
Th. F. might.   248. S. for ; *rest om.*   251, 252. T. D. lette, whette ;
Th. F. let, whet.   *All* despite.   253. S. Aȝeynes ; T. Agaynes ; F. D.
Ayens ; Th. Agaynst.   257. P. of wrath.   258. S. aȝeynes ; T.
agaynes ; F. D. ayens ; Th. agaynst.   260, 262. Th. tel, bel ; *rest* telle,
belle. S. rong ; F. T. D. ronge ; Th. range.   267, 269. S. lond, fond ; *rest*
londe, fonde.   271. Th. D. falshode ; F. S. falshed ; T. falsehede.   276.
Th. D. be ; *rest* ben.

For Crueltè sat in jugëment
Of hastinesse, withoute avysëment,
And bad Disdayn do execute anon
His jugëment, in presence of his foon.　　　280

Attourney noon ne may admitted been
T'ëxcuse Trouthë, ne a word to speke;
To fayth or ooth the juge list not seen,
There is no gayn, but he wil be wreke.
O lord of trouthe, to thee I calle and clepe;　　　285
How may thou see, thus in thy presence,
Withoute mercy, murdred innocence?

Now god, that art of trouthe soverain
And seëst how I lye for trouthe bounde,
So sore knit in loves fyry chain　　　290
Even at the deth, through-girt with many a wounde
That lykly are never for to sounde,
And for my trouthe am dampned to the deeth,
And not abyde, but drawe along the breeth:

Consider and see, in thyn eternal right,　　　295
How that myn herte professed whylom was
For to be trewe with al my fulle might
Only to oon, the whiche now, alas!
Of voluntè, withoute any trespas,
Myn accusours hath taken unto grace,　　　300
And cherissheth hem, my deth for to purchace.

What meneth this? what is this wonder ure
Of purveyauncë, if I shal it calle,
Of god of love, that false hem so assure,
And trewe, alas! doun of the whele ben falle?　　　305
And yet in sothe, this is the worst of alle,
That Falshed wrongfully of Trouthe hath name,
And Trouthe ayenward of Falshed bereth the blame.

This blinde chaunce, this stormy aventure,
In lovë hath most his experience;　　　310
For who that doth with trouthe most his cure

277. S. sat; *rest* sate, satte.　281. F. non ne may; *rest* may non.　283.
D. oth; S. soth; *rest* othe.　285. Th. F. T. P. clepe; D. speke; S. cleke (!).
297. T. D. full*e*; Th. F. ful.　298. Th. S. one; *rest* oon.　299. F. more
(*for* any).　303. Th. cal.　305. Th. fal.　306. Th. al.　307. *All*
the name; *I omit* the.　308. *All* the blame; *read* ber'the.

Shal for his mede finde most offence,
That serveth love with al his diligence;
For who can faynë, under lowliheed,
Ne fayleth not to finde grace and speed.   315

For I loved oon, ful longë sith agoon,
With al my herte, body, and ful might,
And, to be deed, my herte can not goon
From his hest, but holde that he hath hight;
Though I be banisshed out of her sight,   320
And by her mouth dampned that I shal deye,
†To my behest yet I wil ever obeye.

For ever, sithë that the world began,
Who-so list lokë, and in storie rede,
He shal ay finde that the trewe man   325
Was put abakke, wher-as the falshede
Y-furthered was; for Love taketh non hede
To slee the trewe, and hath of hem no charge,
Wher-as the false goth freely at hir large.

I take recorde of Palamides,   330
The trewe man, the noble worthy knight,
That ever loved, and of his payn no relees;
Notwithstonding his manhood and his might
Love unto him did ful greet unright;
For ay the bet he did in chevalrye,   335
The more he was hindred by envye.

And ay the bet he did in every place
Through his knighthood and his besy payne,
The ferther was he from his lady grace,
For to her mercy mighte he never attayne;   340
And to his deth he coude it not refrayne
For no daungere, but ay obey and serve
As he best coude, plainly, til he sterve.

What was the fyne also of Hercules,
For al his conquest and his worthinesse,   345
That was of strengthe alone pereles?

314, 315. D. lowlyheed, speed; *rest* -hede, spede.   322. *All* Vn-to; *read*
To.   323. F. sithe; S. sithen; *rest* sith.   332. *Perhaps omit* his. D.
payn; T. peyn; *rest* payne (peyne).   337. S. bet; F. bette; *rest* better.
338. Th. F. *om. 2nd* his.   339. T. lady; F. ladye; *rest* ladyes.   346.
D. perelees; F. T. S. P. pereles; Th. peerles.

For, lyk as bokes of him list expresse,
He sette pillers, through his hy prowesse,
Away at Gades, for to signifye
That no man mighte him passe in chevalrye.   350

The whiche pillers ben ferre beyonde Inde
Beset of golde, for a remembraunce ;
And, for al that, was he set behinde
With hem that Love liste febly avaunce ;
For [he] him sette last upon a daunce,   355
Ageynes whom helpe may no stryf ;
For al his trouthe, yit he loste his lyf.

Phebus also, for al his persaunt light,
Whan that he wente here in erthe lowe,
Unto the herte with fresh Venus sight   360
Y-wounded was, through Cupydes bowe,
And yet his lady liste him not to knowe.
Though for her love his herte didë blede,
She leet him go, and took of him no hede.

What shal I saye of yonge Piramus?   365
Of trew Tristram, for al his hye renoun?
Of Achilles, or of Antonius?
Of Arcite eke, or of him Palemoun?
What was the endë of hir passioun
But, after sorowe, deeth, and than hir grave?   370
Lo, here the guerdon tha these lovers have!

But false Jason, with his doublenesse,
That was untrewe at Colkos to Medee,
And Theseus, rote of unkindënesse,
And with these two eek the false Enee ;   375
Lo! thus the falsë, ay in oon degrè,
Had in love hir lust and al hir wille ;
And, save falshood, ther was non other skille.

Of Thebes eek the false [knight] Arcyte,
And Demophon †also, for [al] his slouthe,   380
They had hir lust and al that might delyte

---

347. T. liste of hym ; S. can of him.   349. F. Gades ; S. Gadis ; *rest*
Gaddes.   351. Th. P. *om.* ben.   352. S. Y-sett ; D. Sette.   355. *I*
supply he.   357. S. ʒit ; *rest omit.*   360. S. fresch ; *rest omit.*   363.
T. didë ; *rest* did.   368. S. eke ; *rest omit.*   374. F. Tereus (*for*
Theseus).   378. F. falshed ; S. falshede.   379. *I supply* knight.   380.
All eke ; *read* also. *I supply* al.

For al hir falshode and hir greet untrouthe.
Thus ever Love (alas! and that is routhe!)
His false leges forthereth what he may,
And sleeth the trewe ungoodly, day by day.   385

For trewe Adon was slayn with the bore
Amid the forest, in the grene shade;
For Venus love he feltë al the sore.
But Vulcanus with her no mercy made;
The foule chorl had many nightes glade,   390
Wher Mars, her worthy knight, her trewe man,
To finde mercy, comfort noon he can.

Also the yonge fresshe Ipomenes
So lusty free [was], as of his corage,
That for to serve with al his herte he chees   395
Athalans, so fair of hir visage;
But Love, alas! quitte him so his wage
With cruel daunger plainly, at the laste,
That, with the dethe, guerdonles he paste.

Lo! here the fyne of loveres servyse!   400
Lo! how that Love can his servaunts quyte!
Lo! how he can his faythful men despyse,
To slee the trewe, and false to respyte!
Lo! how he doth the swerd of sorowe byte
In hertes, suche as most his lust obeye,   405
To save the false, and do the trewe deye!

For fayth nor ooth, word, ne assuraunce,
Trewe mening, awayte, or besinesse,
Stille port, ne faythful attendaunce,
Manhood, ne might, in armes worthinesse,   410
Pursute of worship, nor no hy prowesse,
In straunge lande ryding, ne travayle,
Ful lyte or nought in lovë doth avayle.

---

382. S. and thair (*for* and hir); *rest omit* thair (=hir).   384. Th. lieges.
386. *So all.*   391. S. worthi kny*ch*t & hir trew; *rest omit* worthi *and* trew.
I follow S.; *but omit* and.   393. F. T. Ipomones; Th. Ypomedes; S. P.
Ypomenes; D. Ipomeus.   394. *I supply* was.   400. F. lovers; T. louys;
rest loues.   403. S. trewe; *rest* trewe men.   405. Th. moost.   407.
D. S. oth; *rest* othe.   409. F. P. S. port; *rest* porte.   411. S. no; *rest*
omit.   413. Th. lytel; P. litill; D. litle; *rest* lyte.

* * *
* * * *   S

Peril of dethe, nother in see ne lande,
Hunger ne thurst, sorowe ne sekenesse,　　　　　　415
Ne grete empryses for to take on hande,
Sheding of blode, ne manful hardinesse,
Ne ofte woundinge at sautes by distresse,
Nor †juparting of lyf, nor deeth also—
Al is for nought, Love taketh no hede therto !　　　420

But lesings, with hir false flaterye,
Through hir falshede, and with hir doublenesse,
With tales newe and many fayned lye,
By fals semblaunt and counterfet humblesse,
Under colour depeynt with stedfastnesse,　　　　　　425
With fraude covered under a pitous face
Accepte been now rathest unto grace,

And can hem-selve now best magnifye
With fayned port and fals presumpcioun ;
They haunce hir cause with fals surquedrye　　　　　430
Under meninge of double entencioun,
To thenken oon in hir opinioun
And saye another ; to sette hemselve alofte
And hinder trouthe, as it is seyn ful ofte.

The whiche thing I bye now al to dere,　　　　　435
Thanked be Venus and the god Cupyde !
As it is sene by myn oppressed chere,
And by his arowes that stiken in my syde,
That, sauf the deth, I nothing abyde
Fro day to day ; alas, the harde whyle !　　　　　440
Whan ever his dart that him list to fyle,

My woful herte for to ryve a-two
For faute of mercy, and lak of pitè
Of her that causeth al my payne and wo
And list not ones, of grace, for to see　　　　　445
Unto my trouthe through her crueltee ;
And, most of alle, yit I me complayne,
That she hath joy to laughen at my peyne !

---

414. F. nother ; *rest* nor.　415. Th. syknesse ; F. sekenesse.　419. D.
Iupardy ; *rest* in partynge (*for* iupartynge) ; *read* juparting ; cf. l. 475.
421. F. fals (*error for* false) ; *rest omit.*　426. S. double (*for* pitous).
429. S. falss ; *rest om.*　435. Th. F. P. bye ; D. bie ; T. bey ; S. by.　437. Th.
T. S. sene ; F. seen ; P. D. seyn.　438. Th. sticken ; P. D. stekyn.　439.
S. P. the ; *rest om.*　447. S. ȝit ; *rest om.*

And wilfully hath [she] my deeth y-sworn
Al giltëlees, and wot no cause why 450
Save for the trouthe that I have had aforn
To her alone to serve faithfully !
O god of lovë ! unto thee I cry,
And to thy blinde double deitee
Of this gret wrongë I compleyne me, 455

And to thy stormy wilful variaunce
Y-meynt with chaunge and greet unstablenesse ;
. Now up, now doun, so renning is thy chaunce,
That thee to truste may be no sikernesse.
I wyte it nothing but thy doublenesse ; 460
And who that is an archer and is †blent
Marketh nothing, but sheteth as he †went.

And for that he hath no discrecioun,
Withoute avys he let his arowe go ;
For lakke of sight, and also of resoun, 465
In his shetinge, it happeth ofte so,
To hurte his frend rather than his fo ;
So doth this god, [and] with his sharpe floon
The trewe sleeth, and let the false goon.

And of his wounding this is the worst of alle, 470
Whan he hurteth, he doth so cruel wreche
And maketh the seke for to crye and calle
Unto his fo, for to been his leche ;
And hard it is, for a man to seche,
Upon the point of dethe in jupardye, 475
Unto his fo, to finde remedye !

Thus fareth it now even by me,
That to my fo, that yaf myn herte a wounde,
Mote aske grace, mercy, and pitè,
And namëly, ther wher non may be founde ! 480
For now my sore my leche wil confounde,

---

449. *I supply* she. S. ysuorn ; *rest om.* y-. 451. Th. *om.* have. 453. T. D. S. aboue (*for* of love) ; *see* l. 454. 461. S. blend (*read* blent) ; *rest* blynde (blinde). 462. S. as he wend (*read* went) ; Th. by wende (!) ; *rest* by wenynge (!). 464. F. T. avise ; D. avice ; S. aviss ; Th. aduyse. 467. S. P. frend ; *rest* frende. 468. B. *begins here. I supply* and. 469. T. lette ; F. leteth ; Th. letteth ; B. D. letith ; S. lattith. 471. B. F. S. he doth ; Th. T. doth to. 475. Th. ieopardye ; S. Iupartye ; F. partie (!) ; B. D. T. Iupardye ; P. Iupard.

And god of kinde so hath set myn ure,
My lyves fo to have my wounde in cure!

Alas! the whyle now that I was born!
Or that I ever saw the brighte sonne!　　　485
For now I see, that ful longe aforn,
Or I was born, my desteny was sponne
By Parcas sustren, to slee me, if they conne;
For they my deth shopen or my sherte
Only for trouthe! I may it not asterte.　　　490

The mighty goddesse also of Nature
That under god hath the governaunce
Of worldly thinges committed to her cure,
Disposed hath, through her wys purveyaunce,
To yeve my lady so moche suffisaunce　　　495
Of al vertues, and therwithal purvyde
To murdre trouthe, hath take Daunger to gyde.

For bountè, beautè, shappe, and semeliheed,
Prudence, wit, passingly fairnesse,
Benigne port, glad chere with lowliheed,　　　500
Of womanheed right plenteous largesse,
Nature did in her fully empresse,
Whan she her wroughte; and alther-last Disdayne,
To hinder trouthe, she made her chamberlayne;

Whan Mistrust also, and Fals-Suspeccioun,　　　505
With Misbeleve, she made for to be
Cheef of counsayl to this conclusioun,
For to exyle Routhe, and eek Pitè,
Out of her court to make Mercy flee,
So that Dispyt now holdeth forth her reyne,　　　510
Through hasty bileve of tales that men feyne.

And thus I am, for my trouthe, alas!
Murdred and slayn with wordes sharpe and kene,
Giltlees, god wot, of al maner trespas,
And lye and blede upon this colde grene.　　　515
Now mercy, swete! mercy, my lyves quene!
And to your grace of mercy yet I preye,
In your servyse that your man may deye!

---

488. Th. systerne.　　489. S. haue schapen (*for* shopen).　　494. F. hath;
Th. haue.　　501. F. B. plentevous.　　Th. largnesse.　　508. Th. trouthe; S.
treuth; *rest* routhe; *see* l. 679.　　514. Th. Gyltlesse; F. Giltles; P. Gylteles.

But if so be that I shal deye algate,
And that I shal non other mercy have,   520
Yet of my dethe let this be the date
That by your wille I was brought to my grave ;
Or hastily, if that you list me save,
My sharpe woundes, that ake so and blede,
Of mercy, charme, and also of womanhede.   525

For other charme, playnly, is ther non
But only mercy, to helpe in this case ;
For though my woundes blede ever in oon,
My lyf, my deeth, standeth in youre grace ;
And though my gilt be nothing, alas !   530
I aske mercy in al my beste entente,
Redy to dye, if that ye assente.

For ther-ayeines shal I never stryve
In worde ne werke ; playnly, I ne may ;
For lever I have than to be alyve   535
To dye soothly, and it be her to pay ;
Ye, though it be this eche same day
Or whan that ever her liste to devyse ;
Suffyceth me to dye in your servyse.

And god, that knowest the thought of every wight 540
Right as it is, in †al thing thou mayst see,
Yet, ere I dye, with all my fulle might
Lowly I pray, to graunte[n] unto me
That ye, goodly, fayre, fresshe, and free,
Which slee me only for defaute of routhe,   545
Or that I dye, ye may knowe my trouthe.

For that, in sothe, suffyseth unto me,
And she it knowe in every circumstaunce ;
And after, I am wel apayd that she
If that hir list, of dethe to do vengeaunce   550
Untó me, that am under her legeaunce ;

523. F. B. P. ye (*for* you .   530. F. B. S. gilt; *rest* gylte (gilte).   533.
S. aȝeynes ; T. agaynst ; F. B. D. ayens ; Th. agaynst.   536. S. ȝow to pay ;
rest her to pay.   537. Th. *om.* eche.   538. T. D liste ; *rest* list.   541.
All euery ; *read* al.   543. *All* graunte (graunt) ; *read* graunten.   545.
Th. onely sle me ; MSS. slee me only.   547. S. vnto ; *rest om.*   548. S.
If (*for* And).   549. S. apaid ; *rest* payd (paid).   550. *For* to *read* shal ?
551. F. P. legeaunce ; Th. D. ligeaunce ; T. lygeaunce.

It sit me not her doom to disobeye,
But, at her luste, wilfully to deye.

Withoute grucching or rebellioun
In wille or worde, hoolly I assent,   555
Or any maner contradiccioun,
Fully to be at her commaundëment ;
And, if I dyë, in my testament
My herte I sende, and my spirit also,
What-so-ever she list, with hem to do.   560

And alder-last unto her womanhede
And to her mercy me I recommaunde,
That lye now here, betwixe hope and drede,
Abyding playnly what she list commaunde.
For utterly, (this nis no demaunde),   565
Welcome to me, whyl me lasteth breeth,
Right at her choise, wher it be lyf or deeth !

In this matere more what mighte I seyn,
Sith in her hande and in her wille is al,
Both lyf and deeth, my joy and al my payn?   570
And fynally, my heste holde I shal,
Til my spirit, by desteny fatal,
Whan that her liste, fro my body wende ;
Have here my trouthe, and thus I make an ende !'

And with that worde he gan syke as sore   575
Lyk as his herte ryve wolde atwayne,
And held his pees, and spak a word no more.
But, for to see his wo and mortal payne,
The teres gonne fro myn eyen rayne
Ful pitously, for very inward routhe   580
That I him saw so languisshing for trouthe.

And al this whyle my-self I kepte cloos
Among the bowes, and my-self gan hyde,
Til, at the laste, the woful man aroos,
And to a logge wente ther besyde,   585
Where, al the May, his custome was t'abyde,

---

553. T. D. luste ; Th. F. B. lust. S. Quherso hir list to do me lyue or deye.
555. S. hoolly ; Th. holy.   560. Th. T. D. lyste ; F. S. P. list.   561. S.
vnto ; *rest* to.   566. S. quhill þat me.   568. Th. mater.   571. F. B.
P. hest.   573. T. liste ; *rest* list (lust).   575. T. sike ; S. to sike ; Th. D.
sygh ; F. B. sile (!).   577. Th. no worde.   581. Th. long wisshing (!). Th. S.
for ; F. B. D. P. for his ; T. for her.   583. S. P. gan ; *rest* gonne (gunne).

Sole, to complaynen of his paynes kene,
Fro yeer to yere, under the bowes grene.

And for bicause that it drow to the night
And that the sonne his ark diurnál   590
Y-passed was, so that his persaunt light,
His brighte bemes and his stremes al,
Were in the wawes of the water fal,
Under 'the bordure of our ocëan,
His char of golde his cours so swiftly ran :   595

And whyl the twylight and the rowes rede
Of Phebus light were dëaurat a lyte,
A penne I took, and gan me faste spede
The woful playntë of this man to wryte
Word by wordë, as he did endyte ;   600
Lyk as I herde, and coude him tho reporte,
I have here set, your hertes to disporte.

If ought be mis, layeth the wyte on me,
For I am worthy for to bere the blame
If any thing [here] misreported be,   605
To make this dytè for to seme lame
Through myn unconning ; but, to sayn the same,
Lyk as this man his complaynt did expresse,
I aske mercy and forgivënesse.

And, as I wroot, me thoughte I saw a-ferre,   610
Fer in the weste, lustely appere
Esperus, the goodly brighte sterre,
So glad, so fair, so persaunt eek of chere,
I mene Venus, with her bemes clere,
That, hevy hertes only to releve,   615
Is wont, of custom, for to shewe at eve.

And I, as faste, fel doun on my knee
And even thus to her gan I to preye :—
'O lady Venus ! so faire upon to see,
Let not this man for his trouthe deye,   620
For that joy thou haddest whan thou leye
With Mars thy knight, whan Vulcanus you fond,
And with a chayne invisible you bond

---

587. S. compleynen ; *rest* complayne.   598. T. faste ; *rest* fast.   605. *I
supply* here.   606. Th. dytte.   611. T. D. weste ; *rest* west.   617. T. D. faste ;
rest fast.   S. D. F. doun ; Th. adowne ; D. T. Adoun.   622. T. you ; *rest om.*

Togider, bothe twayne, in the same whyle
That al the court above celestial   625
At youre shame gan for to laughe and smyle!
A! fairë lady! welwilly founde at al,
Comfort to careful, O goddesse immortal!
Be helping now, and do thy diligence
To let the stremes of thyn influence   630

Descende doun, in forthering of the trouthe,
Namely, of hem that lye in sorowe bounde;
Shew now thy might, and on hir wo have routhe
Er fals Daunger slee hem and confounde.
And specially, let thy might be founde   635
For to socourë, what-so that thou may,
The trewe man that in the herber lay,

And alle trewe forther, for his sake,
O gladde sterre, O lady Venus myne!
And cause his lady him to grace take.   640
Her herte of stele to mercy so enclyne,
Er that thy bemes go up, to declyne,
And er that thou now go fro us adoun,
Fór that love thou haddest to Adoun!'

And whan that she was gon unto her reste,   645
I roos anon, and hoom to bedde wente,
For verily, me thoughte it for the beste;
Prayinge thus, in al my best entente,
That alle trewe, that be with Daunger shente,
With mercy may, in reles of hir payn,   650
Recured be, er May come eft agayn.

And for that I ne may no lenger wake,
Farewel, ye lovers alle, that be trewe!
Praying to god; and thus my leve I take,
That, er the sonne to-morowe be risen newe,   655
And er he have ayein his rosen hewe,
That eche of you may have suche a grace,
His owne lady in armes to embrace.

---

626. S. for to; *rest om.*   627. MSS. welwilly; Th. wyl I (!).   636.
Th. socouer (*misprint*).   645. S. vnto; *rest* to.   647. S. verily; Th. T. D.
wery (!); B. very wery (!); F. werry werry (!); P. very.   650. F. B. reles; T.
D. relese; Th. release; S. relesche.   656. Th. T. S. P. *om.* his.

I mene thus, that, in al honestee,
Withoute more, ye may togider speke   660
What so ye listë, at good libertee,
That eche may to other hir herte breke,
On Jelousyë only to be wreke,
That hath so longe, of malice and envye,
Werreyed Trouthe with his tirannye.   665

Lenvoy.

Princesse, plese it your benignitee
This litel dytè for to have in mynde!
Of womanhedë also for to see
Your trewe man may youre mercy finde;
And Pitè eek, that long hath be behinde,   670
Let him ayein be próvoked to grace;
For, by my trouthe, it is ayeines kinde,
Fals Daunger for to occupye his place!

Go, litel quayre, unto my lyves queen,
And my very hertes soverayne;   675
And be right glad; for she shal thee seen;
Suche is thy grace! But I, alas! in payne
Am left behinde, and not to whom to playne.
For Mercy, Routhe, Grace, and eek Pitè
Exyled be, that I may not attayne   680
Recure to finde of myn adversitè.

Explicit.

---

659. Th. *om.* that.   663. Th. ialousyes; D. Ielosies; *rest* Ielosye.   664.
T. B. P. of; *rest* of his.   665. S. Werreyed; D. Werried; *rest* Werred.
666. MSS. Princes; Th. Pryncesse. Th. pleaseth; F. pleseth; P. plesith
(*read* plese). Th. it to your; *rest om.* to.   667. S. P. for; *rest om.*   669.
Th. D. *om.* trewe.   673. S. for; *rest om.*

IX. THE FLOUR OF CURTESYE.

———◆———

IN Fevrier, whan the frosty mone
  Was horned, ful of Phebus fyry light,
And that she gan to reyse her stremes sone,
Saint Valentyne! upon thy blisful night
Of duëtee, whan glad is every wight,   5
And foules chese (to voyde hir olde sorowe)
Everich his make, upon the nexte morowe;

The same tyme, I herde a larke singe
Ful lustely, agayn the morowe gray——
'Awake, ye lovers, out of your slombringe,   10
This gladde morowe, in al the haste ye may;
Some observaunce doth unto this day,
Your choise ayen of herte to renewe
In confirming, for ever to be trewe!

And ye that be, of chesing, at your large,   15
This lusty day, by custome of nature,
Take upon you the blisful holy charge
To serve lovë, whyl your lyf may dure,
With herte, body, and al your besy cure,
For evermore, as Venus and Cipryde   20
For you disposeth, and the god Cupyde.

For joye owe we playnly to obeye
Unto this lordes mighty ordinaunce,

From Th. (Thynne, ed. 1532). TITLE: Th. The Floure of Curtesy; (ed. 1561 *adds*—made by Ihon Lidgate). *I note here the rejected spellings.*
1. Feverier.   2. firy.   3. streames.   5. dutie.   6. her.
7. Eueryche; next.   9. agayne.   11. glad.   12. dothe.
15. chosyng.   18. whyle; lyfe.   20. Cipride.   22. obey.

And, mercilesse, rather for to deye
Than ever in you be founden variaunce;   25
And, though your lyf be medled with grevaunce,
And, at your herte, closed be your wounde,
Beth alway one, ther-as ye are bounde!'

Thát whan I had herd, and listed longe,
With devout herte, the lusty melodye   30
Of this hevenly comfortable songe
So ágreable, as by harmonye,
I roos anon, and faste gan me hye
Toward a grove, and the way [gan] take
Foules to sene, everich chese his make.   35

And yet I was ful thursty in languisshing;
Myn ague was so fervent in his hete,
Whan Aurora, for drery complayning,
Can distille her cristal teres wete
Upon the soile, with silver dewe so swete;   40
For she [ne] durste, for shame, not apere
Under the light of Phebus bemes clere.

And so, for anguisshe of my paynes kene,
And for constraynte of my sighes sore,
I sette me doun under a laurer grene   45
Ful pitously; and alway more and more,
As I beheld into the holtes horé,
I gan complayne myn inward deedly smerte,
That ay so sore †crampisshed myn herte.

And whyl that I, in my drery payne,   50
Sat, and beheld aboute on every tree
The foules sitten, alway twayne and twayne,
Than thoughte I thus: 'alas! what may this be,
That every foul hath his libertee
Frely to chesen after his desyre   55
Everich his make thus, fro yeer to yere?

---

26. lyfe.   26. closet.   27. there.   29. herde.   30. deuoute.
32. ermonye.   33. rose.   34. Towarde; *supply* gan.   35. eueryche
chose.   39. distyl; (*read* distille); chrystal teeres.   41. *Supply* ne.
42. beames.   45. set; downe.   47. behelde.   48. inwarde.   49.
aye; crampessh at (*read* crampisshed).   50. whyle.   51. Sate; behelde;
tre.   52. sytte (*read* sitten).   53. thought.   54. foule.   55. chose
(*read* chesen).   56. Eueryche; yere to yere.

The sely wrenne, the titmose also,
The litel redbrest, have free eleccioun
To flyen y-ferë and †togider go
Wher-as hem liste, abouten enviroun,   60
As they of kynde have inclinacoun,
And as Nature, emperesse and gyde,
Of every thing, liste to provyde ;

But man aloon, alas ! the harde stounde !
Ful cruelly, by kyndes ordinaunce,   65
Constrayned is, and by statut bounde,
And debarred from alle such plesaunce.
What meneth this ? What is this purveyaunce
Of god above, agayn al right of kynde,
Withoute cause, so narowe man to bynde ? '   70

Thus may I [soothly] seen, and playne, alas !
My woful houre and my disaventure,
That dolefully stonde in the same cas
So fer behyndë, from al helth and cure.
My wounde abydeth lyk a sursanure ;   75
For me Fortune so felly list dispose,
My harm is hid, that I dar not disclose.

For I my herte have set in suche a place
Wher I am never lykly for to spede ;
So fer I am hindred from her grace   80
That, save daunger, I have non other mede.
And thus, alas ! I not who shal me rede
Ne for myn helpe shape remedye,
For Male-bouche, and for false Envye :

The whiche twayne ay stondeth in my wey   85
Maliciously ; and Fals Suspeccioun
Is very causë also that I dey,
Ginning and rote of my distruccioun ;
So that I fele, [as] in conclusioun,

---

57. tytemose.   58. election.   59. togyther (*read* togider).   60.
Where as ; lyst aboute envyron.   61. inclynacion.   62. empresse (*read*
emperesse).   63. lyst.   64. alone.   66. statute.   67. al suche.
69. agayne.   70. Without.   71. *Supply* soothly ; sene.   73. doulfully ;
caas.   74. ferre.   75. lyke.   76. lyste.   77. harme ; dare.   79.
lykely.   80. ferre.   81. none.   83. myne.   85. aye.   86. false
suspection.   88. distruction.   89. *Supply* as ; conclusyon.

With hir traynes that they wol me shende,   90
Of my labour that deth mot make an ende!

Yet, or I dye, with herte, wil, and thought
To god of lovë this avowe I make,
(As I best can, how dere that it be bought,
Wher-so it be, that I slepe or wake,   95
Whyl Boreas doth the leves shake)
As I have hight, playnly, til I sterve,
For wele or wo, that I shal [ay] her serve.

And, for her sake, now this holy tyme,
Saint Valentyne! somwhat shal I wryte   100
Al-though so be that I can not ryme,
Nor curiously by no crafte endyte,
Yet lever I have, that she putte the wyte
In unconning than in negligence,
What-ever I sayë of her excellence.   105

What-ever I saye, it is of duëtee,
In sothfastnesse and no presumpcioun;
This I ensure to you that shal it see,
That it is al under correccioun;
What I reherce in commendacioun   110
Of herë that I shal to you, as blyve,
So as I can, her vertues here discryve. —

¶ Right by example as the somer-sonne
Passeth the sterre with his bemes shene,
And Lucifer among the skyës donne   115
A-morowe sheweth to voyde nightes tene,
So verily, withouten any wene,
My lady passeth (who-so taketh hede)
Al tho alyve, to speke of womanhede.

And as the ruby hath the soverainte   120
Of riche stones and the regalyë;
And [as] the rose, of swetnesse and beautè,
Of fresshe floures, withouten any lyë;
Right so, in sothe, with her goodly yë,

---

91 dethe mote.   94. howe.   95. Where so.   96. Whyle; dothe;
leaues.   98. wel; *supply* ay.   99. nowe.   103. put.   106. say; dute
(*read* duetee).   107. presumpcion.   108. se.   109. correction.   110.
commendacion.   111. her (*read* here).   114. beames.   115. amonge.
122. *Supply* as; swetenesse.   123. without.   124. eye.

She passeth al in bountee and fairnesse, 125
Of maner ekë, and of gentilnesse.

For she is bothe the fairest and the beste,
To reken al in very sothfastnesse ;
For every vertue is in her at reste ;
And furthermore, to speke of stedfastnesse, 130
She is the rotë ; and of seemlinesse
The very mirrour ; and of governaunce
To al example, withouten variaunce.

Of port benigne, and wonder glad of chere,
Having evermore her trewe advertence 135
Alway to reson ; so that her desyre
Is brydeled ay by witte and providence ;
Thereto, of wittë and of hy prudence
She is the wellë, ay devoide of pryde,
That unto vertue her-selven is the gyde ! 140

And over this, in her daliaunce
Lowly she is, discret. wyse, [and secree],
And goodly gladde by attemperaunce,
That every wight, of high and low degree,
Are gladde in herte with her for to be ; 145
Só that, shortly, if I shal not lye,
She named is 'The Flour of Curtesye.'

And there, to speke of femininitee,
The leste mannish in comparisoun,
Goodly abasshed, having ay pitee 150
Of hem that been in tribulacioun ;
For she aloon is consolacioun
To al that arn in mischeef and in nede,
To comforte hem, of her womanhede.

And ay in vertue is her besy charge, 155
Sadde and demure, and but of wordes fewe ;
Dredful also of tonges that ben large,
Eschewing ay hem that listen to hewe
Above hir heed, hir wordes for to shewe,

125. bountie ; fayrenesse.   128. reken (*read* reknen ?).   131. semelynesse.   136. reason.   137. aye.   138. hye.   139. aye.   142. discrete and wyse (*read* discret wyse ; *and supply* secree *for the rime*).   144. lowe.
145. glad.   147. Floure.   148. femynyte (!).   149. mannyshe ; comparison.   150. aye pyte.   151. ben ; trybulacion.   152. alone ; -cion.   153.
arne ; mischefe.   155. aye.   157. Dredeful.   158. aye.   159. her (*twice*.)

Dishonestly to speke of any wight ;   160
She deedly hateth of hem to have a sight.

The herte of whom so honest is and clene,
And her entent so faithful and entere
That she ne may, for al the world, sustene
To suffre her eres any word to here,   165
Of frend nor fo, neither fer ne nere,
Amis resowning, that hinder shulde his name ;
And if she do, she wexeth reed for shame.

So trewëly in mening she is set,
Without chaunging or any doublenesse ;   170
For bountee and beautee ar togider knet
In her personë, under faithfulnesse ;
For void she is of newëfangelnesse ;
In herte ay oon, for ever to perséver
Ther she is set, and never to dissever.   175

I am to rude her vertues everichoon
Cunningly [for] to discryve and wryte ;
For wel ye wot, colour[es] have I noon
Lyk her discrecioun craftely t'endyte ;
For what I sayë, al it is to lyte.   180
Whérfor to you thus I me excuse,
That I aqueynted am not with no muse !

By rethoryke my style to governe,
In her preyse and commendacioun,
I am to blind, so hyly to discerne,   185
Of her goodnesse to make discripcioun,
Save thus I sayë, in conclusioun,
If that I shal shortly [her] commende,
In her is naught that Nature can amende.

For good she is, lyk to Policene,   190
And, in fairnesse, to the quene Helayne ;
Stedfast of herte, as was Dorigene,

---

164. worlde.   165. eeres ; worde.   166. frende ; foe ; ferre.   167.
Amysse.   169. trewly ; is in sette (*om.* in).   171. bountie ; beautie are
togyther knette.   173. voyde ; newfanglenesse (*or read* voide *and* new-
fangelnesse).   174. aye one.   175. There ; sette.   176. euerychone.
177. *Supply* for.   178. colour ; none.   179. Lyke ; to endyte.   180.
say.   181. Wherfore.   184. co*m*mendacion.   185. blynde ; hylye.
186. discrypcion.   187. say ; conclusyon.   188. *Supply* her.   190. lyke.
191. fayrenesse.

And wyfly trouthë, if I shal not fayne:
In constaunce eke and faith, she may attayne
To Cleopatre; and therto as †secree   195
As was of Troye the whyte Antigone;

As Hester meke; lyk Judith of prudence;
Kynde as Alceste or Marcia Catoun;
And to Grisilde lyk in pacience,
And Ariadne, of discrecioun;   200
And to Lucrece, that was of Rome toun,
She may be lykned, as for honestè;
And, for her faith, unto Penelope.

To faire Phyllis and to Hipsiphilee,
For innocencë and for womanhede;   205
For seemlinessë, unto Canacee;
And over this, to speke of goodlihede,
She passeth alle that I can of rede;
For worde and dede, that she naught ne falle,
Acorde in vertue, and her werkes alle.   210

For though that Dydo, with [her] witte sage,
Was in her tyme stedfast to Enee,
Of hastinesse yet she did outrage;
And so for Jason did also Medee.
But my lady is so avisee   215
That, bountee and beautee bothe in her demeyne,
She maketh bountee alway soverayne.

This is to mene, bountee goth afore,
Lad by prudence, and hath the soveraintee;
And beautee folweth, ruled by her lore,   220
That she †n'offendë her in no degree;
So that, in one, this goodly fresshe free
Surmounting al, withouten any were,
Is good and fair, in oon persone y-fere.

And though that I, for very ignoraunce,   225
Ne may discryve her vertues by and by,

---

193. wyfely.   194. faythe.   195. setrone (!); *read* secree (*see note*).
197. lyke.   198. Alcest.   199. lyke.   202. lykened.   203. faythe.
206. semelynesse; Canace.   208. al.   209, 210. fal, al.   211. *Supply*
her.   216. bountie; beautie.   217. bountie.   218. meane bountie
gothe.   220. beautie foloweth.   221. ne fende (!); degre.   222.
fre.   224. fayre; one.

Yet on this day, for a rémembraunce,
Only supported under her mercy,
With quaking hondë, I shal ful humbly
To her hynesse, my rudenes for to quyte,   230
A litel balade here bineth endyte,

Ever as I can suppryse in my herte,
Alway with fere, betwixe drede and shame,
Lest out of lose any word asterte
In this metre, to make it seme lame;   235
Chaucer is deed, that hadde suche a name
Of fair making, that [was], withoute wene,
Fairest in our tonge, as the laurer grene.

We may assaye for to counterfete
His gaye style, but it wil not be;   240
The welle is drye, with the licour swete,
Bothe of Clio and of Caliopè;
And first of al, I wol excuse me
To her, that is [the] ground of goodlihede;
And thus I saye until hir womanhede:—   245

Balade simple.

¶ 'With al my mightë, and my beste entente,
With al the faith that mighty god of kynde
Me yaf, sith he me soule and knowing sente,
I chese, and to this bonde ever I me bynde,
To love you best, whyl I have lyf and mynde':— 250
Thus herde I foules in the dawëninge
Upon the day of saint Valentyne singe.

'Yet chese I, at the ginning, in this entente,
To love you, though I no mercy fynde;
And if you liste I dyed, I wolde assente,   255
As ever twinne I quik out of this lynde!
Suffyseth me to seen your fetheres ynde':—

---

228. Onely.   230. rudenesse.   233. feare; betwyxt.   234. Leste;
worde.   236. had.   237. fayre; *supply* was; without.   239. assay.
240. gay.   241. lycoure.   242. Clye (!).   244. *Supply* the; grounde.
245. say.   246. might; best entent.   247. faythe.   248. yaue; sent.
250. whyle; lyfe.   251. daunynge.   252, 259. saynte Valentyne (? *om.*
saynte).   253. begynnyng (*read* ginning); entent.   255. assent.   256.
quicke; lyne (*misprint*).   257. sene; fethers.

Thus herde I foules in the morweninge
Upon the day of saint Valentyne singe.

'And over this, myn hertes lust to-bente,   260
In honour only of the wodëbynde,
Hoolly I yeve, never to repente
In joye or wo, wher-so that I wynde
Tofore Cupyde, with his eyën blynde':—
The foules alle, whan Tytan did springe,   265
With dévout herte, me thoughte I herde singe!

Lenvoy.

¶ Princesse of beautee, to you I represente
This simple dytè, rude as in makinge,
Of herte and wil faithful in myn entente,
Lyk as, this day, [the] foules herde I singe.   270

Here endeth the Flour of Curtesye.

---

258. mornynge (*for* morweninge).   260. myne ; luste.   261. onely ;
wodde bynde.   262. Holy.   263. where so.   265. al.   266. deuoute
hert ; thought.   267. Lenvoye. beautie ; represent.   269. entent.   270.
Lyke ; *supply* the.   COLOPHON : Floure ; Curtesy.

X. A BALADE; IN COMMENDATION
OF OUR LADY.

———•———

**(A devoute balade by Lidegate of Bury, made at the
reverence of oure lady, Qwene of mercy.— A.)**

A THOUSAND stories coude I mo reherce
Of olde poetes, touching this matere,
How that Cupyde the hertes gan so perce
Of his servauntes, setting hem on fere ;
Lo, here the fyn of th'errour and the were !   5
Lo, here of love the guerdon and grevaunce
That ever with wo his servaunts doth avaunce !

Wherfor now playnly I wol my style dresse
Of one to speke, at nede that wol nat fayle ;
Alas ! for dole, I ne can ne may expresse   10
Her passing pryse, and that is no mervayle.
O wind of grace, now blow into my sayle !
O aureat licour of Cleo, for to wryte
My penne enspyre, of that I wolde endyte !

Alas ! unworthy I am and unable   15
To love suche oon, al women surmounting,
To be benigne to me, and merciable,

From Th. ; *collated with* A. (Ashmole 59) ; *and* Sl. (Sloane 1212). 1. A.
I kouþe to you. 2. A. clerkis (*for* poetes) ; the (*for* this). 3. A. cane
mens hertes presse (!). 4. Th. hem ; A. þeire hertes. Th. in fere ; A. a fuyre.
5. A. With ful daunger payeþe his subgettes hyre. Sl. weere ; Th. fere.
7. Th. Sl. euer ; A. aye. Sl. A. his..doth ; Th. her..do. 8. Th. nowe ; A.
om. Sl. redresse. 10. A. Ellas I ne can ne may not ful expresse. 11.
Th. Sl. and that ; A. the whiche. 12. Th. wynde. Sl. into ; Th. unto. A.
þou blowe nowe to my. 13. Th. auryate ; A. aureate. A. *om.* of. 14.
A. tenspyre of whiche I thenk to wryte. Sl. wold ; Th. wol. 15. A. But sith
I am sonworthy (!). 16. Sl. on ; Th. A. one. 17. A. To ; Th. Sl. But she.

T 2

That is of pitè the welle and eek the spring !
Wherfor of her, in laude and in praysing,
So as I can, supported by her grace,   20
Right thus I say, kneling tofore her face :—

O sterre of sterres, with thy stremes clere,
Sterre of the see, to shipmen light and gyde,
O lusty living, most plesaunt to apere,
Whos brighte bemes the cloudes may not hyde ;   25
O way of lyf to hem that go or ryde,
Haven from tempest, surest up to ryve,
On me have mercy, for thy joyes fyvè !

O rightful rule, O rote of holinesse,
And lightsom lyne of pitè for to playne,   30
Original ginning of grace and al goodnesse,
Clenest conduit of vertue soverayne,
Moder of mercy, our trouble to restrayne,
Chambre and closet clenest of chastitè,
And named herberwe of the deitè !   35

O hoolsom garden, al voyde of wedes wikke,
Cristallin welle, of clennesse clere consigned,
Fructif olyve, of foyles faire and thikke,
And redolent cedre, most dereworthly digned,
Remembre on sinners unto thee assigned   40
Er wikked fendes hir wrathe upon hem wreche ;
Lanterne of light, thou be hir lyves leche !

Paradyse of plesaunce, gladsom to al good,
Benigne braunchelet of the pyne-tree,
Vyneyerd vermayle, refressher of our food,   45

---

18. A. Whiche of pytee is welle.   19. Th. Sl. of ; A. to.   20. Th.
Sl. can ; A. am.   22. A. O souereine sterre.   24. Sl. lemand (*for*
living). Sl. most ; Th. A. moste.   25. Th. Whose bright beames. Th. Sl.
may ; A. cane.   26. A. lyff ; Th. Sl. lyfe.   27. A. frome ; Th. Sl. after.
29. Sl. rote ; Th. A. bote.   31. A. gynnyng of grace and ; Th. Sl. begynn-
ing of grace and al.   32. A. Clennest ; Th. And clenest. Th. Sl. *ins.* most
bef. sovereyne.   33. A. Moder ; Th. Mother.   34. A. al cloose closette ;
Th. Sl. and closet clennest.   35. Th. herbrough ; Sl. herberwe.   A. The
hyest herber (!) of al the.   36. A. holsome ; Th. Sl. closed.   A. *om.* al.   37.
A. Welle cristallyne.   A. Sl. clennesse ; Th. clerenesse.   38. A. Fructyff ;
Th. Fructyfyed.   Th. fayre ; A. so feyre.   39. A. *om.* And.   A. *om.*
most.   40. A *om.* on. Sl. pecchours (*for* sinners).   A. unto ; Th. Sl. that
to the be.   41. Th. Sl. Or wikked ; A. Er foule.   A. on hem þeire wrathe.
Sl. upon ; Th. on.   42. Th. *om.* be.   43. A. Thou Paradys plesante,
gladnesse of goode.   44. A. And benigne braunche.   45. A. Vyneyerde
vermayle ; Th. Sl. Vynarie enuermayled.   Sl. food ; Th. A. bote.

Licour ayein languor, palled that may not be,
Blisful bawme-blossom, byding in bountè,
Thy mantel of mercy on our mischef sprede,
And er wo wake, wrappe us under thy wede !

O rody rosier, flouring withouten spyne,   50
Fountayne filthles, as beryl currant clere,
Som drope of graceful dewe to us propyne ;
Light withoute nebule, shyning in thy spere,
Medecyne to mischeves, pucelle withouten pere,
Flame doun to doleful light of thyn influence   55
On thy servauntes, for thy magnificence !

Of al Christen protectrice and tutele,
Retour of exyled, put in prescripcioun
To hem that erre in the pathe of hir sequele ;
To wery wandred tent and pavilioun,   60
The feynte to fresshe, and the pausacioun ;
Unto unresty bothe reste and remedye,
Fruteful to al tho that in her affye.

To hem that rennen thou art itinerárie,
O blisful bravie to knightes of thy werre ;   65
To wery werkmen thou art diourn denárie,
Mede unto mariners that have sayled ferre ;
Laureat crowne, streming as a sterre
To hem that putte hem in palestre for thy sake,
Cours of her conquest, thou whyte as any lake !   70

Thou mirthe of martyrs, sweter than citole,
Of confessours also richest donatyf,

46. Th. ayen al langour ; A. geyne langoure.   A. palde that ; Th. Sl.
that palled.   47. Sl. Blisful bawme ; A. Thou blessed ; Th. Blysful blomy.
48. Sl. misericord on our myschef. Th. on our myserie ; A. vppon vs spilt thou.
49. Th. awake. A. wake and wrappe vs ay vnder.   50. A. O rede roos
raylling withouten. Th. without.   51. Th. al fylthlesse ; A. om. al. A.
currant as beryle. Th. byrel.   52. Th. Sl. of thy ; I omit thy. A. Grace of thy
dewe til vs thou do propyne.   53. Th. O light ; Sl. Thou lyght. A. Thou
louely light, shynynge in bright spere.   54. A. missers ; Th. mischeues ;
Sl. myscheuows. A. withouten ; Th. without.   55. Th. Flambe ; A. Dryve.
Sl. to ; Th. A. the. A. om. doleful.   56. A. On ; Th. Sl. Remembring.
58. Sl. Retour ; Th. Returne ; A. Reeure. A. Sl. in ; Th. in the.   59.
A. To therroures of the pathe sequele.   60. A. For (for To). Sl. wan-
drid ; Th. forwandred ; A. wandering.   61. So A. Th. To faynte and to
fresshe the.   62. A. To wery wightes ful reste.   63. Th. tho that ; A.
that hem. A. omits ll. 64–119.   64. Th. arte.   66. Sl. thou art ; Th.
she is. Th. diourne.   68. Th. Laureate.   69. Th. put ; palastre.
71. Sl. Thow ; Th. O. Th. myrthe ; swetter ; sytole.   72. Sl. om. also. Th.
donatyfe.

Unto virgynes eternal lauriole,
Afore al women having prerogatyf;
Moder and mayde, bothe widowe and wyf,   75
Of al the worlde is noon but thou alone !
Now, sith thou may, be socour to my mone !

O trusty turtle, trewest of al trewe,
O curteyse columbe, replete of al mekenesse,
O nightingale with thy notes newe,   80
O popinjay, plumed with al clennesse,
O laverok of love, singing with swetnesse,
Phebus, awayting til in thy brest he lighte
Under thy winge at domesday us dighte !

O ruby, rubifyed in the passioun   85
Al of thy sone, among have us in minde,
O stedfast dyamaunt of duracioun,
That fewe feres that tyme might thou finde,
For noon to him was founden half so kinde !
O hardy herte, O loving crëature,   90
What was it but love that made thee so endure ?

Semely saphyre, depe loupe, and blewe ewage,
Stable as the loupe, ewage of pitè,
This is to say, the fresshest of visage,
Thou lovest hem unchaunged that serven thee.   95
And if offence or wrything in hem be,
Thou art ay redy upon hir wo to rewe,
And hem receyvest with herte ful trewe.

O goodly gladded, whan that Gabriel
With joy thee grette that may not be nombred !   100
Or half the blisse who coude wryte or tel
Whan the holy goost to thee was obumbred,
Wherthrough fendes were utterly encombred ?
O wemlees mayde, embelisshed in his birthe,
That man and aungel therof hadden mirthe !   105

---

74. Th. -tyfe.　　75. Th. Mother; wyfe.　　76. Sl. In all this. Sl. noon;
Th. none.　　78. Sl. trewest; Th. truefastest.　　81. Sl. plumed; Th. pured.
82. Sl. larke.　　　83. Sl. in; Th. on.　　83, 84. lyght, dyght.　　　85.
passyon.　　86. Sl. All*e*; Th. *om.* Th. sonne. Sl. among haue us; Th. vs haue
amonge.　87. Sl. dyamaunt; Th. dyametre. 88. Sl. that; Th. any. 89. halfe.
91. the.　　92. Th. saphre (*sic*); Sl. saffyr.　　95. *So* Sl.; Th. unchaunged hem.
96. Sl. writhyng; Th. varyeng.　　　97. arte; her.　　　98. hert; *see note.*
99. gladed.　　100. the.　　102. goste; the.　　103. Sl. vtterly; Th. bytterly.
104. wemlesse. Th. in; Sl. with.

Lo, here the blossom and the budde of glorie,
Of which the prophet spak so longe aforn ;
Lo, here the same that was in memórie
Of Isaie, so longe or she was born ;
Lo, here of David the delicious corn ;   110
Lo, here the ground that list [him] to onbelde,
Becoming man, our raunsom for to yelde !

O glorious vyole, O vytre inviolat !
O fyry Tytan, persing with thy bemes,
Whos vertuous brightnes was in thy brest vibrat,   115
That al the world embelisshed with his lemes !
Conservatrice of kingdomes and remes ;
Of Isaies sede O swete Sunamyte,
Mesure my mourning, myn owne Margaryte !

O sovereignest, sought out of Sion,   120
O punical pome ayens al pestilence ;
And aureat urne, in whom was bouk and boon
The agnelet, that faught for our offence
Ayens the serpent with so high defence
That lyk a lyoun in victorie he was founde ;   125
To him commende us, of mercy most habounde !

O precious perle, withouten any pere,
Cockle with gold dew from above berayned,
Thou busshe unbrent, fyrles set a-fere,
Flambing with fervence, not with hete payned ;   130
Thou during daysye, with no tweder stayned ;
Flees undefouled of gentil Gedeon,
And fructifying yerd thou of Aaron.

---

106. blosme.   107. Th. prophete; Sl. prophetys. Sl. spak so long aforn ;
Th. so longe spake beforne.   109, 110. borne, corne.   111. Th. of lyfe in
to bilde ; Sl. that list to onbelde.   113. Sl. o vitre ; Th. and vyte. Th.
inuyolate.   115. Th. *om.* thy ; vibrate.   116. Sl. his ; Th. the.   117. Sl.
kyngdamys ; Th. kynges dukes. Sl. remys ; Th. realmes.   118. Sl. o ; Th.
om.   120. A. souereine. Th. A. sought ; Sl. sowth. Th. out of ; Sl. of out ;
A. fer oute.   121–127. *In* Sl. *only.*   121. Sl. alle.   122. Sl. auryat ; book
and born (!) ; *see note.*   125. Sl. victory.   126. Sl. moost.   127. Sl. ony.
128. Th. golde dewe ; A. glorie.   129. A. Sl. Thou ; Th. Dewe (!).   Sl.
ferlett (!) set affere ; A. fuyrles thou sette vppon ; Th. fyrelesse fyre set on.
130. Sl. peyned ; A. empeyred (!).   131. Sl. Th. *om.* Thou. A. with ; Th.
that. Th. A. wether. A. disteyned.   132. Th. Fleece. A. gentyle ; Th.
gentylest.   133. Th. Sl. *insert* fayrest *after* fructifyeng (*sic*). A. yerde thowe ;
Th. Sl. the yerde.

Thou misty arke, probatik piscyne,
Laughing Aurora, and of pees olyve;   135
Columpne and base, up bering from abyme;
Why nere I conning, thee for to discryve?
Chosen of Joseph, whom he took to wyve,
Unknowing him, childing by greet mirácle,
And of our manhode trewe tabernacle!   140

---

134. A. Thowe; Sl. Th. The.   Sl. mysti; Th. A. mighty.   Sl. probatyk; Th. probatyfe; A. the probatyf.   135. A. Aurora; Th. aurore.   A. tholyve; Sl. Th. olyue.   136. A. Pillor from base beryng from abysme.   137. A. Why nad I langage.   Sl. the for; A. hir for; Th. here.   138. Th. toke. A. Chosen of god, whome Joseph gaf (!) to wyve.   139. Th. Sl. childyng; A. bare Cryste.   Th. Sl. *om.* greet.   140. Th. And of our manly figure the; Sl. And of oure mar (!) figure; A. And of Ihesus manhode truwe.

XI. TO MY SOVERAIN LADY.

—◦—

I HAVE non English convenient and digne
   Myn hertes hele, lady, thee with t'honoure,
Ivorie clene ; therfore I wol resigne
In-to thyn hand, til thou list socoure
To help my making bothe florisshe and floure ;   5
Than shulde I shewe, in lovë how I brende,
In songes making, thy name to commende.

For if I coude before thyn excellence
Singen in love, I wolde, what I fele,
And ever standen, lady, in thy presence,   10
To shewe in open how I love you wele ;
And sith, although your herte be mad of stele,
To you, withoute any disseveraunce,
J'ay en vous toute ma fiaunce.

Wher might I love ever better besette   15
Than in this lilie, lyking to beholde ?
The lace of love, the bond so wel thou knette,
That I may see thee or myn herte colde,
And or I passe out of my dayes olde,
Tofore singing evermore utterly—   20
'Your eyën two wol slee me sodainly.'

For love I langour, blissed be such seknesse,
Sith it is for you, my hertely suffisaunce ;
I can not elles saye, in my distresse,
So fair oon hath myn herte in governaunce ;   25
And after that I †ginne on esperaunce

From Th. (Thynne, ed. 1532) ; *I note rejected spellings.* 1. none englysshe.
2. heale ; the ; to honour.   3. cleane.   4. thyne hande ; socoure.   5.
helpe ; flour.   6. howe.   8. thyne.   11. howe.   12. made.   13.
withouten ; disceueraunce.   14. tout.   15. Where ; beset.   17. bonde ;
knyt.   18. se the ; myne.   22. sicknesse.   23. Sythe.   24. els say.
25. fayre one ; myne.   26. begynne ; *read* ginne.

With feble entune, though it thyn herte perce,
Yet for thy sake this lettre I do reherce.

God wot, on musike I can not, but I gesse,
(Alas! why so?) that I might say or singe,　　　　30
So love I you, myn own soverain maistresse,
And ever shal, withouten départinge.
Mirrour of beautè, for you out shuld I ringe,
In rémembraunce eke of your eyen clere,
Thus fer from you, my soverain lady dere!　　　　35

So wolde god your love wold me slo,
Sith, for your sake, I singe day by day;
Herte, why nilt thou [never] breke a-two,
Sith with my lady dwellen I ne may?
Thus many a roundel and many a virelay　　　　40
In fresshe Englisshe, whan I me layser finde,
I do recorde, on you to have minde!

Now, lady myn! sith I you love and drede,
And you unchaunged finde, in o degree,
Whos grace ne may flye fro your womanhede,　　　　45
Disdayneth not for to remembre on me!
Myn herte bledeth, for I may nat you see;
And sith ye wot my mening désirous,
Pleurez pur moi, si vous plaist amorous!

What marveyle is, though I in payne be?　　　　50
I am departed from you, my soveraine;
Fortune, alas! *dont vient la destenee,*
That in no wyse I can ne may attayne
To see the beautè of your eyën twayne.
Wherfore I say, for tristesse doth me grame,　　　　55
Tant me fait mal departir de ma dame!

Why nere my wisshing brought to suche esploit
That I might say, for joye of your presence,
' *Ore a mon cuer ce quil veuilloit,*
Ore a mon cuer the highest excellence　　　　60
That ever had wight;' and sith myn advertence

---

27. thyne.　28. letter.　30. wote.　31. owne; maistres.　32. without.
35. ferre.　36. wolde (*twice*).　37. Sythe.　38. nylte; *I supply* never;
breake.　39. Sythe; dwel.　43. Nowe; myne sithe.　44. euer fynde
(*om.* euer).　45. Whose.　47. Myne; se.　48. sithe; wotte; meanyng.
49. Plures; moy.　52. destenie.　53. canne.　54. se.　55. dothe.　56.
male.　58. ioye.　61. sithe myne.

Is in you, reweth on my paynes smerte,
I am so sore wounded to the herte.

To live wel mery, two lovers were y-fere,
So may I say withouten any blame ;   65
If any man [per cas] to wilde were,
I coude him [sonë] teche to be tame ;
Let him go love, and see wher it be game !
For I am brydled unto sobernesse
For her, that is of women cheef princesse.   70

But ever, whan thought shulde my herte embrace,
Than unto me is beste remedye,
Whan I loke on your goodly fresshe face ;
So mery a mirrour coude I never espye ;
And, if I coude, I wolde it magnifye.   75
For never non was [here] so faire y-founde,
To reken hem al, and also Rosamounde.

And fynally, with mouthe and wil present
Of double eye, withoute repentaunce,
Myn herte I yeve you, lady, in this entent,   80
That ye shal hoolly therof have governaunce ;
Taking my leve with hertes obeysaunce,
' Salve, regina !' singing laste of al,
To be our helpe, whan we to thee cal !

Al our lovë is but ydelnesse   85
Save your aloon ; who might therto attayne ?
Who-so wol have a name of gentillesse,
I counsayle him in love that he not fayne.
Thou swete lady ! refut in every payne,
Whos [pitous] mercy most to me avayleth   90
To gye by grace, whan that fortune fayleth.

Nought may be told, withouten any fable,
Your high renome, your womanly beautè ;
Your governaunce, to al worship able,
Putteth every herte in ese in his degree.   95
O violet, O flour desiree,

---

66. *Short line ; I insert* per cas.   67. *Short line ; I insert* sone. for to ;
I omit for.   68. Lette ; se where.   70. chefe.   71. my hert shuld.   72.
best remedy.   74. espy.   76. none ; *I insert* here.   79. without.
81. holy.   82. leaue.   84. the.   86. your loue alone ; *om.* loue.
89. refute.   90. Whose ; *I insert* pitous.   92. tolde.   95. ease.   96. floure.

Sith I am for you so amorous,
Estreynez moy, [lady,] *de cuer joyous!*

With fervent herte my brest hath broste on fyre;
L'ardant espoir que mon cuer poynt, est mort,　　　100
D'avoir l'amour de celle que je desyre,
I mene you, swete, most plesaunt of port,
Et je sai bien que ceo n'est pas mon tort
That for you singe, so as I may, for mone
For your departing; alone I live, alone.　　　105

Though I mighte, I wolde non other chese;
In your servyce, I wolde be founden sad;
Therfore I love no labour that ye lese,
Whan, in longing, sorest ye be stad;
Loke up, ye lovers [alle], and be right glad　　　110
Ayeines sëynt Valentynes day,
For I have chose that never forsake I may!

Explicit.

---

97. Sythe; amerous.　　98. Estreynes; *I insert* lady *to fill out the line.*
99. brost.　　102. meane; porte.　　103. say.　　106. myght; none.
107. sadde.　　109. stadde.　　110. *I supply* alle; gladde.　　111. Ayenst
saynt.　　112. chese (*read* chose).

XII. BALLAD OF GOOD COUNSEL.

CONSIDER wel, with every circumstaunce,
   Of what estat so-ever that thou be—
Riche, strong, or mighty of puissaunce,
Prudent or wyse, discrete or avisee,
The doom of folke in soth thou mayst nat flee ;   5
What-ever that thou do, trust right wel this,
A wikked tonge wol alway deme amis.

For in thy port or in thyn apparayle
If thou be clad or honestly be-seyn,
Anon the people, of malice, wol nat fayle,   10
Without advyce or reson, for to sayn
That thyn array is mad and wrought in vayn ;
What ! suffre hem spekë !—and trust right wel this,
A wikked tonge wol alway deme amis.

Thou wilt to kinges be equipolent,   15
With gretë lordes even and peregal ;
And, if thou be to-torn and al to-rent,
Than wol they say, and jangle over-al,
Thou art a slogard, that never thryvë shal ;
Yet suffre hem spekë !—and trust right wel this,   20
A wikked tonge wol alway deme amis.

From Th. (Thynne's edition, 1532) ; *collated with* Ff. (MS. Ff. 1. 6, Camb. Univ. Library). *Another copy in* H. (Harl. 2251).   1. H. with ; Ff. wiht ; Th. *om.*   2. Ff. H. estat ; Th. estate. Th. *om.* that.   3. Th. stronge. 4. Ff. avisee ; H. avice ; Th. besy.   5. Th. Ff. dome ; H. doome. Th. sothe. H. mayst ; Th. Ff. may. Th. Ff. flye ; H. flee.   6. H. that ; *rest om.* Ff. H. do ; Th. doste. Th. *om.* right.   7. H. Ff. deme ; Th. say.   8. Ff. port ; Th. porte. Th. thyne.   9. *All* cladde. Ff. H. or ; Th. and. Ff. beseyn ; Th. be sayne.   10. Ff. Anon ; Th. Anone (*and so in other places I correct the spelling by the* MSS.).   12. *All* made.   13. Th. H. *om.*. right.   14. Ff. H. deme ; Th. say.   15. Ff. H. wylt ; Th. wolde. Ff. H. equipolent ; Th. equiuolent.   16. Ff. H. grete ; Th. great.   17. Ff. to-torn ; Th. H. torn.   19. Ff. H. Thou ; Th. That thou.   20. Th. H. *om.* right.   21. Ff. H deme ; Th. say.

If thou be fayr, excelling of beautee,
Than wol they say, that thou art amorous;
If thou be foul and ugly on to see,
They wol afferme that thou art vicious,   25
The peple of langage is so dispitous;
Suffre hem spekë, and trust right wel this,
A wikked tonge wol alway deme amis.

And if it fallë that thou take a wyf,
[Than] they wol falsly say, in hir entent,   30
That thou art lykly ever to live in stryf,
Voyd of al rest, without alegëment;
Wyves be maistres, this is hir jugëment;
Yet suffre hem spekë—and trust right wel this,
A wikked tonge wol alway deme amis.   35

And if it so be that, of parfitnesse,
Thou hast avowed to live in chastitee,
Thán wol folk of thy persone expresse
Say thou art impotent t'engendre in thy degree;
And thus, whether thou be chast or deslavee,   40
Suffre hem spekë—and trust right wel this,
A wikked tonge wel alway deme amis.

And if that thou be fat or corpulent,
Than wol they say that thou art a glotoun,
A devourour, or ellës vinolent;   45
If thou be lene or megre of fassioun,
Cal thee a nigard, in hir opinioun;
Yet suffre hem spekë—and trust right wel this,
A wikked tonge wol alway deme amis.

22-35. *So in* H.; Th. Ff. *transpose* ll. 21-28 *and* 29-35. Th. fayre and;
Ff. H. *om.* and. H. excellyng; Ff. Th. excellent.   23. Ff. H. Than; Th.
Yet. *All* amerous.   24. *All* foule.   26. Ff. H. peple of; Th. peoples.
27. *So* Ff.; Th. H. Suffre al their speche and truste (H. deme) wel this.
28. Ff. H. deme ; Th. say.   29. Ff. And yif hit falle ; Th. If it befal.   30.
Insert Than ; *see* l. 23.   31. Ff. Thou art euer lykkely to lyue in stryve.
32. Ff. alleggement.   33. Ff. H. be maistres; Th. hem maystren.   34. *So*
Ff. ; Th. suffren their speche ; *om.* right.   35. Ff. H. deme ; Th. say.   36.
H. And if; Ff. And yif; Th. If. H. it; Th. Ff. *om.* Th. that thou : Ff. H.
om. thou.   37. Ff. H. Thou hast; Th. Haue.   39. Ff. H. Say ; Th. That.
Th. tengendre ; Ff. to gendre.   40. Ff. Th. chaste. Ff. dyslave (*better* deslavee);
Th. delauie.   41. Th. H. *om.* right.   42. Ff. H. deme; Th. say.   43. Th.
om. And.   44. Th. H. *om.* that.   45. Th. H. deuourer ; Ff. devowrer
(*better* devourour).   46. Ff. H. lene or megre ; Th. megre or leane.   47.
Ff. H. her ; Th. H. their.   48. Th. H. *om.* right.   49. Ff. H. deme ; Th. say.

If thou be richë, som wol yeve thee laud,   50
And say, it cometh of prudent governaunce;
And som wol sayen, that it cometh of fraud,
Outher by sleight, or by fals chevisaunce;
To say the worst, folk have so gret plesaunce;
Yet suffre hem sayë—and trust right wel this,   55
A wikked tonge wol alway deme amis.

If thou be sad or sobre of countenaunce,
Men wol say—thou thinkest som tresoun;
And if [that] thou be glad of daliaunce,
Men wol deme it dissolucioun,   60
And calle thy fair speche, adulacioun;
Yet let hem spekë—and trust right wel this,
A wikked tonge wol alway deme amis.

Who that is holy by perfeccioun,
Men, of malyce, wol calle him ipocryte;   65
And who is mery, of clene entencioun,
Men say, in ryot he doth him delyte;
Som mourne in blak; som laughe in clothes whyte;
What! suffre them spekë—and trust right wel this,
A wikked tonge wol alway deme amis.   70

Honest array, men deme, †is pompe and pryde,
And who goth poore, men calle him a wastour;
And who goth [mene], men marke him on every syde,
And saye that he is a spye or a gylour;
Who wasteth, men seyn [that] he hath tresour;   75
Wherfore conclude, and trust [right] wel this,
A wikked tonge wil alway deme amis.

---

50. *All* the. Th. laude; Ff. H. lawde.   52. Ff. Th. say; H. sayne. H.
that; Th. Ff. *om.*   53. Ff. Outher; Th. H. Or.   55. Th. What; Ff. H.
Yit. Ff. Th. say. Th. H. *om.* right.   56. Ff. H. deme; Th. say.   57. *All*
sadde.   58. Ff. tresone; Th. H. treason.   59. *I supply* that.   60. Ff. it is;
Th. H. *om.* is.   61. Th. Callyng; Ff. H. And calle. Th. *om.* thy.   62. Th.
H. *om.* right.   63. Ff. H. deme; Th. say.   64. Ff. H. Who; Th.
And who.   65. Th. him an; Ff. H. *om.* an.   66. Th. who that; Ff. H. *om.*
that.   69. Ff. speke; Th. say. Th. H. *om.* right.   70. Ff. H. deme;
Th. say.   71-77. *In* H. *only.*   71. H. in; *read* is.   72. H. vastour.
73. *I insert* mene; *see note.*   75. H. wastith; *I insert* that.   76. H.
coclude(!); H. *om.* right.

Who speketh mochë, men calle him prudent;
And who debateth, men say, he is hardy;
And who saith litel with gret sentiment,   80
Som men yet wol edwyte him of foly;
Trouth is put down, and up goth flatery;
And who list plainly know the cause of this,
A wikked tonge wol alway deme amis.

For though a man were al-so pacient   85
As was David, through his humilitee,
Or with Salamon in wysdom as prudent,
Or in knighthode egal with Josuë,
Or manly proved as Judas Machabee,
Yet, for al that—trust right wel this,   90
A wicked tonge wol alway deme amis.

And though a man hadde the high prowesse
Of worthy Hector, Troyes champioun,
The love of Troilus or the kindenesse,
Or of Cesar the famous high renoun,   95
With Alisaundres dominacioun,
Yet, for al that—trust right wel this,
A wikked tonge wol alway deme amis.

And though a man of high or low degree
Of Tullius hadde the sugred eloquence,   100
Or of Senek the greet moralitee,
Or of Catoun the foresight or prudence,
Conquest of Charles, Arthurs magnificence,
Yet, for al that—trust right wel this,
A wikked tonge wol alway deme amis.   105

---

78. Ff. H. men calle him; Th. is holden.   79. Th. And who; Ff. H. Who
that. Th. H. say that; Ff. om. that.   80. Th. who that; Ff. H. om. that.
81. Th. men yet; Ff. folke. Ff. H. edwyte; Th. wyte.   82. Ff. H. vp; Th. nowe.
83. H. who; Ff. ho (= who); Th. who that. Ff. H. cause; Th. trouth.   84. So
H. Ff.; Th. It is a wicked tonge that alway saythe amys.   85. Ff. also;
Th. H. as.   86. Th. om. his.   87. H. wisdom; Th. wisedome; Ff.
wysdome.   88. Ff. to; Th. H. with.   91. So Ff. H.; Th. Some wycked
tonge of hym wol say amys.   92. Ff. om. a. All had. Ff. H. om. high.
94. Ff. H. kyndenes; Th. kyndnesse.   96. Th. Wyth al; Ff. H. om. al.
98. So Ff.; Th. Some wycked tonge of hym wol say amys.   99. Ff. H.
And; Th. Or.   101. H. Senek; Ff. Senec; Th. Seneca. Th. great; Ff.
H. om.   102. Ff. or prudence; Th. H. and prouidence.   103. Th. The
conquest; Ff. om. The. Ff. Arthurs; Th. H. Arturs.   105. See note
to 96.

Touching of women the parfit innocence,
Thogh they had of Hestre the mekenes,
Or of Griseldes [the] humble pacience,
Or of Judith the proved stablenes,
Or Policenes virginal clennes,   110
Yit dar I say and truste right wel this,
A wikked tonge wol alway deme amis.

The wyfly trouthë of Penelope,
Though they it hadde in hir possessioun,
Eleynes beautè, the kindnes of Medee,   115
The love unfeyned of Marcia Catoun,
Or of Alcest the trewe affeccioun,
Yit dar I say and truste right wel this,
A wikked tonge wol alway deme amis.

Than sith it is, that no man may eschewe   120
The swerde of tonge, but it wol kerve and byte,
Ful hard it is, a man for to remewe
Out of hir daunger, so they hem delyte
To hindre or slaundre, and also to bakbyte;
For [this] hir study fynally it is   125
And hir plesaunce, alwey to deme amis.

Most noble princes, cherisshers of vertue,
Remembreth you of high discrecioun,
The first vertue, most plesing to Jesu,

106–112. *Not in* Thynne; *from* Ff. H.   106. H. of; Ff. to.   108. Ff. grecildes; H. Gresieldis; *I supply* the.   110. H. Polycenes; Ff. Penilops. 113. H. wyfly; Th. wyfely; Ff. wylfull*e* (!). Th. H. trouth; Ff. trowth; *read* trouthe.   114. Th. had; Ff. H. hadde. Th. her; Ff. thaire; H. theyr.   115. H. Eleynes; Ff. Eleyons; Th. Holynesse (*for* Heleynes). Th. kyndenesse; Ff. kyndnes.   116. Ff. H. loue; Th. lyfe (!). Th. Mertia; Ff. H. Marcia. Th. Caton; Ff. H. and catou*n*.   117. Ff. H. Alcestys (*om.* the). 119. *So* Ff.; Th. A wycked tonge wol say of her amys.   120. Ff. suyth; H. sith; Th. sythen. H. it is; Ff. it; Th. it is so (*om.* that).   121. Ff. wyll (=wol); H. wil; Th. *om.*   122. Ff. H. *om.* for.   123. H. hir; Ff. ar; Th. theyr. Ff. so them hem delyte; Th. him for to aquyte. 124. Ff. Tho (*for* To) hindre sclau*n*der, and also to bacbyte; Th. Wo to the tonges that hem so delyte.   125. Ff. For thayre study fynaly it ys; Th. To hynder or sclaunder, and set theyr study in this (cf. l. 124).   126. Th. And theyr pleasaunces to do and say amis; H. And theyr plesaunce alwey to deme amys; Ff. *has* (*as usual*) A wicked tonge wol alway deme amis. 127. Ff. princesse; Th. princes.   129. Th. and most; Ff. H. *om.* and. Ff. plesing; Th. pleasyng.

(By the wryting and sentence of Catoun),   130
Is a good tonge, in his opinioun ;
Chastyse the révers, and of wysdom do this,
Withdraw your hering from al that deme amis.

---

132. H. revers; Th. reuerse; Ff. reue*r*ce. H. wisdom; Th. Ff. wysdome.
133. H. Voydeth (*for* Withdraw).   Ff. deme; Th. saine.

XIII. BEWARE OF DOUBLENESS.

(Balade made by Lydgatê.)

THIS world is ful of variaunce
   In every thing, who taketh hede,
That faith and trust, and al constaunce,
Exyled ben, this is no drede;
And, save only in womanhede,   5
I can [nat] see no sikernesse;
But for al that, yet, as I rede,
Be-war alway of doublenesse.

Also these fresshe somer-floures
Whyte and rede, blewe and grene,   10
Ben sodainly, with winter-shoures,
Mad feinte and fade, withoute wene;
That trust is non, as ye may seen,
In no-thing, nor no stedfastnesse,
Except in women, thus I mene;   15
Yet ay be-war of doublenesse.

The croked mone, this is no tale,
Som whyle is shene and bright of hewe,
And after that ful derk and pale,
And every moneth chaungeth newe;   20
That, who the verray sothe knewe,
Al thing is bilt on brotelnesse,
Save that these women ay be trewe;
Yet ay be-war of doublenesse.

---

1. *From* F. (Fairfax 16); *collated with* Ed. (ed. 1561). *Also in* A. (Ashmole 59), *in which it is much altered*; *other copies in* Ha. (Harl. 7578), *and*
Ad. (Addit. 16165).   2. F. whoo.   6. *I supply* nat.   9. F. A. these; Ed.
that.   12. F. feynt; Ha. Ed. feinte.   13. F. Ed. sene.   18. F. A. Ad. is
shene; Ed. ishene.   21. F. A. who so; Ha. Ad. Ed. who.   23. Ad. these; *rest om.*

The lusty fresshe somers day,   25
And Phebus with his bemes clere,
Towardes night, they drawe away,
And no lenger liste appere ;
That, in this present lyf now here
Nothing abit in his fairnesse,   30
Save women ay be founde intere
And devoid of doublenesse.

The see eke, with his sterne wawes,
Ech day floweth newe again,
And, by concours of his lawes,   35
The ebbe foloweth, in certain ;
After gret drought ther comth a rain,
That farewel here al stabelnesse,
Save that women be hole and plain ;
Yet ay be-war of doublenesse.   40

Fortunes wheel goth round aboute
A thousand tymes, day and night :
Whos cours standeth ever in doute
For to transmew ; she is so light.
For which adverteth in your sight   45
Th'untrust of worldly fikelnesse,
Save women, which of kindly right
Ne have no tache of doublenesse.

What man may the wind restraine
Or holde a snake by the tail,   50
Or a sliper eel constraine
That it nil voide, withouten fail ;
Or who can dryve so a nail
To make sure new-fangelnesse,
Save women, that can gye hir sail   55
To rowe hir boot with doublenesse.

At every haven they can aryve
Wher-as they wote is good passage ;

---

28. Ha. Ad. no ; F. Ed. non.   29. F. So ; *rest* That.   30. F. abytte ;
Ed. abieth ; Ad. abydeth.   32. *In the margin of* F. Ad.—Per Antifrasim.
36. F. Ad. Ha. foloweth ; Ed. *repeats* floweth *from* l. 34. A. Soone affter that
comthe thebbe certeyne.   38. F. Ha. farewel al her ; Ed. Ad. farewel here al.
48. F. Ad. Ha. haue ; Ed. hath. F. tachche ; Ed. teche.   51. F. slepur ; Ha.
sleper ; Ed. Ad. slipper.   52. A. nyl ; Ad. nil ; Ha. wol ; F. wil ; Ed. will.
53. A. dryve so depe a.   54. Ed. suere.   55, 56. Ad. hir ; Ha. F. her ; Ed. their.

Of innocence, they can not stryve
With wawes nor no rokkes rage;   60
So happy is hir lodemanage,
With nelde and stoon hir cours to dresse,
That Salamon was not so sage
To find in hem no doublenesse.

Therfor who-so hem accuse   65
Of any double entencioun,
To speke, rowne, other to muse,
To pinche at hir condicioun;
Al is but fals collusioun,
I dar right wel the sothe expresse;   70
They have no better proteccioun
But shroude hem under doublenesse.

So wel fortúned is hir chaunce
The dys to turnen up-so-doun,
With sys and sink they can avaunce,   75
And than, by revolucioun,
They sette a fel conclusioun
Of ambes as, in sothfastnesse;
Though clerkes make mencioun
Hir kind is fret with doublenesse.   80

Sampsoun had experience
That women were ful trewe founde,
Whan Dalida, of innocence,
With sheres gan his heer to rounde;
To speke also of Rosamounde   85
And Cleopatras feithfulnesse,
The stories plainly wil confounde
Men that apeche hir doublenesse.

Sengle thing ne is not preised,
Nor oo-fold is of no renoun;   90
In balaunce when they be peised,

---

61. F. happe; Ha. Ed. happy. F. her (=hir); Ed. their. 62. F. nelde;
Ed. Ha. nedle. F. Ha. her; Ed. their. 64. F. Ha. hem; Ed. them. 65.
F. Wherfor; Ed. Ha. Ad. Therefore. MSS. hem; Ed. them. 67. Ed.
rowme (!). 68. F. hyr; Ad. hir; Ha. her; Ed. their. 69. A. Ad. nys
(_for_ is). 71. Ed. better; F. bette; Ha. Ad. bet. 72. MSS. hem;
Ed. them. 73. Ad. Ed. their. 74. F. Ed. turne; Ad. Ha. turnen. 78.
F. Ambes ase; Ad. Ha. aumbes as; Ed. lombes, as (!) 82. F. weren; Ed.
A. were. MSS. founde; Ed. ifound. 84. A. heres; Ad. here; Ed.
heere; F. hede. 87. F. Ad. Ed. The; A. Hir. 88. MSS. hir, her;
Ed. their. 90. F. oo folde; A. oone folde; Ed. ofolde.

For lakke of weght they be bore doun ;
And for this cause of just resoun,
These women alle, of rightwisnesse,
Of chois and free eleccioun   95
Most love eschaunge and doublenesse.

Lenvoy.

O ye women, which been enclyned,
By influence of your nature,
To been as pure as gold y-fyned
In your trouth for to endure,   100
Arm your-self in strong armure
Lest men assaile your sikernesse :
Set on your brest, your-self t'assure,
A mighty sheld of doublenesse.

---

92. F. A. Ad. weght; Ha. wight; Ed. waighte. A. borne.   96. A.
Ad. Haue stuffed hem with doublenesse.   97. A. that (*for* which).   100.
A. In alle youre touches for. Ad. trouthe for tendure.   101. *For* Arm *read*
Armeth ?   102. Ha. assaye.   103. F. A. Ad. tassure; Ed. Ha. to
assure.   104. F. Ed. shelde ; A sheelde.

XIV. A BALADE: WARNING MEN TO BEWARE OF DECEITFUL WOMEN.

———•———

LOKE wel aboute, ye that lovers be;
 Lat nat your lustes lede you to dotage;
Be nat enamoured on al thing that ye see.
Sampson the fort, and Salamon the sage
Deceived were, for al hir gret corage;   5
Men deme hit is right as they see at y;
Bewar therfore; the blinde et many a fly.

I mene, in women, for al hir cheres queinte,
Trust nat to moche; hir trouthë is but geson;
The fairest outward ful wel can they peinte, 10
Hir stedfastnes endureth but a seson;
For they feyn frendlines and worchen treson.
And for they be chaungeáble naturally,
Bewar therfore; the blinde et many a fly.

Though al the world do his besy cure   15
To make women stonde in stablenes,
Hit may nat be, hit is agayn nature;
The world is do whan they lak doublenes;
For they can laughe and love nat; this is expres.
To trust in hem, hit is but fantasy;   20
Bewar therfore; the blind et many a fly.

From Trin. (Trin. Coll. Cam. R. 3. 19), *printed in* Ed. (ed. 1561); T. (Trin. Coll. O. 9. 38); H. (Harl. 2251). 1. Trin. well*e*. T. abowte; Trin. about. 2. Trin. leede. 3. Trin. se. 4. T. H. Salamon; Trin. Salomon. 5. T. her*e* (*read* hir)); Trin. H. theyr (*and elsewhere*). 6. *So* T.; Trin. H. hit right that they se with. T. eye; Trin. ey; H. ye; (*read* y). 7. T. ette, *alt. to* ettyth; Trin. H. eteth (*read* et, *and so elsewhere*). 8. H. T. in; Trin. of. Trin. wemen; queynt. 9. Trin. H. hem nat (T. *om.* hem). Trin. trowth; geason (T. geson). 10. T. full*e*; Trin. H. *om.* Trin. peynt. 12. Trin. feyne. 13. T. be; Trin. ar; H. are. Trin. chaungeabylle. 15–28. *So* T. H.; Trin. *transposes* 15–21 *and* 22–28. 16. Trin. wemen stond; stabylnes. 17. T. H. may; Trin. woll*e*. 18. Trin. doubylnes. 19. Trin. lawgh; expresse. H. *om.* nat. 20. H. T. in; Trin. on. Trin. theym.

What wight on-lyve trusteth in hir cheres
Shal haue at last his guerdon and his mede;
They can shave nerer then rasóurs or sheres;
Al is nat gold that shyneth! Men, take hede;   25
Hir galle is hid under a sugred wede.
Hit is ful hard hir fantasy t'aspy;
Bewar therfore; the blinde et many a fly.

Women, of kinde, have condicions three;
The first is, that they be fulle of deceit;   30
To spinne also hit is hir propertee;
And women have a wonderful conceit,
They wepen ofte, and al is but a sleight,
And whan they list, the tere is in the y;
Bewar therfore; the blinde et many a fly.   35

What thing than eyr is lighter and meveable?
The light, men say, that passeth in a throw;
Al if the light be nat so variable
As is the wind that every wey [can] blow;
And yet, of reson, som men deme and trow   40
Women be lightest of hir company;
Bewar therfore; the blind et many a fly.

In short to say, though al the erth so wan
Were parchëmyn smothe, whyte and scribable,
And the gret see, cleped the occian,   45
Were torned in inke, blakker then is sable,
Ech stik a penne, ech man a scriveyn able,
They coud nat wryte wommannes traitory;
Bewar therfore; the blinde et many a fly.   49

---

22. T. yn; Trin. on. Trin. cherys.   24. T. They; Trin. For wemen.
25. Trin. shynyth.   26. Trin. sugryd.   27. T. harde; Trin. H. queynt.
Trin. to aspy.   29. T. *has the note*: Fallere flere nere tria sunt hec
in muliere. Trin. thre.   30. T. that; Trin. H. *om*.   31. T. hyt; Trin.
om. T. properte; Trin. p*r*opurte.   32. H. haue; T. hath; Trin. *om*. Trin.
conseyte.   33. Trin. H. For they; T. *om*. For. T. wepyth (*read* wepen);
Trin. wepe. T. H. but; Trin. *om*. H. a sleight; T. deceyt; Trin. asteyte;
Ed. a sleite.   34. Trin. teere; ey. 36–42. *In* T. only.   37. T. passyth.
38. T. All yff; waryabylle.   39. T. wynde; ys blow (*alt. to* blowth;
read can blow).   40. T. yut; summen.   41. T. ther (*for* hir).   43.
T. schorte; Trin. sothe. Trin. erthe; wanne.   44. Trin. parchemyne;
scrybabyll*e*.   45. T. H. that clepyd is; Trin. that callyd ys (*read* cleped).
H. *om*. the. Trin. occiane.   46. T. yn; Trin. into; H. to. T. H. is; Trin. *om*.
47. T. H. Eche; Trin. Euery. Trin. yche; abyll*e*. H. scryven; T. Trin.
scriuener.   48. T. They cowde not; Trin. Nat cowde then (!). T. wymmenys;
Trin. womans; H. wommans. T. treytorye; Trin. H. trechery

XV. THREE SAYINGS.

(A). A SAYING OF DAN JOHN.

THER beth four thinges that maketh a man a fool,
 Hónour first putteth him in outrage,
And alder-next solitarie and sool;
The second is unweldy croked age;
Women also bring men in dotage;   5
And mighty wyne, in· many dyvers wyse,
Distempreth folk which [that] ben holden wyse.

(B). YET OF THE SAME.

THER beth four thinges causing gret folye,
Honour first, and [than] unweldy age;
Women and wyne, I dar eek specifye,
Make wyse men [to] fallen in dotage;
Wherfore, by counseil of philosophers sage,   5
In gret honour, lerne this of me,
With thyn estat have [eek] humilitee.

(C). BALADE DE BON CONSAIL.

IF it befalle, that god thee list visyte
With any tourment or adversitee,
Thank first the lord; and [than], thyself to quyte,
Upon suffrauncë and humilitee
Found thou thy quarel, what-ever that it be;   5
Mak thy defence (and thou shalt have no losse)
The rémembraunce of Crist and of his crosse.

A. *From* Stowe (ed. 1561).   1. bethe foure; foole.   3. soole.
7. Distempren (!) ; folke whiche ; *supply* that ; bene.
  B. *From the same.*   1. bene (*read* beth, *as above*) foure·   2. *I supply*
than ; vnwildy.   3. dare eke specify·   4. *I supply* to.   6. learne.
7. thine estate ; *I supply* eek.
  C. *From the same.*   1. befall ; the.   2. aduersite.   3. Thanke ; lorde ;
I supply than ; selfe.   4. humilite.   5. Founde ; quarel.   6. Make.

XVI. LA BELLE DAME SANS MERCY.

TRANSLATED OUT OF FRENCH BY
SIR RICHARD ROS.

———◆———

HALF in a dreme, not fully wel awaked,
   The golden sleep me wrapped under his wing;
Yet nat for-thy I roos, and wel nigh naked,
Al sodaynly my-selve rémembring
Of a matér, leving al other thing   5
Which I shold do, with-outen more delay,
For hem to whom I durst nat disobey.

My charge was this, to translate by and by,
(Al thing forgive), as part of my penaunce,
A book called Belle Dame sans Mercy   10
Which mayster Aleyn made of rémembraunce,
Cheef secretarie with the king of Fraunce.
And ther-upon a whyle I stood musing,
And in my-self gretly imagening

What wyse I shuld performe the sayd processe,   15
Considering by good avysement
Myn unconning and my gret simplenesse,

From Th. (Thynne, ed. 1532); *collated with* F. (Fairfax 16); and H. (Harl. 372). *Also in* Ff. (Camb. Univ. Lib. Ff. 1. 6). *Bad spellings of* Th. *are corrected by the* MSS. TITLE. Th. H. La .. mercy; F. Balade de la Bele Dame sanz mercy. H. *adds*—Translatid .. Ros.   1. Th. F. Halfe; H. Half.   2. F. H. Ff. wrapt.   3. *All* rose.   4. Th. Ff. -selfe; H. F. self.   5. F. matere; H. matier. Th. leuynge.   6. Th. must; F. sholde; H. shold.   7. H. to whom; F. the which; Th. whiche. Th. F. dysobey; H. sey nay.   9. Th. thynge. Ff. part; *rest* parte.   10. Th. F. boke; H. book. Th. La bel; F. la bele; H. *om*. La. H. F. sanz; Th. sauns.   11. Th. Whiche.   12. Th. secratairie; F. secretare; H. secretarie.   13. H. ther-; Th. F. her-. Th. F. stode; H. stood.   14. Th. greatly ymagenynge.   15. Th. shulde; F. H. sholde; Ff. shuld. Th. the; F. H. this.   16. Ff. avysement; *rest* adv.   17. F. H. Ff. Myn; Th. My. F. H. Ff. symplesse.

And ayenward the strait commaundement
Which that I had; and thus, in myn entent,
I was vexed and tourned up and doun;   20
And yet at last, as in conclusioun,

I cast my clothes on, and went my way,
This foresayd charge having in rémembraunce,
Til I cam to a lusty green valey
Ful of floures, to see, a gret plesaunce;   25
And so bolded, with their benygn suffraunce
That rede this book, touching this sayd matere,
Thus I began, if it plese you to here.

NAT long ago, ryding an esy paas,
    I fel in thought, of joy ful desperate   30
With greet disese and payne, so that I was
Of al lovers the most unfortunate,
Sith by his dart most cruel, ful of hate,
The deeth hath take my lady and maistresse,
And left me sole, thus discomfit and mate,   35
Sore languisshing, and in way of distresse.

Than sayd I thus, ‘it falleth me to cesse
Eyther to ryme or ditees for to make,
And I, surely, to make a ful promesse
To laugh no more, but wepe in clothes blake.   40
My joyful tyme, alas! now is it slake,
For in my-self I fele no maner ese;
Let it be written, such fortune I take,
Which neither me, nor non other doth plese.

If it were so, my wil or myn entent   45
Constrayned were a joyful thing to wryte,
Myn pen coud never have knowlege what it ment;
To speke therof my tonge hath no delyte.

---

18. Th. -warde; strayte.   19. Th. myne.   20. Th. downe.   21.
Th. conclusyon.   24. H. in-to. H. green; Th. F. grene.   25. Th.
se; great.   26. F. H. Ff. bolded; Th. boldly. F. benyng; Th. benygne;
H. benyngne.   27. F. H. Ff. That; Th. Whiche. Th. F. boke; H. booke.
H. F. the; Th. Ff. this. Th. *om.* seid.   28. F. H. begynne. Th. please.
(*From this point I silently correct the spelling of* Th.)   33. Th. Ff. by; F. H.
with.   35. Ff. soleyne (*for* sole thus); *perhaps better.*   41. F. H. Ff. is;
Th. doth.   42. F. felde. Th. maner of ease.   43. F. H. I; Th. as I.
44. F. H. Ff. nor doth noon other.   46. F. H. Ff. Were constreyned.   47.
H. Myn eyen; F. Myn eyn; Th. My penne; Ff. My pen. Ff. *neuer* haue
knolege; H. haue knowlege (!); Th. neuer knowe; F. haue no knowlych.

And with my mouth if I laugh moche or lyte,
Myn eyen shold make a countenaunce untrewe;   50
My hert also wold have therof despyte,
The weping teres have so large issewe.

These seke lovers, I leve that to hem longes,
Which lede their lyf in hope of alegeaunce,
That is to say, to make balades and songes,   55
Every of hem, as they fele their grevaunce.
For she that was my joy and my plesaunce,
Whos soule I pray god of his mercy save,
She hath my wil, myn hertes ordinaunce,
Which lyeth here, within this tombe y-grave.   60

Fro this tyme forth, tyme is to hold my pees;
It werieth me this mater for to trete;
Let other lovers put hem-self in prees;
Their seson is, my tyme is now forgete.
Fortune by strength the forcer hath unshet   65
Wherin was sperd al my worldly richesse,
And al the goodes which that I have gete
In my best tyme of youthe and lustinesse.

Love hath me kept under his governaunce;
If I misdid, god graunt me forgifnesse!   70
If I did wel, yet felte I no plesaunce;
It caused neither joy nor hevinesse.
For whan she dyed, that was my good maistresse,
Al my welfare than made the same purchas;
The deeth hath set my boundes, of witnes,   75
Which for no-thing myn hert shal never pas.'

In this gret thought, sore troubled in my mynde,
Aloon thus rood I al the morow-tyde,
Til at the last it happed me to fynde
The place wherin I cast me to abyde   80

---

49. F. H. Ff. And; Th. Tho. Th. *om.* if.   53. F. H. Ff. seke; Th. sicke.
54. Th. Ff. theyr; H. F. her (*often*).   55. F. H. balade or.   60. F. H. Ff.
lyth with hir vndir hir tumbe in graue (Ff. I-graue).   65. Th. Ff. by; F. H.
with. F. hath the forser vnschete.   66. Th. sperde; Ff. spred; F. sprad;
H. spradde (!).   73. Th. H. *om.* good.   74. Th. *om.* Al. H. made than.
75. F. Ff. set; H. sette; Th. shette. F. H. Ff. boundes; Th. bondes.   77.
F. H. thoughtes. Th. *om.* my.   79. F. I (*for* it).   80. H. I purposid
me to bide.

Whan that I had no further for to ryde.
And as I went my logging to purvey,
Right sone I herde, but litel me besyde,
In a gardeyn, wher minstrels gan to play.

With that anon I went me bakker-more;   85
My-self and I, me thought, we were y-now;
But twayn that were my frendes here-before
Had me espyed, and yet I wot nat how.
They come for me; awayward I me drow,
Somwhat by force, somwhat by their request,   90
That in no wyse I coud my-self rescow,
But nede I must come in, and see the feest.

At my coming, the ladies everichoon
Bad me welcome, god wot, right gentilly,
And made me chere, everich by oon and oon,   95
A gret del better than I was worthy;
And, of their grace, shewed me gret curtesy
With good disport, bicause I shuld nat mourne.
That day I bood stille in their company,
Which was to me a gracious sojourne.   100

The bordes were spred in right litel space;
The ladies sat, ech as hem semed best.
Were non that did servyce within that place
But chosen men, right of the goodliest:
And som ther were, peravénture most fresshest,   105
That sawe their juges, sitting ful demure,
Without semblaunt either to most or lest,
Notwithstanding they had hem under cure.

Among al other, oon I gan espy
Which in gret thought ful often com and went   110
As man that had ben ravished utterly,
In his langage nat gretly diligent;

<hr>

81. H. forth to.   83. F. H. Ff. but; Th. a.   84. F. H. gardeyn; Th.
garden.   88. F. *om.* yet I; H. *om.* yet.   89. F. H. come; Th. came.   90.
Th. her; F. H. Ff. their.   92. F. H. nede; Th. nedes.   95. H. F. Ff.
eueryche by one and one; Th. euery one by one.   103. *So* Ff.; H. F. Were
none that serued in that place (!); Th. Ther were no deedly seruaunts in the
place.   105. Ff. *peraunter.*   H. *om.* most.   106. Th. *om.* sitting.
110. F. com; H. come; Th. came.   111. H..F. man; Th. one; Ff. on.

His countenaunce he kept with greet tourment,
But his desyr fer passed his resoun;
For ever his eye went after his entent   115
Ful many a tyme, whan it was no sesoun.

To make good chere, right sore him-self he payned,
And outwardly he fayned greet gladnesse;
To singe also by force he was constrayned
For no plesaunce, but very shamfastnesse;   120
For the complaynt of his most hevinesse
Com to his voice alwey without request,
Lyk as the sowne of birdes doth expresse
Whan they sing loude, in frith or in forest.

Other ther were, that served in the hal,   125
But non lyk him, as after myn advyse;
For he was pale, and somwhat lene with-al;
His speche also trembled in fereful wyse;
And ever aloon, but when he did servyse.
Al blak he ware, and no devyce but playn.   130
Me thought by him, as my wit coud suffyse,
His hert was no-thing in his own demeyn.

To feste hem al he did his diligence,
And wel he couth, right as it semed me.
But evermore, whan he was in presence,   135
His chere was don; it wold non other be.
His scole-maister had suche auctorité
That, al the whyle he bood stille in the place,
Speke coude he nat, but upon her beauté
He loked stil, with right a pitous face.   140

With that, his heed he tourned at the last
For to behold the ladies everichon;
But ever in oon he set his ey stedfast
On her, the which his thought was most upon.

115. Th. F. Ff. went; H. yode.   116. Th. F. Ff. Ful; H. At.   117. Th.
om. good *and* right.   122. F. H. Come; Th. Came.   124. F. H. *om. 2nd* in.
133. F. H. feste; Th. feest.   134. Th. coude; *rest* couth. F. H. *om.* it.
138. Th. H. bode.   143. F. eey; H. yee; Th. eye. Th. F. Ff. stedfast;
H. faste.   144. Th. *om.* the.

And of his eyen the shot I knew anon   145
Which federed was with right humble requestes.
Than to my-self I sayd, ' By god aloon,
Suche oon was I, or that I saw these gestes.'

Out of the prees he went ful esely
To make stable his hevy countenaunce ;   150
And, wit ye wel, he syghed tenderly
For his sorowes and woful remembraunce.
Than in him-self he made his ordinaunce,
And forth-withal com to bringe in the mes ;
But, for to juge his most ruful semblaunce,   155
God wot, it was a pitous entremes !

After diner, anon they hem avaunced
To daunce about, these folkes everichoon ;
And forth-withal this hevy lover daunced
Somtyme with twayn, and somtyme but with oon.   160
Unto hem al his chere was after oon,
Now here, now there, as fel by aventure ;
But ever among, he drew to her aloon
Which he most dredde of living creature.

To myn advyse, good was his purveyaunce   165
Whan he her chase to his maistresse aloon,
If that her hert were set to his plesaunce
As moche as was her beauteous persone.
For who that ever set his trust upon
The réport of the eyen, withouten more,   170
He might be deed and graven under stoon
Or ever he shulde his hertes ese restore.

In her fayled nothing, as I coud gesse,
O wyse nor other, prevy nor apert ;
A garnison she was of al goodnesse   175
To make a frounter for a lovers hert ;

145. F. H. And ; Th. For. Th. Ff. shot ; H. sight ; F. seght.   146. H.
fedired ; F. fedred ; Ff. federid ; Th. fereful.   148. Th. I, or that ; F. ther
that ; H. I that there. Th. iestes.   151. F. H. tendirly ; Th. wonderly..
154. F. H. come ; Th. came.   155. F. H. *om.* most. F. H. ruful ; Ff. rewfull ;
Th. woful. F. H. Ff. semblaunce ; Th. penaunce.   158. F. H. these ; Th. the.
159. F. H. louer ; Th. man he.   160. Th. *om.* but.   166. *All* chase.
168. F. H. beautevous.   169. F. H. that ; Th. so. F. H. set ; Th. setteth.
H. trist.   170. Th. the (*rightly*) ; H. there ; F. Ff. their.   171. F. vndir a.
173. F. H. as ; Th. that.   174. F. Ff. O ; H. On ; Th. One.   F. H. vice. (!).
H. ner (*for* 1st nor). Th. Ff. nor ; H. or ; F. ne. Ff. apert ; Th. H. perte ;
F. pert.   175. Th. garyson. Th. goodlynesse.   176. *All* frounter.

Right yong and fresshe, a woman ful covert;
Assured wel her port and eke her chere,
Wel at her ese, withouten wo or smert,
Al underneth the standard of Daungere.   180

To see the feest, it weried me ful sore;
For hevy joy doth sore the hert travayle.
Out of the prees I me withdrew therfore,
And set me down aloon, behynd a trayle
Ful of leves, to see, a greet mervayle,   185
With grene withies y-bounden wonderly;
The leves were so thik, withouten fayle,
That thorough-out might no man me espy.

To this lady he com ful curteisly
Whan he thought tyme to daunce with her a trace; 190
Sith in an herber made ful pleasauntly
They rested hem, fro thens but litel space.
Nigh hem were none, a certayn of compace,
But only they, as fer as I coud see;
And save the trayle, ther I had chose my place, 195
Ther was no more betwix hem tweyne and me.

I herd the lover syghing wonder sore;
For ay the neer, the sorer it him sought.
His inward payne he coud not kepe in store,
Nor for to speke, so hardy was he nought.   200
His leche was neer, the gretter was his thought;
He mused sore, to conquere his desyre;
For no man may to more penaunce be brought
Than, in his hete, to bringe him to the fyre.

The hert began to swel within his chest,   205
So sore strayned for anguish and for payne
That al to peces almost it to-brest,
Whan bothe at ones so sore it did constrayne;

178. F. H. Ff. her; Th. of (*twice*).   180. Th. standerde : F. standarte ;
H. standart.   183. Th. -drawe; H. -drewh.   184. Th. Ff. alone; F.H. *om.*
186. F. withes; H. Ff. wythyes; Th. wrethes.   188. H. Ff. thorughe; Th.
through; F. thorgh. Th. no man might.   189. Th. this; H. his. F. H. come;
Th. came.   191. Th. Set (*for* Sith). H. herbier.   192. H. them. Th. but a.
193. Th. of a certayne.   195. Th. *om.* And.   196. *So* F. H.; Th. bytwene
hem two.   201. Th. more; H. Ff. neer.   204. Ff. hete; Th. heate; F. H. hert.

* * *
* * * *   X

Desyr was bold, but shame it gan refrayne;
That oon was large, the other was ful cloos;   210
No litel charge was layd on him, certayn,
To kepe suche werre, and have so many foos.

Ful often-tymes to speke him-self he peyned,
But shamfastnesse and drede sayd ever 'nay';
Yet at the last so sore he was constrayned,   215
Whan he ful long had put it in delay,
To his lady right thus than gan he say
With dredful voice, weping, half in a rage :—
'For me was purveyd an unhappy day
Whan I first had a sight of your visage !   220

I suffre payne, god wot, ful hoot brenning,
To cause my deeth, al for my trew servyse;
And I see wel, ye rekke therof nothing,
Nor take no hede of it, in no kins wyse.
But whan I speke after my best avyse,   225
Ye set it nought, but make ther-of a game;
And though I sewe so greet an entrepryse,
It peyreth not your worship nor your fame.

Alas ! what shulde be to you prejudyce
If that a man do love you faithfully   230
To your worship, eschewing every vyce ?
So am I yours, and wil be verily;
I chalenge nought of right, and reson why,
For I am hool submit to your servyse;
Right as ye liste it be, right so wil I,   235
To bynde my-self, where I was in fraunchyse !

Though it be so, that I can nat deserve
To have your grace, but alway live in drede,
Yet suffre me you for to love and serve
Without maugrè of your most goodlihede;   240

---

209. Th. Ff. gan; F. H. can.   210. F. H. The toon.   213-220. F. *omits.*
224. F. H. Ff. kyns; Th. kynde.   225. H. Ff. avise; Th. aduyse.   226.
Th. it at; F. H. *om.* at.   227. H. enterprise.   228. F. H. It; Th. Yet.
229. Th. it be; F. H. *om.* it.   231. Th. Ff. eschewynge; F. H. escusyng.   234.
F. H. to; Th. vnto.   235. *All* ye. Th. Ff. right; F. even; H. euyn.   237.
H. *om.* that.   238. Th. alway; F. H. ay to.   239. F. H. *om.* for.
240. Th. Withouten; F. Without.

Both faith and trouth I give your **womanhede**,
And my servyse, withoute ayein-calling.
Love hath me bounde, withouten **wage** or **mede**,
To be your man, and leve al other thing.'

Whan this lady had herd al this langage,   245
She yaf answere ful softe and demurely,
Without chaunging of colour or corage,
No-thing in haste, but mesurabelly :—
'Me thinketh, sir, your thought is **greet** foly!
Purpose ye not your labour for to cese?   250
For thinketh not, whyl that ye live and I,
In this matére to set your hert in pees!'

Lamant. 'Ther may non make the pees, but only ye,
Which ar the ground and cause of al this werre ;
For with your eyen the letters written be,   255
By which I am defyed and put a-fer.
Your plesaunt look, my verray lode-sterre,
Was made heraud of thilk same défyaunce
Which utterly behight me to forbarre
My faithful trust and al myn affyaunce.'   260

La Dame. 'To live in wo he hath **gret** fantasy
And of his hert also hath slipper holde,
That, only for beholding of an y,
Can nat abyde in pees, as reson wolde!
Other or me if ye list to beholde,   265
Our eyen are made to loke ; why shuld we spare?
I take no kepe, neither of yong nor olde ;
Who feleth smert, I counsayle him be ware!'

Lam. 'If it be so, oon hurte another sore,
In his defaut that feleth the grevaunce,   270
Of very right a man may do no more ;
Yet reson wolde it were in remembraunce.

---

241. H. gif; F. geve.   242. F. H. ayein ; Th. any (!).   243.
F. withouten ; H. withoughtyn ; Th. withoute.   248. F. Ff. mesurabely ;
Th. H. mesurably.   249. Th. Ff. your thought is ; F. H. ye do ful.   251.
Th. thynketh; F. H. think ye. Th. whyles ; H. whil that ; Ff. whils that.
252. F. matere ; H. matier ; Th. mater.   258. F. Ff. dyffiaunce.   259. F. H.
Ff. to forbarre ; Th. for to barre. 262. Th. *om.* hath.   263. Th. eye ; F. eeye ;
H. yee ; (*read* y).   265. F. if that ye lyst to beholde ; H. Ff. if ye liste to
biholde ; Th. if ye list ye may beholde.   267. H. nor ; Th. F. Ff. ne.

And, sith Fortune not only, by her chaunce,
Hath caused me to suffre al this payn,
But your beautè, with al the circumstaunce,	275
Why list ye have me in so greet disdayn?'

La D. 'To your persone ne have I no disdayn,
Nor ever had, trewly! ne nought wil have,
Nor right gret love, nor hatred, in certayn;
Nor your counsayl to know, so god me save!	280
If such beleve be in your mynde y-grave
That litel thing may do you greet plesaunce,
You to begyle, or make you for to rave,
I wil nat cause no suche encomberaunce!'

Lam. 'What ever it be that me hath thus purchased,	285
Wening hath nat disceyved me, certayn,
But fervent love so sore hath me y-chased
That I, unware, am casten in your chayne;
And sith so is, as Fortune list ordayne,
Al my welfare is in your handes falle,	290
In eschewing of more mischévous payn;
Who sonest dyeth, his care is leest of alle.'

La D. 'This sicknesse is right esy to endure,
But fewe people it causeth for to dy;
But what they mene, I know it very sure,	295
Of more comfort to draw the remedy.
Such be there now, playning ful pitously,
That fele, god wot, nat alther-grettest payne;
And if so be, love hurt so grevously,
Lesse harm it were, oon sorowful, than twayne!'	300

Lam. 'Alas, madame! if that it might you plese,
Moche better were, by way of gentilnesse,
Of one sory, to make twayn wel at ese,
Than him to stroy that liveth in distresse!
For my desyr is neither more nor lesse	305
But my servyce to do, for your plesaunce,
In eschewing al maner doublenesse,
To make two joyes in stede of oo grevaunce!'

273. Th. *om.* not. Th. her; F. H. Ff. his.	275. F. H. Ff. But; Th. By (!).
278. H. *om.* trewly. Th. Ff. nought; F. H. neuer.	281. F. beleue; H. bileue;
Th. loue (!).	282. *So* Ff.; H. F. *om.* greet (Th. you dyspleasaunce!).	284. *So*
F. Th.; H. encombrance.	290. F. I-falle; H. y-falle; Ff. falle; Th. fal.	297.
Th. F. Ff. now; H. nought.	302. Th. it were; F. H. *om.* it.	303. F. sorow; H.
sorwe; Th. Ff. sory.	304. F. H. stroye; Th. destroye.	308. F. H. oo; Th. one.

La D. 'Of love I seke neither plesaunce nor ese,
Nor greet desyr, nor right gret affyaunce ;   310
Though ye be seke, it doth me nothing plese ;
Also, I take no hede to your plesaunce.
Chese who-so wil, their hertes to avaunce,
Free am I now, and free wil I endure ;
To be ruled by mannes governaunce   315
For erthely good, nay ! that I you ensure !'

Lam. 'Love, which that joy and sorowe doth departe,
Hath set the ladies out of al servage,
And largëly doth graunt hem, for their parte,
Lordship and rule of every maner age.   320
The poor servaunt nought hath of avauntage
But what he may get only of purchace ;
And he that ones to love doth his homage,
Ful often tyme dere bought is the rechace.'

La D. 'Ladies be nat so simple, thus I mene,   325
So dul of wit, so sotted of foly,
That, for wordes which sayd ben of the splene,
In fayre langage, paynted ful plesauntly,
Which ye and mo holde scoles of dayly,
To make hem of gret wonders to suppose ;   330
But sone they can away their hedes wrye,
And to fair speche lightly their eres close.'

Lam. 'Ther is no man that jangleth busily,
And set his hert and al his mynd therfore,
That by resoun may playne so pitously   335
As he that hath moche hevinesse in store.
Whos heed is hool, and sayth that it is sore,
His fayned chere is hard to kepe in mewe ;
But thought, which is unfayned evermore,
The wordes preveth, as the workes sewe.   340

---

309. Th. Ff. nor ; F. H. ne.   310. F. H. grete desire nor ; Th. haue therin no.
Th. *om.* right.   311. F. H. seke ; Th. sicke.   312. Th. of ; F. H. Ff. to.   313.
F. H. their ; Th. her.   317. Th. that ioy ; F. H. *om.* that.   318. F. H. *om.* al.
319. F. H. their ; Th. her.   320. Th. maner of age.   322. Th. by ; F. H. Ff. of.
Th. purchesse ; F. H. purchace.   324. Th. tymes.   F. *om.* the.   H. dere **his**
richesse bought has.   Ff. rechace ; *rest* richesse.   326. Th. in (*for* 2nd of).
327. F. ben ; Th. be ; H. are.   329. H. scoolys holden dieuly.   330. F. H.
of ; Th. al.   331. F. H. their hedes away.   334. F. set ; Ff. sette ; Th. H.
setteth.   337. F. H. *om.* that.   340. Th. shewe ; F. sue ; H. Ff. sewe.

La D. 'Love is subtel, and hath a greet awayt,
Sharp in worching, in gabbing greet plesaunce,
And can him venge of suche as by disceyt
Wold fele and knowe his secret governaunce;
And maketh hem to obey his ordinaunce   345
By chereful wayes, as in hem is supposed;
But whan they fallen in-to repentaunce,
Than, in a rage, their counsail is disclosed.'

Lam. 'Sith for-as-moche as god and eke nature
Hath †love avaunced to so hye degrè,   350
Moch sharper is the point, this am I sure,
Yet greveth more the faute, wher-ever it be.
Who hath no cold, of hete hath no deyntè,
The toon for the tother asked is expresse;
And of plesaunce knoweth non the certeyntè   355
But it be wonne with thought and hevinesse'

La D. 'As for plesaunce, it is nat alway oon;
That you is swete, I thinke it bitter payne.
Ye may nat me constrayne, nor yet right non,
After your lust, to love that is but vayne.   360
To chalenge love by right was never seyn,
But herte assent, before bond and promyse;
For strength nor force may not atteyne, certayn,
A wil that stant enfeffed in fraunchyse!'

Lam. 'Right fayr lady, god mote I never plese,   365
If I seke other right, as in this case,
But for to shewe you playnly my disese
And your mercy to abyde, and eke your grace.
If I purpose your honour to deface,
Or ever did, god and fortune me shende!   370
And that I never rightwysly purchace
Oon only joy, unto my lyves ende!'

---

341. Th. Ff. awayte; F. H. abayte.   342. F. worching; H. worsching;
Th. workyng.   344. F. H. know and fele.   346. F. H. him; Th. Ff. hem.
347. F. H. when that; Th. *om.* that.   348. F. H. their; Th. her.
350. *All* avaunced loue.   351. Th. sharpe. F. H. this; Th. thus.   352.
F. H. It; Th. Ff. Yet.   354. F. ton; H. toon; Th. one. F. H. the tother;
Th. that other.   355. Th. *om.* the. Th. certeyne (!).   356. F. wonne; H.
wonnen; Th. one (!). F. H. with; Th. in.   358. F. H. is; Th. thinke.   363.
F. nor; H. ner; Th. and. Th. *om.* certayn.   364. F. H. stant; Th. standeth.
F. enfeoffed.   366. Th. *om.* as.   371. F. H. rightwysly; Th. vnryghtfully (!).

La D. 'Ye and other, that swere suche othes faste,
And so condempne and cursen to and fro,
Ful sikerly, ye wene your othes laste   375
No lenger than the wordes ben ago !
And god, and eke his sayntes, laughe also.
In such swering ther is no stedfastnesse,
And these wrecches, that have ful trust therto,
After, they wepe and waylen in distresse.'   380

Lam. 'He hath no corage of a man, trewly,
That secheth plesaunce, worship to despyse ;
Nor to be called forth is not worthy
The erthe to touch the ayre in no-kins wyse.
A trusty hert, a mouth without feyntyse,   385
These ben the strength of every man of name ;
And who that layth his faith for litel pryse,
He leseth bothe his worship and his fame.'

La D. 'A currish herte, a mouth that is curteys,
Ful wel ye wot, they be not according ;   390
Yet feyned chere right sone may hem apeyse
Where of malyce is set al their worching ;
Ful fals semblant they bere and trew mening ;
Their name, their fame, their tonges be but fayned ;
Worship in hem is put in forgetting,   395
Nought repented, nor in no wyse complayned.'

Lam. 'Who thinketh il, no good may him befal ;
God, of his grace, graunt ech man his desert !
But, for his love, among your thoughtes al,
As think upon my woful sorowes smert ;   400
For of my payne, wheder your tender hert
Of swete pitè be not therwith agreved,
And if your grace to me were discovert,
Than, by your mene, sone shulde I be releved.'

---

384. Th. Ff. ayre; F. eir; H. heire.   386. Th. Thus be. F. H. Ff. man of;
Th. maner.   387. F. layth; Th. layeth; H. latith.   388. H. losith.
389. F. Ff. currisch; H. kurressh; Th. cursed.   391. Th. F. right; H. ful.
392. F. H. their; Th. her. F. worchyng; H. werchyng; Th. workynge.   393.
Th. and; F. H. a. F. Th. Ff. semyng; H. menyng.   394. F. H. Their; Th.
Her (*thrice*). Th. *om.* be.   Th. but; F. H. not.   400. H. sorowe.   401.
Th. wheder; Ff. whedre; F. H. wher.   403. F. H. Ff. if; Th. of.   404.
F. Ff. Then; H. Thanne; Th. That.

La D. 'A lightsom herte, a folly of plesaunce   405
Are moch better, the lesse whyl they abyde;
They make you thinke, and bring you in a traunce;
But that seknesse wil sone be remedyed.
Respite your thought, and put al this asyde;
Ful good disportes werieth men al-day;   410
To help nor hurt, my wil is not aplyed;
Who troweth me not, I lete it passe away.'

Lam. 'Who hath a brid, a faucon, or a hound,
That foloweth him, for love, in every place,
He cherissheth him, and kepeth him ful sound;   415
Out of his sight he wil not him enchace.
And I, that set my wittes, in this cace,
On you alone, withouten any chaunge,
Am put under, moch ferther out of grace,
And lesse set by, than other that be straunge.'   420

La D. 'Though I make chere to every man aboute
For my worship, and of myn own fraunchyse,
To you I nil do so, withouten doute,
In eschewing al maner prejudyse.
For wit ye wel, love is so litel wyse,   425
And in beleve so lightly wil be brought,
That he taketh al at his own devyse,
Of thing, god wot, that serveth him of nought.'

Lam. 'If I, by love and by my trew servyse,
Lese the good chere that straungers have alway,   430
Wherof shuld serve my trouth in any wise
Lesse than to hem that come and go al-day,
Which holde of you nothing, that is no nay?
Also in you is lost, to my seming,
Al curtesy, which of resoun wold say   435
That love for love were lawful deserving.'

---

408. Th. sicknesse.   410. Th. disporte. Th. me.   411. Th. Ff. nor;
F. H. ne.   412. F. H. Ff. it; Th. hem.   413. Th. Ff. byrde; F. bride;
H. bridde.   415. H. *om. 2nd* him.   416. F. H. *om. 2nd* him.   419.
Th. farther.   420. F. H. sett lesse.   422. F. H. Ff. of; Th. for.   424.
F. H. of all; Th. Ff. *om.* of.   425. Th. wote; F. H. wytt.   429-716.
Misarranged in F. H.; Th. Ff. *follow the right order.* 429. (Th.) = 669 (F. H.).
F. *om. 2nd* by.   431. F. There-of. F. H. shulde; Th. shal.   432. Th. him
that cometh and goth.   433. Th. holdeth.   434. Th. as to; F. H. Ff. *om.* as.
435. F. H. wolde; Th. Ff. wyl.   436. Th. desyringe (!).

La D. 'Curtesy is alyed wonder nere
To Worship, which him loveth tenderly;
And he wil nat be bounde, for no prayere,
Nor for no gift, I say you verily,　　　　　　440
But his good chere depart ful largely
Where him lyketh, as his conceit wil fal;
Guerdon constrayned, a gift don thankfully,
These twayn may not accord, ne never shal.'

Lam. 'As for guerdon, I seke non in this cace;　445
For that desert, to me it is to hy;
Wherfore I ask your pardon and your grace,
Sith me behoveth deeth, or your mercy.
To give the good where it wanteth, trewly,
That were resoun and a curteys maner;　　　450
And to your own moch better were worthy
Than to straungers, to shewe hem lovely chere.'

La D. 'What cal ye good? Fayn wolde I that I wist!
That pleseth oon, another smerteth sore;
But of his own to large is he that list　　　455
Give moche, and lese al his good fame therfore.
Oon shulde nat make a graunt, litel ne more,
But the request were right wel according;
If worship be not kept and set before,
Al that is left is but a litel thing.'　　　　460

Lam. 'In-to this world was never formed non,
Nor under heven crëature y-bore,
Nor never shal, save only your persone,
To whom your worship toucheth half so sore,
But me, which have no seson, lesse ne more,　465
Of youth ne age, but still in your service;
I have non eyen, no wit, nor mouth in store,
But al be given to the same office.'

---

438. Th. To; F. H. With.　F. H. best and tendyrly; Th. Ff. *om.* best and.
440. F. H. *om.* no.　F. H. Ff. yift; Th. gyftes.　　442. F. Wheryn hym.
443. F. H. Ff. constreynte.　　444. F. H. Ff. may not; Th. ca*n* neuer.　F.
H. ne; Th. Ff. nor.　　445. H. seche; F. beseche.　446. F. H. *om.*
it.　450. Th. a curtyse; Ff. a corteys; F. H. curteysy.　456. Th. *om.* al.
460. H. loste (*for* left).　　461. F. H. Ff. neuer formed (fourmed); Th.
founded neuer.　467. Th. no (*for* non). F. eeyn; H. yeen.　　468. H.
That ne alle ar.

La D. 'A ful gret charge hath he, withouten fayle,
That his worship kepeth in sikernesse;   470
But in daunger he setteth his travayle
That feffeth it with others businesse.
To him that longeth honour and noblesse,
Upon non other shulde nat he awayte;
For of his own so moche hath he the lesse   475
That of other moch folweth the conceyt.'

Lam. 'Your eyen hath set the print which that I fele
Within my hert, that, where-so-ever I go,
If I do thing that sowneth unto wele,
Nedes must it come from you, and fro no mo.   480
Fortune wil thus, that I, for wele or wo,
My lyf endure, your mercy abyding;
And very right wil that I thinke also
Of your worship, above al other thing.'

La D. 'To your worship see wel, for that is nede, 485
That ye spend nat your seson al in vayne;
As touching myn, I rede you take no hede,
By your foly to put your-self in payne.
To overcome is good, and to restrayne
An hert which is disceyved folily.   485
For worse it is to breke than bowe, certayn,
And better bowe than fal to sodaynly!'

Lam. 'Now, fair lady, think, sith it first began
That love hath set myn hert under his cure,
I never might, ne truly I ne can   495
Non other serve, whyle I shal here endure;
In most free wyse therof I make you sure,
Which may not be withdrawe; this is no nay.
I must abyde al maner aventure;
For I may not put to, nor take away.'   500

---

472. F. feoffeth.   474. Th. be (*for* he).   475. F. H. *om.* his.   477-524.
Follows 572 *in* F. H.   477 (Th.) = 525 (F. H.).   478. Th. Ff. so; H. sum;
F. some.   479. H. sowndith.   481. H. Ff. thus; Th. this.   486. F. *om.* ye.
H. F. your sesoun spende not.   488. H. Ff. foly; Th. folly.   489. Th. H.
herte.   H. F. folyly; Th. follyly.   492.   H. F. And; Th. *om.* Th. to fal.
493. H. Th. faire.   494. H. Ff. had (*for* hath).   H. F. your; Th. Ff. his.
495. F. H. I neuer; Th. Ff. It neuer.   496. F. H. whiles.   500. H. F. not;
Ff. nought; Th. neyther.

La D. 'I holde it for no gift, in sothfastnesse,
That oon offreth, where that it is forsake ;
For suche gift is abandoning expresse
That with worship ayein may not be take.
He hath an hert ful fel that list to make   505
A gift lightly, that put is in refuse ;
But he is wyse that such conceyt wil slake,
So that him nede never to study ne muse.'

Lam. 'He shuld nat muse, that hath his service spent
On her which is a lady honourable ;   510
And if I spende my tyme to that entent,
Yet at the leest I am not reprevable
Of feyled hert ; to thinke I am unable,
Or me mistook whan I made this request,
By which love hath, of entreprise notable,   515
So many hertes gotten by conquest.'

La D. 'If that ye list do after my counsayl,
Secheth fairer, and of more higher fame,
Whiche in servyce of love wil you prevayl
After your thought, according to the same.   520
He hurteth both his worship and his name
That folily for twayne him-self wil trouble ;
And he also leseth his after-game
That surely can not sette his poyntes double.'

Lam. 'This your counsayl, by ought that I can see,   525
Is better sayd than don, to myn advyse ;
Though I beleve it not, forgive it me,
Myn herte is suche, so hool without feyntyse,
That it ne may give credence, in no wyse,
To thing which is not sowning unto trouthe ;   530
Other counsayl, it ar but fantasyes,
Save of your grace to shewe pitè and routhe.'

---

501. Th. gyfte; H. yifte.   502. Th. *om.* that.   503. Th. a gifte; H. F.
Ff. *om.* a.   505. H. F. *om.* an. H. hurte ful fele (!).   506. H. F. Ff. in ;
Th. to.   508. H. F. neuer; Th. neyther.   509. H. F. Who; Th. Ff. He.   512.
F. *om.* the. Th. reproveable.   513. F. H. feyled ; Th. fayned.   514. Th.
I mystoke; H. F. Ff. me mystoke.   515. F. entrepris.   516. H. F. goten.   517.
H. Th. liste.   518. F. H. Secheth; Th. Seche a.   519. Th. preuayle.   523.
H. hosithe (*for* leseth).   525-572. *Follows* 716 *in* F. H.   528. H. hoole ;
Th. hole.   529. H. F. it; Th. I.   H. F. *om.* ne.   530. H. soundyng.   531.
H. F. it ar; Th. I se be.   Th. Ff. fantasise ; F. fantasyse ; H. fantaisise.

La D. 'I holde him wyse that worketh folily
And, whan him list, can leve and part therfro ;
But in conning he is to lerne, trewly,   535
That wolde him-self conduite, and can not so.
And he that wil not after counsayl do,
His sute he putteth in desesperaunce ;
And al the good, which that shulde falle him to,
Is left as deed, clene out of rémembraunce.'   540

Lam. 'Yet wil I sewe this mater faithfully
Whyls I may live, what-ever be my chaunce ;
And if it hap that in my trouthe I dy,
That deeth shal not do me no displesaunce.
But whan that I, by your ful hard suffraunce,   545
Shal dy so trew, and with so greet a payne,
Yet shal it do me moche the lesse grevaunce
Than for to live a fals lover, certayne.'

La D. 'Of me get ye right nought, this is no fable,
I nil to you be neither hard nor strayt ;   550
And right wil not, nor maner customable,
To think ye shulde be sure of my conceyt.
Who secheth sorowe, his be the receyt !
Other counsayl can I not fele nor see,
Nor for to lerne I cast not to awayte ;   555
Who wil therto, let him assay, for me !'

Lam. 'Ones must it be assayd, that is no nay,
With such as be of reputacioun,
And of trew love the right devoir to pay
Of free hertes, geten by due raunsoun ;   560
For free wil holdeth this opinioun,
That it is greet duresse and discomfort
To kepe a herte in so strayt a prisoun,
That hath but oon body for his disport.'

---

533. H. F. Ff. folily ; Th. no foly (!).   534. H. Th. parte.   536. F. condyte.
538. Th. Ff. sute ; H. F. suerte.   H. F. in ; Th. in to.   539. Th. *om.* which.
H. F. *om.* that.   540. H. F. Ff. left as ; Th. lost and.   F. dethe (!).   542.
H. Ff. Whils ; Th. Whyles. Th. *om.* may.   544. Th. Than ; H. F. Ff. That.
H. not ; Th. F. *om.*   545. Ff. full ; *rest om.* Th. H. harde.   546. H. triew ;
Th. true. H. grete ; Th. great. F. Ff. *om.* a.   547. F. H. *om.* the ; *read*
mochel less ?   550. H. F. nyl ; Th. wyl. H. Th. harde.   551. Th. no man (*for*
nor maner).   555. Th. cast me not.   556. H. F. ther-to ; Th. therof.   558.
H. F. beth.   559. H. trewe ; Th. true. Ff. devoyr ; H. duetes ; F. dewtis ;
Th. honour.   560. Th. gotten. H. F. due ; Th. dewe.   562. H. grete ;
Th. great. H. Th. -forte.   564. H. F. oo ; Ff. on ; Th. one. H. Th. -porte.

La D. 'I know so many cases mervaylous   565
That I must nede, of resoun, think certayn,
That such entree is wonder perilous,
And yet wel more, the coming bak agayn.
Good or worship therof is seldom seyn;
Wherefore I wil not make no suche aray   570
As for to fynde a plesaunce but barayn,
Whan it shal cost so dere, the first assay.'

Lam. 'Ye have no cause to doute of this matere,
Nor you to meve with no such fantasyes
To put me ferre al-out, as a straungere;   575
For your goodnesse can think and wel avyse,
That I have made a prefe in every wyse
By which my trouth sheweth open evidence;
My long abyding and my trew servyse
May wel be knowen by playn experience.'   580

La D. 'Of very right he may be called trew,
And so must he be take in every place,
That can deserve, and let as he ne knew,
And kepe the good, if he it may purchace.
For who that prayeth or sueth in any case,   585
Right wel ye wot, in that no trouth is preved;
Suche hath ther ben, and are, that geten grace,
And lese it sone, whan they it have acheved.'

Lam. 'If trouth me cause, by vertue soverayne,
To shew good love, and alway fynd contráry,   590
And cherish that which sleeth me with the payne,
This is to me a lovely adversary!
Whan that pitè, which long a-slepe doth tary,
Hath set the fyne of al myn hevinesse,
Yet her comfort, to me most necessary,   595
Shuld set my wil more sure in stablenesse.'

---

565. Ff. H. cases; *rest* causes.   566. H. F. Which; Th. Ff. That.   567.
H. F. Ff. entre; Th. auenture (!).   570. Th. Where I ne wyl make suche.
571. Th. but a; H. F. *om.* a.   573-620. *Follows* 668 *in* H. F.   573.
F. matere; Th. mater.   574. Th. fantasyse; F. fantasise; H. fantesye.   576.
F. Ff. avyse; Th. H. aduyse.   577. H. Ff. prefe; F. preue; Th. prise.
578. H. trouthe; Th. truthe.   579. H. Th. trewe.   581. H. Th. trewe.   583.
H. Ff. deserue; Th. discerne (!).   H. Th. knewe.   585. H. Ff. sueth; F.
seweth; Th. swereth.   587. Th. geten; H. F. getith.   588. H. F. Ff. it haue;
Th. haue it.   590. Th. H. shewe; fynde.   593. H. F. a slepe; Th. on
slepe.   595. Th. H. comforte.   596. Ff. Shuld; H. F. Shulde; Th. Shal.

La D. 'The woful wight, what may he thinke or say?
The contrary of al joy and gladnesse.
A sick body, his thought is al away
From hem that fele no sorowe nor siknesse.   600
Thus hurtes ben of dyvers businesse
Which love hath put to right gret hinderaunce,
And trouthe also put in forgetfulnesse
Whan they so sore begin to sighe askaunce.'

Lam. 'Now god defend but he be havëlesse   605
Of al worship or good that may befal,
That to the werst tourneth, by his lewdnesse,
A gift of grace, or any-thing at al
That his lady vouchsauf upon him cal,
Or cherish him in honourable wyse!   610
In that defaut what-ever he be that fal
Deserveth more than deth to suffre twyse!'

La D. 'There is no juge y-set of such trespace
By which of right oon may recovered be;
Oon curseth fast, another doth manace,   615
Yet dyeth non, as ferre as I can see,
But kepe their cours alway, in oon degrè,
And evermore their labour doth encrese
To bring ladyes, by their gret soteltè,
For others gilte, in sorowe and disese!'   620

Lam. 'Al-be-it so oon do so greet offence,
And be not deed, nor put to no juÿse,
Right wel I wot, him gayneth no defence,
But he must ende in ful mischévous wyse,
And al that ever is good wil him dispyse.   625
For falshed is so ful of cursednesse

599. Th. sycke; H. F. seke. F. *om.* his. H. F. Ff. al awaye; Th. alway.
600. H. Ff. fele; Th. felen. H. sorwe; F. Ff. sorowe; Th. sore.   602. Th.
om. right. Th. hindraunce. 604. H. Ff. so; Th. ful; F. *om.*   605. H. Th.
defende. H. F. haueles; Th. harmlesse (!). 607. Th. *om.* the. 608. Th. gyfte;
H. yifte.   609. Th. Ff. vouchesafe; H. vouchith sauf.   610. H. F. cherissh;
Th. Ff. cherissheth.   611. H. Th. defaute.   613. H. F. of; Th. on. H. Th.
suche.   614. H. one; F. ōn; Th. loue.   615. H. Th. One.   616. H. Th.
none.   617. H. Th. her; *see* 618. Th. course; H. corse. Th. H. one; F. a.
618. H. F. euere newe; Th. Ff. euermore.   Ff. their; Th. theyr; H. there;
F. thair. 619. Th. Ff. their great; H. F. *om.* great. H. F. subtilite; Th. subtelte;
Ff. sotelte. 621–668. *Follows* 524 *in* F. H.   621. F. oone; H. on; Th. one.
Th. dothe; great.   622. H. F. Ff. be; Th. is. H. F. Ff. Iuyse; Th. iustyse.
625. *So* H. F. Ff.; Th. And al euer sayd god wyl.   626. Th. *om.* so.

That high worship shal never have enterpryse
Where it reigneth and hath the wilfulnesse.'

La D. 'Of that have they no greet fere now-a-days,
Suche as wil say, and maynteyne it ther-to, 630
That stedfast trouthe is nothing for to prays
In hem that kepe it long for wele or wo.
Their busy hertes passen to and fro,
They be so wel reclaymed to the lure,
So wel lerned hem to withholde also, 635
And al to chaunge, whan love shuld best endure.'

Lam. 'Whan oon hath set his herte in stable wyse
In suche a place as is both good and trewe,
He shuld not flit, but do forth his servyse
Alway, withouten chaunge of any newe. 640
As sone as love beginneth to remewe,
Al plesaunce goth anon, in litel space;
For my party, al that shal I eschewe,
Whyls that the soule abydeth in his place.'

La D. 'To love trewly ther-as ye ought of right, 645
Ye may not be mistaken, doutëlesse;
But ye be foul deceyved in your sight
By lightly understanding, as I gesse.
Yet may ye wel repele your businesse
And to resoun somwhat have attendaunce, 650
Moch better than to byde, by fol simplesse,
The feble socour of desesperaunce.'

Lam. 'Resoun, counsayl, wisdom, and good avyse
Ben under love arested everichoon,
To which I can accorde in every wyse; 655
For they be not rebel, but stille as stoon;

627. Ff. highe; H. F. her; Th. his. H. F. shal; Th. Ff. may. 629. Th.
great; F. H. *om.* Th. dayse; H. daies. 631. H. preys; Th. prayse.
632. F. H. Ff. for; Th. in. 633. Th. F. Theyr; H. There. 637. Th.
one; H. on; Ff. won. 638. H. Ff. which (*for* as). 643. *So* F. H.; Th. As for
my partie that. 644. Th. Whyle; H. F. Ff. Whils that 645. F. H. ye;
Th. it. 647. Th. H. foule. H. F. deceyued; Th. disceyued. 648. H. F.
lightly; Th. light. 649. H. F. this; Th. Ff. your. 650. H. Ff. sumwhat
haue; Th. haue some. 651. *All* Moche. H. sonner; F. sunner; Th. Ff.
better. Th. to abide. Ff. fole; *rest* foly. Th. simplenes; *rest* simplesse.
653. F. Ff. avyse; Th. H. aduyse. 656. Th. as a; H. F. Ff. *om.* a.

Their wil and myn be medled al in oon,
And therwith bounden with so strong a cheyne
That, as in hem, departing shal be noon,
But pitè breke the mighty bond atwayne.'　　　　　660

La D. 'Who loveth not himself, what-ever he be
In love, he stant forgete in every place;
And of your wo if ye have no pitè,
Others pitè bileve not to purchace;
But beth fully assured in this case,　　　　　665
I am alway under oon ordinaunce,
To have better; trusteth not after grace,
And al that leveth tak to your plesaunce!'

Lam. 'I have my hope so sure and so stedfast
That suche a lady shulde nat fail pitè;　　　　　670
But now, alas! it is shit up so fast,
That Daunger sheweth on me his crueltè.
And if she see the vertue fayle in me
Of trew servyce, then she to fayle also
No wonder were; but this is the suretè,　　　　　675
I must suffre, which way that ever it go.'

La D. 'Leve this purpos, I rede you for the best;
For lenger that ye kepe it thus in vayn,
The lesse ye gete, as of your hertes rest,
And to rejoice it shal ye never attayn.　　　　　680
Whan ye abyde good hope, to make you fayn,
Ye shal be founde asotted in dotage;
And in the ende, ye shal know for certayn,
That hope shal pay the wrecches for their wage!'

Lam. 'Ye say as falleth most for your plesaunce,　　　685
And your power is greet; al this I see;

---

657. H. There. Th. H. one; Ff. won.　659. Th. Ff. as (*rightly*); H. F.
is. Th. H. none.　660. Th. H. bonde.　661. H. Ff. Who loueth; F. Who
love; Th. Ye loue. H. F. hym-; Th. your-.　H. F. he be; Th. ye be.　662.
So H. F. Ff.; Th. That in loue stande.　664. Th. bileue ye; *rest om.* ye.
665. H. F. beth; Th. be.　Th. as in; *rest om.* as.　666. Th. alway;
H. F. alwaies. Th. one; Ff. on; H. an.　667. F. H. trusteth; Th. trust. 668.
Th. H. take.　669-716. *Follows* 428 *in* F. H.　670. Th. lacke; H. F. Ff.
faile.　673. H. faileth.　674. F. H. Ff. then she to; Th. thoughe she do.
675. Th. my; F. H. Ff. the.　H. surtee; F. seurte.　677. H. purpos; Th.
pupose.　678. Th. For the lenger ye. H. F. Ff. thus; Th. is.　680. H. F.
Ff. ye; Th. you.　684. Th. *om.* That.　H. ther; Th. her.　686. Th. great.

But hope shal never out of my rémembraunce,
By whiche I felt so greet adversitè.
For whan nature hath set in you plentè
Of al goodnesse, by vertue and by grace,   690
He never assembled hem, as semeth me,
To put Pitè out of his dwelling-place.'

La D. ' Pitè of right ought to be resonable,
And to no wight of greet disavantage ;
There-as is nede, it shuld be profitable,   695
And to the pitous shewing no damage.
If a lady wil do so greet out-rage
To shewe pitè, and cause her own debate,
Of such pitè cometh dispitous rage,
And of the love also right deedly hate.'   700

Lam. 'To comforte hem that live al comfortlesse,
That is no harm, but worship to your name ;
But ye, that bere an herte of such duresse,
And a fair body formed to the same,
If I durst say, ye winne al this defame   705
By Crueltè, which sitteth you ful il,
But-if Pitè, which may al this attame,
In your high herte may rest and tary stil.'

La D. 'What-ever he be that sayth he loveth me,
And peraventure, I leve that it be so,   710
Ought he be wroth, or shulde I blamed be,
Though I did noght as he wolde have me do ?
If I medled with suche or other mo,
It might be called pitè manerlesse ;
And, afterward if I shulde live in wo,   715
Than to repent it were to late, I gesse.'

Lam. 'O marble herte, and yet more hard, pardè,
Which mercy may nat perce, for no labour,

More strong to bowe than is a mighty tree,
What vayleth you to shewe so greet rigour?   720
Plese it you more to see me dy this hour
Before your eyen, for your disport and play,
Than for to shewe som comfort or socour
To respite deth, that chaseth me alway!'

La D. 'Of your disese ye may have allegeaunce;   725
And as for myn, I lete it over-shake.
Also, ye shal not dye for my plesaunce,
Nor for your hele I can no surety make.
I nil nat hate myn hert for others sake;
Wepe they, laugh they, or sing, this I waraunt,   730
For this mater so wel to undertake
That non of you shal make therof avaunt!'

Lam. 'I can no skil of song; by god aloon,
I have more cause to wepe in your presence;
And wel I wot, avauntour am I noon,   735
For certainly, I love better silence.
Oon shuld nat love by his hertes credence
But he were sure to kepe it secretly;
For avauntour is of no reverence
Whan that his tonge is his most enemy.'   740

La D. 'Male-bouche in courte hath greet commaundement;
Ech man studieth to say the worst he may.
These fals lovers, in this tyme now present,
They serve to boste, to jangle as a jay.
The most secret wil wel that some men say   745
How he mistrusted is on some partyes;
Wherfore to ladies what men speke or pray,
It shuld not be bileved in no wyse.'

---

720. H. F. Ff. vaileth; Th. auayleth. Th. great.   721. H. F. Please; Th.
Pleaseth. Th. H. dye.   722. Th. H. dysporte.   723. H. F. Ff. or; Th. and.
724. Th. H. dethe. H. F. that; Th. whiche.   725. Th. H. disease.   726.
H. F. Ff. shake; Th. slake.   728. Th. heale.   729. H. F. Ff. nyl; Th. wyl.
H. F. Ff. hate myn herte; Th. hurte my selfe.   730. Th. they I; H. F. Ff. this I.
731. H. F. wel to: Th. wyl I.   732. H. F. you; Th. hem.   733. H. noo;
Th. nat. H. F. Ff. song; Th. loue. Th. alone.   735. H. F. Ff. I; Th. ye.
Th. H. wote. Th. none.   737. Th. One; H. On.   739. Th. H. a vauntour;
cf. l. 735.   741. Th. great.   744. H. F. Ff. to boste; Th. best.   745.
H. wil wele; F. Ff. wille wel; Th. ywis. H. F. Ff. that; Th. yet.   746.
H. F. on; Th. in.   F. Th. partyse; Ff. partyes; H. party.   747. H. F.
Ff. what; Th. whan so. Th. say (for pray).   748. H. F. shal; Ff. schuld;
Th. shulde.

Lam. 'Of good and il shal be, and is alway;
The world is such; the erth it is not playn.　　　750
They that be good, the preve sheweth every day,
And otherwyse, gret villany, certayn.
Is it resoun, though oon his tonge distayne
With cursed speche, to do him-self a shame,
That such refuse shuld wrongfully remayne　　　755
Upon the good, renommed in their fame?'

La D. 'Suche as be nought, whan they here tydings newe,
That ech trespas shal lightly have pardoun,
They that purposen to be good and trewe—
Wel set by noble disposicioun　　　760
To continue in good condicioun—
They are the first that fallen in damage,
And ful freely their hertes abandoun
To litel faith, with softe and fayr langage.'

Lam. 'Now knowe I wel, of very certaynte,　　　765
Though oon do trewly, yet shal he be shent,
Sith al maner of justice and pite
Is banisshed out of a ladyes entent.
I can nat see but al is at oo stent,
The good and il, the vyce and eek vertue!　　　770
Suche as be good shal have the punishment
For the trespas of hem that been untrewe!'

La D. 'I have no power you to do grevaunce,
Nor to punisshe non other creature;
But, to eschewe the more encomberaunce,　　　775
To kepe us from you al, I holde it sure.
Fals semblaunce hath a visage ful demure,
Lightly to cacche the ladies in a-wayt;

---

750. Th. H. suche.　Th. Ff. erth; H. F. dethe.　H. F. Ff. it is not; Th. is
not al.　751. H. F. preve: Th. profe.　752. Th. great villony.　753. F. Ff.
Is it; Th. H. It is.　Th. H. one.　755. H. F. refuse.　756. Th. renomed;
H. renommeed. F. H. her (*for* their).　757. Th. here; H. herde.　758. Th.
H. eche.　759. H. purposen; F. porposyn; Th. pursuen.　760. *So* H.
F. Ff.; Th. Wyl not set by none il d.　761. Th. in euery; H. F. *om.* euery.
763. Ff. thair; F. ther; H. theym; Th. the.　F. H. *om.* hertes.　764.
Th. faithe.　Th. Ff. softe and fayre; H. faire and softe.　766. F. H.
Though; Th. Ff. If.　*All* one.　768. H. banshid.　769. H. F. oo; Th. one.
770. Th. the (*for* 1*st* and); H. F. and.　Ff. eke; *rest* eke the.　771. H.
Ff. shal; Th. such.　772. H. F. ben; Ff. beth; Th. lyue.　777. F. H. Ff.
visage; Th. face (!).　778. H. F. Ff. the; Th. these.　Th. H. Ff. a wayte.

Y 2

Wherefore we must, if that we wil endure,
Make right good watch; lo! this is my conceyt.'   780

Lam. 'Sith that of grace oo goodly word aloon
May not be had, but alway kept in store,
I pele to god, for he may here my moon,
Of the duresse, which greveth me so sore.
And of pitè I pleyn me further-more,   785
Which he forgat, in al his ordinaunce,
Or els my lyf to have ended before,
Which he so sone put out of rémembraunce.'

La D. 'My hert, nor I, have don you no forfeyt,
By which ye shulde complayne in any kynde.   790
There hurteth you nothing but your conceyt;
Be juge your-self; for so ye shal it fynde.
Ones for alway let this sinke in your mynde—
That ye desire shal never rejoysed be!
Ye noy me sore, in wasting al this wynde;   795
For I have sayd y-nough, as semeth me.'

Verba Auctoris.

This woful man roos up in al his payne,
And so parted, with weping countenaunce;
His woful hert almost to-brast in twayne,
Ful lyke to dye, forth walking in a traunce,   800
And sayd, 'Now, deeth, com forth! thy-self avaunce,
Or that myn hert forgete his propertè;
And make shorter al this woful penaunce
Of my pore lyfe, ful of adversitè!'

Fro thens he went, but whider wist I nought,   805
Nor to what part he drow, in sothfastnesse;

---

779. F. H. Ff. yf that we wil; Th. if we wyl here.   780. Th. H. co*n*ceyte.
781. F. H. oo; Th. a. Th. worde. H. F. Ff. allone; Th. nat one.   782.
F. H. not: Th. nowe. Th. kepte.   783. H. F. Ff. pele; Th. appele. *All*
mone (*read* moon).   785. H. Ff. pleyne me; F. pleyn me; Th. complayne.
786. Th. H. forgate.   787. H. elles.   788. Ff. H. F. he so sone put; Th. so
sone am put.   789. Th. H. forfeyte.   791. *So* H. F. Ff.; Th. Nothing hurteth
you but your owne conceyte.   792. H. shal ye.   793. H. F. Ones for;
Th. Thus.   794. *So* H.Ff.; *so* F. (*with* the *for* ye); Th. That your desyre
shal neuer recouered be.   796. Th. ynoughe. TITLE; *in* H.   797. Th.
rose; H. rosse. H. F. al in; Th. Ff. in al.   798. Ff. partyd; *rest* departed.
799. Th. to-brast; H. F. Ff. it brest.   800. H. forth walkyng; Th. Ff.
walkynge forth.   801. Th. *om.* Now.   803. Th. Ff. shorter; H. shorte;
F. short.   805. H. Ff. whider; Th. whither.   806. F. party. F. Ff.
drow; H. drowh; Th. drewe.

But he no more was in his ladies thought,
For to the daunce anon she gan her dresse.
And afterward, oon tolde me thus expresse,
He rente his heer, for anguissh and for payne,　　810
And in him-self took so gret hevinesse
That he was deed, within a day or twayne.

Lenvoy.

Ye trew lovers, this I beseche you al,
Such †avantours, flee hem in every wyse,
And as people defamed ye hem cal;　　815
For they, trewly, do you gret prejudyse.
Refus hath mad for al such flateryes
His castelles strong, stuffed with ordinaunce,
For they have had long tyme, by their offyce,
The hool countrè of Love in obeysaunce.　　820

And ye, ladyes, or what estat ye be,
In whom Worship hath chose his dwelling-place,
For goddes love, do no such crueltè,
Namely, to hem that have deserved grace.
Nor in no wyse ne folowe not the trace　　825
Of her, that here is named rightwisly,
Which by resoun, me semeth, in this case
May be called LA BELLE DAME SANS MERCY.

Verba Translatoris.

Go, litel book! god sende thee good passage!
Chese wel thy way; be simple of manere;　　830
Loke thy clothing be lyke thy pilgrimage,
And specially, let this be thy prayere
Un-to hem al that thee wil rede or here,
Wher thou art wrong, after their help to cal
Thee to correcte in any part or al.　　835

---

809. Th. Ff. thus; H. it; F. *om.* 811. Th. great. TITLE; *in.* Th. 813.
H. F. Ff. Ye; Th. The. F. trew; H. trewe; Th. true. Th. thus; H. Ff. this.
814. Ff. aventours; *rest* aventures (*see note*). Th. flie; H. F. fle. 816. Th.
great. 817. Th. *omits this line; from* H. F. Ff. H. F. made. H. F. Ff.
flaterise. 821. Th. H. estate; Ff. astate. 822. H. F. Ff. In; Th. Of. 824.
Ff. haue; F. hath; H. *om.* Th. *omits the line.* 825. H. folwe ye not; F.
folowe ye not; Ff. folowe not; Th. foule not. *After* 828, F. *has*—Explicit la
bele dame sanz mercy; H. F. Verba translatoris. 829. Th. H. Ff. the.
833. H. F. *om.* al. *All* the. 834. Th. hir (*for* their). 835. Th. H. The.

Pray hem also, with· thyn humble servyce,
Thy boldënesse to pardon in this case;
For els thou art not able, in no wyse,
To make thy-self appere in any place.
And furthermore, beseche hem, of their grace,   840
By their favour and supportacioun,
To take in gree this rude translacioun,

The which, god wot, standeth ful destitute
Of eloquence, of metre, and of coloures,
Wild as a beest, naked, without refute,   845
Upon a playne to byde al maner shoures.
I can no more, but aske of hem socoures
At whos request thou mad were in this wyse,
Commaunding me with body and servyse.

Right thus I make an ende of this processe,   850
Beseching him that al hath in balaunce
That no trew man be vexed, causëlesse,
As this man was, which is of rémembraunce;
And al that doon their faythful observaunce,
And in their trouth purpose hem to endure,   855
I pray god sende hem better aventure.

Explicit.

---

837. Th. cace; H. caas.   838. H. elles.   840, 841. Th. her (*for* their).
843. Th. H. wote.   844. Th. *om.* and.   845. H. F. Wilde; Th. Ff. Lyke.
846. Ff. tabyde; Th. to abyde.   847. H. axe.   848. Th. Ff. were made;
F. was made; H. made was.   850. H. F. Ff. processe; Th. prosses.   852.
Th. H. trewe.   854. Th. done her; Ff. do thair; H. dothe here; F. doth
thair.   855. Th. her (*for* their). *After* 856; Th. Explicit; H. Amen.

XVII.

THE TESTAMENT OF CRESSEID.

———◦—◦———

A NE dooly sesoun to ane cairfull dyte
  Suld correspond, and be equivalent.
Richt sa it wes quhen I began to wryte
This tragedy; the wedder richt fervent,
Quhen Aries, in middis of the Lent,   5
Shouris of haill can fra the north discend;
That scantly fra the cauld I micht defend.

Yit nevertheles, within myn orature
I stude, quhen Tytan had his bemis bricht
Withdrawin doun and sylit under cure;   10
And fair Venus, the bewty of the nicht,
Uprais, and set unto the west full richt
Hir goldin face, in oppositioun
Of god Phebus direct discending doun.

Throwout the glas hir bemis brast sa fair   15
That I micht see, on every syde me by,
The northin wind had purifyit the air,
And shed the misty cloudis fra the sky.
The froist freisit, the blastis bitterly
Fra pole Artyk come quhisling loud and shill, 20
And causit me remuf aganis my will.

From E. (Edinburgh edition, 1593); *collated with* Th. (Thyme, ed. 1532).
1. E. Ane; Th. A (*often*). E. doolie; Th. doly. E. to; Th. tyl.   **4.** E.
tragedie (*I substitute* -y *for* -ie).   6. E. Schouris (*I substitute* Sh- *for* Sch-).
7. Th. my3t me defende.   8. E. oratur; Th. orature.   10. Th. scyled.
16. *Both* se.   17. Th. northern.   18. Th. shedde his.   19. Th. frost.
20. E. Artick; Th. Artike. Th. whiskyng.   21. E. remufe; Th. remoue.

For I traistit that Venus, luifis quene,
To quhom sum-tyme I hecht obedience,
My faidit hart of luf sho wald mak grene ;
And therupon, with humbil reverence,   25
I thocht to pray hir hy magnificence ;
But for greit cald as than I lattit was,
And in my chalmer to the fyr can pas.

Thocht luf be hait, yit in ane man of age
It kendillis nocht sa sone as in youthheid,   30
Of quhom the blude is flowing in ane rage ;
And in the auld the curage †douf and deid,
Of quhilk the fyr outward is best remeid,
To help be phisik quhair that nature failit ;
I am expert, for baith I have assailit.   35

I mend the fyr, and beikit me about,
Than tuik ane drink my spreitis to comfort,
And armit me weill fra the cauld thairout.
To cut the winter-nicht, and mak it short,
I tuik ane quair, and left all uther sport,   40
Writtin be worthy Chaucer glorious,
Of fair Cresseid and lusty Troilus.

And thair I fand, efter that Diomeid
Ressavit had that lady bricht of hew,
How Troilus neir out of wit abraid,   45
And weipit soir, with visage paill of hew ;
For quhilk wanhope his teiris can renew,
Quhill †esperans rejoisit him agane :
Thus quhyl in joy he levit, quhyl in pane.

Of hir behest he had greit comforting,   50
Traisting to Troy that sho suld mak retour,
Quhilk he desyrit maist of eirdly thing,
For-quhy sho was his only paramour.

---

24. Th. faded.   28. Th. chambre.   *Both* fyre.   29. E. lufe ; Th. loue.
30. E. youtheid ; Th. youthheed.   32. E. doif ; Th. dull ; *read* douf.   34.
E. phisike.   36. E. mend ; Th. made.   *Both* fyre.   Th. beaked.   37.
E. ane ; Th. I.   40. Th. queare.   42. E. worthy ; Th. lusty.   43. Th.
founde.   45. Th. of his wytte abrede.   46. Th. wepte.   48. Th. esperous ;
E. Esperus.   49. E. quhyle.   Th. and while (*for* 2*nd* quhyl).   51. E. suld ;
Th. wolde.   52. Th. of al erthly.

Bot quhen he saw passit baith day and hour
Of hir gaincome, than sorrow can oppres   55
His woful hart in cair and hevines.

Of his distres me neidis nocht reheirs,
For worthy Chaucer, in the samin buik,
In guidly termis and in joly veirs
Compylit hes his cairis, quha will luik.   60
To brek my sleip ane uther quair I tuik,
In quilk I fand the fatall desteny
Of fair Cresseid, that endit wretchitly.

Quha wait gif all that Chauceir wrait was trew?
Nor I wait nocht gif this narratioun   65
Be authoreist, or fenyeit of the new
Be sum poeit, throw his inventioun,
Maid to report the lamentatioun
And woful end of this lusty Cresseid,
And quhat distres sho thoillit, and quhat deid.   70

Quhen Diomed had all his appetyt,
And mair, fulfillit of this fair lady,
Upon ane uther he set his haill delyt,
And send to hir ane lybel of répudy,
And hir excludit fra his company.   75
Than desolait sho walkit up and doun,
And, sum men sayis, into the court commoun.

O fair Cresseid! the flour and *A-per-se*
Of Troy and Grece, how was thou fortunait,
To change in filth all thy feminitee,   80
And be with fleshly lust sa maculait,
And go amang the Greikis air and lait
Sa giglot-lyk, takand thy foull plesance!
I have pity thee suld fall sic mischance!

---

55. E. ganecome ; Th. gayncome. Th. in (*for* than).   58. Th. in that
same.   63. Th. which ended.   66. Th. authorysed or forged.   67. Th.
Of some ; by (*for* throw).   70. Th. she was in or she deyde.   71. *Both*
appetyte.   73. Th. sette was al his delyte.   74. Th. *om.* of.   77. Th. As
(*for* And) ; in the courte as co*m*mune.   78. Th. Creseyde. *Both* floure.   79.
Th. were.   80. E. feminitie.   82. Th. early (*for* air).   84. Th. the ; E. thow.

Yit nevertheles, quhat-ever men deme or say   85
In scornful langage of thy brukilnes,
I sall excuse, als far-furth as I may,
Thy womanheid, thy wisdom, and fairnes,
The quilk Fortoun hes put to sic distres
As hir pleisit, and na-thing throw the gilt   90
Of thee, throw wikkit langage to be spilt.

This fair lady, in this wys destitut
Of all comfort and consolatioun,
Richt prively, but fellowship, on fut
Disgysit passit far out of the toun   95
Ane myle or twa, unto ane mansioun
Beildit full gay, quhair hir father Calchas,
Quhilk than amang the Greikis dwelland was.

Quhan he hir saw, the caus he can inquyr
Of hir cuming; sho said, syching full soir,   100
'Fra Diomeid had gottin his desyr
He wox wery, and wald of me no moir!'
Quod Calchas, 'Douchter, weip thow not thairfoir;
Peraventure all cummis for the best;
Welcum to me; thow art full deir ane gest.'   105

This auld Calchas, efter the law was tho,
Wes keeper of the tempill, as ane preist,
In quhilk Venus and hir son Cupido
War honourit; and his chalmer was thaim neist;
To quhilk Cresseid, with baill aneuch in breist,   110
Usit to pas, hir prayeris for to say;
Quhill at the last, upon ane solempne day,

As custom was, the pepill far and neir,
Befoir the none, unto the tempill went
With sacrifys devoit in thair maneir.   115

---

86. E. scornefull. E. brukkilnes; Th. brutelnesse.   88. E. wisdome.
91. E. wickit.   92. E. in; Th. on. *Both* wyse destitute.   94. E. but;
Th. without. Th. or refute; E. on fute.   95. E. Disagysit; Th. Dissheuelde.
Th. passed out.   99. E. inquyre; Th. enquyre.   101. *Both* desyre.   108.
E. sone; Th. sonne.   109. E. hir; Th. his. Th. chambre. E. thame; Th.
om.   110. E. aneuch in; Th. enewed.   113. *Both* custome.   115. *Both*
sacrifice. Th. deuout.

But still Cresseid, hevy in hir intent,
In-to the kirk wald not hir-self present,
For giving of the pepil ony deming
Of hir expuls fra Diomeid the king :

But past into ane secreit orature   120
Quhair sho micht weip hir wofull desteny.
Behind hir bak sho cloisit fast the dure,
And on hir knëis bair fell down in hy.
Upon Venus and Cupid angerly
Sho cryit out, and said on this same wys,   125
'Allas! that ever I maid yow sacrifys!

Ye gave me anis ane devyn responsaill
That I suld be the flour of luif in Troy;
Now am I maid an unworthy outwaill,
And all in cair translatit is my joy.   130
Quha sall me gyde? quha sall me now convoy,
Sen I fra Diomeid and nobill Troilus
Am clene excludit, as abject odious?

O fals Cupide, is nane to wyte bot thow
And thy mother, of luf the blind goddes!   135
Ye causit me alwayis understand and trow
The seid of luf was sawin in my face,
And ay grew grene throw your supply and grace.
But now, allas! that seid with froist is slane,
And I fra luifferis left, and all forlane!'   140

Quhen this was said, doun in ane extasy,
Ravishit in spreit, intill ane dream sho fell;
And, be apperance, hard, quhair sho did ly,
Cupid the king ringand ane silver bell,
Quhilk men micht heir fra hevin unto hell;   145
At quhais sound befoir Cupide appeiris
The sevin planetis, discending fra thair spheiris,

---

117. Th. churche.   118. E. givin; Th. gyueng. E. pepill; Th. people.
120. Th. oratore.   122. Th. closed; dore.   124. *Both* Cupide.   125.
Th. *om.* same. *Both* wyse.   126. E. Allace; Th. Alas. *Both* sacrifice.
127. E. devine; Th. diuyne.   132. E. Sen; Th. Sithe.   135. E. lufe; Th.
loue. E. the; Th. that.   136. Th. vnderstande alway.   137. E. lufe;
Th. loue.   138. Th. souple grace.   139. E. allace; Th. alas. Th. frost.
140. Th. louers; -layne. 143. Th. herde.   144. *Both* Cupide. E. ringand;
Th. tynkyng.   145. Th. in-to.   147. Th. speres.

Quhilk hes powèr of all thing generábill
To reull and steir, be thair greit influence,
Wedder and wind and coursis variábill.   150
And first of all Saturn gave his sentence,
Quhilk gave to Cupid litill reverence,
But as ane busteous churl, on his maneir,
Com crabbitly, with auster luik and cheir.

His face fronsit, his lyr was lyk the leid   155
His teith chatterit and cheverit with the chin
His ene drowpit, how, sonkin in his heid
Out of his nois the meldrop fast can rin
With lippis bla, and cheikis leine and thin
The yse-shoklis that fra his hair doun hang   160
Was wonder greit, and as ane speir als lang.

Atour his belt his lyart lokkis lay
Felterit unfair, ourfret with froistis hoir ;
His garmound and his †gyte full gay of gray ;
His widderit weid fra him the wind out woir.   165
Ane busteous bow within his hand he boir ;
Under his gyrdil ane flash of felloun flanis
Fedderit with yse, and heidit with hail-stanis.

Than Juppiter richt fair and amiábill,
God of the starnis in the firmament,   170
And nureis to all thing[is] generábill,
Fra his father Saturn far different,
With burely face, and browis bricht and brent ;
Upon his heid ane garland wonder gay
Of flouris fair, as it had been in May.   175

150. Th. course.   151. *Both* Saturne.   152. *Both* Cupide.   153.
Th. boystous.   E. on ; Th. in.   154. *Both* Come. E. crabitlie ; Th.
crabbedly. Th. austryne.   155. E. frosnit (*for* fronsit) ; Th. frounsed.
E. lyre ; Th. lere. *Both* lyke.   156. Th. sheuered.   157. Th. drouped hole.
158. E. of ; Th. at. Th. myldrop.   159. Th. blo.   160. E. ic-eschoklis ; Th.
yse-yckels.   162. E. Atouir ; Th. Attour.   163. E. ovirfret ; Th. ouerfret ;
read ourfret.   164. Th. garment. E. gyis ; Th. gate ; *see* l. 178.   165.
Th. wyddred ; wore.   166. Th. boustous ; bor[e].   167. E. gyrdill.   Th.
a fasshe (!) ; flayns.   168. Th. holstayns (!).   170. Th. sterres.   171.
Th. norice ; thinge.   172. *Both* Saturne.   173. Th. burly.   174.
Th. wonders.   175. E. bene ; Th. ben.

His voice was cleir, as cristal wer his ene;
As goldin wyr sa glitterand was his hair;
His garmound and his gyte full gay of grene,
With goldin listis gilt on every gair;
Ane burely brand about his middill bair.   180
In his right hand he had ane groundin speir,
Of his father the wraith fra us to weir.

Nixt efter him com Mars, the god of ire,
Of stryf, debait, and all dissensioun;
To chyde and fecht, als feirs as ony fyr;   185
In hard harnes, hewmound and habirgeoun,
And on his hanche ane rousty fell fachioun:
And in his hand he had ane rousty sword,
Wrything his face with mony angry word.

Shaikand his sword, befoir Cupide he com   190
With reid visage and grisly glowrand ene;
And at his mouth ane bullar stude of fome,
Lyk to ane bair quhetting his tuskis kene
Richt tuilyour-lyk, but temperance in tene;
Ane horn he blew, with mony bosteous brag,   195
Quhilk all this warld with weir hes maid to wag.

Than fair Phebus, lanterne and lamp of licht
Of man and beist, baith frute and flourishing,
Tender nuréis, and banisher of nicht,
And of the warld causing, be his moving   200
And influence, lyf in all eirdly thing;
Without comfort of quhom, of force to nocht
Must all ga dy, that in this warld is wrocht.

As king royáll he raid upon his chair,
The quhilk Phaeton gydit sum-tyme unricht;   205
The brichtnes of his face, quhen it was bair,

Nane micht behald for peirsing of his sicht.
This goldin cart with fyry bemes bricht
Four yokkit steidis, full different of hew,
But bait or tyring throw the spheiris drew.   210

The first was soyr, with mane als reid as rois,
Callit Eöy, in-to the orient;
The secund steid to name hecht Ethiös,
Quhytly and paill, and sum-deill ascendent;
The thrid Peros, richt hait and richt fervent;   215
The feird was blak, callit † Philegoney,
Quhilk rollis Phebus down in-to the sey.

Venus was thair present, that goddes gay,
Hir sonnis querrel for to defend, and mak
Hir awin complaint, cled in ane nyce array,   220
The ane half grene, the uther half sabill-blak;
Quhyte hair as gold, kemmit and shed abak;
But in hir face semit greit variance,
Quhyles perfit treuth, and quhylës inconstance.

Under smyling sho was dissimulait,   225
Provocative with blenkis amorous;
And suddanly changit and alterait,
Angry as ony serpent venemous,
Richt pungitive with wordis odious.
Thus variant sho was, quha list tak keip,   230
With ane eye lauch, and with the uther weip:—

In taikning that all fleshly paramour,
Quhilk Venus hes in reull and governance,
Is sum-tyme sweit, sum-tyme bitter and sour,
Richt unstabill, and full of variance,   235
Mingit with cairfull joy, and fals plesance;
Now hait, now cauld; now blyth, now full of wo;
Now grene as leif, now widderit and ago.

---

210. Th. speres.   211. Th. sorde (*for* soyr).   212. *Both* Eoye.   213.
Th. Ethose.   215. Th. Perose; and eke.   216. E. Philologie; Th.
Philologee.   218. E. *om.* gay.   219. Th. *om.* for.   222. Th. kembet.
224. Th. Vhile parfite. E. perfyte.   227. E. suddanely; Th. sodaynly.
228. E. venemous; Th. venomous.   232. Th. tokenyng. 237. E. blyith;
Th. blyth.   238. Th. wyddred.

With buik in hand than com Mercurius,
Richt eloquent and full of rethory;   240
With pólite termis and delicious;
With pen and ink to réport all redy;
Setting sangis, and singand merily.
His hude was reid, heklit atour his croun,
Lyk to ane poeit of the auld fassoun.   245

Boxis he bair with fine electuairis,
And sugerit syropis for digestioun;
Spycis belangand to the pothecairis,
With mony hailsum sweit confectioun;
Doctour in phisik, cled in scarlot goun,   250
And furrit weill, as sic ane aucht to be,
Honest and gude, and not ane word coud le.

Nixt efter him com lady Cynthia,
The last of all, and swiftest in hir spheir,
Of colour blak, buskit with hornis twa,   255
And in the nicht sho listis best appeir;
Haw as the leid, of colour na-thing cleir.
For all hir licht sho borrowis at hir brothir
Titan; for of hir-self sho hes nane uther.

Hir gyte was gray, and full of spottis blak;   260
And on hir breist ane churl paintit ful evin,
Beirand ane bunch of thornis on his bak,
Quhilk for his thift micht clim na nar the hevin.
Thus quhen they gadderit war, thir goddis sevin,
Mercurius they cheisit with ane assent   265
To be foir-speikar in the parliament.

Quha had ben thair, and lyking for to heir
His facound toung and termis exquisyte,
Of rhetorik the praktik he micht leir,
In breif sermone ane pregnant sentence wryte.   270

---

239. *Both* come.   242. E. reddie; Th. redy.   244. E. atouir; Th.
attour.   245. *Both* Lyke.   250. E. phisick. Th. cledde in a scarlet.
252. E. culd lie; Th. couth lye.   253. *Both* come.   254. Th. spere.
256. Th. tapere.   258. E. hir (1); Th. the.   260. E. gyse; Th. gyte.
261. E. churle; Th. chorle.   262. E. bunche; Th. busshe.   263. Th.
theft; no ner.   264. Th. gadred were the.   267. E. bene.   269.
E. rhetorick; Th. rethorike. E. prettick; Th. practyke.

Befoir Cupide vailing his cap a lyte,
Speiris the caus of that vocacioun;
And he anon shew his intencioun.

'Lo!' quod Cupide, 'quha will blaspheme the name
Of his awin god, outhir in word or deid,   275
To all goddis he dois baith lak and shame,
And suld have bitter panis to his meid.
I say this by yonder wretchit Cresseid,
The quhilk throw me was sum-tyme flour of lufe,
Me and my mother starkly can reprufe.   280

Saying, of hir greit infelicitè
I was the caus; and my mother Venus,
Ane blind goddes hir cald, that micht not see,
With slander and defame injurious.
Thus hir leving unclene and lecherous   285
Sho wald returne on me and [on] my mother,
To quhom I shew my grace abone all uther.

And sen ye ar all sevin deificait,
Participant of dévyn sapience,
This greit injúry don to our hy estait   290
Me-think with pane we suld mak recompence;
Was never to goddis don sic violence.
As weill for yow as for myself I say;
Thairfoir ga help to révenge, I yow pray.'

Mercurius to Cupid gave answeir,   295
And said, 'Shir king, my counsall is that ye
Refer yow to the hyest planeit heir,
And tak to him the lawest of degrè,
The pane of Cresseid for to modify;
As god Saturn, with him tak Cynthia.'   300
'I am content,' quod he, 'to tak thay twa.'

---

273. E. anone. E. schew; Th. shewde.   276. E. lak; Th. losse.   278.
E. yone; Th. yonder. Th. wretche Creseyde.   280. E. starklie; Th. she
stately.   281. E. -tie.   283. Th. She called a blynde goddes and myght.
286. E. returne; Th. retorte. E. on; Th. in. *I supply 2nd* on.   287. E.
schew; Th. shewde (*as in* l. 273). Th. aboue.   289. E. devyne; Th.
diuyne.   290. E. iniurie; Th. iniure. *Both* done.   290. E. hie; Th. hye.
292. *Both* goddes done.   295. *Both* Cupide.   299. E. modifie; Th.
modifye.   300. *Both* Saturne.

Than thus proceidit Saturn and the Mone,
Quhen thay the mater rypely had degest;
For the dispyt to Cupid sho had done,
And to Venus oppin and manifest,   305
In all hir lyf with pane to be opprest
And torment sair, with seiknes incurábill,
And to all lovers be abominábill.

This dulefull sentence Saturn tuik on hand,
And passit doun quhair cairfull Cresseid lay;   310
And on hir heid he laid ane frosty wand,
Than lawfully on this wyse can he say;
'Thy greit fairnes, and al thy bewty gay,
Thy wantoun blude, and eik thy goldin hair,
Heir I exclude fra thee for evermair.   315

I change thy mirth into melancholy,
Quhilk is the mother of all pensivenes;
Thy moisture and thy heit in cald and dry;
Thyne insolence, thy play and wantones
To greit diseis: thy pomp and thy riches   320
In mortall neid; and greit penuritie
Thow suffer sall, and as ane beggar die.'

O cruel Saturn, fraward and angry,
Hard is thy dome, and to malicious!
On fair Cresseid quhy hes thow na mercy,   325
Quhilk was sa sweit, gentill, and amorous?
Withdraw thy sentence, and be gracious
As thow was never; so shawis thow thy deid,
Ane wraikfull sentence gevin on fair Cresseid.

Than Cynthia, quhen Saturn past away,   330
Out of hir sait discendit down belyve,
And red ane bill on Cresseid quhair sho lay,
Contening this sentence diffinityve :—

303, 309, 323, 330. *Both* Saturne.   304. *Both* Cupide.   E. scho; Th. that
she.   305. Th. open.   306. *Both* lyfe.   308. E. abhominabill;
Th. abhominable.   309. Th. doleful.   318. E. in; Th. into.   319.
E. and: Th. and thy.   321. E. In; Th. Into.   E. penuritie; Th. -te.
322. Th. shalte.   Th. dye.   324. E. malitious.   325. E. On; Th. Of.
328. Th. sheweth through.   329. Th. *om.* fair.   331. Th. seate.

'Fra heil of body I thee now depryve,
And to thy seiknes sal be na recure,   335
But in dolóur thy dayis to indure.

Thy cristall ene minglit with blude I mak,
Thy voice sa cleir unplesand, hoir, and hace;
Thy lusty lyre ourspred with spottis blak,
And lumpis haw appeirand in thy face.   340
Quhair thow cummis, ilk man sall flee the place;
Thus sall thou go begging fra hous to hous,
With cop and clapper, lyk ane lazarous.'

This dooly dream, this ugly visioun
Brocht to ane end, Cresseid fra it awoik,   345
And all that court and convocatioun
Vanischit away.   Than rais sho up and tuik
Ane poleist glas, and hir shaddow coud luik;
And quhen sho saw hir face sa déformait,
Gif sho in hart was wa aneuch, god wait!   350

Weiping full sair, 'Lo! quhat it is,' quod she,
'With fraward langage for to mufe and steir
Our crabbit goddis, and sa is sene on me!
My blaspheming now have I bocht full deir;
All eirdly joy and mirth I set areir.   355
Allas, this day! Allas, this wofull tyde,
Quhen I began with my goddis to chyde!'

Be this was said, ane child com fra the hall
To warn Cresseid the supper was redy;
First knokkit at the dure, and syne coud call—   360
'Madame, your father biddis you cum in hy;
He has mervell sa lang on grouf ye ly,
And sayis, "Your prayërs been to lang sum-deill;
The goddis wait all your intent full weill."'

334. E. heit; Th. heale.   336. Th. endure.   338. Th. vnplesaunt
heer.   339. Th. lere.   E. ouirspred; Th. ouerspred.   342. E. This;
Th. Thus.   343. Th. cuppe.   *Both* lyke.   344. *Both* dreame. E.
uglye.   347. Th. rose she.   348. Th. polysshed.   E. culd; Th.
couth.   349. E. face; Th. visage.   350. Th. were wo, I ne wyte god
wate.   352. Th. *om.* for.   E. mufe; Th. moue.   353. E. craibit;
Th. crabbed.   355. Th. erthly.   356. E. Allace; Th. Alas.   357.
357. E. for to; Th. *om.* for.   358. E. come; Th. came.   359. *Both* warne.
Th. Creseyde.   E. reddy; Th. redy.   360. E. syne culd; Th. efte couth.
362. E. merwel; Th. marueyle.   363. E. prayers bene; Th. bedes bethe.

Quod sho, 'Fair child, ga to my father deir,   365
And pray him cum to speik with me anon.'
And sa he did, and said, 'Douchter, quhat cheir?'
'Allas!' quod she, 'father, my mirth is gon!'
'How sa?' quod he; and sho can all expone,
As I have tauld, the vengeance and the wrak,   370
For hir trespas, Cupide on hir coud tak.

He luikit on hir ugly lipper face,
The quhilk befor was quhyte as lilly-flour;
Wringand his handis, oftymes he said, Allas!
That he had levit to see that wofull hour!   375
For he knew weill that thair was na succour
To hir seiknes; and that dowblit his pane;
Thus was thair cair aneuch betwix tham twane.

Quhen thay togidder murnit had full lang,
Quod Cresseid, 'Father, I wald not be kend;   380
Thairfoir in secreit wyse ye let me gang
To yon hospítall at the tounis end;
And thidder sum meit, for cheritie, me send
To leif upon; for all mirth in this eird
Is fra me gane; sik is my wikkit weird.'   385

Than in ane mantill and ane bevar hat,
With cop and clapper, wonder prively,
He opnit ane secreit yet, and out thairat
Convoyit hir, that na man suld espy,
Unto ane village half ane myle thairby;   390
Deliverit hir in at the spittail-hous,
And dayly sent hir part of his almous.

Sum knew hir weill, and sum had na knawlege
Of hir, becaus sho was sa déformait
With bylis blak, ourspred in hir visage,   395
And hir fair colour faidit and alterait.

365. *Both* chylde.   366. *Both* anone.   368. *Both* gone.   370.
E. wraik; Th. wrake.   371. E. culd.   372. E. uglye. Th. lepers.
374. Th. *om.* he.   378. Th. ynow. E. thame; Th. he*m*.   380. Th. Creseyde.
382. Th. To yon; E. Unto yone.   383. Th. charite.   384. Th. lyue; erthe.
385. Th. werthe(!).   386. E. Than; Th. Whan(!). Th. Beuer; E. bawar.
387. Th. cuppe.   388. Th. secrete gate.   389. Th. Conueyed.   390.
Th. There to.   393. E. knawledge.   395. E. ovirspred; Th. ouerspred.

Z 2

Yit thay presumit, for hir hy regrait
And still murning, sho was of nobill kin;
With better will thairfoir they tuik hir in.

The day passit, and Phebus went. to rest,   400
The cloudis blak ourquhelmit all the sky;
God wait gif Cresseid was ane sorrowful gest,
Seeing that uncouth fair and herbery.
But meit or drink sho dressit hir to ly
In ane dark corner of the hous allone;   405
And on this wyse, weiping, sho maid hir mone.

The Complaint of Cresseid.

'O sop of sorrow sonken into cair!
O caytive Cresseid! now and ever-mair
   Gane is thy joy and all thy mirth in eird;
Of all blyithnes now art thow blaiknit bair;   410
Thair is na salve may saif thee of thy sair!
   Fell is thy fortoun, wikkit is thy weird;
   Thy blis is baneist, and thy baill on breird!
Under the eirth god gif I gravin wer,
   Quhar nane of Grece nor yit of Troy micht heird! 415

Quhair is thy chalmer, wantounly besene
With burely bed, and bankouris browderit bene,
   Spycis and wynis to thy collatioun;
The cowpis all of gold and silver shene,
The swete meitis servit in plaittis clene,   420
   With saipheron sals of ane gude sessoun;
   Thy gay garmentis, with mony gudely goun,
Thy plesand lawn pinnit with goldin prene?
   All is areir thy greit royáll renoun!

---

397. E. hie; Th. hye.   399. Th. there (*for* thairfoir).   401. E. ovir-
quhelmit; Th. ouerheled.   402.' E. was; Th. were.   403. Th. fare.
405, 406. *Perhaps read* alane, mane.   408. E. cative; Th. caytife. E. for
now; Th. *om.* for.   409. Th. erthe.   410. Th. blake and bare.   411.
Th. helpe (*for* saif thee of).   412. Th. werthe (!).   413. Th. bale vnberd (!).
414. Th. Vnder the great god.   415. Th. men (*for* nane). Th. herd   416.
Th. chambre.   417. Th. burly; bankers brouded.   418. Th. wyne.
419. Th. cuppes.   420. Th. plates.   421. Th. sauery sauce.   423. Th.
pene (!).   424. Th. arere.

Quhair is thy garding, with thir greissis gay   425
And fresshe flouris, quhilk the quene Floray
    Had paintit plesandly in every pane,
Quhair thou was wont full merily in May
To walk, and tak the dew be it was day,
    And heir the merle and mavis mony ane ;   430
    With ladyis fair in carrolling to gane,
And see the royal rinkis in thair array
    In garmentis gay, garnischit on every grane?

Thy greit triumphand fame and hy honour,
Quhair thou was callit of eirdly wichtis flour,   435
    All is decayit ; thy weird is welterit so,
Thy hy estait is turnit in darknes dour !
This lipper ludge tak for thy burelie bour,
    And for thy bed tak now ane bunch of stro.
    For waillit wyne and meitis thou had tho,   440
Tak mowlit breid, peirry, and syder sour ;
    But cop and clapper, now is all ago.

My cleir voice and my courtly carrolling,
Quhair I was wont with ladyis for to sing,
    Is rawk as ruik, full hiddeous, hoir, and hace ;   445
My plesand port all utheris precelling,
Of lustines I was held maist conding ;
    Now is deformit the figour of my face ;
    To luik on it na leid now lyking hes.
Sowpit in syte, I say with sair siching—   450
    Lugeit amang the lipper-leid—"Alas ! "

O ladyis fair of Troy and Grece, attend
My misery, quhilk nane may comprehend,
    My frivoll fortoun, my infelicitie,
My greit mischief, quhilk na man can amend.   455

---

425. Th. thy greces.   430. E. mawis.   432. Th. renkes.   E. array; Th.
ray.   Th. *omits* ll. 433-437.   434, 437. E. hie.   438. Th. leper loge.
E. burelie; Th. goodly.   439. E. bunche; Th. bonch.   441. E. peirrie;
Th. pirate. E. ceder; Th. syder.   442. Th. cuppe.   443. E. *om.* my.
444. Th. *om. this line.*   445. Th. ranke as roke, ful hidous heer.   Th. *om.*
ll. 446, 447.   448. Th. Deformed is.   449. Th. no pleople (*sic*) hath
lykyng (!).   450. Th. Solped in syght.   451. E. Ludgeit; Th. Lyeng.
Th. leper folke.   E. allace; Th. alas.   453. Th. *omits.*   454. Th.
freyle fortune.

Be war in tyme, approchis neir the end,
　And in your mynd ane mirrour mak of me.
　As I am now, peradventure that ye,
For all your micht, may cum to that same end,
　Or ellis war, gif ony war may be.   460

Nocht is your fairnes bot ane faiding flour,
Nocht is your famous laud and hy honour
　Bot wind inflat in uther mennis eiris;
Your roising reid to rotting sall retour.
Exempill mak of me in your memour,   465
　Quhilk of sic thingis wofull witnes beiris.
　All welth in eird away as wind it weiris;
Be war thairfoir; approchis neir the hour;
　Fortoun is fikkil, quhen sho beginnis and steiris.'—

Thus chydand with her drery desteny,   470
Weiping, sho woik the nicht fra end to end,
But all in vane; hir dule, hir cairfull cry
Micht nocht remeid, nor yit hir murning mend.
Ane lipper-lady rais, and till hir wend,
And said, 'Quhy spurnis thou aganis the wall,   475
To sla thyself, and mend na-thing at all?

Sen that thy weiping dowbillis bot thy wo,
I counsall thee mak vertew of ane neid,
To leir to clap thy clapper to and fro,
And †live efter the law of lipper-leid.'   480
Thair was na buit, bot forth with thame sho yeid
Fra place to place, quhill cauld and hounger sair
Compellit hir to be ane rank beggair.

That samin tyme, of Troy the garnisoun,
Quhilk had to chiftane worthy Troilus,   485
Throw jeopardy of weir had strikkin doun
Knichtis of Grece in number mervellous.

With greit triúmph and laud victorious
Agane to Troy richt royally thay raid
The way quhair Cresseid with the lipper baid.   490

Seing that company cum, all with ane stevin
They gaif ane cry, and shuik coppis gude speid;
Said, 'Worthy lordis, for goddis lufe of hevin,
To us lipper part of your almous-deid.'
Than to thair cry nobill Troilus tuik heid;   495
Having pity, neir by the place can pas
Quhair Cresseid sat, nat witting quhat sho was.

Than upon him sho kest up baith her ene,
And with ane blenk it com in-to his thocht
That he sum-tyme hir face befoir had sene;   500
But sho was in sic ply he knew hir nocht.
Yit than hir luik in-to his mind it brocht
The sweit visage and amorous blenking
Of fair Cresseid, sumtyme his awin darling.

Na wonder was, suppois in mynd that he   505
Tuik hir figure sa sone, and lo! now, quhy;
The idole of ane thing in cace may be
Sa deip imprentit in the fantasy,
That it deludis the wittis outwardly,
And sa appeiris in forme and lyke estait   510
Within the mynd as it was figurait.

Ane spark of lufe than till his hart coud spring,
And kendlit all his body in ane fyre;
With hait fevir ane sweit and trimbilling
Him tuik, quhill he was redy to expyre;   515
To beir his sheild his breist began to tyre;
Within ane whyle he changit mony hew,
And nevertheles not ane ane-uther knew.

488. *Both* tryumphe; laude.   489. Th. rode.   490. E. baid; Th. stode.
491. E. thai come; Th. come; *read* cum.   492. Th. shoke cuppes.
493. Th. *om.* Said.   495. Th. her (*for* thair).   496. Th. pyte;
E. pietie.   499. *Both* come.   501. E. plye; Th. plyte.   502. E. it; Th. he.
504. E. awin; Th. owne.   508. Th. enprynted.   512. E. culd; Th. couth.
514. E. fewir; Th. feuer. Th. in swette. *Both* trimbling.   515. E. reddie.
516. Th. brest.   517. Th. many a hewe.

For knichtly pity and memoriall
Of fair Cresseid, ane girdill can he tak,   520
Ane purs of gold and mony gay jowáll,
And in the skirt of Cresseid doun can swak;
Than raid away, and not ane word he spak,
Pensive in hart, quhill he com to the toun,
And for greit cair oft-syis almaist fell doun.   525

The lipper-folk to Cresseid than can draw,
To seè the equall distribucioun
Of the almous; but quhan the gold they saw,
Ilk ane to uther prevely can roun,
And said, 'Yon lord hes mair affectioun,   530
However it be, unto yon lazarous
Than to us all; we knaw be his almous.'

'Quhat lord is yon?' quod sho, 'have ye na feill,
Hes don to us so greit humanitie?'
'Yes,' quod a lipper-man, 'I knaw him weill;   535
Shir Troilus it is, gentill and free'
Quhen Cresseid understude that it was he,
Stiffer than steill thair stert ane bitter stound
Throwout hir hart, and fell doun to the ground.

Quhen sho, ourcom with syching sair and sad,   540
With mony cairfull cry and cald—'Ochane!
Now is my breist with stormy stoundis stad,
Wrappit in wo, ane wretch full will of wane';
Than swounit sho oft or sho coud refrane,
And ever in hir swouning cryit sho thus: 545
'O fals Cresseid, and trew knicht Troilus!

Thy luf, thy lawtee, and thy gentilnes
I countit small in my prosperitie;
Sa elevait I was in wantones,
And clam upon the fickill quheill sa hie;   550

---

519. Th. pyte; E. pietie.   520. Th. gan.   521. Th. many a gay iewel.
522. E. swak; Th. shake.   523. E. *om.* he.   524. E. come; Th. came.
525. E. -syis; Th. -syth.   526. E. can; Th. couth.   527. *Both* se.   529.
E. prewelie; Th. priuely.   530. Th. yon; E. yone.   534. Th. That dothe.
E. humanitie; Th. -te.   536. Th. *ins.* a knight *after* is.   540. E. ovircome;
Th. ouercome.   541. Th. colde atone (!).   542. Th. brest.   543.
Th. *om.* ane; Th. one (*for* wane).   544. Th. Than fel in swoun ful ofte.
E. culd; Th. wolde. Th. fone (!); *for* refrane.   547. E. lufe; Th. loue.
Th. laude and al thy.   549. Th. So effated (*or* essated).

All faith and lufe, I promissit to thee,
Was in the self fickill and frivolous;
O fals Cresseid, and trew knicht Troilus!

For lufe of me thou keipt gude countinence,
Honest and chaist in conversatioun;   555
Of all wemen protectour and defence
Thou was, and helpit thair opinioun.
My mynd, in fleshly foull affectioun,
Was inclynit to lustis lecherous;
Fy! fals Cresseid! O, trew knicht Troilus!   560

Lovers, be war, and tak gude heid about
Quhom that ye lufe, for quhom ye suffer paine;
I lat yow wit, thair is richt few thairout
Quhom ye may traist, to have trew lufe againe;
Preif quhen ye will, your labour is in vaine.   565
Thairfoir I reid ye tak thame as ye find;
For they ar sad as widdercock in wind.

Becaus I knaw the greit unstabilnes
Brukkil as glas, into my-self I say,
Traisting in uther als greit unfaithfulnes,   570
Als unconstant, and als untrew of fay.
Thocht sum be trew, I wait richt few ar thay.
Quha findis treuth, lat him his lady ruse;
Nane but my-self, as now, I will accuse.'

Quhen this was said, with paper sho sat doun,   575
And on this maneir maid hir TESTAMENT:—
'Heir I beteich my corps and carioun
With wormis and with taidis to be rent;
My cop and clapper, and myne ornament,
And all my gold, the lipper-folk sall have,   580
Quhen I am deid, to bury me in grave.

551. Th. promytted.   552. Th. thy selfe; furious (!).   554. Th. countenaunce (*om.* gude).   557. Th. were.   558. E. in; Th. on.   562. E. Quhome; Th. Whom. E. quhome; Th. whan.   563. Th. thrughout.   565. Th. Proue.   569. Th. Brittel; unto.   570. Th. great brutelnesse.   572. Th. Though.   576. Th. maner.   577. E. beteiche; Th. bequeth. Th. corse.   578. Th. toodes.   579. Th. cuppe my.   580. E. the; Th. these.

This royall ring, set with this ruby reid,
Quhilk Troilus in drowry to me send,
To him agane I leif it quhan I am deid,
To mak my cairfull deid unto him kend.   585
Thus I conclude shortly, and mak ane end.
My spreit I leif to Diane, quhair sho dwellis,
To walk with hir in waist woddis and wellis.

O Diomeid ! thow hes baith broche and belt
Quhilk Troilus gave me in takinning   590
Of his trew lufe ! '—And with that word sho swelt.
And sone ane lipper-man tuik of the ring,
Syne buryit hir withoutin tarying.
To Troilus furthwith the ring he bair,
And of Cresseid the deith he can declair.   595

Quhen he had hard hir greit infirmitè,
Hir legacy and lamentatioun,
And how sho endit in sik povertè,
He swelt for wo, and fell doun in ane swoun;
For greit sorrow his hart to birst was boun.   600
Syching full sadly, said, ' I can no moir ;
Sho was untrew, and wo is me thairfoir ! '

Sum said, he maid ane tomb of merbell gray,
And wrait hir name and superscriptioun,
And laid it on hir grave, quhair that sho lay,   605
In goldin letteris, conteining this ressoun :—
' Lo ! fair ladyis, Cresseid of Troyis toun,
Sumtyme countit the flour of womanheid,
Under this stane, late lipper, lyis deid ! '

Now, worthy wemen, in this ballet short,   610
Made for your worship and instructioun,
Of cheritè I monish and exhort,
Ming not your luf with fals deceptioun.
Beir in your mynd this short conclusioun
Of fair Cresseid, as I have said befoir ;   615
Sen sho is deid, I speik of hir no moir.

---

583. E. drowrie; Th. dowry (!).   587. Th. spirite.   590. E. takning;
Th. tokenyng; *read* takinning.   593. E. withouttin.   596. E. infirmitie;
Th. -te.   598. E. povertie; Th. -te.   600. Th. *om.* greit.   605. Th.
where as she.   607. Th. Troy the toun.   612. E. cheritie; Th. charyte.   613.
E. lufe; Th. loue.   614. E. schort; Th. sore (!).   616. E. Sen; Th. Sithe.

XVIII.

THE CUCKOO AND THE NIGHTINGALE;

OR

THE BOOK OF CUPID, GOD OF LOVE.

———•◆•———

THE god of love, a ! *benedicite !*
How mighty and how greet a lord is he !
For he can make of lowe hertes hye,
And of hye lowe, and lyke for to dye,
And harde hertes he can maken free.   5

And he can make, within a litel stounde
Of seke folk ful hole, fresshe and sounde,
And of [the] hole, he can make seke;
And he can binden and unbinden eke
What he wol have bounden or unbounde.   10

To telle his might my wit may not suffyse ;
For he may do al that he wol devyse.
For he can make of wyse folk ful nyce,
And [eke] in lyther folk distroyen vyce ;
And proude hertes he can make agryse.   15

From Th. (Thynne, ed. 1532); *collated with* F. (Fairfax 16); B. (Bodley 638); S. (Arch. Selden, B. 24); T. (Tanner 346); *also in* Ff. (Camb. Univ. Ff. 1. 6).   TITLE : Th. Of the C. and the N.; F. B. The boke of Cupide, god of loue.   1. Th. ah; F. a; S. a. a.   2. Th. Howe; gret; lorde. 4. Th. of his; Ff. S. of hye; F. B. high hertis.   6. F. B. S. Ff. And he; Th. *om.* And.   7. Th. folke; *om.* ful.   8. *I supply* the. S. hole folke.   9. S. And he; *rest om.* And. Th. F. B. bynde; *read* binden.   10. Th. T. That; F. B. Ff. What; S. Quhom.   11. Th. tel; wytte.   12, 13. Th. T. *transpose these lines.*   12. Th. Ff. wol; *rest* can.   13. Th. folke. 14. *I supply* eke. Th. T. *om.* in (S. *has* in-to).   F. lyther; S. lidd*er*; Th. Ff. lythy; T. le þi. Th. folke. Th. T. to distroyen; *rest om.* to.

Shortly, al that ever he' wol he may;
Ageines him ther dar no wight sey nay.
For he can gladde and greve whom him lyketh;
And, who that he wol, he laugheth or he syketh;
And most his might he sheweth ever in May.   20

For every trewe gentil herte free
That with him is, or thinketh for to be,
Ageines May now shal have som steringe
Other to joye, or elles to morninge,
In no sesoun so greet, as thinketh me.   25

For whan they mowe here the briddes singe,
And see the floures and the leves springe,
That bringeth into hertes rémembraunce
A maner ese, medled with grevaunce,
And lusty thoughtes fulle of. greet longinge.   30

And of that longing cometh hevinesse,
And therof groweth ofte greet seknesse,
And al for lak of that that they desyre;
And thus in May ben hertes sette on fyre,
So that they brennen forth in greet distresse.   35

I speke this of feling, trewely;
For, althogh I be old and unlusty,
Yet have I felt of that seknesse, in May,
Bothe hoot and cold, an acces every day,
How sore, y-wis, ther wot no wight but I.   40

---

17. Ff. T. Ageynes; S. Ageynest; Th. Agaynst; F. B. Ayenst.   Th. Ff.
T. *om.* 'ther.   18. Th. glad; *rest* 'glade.   19. Th. loweth. S. *has 2nd*
he; *rest omit.* F. B. don hym laugh or siketh.   20. Th. T. shedeth.   21.
Th. fre.   22. F. B. *om.* for.   23. S. Ff. Aȝeynes; F. B. Ayenst; Th. T.
Agayne. Th. nowe.   24. F. B. Other; S. Outhir; Th. T. Ff. Or. Th.
ioy. F. B. S. T. ellis; Th. els. Th. T. Ff. some mournyng; *rest om.* some.
25. F. B. grette; Ff. S. grete; Th. moche.   26. F. then; *rest* whan (when).
Th. may; T. mai; F. B. S. mow; Ff. mowe. Th. byrdes; S. foulis; *rest* briddes.
27. Th. leaues.   28. Th. T. her (*for* hertes).   29. Th. T. ease; S. ess;
F. B. case (!). Ff. y-medled.   30. Th. ful; Ff. fulle. Th. great.   32.
Th. great sicknesse.   33. S. all; *rest om.* Th. lacke.   35. Th. forthe;
great.   36. S. trewely; Th. trewly.   37. F. B. S. For althogh; Th. T.
If (!). Th. olde.   38. Th. T. I haue; *rest* haue I. Th. felte; sicknesse. Th.
Ff. through; *rest* in.   39. *All* hote. Th. F. B. colde. Th. T. and (!); *for*
an. Th. axes; F. B. acces. 40. Th. Howe; wote.

I am so shaken with the fevers whyte,
Of al this May yet slepte I but a lyte ;
And also it naught lyketh unto me,
That any herte shulde slepy be
In whom that Love his fyry dart wol smyte.   45

But as I lay this other night wakinge,
I thoghte how lovers had a tokeninge,
And among hem it was a comune tale,
That it were good to here the nightingale
Rather than the lewde cukkow singe.   50

And then I thoghte, anon as it was day,
I wolde go som whider to assay
If that I might a nightingalë here ;
For yet had I non herd of al this yere,
And hit was tho the thridde night of May.   55

And than, anon as I the day espyde,
No lenger wolde I in my bedde abyde,
But unto a wode, that was faste by,
I wente forth alone, boldely,
And held my way doun by a broke-syde,   60

Til I com to a launde of whyte and grene ;
So fair oon had I never in[ne] been ;
The ground was grene, y-poudred with daisye,
The floures and the gras y-lyke hye,
Al grene and whyte ; was nothing elles sene.   65

42. Th. T. *om.* yet ; (Ff. *has* ne.) Th. T. slepe ; Ff. S. slepte ; F. B. slept.
43. S. naught likith vnto me ; Th. T. Ff. is not lyke to me ; F. B. is vnlike for
to be. 45. Th. darte. 47. Th. howe. 48. Th. amonge. 50.
Th. cuckowe. 51. Th. thought. 52. T. Ff. whider ; S. quhid*er* ;
F. B. whedir ; Th. where. 54. Th. none herde. F. B. T. this ; Ff. the ;
Th. S. that. 55. S. thridde ; T. thridd ; Th. F. B. thirde. 56. S. than ; *rest
om.* Th. aspyde. 58. Ff. to ; Th. T. vnto ; F. B. into ; S. in. Th. wodde ;
F. B. wode. 59. Th. T. went ; F. B. wente. Th. forthe. Th. boldely ; Ff.
T. boldly ; *rest* priuely. 60. Th. helde. F. B. S. my ; Th. Ff. the ; T. me
the. Th. downe. 61. F. B. come ; S. cam ; Th. T. came (*read* com). 62.
All in ; *read* inne. S. *has* in y-ben. 63, 64. B. *transposes.* 64. F. B.
gras ; S. greses ; Th. greues ; T. Ff. grenes. S. ylike ; F. B. al I-like ; Th.
T. Ff. lyke. 65. Th. els.

Ther sat I doun among the faire floures ;
And saw the briddes trippe out of her boures
Ther-as they had hem rested al the night.
They were so joyful of the dayes light
That they †begonne of May to don hir houres !   70

They coude that servyce al by rote ;
Ther was many a lovely straunge note ;
Some songe loudë, as they hadde pleyned,
And some in other maner vois y-feyned,
And some al out, with al the fulle throte.   75

They proyned hem, and made[n] hem right gay,
And daunseden, and lepten on the spray,
And evermore two and two in-fere ;
Right so as they had chosen hem to-yere
In Feverere, on seint Valentynes day.   80

And eke the river, that I sat upon,
It made suche a noise, as it ron,
Accordaunt with the briddes armonye,
Me thoughte, it was the best[e] melodye
That mighte been y-herd of any mon.   85

And for delyt ther-of, I wot never how,
I fel in suche a slomber and a swow,
Not al a-slepe, ne fully wakinge ;
And in that swow me thoughte I herde singe
That sory brid, the lew[e]de cukkow.   90

---

66. Th. sate ; downe.   67. Th. sawe ; birdes. Th. trippe ; T. trip ;
S. flee ; F. B. crepe.   68. Th. T. Ff. *om.* had. S. thame rested ; *rest* rested
hem.   70. Th. T. *om.* That. *All* began ; *read* begonne. Ff. to don hir ;
Th. T. for to done. F. B. of Mayes ben her houres (!) ; S. on mayes vss
thair houres.   72. S. lusty (*for* lovely). S. straunge ; *rest om.*   73. Ff.
lowe. T. hade ; *rest* had. S. compleyned.   74. Th. voice yfayned.   75.
Ff. S. all (2) ; *rest om.* Th. Ff. T. the ful ; S. fullé ; F. B. a lowde.   76. F. B.
pruned. *All* made ; *read* maden.   80. Th. Feuerere ; T. Feuirȝere ; *rest*
Marche (!). *All* upon ; *read* on.   81. S. eke ; *rest om.*   83. Th. T. with ;
rest to. T. Ff. briddes ; S. birdis ; Th. byrdes ; F. B. foules. S. T. Ff. armonye ;
Th. armony ; F. B. ermonye.   84. Th. thought. *All* best (!).   85. Th.
myght ; yherde.   86. *All* delyte. S. therof ; *rest om.* Th. wotte ; F. B.
note ; S. wote ; T. wot. F. B. ner (*for* never). Th. howe.   87. Th.
swowe ; Ff. swough ; S. slowe (!) ; B. slow (!).   88. F. B. S. on slepe.
89. Th. swowe ; thought.   90. F. B. Ff. That ; *rest* the. F. B. Ff. bridde ;
S. T. brid ; Th. byrde. Th. Cuckowe.

And that was on a tree right fast[e] by;
But who was than evel apayd but I?
'Now god,' quod I, 'that dyëd on the crois
Yeve sorow on thee, and on thy lewde vois!
For litel joye have I now of thy cry.'   95

And as I with the cukkow thus gan chyde,
I herde, in the nexte bush besyde,
A Nightingalë so lustily singe
That with her clere vois she made ringe
Through-out al the grene wode wyde.   100

'A! goode Nightingale!' quod I thenne,
'A litel hast thou been to longe henne;
For here hath been the lew[e]de Cukkow,
And songen songes rather than hast thou;
I pray to god that evel fyr him brenne!'   105

But now I wol you telle a wonder thing:
As longë as I lay in that swowning,
Me thoughte, I wiste what the briddes ment,
And what they seyde, and what was her entent,
And of her speche I hadde good knowing.   110

And than herde I the Nightingale say,
'Now, gode Cukkow! go som-where away,
And let us that can singen dwellen here;
For every wight escheweth thee to here,
Thy songes be so elenge, in good fay!'   115

---

91. *All* fast.   92. Th. yuel apayde.   93. Th. Nowe.   F. B.
vpon (*for* on).   94. Th. the.   95. Th. nowe.   96. Th. cuckowe.
Th. T. thus gan; Ff. now gan; S. gan to; F. B. gan.   97. Th. B. busshe;
Ff. T. bussh; F. busshes (!); S. beugh.   F. B. me beside.   100. Th. T. Ff.
om. out.   Ff. the greues of the wode (*better*)   101. Th. Ah.   Ff. S. thenne;
T. thanne; *rest* then.   102. Th. haste.   Ff. S. T. henne; *rest* hen.   103.
F. B. lewde; S. lewed; T. Ff. loude (!).   (*The line runs badly.*)   104.
F. B. *om.* hast.   105. Th. T. *om.* that.   Th. yuel fyre.   Th. S. her; *rest*
him.   Th. bren; *rest* brenne.   106. Th. nowe; tel.   107. Th. laye.
(*The line runs badly; read* longë *or* swowening.)   108. Th. thought; wyst.
Th. T. what; *rest* al that.   109. Th. sayd.   110. T. hade; *rest* had.
111. Th. *om.* And.   Th. T. there (*for* than).   112. Th. Nowe good.   113.
Th. lette.   114. Th. the.

'What?' quod he, 'what may thee eylen now?
It thinketh me, I singe as wel as thou,
For my song is bothe trewe and playn;
Al-though I can not crakel so in vayn
As thou dost in thy throte, I wot never how.   120

And every wight may understande me;
But, Nightingale, so may they not do thee;
For thou hast many a nyce queinte cry.
I have herd thee seyn, "*ocy! ocy!*"
How mighte I knowe what that shulde be?'   125

'A fole!' quod she, 'wost thou not what it is?
Whan that I say "*ocy! ocy!*" y-wis,
Than mene I that I wolde, wonder fayn,
That alle they were shamfully y-slayn
That menen aught ayeines love amis.   130

And also I wolde alle tho were dede
That thenke not in love hir lyf to lede;
For who that wol the god of love not serve,
I dar wel say, is worthy for to sterve;
And for that skil "*ocy! ocy!*" I grede.'   135

'Ey!' quod the Cukkow, 'this is a queint lawe,
That every wight shal love or be to-drawe!
But I forsake al suchë companye.
For myn entent is neither for to dye,
Ne, whyl I live, in loves yok to drawe.   140

---

116. F. B. she (*for* he). Th. the.   118. Th. songe; playne.   119.
Th. T. And though; *rest* Al-though.   Th. crakel; T. crakil; S. crekill; Ff.
crake; F. B. breke hit (!).   Th. vayne.   120. Th. doest; S. dois; *rest* dost.
Th. Ff. S. neuer; T. not; F. B. ner.   122. Th. done; T. S. Ff. do; F. B.
om. Th. the.   123. Th. haste. Th. T. Ff. nyce queynt(e); S. queynt feyned;
F. B. queint.   124. F. B. S. herd the; T. the herd; Th. the herde.   Th.
sayne; T. seyn; F. B. seye; S. sing.   125. Th. Howe. F. B. Who
myghte wete what; S. Bot quho mycht vnderstand quhat.   126. Th. Ah;
Ff. T. A; *rest* O.   Th. foole; woste. Th. T. Ff. it; *rest* that.   128. Th.
meane; fayne.   129. Ff. alle; S. all; *rest* al. Th. T. Ff. they; *rest* tho. Th.
yslayne.   130. Th. meanen. S. aȝeines; F. B. ayen; T. again; Th. agayne.
131. F. B. al tho were dede; Th. T. Ff. that al tho had the dede.   S. And al
they I wold also were dede.   132. Th. thynke; T. think; S. thinkith; Ff.
thenke; F. B. thenk.   F. B. S. Ff. her lyue in loue.   133. Th. S. who so;
rest om. so. Th. T. Ff. *place* not *after* wol.   134. Th. T. F. B. Ff. he is;
S. *om.* he. Th. Ff. T. *om.* for.   136. Th. Eye; cuckowe. F. B. *insert* ywis
before this.   137. Th. T. Ff. That euery wight shal loue or be to-drawe;
F. B. That eyther I shal love or elles be slawe.   139. Th. myne. F. B.
neyther; S. nouthir; Th. T. Ff. not.   140. Th. T. Ff. Ne neuer; *rest om.*
neuer. Th. T. on; *rest* in.

For lovers ben the folk that been on-lyve
That most disesë han, and most unthryve,
And, most enduren sorow, wo, and care;
And, at the laste, failen of welfare;
What nedeth hit ayeines trouth to stryve?'   145

'What?' quod she, 'thou art out of thy minde!
How might thou in thy cherles herte finde
To speke of loves servaunts in this wyse?
For in this worlde is noon so good servyse
To every wight that gentil is of kinde.   150

For ther-of, trewly, cometh al goodnesse,
Al honóur, and [eke] al gentilnesse,
Worship, esë, and al hertes lust,
Parfit joye, and ful assured trust,
Jolitee, plesauncë, and freshnesse,   155

Lowliheed, and trewe companye,
Seemliheed, largesse, and curtesye,
Drede of shame for to doon amis;
For he that trewly Loves servaunt is
Were lother to be shamed than to dye.   160

And that this is sooth, al that I seye,
In that beleve I wol bothe live and deye,
And Cukkow, so rede I thou do, y-wis.'
'Ye, than,' quod he, 'god let me never have blis
If ever I to that counseyl obeye!   165

---

141. Th. S. ben; Ff. T. bene; F. B. lyven (*for* been).   142. Th. moste
(*twice*); disease.   143. Th. moste. F. B. S. enduren; Th. Ff. T. endure.
144. *So* F. B. (*with* of her *for* of); Th. T. Ff. And leste felen of welfare; S.
And alderlast have felyng of welefare.   145. S. ayeynes; Th. B. ayenst;
F. T. ayens.   146. S. Quhat brid quod. Th. arte.   147. Th. T. Ff.
might thou; F. maist thou; B. S. maistow. Th. Ff. churlnesse; T. clerenes (!);
F. B. cherles hert; S. cheilish hert.   148. Th. seruauntes.   149.
Th. none.   152. S. Honestee estate and all gentilness; Th. T. F. Ff. Al
honour and al gentylnesse; B. Al honour and al gentillesse.   153. Th. ease.
154. Th. Parfyte. F. B. ensured.   155. S. and eke.   156, 157. *All but
the first words transposed in* Th. T.   158. F. B. S. and for; Th. T. Ff. *om.*
and. Th. done.   160. Th. T. Ff. *om.* 1st to.   161. F. B. Ff. *om.*
this. F. B. S. al; Th T. Ff. *om.*   162. Th. T. *om.* bothe.   163. F. B. S.
rede I; Th. T. Ff. I rede. Th. that thou.   164. Th. T. Ff. *om.* Ye. F. B.
she; *rest* he. Th. T. *om.* god.   165. Th. T. vnto; F. B. Ff. S. to. F. B.
thy (*for* that).

* * *
* * * *

Nightingale, thou spekest wonder fayre,
But, for al that, the sooth is the contrayre;
For loving is, in yonge folk, but rage,
And in olde folk hit is a greet dotage;
Who most hit useth, most he shal apeyre.   170

For therof comth disese and hevinesse,
Sorowe and care, and mony a greet seknesse,
Dispyt, debat, [and] anger, and envye,
Repreef and shame, untrust and jelousye,
Pryde and mischeef, povértee, and woodnesse.   175

What! Loving is an office of dispayr,
And oo thing is ther-in that is not fayr;
For who that geteth of love a litel blis,
But-if he be alway therwith, y-wis,
He may ful sone of age have his heyr.   180

And, Nightingale, therfor hold thee ny;
For, leve me wel, for al thy queynte cry,
If thou be fer or longe fro thy make,
Thou shalt be as other that been forsake,
And than[ne] thou shalt hoten as do I!'   185

'Fy!' quod she, 'on thy namë and on thee!
The god of love ne let thee never y-thee!
For thou art wors a thousand-fold than wood.
For many on is ful worthy and ful good,
That had be naught, ne hadde love y-be!   190

---

167. F. B. the sothe; S. full sooth. Th. T. Ff. is the sothe contrayre. 168.
F. B. S. Ff. loving; Th. T. loue. Th. folke. 169. Th. folke; F. B. Ff. *om.*
F. B. hit is; Th. T. *om.* Th. great. 170. Th. moste (*twice*). F. B. he;
S. it; Th. T. Ff. *om.* 171. F. mony an; B. mony a; Th. T. S. Ff. disease
and. 172. Th. So sorowe; *rest om.* So. Th. many a gret. F. B. *om.* greet.
173. Th. Dispyte debate. *I supply* and. 174. F. Repreve and; B. Repreff and;
S. Repref and; Th. T. Deprauyng. 175. Th. T. B. Ff. *om.* 1*st* and. Th.
mischefe. S. pouertee; Ff. pouerte; *rest* pouert. 176. Th. T. Ff. *om.*
What. Th. dispayre. 177. B. T. oo; S. o; F. oon; Th. one. Th. fayre.
178. Th. getteth; S. get (*better*). Th. blysse. 179. F. B. *om.* if. F. B. S.
Ff. therby. 180. Th. heyre; T. eyre; S. aire; F. B. crie (!); Ff. heiere.
181. F. B. therfor Nyghtyngale. Th. therefore holde the nye. 182. Th.
Ff. T. S. queynt; F. B. loude. 183. Th. T. Ff. ferre. F. of (*for* or). 184.
Th. T. S. ben; F. B. be (*read* been). 185. Th. Ff. than; F. B. T. then (*read*
thanne); S. *om.* 186. F. B. shalt thou. 188. Th. T. worse.
Th. folde. 189. Th. one; Ff. on; F. B. *om.* S. ar; *rest* is. 190.
T. hade (*twice*); *rest* had.

For Love his servaunts ever-more amendeth,
And from al evel taches hem defendeth,
And maketh hem to brenne right as fyr
In trouthë and in worshipful desyr,
And, whom him liketh, joye y-nough hem sendeth.'   195

'Thou Nightingale,' he seyde, 'hold thee stille;
For Love hath no resoun but his wille;
For ofte sithe untrewe folk he eseth,
And trewe folk so bitterly displeseth
That, for defaute of grace, he let hem spille.   200

With such a lorde wol I never be;
For he is blind alwey, and may not see;
And whom he hit he not, or whom he fayleth;
And in his court ful selden trouthe avayleth;
Só dyvérs and so wilfúl is he.'   205

Than took I of the Nightingale kepe,
She caste a sigh out of her herte depe,
And seyde, 'Alas! that ever I was bore!
I can, for tene, say not oon word more;'
And right with that she brast out for to wepe.   210

'Alas!' quod she, 'my herte wol to-breke
To heren thus this false brid to speke
Of love, and of his worshipful servyse;
Now, god of love, thou help me in som wyse
That I may on this Cukkow been awreke!'   215

---

191. Th. T. Ff. *put* evermore *after* For. Th. seruauntes; F. B. seruant.
192. Ff. T. euel; S. euell; Th. yuel; F. B. *om* F. tachches; S. stachis (!).
F. B. him.   193. F. B. him. F. B. as eny; T. right as a; Ff. right as; Th.
right in a. S. be brynnyng as a. Th. fyre.   195. Th. whan; T. when;
Ff. whanne (*for* whom). F. B. Ff. him; S. he; Th. T. hem. Th. ioy.   196.
F. B. Ye (*for* Thou). Th. sayd. T. F. B. S. Ff. hold the; Th. be. Th. styl.
197. F. B. S. Ff. his; Th. T. it is. Th. wyl.   198. F. B. Ff. sithe; Th. T.
tyme; S. tymes. Th. folke; easeth.   199. Th. folke. Th. T. Ff. he dis-
pleaseth; *rest om.* he.   200. F. B. And (*for* That). Th. corage; *rest* grace.
Th. spyl.   201-205. *From* F. B. Ff. S.; Th. T. *omit.*   201. Ff. wille; F.
wolde; B. wull; S. wole.   202. F. B. blynde; S. blynd. S. alweye; F. B.
Ff. *om.*   203. Ff. And whom he hit he not, or whom he failith (*best*);
F. B. And whan he lyeth he not, ne whan he fayleth; S. Quhom he hurtith he
note, ne quhom he helith (!).   204. *So* Ff.; F. B. In; S. Into. Ff. S. his;
F. B. this. F. B. selde.   205. F. B. dyuerse.   206. Th. toke.   207. Th.
T. Howe she; F. B. S. *om.* Howe. Th. T. Ff. *om.* herte.   208. Th. sayd.
209. Th. not say one; T. nouȝt sey oo.   210. Th. that worde; *rest om.*
worde. F. B. on (*for* out). Th. *om.* for.   212. Th. leude; Ff. false; *rest*
fals. T. B. brid; Ff. bridde; Th. byrde; S. bird. F. B. Ff. to; *rest om.* 214.
Th. helpe; some.   215. Th. cuckowe ben.

Me thoughte than, that I sterte up anon,
And to the broke I ran, and gat a stoon,
And at the Cukkow hertely I caste;
And he, for drede, fley away ful faste;
And glad was I when that he was a-goon.   220

And evermore the Cukkow, as he fley,
He seyde, 'Farewel! farewel, papinjay!'
As though he hadde scorned, thoughte me;
But ay I hunted him fro tree to tree
Til he was fer al out of sighte awey.   225

And thanne com the Nightingale to me,
And seyde, 'Frend, forsothe I thanke thee
That thou hast lyked me thus to rescowe;
And oon avow to Love I wol avowe,
That al this May I wol thy singer be.'   230

I thanked her, and was right wel apayed;
'Ye,' quod she, 'and be thou not amayed,
Though thou have herd the Cukkow er than me.
For, if I live, it shal amended be
The nexte May, if I be not affrayed.   235

And oon thing I wol rede thee also;
Ne leve thou not the Cukkow, loves fo;
For al that he hath seyd is strong lesinge.'
'Nay,' quod I, 'thérto shal no thing me bringe
Fro love; and yet he doth me mochel wo.'   240

---

216. S. thocht; *rest* thought (*read* thoughte). F. B. S. that I; T. Ff. I; Th. he.   217-219. Th. T. *omit.*   217. S. gat; F. B. gatte.   218. S. hardily; F. B. Ff. hertly.   219. Ff. flye3; F. flyed; B. flye; S. gan flee (*read* fley, *as in* 221).   220. Ff. *om.* when.   Th. agon; T. S. agone; Ff. goon; F. gone; B. gon.   221. F. B. fley; Th. flaye; Ff. S. flay; T. flai.   222. Th. T. *om.* He.   Th. sayd.   Th. popyngaye; F. B. papyngay; S. papalay; Ff. papeiay.   223. T. hade; *rest* had.   F. B. Ff. thoght me; S. as thocht me (*read* thoughte me); Th. me alone (*to rime with* 217).   224, 225. Th. T. *omit.*   225. F. B. Ff. sight away.   226. Th. S. than; F. B. T. then; Ff. thanne.   F. B. T. S. come; Th. Ff. came.   227. F. B. seyde; Th. sayd. Th. the.   228. Th. haste.   F. B. thus; S. for; Th. T. Ff. *om.*   T. rescow; *rest* rescowe.   229. Th. one.   Ff. I wol avowe; F. B. I avowe; Th. T. make I nowe.   S. And rycht anon to loue I wole allowe.   231. Th. apayde; T. apaied.   232. F. B. Ff. S. amayed; Th. T. dismayde.   233. Th. herde.   F. B. er; Th. T. Ff. erst.   235. Ff. nexte; *rest* next.   Th. affrayde; T. affraied.   236. Th. one.   237. S. leue; *rest* loue (!).   Th. cuckowe ne his; F. B. S. *om.* ne his.   238. Th. stronge leasyng.   239. F. B. S. Ff. there (*for* therto).   T. man (*for* thing).   240. F. B. S. Fro; Th. T. Ff. For (!).   *So* Ff. F. B. S.; Th. T. and it hath do me moche (T. myche) wo.

'Ye, use thou,' quod she, 'this medicyne;
Every day this May, or that thou dyne,
Go loke upon the fresshe dayësyë.
And though thou be for wo in poynt to dye,
That shal ful gretly lissen thee of thy pyne.   245

And loke alwey that thou be good and trewe,
And I wol singe oon of my songes newe,
For love of thee, as loude as I may crye;'
And than[ne] she began this song ful hye—
'I shrewe al hem that been of love untrewe!'   250

And whan she hadde songe hit to the ende,
'Nów farewel,' quod she, 'for I mot wende;
And god of love, that can right wel and may,
As mochel joye sende thee this day
As ever yet he any lover sende!'   255

Thus took the Nightingale her leve of me.
I pray to god, he alway with her be,
And joye of love he sende her evermore;
And shilde us fro the Cukkow and his lore;
For ther is noon so fals a brid as he.   260

Forth she fley, the gentil Nightingale,
To al the briddes that were in that dale,
And gat hem alle into a place in-fere,
And them besoughte that they woldë here
Her disese; and thus began her tale :—   265

241. F. B. Yee; S. Ya. S. thou schalt vss. Th. T. Ff. *om.* thou.   242. Ff. F. B. er; *rest* or. Th. T. Ff. *om.* that.   243. F. B. S. fressh flour; Ff. Th. T. *om.* flour. S. dayeseye.   245. Th. greatly. B. lisse; F. Ff. lyssen; Th. T. S. lessen. S. *om.* thee.   246—*end. Lost in* S.   247. Th. one. Ff. my; *rest* the.   248. Th. the.   249. Th. T. Ff. than; F. B. then (*read* thanne). Th. songe.   250. F. B. Ff. hem al. Th. ben; T. bene.   251. Ff. hadde; T. hade; *rest* had.   252. Th. Nowe. F. most; B. must; Th. Ff. mote; T. mot.   254. Ff. mochel; F. B. mekil; T. mykil; Th. moche. Th. the.   255. *So* F. B. Ff.; Th. T. As any yet louer he euer sende. 256. Th. T. Ff. taketh; F. B. toke. Th. leaue.   257. Th. T. Ff. *om.* he. 259. Th. cuckowe.   260. Ff. noon; F. B. non; Th. T. not. T. Ff. brid; F. B. bridde; Th. byrde.   261. F. B. fley; T. fleigh; Ff. fleȝt; Th. flewe. 262. Th. byrdes; *rest* briddes. B. the vale; F. the wale; Th. T. Ff. that dale. 263. Th. T. gate; F. B. gat.   264. *All put* hem *after* besoughte. Ff. bysought; *rest* besoughten (!).   265. Th. T. disease.

'Ye witen wel, it is not fro yow hid
How the Cukkow and I faste have chid
Ever sithen it was dayes light;
I pray yow alle, that ye do me right
Of that foule, false, unkinde brid.'   270

Than spak oo brid for alle, by oon assent,
'This mater asketh good avysement;
For we ben fewe briddes here in-fere.
And sooth it is, the Cukkow is not here;
And therefor we wol have a parlement.   275

And therat shal the Egle be our lord,
And other peres that ben of record,
And the Cukkow shal be after sent.
And ther shal be yeven the jugement,
Or elles we shal make som accord.   280

And this shal be, withouten any nay,
The morow of seynt Valentynes day,
Under a maple that is fayr and grene,
Before the chambre-window of the quene
At Wodestok, upon the grene lay.'   285

She thanked hem, and than her leve took,
And fley into an hawthorn by the brook,
And ther she sat, and song upon that tree,
'Terme of [my] lyf, Love hath with-holde me,'
So loude, that I with that song awook.   290

Explicit Clanvowe.

---

266. Ff. Ye wyten; F. B. Ye knowe.; Th. T. The cuckowe (!). F. B. fro
yow hidde; Th. T. for to hyde (!).   267. F. B. How that; *rest om.* that.
Th. T. Ff. fast; F. B. *om.* Th. chyde; Th. chide; F. B. Ff. chidde.   268.
Th. Ff. daye; *rest* dayes.   269. Th. Ff. praye; *rest* pray (prey). Ff. alle;
rest al.   270. Th. bride; T. Ff. brid; F. B. bridde. 271. Th. o; *rest* oon.
T. all; *rest* al. Th. one; T. oon; F. B. *om.*   273. Th. *om.* fewe. Th.
byrdes.   274. *All* soth. Th. cuckowe.   276. T. Ff. lord; *rest* lorde.
277. T. Ff. record; *rest* recorde.   278. Th. cuckowe.   279. Ff. Th. T.
om. And. Th. There. Th. T. yeue; F. yeuen; B. yeuyn; Ff. youe.   280.
F. B. make summe; Th. T. fynally make.   281. Th. without; *rest*
withouten. Th. T. Ff. *om.* any.   282. F. B. of; Th. T. Ff. after.   283.
Th. T. Ff. a; F. B. the. Th. fayre.   284. Th. wyndowe.   285. Th.
wodestocke; F. B. wodestok.   286. F. B. thanketh. Th. leaue toke.
287. F. B. fleye; Th. T. *om.* Th. T. Ff. an; F. B. a. Th. hauthorne; T.
hauthorn. *All* broke.   288. *All* sate. T. Ff. song; *rest* songe. Th. T.
that; F. B. the; Ff. a. 289. *I supply* my. Th. T. Ff. lyfe; F. B. lyve. *After*
290, Ff. *has* Explicit Clanvowe.

XIX. ENVOY TO ALISON.

O LEWDE book, with thy foole rudenesse,
 Sith thou hast neither beautee n'eloquence,
Who hath thee caused, or yeve thee hardinesse
For to appere in my ladyes presence?
I am ful siker, thou knowest her benivolence   5
Ful ágreable to alle hir obeyinge;
For of al goode she is the best livinge.

Allas! that thou ne haddest worthinesse
To shewe to her som plesaunt sentence,
Sith that she hath, thorough her gentilesse,   10
Accepted thee servant to her digne reverence!
O, me repenteth that I n'had science
And leyser als, to make thee more florisshinge;
For of al goode she is the best livinge.

Beseche her mekely, with al lowlinesse,   15
Though I be fer from her [as] in absence,
To thenke on my trouth to her and stedfastnesse,
And to abregge of my sorwe the violence,
Which caused is wherof knoweth your sapience;
She lyke among to notifye me her lykinge;   20
For of al goode she is the best livinge.

From F. (Fairfax 16); *collated with* T. (Tanner 346); *and* Th. (Thynne, ed. 1532). 1. F. boke; T. Th. booke. Th. foule. 2. *All* beaute. 3. *All* the (*twice*). 5. *So all.* 6. Th. abeyeng (!). 7. F. T. goode; Th. good. Th. best; F. T. beste. 9. *All* som*m*e, some. Th. plesaunt; F. plesant. 10. T. thurugh; F. thorgh; Th. through. 11. *All* the. 12. *All* ne (*before* had). 13. *So all* (*with* the *for* thee). 14. Th. good. Th. best; F. T. beste. 16. *I supply* as. 17. T. Th. trouth; F. trouthe. 18. F. abregge; Th. abrege; T. abrigge. T. sorow; F. sorwes; Th. sorowes. 20. *All* amonge. T. Th. notifye; F. notefye. 21. T. Th. al; F. alle. F. T. goode; Th. good.

Lenvoy.

Aurore of gladnesse, and day of lustinesse,
Lucerne a-night, with hevenly influence
Illumined, rote of beautee and goodnesse,
Suspiries which I effunde in silence,   25
Of grace I beseche, alegge let your wrytinge,
Now of al goode sith ye be best livinge.

Explicit.

Th. Lennoye; T. The Lennoye; F. *om.*   24. Th. T. Illumyned; F.
Enlumyned. F. Rote (*with capital*). *All* beaute. F. and of; Th. T. *om.* of.
25. F. Suspiries; Th. Suspires.   26. T. beseke. Th. alege.   27. F.
goode; Th. T. good. *After* 27 : Th. Explicit; F. T. *om.*

XX. THE FLOWER AND THE LEAF.

WHEN that Phebus his chaire of gold so hy
    Had whirled up the sterry sky aloft,
And in the Bole was entred certainly;
Whan shoures swete of rain discended †soft,
Causing the ground, felë tymes and oft,   5
Up for to give many an hoolsom air,
And every plain was [eek y-]clothed fair

With newe grene, and maketh smalë floures
To springen here and there in feld and mede;
So very good and hoolsom be the shoures   10
That it reneweth, that was old and deede
In winter-tyme; and out of every seede
Springeth the herbë, so that every wight
Of this sesoun wexeth [ful] glad and light.

And I, só glad of the seson swete,   15
Was happed thus upon a certain night;
As I lay in my bed, sleep ful unmete
Was unto me; but, why that I ne might
Rest, I ne wist; for there nas erthly wight,
As I suppose, had more hertës ese   20
Than I, for I n'ad siknesse nor disese.

From Speght's edition (1598); *I note rejected readings.* 1. hie. 3. Boole. 4. sweet; raine; oft (!). 6. wholesome aire. 7. plaine was clothed faire. 8. new greene. small flours. 9. field and in mede. 10. wholsome. 11. renueth. 13. hearbe. 14. season; *I supply* ful. 15. season. 16. certaine. 17. sleepe. 19. earthly. 20. hearts ease. 21. Then; nad sicknesse; disease.

Wherfore I mervail gretly of my-selve,
That I so long withouten sleepë lay;
And up I roos, three houres after twelve,
About the [very] springing of the day,   25
And on I put my gere and myn array;
And to a plesaunt grovë I gan passe,
Long or the brightë sonne uprisen was,

In which were okës grete, streight as a lyne,
Under the which the gras, so fresh of hew,   30
Was newly spronge; and an eight foot or nyne
Every tree wel fro his felawe grew,
With braunches brode, laden with leves new,
That sprongen out ayein the sonnë shene,
Som very rede, and som a glad light grene;   35

Which, as me thought, was right a plesaunt sight.
And eek the briddes song[ës] for to here
Would have rejoised any erthly wight.
And I, that couth not yet, in no manere,
Here the nightingale of al the yere,   40
Ful busily herkned, with herte and ere,
If I her voice perceive coud any-where.

And at the last, a path of litel brede
I found, that gretly had not used be,
For it forgrowen was with gras and weede,   45
That wel unneth a wight [ther] might it see.
Thought I, this path som whider goth, pardè,
And so I folowèd, til it me brought
To right a plesaunt herber, wel y-wrought,

That benched was, and [al] with turves new   50
Freshly turved, wherof the grenë gras
So small, so thik, so short, so fresh of hew,
That most lyk to grene †wol, wot I, it was.

---

22. meruaile greatly; selfe.   24. rose; twelfe.   25. *I supply* very.
26. geare; mine.   27. pleasaunt.   28. bright.   29. great.   30.
grasse.   31. sprong.   32. well; féllow.   33. lade.   34. ayen.
35. Some; red; some.   36. song (*read* songes); fort (*sic*).   38. earthly.
40. Heare; all.   41. Full; herkened; hart and with eare.   43. litle breade.
44. greatly.   45. grasse.   46. well; *I supply* ther.   47. some.   48.
followed till.   49. pleasaunt; well.   50. *I supply* al; turfes.   52. thicke.
53. lyke vnto (*read* to); wel (!; *read* wol).

The hegge also, that yede [as] in compas
And closed in al the grene herbere, 55
With sicamour was set and eglantere,

Writhen in-fere so wel and cunningly
That every braunch and leef grew by mesure,
Plain as a bord, of on height, by and by,
[That] I sy never thing, I you ensure, 60
So wel [y-]don ; for he that took the cure
It [for] to make, I trow, did al his peyn
To make it passe al tho that men have seyn.

And shapen was this herber, roof and al,
As [is] a pretty parlour, and also 65
The hegge as thik as [is] a castle-wal,
That, who that list without to stond or go,
Though he wold al-day pryen to and fro,
He shuld not see if there were any wight
Within or no ; but oon within wel might 70

Perceive al tho that yeden there-without
In the feld, that was on every syde
Covered with corn and gras, that, out of dout,
Though oon wold seeken al the world wyde,
So rich a feld [ne] coud not be espyed 75
[Up]on no cost, as of the quantitee,
For of al good thing ther was [greet] plentee.

And I, that al this plesaunt sight [than] sy,
Thought sodainly I felt so sweet an air
[Come] of the eglantere, that certainly, 80
Ther is no hert, I deme, in such despair,
Ne with [no] thoughtës froward and contrair
So overlaid, but it shuld soone have bote,
If it had onës felt this savour sote.

---

54. *I supply* as.   55. (*Perhaps imperfect*) ; all ; green.   56. eglatere ; *see*
l. 80.   57. Wrethen.   58. branch ; leafe.   59. an (*better* on).   60.
I supply That ; see.   61. done ; tooke.   62. *I supply* for ; all ; peine.   63.
all ; seyne.   64. roofe.   65. *I supply* is.   66. thicke ; *I supply* is ; wall.
67. would all.   69. should.   70. one ; well.   71. all.   72. field.
73. corne ; grasse ; doubt.   74. one would seeke all.   75. field ; *I supply*
ne ; espide.   76. On ; coast ; quantity.   77. all ; *I supply* greet ; plenty.
78. all ; pleasaunt sight sie.   79. aire.   80. *I supply* Come ; eglentere.
81. heart ; dispaire.   82. with thoughts ; contraire.   83. should.   84. soote.

And as I stood and cast asyde myn y,   85
I was ware of the fairest medle-tree
That ever yet in al my lyf I sy,
As full of blossomës as it might be.
Therin a goldfinch leping pretily
Fro bough to bough, and, as him list, he eet   90
Here and there, of buddes and floures sweet.

And to the herber-sydë was joining
This fairë tree, of which I have you told;
And, at the last, the brid began to sing,
Whan he had eten what he etë wold,   95
So passing sweetly, that, by manifold,
It was more plesaunt than I coud devyse;
And whan his song was ended in this wyse,

The nightingale with so mery a note
Answéred him, that al the wodë rong   100
So sodainly, that, as it were a sot,
I stood astonied; so was I with the song
Through ravishèd, that, [un]til late and long
Ne wist I in what place I was, ne where;
And †ay, me thought, she song even by myn ere. 105

Wherfore about I waited busily
On every syde, if I her mightë see;
And, at the last, I gan ful wel aspy
Wher she sat in a fresh green laurer-tree
On the further syde, even right by me,   110
That gave so passing a delicious smel
According to the eglantere ful wel.

Wherof I had so inly greet plesyr
That, as me thought, I surely ravished was
Into Paradyse, where my desyr   115
Was for to be, and no ferther [to] passe

---

85. mine eie.   87. all; life; sie.   88. blosomes.   89. leaping
pretile.   91. buds.   95. eaten; eat.   97. pleasaunt then.   98.
when.   99. merry.   100. all; wood.   101. sote.   103. Thorow;
till.   104. I ne wist (*better* Ne wist I).   105. ayen (!).   106. I waited about.
107. might.   108. full well.   109. greene laurey (*error for* laurer);
see l. 158.   111. smell.   112. eglentere full well.   113. great
pleasure.   115. desire.   116. *I supply* to.

As for that day, and on the sotë gras
I sat me doun; for, as for myn entent,
The birdës song was more convenient,

And more plesaunt to me, by many fold,   120
Than mete or drink, or any other thing;
Thereto the herber was so fresh and cold,
The hoolsom savours eek so comforting
That, as I demed, sith the beginning
Of the world, was never seen, or than,   125
So plesaunt a ground of non erthly man.

And as I sat, the briddës herkning thus,
Me thought that I herd voices sodainly,
The most sweetest and most delicious
That ever any wight, I trow trewly,   130
Herde in †this lyf, for [that] the armony
And sweet accord was in so good musyk,
Thát the voice to angels most was lyk.

At the last, out of a grove even by,   **The Leaf.**
That was right goodly and plesaunt to sight,   135
I sy where there cam singing lustily
A world of ladies; but to tell aright
Their greet beautè, it lyth not in my might,
Ne their array; nevertheless, I shal
Tell you a part, though I speke not of al.   140

†In surcotes whyte, of veluet wel sitting,
They were [y-]clad; and the semes echoon,
As it were a maner garnishing,
Was set with emeraudës, oon and oon,
By and by; but many a richë stoon   145
Was set [up-]on the purfils, out of dout,
Of colors, sleves, and trainës round about;

---

117. grasse.   118. downe; mine.   119. birds.   120. pleasaunt.
121. meat; drinke.   123. wholsome; eke.   126. pleasaunt; none
earthly.   127. birds harkening.   128. heard.   131. Heard; their (*error
for* his); *I supply* that.   132. musike.   133. like.   135. pleasant.
136. sie; came.   138. great beauty; lieth.   139. shall.   140. speake;
all.   141. The (!; *read* In); wele.   142. were clad; echone.   144.
Emerauds one and one.   145. rich.   146. on; purfiles.

As gret[e] perlës, round and orient,
Diamondës fyne and rubies rede,
And many another stoon, of which I †want   150
The namës now; and everich on her hede
A richë fret of gold, which, without drede,
Was ful of statly richë stonës set;
And every lady had a chapëlet

On her hede, of [leves] fresh and grene,   155
So wel [y-]wrought, and so mervéilously,
Thát it was a noble sight to sene;
Some of laurer, and some ful plesaúntly
Had chapëlets of woodbind, and sadly
Some of; agnus-castus ware also   160
Chápëlets fresh; but there were many tho

That daunced and eek song ful soberly;
But al they yede in maner of compas.
But oon ther yede in-mid the company
Sole by her-self; but al folowed the pace   165
[Which] that she kept, whos hevenly-figured face
So plesaunt was, and her wel-shape persòn,
That of beautè she past hem everichon.

And more richly beseen, by manifold,
She was also, in every maner thing;   170
On her heed, ful plesaunt to behold,
A crowne of gold, rich for any king;
A braunch of agnus-castus eek bering
In her hand; and, to my sight, trewly,
She lady was of [al] the company.   175

And she began a roundel lustily,
That Sus le foyl de vert moy men call,
Seen, et mon joly cuer endormi;
And than the company answéred all

---

148. great pearles.   149. Diamouds; red.   150. stone; went (for
want).   151. head.   152. rich; dread.   153. stately rich.   155.
head; I supply leves.   156. wele wrought; meruelously.   158.
pleasantly.   160. were; read ware, as in 335.   161. of tho (om. of).   162.
eke.   163. all; compace.   164. one.   165. Soole; selfe; all followed.   166.
I supply Which; whose heauenly.   167. pleasaunt; wele.   168. beauty;
-one.   169. beseene.   171. head; pleasaunt.   172. goldë (?).   173. eke
bearing.   175. I supply al.   176. roundell lustely.   177. Suse; foyle.
178. Seen (sic); en dormy, before which we should perhaps supply est.

With voice[s] swete entuned and so small,   180
That me thought it the sweetest melody
That ever I herdë in my lyf, soothly.

And thus they came[n], dauncing and singing,
Into the middes of the mede echone,
Before the herber, where I was sitting,   185
And, god wot, me thought I was wel bigon;
For than I might avyse hem, on by on,
Who fairest was, who coud best dance or sing,
Or who most womanly was in al thing.

They had not daunced but a litel throw   190
When that I herd, not fer of, sodainly
So greet a noise of thundring trumpës blow,
As though it shuld have départed the sky;
And, after that, within a whyle I sy
From the same grove, where the ladyes come out, 195
Of men of armës coming such a rout

As al the men on erth had been assembled
In that place, wel horsed for the nones,
Stering so fast, that al the erth[ë] trembled;
But for to speke of riches and [of] stones,   200
And men and hors, I trow, the largë wones
Of Prester John, ne al his tresory
Might not unneth have bought the tenth party!

Of their array who-so list herë more,
I shal reherse, so as I can, a lyte.   205
Out of the grove, that I spak of before,
I sy come first, al in their clokes whyte,
A company, that ware, for their delyt,
Chapëlets fresh of okës cereal
Newly spronge, and trumpets they were al.   210

---

180. voice sweet.   182. heard.   183. came.   186. bigone.   187.
one by one.   189. all.   190. little.   191. heard.   192. great; thundering trumps.   193. skie.   194. sie.   196. comming.   197. all.   198.
wele.   199. all; earth.   200. speake; *I supply* of.   201. horse.   202.
Pretir (!); all.   204. their (*read* hir?); heare.   205. rehearse.   206.
spake.   207. sie; all; their (*read* hir?).   208. were: *read* ware (*as in* 329);
delite.   209. seriall (*for* cereal).   210. sprong; all.

On every trumpe hanging a brood banere
Of fyn tartarium, were ful richly bete ;
Every trumpet his lordës armës †bere ;
About their nekkës, with gret perlës set,
Colers brode ; for cost they would not lete,   215
As it would seme ; for their scochones echoon
Were set about with many a precious stoon.

Their hors-harneys was al whyte also ;
And after hem next, in on company,
Cámë kingës of armës, and no mo,   220
In clokës of whyte cloth of gold, richly ;
Chapelets of greene on their hedes on hy,
The crownës that they on their scochones bere
Were set with perlë, ruby, and saphere,

And eek gret diamondës many on ;   225
But al their hors-harneys and other gere
Was in a sute according, everichon,
As ye have herd the foresayd trumpets were ;
And, by seeming, they were nothing to lere ;
And their gyding they did so manerly.   230
And after hem cam a greet company

Of heraudës and pursevauntës eke
Arrayed in clothës of whyt veluët ;
And hardily, they were nothing to seke
How they [up]on hem shuld the harneys set ;   235
And every man had on a chapëlet ;
Scóchones and eke hors-harneys, indede,
They had in sute of hem that before hem yede.

Next after hem, came in armour bright,
Al save their hedes, seemely knightës nyne ;   240
And every clasp and nail, as to my sight,
Of their harneys, were of red gold fyne ;

---

211. broad.   212. fine; richely.   213. lords; here (*read* bere); *see*
223.   214 (*and often*) : their (*for* hir). neckes; great pearles.   216.
echone.   217. stone.   218. horse; all.   219. them (*for* hem);
one.   220. kings.   222. heads; hye.   223. crowns.   224. pearle.
225. eke great Diamonds; one.   226. all; horse; geare.   227. euerichone.
228. heard.   230. there guiding.   231. great.   232. herauds; pur-
seuaunts.   233. white.   235. on; should.   237. horse.   238. him (*for 2nd*
hem).   240. heads; knights.   241. claspe; naile.   242. their (*for* hir ?); *so*
in 214, 216, 218, 222, 223, 230 (there), 240; &c.

With cloth of gold, and furred with ermyne
Were the trappurës of their stedës strong,
Wyde and large, that to the ground did hong;   245

And every bosse of brydel and peitrel
That they had, was worth, as I would wene,
A thousand pound; and on their hedës, wel
Dressed, were crownës [al] of laurer grene,
The best [y-]mad that ever I had seen;   250
And every knight had after him ryding
Three henshmen, [up]on him awaiting;

Of whiche †the first, upon a short tronchoun,
His lordës helme[t] bar, so richly dight,
That the worst was worth[y] the raunsoun   255
Of a[ny] king; the second a sheld bright
Bar at his nekke; the thridde bar upright
A mighty spere, ful sharpe [y-]ground and kene;
And every child ware, of leves grene,

A fresh chapelet upon his heres bright;   260
And clokes whyte, of fyn veluet they ware;
Their stedës trapped and [a]rayed right
Without[en] difference, as their lordës were.
And after hem, on many a fresh co[u]rsere,
There came of armed knightës such a rout   265
That they besprad the largë feld about.

And al they ware[n], after their degrees,
Chapëlets new, made of laurer grene,
Some of oke, and some of other trees;
Some in their handës berë boughës shene,   270
Some of laurer, and some of okës kene,
Some of hawthorn, and some of woodbind,
And many mo, which I had not in mind.

---

244. their (*for* hir?); *so in* 248, &c.   246. boose (!); bridle; paitrell.   248.
heads well.   249. *I supply* al.   250. made; sene.   252. on.   253. whichc
euery on a.   254. lords helme bare.   255. worth.   256. a (*read* any);
shield.   257. Bare; neck; thred bare.   258. spheare (!); ground.   260.
haires.   261. fine.   were; *read* ware (*as in* 259).   262. steeds; raied.   263.
Without; lords.   265. knights.   266. field.   267. were; *read* waren.
270. honds bare.   272. hauthorne.

And so they came, their hors freshly stering
With bloody sownës of hir trompës loud;   275
Ther sy I many an uncouth disgysing
In the array of these knightës proud;
And at the last, as evenly as they coud,
They took their places in-middes of the mede,
And every knight turned his horse[s] hede   280

To his felawe, and lightly laid a spere
In the [a]rest, and so justës began
On every part about[en], here and there;
Som brak his spere, som drew down hors and man;
About the feld astray the stedës ran;   285
And, to behold their rule and governaunce,
I you ensure, it was a greet plesaunce.

And so the justës last an houre and more;
But tho that crowned were in laurer grene
Wan the pryse; their dintës were so sore   290
That ther was non ayenst hem might sustene;
And [than] the justing al was left of clene;
And fro their hors the †nine alight anon;
And so did al the remnant everichon.

And forth they yede togider, twain and twain,   295
That to behold, it was a worldly sight,
Toward the ladies on the grenë plain,
That song and daunced, as I sayd now right.
The ladies, as soone as they goodly might,
They breke[n] of both the song and dance,   300
And yede to mete hem, with ful glad semblance.

And every lady took, ful womanly,
Bý the hond a knight, and forth they yede
Unto a fair laurer that stood fast by,
With levës lade, the boughës of gret brede;   . 305
And to my dome, there never was, indede,

---

274. horses.   276. sie; disguising.   277. knights.   279. their
(*for* hir? *see* 275); *so in* 286, &c.   280. horse.   281. fellow; speare.
282. rest.   283. about.   284. Some brake; some.   285. field; steeds.
287. great pleasaunce.   290. dints.   291. none.   292. *I supply* than;
all.   293. horse. ninth; *read* nine.   296. worldly (*perhaps read*
worthy).   297. green.   300. brake; they (*error for* the).   301. meet; full.
302. tooke.   304. faire.   305. great.

[A] man that had seen half so fair a tree;
For underneth it there might wel have be

An hundred persons, at their own plesaunce,
Shadowed fro the hete of Phebus bright   310
So that they shuld have felt no [greet] grevaunce
Of rain, ne hail, that hem hurt[ë] might.
The savour eek rejoice would any wight
That had be sick or melancolious,
It was so very good and vertuous.   315

And with gret reverence they †enclyned low
[Un]to the tree, so sote and fair of hew;
And after that, within a litel throw,
†Bigonne they to sing and daunce of-new;
Some song of love, some playning of untrew,   320
Environing the tree that stood upright;
And ever yede a lady and a knight.

And at the last I cast myn eye asyde,   **The Flower.**
And was ware of a lusty company
That came, roming out of the feld wyde,   325
Hond in hond, a knight and a lady;
The ladies alle in surcotes, that richly
Purfyled were with many a riche stoon;
And every knight of greene ware mantles on,

Embrouded wel, so as the surcotes were,   330
And everich had a chapelet on her hede;
Which did right wel upon the shyning here,
Made of goodly floures, whyte and rede.
The knightës eke, that they in hond lede,
In sute of hem, ware chapelets everichon;   335
And hem before went minstrels many on,

As harpës, pypës, lutës, and sautry,
Al in greene; and on their hedës bare
Of dyvers flourës, mad ful craftily,

Al in a sute, goodly chapelets they ware;   340
And so, dauncing, into the mede they fare,
In-mid the which they found a tuft that was
Al oversprad with flourës in compas.

Where[un]to they enclyned everichon
With greet reverence, and that ful humblely;   345
And, at the last[ë], there began anon
A lady for to sing right womanly
A bargaret in praising the daisy;
For, as me thought, among her notës swete,
She sayd, ' *Si doucë est la Margarete.*'   350

Thén they al answéred her infere,
So passingly wel, and so plesauntly,
Thát it was a blisful noise to here.
But I not [how], it happed sodainly,
As, about noon, the sonne so fervently   355
Wex hoot, that [al] the prety tender floures
Had lost the beautè of hir fresh coloures,

For-shronk with hete; the ladies eek to-brent,
That they ne wist where they hem might bestow.
The knightës swelt, for lak of shade ny shent;   360
And after that, within a litel throw,
The wind began so sturdily to blow,
That down goth al the flourës everichon
So that in al the mede there laft not on,

Save suche as socoured were, among the leves,   365
Fro every storme, that might hem assail,
Growing under hegges and thikke greves;
And after that, there came a storm of hail
And rain in-fere, so that, withouten fail,
The ladies ne the knightës n'ade o threed   370
Drye [up]on hem, so dropping was hir weed.

---

344. Whereto.   345. great; humbly.   346. last.   348. daisie.
350. douset & la.   351. all.   352. well; pleasauntly.   354. *I supply*
how.   355. noone.   356. Waxe whote; *I supply* al.   357. beauty.
358. Forshronke; heat; eke.   360. knights; lack; nie.   361. little.
363. down goeth all; euerichone.   364. all; one.   365. succoured.
366. assaile.   367. thicke.   368. storme; haile.   369. raine in
feare; faile.   370. knights.   371. on them so; her.

And when the storm was clene passed away,
Tho [clad] in whyte, that stood under the tree,
They felt[ë] nothing of the grete affray,
That they in greene without had in y-be.   375
To hem they yedë for routh and pitè,
Hem to comfort after their greet disese;
So fain they were the helpless for to ese,

Then was I ware how oon of hem in grene
Had on a crown[ë], rich and wel sitting;   380
Wherfore I demed wel she was a quene,
And tho in greene on her were awaiting,
The ladies then in whyte that were coming
Toward[ës] hem, and the knightës in-fere
Began to comfort hem and make hem chere.   385

The quene in whyte, that was of grete beautè,
Took by the hond the queen that was in grene,
And said, 'Suster, I have right·greet pitè
Of your annoy, and of the troublous tene
Wherein ye and your company have been   390
So long, alas! and, if that it you plese
To go with me, I shal do you the ese

In al the pleisir that I can or may,'
Wherof the tother, humbly as she might,
Thanked her; for in right ill aray   395
She was, with storm and hete, I you behight.
And every lady then, anon-right,
·That were in whyte, oon of hem took in grene
By the hond; which when the knightes had seen,

In lyke wyse, ech of hem took a knight   400
·Clad in grene, and forth with hem they fare
[Un]to an heggë, where they, anon-right,
To make their justës, [lo!] they would not spare
Boughës to hew down, and eek treës square,

372. cleane.   373. *I supply* clad.   374. felt; great.   376. them
(*for* hem).   377. Them (*for* Hem); great disease.   378. faine;
helplesse; ease.   379. one.   380. crown; well.   384. Toward
them; knights.   386. Queen; great beauty.   387. Tooke.   388.
great pity.   390. bene.   391. please.   392. shall; ease.   393. all;
pleasure.   396. heat.   398. one; them.   399. knights; sene.   400.
them.   402. To.   403. iusts; *supply* lo.   404. downe; eke.

Wherewith they made hem stately fyres grete   405
To dry their clothës that were wringing wete.

And after that, of herbës that there grew,
They made, for blisters of the sonne brenning,
Very good and hoolsom ointments new,
Where that they yede, the sick fast anointing;   410
And after that, they yede about gadring
Plesaunt saladës, which they made hem ete,
For to refresh their greet unkindly hete.

The lady of the Leef then gan to pray
Her of the Flour, (for so to my seeming   415
They should[ë] be, as by their [quaint] array),
To soupe with her; and eek, for any thing,
That she should with her al her people bring.
And she ayein, in right goodly manere,
Thanketh her of her most freendly chere,   420

Saying plainly, that she would obey
With al her hert al her commaundëment.
And then anon, without lenger delay,
The lady of the Leef hath oon y-sent
For a palfray, [as] after her intent,   425
Arayed wel and fair in harneys of gold,
For nothing lakked, that to him long shold.

And after that, to al her company
She made to purvey hors and every thing
That they needed; and then, ful lustily,   430
Even by the herber where I was sitting,
They passed al, so plesantly singing,
That it would have comfórted any wight;
But then I sy a passing wonder sight:—

For then the nightingale, that al the day   435
Had in the laurer sete, and did her might
The hool servyse to sing longing to May,

---

405. great.   406. weat.   407. hearbs.   409. wholsome.   410.
annointing.   411. gadering.   412. Pleasaunt; eat.   413. great;
heat.   414. leafe; began (*for* gan).   415. floure.   416. should;
I supply quaint.   417. eke.   418. all.   419. ayen.   420. friendly
cheare.   421. obay.   422. all; hart all.   424. Leafe; one.   425. *I
supply* al.   426. well; faire.   427. lacked; should.   428. all.   429. horse.
432. all; pleasantly.   434. sie.   435. all.   437. whol seruice.

Al sodainly [be]gan to take her flight;
And to the lady of the Leef forthright
She flew, and set her on her hond softly,   440
Which was a thing I marveled of gretly.

The goldfinch eek, that fro the medle-tree
Was fled, for hete, into the bushes cold,
Unto the lady of the Flour gan flee,
And on her hond he set him, as he wold,   445
And plesantly his wingës gan to fold;
And for to sing they pained hem both as sore
As they had do of al the day before.

And so these ladies rood forth a gret pace,
And al the rout of knightës eek in-fere;   450
And I, that had seen al this wonder case,
Thought [that] I would assay, in some manere,
To know fully the trouth of this matere,
And what they were that rood so plesantly.
And, when they were the herber passed by,   455

I drest me forth, and happed to mete anon
Right a fair lady, I you ensure;
And she cam ryding by herself aloon,
Al in whyte, with semblance ful demure.
I salued her, and bad good aventure   460
†Might her befall, as I coud most humbly;
And she answered, 'My doughter, gramercy!'

'Madam,' quod I, 'if that I durst enquere
Of you, I wold fain, of that company,
Wit what they be that past by this herbere?'   465
And she ayein answéred right freendly:
'My fair daughter, al tho that passed hereby
In whyte clothing, be servants everichoon
Unto the Leef, and I my-self am oon.

---

438. gan.   439. leafe.   441. greatly.   442. eke; medill.   443. heat.
444. Flower; fle.   445. hir.   446. pleasantly; wings.   448. all.   449.
rode; great.   450. knights.   451. sene all.   452. *I supply* that.   454.
rode; pleasantly.   457. faire.   458. come; hir selfe alone.   459. All.
460. saluted (*read* salued); bad her good (*omit* her).   461. Must (*read* Might).
464. faine.   465. arbere.   466. ayen; friendly.   467. faire; all.
468. euerichone.   469. Leafe; selfe; one.

See ye not her that crowned is,' quod she,   470
'Al in whyte?' 'Madamë,' quod I, 'yis!'
'That is Diane, goddesse of chastitè;
And, for bicause that she a maiden is,
In her hond the braunch she bereth, this
That *agnus-castus* men call properly;   475
And alle the ladies in her company

Which ye see of that herb[ë] chaplets were,
Be such as han kept †ay hir maidenhede;
And al they that of laurer chaplets bere
Be such as hardy were and †wan, indede,   480
Victorious name which never may be dede.
And al they were so worthy of hir hond,
[As] in hir tyme, that non might hem withstond.

And tho that werë chapelets on hir hede
Of fresh woodbind, be such as never were   485
To love untrew in word, [ne] thought, ne dede,
But ay stedfast; ne for plesaunce, ne fere,
Though that they shuld hir hertës al to-tere,
Would never flit, but ever were stedfast,
Til that their lyves there asunder brast.'   490

'Now, fair madam,' quod I, 'yet I would pray
Your ladiship, if that it might be,
That I might know[ë], by some maner way,
Sith that it hath [y-]lyked your beautè,
The trouth of these ladies for to tel me;   495
What that these knightës be, in rich armour;
And what tho be in grene, and were the flour;

And why that some did reverence to the tree,
And some unto the plot of flourës fair?'
'With right good wil, my fair doughter,' quod she, 500
'Sith your desyr is good and debonair.

---

471. All; yes (*read* yis).   472. goddes; chastity.   476. all.   477.
hearb.   478. kepte; alway (*read* ay); her.   479. beare.   480. manly (*read*
wan).   482. all; ther (*read* hir).   483. *I supply* As; none.   484. weare;
ther (*read* hir).   486. untrue; *I supply* ne.   487. aye; pleasance.   488.
their harts all.   490. Till; their (*read* hir?).   491. faire.   493. know.   494.
liked.   495. tell.   496. knights.   497. weare.   499. faire.   500. will;
doghter.   501. youre desire; debonaire.

Tho nine, crownèd, be very exemplair
Of all honour longing to chivalry,
And thosé, certain, be called the Nine Worthy,

Which ye may see [here] ryding al before,   505
That in hir tyme did many a noble dede,
And, for their worthines, ful oft have bore
The crowne of laurer-leves on their hede,
As ye may in your old[ë] bokes rede ;
And how that he, that was a conquerour,   510
Had by laurer alway his most honour.

And tho that bere boughës in their hond
Of the precious laurer so notáble,
Be such as were, I wol ye understond,
Noble knightës of the Round[ë] Table,   515
And eek the Douseperes honourable ;
Which they bere in signe of victory,
†As witness of their dedes mightily.

Eek there be knightës olde of the Garter,
That in hir tyme did right worthily ;   520
And the honour they did to the laurer
Is, for by [it] they have their laud hoolly,
Their triumph eek, and martial glory ;
Which unto hem is more parfyt richesse
Than any wight imagine can or gesse.   525

For oon leef given of that noble tree
To any wight that hath don worthily,
And it be doon so as it ought to be,
Is more honour then any thing erthly.
Witnesse of Rome that founder was, truly,   530
Of all knighthood and dedës marvelous ;
Record I take of Titus Livius.

And as for her that crowned is in greene,
It is Flora, of these flourës goddesse ;

502. exemplaire.   504. certaine.   505. *I supply* here.   507. their (*read*
hir ? *see* 506) ; *so in* 512, &c.   508. leaues.   509. old bookes.   512. beare.
bowes ; *see* 270.   514. woll.   515. knights ; round.   516. eke ; douseperis.
517. beare.   518. It is (*but read* As).   519. Eke ; knights old.   522.
I supply it ; wholly.   523. eke ; marshall (!).   524. them ; riches.   526.
one leafe.   527, 528. done.   529. earthly.   530. Witnes.   531.
deeds.

And al that here on her awaiting been,   535
It are such [folk] that loved idlenes,
And not delyte [had] of no busines
But for to hunt and hauke, and pley in medes,
And many other such [lyk] idle dedes.

And for the greet delyt and [the] plesaunce   540
They have [un]to the flour, so reverently
They unto it do such [gret] obeisaunce,
As ye may see.' 'Now, fair madame,' quod I,
'If I durst ask what is the cause and why
That knightës have the signe of [al] honour   545
Rather by the Leef than by the Flour?'

'Sothly, doughter,' quod she, 'this is the trouth:
For knightës ever should be persévering,
To seeke honour without feintyse or slouth,
Fro wele to better, in al maner thing;   550
In signe of which, with Levës ay lasting
They be rewarded after their degree,
Whos lusty grene may not appeired be,

But ay keping hir beautè fresh and greene;
For there nis storm [non] that may hem deface,   555
Hail nor snow, wind nor frostës kene;
Wherfore they have this propertè and grace.
And for the Flour within a litel space
Wol be [y-]lost, so simple of natüre
They be, that they no grevance may endure,   560

And every storm wil blow hem sone away,
Ne they last not but [as] for a sesoun,
That tis the cause, the very trouth to say,
That they may not, by no way of resoun,
Be put to no such occupacioun.'   565

---

535. all; beene.   536. *I supply* folk.   537. delite of; busines.   539.
I supply lyk.   540. great delite; *I supply* the; pleasaunce.   541. to;
and so (*omit* and).   542. *I supply* gret.   543. faire.   544. aske.   545.
knights; *I supply* al.   546. leafe; floure.   548. knights.   550. all.
551. leaues aye.   552. their; *read* hir?   553. Whose; green May may (*sic*).
554. aye; their beauty.   555. storme; *I supply* non.   556. Haile; frosts.
557. propertie.   558. floure; little.   559. Woll; lost.   560. greeuance.
561. storme will; them.   562. *I supply* as; season.   563. That if their
(*read* That is the).   564. reason.   565. occupacion.

'Madame,' quod I, 'with al my hool servyse
I thank you now, in my most humble wyse.

For now I am acértainèd throughly
Of every thing I désired to know.'
'I am right glad that I have said, sothly,   570
Ought to your pleysir, if ye wil me trow,'
Quod she ayein, 'but to whom do ye ow
Your servyce? and which wil ye honour,
Tel me, I pray, this yeer, the Leef or Flour?'

'Madame,' quod I, 'though I [be] leest worthy,   575
Unto the Leef I ow myn observaunce.'
'That is,' quod she, 'right wel don, certainly,
And I pray god to honour you avaunce,
And kepe you fro the wikked rémembraunce
Of Male-Bouche, and al his crueltè ;   580
And alle that good and wel-condicioned be.

For here may I no lenger now abyde,
I must folowe the gret[ë] company
That ye may see yonder before you ryde.'
And forth[right], as I couth, most humblely,   585
I took my leve of her as she gan hy
After hem, as fast as ever she might ;
And I drow hoomward, for it was nigh night ;

And put al that I had seen in wryting,
Under support of hem that lust it rede.   590
O litel book, thou art so unconning,
How darst thou put thy-self in prees for drede ?
It is wonder that thou wexest not rede,
Sith that thou wost ful lyte who shal behold
Thy rude langage, ful boistously unfold.   595

Explicit.

---

566. all mine whole.   567. thanke.   571. pleasure; will.   572.
ayen; whome doe; owe.   573. woll.   574. Tell; yeere; leafe or the
flour.   575. I least.   576. leafe; owe mine.   577. well done.
580. male bouch; all; crueltie.   581. all.   583. follow; great.   585.
forth as; humbly.   586. tooke; hie.   587. them.   588. homeward.
589. all.   590. them; it to rede (*omit* to).   591. little booke.   594.
shall.   595. full.

XXI. THE ASSEMBLY OF LADIES.

— ·· —

I N Septembre, at the falling of the leef,
  The fressh sesoun was al-togider doon,
And of the corn was gadered in the sheef;
In a gardyn, about twayn after noon,
Ther were ladyes walking, as was her wone,   5
Foure in nombre, as to my mynd doth falle,
And I the fifte, the simplest of hem alle.

Of gentilwomen fayre ther were also,
Disporting hem, everiche after her gyse,
In crosse-aleys walking, by two and two,   10
And some alone, after her fantasyes.
Thus occupyed we were in dyvers wyse;
And yet, in trouthe, we were not al alone;
Ther were knightës and squyers many one.

'Wherof I served?' oon of hem asked me;   15
I sayde ayein, as it fel in my thought,
'To walke about the mase, in certayntè,
As a woman that [of] nothing rought.'
He asked me ayein—'whom that I sought,
And of my colour why I was so pale?'   20
'Forsothe,' quod I, 'and therby lyth a tale.'

From Th. (Thynne, ed. 1532); *compared with* A. (Addit. 34360); *and* T. (Trin. R. 3. 19). TITLE. Th. The assemble of ladies; T. the Boke callyd Assemble de Damys.   1. A. leef; Th. lefe.   2. Th. ceason.   3. Th. corne; gathered. A. in; Th. T. *om.* A. sheef; Th. shefe.   4. Th. gardyne aboute twayne; noone.   6. Th. mynde dothe fal.   7. Th. fyfthe; A. T. fift. A. T. *om.* the. Th. al.   13. Th. T. al; A. *om.*   16. Th. sayd ayen; A. seyde ageyne.   17. Th. aboute.   18. *I supply* of.   19. Th. ayen; A. ageyn.   21. Th. lythe. [*Henceforward unmarked readings are from* Thynne.]

'That must me wite,' quod he, 'and that anon;
Tel on, let see, and make no tarying.'
'Abyd,' quod I, 'ye been a hasty oon,
I let you wite it is no litel thing.   25
But, for bicause ye have a greet longing
In your desyr, this proces for to here,
I shal you tel the playn of this matere.—

It happed thus, that, in an after-noon,
My felawship and I, by oon assent,   30
Whan al our other besinesse was doon,
To passe our tyme, into this mase we went,
And toke our wayes, eche after our entent;
Some went inward, and †wend they had gon out,
Some stode amid, and loked al about.   35

And, sooth to say, some were ful fer behind,
And right anon as ferforth as the best;
Other ther were, so mased in her mind,
Al wayes were good for hem, bothe eest and west.
Thus went they forth, and had but litel rest;   40
And some, her corage did hem sore assayle,
For very wrath, they did step over the rayle!

And as they sought hem-self thus to and fro,
I gat myself a litel avauntage;
Al for-weried, I might no further go,   45
Though I had won right greet, for my viage.
So com I forth into a strait passage,
Which brought me to an herber fair and grene,
Mad with benches, ful craftily and clene,

That, as me thought, ther might no crëature   50
Devyse a better, by dew proporcioun;
Safe it was closed wel, I you ensure,

---

22. *All* me. A. wite; Th. T. wete. anone.   23. se; taryeng.   24. Abyde;
ben.   25. A. wite; Th. T. wete.   26. great.   27. desyre; processe.
28. playne.   29. noone.   30. one.   31. A. oure; Th. T. *om.* T. A.
besynes was; Th. besynesses were doone.   34. *All* went (*twice*); *read*
wend (=weened).   35. A. amyddis; Th. T. in the myd. aboute.   36.
sothe. A. T. fer; Th. ferre. behynde.   37. ferforthe; beste.   38. mynde.
40. forthe.   41. A. so (*for* sore).   42. wrathe. A. stept (*for* did step).
43. A. thus; T. Th. *om.* -selfe.   44. gate.   46. great.   47. came; A.
com. forthe; strayte.   48. fayre.   49. *All* Made. T. craftyly; A. Th.
crafty.   51. T. dew; Th. dewe; A. *om.*

With masonry of compas enviroun,
Ful secretly, with stayres going doun
Inmiddes the place, with turning wheel, certayn ;   55
And upon that, a pot of marjolain ;

With margarettes growing in ordinaunce,
To shewe hemself, as folk went to and fro,
That to beholde it was a greet plesaunce,
And how they were acompanyed with mo   60
Ne-m'oublie-mies and sovenez also ;
The povre pensees were not disloged there ;
No, no ! god wot, her place was every-where !

The flore beneth was paved faire and smothe
With stones square, of many dyvers hew,   65
So wel joynëd that, for to say the sothe,
Al semed oon (who that non other knew) ;
And underneth, the stremës new and new,
As silver bright, springing in suche a wyse
That, whence it cam, ye coude it not devyse.   70

A litel whyle thus was I al alone,
Beholding wel this délectable place ;
My felawship were coming everichone,
So must me nedes abyde, as for a space.
Rememb[e]ring of many dyvers cace   75
Of tyme passed, musing with sighes depe,
I set me doun, and ther I fel a-slepe.

And, as I slept, me thought ther com to me
A gentilwoman, metely of stature ;
Of greet worship she semed for to be,   80
Atyred wel, not high, but by mesure ;
Her countenaunce ful sad and ful demure ;

---

53. masonrye. A. T. compas ; Th. compace.   54. T. steyers.   55.
whele.   56. potte. A. Margoleyne ; Th. Margelayne ; T. Margelayn.
58. -selfe ; folke.   59. great.   60. howe.   61. A. Ne moubliemies ;
Th. Ne momblysnesse ; T. Ne momblynes. A. souenez ; T. souenes ; Th.
souenesse.   62. *All* penses.   63. A. No no ; Th. T. Ne (!). wote.
64. A. beneth ; Th. T. and benche (!).   Th. smoth.   65. hewe.   67.
one. A. who ; Th. T. *om.* none ; knewe.   68. streames newe and newe.
70. came.   71. A. thus ; Th. T. *om.*   74. muste. T. nedys ; Th. nedest ;
A. nede. A. as ; Th. T. *om.*   76. A. musyng ; Th. T. *om.* 77. downe.   78.
A. com ; Th. came.   80. Th. great.   82. sadde. A. ful (2) ; Th. T. *om.*

Her colours blewe, al that she had upon ;
Ther com no mo [there] but herself aloon.

Her gown was wel embrouded, certainly,   85
With sovenez, after her own devyse ;
On her purfyl her word [was] by and by
Bien et loyalment, as I coud devyse.
Than prayde I her, in every maner wyse
That of her name I might have remembraunce ;   90
She sayd, she called was Persèveraunce.

So furthermore to speke than was I bold,
Where she dwelled, I prayed her for to say ;
And she again ful curteysly me told,
" My dwelling is, and hath ben many a day   95
With a lady."—" What lady, I you pray ? "
" Of greet estate, thus warne I you," quod she ;
"What cal ye her ? "—" Her name is Loyaltè."

" In what offyce stand ye, or in what degrè ? "
Quod I to her, " that wolde I wit right fayn."   100
" I am," quod she, " unworthy though I be,
Of her chambre her ussher, in certayn ;
This rod I bere, as for a token playn,
Lyke as ye know the rule in such servyce
Pertayning is unto the same offyce.   105

She charged me, by her commaundëment,
To warn you and your felawes everichon,
That ye shuld come there as she is present,
For a counsayl, which shal be now anon,
Or seven dayës be comen and gon.   110
And furthermore, she bad that I shuld say
Excuse there might be non, nor [no] delay.

84. A. com ; Th. came. I supply there.   85. gowne. A. embrowded ; T.
enbrowdyd ; Th. enbraudred.   86. A. souenez ; Th. T. stones.   87. A. On ;
Th. T. In. A. the ; Th. T. her.   All worde ; read word was.   88. A.
Bien loielment as I cowde me deuyse.   89. A. euery ; T. many (om. in) ;
Th. any.   91. All was called.   92. A. than ; Th. T. om. bolde.   94.
agayne ; curtesly ; tolde.   95. be.   97. great.   99. stande.   100. A.
wit ; Th. T. wete. A. ful ; Th. T. right. 102. hussher (A. T. vssher) ; certayne.
103. rodde ; beare ; playne.   104. knowe.   105. A. Perteyneng ; Th. T.
Apertaynyng. A. vnto ; Th. T. to.   107. warne ; -one.   108. shulde.
109. counsayle ; nowe anone.   110. gone.   111. shulde.   112. I
supply no.

Another thing was nigh forget behind
Whiche in no wyse I wolde but ye it knew;
Remembre wel, and bere it in your mind,   115
Al your felawes and ye must come in blew,
Every liche able your maters for to sew;
With more, which I pray you thinke upon,
Your wordës on your slevës everichon.

And be not ye abasshed in no wyse,   120
As many been in suche an high presence;
Mak your request as ye can best devyse,
And she gladly wol yeve you audience.
There is no greef, ne no maner offence,
Wherin ye fele that your herte is displesed,   125
But with her help right sone ye shul be esed."

"I am right glad," quod I, "ye tel me this,
But there is non of us that knoweth the way."
"As of your way," quod she, "ye shul not mis,
Ye shul have oon to gyde you, day by day,   130
Of my felawes (I can no better say)
Suche oon as shal tel you the way ful right;
And Diligence this gentilwoman hight.

A woman of right famous governaunce,
And wel cherisshed, I tel you in certayn;   135
Her felawship shal do you greet plesaunce.
Her port is suche, her maners trewe and playn;
She with glad chere wol do her besy payn
To bring you there; now farwel, I have don."
"Abyde," sayd I, "ye may not go so sone."   140

"Why so?" quod she, "and I have fer to go
To yeve warning in many dyvers place
To your felawes, and so to other mo;
And wel ye wot, I have but litel space."

---

113. A. nygh; Th. T. not (!). behynde.   114. knewe.   115. beare.
116. muste; blewe.   119. T. wordys; sleuys.   120. *So* A.; Th. T. be
not abasshed in no maner wyse.   122. Make.   124. grefe.   125. displeased.   126. helpe.   A. shul; Th. T. shal.   eased.   127. T. (*heading*):
Diligence Guyde.   129. A. shul; Th. T. shal.   130. A. shul; Th. T. shal.   A.
one (= oon); Th. T. *om.*   132. one; waye.   135. A. I sey yow for.
136. great.   137. porte; playne.   139. A. T. farewele now have I.   140.
A. quod (for sayd.).   141. ferre.   144. wote.

"Now yet," quod I, "ye must tel me this cace, 145
If we shal any man unto us cal?"
"Not oon," quod she, "may come among you al."

"Not oon," quod I, "ey! *benedicite*!
What have they don? I pray you tel me that!"
"Now, by my lyf, I trow but wel," quod she; 150
"But ever I can bileve there is somwhat,
And, for to say you trouth, more can I nat;
In questiouns I may nothing be large,
I medle no further than is my charge."

"Than thus," quod I, "do me to understand, 155
What place is there this lady is dwelling?"
"Forsothe," quod she, "and oon sought al this land,
Fairer is noon, though it were for a king
Devysed wel, and that in every thing.
The toures hy ful plesaunt shul ye find, 160
With fanes fressh, turning with every wind.

The chambres and parlours both of oo sort,
With bay-windowes, goodly as may be thought,
As for daunsing and other wyse disport;
The galeryes right wonder wel y-wrought, 165
That I wel wot, if ye were thider brought.
And took good hede therof in every wyse,
Ye wold it thinke a very paradyse."

"What hight this place?" quod I; "now say me that."
"Plesaunt Regard," quod she, "to tel you playn." 170
"Of verray trouth," quod I, "and, wot ye what,
It may right wel be called so, certayn;
But furthermore, this wold I wit ful fayn,

---

145. Nowe; A. *om.*   147. one. Th. amonges; A. T. among.   148. A.
Nat one quod I ey; Th. Not one than sayd I eygh; T. Not oon then sayd I O.
149. A. they; Th. T. I. done.   150. Th. Nowe; lyfe.   152. trouthe.
T. A. nat; Th. not.   153. questyons. Th. be to large; A. *om.* to.   154.
A. medle; Th. meddle. A. is (*in later hand*); Th. T. *om.*   155. vnderstande.
157. one; lande.   158. none.   160. hye. A. shul; Th. shal. fynde.
161. A. fanes; Th. phanes; T. vanes. wynde.   162. A. *om.* and. A.
parlours; Th. parlers; T. parlors. A. both; Th. T. *om.* A. oo; Th. T. a.
sorte.   164. disporte.   166. wote.   167. A. toke; Th. T. take.   168.
Th. wol; A. T. wold.   169. A. this; Th. T. the. nowe.   170. regarde;
playne.   171. A. verray; T. *verrey*; Th. verey. wote.   172. A. *om.* right.
173. A. T. ful; Th. right.

What shulde I do as sone as I come there,
And after whom that I may best enquere?"   175

"A gentilwoman, a porter at the yate
There shal ye find; her name is Countenaunce;
If †it so hap ye come erly or late,
Of her were good to have som acquaintaunce.
She can tel how ye shal you best avaunce,   180
And how to come to her ladyes presence;
To her wordës I rede you yeve credence.

Now it is tyme that I depart you fro;
For, in good sooth, I have gret businesse."
"I wot right wel," quod I, "that it is so;   185
And I thank you of your gret gentilnesse.
Your comfort hath yeven me suche hardinesse
That now I shal be bold, withouten fayl,
To do after your ávyse and counsayl."

Thus parted she, and I lefte al aloon;   190
With that I saw, as I beheld asyde,
A woman come, a verray goodly oon;
And forth withal, as I had her aspyed,
Me thought anon, [that] it shuld be the gyde;
And of her name anon I did enquere.   195
Ful womanly she yave me this answere.

"I am," quod she, "a simple crëature
Sent from the court; my name is Diligence.
As sone as I might come, I you ensure,
I taried not, after I had licence;   200
And now that I am come to your presence,
Look, what servyce that I can do or may,
Commaundë me; I can no further say."

I thanked her, and prayed her to come nere,
Because I wold see how she were arayed;   205

---

174. T. shulde I; Th. I shulde; A. shal I.   175. A. that; Th. T. *om.*
176. A. at; Th. T. of.   177. fynde.   178. Th. T. ye (*for* it); A. *om.*
(*but* it *seems required*).   180. *So* A.; Th. T. you tel howe ye shal you.
181. howe. Th. her; A. T. this.   182. A. T. yow; Th. ye. gyue.   183.
Th. *om.* that.   T. depart; Th. parte; A. part.   184. A. T. soth; Th.
faythe. great.   185. wote.   186. thanke; great.   187. comforte.
A. suche; Th. T. *om.*   188. nowe; bolde; fayle.   189. A. auise; Th.
aduyce.   Th. and good; A. T. *om.* good.   198. courte.   201. nowe.
202. A. that; Th. T. *om.*   205. wolde se howe. A. were; Th. T. was.
arayde.

Her gown was blew, dressed in good manere
With her devyse, her word also, that sayd
Tant que je puis; and I was wel apayd;
For than wist I, withouten any more,
It was ful trew, that I had herd before.　　　　210

"Though we took now before a litel space,
It were ful good," quod she, "as I coud gesse."
"How fer," quod I, "have we unto that place?"
"A dayes journey," quod she, "but litel lesse;
Wherfore I redë that we onward dresse;　　　　215
For, I suppose, our felawship is past,
And for nothing I wold that we were last."

Than parted we, at springing of the day,
And forth we wente [a] soft and esy pace,
Til, at the last, we were on our journey　　　　220
So fer onward, that we might see the place.
"Now let us rest," quod I, "a litel space,
And say we, as devoutly as we can,
A *pater-noster* for saint Julian."

"With al my herte, I assent with good wil;　　　　225
Much better shul we spede, whan we have don."
Than taried we, and sayd it every del.
And whan the day was fer gon after noon,
We saw a place, and thider cam we sone,
Which rounde about was closed with a wal,　　　　230
Seming to me ful lyke an hospital.

Ther found I oon, had brought al myn aray,
A gentilwoman of myn aquaintaunce.
"I have mervayl," quod I, "what maner way
Ye had knowlege of al this ordenaunce."　　　　235
"Yis, yis," quod she, "I herd Perséveraunce,

---

207. worde; sayde.　208. apayde.　209. A. For; Th. T. And.　210.
trewe; herde.　211. nowe.　212. coude.　213. Howe farre.　A.
that; Th. T. the.　215. A. onward; Th. T. outwarde.　217. *So* A.;
Th. T. wolde not we were the last.　218. A. parted; Th. T. departed. Th.
T. at the; A. *om.* the.　219. *I supply* a.　T. and an esy.　221. far.
A. onward; Th. T. outwarde. se.　222. Nowe.　225. A. myn hert
quod she I gre me wele (*better*?).　226. A. shul; Th. shal.　227. A.
dele; T. delle; Th. dyl.　228. A. was fer gon; Th. T. was past farre.
229. sawe; came.　230. aboute.　232. founde I one.　233. myne.
234. meruayle.　236. A. Yis yis; Th. Yes yes. herde.

C C 2

How she warned your felawes everichon,
And what aray that ye shulde have upon."

"Now, for my love," quod I, "this I you pray,
Sith ye have take upon you al the payn,   240
That ye wold helpe me on with myn aray;
For wit ye wel, I wold be gon ful fayn."
"Al this prayer nedeth not, certayn;"
Quod she agayn; "com of, and hy you sone,
And ye shal see how wel it shal be doon."   245

"But this I dout me greetly, wot ye what,
That my felawes ben passed by and gon."
"I warant you," quod she, "that ar they nat;
For here they shul assemble everichon.
Notwithstanding, I counsail you anon;   250
Mak you redy, and tary ye no more,
It is no harm, though ye be there afore."

So than I dressed me in myn aray,
And asked her, whether it were wel or no?
"It is right wel," quod she, "unto my pay;   255
Ye nede not care to what place ever ye go."
And whyl that she and I debated so,
Cam Diligence, and saw me al in blew:
"Sister," quod she, "right wel brouk ye your new!"

Than went we forth, and met at aventure   260
A yong woman, an officer seming:
"What is your name," quod I, "good crëature?"
"Discrecioun," quod she, "without lesing."
"And where," quod I, "is your most abyding?"
"I have," quod she, "this office of purchace,   265
Cheef purveyour, that longeth to this place."

237. T. A. your; Th. her. -one.   238. A. that; Th. T. *om.* A. shal.
239. Nowe.   240. A. this (*for* the).   241. wolde; myne.   242.
wolde; gone. A. ful; Th. T. ryght. fayne.   243. certayne.   244.
agayne come; hye.   245. se. A. how wele; Th. T. anone. done.
246. doute; greatly wote.   247. T. byn; A. bien; Th. be. gone.
248. A. waraunt; Th. T. warne.   249. A. T. shul; Th. shal. -one.
250. counsayle; anone.   251. A. ye (*twice*); Th. T. you (*twice*).   252.
harme thoughe. A. afore; Th. T. before.   257. A. while; Th. whyles.
258. Came; sawe; blewe.   259. *All* broke (*for* brouk).   *Before* 260:
Th. T. Discrecyon purvyour.   260. wente.   261. yonge; semynge.
263. Dyscrecyon; lesynge.   264. abydynge.   266. Chefe.

"Fair love," quod I, "in al your ordenaunce,
What is her name that is the herbegere?"
"For sothe," quod she, "her name is Acquaintaunce,
A woman of right gracious manere."   270
Than thus quod I, "What straungers have ye here?"
"But few," quod she, "of high degree ne low;
Ye be the first, as ferforth as I know."

Thus with talës we cam streight to the yate;
This yong woman departed was and gon;   275
Cam Diligence, and knokked fast therat;
"Who is without?" quod Countenaunce anon.
"Trewly," quod I, "fair sister, here is oon!"
"Which oon?" quod she, and therwithal she lough;
"I, Diligence! ye know me wel ynough."   280

Than opened she the yate, and in we go;
With wordës fair she sayd ful gentilly,
"Ye are welcome, ywis! are ye no mo?"
"Nat oon," quod she, "save this woman and I."
"Now than," quod she, "I pray yow hertely,   285
Tak my chambre, as for a whyl, to rest
Til your felawës come, I holde it best."

I thanked her, and forth we gon echon
Til her chambre, without[en] wordës mo.
Cam Diligence, and took her leve anon;   290
"Wher-ever you list," quod I, "now may ye go;
And I thank you right hertely also
Of your labour, for which god do you meed;
I can no more, but Jesu be your speed!"

Than Countenauncë asked me anon,   295
"Your felawship, where ben they now?" quod she.
"For sothe," quod I, "they be coming echon;

Before 267: Th. T. Acquayntaunce herbyger.   267. Fayre.   268.
A. herbegyer; Th. T. herbygere.   272. fewe; hyghe degre; lowe.   273.
knowe.   *Before* 274: Th. Countenaunce porter.   274. came.   275. yonge.
276. Came; therate.   277. anone.   278. Truely; fayre; one.   279.
Whiche one; loughe.   280. knowe; ynoughe.   281. T. yate; A.
Th. gate.   282. fayre.   284. one.   285. Nowe.   286. Take. A. as;
Th. T. *om.* whyle.   288. A. gon; Th. go. A. eche on; Th. T. euerychone.
289. *All* without (!).   290. Came; toke; leaue onone.   291. A. yow;
Th. T. ye. nowe.   292. thanke.   293. laboure; whiche; mede.   294.
spede.   295. anone.   296. A. now; Th. T. *om.*   297. A. eche
one; Th. T. euerychone.

But in certayn, I know nat wher they be,
Without I may hem at this window see.
Here wil I stande, awaytinge ever among,　　300
For, wel I wot, they wil nat now be long."

Thus as I stood musing ful busily,
I thought to take good hede of her aray,
Her gown was blew, this wot I verely,
Of good fasoun, and furred wel with gray;　　305
Upon her sleve her word (this is no nay),
Which sayd thus, as my pennë can endyte,
A moi que je voy, writen with lettres whyte.

Than forth withal she cam streight unto me,
"Your word," quod she, "fayn wold I that I knew."　310
"Forsothe," quod I, "ye shal wel knowe and see,
And for my word, I have non; this is trew.
It is ynough that my clothing be blew,
As here-before I had commaundëment;
And so to do I am right wel content.　　315

But tel me this, I pray you hertely,
The steward here, say me, what is her name?"
"She hight Largesse, I say you suërly;
A fair lady, and of right noble fame.
Whan ye her see, ye wil report the same.　　320
And under her, to bid you welcome al,
There is Belchere, the marshal of the hall.

Now al this whyle that ye here tary stil,
Your own maters ye may wel have in mind.
But tel me this, have ye brought any bil?"　　325
"Ye, ye," quod I, "or els I were behind.
Where is there oon, tel me, that I may find

---

298. *So* A; Th. T. But where they are I knowe no certaynte.　299. wyndowe se.　300. amonge.'　301. A. now; Th. *om.*　302. stode musynge.　304. gowne; blewe; wote.　305. facyon.　306. worde.　307. A. The whiche. 308. A. *O (for A)*. A. lettres; Th. letters.　309. A. Than ferforth as she com. came. A. vnto; Th. to.　310. T. worde; Th. wordes; A. *om.* (*see* 312). fayne.　311. se.　312. worde; none; trewe.　313. ynoughe; blewe.　*Above* 316: Th. Largesse stewarde; T. Belchere Marchall.　318. T. sewerly; Th. surely.　319. fayre. A. right of nobil.　320. se; reporte.　322. A. Bealchiere; T. Belchere; Th. Belchier. A. the (1); Th. T. *om.*　323. Th. Nowe.　324. A. matiers. mynde.　326. A. or; Th. T. and. behynde.　327. one; fynde.

To whom that I may shewe my matters playn?"
"Surely," quod she, " unto the chamberlayn."

"The chamberlayn?" quod I, "[now] say ye trew?" 330
"Ye, verely," sayd she, " by myne advyse;
Be nat aferd; unto her lowly sew."
"It shal be don," quod I, "as ye devyse;
But ye must knowe her name in any wyse?"
"Trewly," quod she, "to tell you in substaunce, 335
Without fayning, her name is Remembraunce.

The secretary yit may not be forget;
For she may do right moche in every thing.
Wherfore I rede, whan ye have with her met,
Your mater hool tel her, without fayning; 340
Ye shal her finde ful good and ful loving."
"Tel me her name," quod I, " of gentilnesse."
"By my good sooth," quod she, " Avysënesse."

"That name," quod I, "for her is passing good;
For every bil and cedule she must see; 345
Now good," quod I, " com, stand there-as I stood;
My felawes be coming; yonder they be."
"Is it [a] jape, or say ye sooth?" quod she.
"In jape? nay, nay; I say you for certain;
See how they come togider, twain and twain!" 350

"Ye say ful sooth," quod she, "that is no nay;
I see coming a goodly company."
"They been such folk," quod I, "I dar wel say,
That list to love; thinke it ful verily.
And, for my love, I pray you faithfully, 355
At any tyme, whan they upon you cal,
That ye wol be good frend unto hem al."

---

328. playne.   329, 330. Chamberlayne.   *Above* 330: Th. T. Remembraunce chamberlayne.   330. *I supply* now.   trewe.   332. aferde. A.
aferd but lowly til hir.   Th. sewe; T. sew; A. shewe.   333. done.   334.
A. me (*for* ye).   335. T. A. tell*e*; Th. shewe.   336. A. T. Without;
Th. Withouten.   *Above* 337: T. Auysen[e]s.   337. A. yit may nat;
Th. T. she may not yet be.   338. A. may do; Th. T. doth.   thynge.
339. A. T. met; Th. ymet.   340. matere hole; faynynge.   341. louynge.
342. A. gentillesse.   343. sothe.   344. A. name; Th. T. *om.*   345.
se.   346. Nowe; come stande; stode.   348. *I supply* a.   sothe.   349.
A. it (*for* you).   certayne.   350. Se; twayne (*twice*).   351. sothe.
A. it (*for* that).   352. se comynge.   353. ben suche folke.   A. I dare
wele; T. I dar*e*; Th. dare I.   354. A. ful; Th. T. *om.*   356. A. T.
yow; Th. me (!).   357. frende.   T. vnto; A. Th. to.

"Of my frendship," quod she, "they shal nat mis,
And for their ese, to put therto my payn."
"God yelde it you!" quod I; "but tel me this,   360
How shal we know who is the chamberlayn?"
"That shal ye wel know by her word, certayn."
"What is her word? Sister, I pray you say."
"*Plus ne purroy*; thus wryteth she alway."

Thus as we stood togider, she and I,   365
Even at the yate my felawes were echon.
So met I hem, as me thought was goodly,
And bad hem welcome al, by on and on.
Than forth cam [lady] Countenaunce anon;
"Ful hertely, fair sisters al," quod she,   370
"Ye be right welcome into this countree.

I counsail you to take a litel rest
In my chambre, if it be your plesaunce.
Whan ye be there, me thinketh for the best
That I go in, and cal Perséveraunce,   375
Because she is oon of your aquaintaunce;
And she also wil tel you every thing
How ye shal be ruled of your coming."

My felawes al and I, by oon avyse,
Were wel agreed to do lyke as she sayd.   380
Than we began to dresse us in our gyse,
That folk shuld see we were nat unpurvayd;
And good wageours among us there we layd,
Which of us was atyred goodliest,
And of us al which shuld be praysed best.   385

The porter cam, and brought Perséveraunce;
She welcomed us in ful curteys manere:
"Think ye nat long," quod she, "your attendaunce;

---

358. frenshyp; mysse.   359. ease; payne.   360. A. telle me; Th.
T. take you.   361. Howe. A. whiche (*for* who). chamberlayne.   362.
worde certaine.   363. worde. A. T. suster.   365. stode.   366. echone.
368. one (*twice*).   369. A. forth com; Th. T. came forth. *I supply* lady.
370. fayre.   372. counsayle.   374. Th. thynketh; Th. A. thynke it.
376. A. oon; Th. T. *om.*   377. thinge.   378. Howe; cominge.   379.
one. A. Avise; Th. T. aduyse.   380. sayde.   381. T. wyse (*for* gyse).
382. folke. A. se; Th. T. say. vnpurueyde.   383. A. wageours; Th. T.
wagers. amonge; layde.   384. most goodlest (*read* goodliest); *see* 452.
385. whiche shulde. A. And whiche of vs al preysed shuld be best.   386.
came.   387. A. ful; T. Th. *om.* A. T. curteys; Th. curtyse.   388.
Thinke. Th. T. of your; A. *om.* of.

I wil go speke unto the herbergere,
That she may purvey for your logging here.   390
Than wil I go unto the chamberlayn
To speke for you, and come anon agayn."

And whan [that] she departed was and gon,
We saw folkës coming without the wal,
So greet people, that nombre coud we non;   395
Ladyes they were and gentilwomen al,
Clothed in blew, echon her word withal;
But for to knowe her word or her devyse,
They cam so thikke, that I might in no wyse.

With that anon cam in Perséveraunce,   400
And where I stood, she cam streight [un]to me.
"Ye been," quod she, "of myne olde acquaintaunce;
You to enquere, the bolder wolde I be;
What word they bere, eche after her degree,
I pray you, tel it me in secret wyse;   405
And I shal kepe it close, on warantyse."

"We been," quod I, "fyve ladies al in-fere,
And gentilwomen foure in company;
Whan they begin to open hir matere,
Than shal ye knowe hir wordës by and by;   410
But as for me, I have non verely,
And so I told Countenaunce here-before;
Al myne aray is blew; what nedeth more?"

"Now than," quod she, "I wol go in agayn,
That ye may have knowlege, what ye shuld do."   415
"In sooth," quod I, "if ye wold take the payn,
Ye did right moch for us, if ye did so.
The rather sped, the soner may we go.
Gret cost alway ther is in tarying;
And long to sewe, it is a wery thing."   420

---

389. A. herbergier; Th. herbigere.   390. A. may; Th. T. *om.* lodginge.
391. chamberlayne.   392. anone agayne.   393. *I supply* that.   394.
sawe; comynge.   395. great; coude; none.   397. echone; worde.
398. worde.   399. Th. T. I ne; A. we (*om.* ne).   400. anone came.
401. stode; came. *All* to.   404. worde.   405. A. pray yow; Th. T. you
pray.   secrete.   407. A. quod I fyve ladies; Th. fyue ladyes quod I.   409,
410. her.   412. tolde.   413. blewe.   414. A. in; Th. T. *om.*   415.
shulde.   416. soth; wolde; payne.   417. moche. T. wold (*for* 2nd did).
418. A. ye (*for* we).   419. Great; tarienge.   420. longe. A. sue. thynge.

Than parted she, and cam again anon;
"Ye must," quod she, "come to the chamberlayn."
"We been," quod I, "now redy everichon
To folowe you whan-ever ye list, certayn.
We have non eloquence, to tel you playn;   425
Beseching you we may be so excused,
Our trew mening, that it be not refused."

Than went we forth, after Perséveraunce,
To see the prees; it was a wonder cace;
There for to passe it was greet comb[e]raunce,   430
The people stood so thikke in every place.
"Now stand ye stil," quod she, "a litel space;
And for your ese somwhat I shal assay,
If I can make you any better way."

And forth she goth among hem everichon,   435
Making a way, that we might thorugh pas
More at our ese; and whan she had so don,
She beckned us to come where-as she was;
So after her we folowed, more and las.
She brought us streight unto the chamberlayn;   440
There left she us, and than she went agayn.

We salued her, as reson wolde it so,
Ful humb[el]ly beseching her goodnesse,
In our maters that we had for to do
That she wold be good lady and maistresse.   445
"Ye be welcome," quod she, "in sothfastnesse,
And see, what I can do you for to plese,
I am redy, that may be to your ese."

We folowed her unto the chambre-dore,
"Sisters," quod she, "come ye in after me."   450
But wite ye wel, there was a paved flore,
The goodliest that any wight might see;

421. came agayne anone.   422. -layne.   423. A. T. We bien quod I
now redy; Th. We be nowe redy quod I.   -one.   424. A. yow (for ye).
certayne.   425. playne.   426. Besechynge.   427. trewe meanynge.
428. wente.   429. se.   430. great combraunce (read comberaunce).
431. stode.   432. Nowe stande.   433. ease.   A. shal I.   435.
amonge; -one.   436. T. thorow; Th. thorugh; A. thurgh.   passe.   437.
ease; done.   438. T. beckenyd; Th. beckende.   A. there (for where).
440. -layne.   441. lefte.   442. T. salutyd.   reason.   443. Th. great;
T. gret; A. om. (after her).   444. A. matiers.   445. wolde.   447.
se; A. so.   please.   448. ease.   451. A. wite; Th. wete; T. wote.
452. se.

And furthermore, about than loked we
On eche corner, and upon every wal,
The which was mad of berel and cristal;   455

Wherein was graven of stories many oon;
First how Phyllis, of womanly pitè,
Deyd pitously, for love of Demophoon.
Nexte after was the story of Tisbee,
How she slew her-self under a tree.   460
Yet saw I more, how in right pitous cas
For Antony was slayn Cleopatras.

That other syde was, how Hawes the shene
Untrewly was disceyved in her bayn.
There was also Annelida the quene,   465
Upon Arcyte how sore she did complayn.
Al these stories were graved there, certayn;
And many mo than I reherce you here;
It were to long to tel you al in-fere.

And, bicause the wallës shone so bright,   470
With fyne umple they were al over-sprad,
To that intent, folk shuld nat hurte hir sight;
And thorugh it the stories might be rad.
Than furthermore I went, as I was lad;
And there I saw, without[en] any fayl,   475
A chayrë set, with ful riche aparayl.

And fyve stages it was set fro the ground,
Of cassidony ful curiously wrought;
With four pomelles of golde, and very round,
Set with saphyrs, as good as coud be thought;   480
That, wot ye what, if it were thorugh sought,
As I suppose, fro this countrey til Inde,
Another suche it were right fer to finde!

---

453. aboute.   454. A. eche a corn*er*.   455. A. The; Th. T. *om*.
made. A. berel; Th. Burel; T. byrall*e*.   456. one.   457. howe.
458. A. Deyd; Th. Dyed. Demophone.   459. Th. Tysbe; A. T. Thesbe.
460. slowe; -selfe.   461. sawe; howe.   Th. T. a right; A. *om*. a.
462. slayne.   463. Th. T. was Hawes the shene; A. was how Enclusene
(? *error for* Melusine).   464. A. Vntriewly was; Th. T. Ful vntrewly.
bayne.   466. howe; complayne.   467. certayne.   469. longe.   470.
shone (= shoon).   471. Th. A. vmple; T. vmpyll*e*.   472. folke
shulde.   473. Th. through; A. thurgh (= thorugh; *see* 436).   475. sawe.
All without. fayle.   476. aparayle.   477. grounde.   479. rounde.
480. coude.   481. wote. T. thorow; A. thurgh (= thorugh; Th. through
(*see* 473).   482. A. til; Th. T. to.   483. farre.

For, wite ye wel, I was right nere that,
So as I durst, beholding by and by;   485
Above ther was a riche cloth of estate,
Wrought with the nedle ful straungëly,
Her word thereon; and thus it said trewly,
A endurer, to tel you in wordës few,
With grete letters, the better I hem knew.   490

Thus as we stode, a dore opened anon;
A gentilwoman, semely of stature,
Beringe a mace, cam out, her-selfe aloon;
Sothly, me thought, a goodly crëature!
She spak nothing to lowde, I you ensure,   495
Nor hastily, but with goodly warning:
"Mak room," quod she, "my lady is coming!"

With that anon I saw Perséveraunce,
How she held up the tapet in her hand.
I saw also, in right good ordinaunce,   500
This greet lady within the tapet stand,
Coming outward, I wol ye understand;
And after her a noble company,
I coud nat tel the nombre sikerly.

Of their namës I wold nothing enquere   505
Further than suche as we wold sewe unto,
Sauf oo lady, which was the chauncellere,
Attemperaunce; sothly her name was so.
For us nedeth with her have moch to do
In our maters, and alway more and more.   510
And, so forth, to tel you furthermore,

Of this lady her beautè to discryve,
My conning is to simple, verely;
For never yet, the dayës of my lyve,

---

484. A. wite; Th. wete; T. wot.   487. T. nedyll*e*.   488. worde.
489. A. *endurer*; Th. T. *endure*. *All* you.   490. great; knewe.   491.
anone.   493. came; alone.   494. Sothely.   495. spake nothynge.
496. A. T. hastely; Th. hastely. warnynge.   497. A. roome; Th. T.
rome. comynge.   498. sawe.   499. helde; hande.   500. sawe.
A. goode; Th. T. goodly.   501. great; stande.   502. -stande.   504.
coude.   505. (*above*): T. Attemperaunce chaunclere. wolde.   506.
wolde. T. sew; A. sue.   507. A. Sauf oo; Th. Saue a.   508. sothely.
509. moche.   510. A. matiers. alwaye.   511. forthe.   513.
connynge.   514. A. dayes of al my.

So inly fair I have non seen, trewly.   515
In her estate, assured utterly,
There wanted naught, I dare you wel assure,
That longed to a goodly crëature.

And furthermore, to speke of her aray,
I shal you tel the maner of her gown ;   520
Of clothe of gold ful riche, it is no nay ;
The colour blew, of a right good fasoun ;
In tabard-wyse the slevës hanging doun ;
And what purfyl there was, and in what wyse,
So as I can, I shal it you devyse.   525

After a sort the coller and the vent,
Lyk as ermyne is mad in purfeling ;
With grete perlës, ful fyne and orient,
They were couchèd, al after oon worching,
With dyamonds in stede of powdering ;   530
The slevës and purfilles of assyse ;
They were [y-]mad [ful] lyke, in every wyse.

Aboute her nekke a sort of fair rubyes,
In whyte floures of right fyne enamayl ;
Upon her heed, set in the freshest wyse,   535
A cercle with gret balays of entayl ;
That, in ernest to speke, withouten fayl,
For yonge and olde, and every maner age,
It was a world to loke on her visage.

Thus coming forth, to sit in her estat,   540
In her presence we kneled down echon,
Presentinge up our billes, and, wot ye what,
Ful humb[el]ly she took hem, by on and on ;

515. fayre. A. none sene ; Th. sene none ; T. noon seen.   517. A. you ;
Th. T. om.   519-532. Missing in A.   520. gowne.   522. coloure
blewe. T. good ; Th. goodly. facyoun.   523. Th. taberde ; T. taberd.
T. doun ; Th. adowne.   526. sorte ; vente (T. vent).   527. T. ermyn ;
Th. Armyne. made ; purfelynge.   528. Th. great ; T. gret.   529.
one worchynge.   530. Th. diamondes ; T. dyamondes. powderynge.
531. T. purfyllys ; Th. purfel (!).   532. Both made lyke (!).   533.
sorte.   534. enamayle.   535. A. fresshest ; Th. T. fayrest.   536.
A. with ; Th. T. of. great ; entayle.   537. A. withouten ; Th. T. without.
fayle.   539. worlde. A. T. loke ; Th. loken.   540. comynge forthe ;
estate.   541. downe. A. eche on ; Th. T. euerychone.   542. A. T.
vp ; Th. om. wote.   543. toke ; one and one.

When we had don, than cam they al anon,
And did the same, eche after her manere,   545
Knelinge at ones, and rysinge al in-fere.

Whan this was don, and she set in her place,
The chamberlayn she did unto her cal;
And she, goodly coming til her a-pace,
Of her entent knowing nothing at al,   550
"Voyd bak the prees," quod she, "up to the wal;
Mak larger roum, but look ye do not tary,
And tak these billës to the secretary."

The chamberlayn did her commaundëment,
And cam agayn, as she was bid to do;   555
The secretary there being present,
The billës were delivered her also,
Not only ours, but many other mo.
Than the lady, with good advyce, agayn
Anon withal called her chamberlayn.   560

"We wol," quod she, "the first thing that ye do,
The secretary, make her come anon
With her billës; and thus we wil also,
In our presence she rede hem everichon,
That we may takë good advyce theron   565
Of the ladyes, that been of our counsayl;
Look this be don, withouten any fayl."

The chamberlayn, whan she wiste her entent,
Anon she did the secretary cal:
"Let your billës," quod she, "be here present,   570
My lady it wil." "Madame," quod she, "I shal."
"And in presence she wil ye rede hem al."
"With good wil; I am redy," quod she,
"At her plesure, whan she commaundeth me."

---

544. done; came; anone.   547. A. Whan; Th. T. And wha*n*.   done.
548. -layne.   549. A. til; T. to; Th. vnto.   551. Voyde backe;
preace.   552. Make. A. larger; Th. T. large. roume; loke.   553.
take; secretarye.   554. -layne.   555. came agayne.   556. -tarye.
558. onely.   559. agayne.   560. -layne.   562. Th. secretarye ye
do make come; A. T. secretary make hir come.   565. maye. A. avise;
T. auyse.   566. counsayle.   567. Loke; done; fayle.   568. A. The
chambrelayn whan she wist; Th. T. Whan the chamberlayne wyste of.   569.
-tarye.   571. A. *om.* it.   572. A. ye rede hem al; T. yow there cal (!);
Th. ye hem cal (!).   573. A. gode.

And upon that was mad an ordinaunce,   575
They that cam first, hir billës shuld be red.
Ful gentelly than sayd Perséveraunce,
"Resoun it wold that they were sonest sped."
Anon withal, upon a tapet spred,
The secretary layde.hem doun echon;   580
Our billës first she redde hem on by on.

The first lady, bering in her devyse
Sans que jamais, thus wroot she in her bil;
Complayning sore and in ful pitous wyse
Of promesse mad with faithful hert and wil   585
And so broken, ayenst al maner skil,
Without desert alwayes on her party;
In this mater desyring remedy.

Her next felawës word was in this wyse,
Une sanz chaungier; and thus she did complayn, 590
Though she had been guerdoned for her servyce,
Yet nothing lyke as she that took the payn;
Wherfore she coude in no wyse her restrayn,
But in this cas sewe until her presence,
As reson woldë, to have recompence.   595

So furthermore, to speke of other twayn,
Oon of hem wroot, after her fantasy,
Oncques puis lever; and, for to tel you plain,
Her complaynt was ful pitous, verely,
For, as she sayd, ther was gret reson why;   600
And, as I can remembre this matere,
I shal you tel the proces, al in-fere.

Her bil was mad, complayninge in her gyse,
That of her joy, her comfort and gladnesse
Was no suretee; for in no maner wyse   605

576. came. Th. shuld; A. T. to. T. red; A. Th. redde.   578. Rayson.
A. T. wold that; Th. wyl. spedde.   579. spredde.   580. -tarie; downe
echone.   581. T. rad. T. theym (=hem); Th. A. *om.* one by one.   582.
bearyng.   583. A. T. in; Th. on.   585. made.   587. deserte; partye.
588. A. matier. Th. T. a remedy; A. *om.* a.   589. A. next felawes word;
Th. T. next folowing her word.   590. A. Une; Th. T. Vng. T. saunz
chaunger. com̄playne.   592. toke; payne.   593. restrayne.   594.
case.   595. reason.   596. twayne.   597. wrote.   598. A. Oncques;
Th. Vncques; T. Vnques. playne.   599. A. grevous (*for* pitous).   600.
great reason.   601. A. And; Th. T. *om.*   602. processe.   603. made.
604. comforte.   605. Th. surete; A. suerte; T. seurte.

She fond therin no point of stablenesse,
Now il, now wel, out of al sikernesse;
Ful humbelly desyringe, of her grace,
Som remedy to shewe her in this cace.

Her felawe made her bil, and thus she sayd,   610
In playning wyse; there-as she loved best,
Whether she were wroth or wel apayd
She might nat see, whan [that] she wold faynest;
And wroth she was, in very ernest;
To tel her word, as ferforth as I wot,   615
Entierment vostre, right thus she wroot.

And upon that she made a greet request
With herte and wil, and al that might be don
As until her that might redresse it best;
For in her mind thus might she finde it sone,   620
The remedy of that, which was her boon;
Rehersing [that] that she had sayd before,
Beseching her it might be so no more.

And in lyk wyse as they had don before,
The gentilwomen of our company   625
Put up hir billës; and, for to tel you more,
Oon of hem wroot *cest sanz dire*, verily;
And her matere hool to specify,
With-in her bil she put it in wryting;
And what it sayd, ye shal have knowleching.   630

It sayd, god wot, and that ful pitously,
Lyke as she was disposed in her hert,
No misfortune that she took grevously;
Al oon to her it was, the joy and smert,
Somtyme no thank for al her good desert.   635

---

606. A. fonde; Th. T. sayd (!).   607. Nowe; wele.   608. Th. humbly;
A. humble (!); *read* humbelly. her high grace; A. *om.* high.   609. A. Som
remedy to chewe (!) in; Th. T. Soone to shewe her remedy in.   610. sayde.
611. playnynge.   612. wrothe. wele apayde.   613. se; wolde. *I supply*
that.   614. wrothe.   615. worde; wote.   616. wrote.   617.
great.   618. done.   620. mynde. A. thus; Th. T. there.   621.
whiche; boone.   622. Rehersynge. *I supply* that.   623. Besechynge.
624. lyke; done.   626. A. vp; Th. T. *om.*   627. One; wrote.   628.
hole. A. Of hir compleynt also the cause why; T. *om. this line.*   629.
writinge.   630. A. knowlachyng; Th. T. knowynge.   631. wote.
632. herte.   633. toke.   634. one. A. til. A. it; Th. T. *om.* smerte.
635. thanke; deserte.

Other comfort she wanted non coming,
And so used, it greved her nothing.

Desyringe her, and lowly béseching,
That she for her wold seke a better way,
As she that had ben, al her dayes living,   640
Stedfast and trew, and so wil be alway.
Of her felawe somwhat I shal you say,
Whos bil was red next after forth, withal;
And what•it ment rehersen you I shal.

En dieu est, she wroot in her devyse;   645
And thus she sayd, withouten any fayl,
Her trouthë might be taken in no wyse
Lyke as she thought, wherfore she had mervayl;
For trouth somtyme was wont to take avayl
In every matere; but al that is ago;   650
The more pitè, that it is suffred so.

Moch more there was, wherof she shuld complayn,
But she thought it to greet encomb[e]raunce
So moch to wryte; and therfore, in certayn,
In god and her she put her affiaunce   655
As in her worde is mad a remembraunce;
Beseching her that she wolde, in this cace,
Shewe unto her the favour of her grace.

The third, she wroot, rehersing her grevaunce,
Ye! wot ye what, a pitous thing to here;   660
For, as me thought, she felt gret displesaunce,
Oon might right wel perceyve it by her chere,
And no wonder; it sat her passing nere.
Yet loth she was to put it in wryting,
But nede wol have his cours in every thing.   665

---

636. comforte. A. wayted; Th. T. wanted. comynge.   637. -thynge.
638. besechynge.   639. A. T. for her wold; Th. wolde for her.   640.
A. al; Th. T. *om.* lyuynge. 641. trewe. A. so; Th. T. *om.* 642. saye.
643. nexte. A. after; Th. T. *om.* forthe. 645. *diu*; wrote. 646. A. any;
Th. T. *om.* fayle. 647. T. takyn; Th. A. take. 648. meruaile. 649.
auayle.   652. shulde.   653. great. *All* encombraunce.   654. moche.
655. Th. T. al her; A. *om.* al.   656. made.   659. wrote.   660. thinge.
661. felte great.   662. A. *om.* right.   663. sate; passynge.   664. lothe;
wrytynge. 665. A. his; T. a; Th. *om.* thinge.

* * *
* * * *   D d

Soyes en sure, this was her word, certayn,
And thus she wroot, but in a litel space;
There she lovëd, her labour was in vayn,
For he was set al in another place;
Ful humblely desyring, in that cace,   670
Som good comfort, her sorow to appese,
That she might livë more at hertes ese.

The fourth surely, me thought, she liked wele,
As in her porte and in her behaving;
And *Bien moneste*, as fer as I coud fele,   675
That was her word, til her wel belonging.
Wherfore to her she prayed, above al thing,
Ful hertely (to say you in substaunce)
That she wold sende her good continuaunce.

"Ye have rehersed me these billës al,   680
But now, let see somwhat of your entent."
"It may so hap, paraventure, ye shal.
Now I pray you, whyle I am here present,
Ye shal, pardè, have knowlege, what I ment.
But thus I say in trouthe, and make no fable,   685
The case itself is inly lamentable.

And wel I wot, that ye wol think the same,
Lyke as I say, whan ye have herd my bil."
"Now good, tel on, I hate you, by saynt Jame!"
"Abyde a whyle; it is nat yet my wil.   690
Yet must ye wite, by reson and by skil,
Sith ye know al that hath be don before:—"
And thus it sayd, without[en] wordes more.

"Nothing so leef as deth to come to me
For fynal ende of my sorowes and payn;   695
What shulde I more desyre, as semë ye?

---

666. A. *Se iour* (for *Soyes*).   worde certayne.   667. wrote.   A. but; Th.
T. *om*.   668. vayne.   670. Th. T. humbly; A. humble (!); *see* 607.
desyrynge.   671. comforte; sorowe.   672. ease.   675. Th. *moneste*;
T. A. *monest*. farre; coude.   676. worde.   678. T. tell (*for* say).
679. wolde.   681. lete se.   683. Nowe.   684. A. T. parde have
knowlache; Th. haue knowlege parde.   686. selfe.   687. wote. A. that;
Th. T. *om*. thinke.   688. herde.   689. Nowe. *All* hate (=hote).   691.
A. wite; Th. T. wete.   reason.   692. A. knowe al that hath be done afore;
Th. T. haue knowlege of that was done before.   693. A. it; Th. T. it is
(*om*. is). *All* without. A. any (*for* wordes).   694. Nothynge. A. lief; T.
leef; Th. lefe.   dethe.   695. payne.

And ye knewe al aforn it for certayn,
I wot ye wolde; and, for to tel you playn,
Without her help that hath al thing in cure
I can nat think that I may longe endure.   700

As for my trouthe, it hath be proved wele,
To say the sothe, I can [you] say no more,
Of ful long tyme, and suffred every dele
In pacience, and kepe it al in store;
Of her goodnesse besechinge her therfore   705
That I might have my thank in suche [a] wyse
As my desert deserveth of justyse."

Whan these billës were rad everichon,
This lady took a good advysement;
And hem to answere, ech by on and on,   710
She thought it was to moche in her entent;
Wherfore she yaf hem in commaundëment,
In her presence to come, bothe oon and al,
To yeve hem there her answer general.

What did she than, suppose ye verely?   715
She spak herself, and sayd in this manere,
"We have wel seen your billës by and by,
And some of hem ful pitous for to here.
We wol therfore ye knowe al this in-fere,
Within short tyme our court of parliment   720
Here shal be holde, in our palays present;

And in al this wherin ye find you greved,
Ther shal ye finde an open remedy
In suche [a] wyse, as ye shul be releved
Of al that ye reherce here, thoroughly.   725
As for the date, ye shul know verily,
That ye may have a space in your coming;
For Diligence shal it tel you by wryting."

697. aforne; certayne.   698. wote.   699. helpe; thinge.   700.
thinke. T. I; Th. A. it.   702. *I supply* you.   703. longe.   706. thanke.
I supply a.   707. deserte. A. deser*v*ith; Th. T. serueth.   708.
-one.   709. A. This lady; Th. T. The ladyes. toke.   710. A. ech;
Th. T. *om.*   712. A. yaf; Th. T. yaue.   T. in; Th. A. *om.*   713. one.
714. A. hem there hir answere; Th. T. hem her answere in.   716. spake;
-selfe.   717. sene.   718. A. T. ful; Th. *om.*   720. shorte; courte.   721.
A. T. paleys.   722. fynde.   724. *I supply* a. A. shul; Th. T. shal.   725.
T. thoroughly; Th. throughly; A. triewly.   726. shal (*see* 724); knowe.
728. *So* Th.; A. shal bryng it yow bi; T. shall hyt yow tell by.

We thanked her in our most humble wyse,
Our felauship, echon by oon assent,   730
Submitting us lowly til her servyse.
For, as we thought, we had our travayl spent
In suche [a] wyse as we helde us content.
Than eche of us took other by the sleve,
And forth withal, as we shuld take our leve.   735

Al sodainly the water sprang anon
In my visage, and therwithal I wook :—
"Where am I now?" thought I; "al this is gon;"
And al amased, up I gan to look.
With that, anon I went and made this book,   740
Thus simpely rehersing the substaunce,
Bicause it shuld not out of remembraunce.'—

'Now verily, your dreem is passing good,
And worthy to be had in rémembraunce ;
For, though I stande here as longe as I stood,   745
It shuld to me be non encomb[e]raunce ;
I took therin so inly greet plesaunce.
But tel me now, what ye the book do cal?
For I must wite.' 'With right good wil ye shal :

As for this book, to say you very right,   750
And of the name to tel the certeyntè,
L'ASSEMBLÈ DE DAMES, thus it hight ;
How think ye?' 'That the name is good, pardè !'
'Now go, farwel ! for they cal after me,
My felawes al, and I must after sone ;   755
Rede wel my dreem ; for now my tale is doon.'

Here endeth the Book of Assemble de Damys.

729. moste.   730. eche one by one.   732. A. vs (*for* 1*st* we).   trauayle.
733. *I supply* a.   734. toke.   735. forthe; shulde.   736. sprange
anone.   737. woke.   738. nowe; gone.   739. A. Al amased vp;
Th. T. Al mased and vp (*read* And al amased up). loke.   740. boke.   741.
All simply.   742. shulde. Th. T. be out; A. out (*om.* be).   743.
Nowe; dreame.   745. stode.   746. shulde; none. *All* encombraunce.
747. toke; great.   748. nowe; boke.   749. A. wite; Th. T. wete.
750. boke.   751. *So* A. ; Th. T. Of the name to tel you in certaynte (T.
certayn).   752. A. La semble ; T. Lassembyll.   753. Howe thynke. A.
the ; Th. T. *om.*   754. Nowe.   756. dreme ; done. COLOPHON : *in* T. *only.*

XXII. A GOODLY BALADE.

——◆◆——

¶ **M**ODER of norture, best beloved of al,
    And fresshest flour, to whom good thrift god sende.
Your child, if it list you me so to cal,
Al be I unable my-self so to pretende,
To your discrecioun I recommende   5
Myn herte and al, with every circumstaunce,
Al hoolly to be under your governaunce.

Most desyre I, and have, and ever shal
Thing, whiche might your hertës ese amende;
Have me excused, my power is but smal;   10
Natheles, of right ye ought[e] to commende
My good[e] will, which fayn wolde entende
To do you service; for al my suffisaunce
Is hoolly to be under your governaunce.

Meulx un: in herte, which never shal apal,   15
Ay fresshe and newe, and right glad to dispende
My tyme in your servyce, what-so befal,
Beseching your excéllence to defende
My simplenesse, if ignoraunce offende
In any wyse; sith that myn affiaunce   20
Is hoolly to be under your governaunce.

From Th. (Thynne's ed. 1532).   TITLE. A goodly balade of Chaucer.
I note here rejected spellings.   3. childe; lust.   4. selfe.   5. discrecion;
recomende.   7. holy.   9. ease.   10. small.   11. Nathelesse; ought.
12. good; whiche fayne.   14. holy.   17. befall.   20. sythe.
21. holy; ben.

¶ Daisy of light! very ground of comfort!
The sonnes doughter ye hight, as I rede;
For when he westreth, farwel your disport!
By your nature anon, right for pure drede   25
Of the rude night, that with his boystous wede
Of derkness shadoweth our emispere,
Than closen ye, my lyves lady dere!

Dawing the day to his kinde resort,
Phebus your fader, with his stremes rede,   30
Adorneth the morow, cónsuming the sort
Of misty cloudës, that wolde overlede
Trewe humble hertës with hir mistihede,
Nere comfort a-dayes, whan eyën clere
Disclose and sprede my lyves lady dere.   35

[*A stanza lost; lines* 36–42.]

¶ *Je vouldray* :—but [the] gret[e] god disposeth
And maketh casuel by his providence
Such thing as mannës frelë wit purposeth;   45
Al for the best, if that our conscience
Nat grucche it, but in humble pacience
It receyve; for god saith, without[e] fable,
A faithful hertë ever is acceptáble.

Cautels who useth gladly, gloseth;   50
To eschewe suche it is right high prudence;
What ye said[e] onës, [now] myn herte opposeth,
"That my wryting japës, in your absence,
Plesed you moche bet than my presence!"
Yet can I more, ye be nat excusáble;   55
A faithful hertë ever is acceptáble.

Quaketh my penne; my spirit supposeth
That in my wryting ye finde wol som offence;
Myn herte welkeneth thus sone, anon it †roseth;
Now hot, now cold, and eft in [al] fervence;   60

---

22. grounde; comforte.   24. disporte.   27. derkenesse.   29. resorte.
30. And Phebus (*I omit* And); father.   31. morowe; sorte.   32. wolden.
34. comforte.   43. great (*read* the grete).   45. Suche; mans (*read*
mannes); witte.   47. grutche.   48. *Read* Receyve it (?); saythe withoute.
52. sayd; *I supply* now.   53. *Read* wryting of iapes (?).   54. Pleased;
better (*read* bet).   58. *Omit* wol (?); some.   59. ryseth (!); *read*
roseth.   60. Nowe hotte, nowe colde; efte; *I supply* al.

That mis is, is caused of negligence
And not of malice; therfor beth merciable;
A faithful hertë ever is acceptáble.

Lenvoy.

¶ Forth, complaynt! forth, lakking eloquence,
 Forth, litel lettre, of endyting lame!   65
 I have besought my ladies sapience
 Of thy behalfe, to accept in game
 Thyn inabilitee; do thou the same!
 Abyd! have more yet; *Je serve Jonesse.*
 Now forth; I close thee, in holy Venus name; 70
 Thee shal unclose my hertes governeresse.

Finis.

---

61. mysse.   62. therfore bethe.   64. *Headed* Lenuoye.   Forthe;
forthe lackyng.   65. Forthe.   68. inabylite.   69. Iouesse.
70. Nowe; the.   71. The.

XXIII. GO FORTH, KING.

REX sine sapiencia: Episcopus sine doctrina.
Dominus sine consilio: Mulier sine castitate.
Miles sine probitate: Iudex sine Iusticia.
Diues sine elemosina: Populus sine lege.
Senex sine religione: Seruus sine timore.
Pauper superbus: Adolescens sine obediencia.

GO forth, king, rule thee by sapience;
   Bishop, be able to minister doctryne;
Lord, to trew consayl yeve audience;
Womanheed, to chastitè ever enclyne;
Knight, let thy dedes worship determyne;   5
Be rightwis, jugè, in saving thy name;
Rich, do almesse, lest thou lese blis with shame.

People, obey your king and the lawe;
Age, be thou ruled by good religioun;
Trew servant, be dredful, and keep thee under awe,   10
And thou, povre, fy on presumpcioun;
Inobedience to youth is utter distruccioun;
Remembre you how god hath set you, lo!
And do your part, as ye be ordained to.

From Th. (Thynne, ed. 1532); *I give rejected spellings.*   1. forthe; the.
2. Bishoppe.   3. Lorde; trewe counsayle.   4. Womanhede.   5. lette.
6. rightous (*read* rightwis); iuge.   7. blysse.   9. relygion.   10.
Trewe; dredeful; kepe.   11. poore; presumption.   12. distruction.
13. howe.   14. parte.

XXIV. THE COURT OF LOVE.

——••——

WITH timerous hert and trembling hand of drede,
    Of cunning naked, bare of eloquence,
Unto the flour of port in womanhede
I write, as he that non intelligence
Of metres hath, ne floures of sentence ;   5
Sauf that me list my writing to convey,
In that I can to please her hygh nobley.

The blosmes fresshe of Tullius garden soote
Present thaim not, my mater for to borne :
Poemes of Virgil taken here no rote,   10
Ne crafte of Galfrid may not here sojorne :
Why nam I cunning? O well may I morne,
For lak of science that I can-not write
Unto the princes of my life a-right

No termes digne unto her excellence,   15
So is she sprong of noble stirpe and high :
A world of honour and of reverence
There is in her, this wil I testifie.
Calliope, thou sister wise and sly,
And thou, Minerva, guyde me with thy grace,   20
That langage rude my mater not deface.

Thy suger-dropes swete of Elicon
Distill in me, thou gentle Muse, I pray ;
And thee, Melpomene, I calle anon,
Of ignoraunce the mist to chace away ;   25
And give me grace so for to write and sey,

From MS. Trin. R. 3. 19, fol. 128 ; *collated with the print of the same in*
(S.) Stowe's *edition* (1561). *I note some rejected readings of the* MS.   1.
tyme*ros* ; tremlyng.   3. poort.   4. none.   9. matere.   10. Poemys ;
Virgile.   11. Galfride.   15. termys.   17. honoure.   18. wille ;
S. wil.   19, 20, 23. thowe.   24. the ; anone.   25. miste.

That she, my lady, of her worthinesse,
Accepte in gree this litel short tretesse,

That is entitled thus, 'THE COURT OF LOVE.'
And ye that ben metriciens me excuse,   30
I you besech, for Venus sake above;
For what I mene in this ye need not muse:
And if so be my lady it refuse
For lak of ornat speche, I wold be wo,
That I presume to her to writen so.   35

But myn entent and all my besy cure
Is for to write this tretesse, as I can,
Unto my lady, stable, true, and sure,
Feithfull and kind, sith first that she began
Me to accept in service as her man: 40
To her be all the plesure of this boke,
That, whan her like, she may it rede and loke.

WHEN I was yong, at eighteen yere of age,
    Lusty and light, desirous of pleasaunce,
Approching on full sadde and ripe corage,   45
Love arted me to do myn observaunce
To his astate, and doon him obeysaunce,
Commaunding me the Court of Love to see,
A lite beside the mount of Citharee,

There Citherea goddesse was and quene   50
Honoured highly for her majestee;
And eke her sone, the mighty god, I wene,
Cupid the blind, that for his dignitee
A thousand lovers worship on their knee;
There was I bid, on pain of death, t'apere,   55
By Mercury, the winged messengere.

So than I went by straunge and fer contrees,
Enquiring ay what costes †to it drew,
The Court of Love: and thiderward, as bees,
At last I sey the peple gan pursue: 60
Anon, me thought, som wight was there that knew
Where that the court was holden, ferre or ny,
And after thaim ful fast I gan me hy.

---

28. litill.   29. courte.   30. bene.   31. beseche.   32. whate; nede.
34. woo.   35. soo.   36. myne.   39. kynde.   41. pleasure.
48. courte.   49. mounte.   51. maiestie.   52. sonne.   53. Cupyde;
blynde; dignyte.   54. theire kne.   55. bidde; S. bid. in (*read* on).
to pere (*read* tapere).   56. Marcury.   57. be; S. by. ferre.   58. whate;
that it drewe (*read* to it drew).   59. courte.   60. se (*read* sey).   61.
knewe.   62. courte; nye.   63. fulle faste; hie.

Anone as I theim overtook, I said,
'Hail, frendes! whider purpose ye to wend?' 65
'Forsooth,' quod oon that answered lich a maid,
'To Loves Court now go we, gentill frend.'
'Where is that place,' quod I, 'my felowe hend?'
'At Citheron, sir,' seid he, 'without dowte,
The King of Love, and all his noble rowte, 70

Dwelling within a castell ryally.'
So than apace I jorned forth among,
And as he seid, so fond I there truly.
For I beheld the towres high and strong,
And high pinácles, large of hight and long, 75
With plate of gold bespred on every side,
And presious stones, the stone-werk for to hide.

No saphir ind, no rubè riche of price,
There lakked than, nor emeraud so grene,
Baleis Turkeis, ne thing to my devise, 80
That may the castell maken for to shene:
All was as bright as sterres in winter been;
And Phebus shoon, to make his pees agayn,
For trespas doon to high estates tweyn,

Venus and Mars, the god and goddesse clere, 85
Whan he theim found in armes cheined fast:
Venus was then full sad of herte and chere.
But Phebus bemes, streight as is the mast,
Upon the castell ginneth he to cast,
To plese the lady, princesse of that place, 90
In signe he loketh aftir Loves grace.

For there,nis god in heven or helle, y-wis,
But he hath ben right soget unto Love:
Jove, Pluto, or what-so-ever he is,
Ne creature in erth, or yet above; 95
Of thise the révers may no wight approve.
But furthermore, the castell to descry,
Yet saw I never non so large and high.

For unto heven it streccheth, I suppose,
Within and out depeynted wonderly, 100

---

64. overtoke; seide.   65. Haile; wende.   66. Forsothe; one; mayde.
67. courte nowe goo.   71. withynne.   74. behelde.   76. bespredde.
77. stone; S. stones. werke.   79. thanne; emerawde.   80. Bales turkes.
82. bene.   83. shone; pease.   84. trespace; tweyne.   86. founde; faste.
87. harte.   88. maste.   89. gynith; S. ginneth.   90. please.   94.
whate.   97. discrive; S. descrie.   98. sawe; none.   100. Withynne;
oute.

With many a thousand daisy, rede as rose,
And white also, this saw I verily:
But what tho daises might do signify,
Can I not tell, sauf that the quenes flour
Alceste it was that kept there her sojour;   105

Which under Venus lady was and quene,
And Admete king and soverain of that place,
To whom obeyed the ladies gode ninetene,
With many a thowsand other, bright of face.
And yong men fele came forth with lusty pace,   110
And aged eke, their homage to dispose;
But what thay were, I coud not well disclose.

Yet ner and ner furth in I gan me dresse
Into an halle of noble apparaile,
With arras spred and cloth of gold, I gesse,   115
And other silk of esier availe:
Under the cloth of their estate, saunz faile,
The king and quene ther sat, as I beheld:
It passed joye of Helisee the feld.

There saintes have their comming and resort,   120
To seen the king so ryally beseyn,
In purple clad, and eke the quene in sort:
And on their hedes saw I crownes tweyn,
With stones fret, so that it was no payn,
Withouten mete and drink, to stand and see   125
The kinges honour and the ryaltee.

And for to trete of states with the king,
That been of councell chief, and with the quene,
The king had Daunger ner to him standing,
The Quene of Love, Disdain, and that was seen: 130
For by the feith I shall to god, I wene,
Was never straunger [non] in her degree
Than was the quene in casting of her ee.

And as I stood perceiving her apart,
And eke the bemes shyning of her yen,   135
Me thought thay were shapen lich a dart,
Sherp and persing, smale, and streight as lyne.
And all her here, it shoon as gold so fyne,

---

102. sawe; verely.   103. whate; deyses; signifie.   104. floure.
105. yit; S. it. kepte; soioure.   108. obeide.   111, 117. theire.
112. whate; cowde.   113. nere (*twice*).   116. silke.   119. Helise.
121. beseen.   123. theire; sawe; twayn.   124. frett; payne.   125.
drynke.   126. ryaltie; S. rialtee.   128. bene.   129. nere.   130.
disdeyne.   132. *I supply* non.   133. ye; S. eye.   134. stode.
136. shapyn liche; darte.   137. Sherpe.   138. shone.

Dishevel, crisp, down hinging at her bak
A yarde in length : and soothly than I spak :— 140

'O bright Regina, who made thee so fair?
Who made thy colour vermelet and white?
Where woneth that god? how fer above the eyr?
Greet was his craft, and greet was his delyt.
Now marvel I nothing that ye do hight 145
The Quene of Love, and occupy the place
Of Citharee : now, sweet lady, thy grace.'

In mewet spak I, so that nought astert,
By no condicion, word that might be herd;
B[ut] in myn inward thought I gan advert, 150
And oft I seid, 'My wit is dulle and hard :'
For with her bewtee, thus, god wot, I ferd
As doth the man y-ravisshed with sight,
When I beheld her cristall yen so bright,

No respect having what was best to doon; 155
Till right anon, beholding here and there,
I spied a frend of myne, and that full soon,
A gentilwoman, was the chamberer
Unto the quene, that hote, as ye shall here,
Philobone, that lovëd all her life : 160
Whan she me sey, she led me furth as blyfe;

And me demaunded how and in what wise
I thider com, and what myne erand was?
'To seen the court,' quod I, 'and all the guyse;
And eke to sue for pardon and for grace, 165
And mercy ask for all my greet trespace,
That I non erst com to the Court of Love :
Foryeve me this, ye goddes all above!'

'That is well seid,' quod Philobone, 'in-dede :
But were ye not assomoned to apere 170
By Mercury? For that is all my drede.'
'Yes, gentil fair,' quod I, 'now am I here;
Ye, yit what tho, though that be true, my dere?'
'Of your free will ye shuld have come unsent :
For ye did not, I deme ye will be shent. 175

---

139. Disshivill crispe downe.   140. southly; spake.   141. the; faire.
143. weneth (S. wōneth).   howe; eyre.   144. Grete; crafte; grete; delite.
146. occupie.   147. Cithare; nowe swete.   148. spake.   149. worde;
harde.   150. myne; aduerte.   151. witte; harde.   152. bewtie; ferde.
154. Whenne.   155. whate.   157. sone.   162. howe; whate.   163.
come; whate.   164. sene; Courte.   166. aske; grete.   167. none;
come; courte.   171. Mercurius (see l. 56).   172. gentill feire; nowe.
173. whate thowe; S. what tho (i. e. then).   174. youre fre wille.   175.
dide; wille.

For ye that reign in youth and lustinesse,
Pampired with ese, and †jolif in your age,
Your dewtee is, as fer as I can gesse,
To Loves Court to dressen your viage,
As sone as Nature maketh you so sage,   180
That ye may know a woman from a swan,
Or whan your foot is growen half a span.

But sith that ye, by wilful necligence,
This eighteen yere have kept yourself at large,
The gretter is your trespace and offence,   185
And in your nek ye moot bere all the charge:
For better were ye ben withouten barge,
Amiddë see, in tempest and in rain,
Than byden here, receiving woo and pain,

That ordeined is for such as thaim absent   190
Fro Loves Court by yeres long and fele.
I ley my lyf ye shall full soon repent;
For Love will reyve your colour, lust, and hele:
Eke ye must bait on many an hevy mele:
No force, y-wis, I stired you long agoon   195
To draw to court,' quod litell Philobon.

'Ye shall well see how rough and angry face
The King of Love will shew, when ye him see;
By myn advyse kneel down and ask him grace,
Eschewing perell and adversitee;   200
For well I wot it wol non other be,
Comfort is non, ne counsel to your ese;
Why will ye than the King of Love displese?'

'O mercy, god,' quod ich, 'I me repent,
Caitif and wrecche in hert, in wille, and thought!   205
And aftir this shall be myne hole entent
To serve and plese, how dere that love be bought:
Yit, sith I have myn own penaunce y-sought,
With humble spirit shall I it receive,
Though that the King of Love my life bereyve.   210

---

176. reigne.   177. ease.   ioylof; S. ialous (*read* iolif).   178. Youre
dewtie; ferre; canne.   179. courte; youre.   181. knowe.   182.
whanne youre fote; spanne.   183. be (*for* by); wilfull.   184. kepte
youre.   185. youre (*often*).   186. motte.   188. S. Amidde the
sea. rayne.   189. That (!); S. Then. payne.   190. suche; absente.
191. courte.   192. sone.   193. wille; youre coloure.   194. most
bayte.   195. agoone.   196. drawe; Courte.   197. se howe rowhe (S.
rough).   198. shewe; se.   199. myne; knele downe; aske.   201. welle;
wolle none.   202. Comforte; none; councell; youre ease.   203. wille;
thanne.   204. Iche.   207. please howe.   208. myne owen.   209. sprite.

And though that fervent loves qualitè
In me did never worch truly, yit I
With all obeisaunce and humilitè,
And benign hert, shall serve him til I dye :
And he that Lord of †might is, grete and highe,　　215
Right as him list me chastice and correct,
And punish me, with trespace thus enfect.'

Thise wordes seid, she caught me by the lap,
And led me furth intill a temple round,
Large and wyde : and, as my blessed hap　　220
And good avénture was, right sone I found
A tabernacle reised from the ground,
Where Venus sat, and Cupid by her syde ;
Yet half for drede I gan my visage hyde.

And eft again I loked and beheld,　　225
Seeing full sundry peple in the place,
And mister folk, and som that might not weld
Their limmes well, me thought a wonder cas ;
The temple shoon with windows all of glas,
Bright as the day, with many a fair image ;　　230
And there I sey the fresh quene of Cartage,

Dido, that brent her bewtee for the love
Of fals Eneas ; and the weymenting
Of hir, Anelida, true as turtill-dove,
To Arcite fals : and there was in peinting　　235
Of many a prince, and many a doughty king,
Whose marterdom was shewed about the walles ;
And how that fele for love had suffered falles.

But sore I was abasshed and astonied
Of all tho folk that there were in that tyde ;　　240
And than I asked where thay had [y-]woned :
'In dyvers courtes,' quod she, 'here besyde.'
In sondry clothing, mantil-wyse full wyde,
They were arrayed, and did their sacrifice
Unto the god and goddesse in their guyse.　　245

'†Lo ! yonder folk,' quod she, 'that knele in blew,
They were the colour ay, and ever shall,

---

211. the ; S. that.　212. worche.　214. benigne harte.　215. myghtes
(*read* might is).　216. lyste ; correcte.　217. punyssh ; enfecte.　221.
gode ; founde.　222. grounde.　223. cupide.　225. behild ; S.
behelde.　226. Seyng.　227. folke ; wild (S. welde).　228. Theire ; wele ;
case.　229. shone ; wyndowes ; glasse.　230. feire.　231. fressh.
232. bewtie.　235. penytyng (!).　237. aboute.　238. howe ; feale.
239. stonyed ; S. astonied.　240. thoo folke.　241. hade.　244, 245.
theire.　246. To (!) ; *read* Lo ; folke ; blewe.　247. coloure.

In sign they were, and ever will be trew
Withouten chaunge : and sothly, yonder all
That ben in blak, with morning cry and call   250
Unto the goddes, for their loves been
Som fer, som dede, som all to sherpe and kene.'

'Ye, than,' quod I, 'what doon thise prestes here,
Nonnes and hermits, freres, and all thoo
That sit in white, in russet, and in grene?'   255
'For-soth,' quod she, 'they wailen of their wo.'
'O mercy, lord! may thay so come and go
Freely to court, and have such libertee?'
'Ye, men of ech condicion and degree,

And women eke: for truly, there is non   260
Excepcion mad, ne never was ne may :
This court is ope and free for everichon,
The King of Love he will nat say thaim nay :
He taketh all, in poore or riche array,
That meekly sewe unto his excellence   265
With all their herte and all their reverence.'

And, walking thus about with Philobone,
I sey where cam a messenger in hy
Streight from the king, which let commaund anon,
Through-out the court to make an ho and cry :   270
'A! new-come folk, abyde! and wot ye why?
The kinges lust is for to seen you soon :
Com ner, let see! his will mot need be doon.'

Than gan I me present to-fore the king,
Trembling for fere, with visage pale of hew,   275
And many a lover with me was kneling,
Abasshed sore, till unto tyme thay knew
The sentence yeve of his entent full trew :
And at the last the king hath me behold
With stern visage, and seid, 'What doth this old,   280

Thus fer y-stope in yeres, come so late
Unto the court?' 'For-soth, my liege,' quod I,
'An hundred tyme I have ben at the gate

---

248. signe.   249. southly.   250. calle.   251. bene.   252. ferre ;
sherpe.   253. whate done.   254. hermytes.   256. theire woo.   257. goo.
258. Frely ; suche libertie.   259. eche.   260. none.   261. made.
262. courte ; fre ; euerichone.   263. wille.   264. arraye.   265. mekely.
266. theire harte.   267. aboute.   268. se ; come ; high (S. hie).   269.
commaunde.   270. -oute ; courte ; crye.   271. newe ; wote ; whye.
272. luste ; youe sone.   273. Come nere ; se ; wille mote nede ; done.
275. Tremelyng (S. Trembling) ; hewe.   277. unto the tyme (om. the) ;
knewe.   278. yove (S. yeue) ; trewe.   279. laste.   280. sterne ; whate.
281. ferre.   282. courte.

Afore this tyme, yit coud I never espy
Of myn acqueyntaunce any with mine y ;   285
And shamefastnes away me gan to chace ;
But now I me submit unto your grace.'

'Well ! all is perdoned, with condicion
That thou be trew from hensforth to thy might,
And serven Love in thyn entencion :   290
Swere this, and than, as fer as it is right,
Thou shalt have grace here in my quenes sight.'
'Yis, by the feith I ow your crown, I swere,
Though Deth therfore me thirlith with his spere !'

And whan the king had seen us everichoon,   295
He let commaunde an officer in hy
To take our feith, and shew us, oon by oon,
The statuts of the court full besily.
Anon the book was leid before their y,
To rede and see what thing we must observe   300
In Loves Court, till that we dye and sterve.

A ND, for that I was lettred, there I red
     The statuts hole of Loves Court and hall :
The *first* statut that on the boke was spred,
Was, To be true in thought and dedes all   305
Unto the King of Love, the Lord ryall ;
And to the Quene, as feithful and as kind,
As I coud think with herte, and will and mind.

The *secund* statut, Secretly to kepe
Councell of love, nat blowing every-where   310
All that I know, and let it sink †or flete ;
It may not sown in every wightes ere :
Exyling slaunder ay for dred and fere,
And to my lady, which I love and serve,
Be true and kind, her grace for to deserve.   315

The *thrid* statut was clerely write also,
Withouten chaunge to live and dye the same,
Non other love to take, for wele ne wo,

284. coude ; espye.   285. myne ; eny ; myne ye.   286. gane.   287.
nowe ; submytte.   289. thowe ; trewe.   290. seruen (!) ; thyne.   291.
thanne.   292. Thowe shalte.   293. owe youre crowne.   295. sene ;
eueryghone.   296. hie.   297. oure ; shewe ; one by one.   298.
statutis ; courte.   299. boke ; leide ; her (S. their) ; ye.   300. se whate ;
most.   301. courte.   302. redde.   303. statutis ; courte ; halle.   304.
firste statute.   307. kynde.   308. coude thynke ; harte ; wille ; mynde.   309.
secunde statute secretely.   311. knowe ; and (*read* or).   312. sowne.   315.
kynde.   316. thridde statute.   317. *om.* the (*supplied in* S.).   318.
None ; woo.

      * * *
    * * * *   E e

For brind delyt, for ernest nor for game:
Without repent, for laughing or for grame,
To byden still in full perseveraunce:
Al this was hole the kinges ordinaunce.

The *fourth* statut, To purchace ever to here,
And stiren folk to love, and beten fyr
On Venus awter, here about and there,
And preche to thaim of love and hot desyr,
And tell how love will quyten well their hire:
This must be kept; and loth me to displese:
If love be wroth, passe forby is an ese.

The *fifth* statut, Not to be daungerous,
If that a thought wold reyve me of my slepe:
Nor of a sight to be over squeymous;
And so, verily, this statut was to kepe,
To turne and walowe in my bed and wepe,
When that my lady, of her crueltè,
Wold from her herte exylen all pitè.

The *sixt* statut, it was for me to use,
Alone to wander, voide of company,
And on my ladys bewtee for to muse,
And to think [it] no force to live or dye;
And eft again to think the remedy,
How to her grace I might anon attain,
And tell my wo unto my souverain.

The *seventh* statut was, To be pacient,
Whether my lady joyfull were or wroth;
For wordes glad or hevy, diligent,
Wheder that she me helden lefe or loth:
And hereupon I put was to myn oth,
Her for to serve, and lowly to obey,
Shewing my chere, ye, twenty sith a-day.

The *eighth* statut, to my rememb[e]raunce,
Was, To speke, and pray my lady dere,
With hourly labour and gret attendaunce,
Me for to love with all her herte entere,
And me desyre, and make me joyfull chere,

320

325

330

335

340

345

350

355

319. brynde delite. 320. Withoute. 323. statute. 324. folke; fire.
325. aboute. 326. hote desire. 327. howe. 328. kepte; displease.
329. ease. 330. statute. 332. squymouse. 333. veryeuly (S. verely);
statute. 335. crueltie. 336. harte exilyn. 337. statute. 339.
bewtie. 340. thinke; *I supply* it. 341. thynke. 342. Howe.
343. woo. 344. statute. 347. helden (*sic*). 348. othe. 350.
And shewing (*om.* And). 351. statute. 353. hourely laboure; grete
attendaunce (S. entteɴdaunce). 354. harte entier.

Right as she is, surmounting every faire,
Of bewtie well, and gentill debonaire.

The *ninth* statut, with lettres writ of gold,
This was the sentence, How that I and all
Shuld ever dred to be to over-bold   360
Her to displese ; and truly, so I shall ;
But ben content for thing[es] that may falle,
And meekly take her chastisement and yerd,
And to offende her ever ben aferd.

The *tenth* statut was, Egally discern   365
By-twene thy lady and thyn abilitee,
And think, thy-self art never like to yern,
By right, her mercy, nor of equitee,
But of her grace and womanly pitee :
For though thy-self be noble in thy strene,   370
A thowsand-fold more nobill is thy quene,

Thy lyves lady, and thy souverayn,
That hath thyn herte all hole in governaunce.
Thou mayst no wyse hit taken to disdayn,
To put thee humbly at her ordinaunce,   375
And give her free the rein of her plesaunce ;
For libertee is thing that women loke,
And truly, els the mater is a-croke.

The *eleventh* statut, Thy signes for to †con
With y and finger, and with smyles soft,   380
And low to cough, and alway for to shon,
For dred of spyes, for to winken oft :
But secretly to bring a sigh a-loft,
And eke beware of over-moch resort ;
For that, paraventure, spilleth al thy sport.   385

The *twelfth* statut remember to observe :
For al the pain thow hast for love and wo,
All is to lite her mercy to deserve,
Thow must then think, where-ever thou ryde or go ;
And mortall woundes suffer thow also,   390
All for her sake, and thinke it well beset
Upon thy love, for it may be no bet.

---

356. fire ; S. faire.   357. debonayre.   358. statute.   361. displease.
363. mekely ; yerde.   365. statute ; discerne.   367. thynke ; arte ; yerne.
373. thyne harte.   374. disdayne.   375. the.   376. yf (S. giue) ;
reyne.   377. libertie.   378. ellis.   379. statute. knowe (*read*
con).   380. Ie (*for* y).   381. lowe ; kowigh (*for* cough).   382.
ofte.   383. bring vp (*om.* vp).   384. moche resorte.   385. sporte.
386. statute.   387. payne ; haste.   389. thou *or* thon (S. then) ;
thynke ; goo.   392. bette.

The *thirteenth* statut, Whylom is to thinke,
What thing may best thy lady lyke and plese,
And in thyn hertes botom let it sinke :   395
Som thing devise, and take [it] for thyn ese,
And send it her, that may her herte †apese :
Some hert, or ring, or lettre, or device,
Or precious stone ; but spare not for no price.

The *fourteenth* statut eke thou shalt assay   400
Fermly to kepe the most part of thy lyfe :
Wish that thy lady in thyne armes lay,
And nightly dreme, thow hast thy hertes wyfe
Swetely in armes, straining her as blyfe :
And whan thou seest it is but fantasy,   405
See that thow sing not over merily,

For to moche joye hath oft a wofull end.
It longith eke, this statut for to hold,
To deme thy lady evermore thy frend,
And think thyself in no wyse a cocold.   410
In every thing she doth but as she shold :
Construe the best, beleve no tales newe,
For many a lie is told, that semeth full trewe.

But think that she, so bounteous and fair,
Coud not be fals : imagine this algate ;   415
And think that tonges wikke wold her appair,
Slaundering her name and worshipfull estat,
And lovers true to setten at debat :
And though thow seest a faut right at thyne y,
Excuse it blyve, and glose it pretily.   420

The *fifteenth* statut, Use to swere and stare,
And counterfet a lesing hardely,
To save thy ladys honour every-where,
And put thyself to fight [for her] boldly :
Sey she is good, virtuous, and gostly,   425
Clere of entent, and herte, and thought and wille ;
And argue not, for reson ne for skille,

---

393. statute.   394. Whate; please.   395. thyne hartes.   396. think ;
I supply it ; thyne ease.   397. sent (*read* send) ; harte pease (*read* herte
apese).   398. letre ; devise.   400. statute ; shalte.   401. Formely ; parte.
402. Wisshe.   403. thy nyghtes hart*es* wife (*om.* nyghtes).   405. whanne.
406. merely.   408. statute.   409. frende.   410. thynke.   411.
shuld.   412. beste.   413. semyth (S. semth).   414. thinke ; fayre.
415. Cowde.   416. thinke ; wykked (*read* wikke) ; appaier.   417.
Sklaunderyng ; estate.   418. debate.   419. fawte ; thyne ye.   421.
statute.   422. counterfete.   423. honoure ; -whare.   424. *I supply* for her ;
boldely.   425. gode ; gostely.   426. harte.

Agayn thy ladys plesir ne entent,
For love wil not be countrepleted, indede:
Sey as she seith, than shalt thou not be shent,   430
The crow is whyte; ye, truly, so I rede:
And ay what thing that she thee will forbede,
Eschew all that, and give her sovereintee,
Her appetyt folow in all degree.

The *sixteenth* statut, kepe it if thow may:—   435
Seven sith at night thy lady for to plese,
And seven at midnight, seven at morow-day;
And drink a cawdell erly for thyn ese.
Do this, and kepe thyn hede from all disese,
And win the garland here of lovers all,   440
That ever come in court, or ever shall.

Ful few, think I, this statut hold and kepe;
But truly, this my reson giveth me fele,
That som lovers shuld rather fall aslepe,
Than take on hand to plese so oft and wele.   445
There lay non oth to this statut a-dele,
But kepe who might, as gave him his corage:
Now get this garland, lusty folk of age.

Now win who may, ye lusty folk of youth,
This garland fresh, of floures rede and whyte,   450
Purpill and blewe, and colours †ful uncouth,
And I shal croune him king of all delyt!
In al the court there was not, to my sight,
A lover trew, that he ne was adred,
When he expresse hath herd the statut red.   455

The *seventeenth* statut, Whan age approchith on,
And lust is leid, and all the fire is queint,
As freshly than thou shalt begin to fon,
And dote in love, and all her image paint
In rémembraunce, til thou begin to faint,   460
†As in the first seson thyn hert began:
And her desire, though thou ne may ne can

---

428. Agayne; plesire.   429. wille.   430. shalte thowe.   431.
crowe.   432. whate; the wille forbidde.   433. Eschewe; souerentie.
434. Hir appetide felawe (*sic*; S. appetite folowe).   435. statute.   436.
please.   437. morowe.   438. drynke; thyne ease.   439. thyne; dyssease.
440. wynne; alle.   441. courte; shalle.   442. fewe thynke; statute.
443. reason.   445. please; ofte.   446. none othe; statute.   448. Nowe;
garlant; folke.   449. (*From this point, I cease to give minute corrections of
spelling, such as are given above.*)   451. fel (*read* ful).   452. delite.   455.
hard; statute redde.   458. fonne.   460. In the remembraunce (*I omit* the).
461. And (*read* As).

Perform thy living actuell, and lust;
Regester this in thy rememb[e]raunce:
Eke when thou mayst not kepe thy thing from rust,   465
†Yit speke and talk of plesaunt daliaunce;
For that shall make thyn hert rejoise and daunce.
And when thou mayst no more the game assay,
The statut †bit thee pray for hem that may.

The *eighteenth* statut, hoolly to commend,   470
To plese thy lady, is, That thou eschewe
With sluttishness thy-self for to offend;
Be jolif, fresh, and fete, with thinges newe,
Courtly with maner, this is all thy due,
Gentill of port, and loving clenlinesse;   475
This is the thing that lyketh thy maistresse.

And not to wander lich a dulled ass,
Ragged and torn, disgysed in array,
Ribaud in speche, or out of mesure pass,
Thy bound exceding; think on this alway: 480
For women †been of tender hertes ay,
And lightly set their plesire in a place;
Whan they misthink, they lightly let it passe.

The *nineteenth* statut, Mete and drink forgete:
Ech other day, see that thou fast for love,   485
For in the court they live withouten mete,
Sauf such as cometh from Venus all above;
They take non heed, in pain of greet reprove,
Of mete and drink, for that is all in vain;
Only they live by sight of their soverain.   490

The *twentieth* statut, last of everichoon,
Enroll it in thyn hertes privitee;
To wring and wail, to turn, and sigh and grone,
When that thy lady absent is from thee;
And eke renew the wordes [all] that she   495
Bitween you twain hath seid, and all the chere
That thee hath mad thy lyves lady dere.

And see thyn herte in quiet ne in rest
Sojorn, to tyme thou seen thy lady eft;
But wher she won by south, or est, or west,   500
With all thy force, now see it be not left:

---

466. It (*read* Yit).   468. gam; S. game.   469. bidde (*read* bit).   470.
holy.   471. please.   476. mastresse.   481. but (!); *read* been.   483.
the (*for* 1*st* they; S. thei).   490. be (*for* by). MS. savioure (!); S. soueraine.
492. hartes.   495. MS. revowe; S. renewe; *I supply* all.   497. made.
499. sene (!).   500. wonne; S. won. be (*for* by).

Be diligent, till tyme thy lyfe be reft,
In that thou mayst, thy lady for to see;
This statut was of old antiquitee.

An officer of high auctoritee,   505
Cleped Rigour, made us swere anon:
He nas corrupt with parcialitee,
Favour, prayer, ne gold that cherely shoon;
'Ye shall,' quod he, 'now sweren here echoon,
Yong and old, to kepe, in that †ye may,   510
The statuts truly, all, aftir this day.'

O god, thought I, hard is to make this oth!
But to my pouer shall I thaim observe;
In all this world nas mater half so loth,
To swere for all; for though my body sterve,   515
I have no might the hole for to reserve.
But herkin now the cace how it befell:
After my oth was mad, the trouth to tell,

I turned leves, loking on this boke,
Where other statuts were of women shene;   520
And right furthwith Rigour on me gan loke
Full angrily, and seid unto the quene
I traitour was, and charged me let been:
'There may no man,' quod he, 'the statut[s] know,
That long to woman, hy degree ne low.   525

In secret wyse thay kepten been full close,
They sowne echon to libertie, my frend;
Plesaunt thay be, and to their own purpose;
There wot no wight of thaim, but god and fend,
Ne naught shall wit, unto the worldes end.   530
The quene hath yeve me charge, in pain to dye,
Never to rede ne seen thaim with myn ye.

For men shall not so nere of councell ben,
With womanhode, ne knowen of her gyse,
Ne what they think, ne of their wit th'engyn;   535
I me report to Salamon the wyse,
And mighty Sampson, which begyled thryes
With Dalida was: he wot that, in a throw,
There may no man statut of women knowe.

---

508. cherely (S. clerely); shone.   510. they (*read* ye).   517. herkyn.
518. othe; made.   519. loues (!); S. leaues.   523. bene.   524. statute
(*read* statuts; *see* 520).   525. hie.   526. kepten ben.   527. ecchone.
528. owen.   531. youe; S. yeue.   534. guyse.   535. thengene.

For it paravénture may right so befall,   540
That they be bound by nature to disceive,
And spinne, and wepe, and sugre strewe on gall,
The hert of man to ravissh and to reyve,
And whet their tong as sharp as swerd or gleyve :
It may betyde, this is their ordinaunce;   545
So must they lowly doon the observaunce,

And kepe the statut yeven thaim of kind,
Or such as love hath yeve hem in their lyfe.
Men may not wete why turneth every wind,
Nor waxen wyse, nor ben inquisityf   550
To know secret of maid, widow, or wyfe ;
For they their statutes have to thaim reserved,
And never man to know thaim hath deserved.

Now dress you furth, the god of Love you gyde !'
Quod Rigour than, 'and seek the temple bright   555
Of Cither[e]a, goddess here besyde;
Beseche her, by [the] influence and might
Of al her vertue, you to teche a-right,
How for to serve your ladies, and to plese,
Ye that ben sped, and set your hert in ese.   560

And ye that ben unpurveyed, †pray her eke
Comfort you soon with grace and destinee,
That ye may set your hert there ye may lyke,
In suche a place, that it to love may be
Honour and worship, and felicitee   565
To you for ay. Now goth, by one assent.'
'Graunt mercy, sir !' quod we, and furth we went

Devoutly, soft and esy pace, to see
Venus the goddes image, all of gold :
And there we founde a thousand on their knee,   570
Sum freshe and feire, som dedely to behold,
In sondry mantils new, and som were old,
Som painted were with flames rede as fire,
Outward to shew their inward hoot desire :

With dolefull chere, full fele in their complaint   575
Cried 'Lady Venus, rewe upon our sore!
Receive our billes, with teres all bedreint;
We may not wepe, there is no more in store;

---

541. be (*for* by).   542. sugre.   543. hart.   547. youen; S. yeuen.
548. Or; S. Of.   yove; S. yeue.   551. widue; S. widowe.   552. Or (!);
S. For.   554. guyde.   556. Cithera.   557. *I supply* the; enfluence.
559. ladis (S. ladies); please.   560. hart; ease.   561. prayer (*for* pray
her).   563. hart.   565. filicite.   574. hote.   575. feele; S. fele.

But wo and pain us frettith more and more:
Thou †blisful planet, lovers sterre so shene,   580
Have rowth on us, that sigh and carefull been;

And ponish, Lady, grevously, we pray,
The false untrew with counterfet plesaunce,
That made their oth, be trew to live or dey,
With chere assured, and with countenaunce;   585
And falsly now thay foten loves daunce,
Barein of rewth, untrue of that they seid,
Now that their lust and plesire is alleyd.'

Yet eft again, a thousand milion,
Rejoysing, love, leding their life in blis: 590
They seid:—' Venus, redresse of all division,
Goddes eterne, thy name †y-heried is!
By loves bond is knit all thing, y-wis,
Best unto best, the erth to water wan,
Bird unto bird, and woman unto man;   595

This is the lyfe of joye that we ben in,
Resembling lyfe of hevenly paradyse;
Love is exyler ay of vice and sin;
Love maketh hertes lusty to devyse;
Honour and grace have thay, in every wyse,   600
That been to loves law obedient;
Love makith folk benigne and diligent;

Ay stering theim to drede[n] vice and shame:
In their degree it maketh thaim honorable;
And swete it is of love [to] bere the name,   605
So that his love be feithfull, true, and stable:
Love prunith him, to semen amiable;
Love hath no faut, there it is exercysed,
But sole with theim that have all love dispised.

Honour to thee, celestiall and clere   610
Goddes of love, and to thy celsitude,
That yevest us light so fer down from thy spere,
Persing our hertes with thy pulcritude!
Comparison non of similitude
May to thy grace be mad in no degree,   615
That hast us set with love in unitee.

---

579. woo.   580. blessedfull; S. blissedful.   581. bene.   582.
ponysshe. 583. counterfete. 584. dye; S. deie. 587. Baron (*read* Barein);
S. Barain.   588. alleide.   590. blisse.   592. eternel (*read* eterne);
I-hired (*read* y-heried).   594. wanne.   595. woman vnto woman (!);
S. woman unto man.   599, 613. hartes.   605. *I supply* to.   608.
faute; excercised.   611. celcitude.   614. Compersion; S. Comparison.
615. made.

Gret cause have we to praise thy name and thee,
For [that] through thee we live in joye and blisse.
Blessed be thou, most souverain to see!
Thy holy court of gladness may not misse: 620
A thousand sith we may rejoise in this,
That we ben thyn with harte and all y-fere,
Enflamed with thy grace, and hevinly fere.'

Musing of tho that spakin in this wyse,
I me bethought in my rememb[e]raunce   625
Myne orison right goodly to devyse,
And plesauntly, with hartes obeisaunce,
Beseech the goddes voiden my grevaunce;
For I loved eke, sauf that I wist nat where;
Yet down I set, and seid as ye shall here.   630

'Fairest of all that ever were or be!
†Lucerne and light to pensif crëature!
Myn hole affiaunce, and my lady free,
My goddes bright, my fortune and my ure,
I yeve and yeld my hart to thee full sure,   635
Humbly beseching, lady, of thy grace
Me to bestowe into som blessed place.

And here I vow me feithfull, true, and kind,
Without offence of mutabilitee,
Humbly to serve, whyl I have wit and mind,   640
Myn hole affiaunce, and my lady free!
In thilkë place, there ye me sign to be:
And, sith this thing of newe is yeve me, ay
To love and serve, needly must I obey.

Be merciable with thy fire of grace,   645
And fix myne hert there bewtie is and routh,
For hote I love, determine in no place,
Sauf only this, by god and by my trouth,
Trowbled I was with slomber, slepe, and slouth
This other night, and in a visioun   650
I sey a woman romen up and down,

Of mene stature, and seemly to behold,
Lusty and fresh, demure of countynaunce,
Yong and wel shap, with here [that] shoon as gold,
With yen as cristall, farced with plesaunce;   655

---

618. *I supply* that.   626. godely.   628. Beseche.   632. Lucorne;
S. Liquor (!).   634. vse (!); S. vre.   635. harte.   637. blissed; S.
blessed.   643. yove (S. yeue); to me (S. me aie, *which seems better*).   644.
and nedely most (*om.* and).   648. be (*for* 1st by).   650. vision.   651.
se (*read* sey).   654. *I supply* that; shone.   655. fercid.

And she gan stir myne harte a lite to daunce;
But sodenly she vanissh gan right there:
Thus I may sey, I love and wot not where.

For what she is, ne her dwelling I not,
And yet I fele that love distraineth me: 660
Might ich her know, that wold I fain, god wot,
Serve and obey with all benignitee.
And if that other be my destinee,
So that no wyse I shall her never see,
Than graunt me her that best may lyken me,   665

With glad rejoyse to live in parfit hele,
Devoide of wrath, repent, or variaunce;
And able me to do that may be wele
Unto my lady, with hertes hy plesaunce:
And, mighty goddes! through thy purviaunce   670
My wit, my thought, my lust and love so gyde,
That to thyne honour I may me provyde

To set myne herte in place there I may lyke,
And gladly serve with all affeccioun.
Gret is the pain which at myn hert doth stik,   675
Till I be sped by thyn eleccioun:
Help, lady goddes! that possessioun
I might of her have, that in all my lyfe
I clepen shall my quene and hertes wife.

And in the Court of Love to dwell for ay   680
My wille it is, and don thee sacrifice:
Daily with Diane eke to fight and fray,
And holden werre, as might well me suffice:
That goddes chaste I kepen in no wyse
To serve; a fig for all her chastitee!   685
Her lawe is for religiositee.'

And thus gan finish preyer, lawde, and preise,
Which that I yove to Venus on my knee,
And in myne hert to ponder and to peise,
I gave anon hir image fressh bewtie;   690
'Heil to that figure sweet! and heil to thee,
Cupide,' quod I, and rose and yede my way;
And in the temple as I yede I sey

---

663. by; S. be.   669. hartes hie.   671. guyde.   673. harte.
674. affeccion.   675. hart; styke.   679. hart*es*.   682. for to (*om.*
for).   684. in kepen (!); S. I kepen.   687. preice.   689. harte; peice.

A shryne sormownting all in stones riche,
Of which the force was plesaunce to myn y,   695
With diamant or saphire; never liche
I have non seyn, ne wrought so wonderly.
So whan I met with Philobone, in hy
I gan demaund, 'Who[s] is this sepulture?'
'Forsoth,' quod she, 'a tender creature   700

Is shryned there, and Pitè is her name.
She saw an egle wreke him on a fly,
And pluk his wing, and eke him, in his game,
And tender herte of that hath made her dy:
Eke she wold wepe, and morn right pitously   705
To seen a lover suffre gret destresse.
In all the court nas non that, as I gesse,

That coude a lover †half so well availe,
Ne of his wo the torment or the rage
†Aslaken, for he was sure, withouten faile,   710
That of his grief she coud the hete aswage.
In sted of Pitè, spedeth hot corage
The maters all of court, now she is dede;
I me report in this to womanhede.

For weile and wepe, and crye, and speke, and pray,—   715
Women wold not have pitè on thy plaint;
Ne by that mene to ese thyn hart convey,
But thee receiven for their own talent:
And sey, that Pitè causith thee, in consent
Of rewth, to take thy service and thy pain   720
In that thow mayst, to plese thy souverain.

But this is councell, keep it secretly;'
Quod she, 'I nold, for all the world abowt,
The Quene of Love it wist; and wit ye why?
For if by me this matter springen out,   725
In court no lenger shuld I, owt of dowt,
Dwellen, but shame in all my life endry:
Now kepe it close,' quod she, 'this hardely.

Well, all is well! Now shall ye seen,' she seid,
'The feirest lady under son that is: 730

---

695. ye. 697. wounderly. 698. hie. 699. Who; *read* Whos. 704. harte.
705. piteously; S. pitously.   708. haue (!); *read* half.   710. Assliken
(*read* Aslaken); S. Asken (!).   711. gryfe; S. grief. 714. womanhode (!).
717. meane; ease.   718. owen.   721. please.   724. witte.   725.
spryngen (*sic*).   726. dowte.   729. sene.   730. sonne.

Come on with me, demene you liche a maid,
With shamefast dred, for ye shall spede, y-wis,
With her that is the mir[th] and joy and blis:
But sumwhat straunge and sad of her demene
She is, be ware your countenaunce be sene,　　　　735

Nor over light, ne recheless, ne to bold,
Ne malapert, ne rinning with your tong;
For she will you abeisen and behold,
And you demaund, why ye were hens so long
Out of this court, without resort among:　　　　740
And Rosiall her name is hote aright,
Whose harte †as yet [is] yeven to no wight.

And ye also ben, as I understond,
With love but light avaunced, by your word;
Might ye, by hap, your fredom maken bond,　　　　745
And fall in grace with her, and wele accord,
Well might ye thank the god of Love and lord;
For she that ye sawe in your dreme appere,
To love suche one, what are †ye than the nere?

Yit wot ye what? as my rememb[e]raunce　　　　750
Me yevith now, ye fayn, where that ye sey
That ye with love had never acqueintaunce,
Sauf in your dreme right late this other day:
Why, yis, parde! my life, that durst I lay,
That ye were caught upon an heth, when I　　　　755
Saw you complain, and sigh full pitously;

Within an erber, and a garden fair
With floures growe, and herbes vertuous,
Of which the savour swete was and the eyr,
There were your-self full hoot and amorous:　　　　760
Y-wis, ye ben to nice and daungerous;
A! wold ye now repent, and love som new?'—
'Nay, by my trouth,' I seid, 'I never knew

The goodly wight, whos I shall be for ay:
Guyde me the lord that love hath made and me.'　　　　765

---

731. demeane.　　732. spede; S. speke (*a needless alteration*).　　733.
MS. mir and ioye and blisse; S. mirrour ioye and blisse.　　738. abeisen.
740. withouten.　　742. is (*read* as); *supply* is; youen (S. yeuon).　　745. be;
S. by.　　747. think; S. thanke.　　749. the (= þe, *error for* ye); S. thei (!).
751. fayne.　　755. opon.　　756. piteously; S. pitously.　　757. faier.　　758.
vertuse (*sic*).　　759. heire (!).　　760. ote (!); S. hote.　　764. godely; whoes.

But furth we went in-till a chambre gay,
There was Rosiall, womanly to see,
Whose stremes sotell-persing of her ee
Myn hart gan thrill for bewtie in the stound :
'Alas,' quod I, 'who hath me yeve this wound?'   770

And than I dred to speke, till at the last
I gret the lady reverently and wele,
Whan that my sigh was gon and over-past ;
And down on knees full humbly gan I knele,
Beseching her my fervent wo to kele,   775
For there I took full purpose in my mind,
Unto her grace my painfull hart to bind.

For if I shall all fully her discryve,
Her hede was round, by compace of nature,
Her here as gold,—she passed all on-lyve,—   780
And lily forhede had this crëature,
With lovelich browes, flawe, of colour pure,
Bytwene the which was mene disseveraunce
From every brow, to shewe[n] a distaunce.

Her nose directed streight, and even as lyne,   785
With fourm and shap therto convenient,
In which the goddes milk-whyt path doth shine ;
And eke her yen ben bright and orient
As is the smaragde, unto my juggement,
Or yet thise sterres hevenly, smale and bright ;   790
Her visage is of lovely rede and whyte.

Her mouth is short, and shit in litell space,
Flaming somdele, not over-rede, I mene,
With pregnant lippes, and thik to kiss, percas ;
(For lippes thin, not fat, but ever lene,   795
They serve of naught, they be not worth a bene ;
For if the basse ben full, there is delyt,
Maximian truly thus doth he wryte.)

But to my purpose :—I sey, whyte as snow
Ben all her teeth, and in order thay stond   800
Of oon stature ; and eke hir breth, I trow,
Surmounteth alle odours that ever I fond
In sweetnes ; and her body, face, and hond
Ben sharply slender, so that from the hede
Unto the fote, all is but womanhede.   805

---

768. ye (*read* ee).   769. harte.   770. you (!) ; S. yeue.   772. grete.
776. toke.   777. harte.   781. lylly.   782. loueliessh (!) ; S. liuelishe.
flawe (*for* flave).   794. prengnaunte.   800. stand.   801. one.   802.
oders (!) ; S. odours ; found.   803. switnesse ; S. swetenesse.

I hold my pees of other thinges hid :—
Here shall my soul, and not my tong, bewray :—
But how she was arrayed, if ye me bid,
That shall I well discover you and say :
A bend of gold and silk, full fressh and gay ; 810
With here in tresse[s], browdered full well,
Right smothly kept, and shyning every-del.

About her nek a flour of fressh devyse
With rubies set, that lusty were to sene ;
And she in gown was, light and somer-wyse, 815
Shapen full wele, the colour was of grene,
With aureat seint about her sydes clene,
With dyvers stones, precious and riche :—
Thus was she rayed, yet saugh I never her liche.

For if that Jove had [but] this lady seyn, 820
Tho Calixto ne [yet] Alcmenia,
Thay never hadden in his armes leyn ;
Ne he had loved the faire Europa ;
Ye, ne yet Dane ne Antiopa !
For al their bewtie stood in Rosiall ; 825
She semed lich a thing celestiall

In bowntè, favor, port, and semliness,
Plesaunt of figure, mirrour of delyt,
Gracious to sene, and rote of gentilness,
With angel visage, lusty rede and white : 830
There was not lak, sauf daunger had a lite
This goodly fressh in rule and governaunce ;
And somdel straunge she was, for her plesaunce.

And truly sone I took my leve and went,
Whan she had me enquyred what I was ; 835
For more and more impressen gan the dent
Of Loves dart, whyl I beheld her face ;
And eft again I com to seken grace,
And up I put my bill, with sentence clere
That folwith aftir ; rede and ye shall here. 840

'O ye [the] fressh, of [all] bewtie the rote,
That nature hath fourmed so wele and made
Princesse and Quene ! and ye that may do bote
Of all my langour with your wordes glad !

---

806. pease ; hidde.   807. bewry ; S. bewraie.   · 808. bidde.   811.
her intresse (*read* here in tresses).   812. kepte (*perhaps for* kempt).   820.
I supply but.   821. *I supply* yet.   MS. alcenia (!).   823. eurosa (!).
825. stode.   828. delite.   832. godely.   834. toke.   840.
folowith.   841. *I supply* the *and* all.   843. I (!) ; S. ye.

Ye wounded me, ye made me wo-bestad;   845
Of grace redress my mortall †grief, as ye
Of all myne †harm the verrey causer be.

Now am I caught, and unwar sodenly,
With persant stremes of your yën clere,
Subject to ben, and serven you meekly,   850
And all your man, y-wis, my lady dere,
Abiding grace, of which I you requere,
That merciles ye cause me not to sterve;
But guerdon me, liche as I may deserve.

For, by my troth, the dayes of my breth   855
I am and will be youre in wille and hert,
Pacient and meek, for you to suffre deth
If it require; now rewe upon my smert;
And this I swere, I never shall out-stert
From Loves Court for none adversitee,   860
So ye wold rewe on my distresse and me.

My destinee, †my fate, and ure I bliss,
That have me set to ben obedient
Only to you, the flour of all, y-wis:
I trust to Venus never to repent;   865
For ever redy, glad, and diligent
Ye shall me finde in service to your grace,
Till deth my lyfe out of my body race.

Humble unto your excellence so digne,
Enforcing ay my wittes and delyt   870
To serve and plese with glad herte and benigne,
And ben as Troilus, [old] Troyes knight,
Or Antony for Cleopatre bright,
And never you me thinkes to reney:
This shall I kepe unto myne ending-day.   875

Enprent my speche in your memorial
Sadly, my princess, salve of all my sore!
And think that, for I wold becomen thrall,
And ben your own, as I have seyd before,
Ye must of pity cherissh more and more   880
Your man, and tender aftir his desert,
And yive him corage for to ben expert.

---

846. give (!); *read* grief.   847. harte (!); *read* harm.   850. mekely.
852. require (!).   856. harte.   857. meke.   862. and me (S.
me); *read* my.   868. rase.   870. delite.   871. please; harte.   872.
I supply old.   874. thynkes (*sic*).   876. Eprent (*for* Enprent).   878.
becom*m*en.   879. owyn; S. owne.   880. most.   882. yf (= yif);
S. giue.

For where that oon hath set his herte on fire,
And findeth nether refut ne plesaunce,
Ne word of comfort, deth will quyte his hire.   885
Allas ! that there is none allegeaunce
Of all their wo ! allas, the gret grevaunce
To love unloved ! But ye, my Lady dere,
In other wyse may govern this matere.'

'Truly, gramercy, frend, of your good will,   890
And of your profer in your humble wyse !
But for your service, take and kepe it still.
And where ye say, I ought you well cheryse,
And of your gref the remedy devyse,
I know not why : I nam acqueinted well   895
With you, ne wot not sothly where ye dwell.'

'In art of love †I wryte, and songes make,
That may be song in honour of the King
And Quene of Love ; and than I undertake,
He that is sad shall than full mery sing.   900
And daunger[o]us not ben in every thing
Beseche I you, but seen my will and rede,
And let your aunswer put me out of drede.'

'What is your name ? reherse it here, I pray,
Of whens and where, of what condicion   905
That ye ben of ? Let see, com of and say !
Fain wold I know your disposicion :—
Ye have put on your old entencion ;
But what ye mene to servë me I noot,
Sauf that ye say ye love me wonder hoot.'   910

'My name ? alas, my hert, why [make it straunge ?]
Philogenet I cald am fer and nere,
Of Cambrige clerk, that never think to chaunge
Fro you that with your hevenly stremes clere
Ravissh myne herte and gost and all in-fere :   915
This is the first, I write my bill for grace,
Me think, I see som mercy in your face.

And what I mene, by god that al hath wrought,
My bill, that maketh finall mencion,
That ye ben, lady, in myne inward thought   920

---

883. one; harte.   884. refute.   886. allegaunce (!).   890. gode wille.
893. cheryssh.   894. gref.   896. southly.   897. and (!); *read* I.
902. sene (*sic*).   908. vppon; *read* on.   909. nete (*error for* note =
noot).   910. hete (*error for* hote = hoot).   911. hart why (*rest of
line blank*; *I supply* make it straunge).   914. For (!); S. Fro.   915.
harte.   918. goddes (S. gods); *read* god.

Of all myne hert without offencion,
That I best love, and have, sith I begon
To draw to court. Lo, than! what might I say?
I yeld me here, [lo!] unto your nobley.

And if that I offend, or wilfully   925
By pompe of hart your precept disobey,
Or doon again your will unskillfully,
Or greven you, for ernest or for play,
Correct ye me right sharply than, I pray,
As it is sene unto your womanhede,   930
And rewe on me, or ellis I nam but dede.'

' Nay, god forbede to feffe you so with grace,
And for a worde of sugred eloquence,
To have compassion in so litell space!
Than were it tyme that som of us were hens!   935
Ye shall not find in me suche insolence.
Ay? what is this? may ye not suffer sight?
How may ye loke upon the candill-light,

That clere[r] is and hotter than myn y?
And yet ye seid, the bemes perse and frete:—   940
How shall ye than the candel-[l]ight endry?
For wel wot ye, that hath the sharper hete.
And there ye bid me you correct and bete,
If ye offend,—nay, that may not be doon:
There come but few that speden here so soon.   945

Withdraw your y, withdraw from presens eke:
Hurt not yourself, through foly, with a loke;
I wold be sory so to make you seke:
A woman shuld be ware eke whom she toke:
Ye beth a clark:—go serchen [in] my boke,   950
If any women ben so light to win:
Nay, byde a whyl, though ye were all my kin.

So soon ye may not win myne harte, in trouth
The gyse of court will seen your stedfastness,
And as ye don, to have upon you rewth.   955
Your own desert, and lowly gentilness,
That will reward you joy for heviness;
And though ye waxen pale, and grene and dede,
Ye must it use a while, withouten drede,

---

921. harte.   922. beganne.   924. *I supply* lo; nobly (S. nobleye).
927. done (*sic*).   928. growen (*sic*); S. greuen.   939. clere; hatter
(S. hotter); ye.   944, 945. done, sone.   946. ye.   948. syke; *read*
seke.   950. serchynne; *read* serchen in.   951. wynne.   952. abide
(*read* byde); thowe; kynne.   954. guyse.   955. rewth.   956. owen;
lawly.   958. thowe.   959. most.

And it accept, and grucchen in no wyse;   960
But where as ye me hastily desyre
To been to love, me think, ye be not wyse.
Cese of your language! cese, I you requyre!
For he that hath this twenty yere ben here
May not obtayn; than marveile I that ye   965
Be now so bold, of love to trete with me.'

'Ah! mercy, hart, my lady and my love,
My rightwyse princesse and my lyves guyde!
Now may I playn to Venus all above,
That rewthles ye me †give these woundes wyde!   970
What have I don? why may it not betyde,
That for my trouth I may received be?
Alas! your daunger and your crueltè!

In wofull hour I got was, welaway!
In wofull hour [y-]fostred and y-fed,   ·975
In wofull hour y-born, that I ne may
My supplicacion swetely have y-sped!
The frosty grave and cold must be my bedde,
Without ye list your grace and mercy shewe,
Deth with his axe so faste on me doth hewe.   980

So greet disese and in so litell whyle,
So litell joy, that felte I never yet;
And at my wo Fortune ginneth to smyle,
That never erst I felt so harde a fit:
Confounded ben my spirits and my wit,   985
Till that my lady take me to her cure,
Which I love best of erthely crëature.

But that I lyke, that may I not com by;
Of that I playn, that have I habondaunce;
Sorrow and thought, thay sit me wounder ny;   990
Me is withhold that might be my plesaunce:
Yet turne again, my worldly suffisaunce!
O lady bright! and save your feithfull true,
And, er I die, yet on[e]s upon me rewe.'

With that I fell in sounde, and dede as stone,   995
With colour slain, and wan as assh[es] pale;

---

963. Cease (*twice*).   965. optayne.   968. rightwose (!).   970.
ye may gise (*or* gife) this wounder wide (*no sense*).   973. Alas thanne youre
(*om.* thanne); crueltie.   974. gote.   975. fostered and Ifedde.   977.
Ispedde.   984. arst.   985. spritis.   993. sauf.   994. ar (*for* er).

And by the hand she caught me up anon,
'Aryse,' quod she, 'what? have ye dronken dwale?
Why slepen ye? it is no nightertale.'
'Now mercy, swete,' quod I, y-wis affrayed: 1000
'What thing,' quod she, 'hath mad you so dismayed?

Now wot I well that ye a lover be,
Your hewe is witnesse in this thing,' she seid:
'If ye were secret, [ye] might know,' quod she,
'Curteise and kind, all this shuld be allayed: 1005
And now, myn herte! all that I have misseid,
I shall amend, and set your harte in ese.'
'That word it is,' quod I, 'that doth me plese.'

'But this I charge, that ye the statuts kepe,
And breke thaim not for sloth nor ignoraunce.'   1010
With that she gan to smyle and laughen depe.
'Y-wis,' quod I, 'I will do your plesaunce;
The sixteenth statut doth me grete grevaunce,
But ye must that relesse or modifie.'
'I graunt,' quod she, 'and so I will truly.'   1015

And softly than her colour gan appeare,
As rose so rede, through-out her visage all,
Wherefore me think it is according here,
That she of right be cleped Rosiall.
Thus have I won, with wordes grete and small,   1020
Some goodly word of hir that I love best,
And trust she shall yit set myne harte in rest.

*   *   *   *   *   *

'GOTH on,' she seid to Philobone, 'and take
This man with you, and lede him all abowt
Within the court, and shew him, for my sake,   1025
What lovers dwell withinne, and all the rowte
Of officers; for he is, out of dowte,
A straunger yit:'—'Come on,' quod Philobone,
'Philogenet, with me now must ye gon.'

And stalking soft with esy pace, I saw   1030
About the king [ther] stonden environ,

---

998. Aryse anon quod (*om.* anon).   999. nytirtale.   1001. made.
1004. *I supply* ye.   1006. myne harte.   1007. harte; ease.   1008.
please.   1009. steutes (!); *error for* statuts.   1014. most.   1018. thynke
that it (*I omit* that).   1021. godely.   1023. phelobone.   1027. officers
him shewe for (*om.* him shewe).   1030. easy pase.   1031. *I supply* ther.

Attendaunce, Diligence, and their felaw
Fortherer, Esperaunce, and many oon ;
Dred-to-offend there stood, and not aloon ;
For there was eke the cruell adversair,   1035
The lovers fo, that cleped is Dispair,

Which unto me spak angrely and fell,
And said, my lady me deceiven shall :
'Trowest thow,' quod she, 'that all that she did tell,
Is true? Nay, nay, but under hony gall!   1040
Thy birth and †hers, [they] be nothing egall :
Cast of thyn hart, for all her wordes whyte,
For in good faith she lovith thee but a lyte.

And eek remember, thyn habilite
May not compare with hir, this well thow wot.'   1045
Ye, than cam Hope and said, 'My frend, let be !
Beleve him not: Dispair, he ginneth dote.'
'Alas,' quod I, 'here is both cold and hot :
The tone me biddeth love, the toder nay;
Thus wot I not what me is best to say.   1050

But well wot I, my lady graunted me,
Truly to be my woundes remedy ;
Her gentilness may not infected be
With dobleness, thus trust I till I dy.'
So cast I void Dispaires company,   1055
And taken Hope to councell and to frend.
'Ye, kepe that wele,' quod Philobone, 'in mind.'

And there besyde, within a bay-window,
Stood oon in grene, full large of brede and length,
His berd as blak as fethers of the crow ;   1060
His name was Lust, of wounder might and strength ;
And with Delyt to argue there he thenkth,
For this was all his [hool] opinion,
That love was sin ! and so he hath begon

To reson fast, and legge auctoritè :   1065
'Nay,' quod Delyt, 'love is a vertue clere,
And from the soule his progress holdeth he :

1032. felowe.   1033. asperaunce.   1034. stode.   1035. adu*er*sary (!).
1036. displesire (!); *for* Despair (*see* l. 1047).   1038. dysseyuene (!); *error
for* dysseyuen.   1039. Throwest (!) ; S. Trowest.   1041. his (!); *read*
hers ; *I supply* they.   1043. gode ; louith.   1048. hote.   1054. dye.
1059. Stode one.   1062. thynketh; S. thinkth.   1063. *I supply* hool.
1064. synne ; begonne.   1065. reason.   1066. delite.

Blind appetyt of lust doth often stere,
And that is sin : for reson lakketh there,
For thow [dost] think thy neighbours wyfe to win :　　1070
Yit think it well that love may not be sin ;

For god and seint, they love right verely,
Void of all sin and vice: this knowe I wele,
Affeccion of flessh is sin, truly ;
But verray love is vertue, as I fele,　　　　　　　1075
For love may not thy freil desire akele :
For [verray] love is love withouten sin.'
'Now stint,' quoth Lust, 'thow spekest not worth a pin.'

And there I left thaim in their arguing,
Roming ferther in the castell wyde,　　　　　　　1080
And in a corner Lier stood talking
Of lesings fast, with Flatery there besyde ;
He seid that women were attire of pryde,
And men were founde of nature variaunt,
And coud be false, and shewen beau semblaunt.　　1085

Than Flatery bespake and seid, y-wis :
'See, so she goth on patens faire and fete,
Hit doth right wele : what pretty man is this
That rometh here? Now truly, drink ne mete
Nede I not have ; myne hart for joye doth bete　　1090
Him to behold, so is he goodly fressh :
It semeth for love his harte is tender nessh.'

This is the court of lusty folk and glad,
And wel becometh their habit and array :
O why be som so sorry and so sad,　　　　　　　1095
Complaining thus in blak and whyte and gray?
Freres they ben, and monkes, in good fay :
Alas, for rewth ! greet dole it is to seen,
To see thaim thus bewaile and sory been.

See how they cry and wring their handes whyte,　　1100
For they so sone went to religion !
And eke the nonnes, with vaile and wimple plight,

1068. appityde (!) ; stirre (S. stere).　1069. synne ; reason.　1070. *I supply*
dost ; do wyn (*read* to win).　1071. synne.　1072. verely.　1073.
synne ; vise.　1074. synne.　1076. For verray loue may not thy freyle
desire akkele (*too long*).　1077. *I supply* verray ; synne.　1078. pynne.
1081. stode.　1083. woman (!).　1085. beawe.　1089. her ; S. here.
1091. godely.　1094. abite.　1097. gode.　1098. sene.　1099. bene.

There thought that they ben in confusion :
'Alas,' thay sayn, 'we fayn perfeccion,
In clothes wide, and lak our libertè ;   1105
But all the sin mote on our frendes be.

For, Venus wot, we wold as fayn as ye,
That ben attired here and wel besene,
Desiren man, and love in our degree,
Ferme and feithfull, right as wold the quene :   1110
Our frendes wikke, in tender youth and grene,
Ayenst our will made us religious ;
That is the cause we morne and wailen thus.'

Than seid the monks and freres in the tyde,
'Wel may we curse our abbeys and our place,   1115
Our statuts sharp, to sing in copes wyde,
Chastly to kepe us out of loves grace,
And never to fele comfort ne solace ;
Yet suffre we the hete of loves fire,
And after than other haply we desire.   1120

O Fortune cursed, why now and wherefore
Hast thow,' they seid, ' beraft us libertè,
Sith nature yave us instrument in store,
And appetyt to love and lovers be ?
Why mot we suffer suche adversitè,   1125
Diane to serve, and Venus to refuse ?
Ful often sith this matier doth us muse.

We serve and honour, sore ayenst our will,
Of chastitè the goddes and the quene ;
Us leffer were with Venus byden still,   1130
And have reward for love, and soget been
Unto thise women courtly, fressh, and shene.
Fortune, we curse thy whele of variaunce !
There we were wele, thou revest our plesaunce.'

Thus leve I thaim, with voice of pleint and care,   1135
In raging wo crying ful pitously ;
And as I yede, full naked and full bare
Some I behold, looking dispitously,
On povertè that dedely cast their y ;
And 'Welaway !' they cried, and were not fain,   1140
For they ne might their glad desire attain.

1106. synne.   1108. hire (!) ; S. here.   1114. monke ; *read* monks.   1115.
course (S. curse) ; abbes.   1120. aftir than other happly.   1122. libartie.
1124. appetide (!).   1127. matiers (!).   1134. revist.   1136. woo ; petiously.
1138. beholde (*perhaps read* beheld) ; dispiteously.   1139. ye.

For lak of richesse worldely and of †gode,
They banne and curse, and wepe, and sein, ' Alas,
That poverte hath us hent that whylom stode
At hartis ese, and free and in good case !   1145
But now we dar not shew our-self in place,
Ne us embolde to duelle in company,
There-as our hart wold love right faithfully.'

And yet againward shryked every nonne,
The prang of love so straineth thaim to cry :   1150
' Now wo the tyme,' quod thay, ' that we be boun !
This hateful ordre nyse will don us dy !
We sigh and sobbe, and bleden inwardly,
Freting our-self with thought and hard complaint,
That ney for love we waxen wode and faint.'   1155

And as I stood beholding here and there,
I was war of a sort full languisshing,
Savage and wild of loking and of chere,
Their mantels and their clothës ay tering ;
And oft thay were of nature complaining,   1160
For they their members lakked, fote and hand,
With visage wry and blind, I understand.

They lakked shap, and beautie to preferre
Theim-self in love : and seid, that god and kind
Hath forged thaim to worshippen the sterre,   1165
Venus. the bright, and leften all behind
His other werkes clene and out of mind :
' For other have their full shape and bewtee,
And we,'.quod they, ' ben in deformitè.'

And nye to thaim there was a company,   1170
That have the susters waried and misseid ;
I mene, the three of fatall destinè,
That be our †werdes ; and sone, in a brayd,
Out gan they cry as they had been affrayd,
' We curse,' quod thay, ' that ever hath nature   1175
Y-formed us, this wofull lyfe t'endure !'

And there he was contrite, and gan repent,
Confessing hole the wound that Citherè
Hath with the dart of hot desire him sent,
And how that he to love must subjet be :   1180

1142. gold (!) ; *read* gode *or* good.   1145. eas ; gode.   1146. *Not in
the* MS. ; *supplied by* Stowe.   1150. prange (*and so in* S.).   1151. woo ;
boune.   1152. dye.   1156. stode.   1157. ware.   1159. mantaylles.
1161. there ; S. their.   1168. shappe ; bewtie.   1173. wordes (!).
·1176. to endure.   1177. *Sic.*   1179. sent ; *perhaps read* shent.

Than held he all his skornes vanitè,
And seid, that lovers lede a blisful lyfe,
Yong men and old, and widow, maid and wyfe.

'Bereve †me, goddesse,' quod he, '[of] thy might,
My skornes all and skoffes, that I have   1185
No power forth, to mokken any wight,
That in thy service dwell : for I did rave :
This know I well right now, so god me save,
And I shal be the chief post of thy feith,
And love uphold, the révers who-so seith.'   1190

Dissemble stood not fer from him in trouth,
With party mantill, party hood and hose ;
And said, he had upon his lady rowth,
And thus he wound him in, and gan to glose
Of his entent full doble, I suppose :   1195
And al the world, he seid, he loved it wele ;
But ay, me thoughte, he loved her nere a dele.

Eek Shamefastness was there, as I took hede,
That blusshed rede, and durst nat ben a-knowe
She lover was, for thereof had she drede ;   1200
She stood and hing her visage down alowe ;
But suche a sight it was to sene, I trow,
†As of these roses rody on their stalk :
There cowd no wight her spy to speke or talk

In loves art, so gan she to abasshe,   1205
Ne durst not utter all her privitè :
Many a stripe and many a grevous lasshe
She gave to thaim that wolden loveres be,
And hindered sore the simpill comonaltè,
That in no wyse durst grace and mercy crave ;   1210
For were not she, they need but ask and have ;

Where if they now approchin for to speke,
Than Shamefastness returnith thaim again :
Thay think, if †we our secret councell breke,
Our ladies will have scorn on us, certain,   1215
And [per]aventure thinken greet disdain :
Thus Shamefastness may bringin in Dispeir,
Whan she is dede, the toder will be heir.

1182. blissed full (!).   1183. widue.   1184. my (read me) ; I supply of.
1186. forth (S. for).   1187. ded (for did).   1189. Chife.   1192.
hode.   1198. toke.   1199. blasshed (for blusshed) ; darst (for durst).
1203. And (!) ; read As.   1205. harte (!) ; for art.   1206. previte,
1208. gaven (!).   1209. comonaltie.   1211. nede.   1214. thay
(read we) ; secrites (!).   1215. ladys ; certen.   1216. I supply per-.
1217, 1218. bryngyn ; dispeire ; heire.

Com forth, Avaunter! now I ring thy bell!
I spyed him sone; to god I make a-vowe,   1220
He loked blak as fendes doth in hell :—
'The first,' quod he, 'that ever [I] did †wowe,
Within a word she com, I wot not how,
So that in armes was my lady free ;
And so hath ben a thousand mo than she.   1225

In Englond, Bretain, Spain, and Pycardie,
Arteys, and Fraunce, and up in hy Holand,
In Burgoyne, Naples, and [in] Italy,
Naverne, and Grece, and up in hethen land,
Was never woman yit that wold withstand   1230
To ben at myn commaundement, whan I wold :
I lakked neither silver, coin, ne gold.

And there I met with this estate and that;
And here I broched her, and here, I trow :
Lo! there goth oon of myne ; and wot ye what?   1235
Yon fressh attired have I leyd full low ;
And such oon yonder eke right well I know :
I kept the statut whan we lay y-fere ;
And yet yon same hath made me right good chere.'

Thus hath Avaunter blowen every-where   1240
Al that he knowith, and more, a thousand-fold ;
His auncetrye of kin was to Lière,
For firste he makith promise for to hold
His ladies councell, and it not unfold ;
Wherfore, the secret when he doth unshit,   1245
Than lyeth he, that all the world may wit.

For falsing so his promise and behest,
I wounder sore he hath such fantasie ;
He lakketh wit, I trowe, or is a best,
That can no bet him-self with reson gy.   1250
By myn advice, Love shal be contrarie
To his availe, and him eke dishonoure,
So that in court he shall no more sojoure.

'Take hede,' quod she, this litell Philobone,
'Where Envy rokketh in the corner yond,   1255
And sitteth dirk ; and ye shall see anone
His lenë bodie, fading face and hond;

1222. firste; *I supply* I; ded vowe.   1228. *I supply* in.   1229. lond.   1230.
withstond.   1233. the (!); S. this.   1235. goith one; wotte ; whate.
1236. Yonne.   1237. one.   1242. kynne; lier.   1244. ladys.   1245.
vnshitte.   1246. That leith ; S. Than lieth ; witte.   1248. fantasie.
1250. canne; bette ; reason guy.   1251. Be (*for* By).   1253. soiorne (!);
S. soioure.   1255. rokketh (*perhaps read* rouketh) ; Cornor (!).

Him-self he fretteth, as I understond;
Witnesse of Ovid Methamorphosose;
The lovers fo he is, I wil not glose.   1260

For where a lover thinketh him promote,
Envy will grucch, repyning at his wele;
Hit swelleth sore about his hartes rote,
That in no wyse he can not live in hele;
And if the feithfull to his lady stele,   1265
Envy will noise and ring it round aboute,
And sey moche worse than don is, out of dowte.'

And Prevy Thought, rejoysing of him-self,
Stood not fer thens in habit mervelous;
'Yon is,' thought [I], 'som spirit or some elf,   1270
His sotill image is so curious:
How is,' quod I, 'that he is shaded thus
With yonder cloth, I not of what colour?'
And nere I went, and gan to lere and pore,

And frayned him [a] question full hard.   1275
'What is,' quod I, 'the thing thou lovest best?
Or what is boot unto thy paines hard?
Me think, thow livest here in grete unrest;
Thow wandrest ay from south to est and west,
And est to north; as fer as I can see,   1280
There is no place in court may holden thee.

Whom folowest thow? where is thy harte y-set?
But my demaunde asoile, I thee require.'
'Me thought,' quod he, 'no crëature may let
†Me to ben here, and where-as I desire: 1285
For where-as absence hath don out the fire,
My mery thought it kindleth yet again,
That bodily, me think, with my souverain

I stand and speke, and laugh, and kisse, and halse,
So that my thought comforteth me full oft: 1290
I think, god wot, though all the world be false,
I will be trewe; I think also how soft
My lady is in speche, and this on-loft
Bringeth myn hart †to joye and [greet] gladnesse;
This prevey thought alayeth myne hevinesse.   1295

1259. methamorphosees; S. Methamorphosose.   1260. foo; gloose.
1263. hartes.   1269. Stode; ferre; abite.   1270. Yonne; *I supply* I;
sprite.   1271. corious; S. curious.   1275. *I supply* a.   1277.
bote.   1280. ferre; canne.   1285. Nowe; *read* Me.   1287.
kyndelith.   1288. bodely.   1294. from (!); *read* to; *I supply* greet.

And what I thinke, or where to be, no man
In all this erth can tell, y-wis, but I :
And eke there nis no swallow swift, ne swan
So wight of wing, ne half [so] yern can fly ;
For I can been, and that right sodenly,   1300
In heven, in helle, in paradise, and here,
And with my lady, whan I will desire.

I am of councell ferre and wyde, I wot,
With lord and lady, and their previtè
I wot it all; but be it cold or hot,   1305
They shall not speke without licence of me,
I mene, in suche as sesonable be ;
For first the thing is thought within the hert,
Ere any word out from the mouth astert.'

And with that word Thought bad farewell and yede : 1310
Eke furth went I to seen the courtes gyse :
And at the dore cam in, so god me spede,
†Twey courteours of age and of assyse
Liche high, and brode, and, as I me advyse,
The Golden Love, and Leden Love thay hight : 1315
The ton was sad, the toder glad and light.

[*Some stanzas lost.*]

'Yis ! draw your hart, with all your force and might,
To lustiness, and been as ye have seid ;
And think that I no drop of favour hight,
Ne never had to your desire obeyd,   1320
Till sodenly, me thought, me was affrayed,
To seen you wax so dede of countenaunce ;
And Pitè bad me don you some plasaunce.

Out of her shryne she roos from deth to lyve,
And in myne ere full prevely she spak,   1325
" Doth not your servaunt hens away to dryve,
Rosiall," quod she ; and than myn harte [it] brak,
For tender †treuth : and where I found moch lak
In your persoune, †than I my-self bethought,
And seid, " This is the man myne harte hath sought."' 1330

1299. *I supply* so. 1302. laday (!) ; S. lady. 1305. hoote or cold.
1306. withouten. 1307, 1308. harte, astarte. 1311. sene ; cortis guyse.
1313. Twenty (!) ; *read* Twey. 1316. The tone. 1320. vnto ; *read*
to. 1322. sene. 1323. pleasaunce. 1324. shyne (S. shrine) ; rose.
1325. eke (!) ; S. eare. 1327. *I supply* it ; blak (*for* brak). 1328. reiche
(*read* reuth). 1329. and I me ; *read* than I myself.

'Gramercy, Pitè! might I †but suffice
To yeve the lawde unto thy shryne of gold,
God wot, I wold; for sith that ††thou did rise
From deth to lyve for me, I am behold
To †thanken you a thousand tymes told,   1335
And eke my lady Rosiall the shene,
Which hath in comfort set myn harte, I wene.

And here I make myn protestacion,
And depely swere, as [to] myn power, to been
Feithfull, devoid of variacion,   1340
And her forbere in anger or in tene,
And serviceable to my worldes quene,
With al my reson and intelligence,
To don her honour high and reverence.'

I had not spoke so sone the word, but she,   1345
My souverain, did thank me hartily,
And seid, 'Abyde, ye shall dwell still with me
Till seson come of May; for than, truly,
The King of Love and all his company
Shall hold his fest full ryally and well:'   1350
And there I bode till that the seson fell.

———+·+———

ON May-day, whan the lark began to ryse,
   To matens went the lusty nightingale
Within a temple shapen hawthorn-wise;
He might not slepe in all the nightertale,   1355
But 'Domine labia,' gan he crye and gale,
'My lippes open, Lord of Love, I crye,
And let my mouth thy preising now bewrye.'

The eagle sang 'Venite, bodies all,
And let us joye to love that is our helth.'   1360
And to the deske anon they gan to fall,
And who come late, he pressed in by stelth:
Than seid the fawcon, our own hartis welth,
'Domine, Dominus noster, I wot,
Ye be the god that don us bren thus hot.'   1365

1331. not (!); *read* but.   1333. she (*sic*); *read* thou.   1335. taken (!);
S. thanken.   1339. *I supply* to.   1341. heree (!); *for* her.   1343.
reason.   1348, 1351. season.   1358. bewreye; S. bewrye.   1362. preced.
1363. oure owen.   1365. brenne; hote.

'*Celi enarrant*,' said the popingay,
'Your might is told in heven and firmament.'
And than came in the goldfinch fresh and gay,
And said this psalm with hertly glad intent,
'*Domini est terra* ; this Laten intent,   1370
The god of Love hath erth in governaunce :'
And than the wren gan skippen and to daunce.

'*Jube, Domine*, Lord of Love, I pray
Commaund me well this lesson for to rede;
This legend is of all that wolden dey   1375
Marters for love; god yive the sowles spede !
And to thee, Venus, †sing we, out of drede,
By influence of all thy vertue grete,
Beseching thee to kepe us in our hete.'

The second lesson robin redebrest sang,   1380
'Hail to the god and goddess of our lay ! '
And to the lectorn †amorously he sprang :—
'Hail,' quod [he] eke, 'O fresh seson of May,
Our moneth glad that singen on the spray !
Hail to the floures, rede, and whyte, and blewe,   1385
Which by their vertue make our lustes newe ! '

The thrid lesson the turtill-dove took up,
And therat lough the mavis [as] in scorn :
He said, 'O god, as mot I dyne or sup,
This folissh dove will give us all an horn !   1390
There been right here a thousand better born,
To rede this lesson, which, as well as he,
And eke as hot, can love in all degree.'

The turtill-dove said, 'Welcom, welcom, May,
Gladsom and light to loveres that ben trewe !   1395
I thank thee, Lord of Love, that doth purvey
For\ me to rede this lesson all of dewe ;
For, in gode sooth, of corage I †pursue
To serve my make till deth us must depart :'
And than '*Tu autem*' sang he all apart.   1400

'*Te deum amoris*,' sang the thrustell-cok :
Tuball him-self, the first musician,
With key of armony coude not unlok
So swete [a] tewne as that the thrustill can :

1366. Cely enarant. 1369. thus (! ; S. this); hartily. 1375. dye. 1376.
yf (*for* yive).   1377. signe (!).   1382. amoryly (!); sprong.   1383.
I supply he.   1384. *Sic*.   1386. maketh; *read* make.   1387. toke.
1388. *I supply* as.   1389. mut; dyene; suppe.   1390. gife.   1398.
south ; purpose (!); *read* pursue.   1399. most.   1400. tue (!).   1403.
on-lok.   1404. *I supply* a.

'The Lord of Love we praisen,' quod he than,   1405
'And so don all the fowles, grete and lyte;
Honour we May, in fals lovers dispyte.'

'*Dominus regnavit*,' seid the pecok there,
'The Lord of Love, that mighty prince, y-wis,
He hath received her[e] and every-where: 1410
Now *Jubilate* †sing:'—'What meneth this?'
Seid than the linet; 'welcom, Lord of blisse!'
Out-stert the owl with '*Benedicite*,
What meneth al this mery fare?' quod he.

'*Laudate*,' sang the lark with voice full shrill;   1415
And eke the kite, ' *O admirabile;*
This quere will throgh myne eris pers and thrill;
But what? welcom this May seson,' quod he;
'And honour to the Lord of Love mot be,
That hath this feest so solemn and so high:'   1420
'*Amen*,' seid all; and so seid eke the pye.

And furth the cokkow gan procede anon,
With '*Benedictus*' thanking god in hast,
That in this May wold visite thaim echon,
And gladden thaim all whyl the fest shall last: 1425
And therewithall a-loughter out he brast,
'I thank it god that I shuld end the song,
And all the service which hath been so long.'

Thus sang thay all the service of the fest,
And that was don right erly, to my dome;   1430
And furth goth all the Court, both most and lest,
To feche the floures fressh, and braunche and blome;
And namly, hawthorn brought both page and grome.
With fressh garlandës, partie blewe and whyte,
And thaim rejoysen in their greet delyt.   1435

Eke eche at other threw the floures bright,
The prymerose, the violet, the gold;
So than, as I beheld the ryall sight,
My lady gan me sodenly behold,
And with a trew-love, plited many-fold,   1440
She smoot me through the [very] hert as blyve;
And Venus yet I thanke I am alyve.

1406. light; *read* lyte.   1411. sang (!); *read* sing.   1412. lynette.
1416. kiȝt; S. kight.   1417. throwe.   1418. season.   1420. solempne.
1425. lest.   1431. goith.   1432. bleme (!).   1434. garlantis.   1435.
reioyson; theire grete delite.   1441. smote; thrugh; *I supply* very; harte.

XXV. VIRELAI.

———•+•———

A LONE walking, In thought pleyning,
   And sore sighing, All desolate,
Me remembring Of my living,
My deth wishing Bothe erly and late.

Infortunate Is so my fate   5
That, wote ye what? Out of mesure
My lyf I hate Thus desperate ;
In pore estate Do I endure.

Of other cure Am I nat sure,
Thus to endure Is hard, certain ;   10
Such is my ure, I yow ensure ;
What creature May have more pain ?

My trouth so pleyn Is take in veyn,
And gret disdeyn In remembraunce ;
Yet I full feyn Wold me compleyn   15
Me to absteyn From this penaunce.

But in substaunce Noon allegeaunce
Of my grevaunce Can I nat finde ;
Right so my chaunce With displesaunce
Doth me avaunce ; And thus an ende. 20

Explicit.

From Trin. (Trin. Coll. Cam. R. 3. 19) ; *collated with* S. (Stowe's ed. 1561).
4. S. death. Trin. wyssyng ; S. wishyng. S. early. 5. Trin. soo ; S. so.
6. Trin. whate Oute. S. measure. 7. Trin. lyfe ; S. life. 8. Trin.
In suche pore (I *omit* suche). S. Doe. 9. S. not. 12. S. Maie.
13. S. truthe ; plain ; vain. 14. S. greate disdain. 15. Trin. feyne ;
S. faine. S. Would. Trin. compleyne ; S. complaine. 16. Trin. absteyne ;
S. abstaine. 17. S. None. 18. S. not. 20. S. Doeth.

XXVI. PROSPERITY.

———◆◆———

R ICHT as povert causith sobirnes,
    And febilnes enforcith contenence,
Richt so prosperitee and gret riches
The moder is of vice and negligence;
And powere also causith insolence;   5
And honour oftsiss chaungith gude thewis;
Thare is no more perilous pestilence
Than hie estate geven unto schrewis.
                  Quod Chaucere.

XXVII. LEAULTE VAULT RICHESSE.

———◆◆———

T HIS warldly joy is only fantasy,
    Of quhich non erdly wicht can be content;
Quho most has wit, lest suld in it affy,
Quho taistis it most, most sall him repent;
Quhat valis all this richess and this rent,   5
Sen no man wat quho sall his tresour have?
Presume nocht gevin that god has don but lent,
Within schort tyme the quhiche he thinkis to crave.

Leaulte vault richesse.

XXVI. *From* MS. Arch. Seld. B. 24, fol. 119; *I give rejected spellings.*
3. Ry*ch*t; grete.   7. pe*r*ilouss.
    XXVII. *From* MS. Arch. Seld. B. 24, fol. 138; *I give rejected spellings.*
1. Ioy; onely.   3. leste.   6. wate.   7. done.   9. richess.

XXVIII. SAYINGS PRINTED BY CAXTON.

1. WHAN feyth failleth in prestes sawes,
    And lordes hestes ar holden for lawes,
And robbery is holden purchas,
And lechery is holden solas,
Than shal the lond of Albyon   5
Be brought to grete confusioun.

2. Hit falleth for every gentilman
To saye the best that he can
In [every] mannes absence,
And the soth in his presence.   10

3. Hit cometh by kynde of gentil blode
To cast away al hevines,
And gadre to-gidre wordes good;
The werk of wisdom berith witnes.

Et sic est finis.

XXIX. BALADE IN PRAISE OF CHAUCER.

MASTER Geffray Chauser, that now lyth in grave,
    The nobyll rethoricien, and poet of Gret Bretayne,
That worthy was the lawrer of poetry have
For thys hys labour, and the palme attayne;
Whych furst made to dystyll and reyne   5
The gold dew-dropys of speche and eloquence
In-to Englyssh tong, thorow hys excellence.

Explicit.

XXVIII. *From* Caxton's print of Chaucer's Anelida, &c.; see vol. i. p. 46.
Also in ed. 1542, in later spelling   7. Cx. euery.   9. *I supply* every.
12. Cx. heuynes.   14. Cx. wisedom.
    XXIX. *From* MS. Trin. R. 3. 19, fol. 25; *also in* Stowe (ed. 1561).
1. MS. Chausers; Stowe, Chauser.   2. Rethoricion (!).   6. elloquence.

NOTES.

I. THE TESTAMENT OF LOVE.

THE text is from Thynne's first edition (1532); the later reprints are of inferior value. No MS. of this piece is known. Rejected spellings are given at the bottom of each page. Conjectural emendations are marked by a prefixed obelus (†). In many places, words or letters are supplied, within square brackets, to complete or improve the sense. For further discussion of this piece, see the Introduction.

BOOK I.

Prologue. 1. The initial letters of the chapters in Book I. form the words MARGARETE OF. See the Introduction.

3. *by queynt knitting coloures*, by curious fine phrases, that 'knit' or join the words or verses together. For *coloures*=fine phrases, cf. Ch., HF. 859; C. T., E 16, F 726.

7. *for*, because, seeing that; *boystous*, rough, plain, unadorned; cf. l. 12. The Glossary in vol. vi should be compared for further illustration of the more difficult words.

19. *for the first leudnesse*, on account of the former lack of skill.

21. *yeve sight*, enable men to see clearly.

30. *conne jumpere suche termes*, know how to jumble such terms together. *Jumpere* should rather be spelt *jumpre*; cf. *jompre* in the Gloss. to Chaucer. For such words, see the Glossary appended to the present volume.

but as, except as the jay chatters English; i.e. without understanding it; cf. Ch. Prol. 642.

43. *necessaries to cacche*, to lay hold of necessary ideas. Throughout this treatise, we frequently find the verb placed *after* the substantive which it governs, or relegated to the end of the clause or sentence. This absurd affectation often greatly obscures the sense.

45. The insertion of the words *perfeccion is* is absolutely necessary to the sense; cf. ll. 47, 50. For the general argument, cf. Ch. Boeth. iii.

proses 10 and 11, where 'perfection' is represented by *suffisaunce*, as, e.g., in iii. pr. 11. l. 18.

50. Aristotle's Metaphysics begins with the words : πάντες ἄνθρωποι τοῦ εἰδέναι ὀρέγονται φύσει, all men by nature are actuated by the desire of knowledge. The reference to this passage is explicitly given in the Romans of Partenay, ll. 78-87 ; and it was doubtless a much worn quotation. And see l. 64 below.

58. *sightful and knowing*, visible and capable of being known.

61. *David*. The whole of this sentence is so hopelessly corrupt that I can but give it up. Possibly there is a reference to Ps. cxxxix. 14. *me in makinge* may be put for 'in makinge me.' *Tune* is probably a misprint for *time* ; *lent* may be an error for *sent* ; but the whole is hopelessly wrong.

64. Apparently derived from Aristotle, De Animalibus, bk. i. c. 5. The general sense is that created things like to know both their creator and the causes of natural things akin to them (οἰκεῖα).

67. *Considred* ; i. e. the forms of natural things and their creation being considered, men should have a great natural love to the Workman that made them.

68. *me* is frequently written for *men*, the unemphatic form of *man*, in the impersonal sense of 'one' or 'people' ; thus, in King Horn, ed. Morris, 366, 'ne recche i what *me* telle' means 'I care not what people may say.' Strict grammar requires the form *him* for *hem* in l. 69, as *me* is properly singular ; but the use of *hem* is natural enough in this passage, as *me* really signifies created beings in general. Cf. *me* in ch. i. l. 18 below.

80. *Styx* is not 'a pit,' but a river. The error is Chaucer's ; cf. 'Stix, the put of helle,' in Troil. iv. 1540. Observe the expression—'Stygiamque paludem' ; Vergil, Aen. vi. 323.

86. I. e. 'rend the sword out of the hands of Hercules, and set Hercules' pillars at Gades a mile further onward.' For the latter allusion, see Ch. vol. ii. p. lv ; it may have been taken from Guido delle Colonne. And see Poem VIII (below), l. 349. *Gades*, now Cadiz.

89. *the spere*, the spear. There seems to be some confusion here. It was King Arthur who drew the magic sword out of the stone, after 150 knights had failed in the attempt ; see Merlin, ed. Wheatley (E. E. T. S.), pp. 100-3. Alexander's task was to untie the Gordian knot.

90. *And that* ; 'and who says that, surpassing all wonders, he will be master of France by might, whereas even King Edward III could not conquer all of it.' An interesting allusion.

96. *unconninge*, ignorance. There is an unpublished treatise called 'The Cloud of Unknowing'; but it is probably not here alluded to.

98. *gadered*, gathered. Thynne almost invariably commits the anachronism of spelling the words *gader, fader, moder, togider*, and the like, with *th* ; and I have usually set him right, marking such corrections with a prefixed obelus (†). Cf. *weder* in l. 123 below.

100. *rekes*, ricks. The idea is from Chaucer, L. G. W. 73-4.

101, 102. *his reson*, the reason of him. *hayne*, hatred.

110. *Boëce*, Boethius. No doubt the author simply consulted Chaucer's translation. See the Introduction.

115. *slye*, cunning ; evidently alluding to the parable of the unjust steward.

117. *Aristotle*. The allusion appears to be to the Nicomachean Ethics, bk. i. c. 7 : δόξειε δ' ἂν παντὸς εἶναι προαγαγεῖν, . . . παντὸς γὰρ προσθεῖναι τὸ ἐλλεῖπον.

122. *betiden*, happened to me ; the *i* is short. This sudden transition to the mention of the author's pilgrimage suggests that a portion of the Prologue is missing here.

Chap. I. 1. Copied from Ch. Boeth. bk. i. met. i. ll. 1, 2.

12. *thing* seems to mean 'person' ; the person that cannot now embrace me when I wish for comfort.

15. *prison* ; probably not a material prison. The author, in imitation of Boethius, imagines himself to be imprisoned. At p. 144, l. 132, he is 'in good plite,' i. e. well off. Cf. note to ch. iii. 116.

16. *caitived*, kept as a captive ; the correction of *caytisned* (with f for *s*) to *caytifued* (better spelt *caitived*) is obvious, and is given in the New E. Dict., s. v. *Caitive*.

17, 18. *Straunge*, a strange one, some stranger ; *me*, one, really meaning 'myself' ; *he shulde*, it ought to be.

21, 22. *bewent*, turned aside ; see New E. Dict., s. v. *Bewend*. The reading *bewet*, i. e. profusely wetted, occurs (by misprinting) in later editions, and is adopted in the New E. Dict., s. v. *Bewet*. It is obviously wrong.

23. *of hem*, by them ; these words, in the construction, follow *enlumined*. The very frequent inversion of phrases in this piece tends greatly to obscure the sense of it.

24. *Margarite precious*, a precious pearl. Gems were formerly credited with 'virtues' ; thus Philip de Thaun, in his Bestiary (ed. Wright, l. 1503), says of the pearl—

'A mult choses pot valier, ki cestes peres pot aveir,' &c., or, in Wright's translation : 'For him who can have this stone, it will be of force against many things ; there will never be any infirmity, except death, from which a person will not come to health, who will drink it with dew, if he has true faith.' See l. 133 below.

28. *twinkling in your disese*, a small matter tending to your discomfort. Here *disese*=dis-ease, want of ease. Cf. l. 31 below.

42. 'It is so high,' &c. The implied subject to which *it* refers is *paradise*, where the author's *Eve* is supposed to be. Hence the sense is :—'paradise is so far away from the place where I am lying and from the common earth, that no cable (let down from it) can reach me.'

59. *ferdnes* is obviously the right word, though misprinted *frendes*. It signifies 'fear,' and occurs again in ch. ii. ll. 9, 16 ; besides, it is again misprinted as *frendes* in the same chapter, l. 13.

63. *weyved* is an obvious correction for *veyned* ; see the Glossary.

70. *mercy passeth right*, your mercy exceeds your justice. This was a proverbial phrase, or, as it is called in the next clause, a ' proposition.'

79. *flitte*, stir, be moved ; 'not even the least bit.'

80. *souded* (misprinted *sonded* by Thynne), fixed ; cf. Ch. C.T., B 1769. From O. F. *souder*, Lat. *solidare*.

83. *do*, cause ; 'cause the lucky throw of comfort to fall upward '; alluding to dice-play.

96. *wolde conne*, would like to be able to.

99, 100. *me weninge*, when I was expecting. *ther-as*, whereas.

116. *no force*, it does not matter ; no matter for that.

117-20. Evidently corrupt, even when we read *flowing* for *folowing*, and *of al* for *by al*. Perhaps *ther* in l. 119 should be *they* ; giving the sense :—'but they (thy virtues) are wonderful, I know not which (of them it is) that prevents the flood,' &c. Even so, a clause is lacking after *vertues* in l. 118.

126. Thynne has *ioleynynge* for *ioleyuynge*, i. e. *joleyving*, cheering, making joyous. The word is not given in Stratmann or in Mätzner, but Godefroy has the corresponding O. F. verb *joliver*, to caress.

Chap. II. 18. *a lady* ; this is evidently copied from Boethius ; see Ch. Boeth. bk. i. pr. 1. l. 3. The visitor to the prison of Boethius was named Philosophy ; the visitor in the present case is Love, personified as a female ; see l. 53 below.

20. *blustringe*, glance. But the word is not known in this sense, and there is evidently some mistake here. I have no doubt that the right word is *blushinge* ; for the M.E. *blusshen* was often used in the sense of 'to cast a glance, give a look, glance with the eye '; as duly noted in the New E. Dict., s.v. *Blush*. The word was probably written *blusch-inge* in Thynne's MS., with a *c* exactly (as often) like a *t*. If he misread it as *blusthinge*, he may easily have altered it to *blustringe*.

32. *neighe*, approach ; governing *me*.

37. *O my nory*, O my pupil ! Copied from Ch. Boeth. bk. i. pr. 3. l. 10 ; cf. the same, bk. iii. pr. 11. l. 160. In l. 51 below, we have *my disciple*.

60. *by thyn owne vyse*, by thine own resolve ; i.e. of thine own accord ; see *Advice* in the New E. Dict. § 6. *Vyse* is put for *avyse*, the syllable *a* being dropped. Halliwell notes that *vice*, with the sense of 'advice,' is still in use.

64. 'Because it comforts me to think on past gladness, it (also) vexes me again to be doing so.' Clumsily expressed ; and borrowed from Ch. Boeth. bk. ii. pr. 4. ll. 4-7.

74-84. From Matt. xviii. 12 ; Luke, xv. 4 ; John, x. 11.

92. Love was kind to Paris, because he succeeded in gaining Helen. Jason was false to Love, because he deserted Hypsipyle and Medea. It is probable that *false* is misprinted for *faire* in l. 93 ; otherwise there is no contrast, as is implied by *for*.

93. *Sesars sonke* (*sic*) should probably be *Cesars swink*, i.e. Caesar's toil. I adopt this reading to make sense ; but it is not at all clear why Caesar should have been selected as the type of a successful lover.

95. *loveday*, a day of reconciliation ; see note to Ch. C. T., A 258.

96. 'And chose a maid to be umpire between God and man'; alluding to the Virgin Mary.

114–5. *cause, causing*, the primary cause, originating these things and many others besides. See note to Troil. iv. 829.

123–4. *wo is him*; Lat. ve soli, Eccl. iv. 10; quoted in Troil. i. 694.

125. Cf. 'weep with them that weep'; Rom. xii. 15.

138. Here the author bemoans his losses and heavy expenses.

143. For *wolde endeynous* I here read *wolde ben deynous,* i.e. would be disdainful ; see *Deynous* in the Gloss. to Chaucer. The New E. Dict. adopts the reading *wolde [be] endeynous,* with the same sense; but no other example of the adj. *endeynous* is known, and it is an awkward formation. However, there are five examples of the verb *endeign,* meaning 'to be indignant'; see Wyclif, Gen. xviii. 30; Ex. xxxii. 22; Is. lvii. 6; Job, xxxii. 2; Wisd. xii. 27.

166. Copied from Troil. iv. 460-1 :—

'But canstow playen raket, to and fro,
  Netle in, dokke out, now this, now that, Pandare?'

See the note on the latter line.

Wethercocke is a late spelling; the proper M.E. spelling is *wedercokke,* from a nom. *wedercok,* which appears in the poem Against Women Unconstant, l. 12.

173. *a*, an unemphatic form of *have*; 'thou wouldest have made me.'

180. *voyde*, do away with. *webbes*; the *web,* also called *the pin and web,* or *the web and pin,* is a disease of the eyes, now known as cataract. See Nares, s.v. *Pin*; Florio's Ital. Dict., s.v. *Cateratta*; the New E. Dict., s.v. *Cataract*; King Lear, iii. 4. 122 ; Winter's Tale, i. 2. 291.

191, 192. *truste on Mars,* trust to Mars, i.e. be ready with wager of battle; alluding to the common practice of appealing to arms when a speaker's truthfulness was called in question. See ch. vii. 10 below (p. 31).

Chap. III. 14. *Come of,* lit. come off; but it is remarkable that this phrase is used in M.E. where we should now say rather 'come on !' See note to Troil. ii. 1738.

21. *mayst thou,* canst thou do (or act)?

25–7. 'I never yet set any one to serve anywhere who did not succeed in his service.'

32. 'the nut in every nook.' Perhaps *on* should be *in*.

37–8. There is some corruption here. I insert *Tho gan I* to help out the sense, but it remains partially obscure. Perhaps the sense is :— 'Often one does what one does not wish to do, being stirred to do so by the opinion of others, who wanted me to stay at home; whereupon I suddenly began to wish to travel.' He would rather have stayed at home; but when he found that others wanted him to do so, he perversely began to wish to travel.

39. *the wynding of the erthe*; an obscure expression; perhaps 'the envelopment of the earth in snow.'

40. ' I walked through woods in which were broad ways, and (then) by small paths which the swine had made, being lanes with by-paths for seeking (there) their beech-mast.'

42. *ladels*, by-paths (?). No other example of the word appears. I guess it to be a diminutive of M.E. *lade*, a path, road, which occurs in the Ormulum; see Stratmann. Perhaps it is a mere misprint for *lades*.

44, 45. *gonne to wilde*, began to grow wild; cf. *ginne ayen waxe ramage*, in l. 48, with the like sense. I know of no other example of the verb *to wilde*.

52. *shippe*, ship; not, however, a real ship, but an allegorical one named Travail, i.e. Danger; see ll. 55, 75 below. *many* is here used in place of *meynee*, referring to the ship's company; some of whom had the allegorical names of Sight, Lust, Thought, and Will. The 'ship' is a common symbol of this present life, in which we are surrounded by perils; compare the parable of 'the wagging boat' in P. Plowm. C. xi. 32, and the long note to that line.

58. *old hate*; probably borrowed from Ch. Pers. Tale, I 562; see the note.

64. *avowing*, vowing; because persons in peril used to vow to perform pilgrimages.

75. *my ship was out of mynde*, i.e. I forgot all about my previous danger.

84. *the man*, the merchant-man in Matt. xiii. 45.

105. *enmoysed*, comforted. *Enmoise* or *emmoise* is a variant of M.E. *amese*, *ameise*, from O.F. *amaiser*, *amaisier*, to pacify, appease, render gentle (Godefroy); answering to the Low Lat. type *ad-mitiare* from *mitis*, gentle. See *Amese* in the New E. Dict. No other example of the form *enmoyse* is known.

111. *of nothing now may serve*, is now of no use (to you).

116. *prison*; the author has forgotten all about his adventure in the ship, and is now back in prison, as in ch. i.

118. *renyant forjuged*, a denier (of his guilt) who has been wrong-fully condemned.

121. *suche grace and non hap*, such favour and no mere luck.

124. *let-games*; probably from Troil. iii. 527; spoilers of sport or happiness. *wayters*, watchers, watch-men, guards.

131. *nothing as ye shulde*, not at all as you ought to do.

148. *feld*, felled, put down, done away with.

153-4. *For he . . . suffer*, a perfect alliterative line; imitated from P. Plowm. C. xxi. 212 :—'For wot no wight what wele is, that never wo suffrede.' Clearly quoted from memory; cf. notes to bk. ii. ch. 9. 178, and ch. 13. 86.

157. *happy hevinesse*, fortunate grief; a parallel expression to *lyking tene*, i.e. pleasing vexation, in l. 158. These contradictory phrases were much affected by way of rhetorical flourish. For a long passage of this character, cf. Rom. Rose, 4703–50.

158. *harse* is almost certainly a misprint for *harme*; then *goodly* *harme* means much the same as *lyking tene* (see note above). So, in Rom. Rose, 4710, 4733, 4743, we find mention of 'a sweet peril,' 'a joyous pain,' and 'a sweet hell.'

Chap. IV. 2. *semed they boren*, they seemed to bore; *boren* being in the infin. mood.

18. For *or* read *for*, to make sense; *for of disese*, for out of such distress come gladness and joy, so poured out by means of a full vessel, that such gladness quenches the feeling of former sorrows. Here *gladnesse and joy* is spoken of as being all one thing, governing the singular verb *is*, and being alluded to as *it*.

25. *commensal*, table-companion; from F. *commensal*, given in Cotgrave. See the New E. Dict.

27. *soukinges*, suckings, draughts of milk; cf. Ch. Boeth. bk. i. pr. 2. l. 4.

36. *clothe*, cloth. This circumstance is copied from Ch. Boeth. bk. i. pr. 2. l. 19.

42. This reference to Love, as controlling the universe, is borrowed from Boeth. bk. ii. met. 8.

47. Read *werne* (refuse) and *wol* (will); 'yet all things desire that you should refuse help to no one who is willing to do as you direct him.'

56. *every thing in coming*, every future thing. *contingent*, of uncertain occurrence; the earliest known quotation for this use of the word in English.

61-2. *many let-games*; repeated from above, ch. iii. ll. 124-8. *thy moeble*; from the same, ll. 131-2.

64. *by the first*, with reference to your first question; so also *by that other*, with reference to your second question, in l. 71.

Chap. V. 8. Acrisius shut his daughter Danaë up in a tower, to keep her safe; nevertheless she became the mother of Perseus, who afterwards killed Acrisius accidentally.

14. *entremellen*, intermingle hearts after merely seeing each other.

16. *beestes*, animals, beings; not used contemptuously; equivalent to *living people* in ll. 17, 18.

20. *esployte*, success, achievement; see *Exploit* in the New E. Dict.

29. Supply *don*; 'and I will cause him to come to bliss, as being one of my own servants.'

35. *and in-to water*, and jumps into the water and immediately comes up to breathe; like an unsuccessful diver.

37. *A tree*, &c.; a common illustration; cf. Troil. i. 964.

43. *this countrè*; a common saying; cf. Troil. ii. 28 (and note), 42. And see l. 47 below.

45. 'the salve that he healed his heel with.' From HF. 290.

71. *jangelers*; referring to l. 19 above. *lokers*; referring to *overlokers*; in ch. iii. l. 128.

72. *wayters*; referring to ch. iii. l. 128.

77. 'It is sometimes wise to feign flight.' Cf. P. Plowman, C. xxii. 103.

85. *cornes*, grains of corn. I supply *bare*, i. e. empty.

86-7. *Who*, &c.; a proverb; from Troil. v. 784.

87-8. *After grete stormes*; see note to P. Plowman, C. xxi. 454.

92. *grobbed*, grubbed; i. e. dug about. Cf. Isaiah, v. 2.

95. *a*, have (as before). *Lya*, Leah; Lat. *Lia*, in Gen. xxix. 17 (Vulgate).

103. *eighteth*, eighth; an extraordinary perversion of the notion of the sabbatical year. So below, in l. 104, we are informed that the number of workdays is *seven*; and that, in Christian countries, the day of rest is the eighth day in the week! *kinrest*, rest for the *kin* or people; a general day of rest. I know of no other example of this somewhat clumsy compound.

110. *sothed*, verified; referring to Luke, xiv. 29.

113. *conisance*, badge. Badges for retainers were very common at this date. See Notes to Richard the Redeless, ii. 2.

117-9. Copied from P. Plowman, C. vii. 24, 25 :—

> 'Lauhynge al aloude, for lewede men sholde
> *Wene* that ich were *witty*, and *wyser than anothere*;
> *Scorner* and unskilful to hem that *skil* shewed.'

As these lines are not found in the earlier versions, it follows that the author was acquainted with the *latest* version.

124. *a bridge*; i. e. to serve by way of retreat for such as trust them. *wolves*, destroyers; here meant as a complimentary epithet.

127. This idea, of Jupiter's promotion, from being a bull, to being the mate of Europa, is extremely odd; still more so is that of the promotion of Aeneas from being in hell (l. 129). Cf. *Europe* in Troil. iii. 722.

128. *lowest degrè*; not true, as Caesar's father was praetor, and his aunt married Marius. But cf. C. T., B 3862.

Chap. VI. 8. *enfame*, infamy, obloquy; from Lat. *infamia*. Godefroy gives *enfamer*, to dishonour. The word only occurs in the present treatise; see ll. 6, 7, 15.

12. From Prov. xxvii. 6: 'Meliora sunt vulnera diligentis quam fraudulenta oscula odientis.'

17. Cf. Ch. Boeth. bk. iii. pr. 6. ll. 5-13.

23. Cf. the same; bk. iv. pr. 7. ll. 34-42.

27. Cf. the same; bk. ii. pr. 5. ll. 121, 122.

30. Cf. the same; bk. iv. pr. 6. ll. 184-191.

48. *Zedeoreys* (or *ȝedeoreys*). I can find nothing resembling this strange name, nor any trace of its owner's dealings with Hannibal.

53. The (possibly imaginary) autobiographical details here supplied have been strangely handled for the purpose of insertion into the life of Chaucer, with which they have nothing to do. See Morris's Chaucer, vol. i. p. 32 (Aldine edition). The author tells us very little, except that tumults took place in London, of which he was a native, and that he had knowledge of some secret which he was pressed to betray, and did so in order to serve his own purposes.

77-8. From Chaucer, Troil. v. 6, 7 :—   *p* 27

> —'shal dwelle in pyne
> Til Lachesis his threed no lenger twyne.'

107. Referring to John, xiv. 27.

114. *Athenes* ; Athene was the goddess who maintained the authority of law and order, and in this sense was 'a god of peace.' But she was certainly also a goddess of battles.

139. *mighty senatoures.* It has been conjectured that the reference is to John of Gaunt. In the Annals of England, under the date 1384, it is noted that ' John of Northampton, a vehement partisan of the duke, is tried and sentenced to imprisonment and forfeiture. An attempt is also made to put the duke on his trial.' John of Northampton had been mayor of London in 1382, when there was a dispute between the court and the citizens regarding his election ; perhaps the words *comen eleccion* (common election), in l. 125 above, may refer to this trouble; so also *free eleccion* in l. 140. In l. 143 we must read *fate*, not *face* ; the confusion between *c* and *t* is endless. Perhaps *governours* in l. 144 should be *governour*, as in l. 147. Note that the author seems to condemn the disturbers of the peace.

157. *coarted by payninge dures*, constrained by painful duress (or tːrture).

165. *sacrament*, my oath of allegiance. Note that the author takes credit for giving evidence *against* the riotous people ; for which the populace condemned him as a liar (l. 171).

178. *passed*, surpassed (every one), in giving me an infamous character.

181. *reply*, i.e. to subvert, entirely alter, recall ; lit. to fold or bend back.

189. Here the author says, more plainly, that he became unpopular for revealing a conspiracy.

193. *out of denwere*, out of doubt, without doubt. Such is clearly the sense ; but the word *denwere* is rejected from the New E. Dict., as it is not otherwise known, and its form is suspicious. It is also omitted in Webster and in the Century Dictionary. Bailey has '*denwere*, doubt,' taken from Speght's Chaucer, and derived from this very passage. Hence Chatterton obtained the word, which he was glad to employ. It occurs, for instance, in his poem of Goddwyn, ed. Skeat, vol. ii. p. 100 :—

> —' No *denwere* in my breast I of them feel.'

The right phrase is simply *out of were* ; cf. 'withoute were' in the Book of the Duchess, 1295. I think the letters *den* may have been prefixed accidentally. The line, as printed in Thynne, stands thus : ' denwere al the sothe knowe of these thinges.' I suggest that *den* is an error for *don*, and the word *don* ought to come at the *end* of the line (after *thinges*) instead of at the beginning. This would give the readings 'out of were' and 'these thinges don in acte'; both of which are improvements.

194. *but as,* only as, exactly as.

198. *clerkes,* i. e. Chaucer, HF. 350 ; Vergil, Aen. iv. 174.

200. *of mene,* make mention of. Cf. 'hit is a schep[h]erde *that I of mene*'; Ancient Metrical Tales, ed. Hartshorne, p. 74.

Chap. VII. 10. *profered,* offered wager of battle ; hence the mention of *Mars* in l. 11. Cf. note to ch. ii. 191 above, p. 455.

23. *he,* i. e. thine adversary shall bring dishonour upon you in no way.

34. *Indifferent,* impartial. *who,* whoever.

38. *discovered,* betrayed ; so that the author admits that he betrayed his mistress.

46. *that sacrament,* that the oath to which you swore, viz. when you were charged upon your oath to tell the truth. That is, his oath in the court of justice made him break his private oath.

49. *trewe* is certainly an error for *trewthe*; the statement is copied from Jer. iv. 2 :—'Et iurabis . . . in veritate, et in iudicio, et in justitia.' So in l. 58 below, we have: 'in jugement, *in trouthe,* and rightwisenesse'; and in l. 53—'for a man to say truth, unless judgement and righteousness accompany it, he is forsworn.'

54. *serment,* oath ; as in l. 52 : referring to Matt. xiv. 7.

56. 'Moreover, it is sometimes forbidden to say truth rightfully— except in a trial—because all truths are not to be disclosed.'

60. *that worde:* 'melius mori quam male vivere'; for which see P. Plowman, C. xviii. 40. Somewhat altered from Tobit, iii. 6 :— 'expedit mihi mori magis quam vivere.'

61, 62. *al,* although. *enfame,* dishonour ; as in vi. 3 (see note, p. 458).

63. *whan,* yet when.

73. *legen,* short for *alegen* ; 'allege against others.'

75. Here misprinted ; *read* :—'may it be sayd, "in that thinge this man thou demest,"' &c. From Rom. ii. 1 ; 'in quo enim iudicas alterum, teipsum condemnas.'

83. *shrewe,* wicked man, i. e. Ham ; Gen. ix. 22.

101. *emprisonned*; so in Thynne ; better, *emprisouned.*

104. *brige,* contention, struggle, trouble ; see note to Ch. C. T., B 2872.

105. *after thyne helpes,* for your aid ; i. e. to receive assistance from you.

108. *Selande,* Zealand, Zeeland. The port of Middleburg, in the isle of Walcheren, was familiar to the English ; cf. note to C. T., Prol. 277. The reference must be to some companions of the author who had fled to Zealand to be out of the way of prosecution. *rydinge,* expedition on horseback, journey.

109, 110. *for thy chambre,* to pay the rent of your room. *renter,* landlord ; 'unknown to the landlord.'

112. *helpe of unkyndnesse,* relieve from unkind treatment.

115-6. *fleddest*, didst avoid. *privité to counsayle*, knowledge of a secret.

120-1. Cf. Ch. Boeth. bk. ii. pr. 8. ll. 31-3.

Chap. VIII. 1. *Eft*, again. Thynne prints *Ofte*, which does not give the sense required. Fortunately, we know that the first letter *must* be E, in order that the initial letters of the Prologue and chapters I. to VIII. may give the word MARGARETE. The reading *Ofte* would turn this into MARGARETO.

4, 5. From Ch. Troil. iv. 3 ; Boeth. bk. ii. pr. 8. ll. 19-21.

13. *and thou*, if thou. Cf. Matt. xviii. 12.

27. *in their mouthes*, into their mouths ; Matt. xii. 34.

31. *leve for no wight*, cease not on any one's account.

32. *use Jacobs wordes.* The allusion seems to be to the conciliatory conduct of Jacob towards Esau ; Gen. xxxiii. 8, 10, 11. Similarly the author is to be patient, and to say—'I will endure my lady's wrath, which I have deserved,' &c.

41. *sowe hem*, to sew them together again. *at his worshippe*, in honour of him ; but I can find no antecedent to *his*. Perhaps for *his* we should read *her*.

44. The text has *forgoing al errour distroyeng causeth* ; but *distroyeng* (which may have been a gloss upon *forgoing*) is superfluous, and *al* should be *of*. But *forgoing* means rather 'abandonment.'

55. *passest*, surpassest.   59. *by*, with reference to.

61. Hector, according to Guido delle Colonne, gave counsel against going to war with the Greeks, but was overborne by Paris. See the alliterative Destruction of Troy, ed. Panton and Donaldson (E. E. T. S.), Book VI ; or Lydgate's Siege of Troye, ch. xii.

65. *leveth*, neglects to oppose what is wrong.

66. The modern proverb is : 'silence gives consent.' Ray gives, as the Latin equivalent, 'qui tacet consentire videtur (inquiunt iuris consulti).' This is the exact form which is here translated.

73. Alluding to the canticle 'Exultet' sung upon Easter Eve, in the Sarum Missal :—'O certe necessarium Ade peccatum.' See note to P. Plowman, C. viii. 126 (or B. v. 491).

80. *lurken*, creep into lurking-holes, slink away.

95. *centre*, central point ; from Ch. Boeth. bk. ii. pr. 7. ll. 18-20. The whole passage (ll. 94-105) is imitated from the same 'prose' of Boethius.

103. *London* is substituted for 'Rome' in Chaucer's Boethius. Chaucer has—'may thanne the glorie of a singuler Romaine strecchen thider as the fame of the name of Rome may nat climben or passen?' See the last note.

112-6. From Ch. Boethius, bk. ii. pr. 7. 58-62.

116-25. From the same, ll. 65-79. Thus, in l. 123, the word *ofte* (in Thynne) is a misprint for *of the*; for Chaucer has—'For of thinges that han ende may be maked comparisoun.' The whole passage shews that the author consulted Chaucer's translation of Boethius rather than the Latin text.

127. *and thou canst nothing don aright*; literally from Chaucer: 'Ye men, certes, *ne conne don nothing aright*'; Boeth. bk. ii. pr. 7. 79. *but thou desyre the rumour therof be heled and in every wightes ere;* corresponds to Chaucer's—'but-yif it be for the audience of the people and for ydel rumours'; Boeth. bk. ii. pr. 7. 80. Hence *heled* (lit. hidden) is quite inadmissible; the right reading is probably *deled*, i. e. dealt round.

134. The words supplied are necessary; they dropped out owing to the repetition of *vertue*.

135-6. Again copied from Ch. Boeth. bk. ii. pr. 7. 106: 'the sowle .. unbounden fro the prison of the erthe.'

Chap. IX. 13. *than leveth there*, then it remains.

15. *for thy moebles*, because thy goods.

20. This proverb is given by Hazlitt in the form—

> 'Who-so heweth over-high,
> The chips will fall in his eye.'

Cf. 'one looketh high as one that feareth no chips'; Lyly's Euphues, ed. Arber, p. 467. And see IX. 158 (p. 270).

34. From Chaucer, Boeth. bk. i. pr. 4. 186. The saying is attributed to Pythagoras; see the passage in Chaucer, and the note upon it.

39. *a this halfe god*, on this side of God, i. e. here below; a strange expression. So again in bk. ii. ch. 13. 23.

46. *the foure elementes*, earth, air, fire, and water; see notes to Ch. C. T., A 420, 1247, G 1460. *Al universitee*, the whole universe; hence man was called the microcosm, or the universe in little; see Coriolanus, ii. 1. 68.

64. *I sette now*, I will now suppose the most difficult case; suppose that thou shouldst die in my service.

71. *in this persone*; read *on this persone*; or else, perhaps, *in this prisoune*.

86. *til deth hem departe*; according to the phrase 'till death us depart' in the Marriage Service, now ingeniously altered to 'till death us *do part*.'

96. 'and although they both break the agreement.'

98, 99. *accord*, betrothal. *the rose*, i.e. of virginity; as in the Romance of the Rose, when interpreted.

99, 100. *Marye his spouse.* But the Vulgate has; 'Surge, et accipe puerum et *matrem eius*'; Matt. ii. 13. The author must have been thinking of Matt. i. 18: 'Cum esset *desponsata* mater eius Maria Ioseph.'

113. *al being thinges*, all things that exist.

118. *prophete*; David, in Ps. xcvi. 5: (xcv. 5 in the Vulgate): 'omnes dii gentium daemonia.'

129. This refers back to ch. iv. 71-2, ch. ix. 14, 20, 56.

Chap. X. 5. *last objeccion*; i.e. his poverty, see ch. iii. 131, iv. 73, ix. 14.

12-8. Imitated from Ch. Boeth. bk. i. pr. 4. 200-17.

18. *sayd*, i.e. it is said of him.

19. *aver*, property, wealth; 'lo! how the false man, for the sake of his wealth, is accounted true!'

20. *dignitees*; cf. Ch. Boeth. bk. ii. pr. 6.

21. *were he out*, if he were not in office; cf. l. 23.

26-37. Cf. Ch. Boeth. bk. i. met. 5. 22-39. Thus, *slydinge chaunges* in l. 31 answers to Chaucer's *slydinge fortune* (l. 24); and *that arn a fayr parcel of the erthe*, in l. 32, to *a fayr party of so grete a werk* (l. 38); and yet again, *thou that knittest*, in l. 35, to *what so ever thou be that knittest* (l. 36).

37-40. From Ch. Boeth. bk. i. met 5. 27-30.

64-7. From the same; bk. ii. pr. 2. 7-12.

71-6. From the same; bk. ii. pr. 2. 23-5.

76-80. Cf. the argument in the same; bk. iii. pr. 3.

85-120. From Ch. Boeth. bk. ii. pr. 8. For literal imitations, compare *the other haleth him to vertue by the hookes of thoughtes* (l. 104-5) with Chaucer's 'the contrarious Fortune... haleth hem ayein as with an hooke' (l. 21); and *Is nat a greet good... for to knowe the hertes of thy sothfast frendes* (ll. 107-9) with Chaucer's 'wenest thou thanne that thou oughtest to leten this a litel thing, that this . . . Fortune hath discovered to thee the thoughtes of thy trewe frendes' (l. 22). Also ll. 114-6 with Chaucer (ll. 28-31).

126. *let us singen*; in imitation of the Metres in Boethius, which break the prose part of the treatise at frequent intervals. Cf. 'and bigan anon to singen right thus'; Boeth. bk. iii. pr. 9. 149.

BOOK II.

Chap. I. The initials of the fourteen Chapters in this Book give the words: VIRTW HAVE MERCI. Thynne has not preserved the right division, but makes *fifteen* chapters, giving the words: VIRTW HAVE MCTRCI. I have set this right, by making Chap. XI begin with 'Every.' Thynne makes Chapter XI begin with 'Certayn,' p. 86, l. 133, and another Chapter begin with 'Trewly,' p. 89, l. 82. This cannot be right, because the latter word, 'Trewly,' belongs to the last clause of a sentence; and the Chapter thus beginning would have the unusually small number of 57 lines.

1. Chapter I really forms a Prologue to the Second Book, interrupting our progress. At the end of Book I we are told that Love is about to sing, but her song begins with Chap. II. Hence this first Chapter must be regarded as a digression, in which the author reviews what has gone before (ll. 10-3), and anticipates what is to come (l. 61).

9. *steering*, government (of God). *otherwysed*, changed, varied; an extraordinary form.

12, 13. *after as*, according as. *hildeth*, outpours.

14-8. There is clearly much corruption in this unintelligible and imperfect sentence.   The reference to 'the Roman emperor' is mysterious.

21. *woweth*; so in Thynne, but probably an error for *waweth*, i. e. move, shift; see *waȝien* in Stratmann.

23. *phane*, vane; cf. 'chaunging as a vane'; Ch. C. T., E 996.

34. *irrecuperable*, irrecoverable; *irrecuperabilis* is used by Tertullian (Lewis and Short).

40. *armes*; this refers, possibly, to the struggle between the pope and anti-pope, after the year 1378.

51-2. *lovers clerk*, clerk of lovers; but perhaps an error for *Loves clerk*; cf. Troil. iii. 41.

62-3. *ryder and goer*, rider on horseback and walker on foot.

77. Translated from 'Fides non habet meritum ubi humana ratio praebet experimentum'; as quoted in P. Plowman, C. xii. 160. This is slightly altered from a saying of St. Gregory (xl. Homil. in Evangelium, lib. ii. homil. 26) — 'nec fides humana habet meritum cui humana ratio praebet experimentum.' See note to P. Plowman (as above).

83. *as by a glasse*, as in a mirror; 1 Cor. xiii. 12.

93. *cockle*, tares. This seems to refer to the Lollards, as puns upon the words *Lollard* and *lolia* were very rife at this period. If so, the author had ceased to approve of Lollard notions. In l. 94, *love* seems to mean Christian charity, in its highest sense; hence it is called, in l. 95, the most precious thing in nature.

96, 97. The passage seems corrupt, and I cannot quite see what is meant. Perhaps read: 'with many eke-names, [and] that [to] other thinges that the soule [seketh after, men] yeven the ilke noble name.' The comma after *kynde* in l. 96 represents a down-stroke (equivalent to a comma) in Thynne; but it is not wanted.

99. *to thee*, i. e. to the 'Margaret of virtue' whose name appears as an acrostic at the head of the Chapters in Book I. and Chapters I–V of Book II; moreover, we find at last that Margaret signifies Holy Church, to which the treatise is accordingly dedicated. *tytled of Loves name*, entitled the Testament of Love.

103. *inseëres*, lookers into it, readers.

104. *Every thing*; with respect to everything to which appertains a cause which is wrought with a view to its accomplishment, Aristotle supposes that the doing of everything is, in a manner, its final cause. 'Final cause' is a technical term, explained in the New E. Dict. as 'a term introduced into philosophical language by the schoolmen as a translation of Aristotle's fourth cause, τὸ οὗ ἕνεκα or τέλος, the end or purpose for which a thing is done, viewed as the cause of the act; especially as applied in Natural Theology to the design, purpose, or end of the arrangements of the universe.' The phrase 'the end in view' comes near to expressing it, and will serve to explain 'A final cause' in the next clause.

107. *is finally to thilke ende*, is done with a view to that result.

109. After *so*, understand 'is it with regard to.'

110. *the cause*, the cause whereby I am directed, and that for which I ought to write it, are both alike noble.

113. *this leude*, &c.; I have set about learning this alphabet; for I cannot, as yet, go beyond counting up to three.

115. *in joininge*, &c.; by proceeding to the joining together of syllables.

124. *in bright whele*, in (its) bright circuit. Chaucer has *wheel* in the sense of orbit; HF. 1450.

126. *another tretyse.* As to this proposed treatise nothing is known. Perhaps it never was written.

Chap. II. 2. *in Latin.* This suggests that the present chapter may be adapted from some Latin original; especially as the author only gives the *sentence* or general drift of it. But the remark may mean nothing, and the tone of the chapter is wholly medieval.

24. *Saturnes sphere*, Saturn's orbit; the supposed outer boundary of the spheres of the seven planets.

27. *me have*, possess me (i.e. love), since Love is the speaker; i.e. they think they can procure men's love by heaping up wealth.

28. Perhaps place the comma after *sowed* (sewn), not after *sakke*.

29. *pannes*, better spelt *panes*; see *pane* in Stratmann. From O.F. *pan*, *panne*, Lat. *pannus*, a cloth, garment, robe. *mouled*, become mouldy; the very form from which the mod. E. *mould-y* has been evolved; see *muwlen* in Stratmann, and *mouldy* in my Etym. Dict. (Supplement). *whicche*, chest, from A.S. *hwæcca*; see P. Plowm. A. iv. 102, where some copies have *huche*, a hutch, a word of French origin. Thus *pannes mouled in a whicche* signifies garments that have become mouldy in a chest. See note to C. T., C 734.

30. *presse*, a clothes-press; observe the context.

35. *seventh*; perhaps an error for *thirde*; cf. 'percussa est tertia pars solis'; Rev. viii. 12. He is referring to the primitive days of the Church, when 'the pope went afoot.'

40. *defended*, forbade (opposed) those taxations. See *Taylage* in Ch. Glossary.

42. *maryed*, caused to be married; cf. P. Plowman, B. vii. 29.

47. *symonye*, simony; cf. note to P. Plowman, C. iii. 63.

48. Observe the rimes: *achates*, *debates*; *wronges*, *songes*.

49. *for his wronges*, on account of the wrongs which he commits. *personer*, better *parsoner* or *parcener*, participant, sharer; i.e. the steward, courtier, escheator, and idle minstrel, all get something. See *parcener* in Stratmann.

50. 'And each one gets his prebend (or share) all for himself, with which many thrifty people ought to profit.'

51. *behynde*, behindhand; even these wicked people are neglected, in comparison with the *losengeour*, or flatterer.

52. Note the rimes, *forsake*, *take. it acordeth*, it agrees, it is all consistent; see note to l. 74 below.

* * *
* * * *

H h

55. *at matins*; cf. P. Plowm. C. i. 125, viii. 27.

56. *bene-breed*, bean-bread; cf. P. Plowm. C. ix. 327.

57, 58. Cf. P. Plowman, C. vi. 160-5.

60. *shete*, a sheet, instead of a napkin to cover the bread; *god* refers to the eucharist.

62. *a clergion*, a chorister-boy; see Ch. C. T., B 1693, and the note.

65. *broken*, torn; as in P. Plowm. B. v. 108, ix. 91.

66. *good houndes*; cf. P. Plowm. C. vi. 161-5.

69. *dolven*, buried; 'because they (the poor) always crave an alms, and never make an offering, they (the priests) would like to see them dead and buried.'

69. *legistres*, lawyers; 'legistres of bothe the lawes,' P. Plowm. B. vii. 14.

71. 'For then wrong and force would not be worth a haw anywhere.' Before *plesen* something seems lost; perhaps read—'and [thou canst] plesen,' i. e. and you can please no one, unless those oppressive and wrong-doing lawyers are in power and full action.'

74. *ryme*, rime. The reference is not to actual jingle of rime, but to a proverb then current. In a poem by Lydgate in MS. Harl. 2251 (fol. 26), beginning—'Alle thynge in kynde desirith thynge i-like,' the refrain to every stanza runs thus:—'It may wele ryme, but it accordith nought'; see his Minor Poems, ed. Halliwell, p. 55. The sense is that unlike things may be brought together, like riming words, but they will not on that account agree. So here: such things may seem, to all appearance, congruous, but they are really inconsistent. Cf. note to l. 52 above.

79. *beestly wit*, animal intelligence.

99. *cosinage*, those who are my relatives.

104. *behynde*, behindhand, in the rear. *passe*, to surpass, be prominent.

109. *comeden* is false grammar for *comen*, came; perhaps it is a misprint. The reference is to Gen. ix. 27: 'God shall enlarge Japheth ... and Canaan shall be his servant.' The author has turned *Canaan* into *Cayn*, and has further confused Canaan with his father Ham!

112. *gentilesse*; cf. Ch. Boeth. bk. iii. pr. 6. 31-4; C. T., D 1109.

116. *Perdicas*, Perdiccas, son of Orontes, a famous general under Alexander the Great. This king, on his death-bed, is said to have taken the royal signet-ring from his finger and to have given it to Perdiccas. After Alexander's death, Perdiccas held the chief authority under the new king Arrhidaeus; and it was really Arrhidaeus (not Perdiccas) who was the son of a *tombestere*, or female dancer, and of Philip of Macedonia; so that he was Alexander's half brother. The dancer's name was Philinna, of Larissa. In the Romance of Alexander, the dying king bequeaths to Perdiccas the kingdom of Greece; cf. note to bk. iii. c. ii. l. 25. Hence the confusion.

122. Copied from Ch. Boeth. bk. iii. met. 6 :—' Al the linage of men that ben in erthe ben of semblable birthe. On allone is fader of thinges . . . Why noisen ye or bosten of your eldres? For yif thou loke your biginninge, and god your auctor and maker,' &c.

135. *one*; i. e. the Virgin Mary.

139. After *secte*, supply *I* :—'that, in any respect, I may so hold an opinion against her sex.' *Secte* is properly 'suite'; but here means *sex*; cf. l. 134.

140. *in hem*, in them, i. e. in women. And so in l. 141.

Chap. III. 8. *victorie of strength*; because, according to the first book of Esdras, iv. 14, 15, women are the strongest of all things.

9. *Esdram*, accus. of Esdras, with reference to the first book of Esdras, called 'liber Esdrae tertius' in the Vulgate.

9, 10. *whos lordship al lignes*. Something is lost here; *lordship* comes at the end of a line; perhaps the insertion of *passeth* will give some sort of sense ; *whos lordship* [*passeth*] *al lignes*, whose lordship surpasses all lines. But *lignes* is probably a corrupt reading.

10. *who is*, i. e. who is it that? The Vulgate has : 'Quis est ergo qui dominatur eorum? Nonne mulieres genuerunt regem,' &c. But the A. V. has : 'Who is it then that ruleth them, or hath the lordship over them? Are they not women? Women have borne the king,' &c. This translates a text in which *mulieres* has been repeated.

17-21. From 1 Esdras, iv. 15-7: 'Women have borne the king and all the people that bear rule by sea and land. Even of them came they : and they nourished them up that planted the vineyards, from whence the wine cometh. These also make garments [Lat. *stolas*] for men ; these bring glory unto men ; and without women cannot men be.'

21-5. Adapted from 1 Esdras, iv. 18, 19.

30. 'That by no way can they refuse his desire to one that asks well.'

32. *of your sectes*, of your followers, of those of your sex. Cf. chap. 2. 139 above, and the note.

38. *wenen*, imagine that your promises are all gospel-truth ; cf. Legend of Good Women, 326 (earlier version).

41. *so maked*; 'and that (i. e. the male sex) is so made sovereign and to be entreated, that was previously servant and used the voice of prayer.' Men begin by entreating, and women then surrender their sovereignty.

43. *trewe*; used ironically ; i. e. untrue.

45, 46. *what thing to women it is*, what a thing it is for women. Ll. 45-58 are borrowed, sometimes word for word, from Ch. HF. 269-85. See note to l. 70 below, and the Introduction, § 11.

47. 'All that glisters is not gold' ; see Ch. C. T., G 962, and the note. But it is here copied from Ch. HF. 272.

55. *whistel*, pipe. Cf. note to P. Plowm. B. xv. 467.

60. *is put*, i. e. she (each one of them) is led to suppose.

63, 64. Copied from Ch. HF. 305–10.

67. *they*, i. e. women ; cf. l. 58.   So also in l. 68.

68. *ye*, i. e. ye men ; so also *you* in l. 69.

70–81. Expanded from Ch. HF. 332–59 ; observe how some phrases are preserved.

91. 'Faciamus ei adiutorium simile sibi'; Gen. ii. 18.

92. *this tree*, i. e. Eve, womankind.   So in l. 96.

100. 'What is heaven the worse, though Saracens lie concerning it?'

111. *dames*, mothers; cf. Ch. Boeth. bk. ii. met. 6. 1–9.

114. *way*, path ; *it lightly passe*, easily go along it.

115. This proverb is copied from Ch. HF. 290–1 ; just as the proverb in l. 47 is from the same, l. 272.   Compare p. 22, ll. 44–5.

131–2. Obscure ; and apparently imperfect.

Chap. IV. 2. Either *my* or *to me* should be struck out.

4–8. From Ch. Boeth. bk. iii. pr. 2. 3–8.   **14–6.** From the same, 8–12.

20–1. *by wayes of riches* ; cf. *richesses* in Ch. Boeth. bk. iii. pr. 2. 20 ; so also *dignite* answers to *digne* of *reverence* in the same, l. 21 ; *power* occurs in the same, l. 24 ; and *renomè* answers to *rencun* in l. 26.

21. *wening me*, seeing that I supposed.

22. *turneth* ; 'it goes against the hair.'   We now say—'against the grain.'

45. The words between square brackets must be supplied.

55. *holden for absolute*, considered as free, separate, or detached ; as in Ch. Boeth. bk. v. pr. 6. 169.

56. *leveth in*, there remain in, i. e. remain for consideration, remain to be considered.   When 'bestial' living is set aside, 'manly' and 'resonable' are left.

61. *riches*, &c. ; from Boethius.   See *riches* discussed in Ch. Boeth. bk. ii. pr. 5 ; *dignitè*, in pr. 6 ; *renomè*, or fame, in pr. 7 ; and *power*, along with *dignitè*, in pr. 6.

99. *as a litel assay*, as if for a short trial, for a while.

100. *songedest*, didst dream ; from F. *songer*.   I know of no other example of this verb in English.   However, Langland has *songewarie*, interpretation of dreams, P. Plowman, C. x. 302.

113. *thy king* ; presumably, Richard II ; cf. l. 120.

116. *to òblige*, to subject thy body to deeds of arms, to offer to fight judicially ; as already said above ; cf. bk. i. c. 7. 10.

138. 'Love and the bliss already spoken of above (cf. 'the parfit blisse of love,' bk. ii. c. 1. 79) shall be called "the knot" in the heart.' This definition of "the knot," viz. as being the perfect bliss or full fruition of love, should be noted ; because, in later chapters, the author continually uses the phrase "the knot," without explaining what he means by it.   It answers to 'sovereyn blisfulnesse' in Chaucer's Boethius.

141. *inpossession* is all one word, but is clearly an error.   The right word is certainly *imposition*.   The Lat. *impositio* was a grammatical term, used by Varro, signifying the *imposing* of a name, or the application of a name to an object; and the same sense of O. F. *imposition* appears in a quotation given by Godefroy. It is just the word required. When Love declares that she shall give the name of "the knot" to the perfect bliss of love, the author replies, 'I shall well understand the application of this name,' i. e. what you mean by it; cf. l. 149.

147. *A goddes halfe*, lit. on the side of God; with much the same sense as in God's name; see Ch. C. T., D 50.

Chap. V. 3. *richesse* is singular; it was probably Thynne who put the following verbs into plural forms.

5. *Aristotle*. Perhaps the reference is to the Nicomachean Ethics, i. 1.

15-20. The argument is from Ch. Boeth. bk. ii. pr. 5. 84, 122.

57, 58. From Ch. Boeth. bk. ii. pr. 5. 45-7.

65. Cf. 'Why embracest thou straunge goodes as they weren thyne?' Ch. Boeth. bk. ii. pr. 5. 50.

67-77. From Ch. Boeth. bk. ii. pr. 5. 52-69.

79-110. From the same; ll. 71-80; 88-133.

Chap. VI. Suggested by Ch. Boeth. bk. ii. pr. 6.

11-4. From the same, 57, 58; 54-7; 62-4.

25. *dignites ... is as the sonne*; the verb *is* agrees with the latter substantive *sonne*.

26-9. From the same as above, 4-6; the author substitutes *wilde fyre* for Chaucer's *flaumbe of Ethna*.

30. Cf. Ch. Boeth. bk. ii. pr. 6. 75-8.

38. Perhaps read *dignitè in suche thing tene y-wrought*; 'as dignity in such a case wrought harm, so, on the contrary, the substance in dignity, being changed, rallied (so as) to bring in again a good condition in its effect.' Obscure. 'Dignities' are further discussed in Boeth. bk. iii. pr. 4.

74-7. Cf. Ch. Boeth. bk. iii. pr. 4. 64-70. ·

78. *Nero*. The name was evidently suggested by the mention of Nero immediately after the end of Boeth. bk. iii. pr. 4 (viz. in met. 4); but the story of Nero killing his mother is from an earlier passage in Boethius, viz. bk. ii. met. 6.

81. *king John*. By asserting his 'dignity' as king against prince Arthur, he brought about a war in which the greater part of the French possessions of the crown were lost.

82. *nedeth in a person*, are necessary for a man.

99. *such maner planettes*, planets such as those; referring to the sun and moon mentioned just above; ll. 87, 91. The sun and moon were then accounted as being among the seven planets.

100-1. 'That have any desire for such (ill) shining planets to appear any more in that way.'

117-8. *I not*, I do not know. *and thou see*, if thou shouldst see. Cf. Ch. Boeth. bk. iii. pr. 4. 22-7.

123-8. From Ch. Boeth. bk. iii. pr. 4. 31-9.

127. *besmyteth*, contaminates, defiles. Note that the author is here reproducing Chaucer's *bispotten and defoulen* (pr. 4. 38). The word is

noted in Stratmann, because the A. S. *besmītan*, in this sense, occurs in Mark, vii. 15. The form *besmitten* is commoner, four examples of it being given in the New E. Dict., s. v. *besmit*. The verb *besmite* has escaped recognition there, because the present passage has not been noted. So also, in the next line, *smyteth* has a like sense. *Smitted* occurs in Troilus, v. 1545.

129. *fyr*, fire ; from Ch. Boeth. bk. iii. pr. 4. 47.

132-4. From the same ; ll. 48-53.

138. The sentence is incomplete and gives no sense ; probably a clause has dropped out after the word *goodnesse*. I cannot set it right.

143-5. Imitated from Ch. Boeth. bk. iii. pr. 4. 55-7.

153-6. Suggested by the same ; ll. 64-70.

164. Cf. 'leve hem in [*or* on] thy lift hand' ; P. Plowman, C. viii. 225.

Chap. **VII.** Suggested by Ch. Boeth. bk. iii. pr. 5.

8. *Nero* ; from the same, bk. iii. met. 4. 4, 5.

14. *ensamples* ; answers to *ensaumples* in the same, bk. iii. pr. 5. 4.

17. *Henry Curtmantil*, Henry II. 'Henry short mantell, or Henry the seconde' ; Fabyan, ed. Ellis, p. 260. 'In his fifty-fifth year he thus miserably expired, and his son Geoffrey of Lincoln with difficulty found any one to attend to his funeral ; the attendants had all fled away with everything valuable that they could lay their hands on' ; Miss Yonge, Cameos from English History (1869) ; p. 180.

20. Copied *without material alteration* from Ch. Boeth. bk. iii. pr. 5. 5-7.

23. *power of rëalmes* ; from the same, l. 7.

30-9. Copied, in part literally, from Ch. Boeth. bk. iii. pr. 5. 8-17.

39-42. From the same ; ll. 20-5.

50-2. Cf. 'Holdest thou thanne thilke man be mighty, that thou seest that he wolde don that he may nat don ?' the same ; ll. 23-5.

72. *overthrowen* would be better grammar.

74-8. From the same prose, ll. 25-9.

78. *warnisshed*, guarded. *warnishe*, guard ; *the hour of warnishe*, the time of his being guarded.

81. *famulers*, household servants ; borrowed from Chaucer's *familieres* in the same prose, l. 29.

82. *sypher*, cipher in arithmetic. Though in itself it signifies nothing, yet appended to a preceding figure it gives that figure a tenfold value. Cf. Richard the Redeless, iv. 53-4 :—

> 'Than satte summe as siphre doth in awgrym
> That noteth a place, and no-thing availeth.'

92. *the blynde* ; alluding to a common fable.

95-6. From Ch. Boeth. bk. iii. pr. 5. 32-4.

98-9 ; 101-3. From the same ; ll. 41-6.

105-8. From the same, ll. 48-51.

109-12. From Ch. Boeth. bk. iii. met. 5.

114-6. Here the author suddenly dashes off to another book of Boethius ; see bk. ii. pr. 6. 44-5.

117. *Buserus*; Chaucer has *Busirides* in his text of Boethius, bk. ii. pr. 6. 47 (whose text our author here follows); but *Busirus* in the Monkes Tale, B 3293. The true name is *Busiris*, of which *Busiridis* is the genitive case. Chaucer evolved the form *Busirides* out of the accusative *Busiridem* in Boethius. See note in vol. ii. p. 433.

118. *Hugest*; substituted for the example of Regulus in Boethius. Hugest is probably an error for Hengest, i.e. Hengist. The story of his slaughter of the Britons at Stonehenge by a shameful treachery is famous ; he certainly 'betrayed many men.' See Fabyan, ed. Ellis, p. 66 ; Rob. of Gloucester, l. 2651 (ed. Hearne, p. 124). The story of his death is not inconsistent with the text. Rob. of Gloucester, at l. 2957 (ed. Hearne, p. 140) tells how he was suddenly seized, in a battle, by Eldol, earl of Gloucester, who cried out for help; many came to his assistance, and Hengist was taken alive. Shortly afterwards, at the instance of Eldad, bishop of Gloucester, Eldol led him out of the town of Corneboru, and smote his head off. Eldad's verdict was :—

'Also doth by this mon that so moche wo ath y-do,
    So mony child y-mad faderles, dighteth him al-so.'

The name of his betrayer or capturer is given as *Collo* in our text ; but proper names take so many forms that it is not much to go by. Thus, the very name which is given as *Eldol* in one MS. of Robert of Gloucester (l. 2679) appears as *Cadel* in another. Fabyan calls him *Edolf* (p. 66), and makes him Earl of Chester. Layamon (ed. Madden, ii. 268) calls him *Aldolf*.

120. 'Omnes enim, qui acceperint gladium, gladio peribunt'; Matt. xxvi. 52.

122. *huisht*, hushed, silent ; cf. *hust* in Ch. Boeth. bk. ii. met. 5. 16.

130-2. Cf. the same, bk. iv. pr. 2. 31-4.

132. 'But then, as for him who could make you wretched, if he wished it, thou canst not resist it.' The sentence appears to be incomplete.

135. *flye*, fly ; substituted for Chaucer's *mous* ; see his Boeth. bk. ii. pr. 6. 22-4.

139-42. From the same, ll. 25-9.

148-9. *Why there*, i.e. 'wherefore (viz. by help of these things) there is no way,' &c. Cf. 'Now is it no doute thanne that thise weyes ne ben a maner misledinges to blisfulnesse'; Ch. Boeth. bk. iii. pr. 8. 1-2.

Chap. VIII. 5. *renomè*, renown ; answering to *glori* and *renoun* in Ch. Boeth. bk. iii. pr. 6. 1, 6. But there is not much imitation of Chaucer in the former part of this chapter.

37. *abouten*, round about ; i. e. you have proved a contradiction.

39. *acorden*, agree ; *by lacking*, with respect to blame and praise.

42. *elementes*, the four elements. Sir T. Elyot's Castel of Helthe (1539) presents the usual strange medieval notions on medicine. He begins by saying that we must consider the things natural, the things not natural, and the things against nature. The things natural are seven, viz. elements, complexions, humours, members, powers, operations, and spirits. ' The Elementes be those originall thynges vnmyxt and vncompounde, of whose temperance and myxture all other thynges, hauynge corporalle substance, be compacte : Of them be foure, that is to saye, Erthe, Water, Ayre, and Fyre.

ERTHE is the moost grosse and ponderouse element, and of her proper nature is *colde* and *drye*.

WATER is more subtyll and lyght thanne erthe, but in respect of Ayre and Fyre, it is grosse and heuye, and of hir proper Nature is *colde* and *moyste*.

AYRE is more lyghte and subtylle than the other two, and beinge not altered with any exteriour cause, is properly *hotte* and *moyste*.

FYRE is absolutely lyght and clere, and is the clarifier of other elementes, if they be vyciate or out of their naturall temperaunce, and is properly *hotte* and *drye*.' Cf. Ch. Boeth. bk. iii. met. 9. 13–7.

50. *oned*, united ; see the last note.

52. *erthe* (see the footnote) is an obvious error for *eyre* ; so also in l. 53. But the whole of the argument is ridiculous.

68–9. Copied from Ch. Boeth. bk. iii. pr. 6. 3–4. From the Andromache of Euripides, l. 319 ; see the note in vol. ii. p. 439.

69–71. From Chaucer, as above, ll. 5–9.

75–81. From the same, ll. 9–17.

82. *obstacles* ; they are enumerated in bk. i. c. 8. l. 98 (p. 37).

85–7 ; 89–97. From Chaucer, bk. iii. pr. 6. ll. 21–34.

99. I do not know the source of this saying. Cf. C.T., D 1109–12.

102–7. From Ch. Boeth. bk. iii. pr. 8. 26–35.

104–5. *fayre and foule*, handsome and ugly men ; *hewe*, beauty.

107–10. *thilke—knotte* ; equivalent to 'they ne ben nat weyes ne pathes that bringen men to blisfulnesse' ; Ch., as above, ll. 42–3.

122. Cf. 'But alday fayleth thing that fooles wenden' ; certainly the right reading of Troil. i. 217 ; see note on the line ; vol. ii. p. 463.

124. *the sterre*, the star of the Southern pole ; so in the next line, the Northern pole-star.

126. *out-waye-going*, going out of the way, error of conduct ; which may be called, as it were, 'imprisonment,' or 'banishment.' It is called *Deviacion* in bk. iii. ch. i. 6, which see.

127. *falsed*, proved false, gave way.

130. Cf. ' It suffyseth that I have shewed hiderto the forme of false welefulness' ; Ch. Boeth. bk. iii. pr. 9. 1. With line 131, cf. the same, ll. 5–7.

Chap. IX. 1-5. Cf. Ch. Boeth. bk. iii. pr. 9. 9-11.

9. The 'harmony' or music of the spheres; see Troil. v. 1812-3; Parl. Foules, 59-63, and the note in vol. i. p. 507.

37-8. *sugre ... soot*; cf. 'sucre be or soot,' Troil. iii. 1194; and 'in her hony galle'; C. T., B 3537.

54. *Flebring*; omitted in the New E. Dict., as being a false form; there is no such word. Mr. Bradley suggests *flekring* or *flekering*, which is probable enough. The M. E. *flekeren*, also spelt *flikeren*, meant not only to flutter, but to be in doubt, to vacillate, and even to caress. We may take it to mean 'light speech' or 'gossip.'

65. 'Good and yvel ben two contraries'; Ch. Boeth. bk. iv. pr. 2. 10.

74. *in that mores*, in the possession of that greater thing.

77-8. Cf. l. 81 below. Hence the sense is: 'and that thing which belongs to it (i. e. to the knot, ought to incline to its superior cause out of honour and good-will.' But it is clumsy enough; and even to get this sense (which seems to have been that intended) we must alter *mores* to *more*. The form was probably miswritten *mores* here owing to the occurrence of *mores* just above (l. 74) and just below l. 79). It proceeds thus :—'otherwise, it is rebellious, and ought to be rejected from protection by its superior.'

116. From Troil. iii. 1656-9.

129-38. Perhaps the finest passage in the treatise, but not very original. Cf. P. Plowman, C. xxi. 456-7; Ch. Boeth. bk. iv. met. 6. 20-3.

133. Cf. 'ones a yere al thinges renovelen'; Ch. C. T., I 1027.

134. Cf. 'To be gayer than the heven'; Book of the Duch. 407.

139. Imitated from Ch. Boeth. bk. ii. pr. 2. 54-5; but with the substitution of 'garmentes' for 'tonnes.'

143. *proverbe*, proverb. 'When bale is hext (highest), then bote is next'; Proverbs of Hending; see notes to Gamelyn, ll. 32, 631, in vol. v. pp. 478, 486. For *hext* our author substitutes *a nyebore*, i. e. a neighbour, nigh at hand.

151. The truth of astrology is here assumed.

155-70. I suspect that this account of the days of the week (though no doubt familiar in those days to many) was really copied from Chaucer's Treatise on the Astrolabe, part ii. sect. 12 (vol. iii. p. 197). For it contains a remarkable blunder. The word *noon* in l. 163 should, of course, be *midnight*; but, as Chaucer omits to say when the first planetary hour of the day occurs, the author was left to himself in regard to this point. Few people understand *why* the day after Sunday must needs be Monday; yet it is very simple. The principle is given in the footnote to vol. iii. p. 197 (cf. vol. v. p. 86), but may here be stated a little more plainly. The earth being taken as the centre of the planetary system, the planets are arranged in the order of the radii of their orbits. The nearest planet is the Moon, then Mercury, Venus, the Sun, Mars, Jupiter, and Saturn. These were arranged by the astrologers in the *reverse* order; viz. Saturn, Jupiter,

Mars, Sun, Venus, Mercury, Moon; after which the rotation began over again, Saturn, Jupiter, Mars, &c.; as before. If we now divide Sunday into twenty-four hours, and assign the *first* of these to the Sun, the *second* to Venus (next in rotation), the *third* to Mercury, and so on, the *eighth* hour will again fall to the Sun, and so will the *fifteenth* and the *twenty-second.* Consequently, the *twenty-third* (like the *second*) belongs to Venus, the *twenty-fourth* to Mercury, and the *twenty-fifth* to the Moon. But the twenty-fifth hour is the first hour of the new day, which is therefore the day of the Moon. And so throughout.

Since the twenty-second hour belongs to the Sun, and the twenty-fifth to the Moon, the planetary interval from day to day is really obtained by pitching upon every *third* planet in the series, i.e. by skipping two. Hence the order of ruling planets for each day (which rule depends upon the assignment of the *first* hour) is obviously—the Sun, the Moon, Mars, Mercury, Jupiter, Venus, Saturn; or, in Anglo-Saxon terminology, the Sun, the Moon, Tīw, Wōden, Thunor (Thur), Frige, and Sætern (Sæter).

178. Cf. 'here wo into wele wende mote atte laste'; P. Plowman, C. xxi. 210. See notes to ch. 13. 86 below, and bk. i. 3. 153.

180. Cf. Troil. iv. 836, and the note (vol. ii. p. 490).

196. *slawe,* slain; the usual expression; cf. Compl. of Mars, 186; Compl. unto Pitè, 112.

Chap. X. 1-6. Cf. Ch. Boeth. bk. iii. pr. 9. 1-4; pr. 10. 1-4.

7. *three lyves;* as mentioned above, bk. ii. ch. 4. 44-6.

18. *firste sayde;* viz. in bk. ii. ch. 4. 56.

28-34. Borrowed from Ch. Boeth. bk. iii. met. 7.

37. *a fair parcel.* Similarly, Boethius recites his former good fortune; bk. ii. pr. 3. 20-43.

45. He insists that he was only a servant of conspirators; he would have nothing to do with the plot (l. 50); yet he repented of it (l. 49); and it is clear that he betrayed it (bk. i. ch. 6. l. 189).

58. *farn,* for *faren,* fared. *Fortune*; cf. the complaints of Boethius, bk. i. met. 1. 19; pr. 4. 8; bk. ii. met. 1.

68-71. From Ch. Boeth. bk. ii. pr. 4. 57-61.

81-3. From the same; bk. ii. pr. 4. 122; pr. 3. 61.

84-7. From the same; pr. 4. 127-32.

88-105. From the same; pr. 3. 48-63.

96. *both,* booth; Chaucer has *tabernacle*; pr. 3. 56.

105-10; 115-20. From the same; bk. ii. pr. 4. 33-42.

126-9. From the same; ll. 43-7.

133. Here begins a new chapter in Thynne; with a large capital C. See note to book ii. ch. i.

148-50. From Ch. Boeth. bk. ii. pr. 4. 97-101.

155. 'The soules of men ne mowe nat deyen in no wyse'; the same, ll. 122-3.

163. *oon of three*; see ch. 10. 10 above (p. 83).

Chap. XI. 11-3. Not in character; the author forgets that Love is supposed to be the speaker, and speaks in his own person.

40-8. From Ch. Boeth. bk. iii. met. 8. 3-7, 16-8; pr. ix. 12-16, 66-70; somewhat varied.

56. *over his soule*; cf. 'but only upon his body'; the same, bk. ii. pr. 6. 31.

56-69. The general idea corresponds with the same, bk. iii. pr. 9. I observe no verbal resemblance.

82. Thynne begins a new chapter here, with a large capital T. See note to bk. ii. ch. i.

93. *Plato.* This story is told of Socrates, and is given in the note to C. T., I 670, in vol. v. p. 466; from Seneca, De Ira, lib. i. c. 15.

111. *conclude* seems here to mean 'include,' as in C. T., G 429.

121. *habit .. monk*; 'Cucullus non facit monachum'; a common medieval proverb; see Rom. Rose, 6192, and the note.

125. *cordiacle* is Thynne's misprint for *cardiacle*; cf. 'That I almost have caught a cardiacle'; C.T., C 313.

Chap. XII. 8. *in place*, i. e. present; *chafinge*, warming.

14. *neigheth*, approaches; *and it .. be*, if it can be.

17. *Donet*, primer, elementary book of instruction; named from *Donatus*, the grammarian; see note to P. Plowman, C. vii. 215.

32. *muskle*; referring to bk. i. ch. 3. 78.

35. *excellence of coloures*, its (outward) blue colour. Blue was the emblem of constancy and truth; see note to C. T., F 644 (vol. v. p. 386). For *coloures* we should rather read *colour*; the same error occurs in l. 43 below (see footnote).

45. 'When pleasant weather is above.'

46. 'Betokening steadfastness (continuance) in peace'; cf. note to l. 35 above.

47. The following is Pliny's account of the Pearl, as translated by Holland; bk. ix. c. 35.

'This shell-fish which is the mother of Pearle, differs not much in the manner of breeding and generation from the Oysters; for when the season of the yeare requireth that they should engender, they seeme to yawne and gape, and so do open wide; and then (by report) they conceive a certaine moist dew as seed, wherewith they swell and grow big; . . . and the fruit of these shell-fishes are the Pear[l]es, better or worse, great or small, according to the qualitie and quantitie of the dew which they receiued. For if the dew were pure and cleare which went into them, then are the Pearles white, faire, and Orient: but if grosse and troubled, the Pearles likewise are dimme, foule, and duskish; . . . according as the morning is faire, so are they cleere; but otherwise, if it were misty and cloudy, they also will be thicke and muddy in colour.'

50. The sense of *Margaryte* in *this* passage is the visible church of Christ, as the context shews. In book iii. ch. 9. 160, the author tells us that it signifies 'grace, lerning, or wisdom of god, or els *holy church.*'

52. *mekenesse,* humility; cf. l. 63. The church is descended from Christ, who is the heavenly dew.

56. *reduced in-to good,* connected with good ; *mene,* intermediate.

58. *beestes,* living things that cannot move; the very word used by Chaucer, Boeth. bk. v. pr. 5. 20; compare the passage.

64. There is something wrong ; either *discendeth* should be *discended,* or we should understand *and* before *to* ; and perhaps *downe* should be *dewe*; cf. l. 68. The reference seems to be to the Incarnation.

68. Here the Protean word *Margaryte* means ' the wisdom of god,' judging by the context ; see note to l. 50 above.

78. This does not mean ' I would have explained it better,' but ' I should like to have it better explained.'

86. *Margaryte* here means the visible church, as before (l. 50) ; to the end of the chapter.

91. *welde,* possess ; and all that he now possesses is his life.

108. *yvel spekers*; this seems to allude to the Lollards, who ought (he says) to be ' stopped and ashamed.'

114. This shews that Margarete does not mean a woman ; for it is declared to be as precious as a woman, to whom it is likened.

121. *deedly,* mortal. Hence Margarete does not mean the church in general, but the visible church at the time of writing, the church militant.

Chap. XIII. 11. ' To be evil, is to be nothing.' The general argument follows Ch. Boeth. bk. iv. pr. 2. 143–94, and pr. 4.

23. *a this halfe,* on this side of, under ; cf. note to bk. i. ch. 9. 39.

30. *determinison,* determination ; a correct form. Cf. *venison* from Lat. acc. *uenationem.* Accordingly, the O. F. forms were *determinaison, -eson, -oison,* as given by Godefroy. He supplies the example : ' Definicio, difinicion ou *determineson,*' from an old glossary. Hence *determination* is here used in the sense of ' definition,' as is obvious from the context. Thynne prints *determission,* which makes nonsense ; and there is no such word. The present passage is entered in the New E. Dict. under *determission,* with the suggestion that it is an error ; it might have been better to enter it under *determinison* (or *-eson*) ; but it is always difficult to know how to deal with these mistakes of printers and editors.

33. *your-selfe sayd*; referring to l. 4 above.

35. *y-sayd good,* called ' good.'

40. *participacion*; from Ch. Boeth. bk. iii. pr. 10. 110.

43. *Austen,* St. Augustin ; and so Pope, Essay on Man, i. 294 :— ' One truth is clear, Whatever is, is right.'

49. *Boece,* Boethius ; whom the author here mentions just once more ; see his former allusion in bk. i. prologue, 110. The reference is to bk. iii. pr. 10. 153–84.

53. *apeted to,* sought after, longed for, desired. *Apete* is a correct form, as it represents an O. F. **apeter* ; but the usual O. F. form is *appeter* (Littré, s. v. *appéter*), from Lat. *appetere.* See New E. Dict., s. v. *Appete,* where a quotation is given from Chaucer, L. G. W. 1582.

But the right reading in that line is surely *appetyteth*, as *appeteth* will not scan; unless we strongly accent the initial *As*. See vol. ii. p. 137, l. 1582 and footnote, and the note to the line, at p. 328.

56. *This* stands for *This is*, as usual; see notes to C. T., A 1091, E 56.

71. *betterer*, better; not necessarily a misprint. The form *bettyrer* occurs in the Catholicon Anglicum.

72. *his kyndely place*, its natural position; cf. Ch. Boeth. bk. iii. pr. 11. 100-2.

77. *blacke*; cf. Troil. i. 642.

82. *yeven by the ayre*, endowed by the air with little goodness and virtue; because the dew that produced the pearl fell through the air; see note to ch. xii. 47 above. Hence *matier* is material, viz. the dew.

86. *unpees*, war. The general argument, with the contrast of colours above mentioned, occurs in P. Plowman, C. xxi. 209-21; cf. also ll. 144-66. Of these lines, ll. 210 and 212 have already been explicitly cited above: see notes to bk. i. ch. 3. 153, and to bk. ii. ch. 9. 178.

92. *Pallas*; we should have expected 'Minerva'; however, *Pallas* occurs five times in Troilus.

94. *and Mercurie*, if Mercury; but it is obscure.

99. *a dewe and a deblys*. Under *Adieu*, in the New E. Dict., we find: '*fig.* an expression of regret at the loss or departure of anything; or a mere exclamatory recognition of its disappearance;=away, no longer, no more, all is over with. *c.* 1400 *Test. Love* ii. (1560) 292/1. Adewe and adewe blis.'

Something has gone wrong here; the edition of 1561 (not 1560) has, at fol. 306, back (not 292) the reading 'a dewe and a deblis'; as in the text. The same reading occurs in all the earlier black-letter editions and in Chalmers; there being no other authority except Thynne. I do not understand the passage; the apparent sense is: 'his name is given *a dieu* and to devils'; i. e. (I suppose) is renounced. *Deblis* for 'devils' is a possible form; at any rate, we find *deblet*, *deblerie*, for *devilet* and *diablerie*; see New E. Dict., under *Dablet* and *Deblerie*.

115-6. 'That which is good, seems to me to be wholly good.' This is extremely significant. 'The church is good, and therefore wholly good,' is evidently intended. In other words, it needs no reform; the Lollards should let it 'alone. In ch. 14. 24, he plainly speaks of 'heretics,' and of the errors of 'mismeninge people.'

130. *leve*, believe. L. 120 shews that he hopes for mercy and pity; we may safely conclude that he had been a Lollard once. Cf. ch. 14. 2-4.

Chap. XIV. 6. *Proverbes.* He refers to Prov. vii. 7-22: 'Considero uecordem iuuenem, qui . . . graditur in obscuro, in noctis tenebris; et ecce occurrit illi mulier ornatu meretricio, praeparata ad capiendas animas, garrula et uaga, quietis impatiens . . . dicens . . . ueni, inebriemur uberibus, et fruamur cupitis amplexibus . . . statim eam sequitur quasi bos ductus ad uictimam.'

25. *skleren and wimplen*, veil and cover over. He probably found

the word *skleire*, a veil, in P. Plowman, C. ix. 5 (cf. also B. vi. 7, A. vii. 7), as that is the only known example of the substantive. The verb occurs here only. Other spellings of *skleire*, sb., in the MSS., are *sklayre, scleyre, slaire, skleir, sleire, sleyre*. Cf. Du. *sluier*, G. *Schleier*.

29. *by experience* ; i.e. the author had himself been inclined to ' heresy ' ; he was even in danger of ' never returning ' (l. 38).

36. *weyved*, rejected ; he had rejected temptations to Lollardry.

38. *shewed thee thy Margarite* ; meaning (I suppose) shewn thee the excellence of the church as it is.

40. *Siloë*, Siloam. It is a wonder where the author found this description of the waters of the pool of Siloam ; but I much suspect that it arose from a gross misunderstanding of Isaiah, viii. 6, 7, thus :— ' the waters of Shiloah that go softly . . . shall come up over all his channels, and go over all his banks.' In the Vulgate : ' aquas Siloë, quae uadunt cum silentio . . . ascendet super omnes riuos eius, et fluet super uniuersas ripas eius.' Hence *cankes* in l. 44 is certainly an error for *bankes* ; the initial *c* was caught from the preceding *circuit*.

46. After *Mercurius* supply *servaunts* or *children*. The children or servants of Mercury mean the clerks or writers. The expression is taken from Ch. C. T., D 697 :—

> ' The children of Mercurie and of Venus
> Ben in hir wirking ful contrarious.'

47. *Veneriens*, followers of Venus ; taken from Ch. C. T., D 609.

52. *that ben fallas* ; that is to say, deceptions. See *Fallace* in the New E. Dict.

60. *sote of the smoke*, soot of the smoke of the fire prepared for the sacrificed ox ; ' bos ductus ad uictimam'; Prov. vii. 22.

61. *it founde*, didst find it ; referring, apparently, to *thy langoring deth*.

67-8. *thilke Margaryte*, the church ; by serving which he was to be delivered from danger, by means of his amendment.

70. *disese*, misery, discomfort ; because he had to do penance.

74. He had formerly sinned against the church.

80. ' And yet thou didst expect to have been rejected for ever.'

83. *lache*, loosen (it) ; from O. F. *lascher*, to loosen, relax. Or it may mean ' turn cowardly.'

85. ' Inueni Dauid seruum meum ; oleo sancto meo unxi eum ' ; Ps. lxxxix. 20 (lxxxviii. 21, Vulgate).

93. *openly* ; hence the author had publicly recanted.

BOOK III.

Chap. I. This chapter is really a Prologue to the Third Book.

2. *discrete*, separate ; *tellinge*, counting.

3. *Three* was considered a perfect number ; see below.

6. Time was divided into three ages ; first, the age of Error, before the coming of Christ ; all that died then went to hell, whence some

were rescued by Christ when He descended thither. The second, the age of Grace, from the time of Christ's coming till His second advent. The third, the age of Joy, enduring for ever in heaven.

Deviacion ; Thynne prints *Demacion*, an obvious error for *Deuiacion* (*m* for *ui*) ; in l. 26, it is replaced by *Errour of misgoinge*, which has the same sense, and in bk. ii. ch. 8. 126, it is called *out-wayegoing*. The New E. Dict. has no quotation for *deviation* older than 1603 ; but here we find it.

25. I. e. Book I treats of Error or Deviation ; Book II, of Grace ; and Book III, of Joy.

28. *whiche is faylinge without desert*, which is failure without merit ; these words are out of place here, and perhaps belong to the preceding clause (after *shewed* in l. 26). *thilke*, &c. ; amending that first fault.

29. Perhaps for *and* read *an* ; it refers to guidance into the right path.

37. He says that the English alter the name *Margarite-perle* into *Margery-perle*, whereas Latin, French, and many other languages keep the true form. Cf. Lat. *margarita*, O. F. *marguerite, margarete,* Gk. μαργαρίτης, Pers. *marwārīd*, Arab. *marjān* ; all from Skt. *manjarī*, a pearl.

45. *the more Britayne*, greater Britain (England and Scotland), as distinguished from lesser Britain (Brittany) ; see note to bk. ii. ch. 12. 47 above. Pliny says (tr. by Holland, bk. ix. c. 35) :—' In Brittaine it is certain that some [pearls] do grow ; but they be small, dim of colour, and nothing orient.'

56. *conninge*, certain knowledge ; *opinion*, uncertain knowledge, supposition ; as he proceeds to say.

62. We thus learn that it was at this date an open question, whether the sun was bigger than the earth ; there were some who imagined it to be so.

68. He here mentions the *quadrivium*, or group of four of the seven sciences, viz. arithmetic, geometry, music, and astronomy ; see note to P. Plowman, C. xii. 98.

73. These are the four cardinal virtues, Prudence, Justice, Temperance, and Fortitude ; see note to P. Plowman, C. i. 131.

79. Why 'two things' are mentioned, is not clear. It was usual to introduce here the *trivium*, or second group of the seven arts (see note to l. 68) ; which contained logic, grammar, and rhetoric. For the two former he has substituted 'art,' the general term.

99. *twey*, two ; viz. *natural* and *reasonable* ; cf. l. 53. The third is *moral*. Hence we have the following scheme.

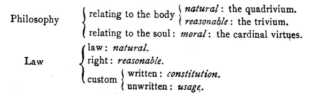

122. I. e. 'so that harm, (as punishment) for harm, should restrain evil-doers by the bridle of fear.'

125. *contraioustee of,* that which is contrary to.

130. *and unworthy,* even if they be unworthy.

professe and reguler; the 'professed' were such as, after a year of probation, had been received into a monastic order; the 'regular' were such as were bound by the three monastic vows of poverty, chastity, and obedience.

131. *obediencer,* bound by obedience; used adjectivally; cf. Low Lat. *obedientiarius.*

134. Thus the author was himself bound by monastic vows, and was one of the 'regular' clergy.

146-7. *abouten,* about (me), near at hand.   *eche,* to increase, lengthen.

156. *refrete,* refrain, burden of a song; O. F. *refrait, refret* (Godefroy). 'Sobs are a ready (ever-present) refrain in its meditations'; where *his* (its) refers to *goost,* or spirit, in l. 155.

157-8. *comming about I not than,* recurring I know not when. For *than* read *whan,* to make sense.

160. *he,* Christ; referring to Matt. xxi. 16.

161. *whos spirit*; 'Spiritus ubi uult spirat'; John, iii. 8; 'Spiritus, diuidens singulis prout uult'; 1 Cor. xii. 11.

170. *wyte that,* lay the blame for that upon. Such is the right idiom; cf. 'Wyte it the ale of Southwerk, I yow preye'; Ch. C. T., A 3140. Thynne prints *with* for *wite* or *wyte,* making nonsense of the passage.

Chap. II. 14. *lybel of departicion,* bill (or writ) of separation; taken from *libellum repudii* in Matt. v. 31, which Wyclif translates by 'a libel of forsakyng.'

16. 'I find, in no law, (provision for) recompensing and rewarding in a bounteous way, those who are guilty, according to their deserts.'

19. *Paulyn,* Paulinus. But there is some mistake. Perhaps he refers to L. Aemilius Paulus, brother of M. Aemilius Lepidus the Triumvir. This Paulus was once a determined enemy of Caesar, but was won over to his side by a large bribe.

21-3. I cannot explain or understand this clause; something seems to be omitted, to which it refers.

23. Julius Caesar was accounted as following Cato in justice. The statement is obscure.

25. Perdiccas, according to the romances, succeeded Alexander the Great; see note to Bk. ii. c. 2. 116. I do not find the anecdote referring to Porus. It is not improbable that the author was thinking of Philip the physician, who revealed to Alexander 'a privy hate' entertained against that monarch by Parmenion; see the Wars of Alexander, ed. Skeat, 2559-83.

49. *right as mater.* Cf. 'sicut ad formam de forma procedere materiam notum est'; an often quoted passage in Guido delle

Colonne's Historia Troiae ; see note to Legend of Good Women, 1582
(vol. iii. p. 329).

65. *and right,* if right-doing were not in the original working.

82. *muste do good nedes,* must necessarily do good.

87. *ende,* object. The reference seems to be to Aristotle, Nicomachean Ethics, bk. i. c. 1, c. 2, or c. 5.

90. *goodly,* with a good motive. In l. 99, it simply means 'a good
motive.'

112. *praysing ne lacking,* praise nor blame.

115. The Latin would be *nemo inuite beatus;* but I do not know
where to find it.

128. *free arbitrement,* Lat. liberum arbitrium; introduced in order
to lead up to a discussion of free will, necessity, and providence; as
in Boeth. bk. v.

140. *closing,* including, implying.

154-60. Cf. Ch. Boeth. bk. v. pr. 3. 1-18.

Chap. III. Cf. Ch. Boeth. bk. v. pr. 3 and pr. 4.

26. Cf. the same, pr. iii. 29, and the context.

58. *for I love,* i. e. because (or since) I love.

74. *commende,* coming ; probably the original MS. had *command,*
the Northern form. We have a similar form *lykende,* in l. 133 below.
In ll. 82, 83, the usual form *comming* appears.

82-3. In many places, *comming* is used nearly with the sense of
'future'; cf. ll. 177-8.

126. Here again we have the usual ridiculous contradictions ; the
sense is—'being wet, I burn; without wasting, I fade.' Cf. Rom.
Rose, Eng. version, 4703-50.

128. Thynne has (here and in ch. 6. 147, p. 132) *vnbyde,* an obvious
error for *onbyde,* i. e. abide, remain ; see ch. 7. 161, 163.

131. 'God grant (that) that thing may soon draw nigh to thee.'
Neigh is here a verb, as in Bk. ii. ch. 12. 14.

164. *that,* that which ; *with nothing,* yet not so as to be constrained
by anything else.

171. *rysinge of the sonne,* rising of the sun ; this example is borrowed
from Ch. Boeth. bk. v. pr. 6. 103, 165.

Chap. IV. Cf. Ch. Boeth. bk. v. pr. 6. 157-89.

29. *and nedeful is,* 'and it is necessary that, in order to desire
(a thing), he may also *not* desire (it)'; otherwise, he does not make
any choice.

30-1. The words 'But thilke . . . the same to wilne' are *repeated* in
Thynne's edition, to the destruction of the sense.

59. *as now,* present ; cf. Boeth. bk. v. pr. 6. 28-32.

96-9. A clear case of reasoning in a circle.

112. 'Constituisti terminos eius, qui praeteriri non poterunt'; Job,
xiv. 5.

121-6. See Rom. viii. 29, 30. *conformes;* the Vulgate has : ' Nam
quos praesciuit, et praedestinauit *conformes* fieri imaginis Filii sui.'

129. Cf. Ch. Boeth. bk. v. pr. 6. 35, 71-8.

140. Cf. the same, 12-9, 28-33, &c.

152. Referring to ll. 121-6 above.

165. *close and one*, are closed and united; here *close* and *one* seem to be verbs.

169. *by*, with reference to.

198-9. *no art*, in no way (?); but surely an error for *nat*, as *wrytest nat* is repeated in l. 200.

206. *defendeth*, 'forbids something to be movable,' &c.

220. Too obscure to deserve the encomium for perspicuity which follows in ll. 222-5.

232. *for right*, &c.; 'for nothing at all exists there (i. e. in eternity) after the manner of that which is temporal.'

243. *ben to ben*, are to come because of God's knowledge.

249. *philosophical poete*; Chaucer, because he translated The Consolation of Philosophy, and introduced passages from it into his poem of Troilus, notably in Book iv. 963-6, 974-1078.   In l. 254, Troilus is expressly mentioned.   Most likely, the allusion is to Bk. iv. 974-1078; although this deals rather with predestination than with the origin of evil.

257. *storiers*, gen. pl. of *storier*, a teller of a story; cf. O. F. *historieur*, an historian (Godefroy).   Thynne prints *starieres*; which gives no sense.

262. *two the laste*, the last two; chapters 13 and 14; but chapter 14 has little to do with the subject.

Chap. V. 4. 'Or as an ook comth of a litel spyr'; Troil. ii. 1335.

33-7. The word *welked* occurs twice in Chaucer, C. T., C 738, D 277; and *wiver* once, Troil. iii. 1010.

57. *with yvel .. acomered*, desires not to be encumbered with evil.

63. 'Why, as soon as one has sprung up on high, does not the other spring up also?'   Here 'one' and 'the other' seem to refer to 'will' and 'bliss'; cf. ll. 16, 17, 70, 71.

73-6. Cf. HF. 737-46; Boeth. bk. iii. pr. 11. 98-101.

Chap. VI. 4-7. Imitated from Ch. Boeth. bk. i. met. 6. 5-11.

10. *seconde boke*; cf. Book ii. ch. 11. 51-69, 102.

12. *setling*; misprinted *setteles*; but see *setling* in ch. 5. l. 23.

17. He here contemplates the possibility of yielding to persecution and threats.

50-1. The *five wits* are the five senses; P. Plowman, C. ii. 15, and the note.

60. *aptes*, natural tendencies; used here only; see New E. Dict.

64. *terme of equivocas*, terms of like signification; *terme* being an error for *termes*.   Answering to Lat. *uerba aequiuoca*, words of like signification; Isidore, Orig. ii. 26 (Lewis and Short).   *Equivocas* is formed by adding the Eng. pl. *-s* to the Lat. neuter plural (New E. Dict.).

Cf. the passage in P. Plowman, where *Liberum-arbitrium* recites his names; C. xvii. 201. The first name, 'instrument of willing,' corresponds to *animus*: '*dum uult, animus est*'; but the rest vary.

68. *reson.* Compare the same passage: '*dum iudicat, racio est.*'

73. Compare the same: '*dum recolit, memoria est.*'

77. *affeccion*: a disposition to wish for sleep.

90. *that lambes*, who scorn and despise lambs.   !

104. Thynne has *vs*, which is a not uncommon spelling of 'use.' I merely print 'us[e]' because *us* looks so unintelligible. In l. 103, the word is *usage*; in l. 110, we have *use*.

140. *thinges*; viz. riches, honour, and power; discussed in Book ii. chapters 5-7.

147. *onbyde*, misprinted *unbyde*; see note above, to ch. 3. 128.

Chap. VII. 11. The idea of this Tree is copied from P. Plowman, C. xix. 4-14. Thus in l. 11, the ground in which the tree grows is said to be 'ful in thyne herte'; and in P. Plowman, the tree grows in *cor-hominis*, the heart of man. In P. Plowman, the tree is called True-love, the blossoms are Benign-Speech (cf. l. 16), and thé fruits are deeds of Charity. See note to l. 69 below.

38. Cf. 'As, wry the gleed, and hotter is the fyr'; Legend of Good Women, 735.

50. *pype*; see Troil. v. 1433; C. T., A 1838 (and note).

53. *no wode lay use*, sing no mad song.

59. *Aristotel.* The reference appears to be to Aristotle, De Interpretatione (περὶ ἑρμηνείας), ch. 1. *Voice* seems to mean 'a word unrelated to a sentence,' i. e. not related to something else as forming part of a sentence.

69. So in P. Plowman, C. xix. 29, the tree is attacked by three wicked winds; especially 'in flouryng-tyme,' l. 35.

97. *A marchaunt*; so in Chaucer, C. T., G 945-50.

99. *So ofte*; from Ch. Troil. ii. 1380-3; note the epithet *happy*, the use of the sb. *sweigh* or *swaye*, and the phrase *come al at ones*, in both passages.

101. Cf. 'Gutta cauat lapidem'; Ovid, Ex Ponto, iv. 10. 5.

lethy, weak; see Prompt. Parv., and Gloss. to P. Plowman.

117-121. Compare Bk. iii. ch. 2. 122-9.

123. 'Quod debuimus facere, fecimus'; Luke, xvii. 10.

145. *al is*, it is all to be accounted to her wholly. *To wyte* usually has a bad sense; as implying blame.

160. *this lady*; i. e. Heavenly Love suddenly took up its place in his heart. This is rather inartistic; no wonder that the author was much astonished at such a proceeding (ch. 8. 2 below). This of course puts an end to the dialogue, but in Thynne's misarranged print the lady speaks to him again, as if it were *out of his heart!*

Chap. VIII. 7. *lynes*, written lines of writing, which he imagines to be imprinted on his understanding; see ll. 8, 13, 14 below.

10. *me might*, one might; *me* for *men = man*, as often.

21. *but for*, except because; so in l. **22.** *wol*, desires.

42. *owe I not alowe*, I ought not to applaud.

46. *it make*, cause it (to be so); as in Troil. ii. 959.

91. 'Quia Christi bonus odor sumus Deo, in iis qui salui fiunt; . . .
aliis quidem odor mortis in mortem'; 2 Cor. ii. 15-6.

120. *ne had*, had; disregarding *ne*, which is inserted after the word
denyed.

123. *without . . . nede*, without any kind of necessity.

125. *him nedeth*, something is lacking to him.

146. *forward*, thenceforward, afterwards.

155-6. *in his owne comodité*, in what is suitable for him; *comodites*, desires that are suitable.   The examples of the word in this
passage are older than any given, s.v. *Commodity*, in the New E. Dict.
Cf. ll. 159, 165.

Chap. IX. 7. *destenee*, destiny; cf. Ch. Boeth. bk. iv. pr. 6. 39, 44.

12. *non inconvenient*, convenient; i. e. befitting.

21. *chapitre*, chapter; viz. ch. 3 of Book iii.

46. Here Thynne's text returns to the right order.

52. The author now concludes his work with a prayer and a short
recommendation of his book to the reader. Ll. 58-61 speak of its
imperfections; ll. 61-6 tell us that the effort of writing it has done
him good.   In ll. 67-75 he anticipates future freedom from anxiety, and
continuance 'in good plight.'   He was then evidently unaware that his
death was near at hand.

86. ' My dull wit is hindred by the stepmother named Forgetfulness.'   A curious expression.

92. *horisons*, put for *orisons*, prayers.

98. *sightful*, visible; an obvious allusion to the eucharist (l. 100).
Similarly, a gem denotes a pearl, or 'margaret'; and Margaret (a
woman's name) denotes grace, learning, or wisdom of God, or else
holy church.

104. From John, vi. 63.

107. From 2 Cor. iii. 6.

109, 110. Printed as prose in Thynne; but two riming verses seem
to be intended.   If so, *al-le* is dissyllabic.

II. THE PLOWMAN'S TALE.

Numerous references are given to Pierce the Ploughman's Crede,
ed. Skeat (E.E.T.S.); a poem by the same author. See the Introduction.

9. *tabard*; a ploughman's loose frock; as in Ch. C. T., A 541.

11. *saynt Thomas*; i. e. his shrine at Canterbury.

30. *therwith to fynd*, to provide for thereby.

40. *queynt*, quenched; because, in the solemn form of excommuni-
cation used in the Romish church, a bell was tolled, the book of offices

for the purpose was used, and three candles were extinguished.   See
Nares, s. v. *Bell, Book, and Candle.*   Cf. ll. 165, 1241.

44. Four lines are here lost, the stanza being incomplete.   We
might supply them thus :—

> They have the loof and we the crust,
> They eten more than kinde hath craved ;
> They been ungentle and unjust,
> With sinners shullen such be graved.

53. *stryf,* strife.   The struggle was between the secular and regular
clergy on the one hand, and the Lollards on the other ; see ll. 61-76.
Each side accused the other of falseness, and the author hopes that the
falser of them may suffer shame.   He evidently sides with the Lollards ;
but, not caring to decide so weighty a question for himself, he contrives that the dispute shall be carried on by two birds, the Griffin and
the Pelican.

55. *sedes,* seeds.   The Lollards were accused of sowing tares (*lolia*).
The author hints that seeds were sown by *both* of the contending
parties.

57. *some* ; referring rather to the sowers than to the seeds.   In any
case, it refers to the two parties.

58. *souple* ; the text has *souble,* which is an obvious error.   The
O. F. *souple* means ' humble,' which is the sense here intended.

71. *a-cale,* chilled, frozen ; cf. note to P. Plowman, C. xxi. 439 ; and
see the New E. Dict.

72. *ever in oon,* always in the same condition, without increasing in
wealth.

73. *I-cleped,* called ; the old text has *Iclepeth,* but some editions
make this obvious correction.   *lollers,* idle fellows ; see the note to
P. Plowman, C. x. 213.

74. ' Whoever looks on them (sees that) they are the reverse of tall.'
Cf. ' a *tall* fellow,' and ' a *tall* man of his hands ' in Shakespeare.

81. *wro,* nook ; see *wrā* in Stratmann.

86. *Griffon,* griffin ; a fabulous monster with the head and wings of
an eagle, and the hinder parts of a lion ; with probable reference to
the Vulture.   ' In that contre ben many *griffounes* . . . thei han the
body upward as an egle, and benethe as a lyoun . . . But o griffoun
is more strong thanne .viij. lyouns ' ; Mandeville's Travels ; ch. xxvi.
See l. 1317 below.

87. ' A Pelican laid his lure to (attracted to him) these lollers.'   The
Pelican was supposed to feed its young with blood which it drew from
its own breast by wounding it, and was early considered as the type of
Christian love or Charity, or of Christ himself ; see l. 1293.   See the
illustration at p. 172 of Legends of the Holy Rood, ed. Morris.   Hence it
is here supposed to plead on behalf of meekness, in the long passages
contained in ll. 95-716,   719-988,   991-1072,   1110-32,   1177-232,
1245-68.   The Pelican is responsible for the greater part of the

poem, as the author distinctly says in l. 1373. Anything that is amiss, we are told, must be put down to the Pelican; the author is irresponsible, as it is only a fable.

106. *pelure*, costly fur ; also spelt *pellour* ; but *pylloure* (as in the old text) is a bad spelling. See Gloss. to P. Plowman.

111. *batail*, battle. It was notorious that William Spenser, bishop of Norwich, used to lead military expeditions. Thus he led one such expedition into Flanders, in 1382. Cf. l. 128.

129. 'God is not the master of them that consider no man equal to them.'

130. *peragall*, equal; spelt 'peragal' or 'paragal' in Rich. the Redeless, i. 71. The old text has *permagall*, where the *m* is clearly for *in*; the spelling *peringall* being intended. Godefroy has O. F. *parivel*, also *parigal, paregal, perigal, paringal* [with intrusive *n*], 'adj. et s., tout à fait ègal, tout à fait semblable.' From Lat. *per-aequalis.*

135. 'Painted and adorned with colours.' Cf. 'peynt and portred '; P. Pl. Crede, 192 ; 'portreid and paynt,' 121.

139. *boystous*, rough. The O. F. *boistous* meant 'lame' (F. *boiteux*); but Godefroy shews, in his Supplement, that it was also applied to a very rough road (as being likely to lame one); hence, generally, rough, and finally, rude, noisy, as in the E. *boisterous*; a word of which the etymology has not yet been fully accounted for, but may be thus explained.

159. *perrey*, precious stones, jewellery; see *Perree* in the Glossary (vol. vi). The old text has *pyrrey.*

162. *gown*, an obvious correction ; old text, *gold*, repeated from l. 161. For 'grene gownes,' see l. 925 below.

178. This line seems to be corrupt.

186. *crallit*, curled, twisted ; cf. *crulle* in Chaucer ; see New E. Dict.

187. *gold-mastling* is a compound word, and should have been printed with a hyphen. It means the same as *latoun*, unless *latoun* was an imitation of an older and richer alloy. Thus, in Wright's A. S. Vocabularies, we find : '*Auricalcum*, goldmæslinc,' col. 334, 10 ; '*Auricalcum*, goldmestling,' col. 550, 34 ; '*Auricalcum, Anglice* latoun,' col. 567, 5. As to *latoun*, see note in vol. v. p. 270. Cf. A. S. *mæstling*, G. *Messing*; words of uncertain origin.

193-4. Cf. 1 John, iv. 3. *admirall*, prince, chief.

198. *demed*; an easy correction ; old text, *done*, which will not scan.

201. *All-holyest*, i. e. *Sanctissimus* (l. 230) ; a title given to the head of a religious order.

208. 'The very thing which Christ forbad to the apostles.'

212. 'They regard him (the pope) as wholly omnipotent.'

213-6. *He*, the Pope. *another*, (apparently) a head of a religious order, an abbot or prior. *mystere*, ministry, office.

220. 'He reserves nothing at all '; *opin*, open, a thing that is free ; *joint*, a thing that is connected.

226. *An angell*; see Rev. xxii. 9.

235. Read *Christ his*; 'Christ keep his people from them'; the printer evidently regarded *Christ his* as a form of the genitive case. The proper sense of *wisse* is guide, or direct.

242. *which of hem*, which of the two popes. The rival popes were Boniface IX, elected Nov. 2, 1389, and Benedict XIII, elected Sept. 28, 1394. Clement VIII, predecessor of the latter, died Sept. 16, 1394.

245. 'Omnes enim, qui acceperint gladium, gladio peribunt'; Matt. xxvi. 52.

255. Swearing was a dismembering of Christ; see note to C. T., C 474 (vol. v. p. 275).

264. 'But curse all that oppose them.'

275. 'But he, who so acquires it, shall part from it.'

281. *rent*, income, profit; the method of doing this is explained in The Freres Tale, D 1371-4.

282. 'They anoint the sheep's sore'; as a shepherd does with tar; see *Tar-box* in Halliwell; and cf. l. 707.

293. *Maximien*; Galerius Valerius Maximianus, usually called Galerius; emperor of Rome, 305-11; a cruel persecutor of the Christians.

297. 'They follow Christ (who went upward) to heaven, just as a bucket (that goes downward) into a well.' Said ironically; their ascent towards heaven is in a downward direction; cf. l. 402. *wall* for 'well' is rare, but not unexampled; cf. *walle-stream*, well-stream, in Layamon, vol. i. p. 121, and see *walle* in Stratmann.

305. 'The truth has (often) slain such men.'

306. 'They comb their "crockets" with a crystal comb.' A *crocket* was a curl or roll of hair, as formerly worn; see the New E. Dict. There is a lost romance entitled 'King Adelstane with gilden kroket'; see footnote to Havelok, ed. Skeat, p. vi. Sir F. Madden remarks that 'the term *crocket* points out the period [i. e. the earliest possible date] of the poem's composition, since the fashion of wearing those large rolls of hair so called, only arose at the latter end of the reign of Henry III.'

321. Cf. 'turpis lucri'; Tit. i. 7, 11; 1 Pet. v. 2.

322. *meynall*, perhaps better spelt *meyneall*. It is the adj. formed from M. E. *meynee*, a household, and is the same word as mod. E. *menial*. Wyclif uses *meyneal* to translate Lat. *domesticam* in Rom. xvi. 5. The sense here is—the exaction of tithes is, with these masters, a household business, a part of their usual domestic arrangements.

325. Lit. 'They betake to farm to their sumners,' i. e. they farm out to their sumners the power of harming people as much as they can; they let their sumners make exactions. The method of doing this is fully exposed in Chaucer's Freres Tale. Cf. ll. 328, 725.

333. 'Such rascals are sure to slander men, in order to induce them to win their favour'; i. e. by compounding.

338. *call*, caul or head-dress, richly ornamented, and therefore expensive; see note to C. T., D 1018 (vol. v. p. 318).

375. 'Or, to commit such a tool (instrument) to such cursed men.'

402. 'As good a bishop as is my horse Ball.' Said ironically; 'no better a bishop than,' &c. Ball was, and still is, a very common name for a horse.

406. *nothing*, not at all, not a whit.

410. Old text, *one fors*, with *s* attached to the wrong word.

417-8. *goodes*, property. *somme totall*, sum total of wealth.

421, 431. *for Christes love*, for love of Christ. The words *forsake* in l. 421, and *wake* in l. 431, are used ironically.

434. *Lamuall*, Lemuel; who was a king; Prov. xxxi. 1.

443. *the stoon*, the rock; Matt. xvi. 18; cf. 1 Cor. x. 4.

445. *croysery*, crusade, as in Rob. of Glouc. 9938. No serious crusade was intended at this time; however, the author affirms that the rival popes discouraged the idea; for each wanted men to fight for him.

464. *hye seet*, sat aloft; the form *seet* occurs in Ch. C. T., A 2075.

471. *fettes*, fetch; observe the use of this Northern plural.

473. 'Their servants are unfaithful [or unserviceable] to them unless they can double their rental.'

477. The author can find no more rimes to rime with *fall*, so he proceeds to 'shew' or propose another word, viz. *amend*.

487. 'They tell men nothing, nor (explain) how; yet, in God's word, they tell of (or count) many a slip, or omission,' i. e. find errors in the Scriptures. See *Balk* in the New E. Dict.

490. *offrend*; O. F. *offrende*; cf. '*Offrande*, an offering'; Cotgrave.

520. Read *punishěments*, as in the old edition; it is a word of four syllables; from O. F. *punissement* (Godefroy), which often appears in verse as a word of four syllables.

531. 'They hate guests of the poor,' i. e. hate to entertain them; cf. l. 747.

542. *careckes*, characters, signs, marks; see the New E. Dict.

567. 'One, to curse to hell; the other, to slay men here (on earth)'; cf. Luke, xxii. 38.

575. 'A sword is no implement to guard sheep with, except for shepherds that would devour the sheep.' In later English, at any rate, a *sheep-biter* meant a thief (Halliwell). Cf. l. 583.

594. *untrend*, unrolled; not rolled up, but freshly pulled off.

605. *Sathan*, Satan; Heb. *sātān*, adversary, opponent.

610. Read *reprende*; cf. *comprende* in Chaucer.

625. *ensyse*, variant of *assyse*, fashion, sort; 'they are, surely, of the same sort.' See *Assize*, sect. 8, in the New E. Dict. Bailey gives: '*Ensise*, quality, stamp; *Old word*'; with reference, doubtless, to this very line. Cf. *assyse*, fashion, manner, in l. 843 below.

626. *frend*, evidently put for *fremde*, strange, foreign, averse; which was difficult to pronounce.

633. Read *maundements*, i. e. commandments (trisyllabic). The form

commaundementes is too long for the line. See *mandement* in Strat-mann and in Chaucer.

642. *to prison.* Evidently written before 1401, when Lollards were frequently sent to the stake for heresy. Cf. l. 650; and see note to l. 827.

645. 'The king's law will judge no man angrily, without allowing the accused to answer.'

661. *testament*, a will; the friars had much to do with the making of wills.

681. 'For they (the people) are faster in their bonds, worse beaten, and more bitterly burnt than is known to the king.' For the word *brent*, see note to l. 827.

693. *The emperour*; Constantine, according to a legend which the Lollards loved to repeat; see the full note to P. Plowman, C. xviii. 220.

695. *sely kyme*, innocent (or silly) wretch. *Kyme* answers to an A.S. *cȳma=*kūm-ja, lit. 'one who laments,' from the verb found in O.H.G. *kūmjan*, to lament, *chū-mo*, a lament; cf. Gk. γόος, wailing; Skt. *gu*, to sound. See O.H.G. *cūm*, *cūmjan* in Schade; and the Idg. root *gu*, in Fick.

723. 'A title of dignity, to be as a play-mate to them'; a curious expression. Godefroy gives O. F. '*personage*, s.m., dignité, bénéfice ecclésiastique; en particulier personnat, dignité ecclésiastique qui donnait quelque prééminence au *chanoine* qui en était revêtu dans le chapitre auquel il appartenait.' Cotgrave has: '*Personat*, a place, or title of honour, enjoyed by a beneficed person, without any manner of jurisdiction, in the church.'

724. Possibly copied from P. Plowman, B. prol. 92 :—' Somme serven the king, and his silver tellen.' These ecclesiastics often busied themselves in the law-courts, to their great profit. Cf. l. 790.

725. 'And let out to farm all that business.'

743. *builde*; so in P. Pl. Crede, 118 : 'For we buldeth a burwgh, a brod and a large.' Cf. Wyclif's Works, ed. Arnold, iii. 380.

748. 'Nor (will they) send anything to Him who hath given them everything.'

759. *gigges*, concubines; see Stratmann. Roquefort has : '*Gigues*, fille gaie, vive.' Cf. *giglot* in Shakespeare. (Initial *g* is here sounded as *j*.)

760. 'And provide them with fine clothes.'

773. Here all the 'seven sins' are mentioned except gluttony.

780. 'The wisdom of such willers is not worth a needle.'

791. *jay*; so also in Chaucer, C. T., A 642.

801. *maynteyners*, abettors of wrongdoers; see note to P. Plowman, B. iii. 90.

827. *brent*, burnt; still more strongly put in l. 1234. That heretics were sometimes burnt before 1401, is certain from Wyclif's Sermons, ed. Arnold, vol. i. pp. x, 205, as compared with p. 354. There is a case given in Bracton of a man who was burnt as early as in the reign of

Henry III. See the whole subject discussed in my edition of P. Plowman (E. E. T. S.), in the Pref. to B-text, p. v, Pref. to C-text, pp. xi–xiv, and the note to B. xv. 81, where Langland has 'ledeth me to brennynge.' Observe that the king is here spoken of as not presuming to burn heretics.

855. The seven sacraments of the Romish church; cf. l. 875.

856. Compare—'And also y sey coveitise *catel to fongen*'; P. Pl. Crede, 146.

857. 'They want to meddle in everything, and to perform matters amiss is their amusement.'

868. *sturte*, variant of *sterte*, start up; *stryve*, struggle.

870. *at the nale* = *at then ale*, at the ale-house; cf. note to P. Plowman, C. i. 43.

871. Cf. 'At marketts and miracles we medleth us nevere'; P. Pl. Crede, 107.

872. 'They dance and hoot with the cry of "heave and hale."' *Heave* is here to use exertion; cf. Troil. ii. 1289; and *hale* is to haul or pull. *Heave and hale*, or *heave and hoe*, was a cry used for men to pull all together; hence *with heve and hale* just corresponds to the modern 'with might and main.' Cotgrave has (s.v. *Cor*) the phrase: '*À cor et à cry*, by proclamation; also, by might and maine, with heave and hoe, eagerly, vehemently, seriously.'

878. *they*, i.e. the husbands; *sory*, aggrieved.

880. *For*, for fear of being summoned.

893. *stocke*, i.e. some image of a saint. An image of a favourite saint was honoured with many candles burning before it; whilst other saints were left in the dark, because they could work no miracles. The most favourite image was that of Mary; see l. 902, and cf. P. Pl. Crede, 79.

915. 'And alle povere in gost god himself blisseth'; P. Pl. Crede, 521.

918. *Baudriks*, belts; *baselardes*, short swords, sometimes curved. See note to P. Plowman, C. iv. 461.

927. *counten* . . *of gownes*, they think much (*counten*) of scarlet and green gowns, that must be made in the latest fashion, in order to embrace and kiss the damsels. An awkward sentence.

929. *sewe*, sue, suit, lit. follow; unless it be for *schewe*, i.e. shew.

930. *pykes*, peaks. Long-peaked shoes were much in fashion; cf. note to P. Plowman, C. xxiii. 219.

941. 'Such men will ask them (i.e. those that confess to them) for money for shriving them.' *is* = *es*, them; a curious form of the plural pronoun of the third person; see *es* in Stratmann.

942. 'And they desire men to creep to the cross.' 'Creeping to the cross' was an old ceremony of penance, most practised on Good Friday; see note to P. Plowman, C. xxi. 475.

943. *askes*, ashes; alluding to the sacrament of penance. For all other sacraments (as baptism, confirmation, holy orders, the eucharist, matrimony, and extreme unction) men had to pay.

955. *sans .. dyre*, without (saying) 'if I may say so.' That is, *ose je dyre*, (dare I say it) is an apologetic phrase for introducing an unpalatable remark.

957. 'Either they give the bishops (some reason) why.'

961. *agryse*, dread, here used in an imperative sense; 'let such men dread God's anger.' Cf. ll. 964, 1216.

979. *for he*, because he would fain earn something.

993. *Benet*, Benedict; cf. Ch. C. T., A 173, and note.

1002. Cf. 'Of double worstede y-dight'; P. Pl. Crede, 228.

1035. Compare—'And his syre a soutere' (cobbler); P. Pl. Crede, 752.

1042-4. *honged*, hung upon, followed after. Cf. 'opon the plow hongen,' P. Pl. Crede, 421. And compare also the same, 784-8.

1050. The line is imperfect. I have supplied *but*, but the right word is *not*. For *cherelich* means 'expensive' or 'prodigal,' from O. F. *cher*, dear. This we know from the occurrence of the same rare form as an adverb in P. Pl. Crede, 582; where the sense is—'but to maintain his chamber as expensively (*chereliche*) as a chieftain.' See *cherely* in the New E. Dict. The parallel phrase *not lordlych* occurs in l. 1052.

1066. *Crede*, i. e. Pierce the Ploughman's Crede, written shortly before by the same author, and describing at length the four orders of friars.

1089. *sad*, sated, tired. The more usual old sense was 'staid.'

1097. 'If they were poor, filthy, and dirty.'

1102. *honest*, honourable, worthy of respect; cf. l. 1105.

1115. *Maysters*, masters; Matt. xxiii. 10. Cf. P. Pl. Crede, 574 6, 838; and C. T., D 2185, and the note (vol. v. p. 340).

1135. Read *leve*, not *lyve*; *with hir leve*, with what is permitted to them. For *leve* (leave), see l. 1238.

1153. *For ye woll*, because you wish to.

1166. *distaunce*, disagreement, strife; see Mätzner.

1174. 'Why do ye meddle, who have nothing to do with it?'

1189. *lette*, to prevent men from living in that way.

1193. *soule-hele*, salvation for the soul.

1200. Pronounce *this is* as *this*.

1212. *Wedding*, matrimony; considered as a sacrament.

1222. 'subject or accident'; cf. note to C. T., C 539.

1231. The line should end with a semicolon.

1244. 'Unless ye will act otherwise.'

1271. *cockes*, euphemistic for *goddes*.

1272. *doule*, small feather, down-feather. I derive it from O. F. *doulle*, variant of *douille*, soft, something soft, from Lat. *ductilis*. Hence it meant something downy, and, in particular, the 'down-feather' of a bird. This is clearly the sense in Shakespeare also, where Ariel uses the expression—'one *dowle* that's in my plume'; Temp. iii. 3. 65; i. e. one down-feather (small feather) that is in my plumage. Dr. Schmidt is in doubt whether *plume* here means 'plumage,' but the stage-direction expressly says that 'Ariel enters like a harpy, and claps his *wings* upon the table.' It is very interesting to see how well this passage illustrates Shakespeare. See Mr. Wright's note for other passages where *dowl* means 'soft down.' Of course, the words *dowl* and *down* are in no way connected. See my note in Phil. Soc. Trans. 1888-90, p. 3.

1280. *God wolde*, i.e. oh! that it might be God's will. Cf. *would God*, Numb. xi. 29 ; Deut. xxviii. 67 ; 2 Kings, v. 3 ; Rich. II, iv. 1. 117.

1293. Christ was likened to the pelican ; see note to l. 87.

1305. *The foul*, the former or *bird*-like part of the griffin ; see note to l. 86, and cf. l. 1317.

1315. 'Because bribery may break God's prohibition.'

1317. Referring to the form of the griffin ; see notes to ll. 86, 1305.

1336. *Y-gurd*, lit. girt ; hence, prepared, ready.

1339. *ly*, lie, i.e. deceive ; because the lapwing tries to delude those who search for its nest.

1340. *for-gerd*, destroyed, utterly done away with ; from M. E. *for-garen*.

1343. *the Phenix*. The Phœnix is here supposed, as being an unique bird, to be the king or master of all birds, and to execute vengeance on evil-doers.

1359. The sense of *of* is here uncertain. Perhaps *of flight* means 'as regards my flight,' and so 'to protect my flight.'

1361. This line is somewhat 'set back,' as in the original. But there seems to be no reason for it.

1362. The original has: 'And the lambe that slayn was' ; imperfect.

1367. Here the author speaks for himself, and excuses the Pelican's language.

III. JACK UPLAND.

To this piece, which is an attack upon the friars, a reply was made by one of them (probably a Dominican, see notes to ll. 100, 130), which is printed at length in Wright's Political Poems and Songs (Record Series), vol. ii. pp. 39-114 ; together with a rejoinder by Jack Upland, printed on the same pages. The friar's reply is often cited in the Notes below, where the number refers to the page of the above-named volume. See further in the Introduction.

1. *Jack Uplande*, Jack the Countryman, a nickname for one who is supposed to have had but little education ; cf. the *Plowman's* Tale.

6. *fellest folk*, the wickedest people ; referring to the friars.

7. The friar's reply copies several of these expressions: thus we find—' On wounder wise, seith Jak, freres, ye ben growun ' ; p. 42.

8. ' sowen in youre sectes of *Anticristis* hondes ' ; p. 42.

9. *not obedient* ; 'unboxom *to bishopis*, not *lege men to kynges*' ; p. 42. The friar asserts that they *do* obey the bishops ; but carefully adds—'although not so fer forth as seculer preestes ' ; p. 44.

11. '*wede, corn, ne gras*, wil ye not hewen'; p. 42; repeated on p. 44. The friar retorts that they are not expected to cleanse ditches, like a Jack Upland; p. 44. We thus learn that *woode* in l. 11 is almost certainly an error for *weede*.

15. *where to been*, where they will (hereafter) go to.

21. See 1 Cor. xiii. 1-3.

27. *skilfully*, reasonably; *skill* often has the sense of reason.

28. The friar evades the question as to the number of orders, and replies that he is of Christ's order; pp. 59-61.

35. Reply: St. James makes mention of two kinds of life, the active and the contemplative; we belong to the latter; pp. 63-6.

37. *apostata*, apostate; a term applied to a friar who left his order (see l. 42) *after* his year of probation had been completed, or else (see l. 42) after a probation of three months. See ll. 273-5, and 310-2 below; and the note to P. Plowman, C. ii. 98 (B. i. 104). The question here put was not answered.

40 1. Reply: it is shocking to speak of men leaving their wives like this; we are not wedded to our habit any more than a priest is to his tonsure; p. 67.

44. Reply: no. We are only punished for leaving off our habits because it implies forsaking of our rule. Our habits are not sendal, nor satin nor golden; pp. 67-8.

50. Reply: what, Jack, does your tippet mean? My wide cope signifies charity. My hood, patience in adversity. The scapulary denotes obedience to our superiors. As for the knotted girdle, ask the Franciscans; pp. 68-71.

52. Reply: Why do most of the Lollards wear gray clothes? p. 71.

58. No reply to this question.

60. Reply: see Eccles. iii. 7; Prov. xxv. 28; p. 71.

62. Reply: a question rather for monks than friars. Why do you not put your dining-table in your cow-house? p. 72.

65. Reply: perhaps some of us go to Rome for dispensations, but most of us have need to stay at home, to keep watch over Lollards; p. 73.

70. Reply: you have forgotten the text, 2 Cor. vi. 9; p. 74.

74. Reply: Christ, at His transfiguration, had only three witnesses from among His apostles. And He chose only twelve apostles, out of His many followers; and see Prov. xii. 15; p. 75.

77. Reply: a man is better than a beast; yet even for your beasts you make cattle-sheds and stables. Our houses are often poor ones. Did you ever see any that resembled the Tower, or Windsor Castle, or Woodstock? Your lies are shameless; pp. 77-8. I note here Jack Upland's rejoinder; he says that he does not object to the friars having houses, but he objects to the needless grandeur of them; for it does not follow that a man who drinks a quart of wine must therefore proceed to drink a gallon; p. 76.

83. Reply: you say that we let the whole realm to farm. Why, it

is not ours at all! It belongs to the king. We have no more estate in the country than you have in heaven; pp. 78-9. The incompleteness of this reply is amazing.

86. The original reading must have been different here. The friar puts the question thus: Why do you pay no tribute to the king, whereas Christ paid tribute to the emperor? Reply: Christ did not pay it as a debt, but only to perform the law in meekness. The Jewish priests did not pay taxes like the commons. Priests may pay if they are willing, but not friars; pp. 79, 80.

90. Reply: we are glad to have the prayers of the poor, if their letters of fraternity are genuine; but we do not desire *your* paternosters; p. 80.

92. Reply: we do not make men more perfect than their baptism makes them; p. 81.

95. Reply: the golden trental, ' that now is purchasid of preestis out of freris hondis,' delivers no soul, except as it is deserved; p. 81. See note to Ch. C. T., D 1717 (vol. v. p. 331).

100. Reply: you are quite mistaken. Perhaps some Carmelite told you this, or some Franciscan. The Austin friars and the Dominicans do not say so; p. 82.

105. Reply: if you accuse us of stealing children, Christ practically did the same, by enticing disciples to follow him. See Matt. xix. 21; Luke, xiv. 33; John, xv. 19. To win souls is no robbery; pp. 83-4.

109. *undernime*, reprove. Reply: according to you, not even the king should maintain any discipline. The pope has a prison; and so has the bishop of Canterbury, and the bishop of London. But you do not like prisons, for you often experience them; pp. 85-6.

114. Reply: burial is *not* a sacrament, as you say. You contradict yourself; p. 86.

116. Reply: if, as you say, we never shrive the poor, why are parish-priests so angry with us for doing so? p. 87. Cf. note to P. Plowman, C. xiii. 21. Questions 26, 27, and 28 are passed over.

127. Reply: we do right to live of the gospel; see 1 Cor. ix. 14; Luke, x. 7; Rom. xv. 26.

130. Reply: God knows how much good the preaching of the friars has wrought; p. 89. The Dominicans especially were proud of their preaching.

133. The friar here remarks that the Wycliffites are heretics, and ought to be burnt; p. 90. The same remark is all the answer made to question 32.

141. Reply: the friars do not *sell* the mass; they only freely give it to those who freely give to them. Even if we did sell it, surely the parish-priests receive money for the same; this is not simony; pp. 93-5. See note to Ch. C. T., D 1749; vol. v. p. 333.

149. Reply: we write down the names only to help our *own* memories; for special prayers are very profitable for souls; pp. 99, 100. See note to Ch. C. T., D 1741; vol. v. p. 332.

153. *berest god in honde,* accusest Christ.   Reply: Christ was lord of all spiritually ; but, as a man, he was needy.   David says of Him, 'I am poor and needy, yet the Lord thinketh upon me'; Ps. xl. 17. I refer you to Matt. viii. 20 ; pp. 95-8.

156. No special answer is given to questions 36-9.

187. Reply: you expect your servant to call you 'master.'   It is not the being called 'master,' but ambition, that Christ forbids ; pp. 100-1. Cf. note to Ch. C. T., D 2185 ; vol. v. p. 340.

189. The reply is singular, to the effect that pope John XXIV wrote against this matter, and the friars Minors (Franciscans) against him. 'Examyne her actis, and loke who hath the beter ; and knowe noon other ordre this perfitnesse approveth' ; p. 101.

208. There is no reply to question 42.

211. Reply ; going two and two together is a scriptural custom. Barnabas and Paul did so.   So did Paul and Timothy.   Besides, there were *two* tables in the law, *two* cherubim in the temple, and *two* in the tabernacle.   It was not good for Adam to be *alone* ; pp. 101-3. Cf. note to P. Plowman, C. xi. 8 ; and to Chaucer, C. T., C 1740.

213. There seems to be no reply to questions 44-8.

246. As regards question 49, the friar replies to ll. 249-51, saying that, according to this, no one could pray for any one ; for we cannot tell his future destiny ; p. 103.   Cf. note to Ch. C. T., D 2126 ; vol. v. p 339.

258. Questions 50 and 51 do not seem to be noticed.   Question 52 is partly answered in the reply to question 22.   See l. 105.

277. Reply : you admit (l. 283) that God made *all things* according to weight, number, and measure.   But a friar is *something* ; ergo, God made friars according to weight, &c.   Why are priests so numerous ? As to a man's hand (l. 287), the number of fingers is fixed, and an extra finger is monstrous.   But neither God nor holy church have fixed the number of priests or friars.   'Many hondis togider maken light werk' ; pp. 105-6.   Cf. note to P. Plowman, C. xxiii. 270.

At this point the friar introduces a subject not discussed in the copy of Jack Upland here printed, viz. the subject of transubstantiation. He says that Jack accuses the friars of saying that the bread is not Christ's body, but mere roundness and whiteness, and accident without subject ; and Wyclif is adduced as saying that it remains material bread, and only Christ's body in a figurative sense ; pp. 106-10.   The rest of the friar's reply (which goes but little further) is inapplicable to our text, so that the latter part of the treatise, ll. 294-end, is left unanswered.   Perhaps sections 54-64 were, at first, a somewhat later addition.

296. This has been partly said before ; see l. 77 above.

310. It was thought that to die in a friar's habit increased a man's chance of salvation ; see l. 100 above.

320. Cf. note to P. Plowman, C. xiii. 21.   See l. 246 above.

336. Cf. P. Plowman, C. xxiii. 323-72.

368. This enquiry takes up a large portion of the Ploughman's Crede. The jealousy of one order against the other was very remarkable. See note to l. 100 above.

399. See James, i. 27 ; cf. l. 36 above.

411. See Matt. xi. 30. Wyclif has—' For my yok is *softe*, and my charge light.'

421. The Franciscans claimed that St. Francis sat in heaven above the Seraphim, upon the throne from which Lucifer fell ; see note to P. Plowman, C. ii. 105 (B. i. 105).

424–7. Evidently intended for four alliterative lines, but the third is too long ; read—' And whan ye han soiled that I saide,' &c. Again, the first is too short ; read—' Go, *frere*, now forth,' &c.

430. *even-Christen*, fellow-Christian ; see Gloss. to P. Plowman.

433. ' Benefac humili, et non dederis impio : prohibe panes illi dari, ne in ipsis potentior te sit'; Ecclus. xii. 6.

IV. GOWER : THE PRAISE OF PEACE.

This piece has no English title except that printed at p. 205 ; for the Latin title, see p. 216. See the Introduction.

12, 13. Henry founded his title on conquest, hereditary right, and election. The first of these is referred to in ll. 9, 10 ; the second, in l. 12 ; and the third, in l. 13. See note in vol. i. p. 564, to XIX. 23.

17. *boun*, ready ; better than the reading *bounde*.

21. I note here an unimportant variation. For *this is*, the MS. has *is this*.

27. I find that there is no need to insert *the*. Read *requeste*, in three syllables, as it really had a final *e*, being a feminine substantive. Cf. ' Et lor *requestë* refaison ' ; Rom. Rose, 4767. *Requeste* is trisyllabic in Troil. iv. 57 ; L. Good Wom. 448.

36. According to the romance of Alexander, the god Serapis, appearing in a dream, told him that his great deeds would be remembered for ever. Before this, Alexander had told his men that he hoped to conquer all the earth—' with the graunt of my god.' See Wars of Alexander, ed. Skeat, ll. 990, 1095.

57. This obviously refers to Bolingbroke's invasion, when he came, as he said, to claim his inheritance ; cf. l. 65.

81. *Of pestilence*, out of pestilence, to free him from pestilence.

86. *lyf*, person, man ; lit. ' living soul.' Common in P. Plowman.

174, 179. Matt. v. 9 ; John, xiv. 27.

185. *out of herre*, out of (off) the hinge ; like mod. E. ' out of joint.' A favourite phrase of Gower's ; see his Conf. Amant. ii. 139 ; iii. 43, 52, 203, 211.

197. Knights were expected to defend the faith ; see note to P. Plowman, C. ix. 26. Cf. ll. 243–5.

202. I supply *alday* (i. e. continually) to complete the line.

204. *wayted*, watched, carefully guarded; in contrast to l. 207.

211. For *any* perhaps read *a*; the line runs badly.

218. ' It is easier to keep a thing than acquire it.'

236. *assysed*, appointed; as in Conf. Amant. i. 181; iii. 228.

251. ' Let men be armed to fight against the Saracens.'

253. Three points; stated in ll. 254, 261-2, and 268; i. e. the church is divided; Christian nations are at variance; and the heathen threaten us.

281-3. These are the nine worthies; of whom three were heathen (281), three Jewish (282), and three Christian (283); as noted in Reliquiæ Antiquæ, i. 287. Sometimes they varied; thus Shakespeare introduces Hercules and Pompey among the number; L. L. L. v. 2. 538. *Machabeus*, Judas Maccabeus. *Godfray*, Godfrey of Bouillon. *Arthus*, King Arthur.

294. For *men*, MS. T. has *pes=pees*; which perhaps is better.

295. For *tennes*, as in Thynne, the Trentham MS. has the older spelling *tenetz*, which gives the etymology of ' tennis.' *Tenetz* is the imperative plural of the verb *tenir*, and must have been a cry frequently used in the *jeu de paume*; probably it was used to call attention, like the modern 'play!' This is the earliest passage in which the word occurs. ' No one can tell whether he will win or lose a " chace " at tennis, till the ball has run its course.' *Chace* is a term 'applied to the second impact on the floor (or in a gallery of a ball which the opponent has failed or declined to return; the value of which is determined by the nearness of the spot of impact to the end wall. If the opponent, on both sides being changed, can " better " this stroke (i. e. cause his ball to rebound nearer the wall) he wins and scores it; if not, it is scored by the first player; until it is so decided, the " chace " is a stroke in abeyance'; New E. Dict.

306. *be gete*, be gotten, be obtained; *begete* gives no sense.

323. *lyf*, life; not as in l. 86. See 1 Cor. xiii. 1.

330. *Cassodore*, Cassiodorus. Magnus Aurelius Cassiodorus, born about A. D. 468, was a statesman and author; his chief work being his *Variarum Epistolarum Libri XII*, which is six times quoted in Chaucer's Tale of Melibeus. Gower, in his Conf. Amantis, iii. 191, quotes this very passage again; thus—

> ' Cassiodore in his aprise telleth,
> The regne is sauf, where pitè dwelleth.'

I find : ' Pietas est quae regit et celos '; Cass. *Var.* xi. 40.

332. *assysed*, fixed, set; cf. l. 236. Unless it means assessed, rated; a sense which is also found in Gower, viz. in his Conf. Amant. i. 5; see the New E. Dict. The passage is a little obscure.

336. ' On account of which mercy should turn aside.'

339. *Constantyn*, Constantine the Great, Roman emperor from A. D. 306 to 337. Eusebius wrote a life of him in four books, which is rather a panegyric than a biography. The story here told is hardly consistent

* * *
* * * *   K k

with the facts, as Constantine caused the death of his own son Crispus and of young Licinius ; as to which Gibbon (c. xviii) remarks that 'the courtly bishop, who has celebrated in an elaborate work the virtues and pieties of his hero, observes a prudent silence on the subject of these tragic events.' In his Conf. Amantis, iii. 192, Gower again says :—

> 'Thus saide whylom Constantyn :—
> What emperour that is enclyn
> To pitè for to be servaunt,
> Of al the worldes remenaunt
> He is worthy to ben a lord.'

But the particular story about the 'yonge children' to which Gower here alludes is given at length in the Conf. Amantis, bk. ii. vol. i. pp. 266-77. Very briefly, it comes to this. Constantine, while still a heathen, was afflicted with leprosy. The physicians said he could only be healed by bathing in the blood of young children. On due reflection, he preferred to retain his leprosy ; whereupon, he was directed in a vision to apply to pope Silvester, who converted him and baptised him ; and he was cured of his leprosy when immersed in the baptismal font. The whole city followed the emperor's example, and was converted to Christianity. This explains ll. 354-5 :—'so that the dear ones, (converted) from being the hateful ones who had formerly been at enmity with Christ,' &c.

363. For *debated*, MS. T. has *deleated*, for *delated*, i. e. deferred ; see *Dilate* in the New E. Dict.

380. 'these other Christian princes' ; viz. in particular, Charles VI, king of France, and Robert III, king of Scotland.

393. These interesting lines tell us that blindness befell the poet in the first year of Henry IV (Sept. 30, 1399—Sept. 29, 1400) ; and we gather that the present poem was meant to be his last. As a matter of fact, he wrote a still later couplet in the following words :—

> 'Henrici regis annus fuit ille secundus
> Scribere dum cesso, sum quia cecus ego.'

These lines occur in MSS. of his Vox Clamantis ; see Morley, Eng. Writers, iv. 157. Notwithstanding his infirmity, Gower survived till the autumn of 1408 ; and was interred, as is well known, in the church of St. Mary Overies—now St. Saviour's—in Southwark, towards the rebuilding of which he had liberally contributed.

It appears that negotiations for peace, both with Scotland and France, were being prosecuted in the latter part of 1399 ; see Wylie, History of Henry IV, i. 82, 86. It is also probable that Gower must have written the 'Praise of Peace' before the death of Richard II in Feb. 1400, as he makes no allusion to that event, nor to the dangerous conspiracy against Henry's life in the early part of January. For these reasons, we may safely date the poem in the end of the year 1399.

V. THOMAS HOCCLEVE: THE LETTER OF CUPID.

This poem is imitated, rather than translated, from the French poem entitled L'Epistre au Dieu d'Amours, written by Christine de Pisan in May, 1399; printed in Œuvres Poétiques de Christine de Pisan, publiées par Maurice Roy, ii. 1-27; Société des Anciens Textes Français, 1891. Hoccleve even rearranges some of the material; and Dr. Furnivall has printed all the lines of the original of which the English poet has made use, in the Notes to his edition of Hoccleve's Works, published for the Early English Text Society, in 1892. It thus appears that the lines of Christine's poem are to be taken in the following order: 1-116, 537-54, 126-30, 531-4, 131-96, 721-5, 259-520, 321-5, 271-4, 387-460, 643-77, 608-23, 559-75, 759-800. The following stanzas, on the other hand, are wholly Hoccleve's own: 71-7, 92-8, 127-33, 141-7, 162-8, 176-89, 267-73, 316-29, 379-434. The last set extends to 56 lines.

Cupid, god of Love, is supposed to write a letter to all lovers, who are his subjects, reproving men for their slander and ill-treatment of women, and defending women against all that is alleged against them. In fact, it is a reply, by Christine de Pisan, to the numerous severe things that Jean de Meun had said about women in the famous Roman de la Rose. He is expressly mentioned by name in l. 281.

I here quote, as a specimen, the first 7 lines of the original, answering to Hoccleve's first stanza—

> ' Cupido, roy par la grace de lui,
> Dieu des amans, sans aide de nullui,
> Regnant en l'air du ciel tres reluisant,
> Filz de Venus la deesse poissant,
> Sire d'amours et de tous ses obgiez,
> A tous vos vrais loiaulx servans subgiez,
> Salut, Amour, Familiarite ! '

5. ' Son of the goddess Cithera,' i.e. Venus. Cithera is an alternative spelling of Citherea, occurring in the Cambridge and Petworth MSS. of the Cant. Tales, A 2215. For the construction, see note to Ch. C. T., F 209.

16. *Albion*. Of course Hoccleve has adapted the poem for English readers. The original has :—' Sur tous païs se complaignent de *France.*'

28. I read *mot* for the sake of the grammar and scansion; the MSS. have *most*, bad spelling for *most-e*, the past tense. But *moot* occurs, correctly, as the emphatic form of *mot*, in l. 35. Cf. l. 410.

30. *As doth*, pray, do; a common idiom; see note to C. T., E 7.

37. *man*, i. e. 'human being'; used generally, and including women.

38. ' When no word can proceed out of his mouth but such as may reasonably please any one, it apparently comes from the heart.'

50. 'Has the pot by the handle'; i.e. holds it securely.

54. Note the accentuation: 'Aný womán.' This accentuation of words on the latter syllable in rather unlikely cases, is a marked peculiarity of Hoccleve's verse. Cf. *womán* in l. 79, *journéy* in l. 106; *axíng* in l. 122, *purpós* in l. 130. Cf. *wommán* in l. 170 with *wómman* in l. 174.

71. *To here*? to her? Dr. Furnivall notes that Hoccleve frequently makes *here* dissyllabic, when it represents the personal pronoun. Cf. l. 70; and see his Preface, p. xli. The reading 'To hir name yet was yt no reprefe,' given in Dr. Furnivall's edition from one MS. only, affords no sense, and will not scan, as *name* is properly dissyllabic.

90. *souneth in-to*, tends to; cf. note to C. T., B 3157.

95. 'They procure such assistants as have a double face.' The accentuation of *prócuren* on the *o* was at this time common; we even find the form *proker* (see Stratmann).

120-2. *wolde . . . Men wiste*, would like men to know.

131. 'Unless he be so far advanced in madness as to spoil all with open coarseness; for *that*, as I suppose, women do not like.'

145. 'Reason follows it so slowly and leisurely.'

184. *dishonest*, unworthy of honour, blameworthy. Ray gives the proverb—'it's an ill bird that bewrays its own nest'; and compares the Greek—τὸν οἴκοι θησαυρὸν διαβάλλειν.

192. *lakken*, blame, find fault with; as in Chaucer.

196. *bilowen*, lied against; pp. of *biléoȝen*, A. S. *biléogan*.

204. Alluding to Ovid's *Remedium Amoris*. Cf. Ch. C. T., D 688–710.

215. 'They say, it is profitable to consider peril.'

225. Rather close to the original French :—

> 'Et aucuns sont qui iadis en mes las
> Furent tenus, mais il sont d'amer las,
> Ou par vieillece ou deffaulte de cuer,
> Si ne veulent plus amer a nul fuer,
> Et convenant m'ont de tous poins nyé,
> Moẏ et mon fait guerpy et renié,
> Comme mauvais serviteurs et rebelles.'

257. *hente*, caught; *in hir daunger*, under their control, within their power.

258. It was thought that one poison would expel another; see P. Plowman, C. xxi. 156-8, and the notes.

272. 'It cannot long abide upon one object.'

281. Jean de Meun, author of the latter and more satirical part of the famous Roman de la Rose; see vol. i.

298. 'They are not so void of constancy.' Read *cónstaunce*.

302. See Ch. Legend of Good Women, 1580.

305. *wold*, desired; pp. of *willen*; see note to C. T., B 2615.

309. See Ch. Legend of Good Women, 924.

316–29. These two stanzas are wholly original. Hoccleve, remembering that the examples of Medea and Dido both occur in Chaucer's Legend of Good Women, here takes occasion to make an express reference to that work, which he here calls 'my Legende of Martres.' *My* refers to Cupid ; *Legend,* to Chaucer's title ; and *Martres,* to the Latin titles to some of the Legends. Thus the Legend of Hypsipyle and Medea is entitled—'Incipit Legenda Ysiphile et Medee, *Martirum.*' Instead of *Martres,* Thynne has the ridiculous reading *Natures,* which the editions carefully retain.

357. 'And, had it not been for the devil,' &c.

360. *her,* the serpent. There was a legend that the serpent had the face of a beautiful virgin. See Ch. C. T., B 360, and note ; P. Plowman, B. xviii. 335, and note.

379–434. These eight stanzas are all Hoccleve's own.

393. *happy to,* fortunate for ; because it brought about Christ's incarnation. The allusion is to the oft-quoted sentence—'O *felix culpa,* O necessarium peccatum Ade,' from the Sarum missal. See note to P. Plowman, C. viii. 126. Cf. l. 396.

421. The day of St. Margaret, Virgin and Martyr, was July 20, in the Latin Church. See the edition of Seinte Marherete, by O. Cockayne, E. E. T. S., 1866.

428. *I,* i. e. Cupid. This stanza is spoken by Cupid, in his own character ; cf. l. 431. In l. 464, he assumes the royal style of *we.* It is, moreover, obvious that this stanza would hardly have been approved of by Chrístine.

473–6. Imitated from the closing lines of Christine's poem :—

> 'Donné en l'air, en nostre grant palais,
> Le jour de May la solempnée feste
> Ou les amans nous font mainte requeste,
> L'An de grace Mil trois cens quate vins
> Et dix et neuf, present dieux et divins,' &c.

It thus appears that 'the lusty month of May,' in l. 472, is merely copied from the French ; but, to the fortunate circumstance that Christine gives the exact date of her poem as 1399, we owe the fact that Hoccleve likewise gives the exact date of his poem as being 1402.

VI. THOMAS HOCCLEVE: TO THE KING; AND TO THE KNIGHTS OF THE GARTER.

These two Balades, each of 32 lines, are written in a highly artificial metre ; for, in each case, the four stanzas of which each consists shew the same rimes throughout. The riming syllables in Balade 1 are *-esse, -our,* and *-alle* ; and in Balade 2, are *-ame, -aunce,* and *-ee.* A similar example of metrical arrangement occurs in Chaucer's Balade to Rosemounde.

2. *king*, Henry V, as we see from the French title.

3. *Justinian*; emperor of Constantinople, A. D. 527–65, whose fame rests upon the justly celebrated Justinian Code of laws. The reference, fortunately, is explained by Hoccleve himself, in a longer Balade concerning Sir John Oldcastel, printed in *Anglia*, v. 23; and again in Hoccleve's Poems, ed. Furnivall, p. 8. Hoccleve is praising Justinian's orthodoxy, to which (as he tells us) Henry V was heir; and the exact reference is to the following clause in one of Justinian's laws, which is quoted in full in the margin of the Balade above mentioned; see *Anglia*, v. 28; or Poems, ed. Furnivall, p. 14. 'Nemo clericus vel militaris, vel cuiuslibet alterius conditionis *de fide Christiana* publice turbis coadunatis et audientibus tractare conetur,' &c. So that Justinian's 'devout tenderness in the faith' was exhibited by repressing religious discussion; cf. l. 27. See Gibbon's Roman Empire, ch. 44.

5. *the Garter.* The noble Order of the Garter was founded by Edward III on St. George's day, Apr. 23, 1349; cf. l. 54.

10. *Constantyn.* He now proceeds to liken Henry V to Constantine the Great, who was a great supporter of the church; see note above, to Poem no. IV, l. 339. Cf. *Anglia*, v. 29; or Poems, ed. Furnivall, p. 15; st. 28.

15. *do forth*, proceed, continue to do as you have done in the past. Not a common expression; see *forth* in Mätzner.

18. Very characteristic of Hoccleve; the accents required by the verse are thrown upon the weak words *your* and *the*. But perhaps *your* is emphatic. Cf. *fully* in l. 20, *á sharp*, 21.

30. Hoccleve is clearly urging the King to repress Lollardry.

37. 'God would have it so; and your allegiance would also have it so.' This is explained in a sidenote in the margin: 'quia Rex illam iustissimam partem tenet.' That is, the lords ought to put down heresy, because their master the king was against it.

41. *Your style*, your motto; the famous 'Honi soit qui mal y pense.' Hence *shame* here means scandal; but *foos to shame* is an awkward expression in this connexion.

47. *nuisaunce*, annoyance; referring to heresy; cf. l. 50.

52. *Slepe nat this*, be not sleepy about this; a rare construction.

58. *norice of distaunce*, nurse of debate or strife.

60. 'Variation from the faith would be a damnable thing.'

64. The remark—*Cest tout*—instead of the usual word *explicit*, occurs at the end of several poems by Hoccleve; see his Poems, ed. Furnivall, pp. 8, 24, 47, 51, 57, 58, 61, 62, 64, &c.

VII. HENRY SCOGAN: A MORAL BALADE.

For remarks upon the heading of this poem, see the Introduction.

3. *Sende*; that is, he did not come and recite the poem himself.

8. This reminds us of the Knight's appeal: 'Now late us ryde, *and herkneth what I seye*'; C. T., A 855.

30. *to queme*, according to your pleasure. *Queme* is here a substantive; see Stratmann. Cf. *to pay* in Chaucer.

49. *Tak'th* is monosyllabic, as in l. 57. So also *Think'th*, in l. 59.

51. From James, ii. 17.

56. 'To the honour of your life and the benefit of your soul.'

65. The exclamation shews that Chaucer was then dead.

67. The quotation is inexact; cf. ll. 120, 121 below. The reference is to the Wyf of Bathes Tale, D 1121 :—

> 'Yet may they [our eldres] nat biquethe us, for no-thing,
> To noon of us hir virtuous living.'

81. Read *Think'th*; so also *Dryv'th* in l. 86; *Tak'th* in l. 89.

97. Here the quotation, again from the Wyf of Bathes Tale (D 1131), is very close :—

> 'For of our eldres may we no-thing clayme
> But temporel thing, that man may hurte and mayme.'

100. 'Therefore God is the source of virtuous nobleness.' This depends on a passage in Boethius, bk. iii. met. 6. l. 2; see notes to poem XIV, in vol. i. pp. 553–5.

105. See this poem of Chaucer's in vol. i. p. 392.

143. *ful rage*, very fierce. But I know of no other example of *rage* as an adjective.

146. *kalends*, the beginning; as in Troil. v. 1634.

150. The passage in Boethius is in Book i. met. 6. 11–15. Cf. Ch. vol. ii. p. 19.

> 'Nec quaeras auida manu Vernos stringere palmites,
> Vuis si libeat frui : Autumno potius sua
> Bacchus munera contulit.'

166. From Chaucer, Wyf of Bathes Tale, D 1165 :—

> 'Thenketh how noble, as seith Valerius,
> Was thilke Tullius Hostilius,
> That out of povert roos to heigh noblesse.'

And Chaucer found it in Valerius Maximus, iii. 4; see vol. v. p. 320.

168. From Chaucer, Monkes Tale, B 3862. But it may be doubted if Caesar's alleged poverty is an historical fact. Cf. p. 24, l. 128 (above).

174. Read the story of Nero in the Monkes Tale, B 3653; that of Balthasar (Belshazzar) in the same, B 3373; and that of Antiochus in the same, B 3765. Compare the lines in B 3800–1 :—

> 'For he so sore fil out of his char
> That it his limes and his skin to-tar.'

187. 'I should be sorry, if ye choose amiss.'

VIII. JOHN LYDGATE; COMPLAINT OF THE BLACK KNIGHT.

There are some excellent notes relative to this poem in Schick's edition of Lydgate's *Temple of Glas* (E. E. T. S.); I refer to them below as 'Schick, T. G.'

4. *Bole*, Bull. The sun entered Taurus, in the fifteenth century, just before the middle of April. Hence the phrase *Amid the Bole* refers, not to the first degree of the sign, but (literally) to the *middle* of it. The reference must be to May 1, when the sun had just passed a little beyond the middle (or 15th degree) of Taurus.

Even here we trace the influence of Chaucer's translation of the Romaunt of the Rose; for which see notes to ll. 36, 74 below. Chaucer reiterates the mention of *May*, R. R. 49, 51, 55, 74, 86; and ll. 1 and 2 of the present poem answer to R. R. 53-56:—

> 'For ther is neither busk ne hay
> *In May*, that it nil shrouded been,
> And it with newe leves wreen.'

12. *with seint Johan*, with St. John for their security or protection; probably suggested by The Compleynt of Mars, l. 9, which opens in a similar strain; cf. note to C. T., F 596; vol. v. p. 385.

15, 16. Compare Rom. Rose (Chaucer's version), ll. 94-5.

21. *halt*, holds, constrains; the present tense.

22, 23. Compare Rom. Rose (Chaucer's version), ll. 100-1.

28. Lydgate is fond of calling the sun *Tytan*; Chaucer has the name only once; in Troil. iii. 1464. Lydgate is here thinking of the passage in the Knightes Tale, A 1493-6, about *fyry Phebus*. Note that he is fond of the word *persaunt*; see ll. 358, 591, 613; cf. Schick, note to T. G. 328.

33. It is odd that no MS. has the form *splayen*; yet the final *n* is required for the metre, or, at any rate, to save an hiatus.

36. Lydgate here copies l. 134 of the English Romaunt of the Rose— 'The river-syde costeying'—and is a witness to the genuineness of Frag- ment A of that poem; as appears more clearly below; see note to l. 75. The whole passage seems founded upon the Romaunt; for this walk by the river brings him to a *park* (a *garden* in the Romaunt) enclosed by a wall that had a small gate in it. It is further obvious that l. 42 is borrowed from l. 122 of the Parliament of Foules—'Right of a park walled with grene stoon.' I may remark here that I have seen a wall constructed of red sandstone so entirely covered with a very minute kind of vegetable growth as to present to the eye a bright green surface.

40. *gate smal*; usually called a *wiket* in similar poems; see Rom. Rose, 528, and Schick, note to T. G. 39.

43-49. This stanza answers to Rom. Rose, ll. 105-8, 78-9.

52. *celúred*, canopied, over-arched (New E. Dict.).

53–6. Cf. Rom. Rose, 1398–1400.

57. *attempre*, temperate; observe that this word occurs in the Rom. Rose, l. 131 (only three lines above the line quoted in the note to l. 36), where the F. text has *atrempee*.

62. *take*, take effect, take hold, become set; an early example of this curious intransitive use of the verb.

63. ' Ready for (men) to shake off the fruit.'

64. *Daphne*. Cf. Troil. iii. 726 :—' O Phebus, thenk whan Dane hirselven shette *Under the bark, and laurer wex* for drede.' And cf. C. T., A 2062 ; and Schick, note to T. G. 115.

66. *myrre*; see Troil. iv. 1138–9.

67. Cf. the mention of laurel, pine, and cedar in Rom. Rose, 1313–4.

68. The resemblance of *philbert* (Philibert's nut) to Phyllis is accidental, but it was then believed that the connexion was real; merely because Vergil has ' Phyllis amat corylos ' ; Ecl. vii. 63. Thus Gower has (Conf. Amant. ii. 30) :—

> ' And, after Phillis, *philiberd*
> This tree was called in the yerd '—

and he gives the story of Phyllis and Demophon, saying that Phyllis hanged herself on a nut-tree. See the Legend of Good Women, 2557. Pliny alludes to ' the almond-tree whereon ladie Phyllis hanged herselfe ' ; Nat. Hist. xvi. 26 (in Holland's translation). See further in Schick, note to T. G. 86.

71. *hawethorn*; often mentioned in poems of this period; see Schick, note to T. G. 505. Cf. XX. 272, p. 369 ; XXIV. 1433, p. 447.

74, 75. The list of trees was evidently suggested by the Rom. Rose ; see Chaucer's translation, 1379–86. Hence the next thing mentioned is a *well*; see the same, ll. 1409–11, 109–30. Note that the water was *cold*, as in R. R. 116; *under a hill*, as in R. R. 114; and ran over *gravel*, as in R. R. 127, 1556. And then note the same, 1417–20 :—

> ' About the *brinkes* of thise welles,
> And by the stremes over-al elles
> *Sprang up the gras*, as thikke y-set
> And *softe as any veluët*.'

It is remarkable that the French original merely has ' Poignoit l'erbe freschete et drue,' without any mention of *softe* or of *veluët*. It thus becomes clear that Lydgate is actually quoting *Chaucer's version*.

81. The reading seems to be *lustily cam springing*; it would be a great improvement to transpose the words, and read *cam lustily springing*. Cf. ' Abouten it is gras springing '; R. R. 1563.

82. Cf. ' That shadwed was with braunches grene '; R. R. 1511.

87. *Narcisus*, Narcissus; introduced as a matter of course, because he is here mentioned in the Romaunt; see R. R. 1468—' Here starf the faire Narcisus.'

88. *Cupyde*; cf. R. R. 1523—'Wel couthe Love him wreke tho. And see the same, 1601-29.

89. Cf. R. R. 1617—'Hath sowen there of love the seed.'

92. *pitte*, i. e. well of Helicon, most likely ; which Chaucer mixed up with the Castalian spring on Parnassus ; see note to Anelida, 15. And cf. *the Pegasee* in C. T., F 207 ; and 'I sleep never on the mount of Pernaso,' F 721.

95. *Dyane*, Diana; see C. T., A 2065-6.

97. *his houndes*, his *own* dogs ; not *her*, as in several MSS. For see C. T., A 2067—'his houndes have him caught.'

102. *pensifheed*, pensiveness ; common in Lydgate ; see Schick, note to T. G. 2.

103. Cf. 'To drinke and fresshe him wel withalle'; R. R. 1513.

107-12. Suggested by R. R. 1507-16 ; especially 1515-6.

127. 'Of gras and *floures, inde* and pers'; R. R. 67. And compare l. 126 with R. R. 68.

129. *hulfere*, holly ; Icel. *hulfr*, dogwood. Spelt *hulwur, huluyr* in the Prompt. Parv. 'The holly is still called in Norfolk *hulver*, and in Suffolk *hulva*' ; Way. Cotgrave has :—'*Houx*, the holly, holme, or hulver-tree.' Also '*Petit houx*, kneehulver, butchers broom.'

131. MS. P. has *of colour*; which suggests the reading—'In blakke and whyte, of colour pale and wan' ; but this, though a better line, cannot stand, as it makes the words *also of his hewe* in l. 132 superfluous; indeed l. 132 then becomes unmeaning.

136. *accesse*, feverish attack ; see Schick, note to T. G. 358.

151. *ure*, destiny ; O. F. *eur*, Lat. *augurium* ; cf. F. *mal-heur*. See l. 302 below, and Barbour's Bruce, i. 312.

154. *among*; so in all the copies ; *among as*, whilst.

161. *ado*, to do ; put for *at do* ; a Northern idiom.

168. *awhaped*, stupefied : see Gloss. in vol. vi. *amat*, dismayed. Cf. Schick, note to T. G. 401.

169. *sitting*, suitable ; cf. R. R. 986.

172. *grounde* (dissyllabic) improves the line ; but *ground* is the correct form.

176. Here the Ashmole MS. inserts 'La compleynt du Chiualier'; but wrongly. For see l. 218.

178. *Niobe*; mentioned in Troil. i. 699. So *woful Myrre*, Troil. iv. 1139.

227. *cheste*, receptacle ; '*cheste* of every care'; Troil. v. 1368.

229. Cf. Troil. i. 420; also Rom. Rose, 4746-50.

233. *fro*, from being, after being.

250. *Daunger*; see Schick, note to T. G. 156.

253. Cf. 'his arwes .. fyle'; Parl. Foules, 212.

260. *Male-Bouche*, Evil Tongue ; cf. R. R. 7357, &c.; where Fragment C has 'Wikkid-Tonge,' the F. original has *Male Bouche*. Cf. IX. 84 (p. 269). See Schick, note to T. G. 153.

274-6. *forjuged* and *excused* only give an assonance, not a rime.

291. *through-girt ... wounde*; from C. T., A 1010.

303. *purveyaunce*, providence; a reminiscence of the argument in Troil. iv. 961, &c.

304. *god*; for *the god*; but the article is unnecessary; see Schick, note to T. G. 132.

305. 'And true men have fallen off the wheel'; i.e. the wheel of Fortune; cf. Troil. iv. 6.

330. *Palamides*, Palamedes. There were two different heroes of this name. One was the son of Nauplius, king of Euboea, who lost his life before Troy, by the artifices of Ulysses. It is said that Ulysses, envious of his fame, forged a letter to him purporting to come from Priam, and then accused him of treachery; whereupon he was condemned to be stoned to death. But the reference is rather to a much later hero, the unsuccessful lover of La bele Isoude. He was defeated by the celebrated knight Sir Tristram, who made him promise to resign his pretensions to the lady; a promise which he did not keep. See Sir T. Malory, Morte Arthure, bk. viii. c. 10, &c.

344. *Hercules*. See the Monkes Tale, B 3285.

349. *Gades*, Cadiz; where, according to Guido, Hercules set up some columns or pillars, to shew that he had come to the end of the world. There is an extraordinary confusion as to the locality and maker of these pillars. Lydgate here follows the account in the Alexander romances, viz. that Alexander set up a pillar of marble in the furthest end of India (l. 351); on which was inscribed—'Ego Alexander Philippi Macedonis post obitum Darii usque ad hunc locum expugnando viriliter militaui'; see Alexander and Dindimus, ed. Skeat, p. 42. Lydgate has confused the two accounts.

354. Copied from Troil. i. 518 :—' Of hem that Love list febly for to avaunce'; which is preceded by 'he may goon in the daunce'; see the next line.

358. *Phebus*. Cf. 'Whan Phebus dwelled here in this erthe adoun'; C. T., H 1. Lydgate is not, however, referring to the story in the Manciples Tale, but rather to the hopeless love of Phoebus for the daughter of Admetus; for which see Troil. i. 659-65. Cf. Schick, note to T. G. 112.

365. *Piramus*. See Legend of Good Women, 724; and Schick, note to T. G. 80.

366. *Tristram*. See notes to Parl. Foules, 288, and to Rosamounde, 20; and to Temple of Glas, ed. Schick, l. 77.

367. Achilles fell in love with Polyxena, a daughter of Priam, according to Guido; see note to Book of the Duch. 1070; and Schick, note to T. G. 94. *Antonius*, Antony; see Legend of Good Women, 588.

368. See the Knightes Tale; but it is a little extraordinary that Lydgate should instance Palamon here.

372. *Jason*; see Legend of Good Women, 1580. For *Theseus*, see the same, 1945; and for *Enee* (Aeneas), the same, 924.

379. An interesting allusion, as the story of the false Arcite was of Chaucer's invention ; see his Anelida.

380. *Demophon* ; already mentioned above, l. 70.

386. *Adon*, Adonis ; see Troil. iii. 721 ; C. T., A 2224.

390. *chorl*, churl ; Vulcan ; cf. C. T., A 2222, and Compl. of Mars.

393. *Ipomenes*, Hippomenes, the conqueror of Atalanta in the foot-race ; and therefore *not* 'guerdonles.' He is thinking of Meleager, the unsuccessful lover of the *other* Atalanta, her of Calydon. Chaucer seems likewise to have confused these stories ; see note to Parl. Foules, 286 ; and cf. C. T., A 2070-2.

412. Cf. Book Duch. 1024, and my note ; and Schick, note to T. G. 169.

419. The correction is obvious. The scribes read *iupartyng* as *inpartyng* and then made it into two words. Cf. l. 475. Chaucer has *juparten*, Troil. iv. 1566.

458. ' So variable is thy chance ' ; cf. C. T., B 125, and the note.

461. *blent*, blinded. Evidently the right reading, for which MS. S. has *blend*. This was turned into *blynde*, destroying the rime.

462. *went*, weeneth, weens, supposes, guesses ; he shoots by guess. Evidently the right word, for which MS. S. has *wend*. But it was easily misunderstood, and most MSS. have *by wenynge*, which preserves the sense, but destroys the rime. Cf. *let*=lets, in l. 464.

480. This line resembles l. 229 of the Temple of Glas.

484. For references to similar lines, see Schick, note to T. G. 60.

488. *Parcas*, Parcae, the Fates ; the form is copied from Troil. v. 3. Lines 486-9 are reminiscences of Troil. iii. 734 and C. T., A 1566.

491. Nature is the deputy of God ; see P. F. 379, and note ; C. T., C 20.

512. With the following stanzas compare Chaucer's Complaint to his Lady, and An Amorous Complaint.

525. ' Out of your mercy and womanliness, charm my sharp wounds.'

554. A stock line of Lydgate's ; it occurs twice in the Temple of Glas, ll. 424, 879.

574. Here the Knight's Complaint ends.

590. ' Parfourned hath the sonne his ark diurne ' ; C. T., E 1795.

596. Cf. ' among yon rowes rede ' ; Compl. Mars, 2.

597. *deaurat*, gilded, of a golden colour ; see *Deaurate* in the New E. Dict.

612. *Esperus*, Hesperus, the evening-star, the planet Venus. See note to Boeth. bk. i. m. 5. 9.

621. Cf. C. T., A 2383, 2389 ; and Temple of Glas, 126-8.

627. ' Venus I mene, the *wel-willy* planete ' ; Troil. iii. 1257. Cf. *gude-willy* in Burns.

644. ' For thilke love thou haddest to Adoun ' ; C. T., A 2224.

647. MS. B. has *for very wery*, meaning ' because I was very weary,' which is a possible expression ; see Schick, note to T. G. 632 ; but *verily* seems better, as otherwise the line is cumbersome.

663. *Jelousye* ; cf. Parl. Foules, 252.

IX. JOHN LYDGATE: THE FLOUR OF CURTESYE.

I know of no MS. copy of this piece.

4. Valentine's day is Feb. 14; cf. Parl. Foules, 309–11.

8. *larke*; cf. the song of the bird in Compl. Mars, 13-21.

20. *Cipryde*, really the same as Venus, but here distinguished; see Parl. Foules, 277.

38. Apparently accented as 'Aúrorà'; Ch. has Auróra, L. G. W. 774.

49. *crampessh at* must be *crampisshed*, i. e. constrained painfully, tortured; see note to Anelida, 171 (vol. i. p. 535).

62. Imitated from Parl. Foules, 379–89.

75. *sursanure*; a wound healed outwardly only; cf. note to C. T., F 1113.

84. *Male-bouche*, Evil Tongue, Slander; from the Roman de la Rose. See VIII. 260 above.

96. *Boreas*, only mentioned by Ch. in his Boethius, bk. i. m. 5. 17, m. 3. 8.

113. *somer-sonne*; imitated from the Book of the Duch. 821-4.

125. 'To speke of bountè or of gentilles,' &c.; T. G. 287.

140. 'To alle hir werkes virtu is hir gyde'; C. T., B 164.

158. Alluding to the proverb—'He that hews above his head, the chips fall in his eye'; which is a warning to men who attack their betters. See I. i. 9. 20, and the note (p. 462).

190-3. *Policene*, Polyxena; cf. note to VIII. 367. *Helayne*, Helen. *Dorigene*; see Frankleyns Tale, F 815.

195. *Cleopatre*; see the first legend in the Legend of Good Women. *secree*, secret, able to keep secrets; a praiseworthy attribute; cf. Parl. of Foules, 395; and Lydgate's Temple of Glas, 294-5 :—

> 'and mirrour eke was she
> Of *secrenes*, of trouth, of faythfulnes.'

It is obvious that the extraordinary word *setrone* (see the footnote) arose from a desire on the part of the scribe to secure a rime for the name in the next line, which he must have imagined to be *An-ti-góne*, in *three* syllables, with a mute final *e*! This turned *secree* into *secrone*, which Thynne probably misread as *setrone*, since *c* and *t* are alike in many MSS. But there are no such words as *secrone* or *setrone*; and *secree* must be restored, because *An-ti-go-ne* is a word of four syllables. We know whence Lydgate obtained his 'white Antigone'; it was from Troilus, ii. 887, where we find 'fresshe Antigone the whyte.' Antigone was Criseyde's niece, and was so 'secree' that Pandarus considered her to be the most fitting person to accompany Criseyde when she visited Troilus (Troil. ii. 1563), and again when she came to visit Pandarus himself (iii. 597).

197. *Hester*, Esther; see Book Duch. 987; but especially Legend of

Good Women, 250 : 'Ester, lay thou thy *mekenesse* al adoun.' *Judith* ; cf. Cant. Tales, B 939, 2289, 3761, E 1366.

198. *Alceste*, Alcestis ; see L. G. W. 432, 511, 518. *Marcia Catoun*, Martia, daughter of Cato of Utica ; see note to L. G. W. 252 (vol. iii. p. 298).

199. *Grisilde* ; the Griselda of the Clerkes Tale. Again mentioned by Lydgate in the Temple of Glas, 75, 405, and elsewhere ; see Schick's note to T. G. l. 75.

200, 201. *Ariadne* ; see L. G. W. 268, 2078, &c. *Lucrece*, Lucretia ; see the same, 1680 ; especially l. 1691 :—'this Lucresse, that starf *at Rome toun.*'

203. *Penelope* ; see note to L. G. W. 252.

204. *Phyllis, Hipsiphilee* ; both in L. G. W. ; 2394, 1368.

206. *Canacee* ; may be either the Canace mentioned in L. G. W. 265, or the heroine of the Squieres Tale ; probably the latter. See Schick, note to l. 137 of the Temple of Glas.

209. *naught*, not. *falle*, stoop, droop ; hence, fail.

211-3. Dido slew herself ; see L. G. W. 1351.

214. *Medee*, Medea ; see L. G. W. 1580. But Chaucer does not there relate how Medea committed any 'outrage.' However, he refers to her murder of her children in the Cant. Tales, B 72.

216. 'That, while goodness and beauty are both under her dominion, she makes goodness have always the upper hand.' See l. 218.

221. Read *n'offende*, offend not. Probably the MS. had *nofende*, which Thynne turned into *ne fende*.

229. It is remarkable how often Lydgate describes his hand as 'quaking' ; see Schick's note to the Temple of Glas, 947. Chaucer's hand quaked but once ; Troil. iv. 14. Cf. note to XXII. 57 (p. 539).

232. *suppryse*, undertake, endeavour to do. *Suppryse* is from O. F. *sousprendre*, for which Godefroy gives the occasional sense 'entre-prendre.'

234. *lose*, praise ; *out of lose*, out of praise, discreditable.

236. Perhaps this means that Chaucer's decease was a very recent event. Schick proposes to date this piece between 1400 and 1402.

242. Chaucer invokes Clio at the beginning of Troilus, bk. ii. (l. 8) ; and Calliope at the beginning of bk. iii. (l. 45).

251. Cf. Compl. Mars, 13, 14. The metre almost seems to require an accent on the second syllable of *Valentyn*, with suppressed final *e* ; but a much more pleasing line, though less regular, can be made by distributing the pauses artificially thus : Upón . the dáy of . saint Válen . týne . sínge. The word *saint* is altogether unemphatic ; cf. ll. 4, 100.

257. *fetheres ynde*, blue feathers ; possibly with a reference to blue as being the colour of constancy. Cf. *floures inde* ; VIII. 127.

261. The woodbine is an emblem of constancy, as it clings to its support ; cf. XX. 485-7.

X. IN COMMENDATION OF OUR LADY.

4, 5. In l. 4, *fere* is the Kentish form of 'fire.' In l. 5, Thynne again prints *fere*, but MS. A. has *hyre* (not a rime), and MS. Sl. has *were*, which means 'doubt,' and is the right word.

7. For *her*, we must read *his*, as in l. 4. The reference is to Love or Cupid; see VIII. 354, and the note.

12. Cf. 'O wind, O wind, the weder ginneth clere,' &c.; Troil. ii. 2. Observe that Chaucer invokes *Cleo* (Clio) in his next stanza.

22. We may compare this invocation with Chaucer's ABC, and his introduction to the Second Nonnes Tale; but there is not much resemblance. Observe the free use of alliteration throughout ll. 22-141.

24. 'O pleasant ever-living one' seems to be meant; but it is very obscure. Notice that the excellent Sloane MS. has *O lusty lemand* (=*leming*), O pleasant shining one. Perhaps we should read *leming* for *living*; cf. l. 25.

27. Cf. 'Haven of refut'; ABC, 14. *up to ryve*, to arrive at; see *rive* in Halliwell.

28. The five joys of the Virgin are occasionally alluded to. See the poem on this subject in An Old Eng. Miscellany, ed. Morris, p. 87. The five joys were (1) at the Annunciation; (2) when she bore Christ; (3) when Christ rose from the dead; (4) when she saw Him ascend into heaven; (5) at her own Assumption into heaven.

30. 'And cheering course, for one to complain to for pity.' Very obscure.

52. *propyne*, give to drink; a usage found in the Vulgate version of Jer. xxv. 15 : 'Sume calicem . . . et *propinabis* de illo cunctis gentibus.'

56. Cf. *magnificence* in Ch. Sec. Nonnes Tale, G 50.

58. *put in prescripcioun*, i. e. prescribed, recommended.

60. Cf. 'I flee for socour to thy tente'; ABC, 41.

64. *itineráríe*, a description of the way.

65. *bravie*, prize, especially in an athletic contest; Lat. *brauium*, Gk. βραβεῖον, in 1 Cor. ix. 24. See note to C. T., D 75.

66. *diourn denárie*, daily pay, as of a penny a day; referring to Matt. xx. 2 : 'Conventione autem facta cum operariis ex *denario diurno.*'

68. *Laureat crowne*, crown of laurel.

69. *palestre*, a wrestling-match; cf. Troil. v. 304.

70. *lake*, fine white linen cloth; as in C. T., B 2048.

71. *citole*, harp; as in C. T., A 1959.

78. 'The wedded turtel, with her herte trewe'; Parl. Foules, 355.

83. *Phebus*; here used, in an extraordinary manner, of the Holy Spirit, as being the spirit of wisdom; perhaps suggested by the mention of the *columbe* (or dove) in l. 79.

87. Here Thynne prints *dyametre*, but the Sloane MS. corrects him.

88. *Fewe feres*, few companions; i. e. few equals.

92, 93. *loupe*; cf. F. *loupe*, an excrescence, fleshy kernel, knot in wood, lens, knob. It was also a term in jewellery. Littré has : 'pierre précieuse que la nature n'a pas achevée. Loupe de saphir, loupe de rubis, certaines parties imparfaites et grossières qui se trouvent quelquefois dans ces pierres.' Hence it is not a very happy epithet, but Lydgate must have meant it in a good sense, as expressing the densest portion of a jewel ; hence his 'stable (i. e. firm) as the loupe.' Similarly he explains *ewage* as being 'fresshest of visage,' i. e. clearest in appearance. *Ewage* was a term applied to a jacinth of the colour of sea-water; see New E. Dict. and P. Plowman, B. ii. 14 ; but it is here described as *blue*, and must therefore refer to a stone of the colour of water in a lake.

98. Read *hértè* for the scansion; but it is a bad line. It runs :—
And hém . recéyvest . wíth . hértè . ful tréwe.

99. *gladded*, gladdened ; referring to the Annunciation.

102. *obumbred*, spread like a shadow; 'uirtus Altissimi *obumbrabit* tibi'; Luke, i. 35. This explains *to thee*, which answers to *tibi*.

106. This stanza refers to Christ rather than to Mary ; see l. 112. But Mary is referred to as the *ground* on which He built (l. 111).

107. Cf. Isaiah, xi. 1 ; Jerem. xxiii. 5.

110. *corn*, grain; 'suscitabo Dauid germen iustum'; Jer. xxiii. 5. Cf. 'ex semine Dauid uenit Christus; John, vii. 42.

111. *ground*; the ground upon which it pleased Him to build. Referring to Mary.

113. *vytre*, glass; Lat. *uitreum*. The Virgin was often likened to glass ; sun-rays pass through it, and leave it pure.

114. *Tytan*, sun ; curiously applied. Christ seems to be meant; see l. 116. But *thy* in l. 115 again refers to Mary. Hence, in l. 114 (as in 116) we should read *his* for *thy*.

118. *Sunamyte*, Shunammite ; Lat. *Sunamitis*, 2 Kings, iv. 25. She was an emblem of the Virgin, because her son was raised from the dead.

119. *Mesure*, moderate, assuage. *Margaryte*, pearl ; as an epithet of the Virgin.

121. *punical pome*, pomegranate ; Pliny has *Punicum malum* in this sense ; Nat. Hist. xiii. 19.

122. *bouk and boon*, body and bone ; see *Bouk* in the New E. Dict.

123. *agnelet*, little lamb ; not in the New E. Dict., because this stanza is now first printed.

126. *habounde*, abundant ; of this adj. the New E. Dict. gives two examples.

128. *Cockle*, shell ; referring to the shell in which the pearl was supposed to be generated by dew. See note to I. ii. 12. 47, p. 475.

129. 'O bush unbrent'; C. T., B 1658 ; see the note. *fyrles*, set on fire without any fire (i. e. without visible cause).

132. Referring to Gideon's fleece ; Judges, vi. 39.

133. Referring to Aaron's rod that budded ; Heb. ix. 4.

134. *misty*, mystic; cf. 'mysty, *misticus*,' in Prompt. Parv.
arke, ark; the ark of the covenant.
probatik; certainly the right reading (as in MS. Sl.), instead of
probatyf or *probatyfe*, as in A. and Thynne. The reference is to the
O. F. phrase *piscine probatique*, which Godefroy explains as being
a cistern of water, near Solomon's temple, in which the sheep were
washed before being sacrificed. The phrase was borrowed immediately from the Vulgate version of John v. 2 : 'Est autem Ierosolymis
probatica piscina, quae cognominatur hebraice Bethsaida'; i. e. the
reference is to the well-known pool of Bethesda. The Greek has :
ἐπὶ τῇ προβατικῇ κολυμβίθρα. The etymology is obvious, from Gk.
πρόβατον, a sheep. We may translate the phrase by 'sheep-cleansing
pool.' Cotgrave explains it very well; he has : '*piscine probatique*,
a pond for the washing of the sheep that were, by the Law, to be
sacrificed.'

135. *Aurora*, dawn; mentioned in Ch. L. G. W. 774. Cf. 'al the
orient *laugheth*'; C. T., A 1494. And cf. 'Th'olyve of pees'; Parl.
Foules, 181.

136. 'Column, with its base, which bears up (or supports) out of the
abysmal depth.'

137. 'Why could I not be skilful?'

140. I make up this line as best I can; the readings are all bad.
Note that, at this point, the MS. copies come to an end, and so does
the alliteration. Poem no. XI is joined on to no. X in Thynne without
any break, but is obviously a different piece, addressed to an earthly
mistress.

XI. TO MY SOVERAIN LADY.

1. Imitated from C. T., B 778 : 'I ne have noon English digne,' &c.
Cf. l. 41. And see the Introduction.

8. 'For if I could sing what I feel in love, I would (gladly do so).'

14. 'I have all my trust in thee.' The scansion is got by grouping
the syllables thus : J'áy . en vóus . tóute . má . fiáunce. It is a line of
the Lydgate type, in which the first syllable in the normal line,
and the first syllable after the cæsura, are alike dropped.

17. *thou knette*, mayst thou knit; the subj. or optative mood.

21. This quotation is most interesting, being taken from the first line
in 'Merciless Beauty'; Ch. Minor Poems; no. XI. Cf. l. 54.

23. *it is*; pronounced either as *it's* or '*t is*. The latter sounds better.

26. The substitution of *ginne* for *beginne* much improves the line.
on esperaunce, in hope.

44. *in o degree*, (being) always in one state.

49. 'Weep for me, if a lover pleases you.'

56. 'So much it grieves to be away from my lady.'

59. 'Now my heart has what it wished for.'

* * *
* * * *   L l

64. *were*, should be, ought to be (subjunctive).

68. *go love*, go and love, learn to love. *wher*, whether.

77. *and also*, including. The 'fair' Rosamond is mentioned in P. Plowman, B. xii. 48 ; which shews that her name was proverbial.

98. 'Embrace me closely with a joyful heart.'

100. 'The ardent hope that pricks my heart, is dead ; the hope—to gain the love of her whom I desire.'

103. 'And I know well that it is not my fault ; (the fault of me) who sing for you, as I may, by way of lament at your departure.' O. F. *sai*, I know, is a correct form.

107. *sad*, fixed, resolute, firm, constant.

XII. BALLAD OF GOOD COUNSEL.

7. Cf. Prov. xvii. 20 : 'He that hath a perverse tongue falleth into mischief.'

15. *equipolent*, equal in power; used by Hoccleve (New E. Dict.).

16. *peregal*, the same as *paregal*, fully equal ; Troil. v. 840.

22. I follow the order of stanzas in MS. H. (Harl. 2251), which is more complete than any other copy, as it alone contains ll. 71-7. Th. and Ff. transpose this stanza and the next one.

23. *amorous* is evidently used as a term of disparagement, i. e. 'wanton.'

33. *this is*; pronounced as *this*, as often elsewhere.

40. *deslavee*, loose, unchaste ; see Gloss. to Chaucer.

45. Accent *dévourour* on the first syllable.

60. *dissolucioun*, dissolute behaviour.

71-7. In Harl. 2251 only. In l. 71, read *is*; the MS. has *in*.

73. The missing word is obviously *mene*, i. e. middling ; missed because the similar word *men* happened to follow it.

78. *prudent* seems here to be used in a bad sense ; cf. mod. E. 'knowing.'

86. In the course of ll. 86-103, Lydgate contrives to mention all the Nine Worthies except Godfrey of Bouillon ; i. e. he mentions David, Joshua, Judas Maccabaeus, Hector, Julius Caesar, Alexander, Charles (Charlemagne), and King Arthur. His other examples are Solomon, Troilus, Tullius Cicero, Seneca, and Cato ; all well known.

96. Thynne has—'With *al* Alisaundres.' The word *al* is needless, and probably due to repeating the first syllable of *Alisaundre*.

107. We now come to examples of famous women. *Hestre* is Esther, and *Griseldes*, the Grisildis of Chaucer's Clerkes Tale. Others are Judith (in the Apocrypha), Polyxena, Penelope, Helen, Medea, Marcia the daughter of Marcus Cato Uticensis (see note to Legend of Good Women, 252), and Alcestis. They are all taken from Chaucer ; Esther, Polyxena, Penelope, Helen, 'Marcia Catoun,' are all mentioned in the 'Balade' in Legend of Good Women, Prologue, B-text, 249-69 ;

and Alcestis is the heroine of the same Prologue. The Legend contains the story of Medea at length ; and Judith is celebrated in the Monkes Tale. See the similar list in IX. 190-210.

110. For *Policenes*, Ff. has *Pen:lops* (!) ; but Penelope is mentioned in l. 113. *Policenes* is right ; see IX. 190.

115. For *Eleynes*, the printed editions have the astonishing reading *Holynesse*, a strange perversion of *Heleynes*.

121. *kerve*, cut ; suggested by Chaucer's use of *forkerveth* in the Manciple's Tale, H 340. This is tolerably certain, as in l. 129 he again refers to the same Tale, H 332-4.

130. Chaucer does not mention Cato ; he merely says—'Thus lerne children whan that they ben yonge.' Both Chaucer and Lydgate had no doubt been taught some of the sayings of Dionysius Cato in their youth ; for see Troil. iii. 293-4. This particular precept occurs in the third distich in Cato's first book ; i. e. almost at the very beginning. See note to C. T., H 332 (vol. v. p. 443).

XIII. BEWARE OF DOUBLENESS.

This piece is gently ironical throughout, as, for example, in ll. 15, 23, 31, 39, 47, &c.

30. *abit*, abideth, abides, remains, is constant.

32 (footnote). The remark in the margin—' Per antifrasim '—simply means that the text is ironical.

48. *tache*, defect ; this is Shakespeare's *touch*, in the same sense ; Troilus and Cressida, iii. 3. 175.

51. *sliper*, slippery ; A. S. *slipor* ; as in XVI. 262. Cf. HF. 2154, and the note.

55. ' Who can (so) guide their sail as to row their boat with craft.' Not clearly put. Is there a reference to Wade's boat ? Cf. C. T., E 1424, and the note. The irony seems here to be dropped, as in ll. 71, 79.

75. *sys and sink*, six and five, a winning throw at hazard ; see C. T., B 124, and the note. *avaunce*, get profit, make gain.

77, 78. Here *sette* seems to mean 'lay a stake upon,' in the game of hazard ; when, if the player throws double aces (*ambes as*), he loses ; see the note on C. T., B 124 as above ; and see *Ambs-Ace* in the New E. Dict. It is amusing to find that Stowe so wholly misunderstood the text as to print *lombes, as* (see footnote on p. 293) ; for *lombes* means 'lambs'!

83. *innocence* is, I suppose, to be taken ironically ; but the constancy of Rosamond and Cleopatra is appealed to as being real. For the ballad of 'Fair Rosamond,' see Percy's Reliques of Ancient Poetry.

'Her chiefest foes did plaine confesse
    She was a glorious wight.'

89, 90. *sengle*, single. *oo-fold*, one-fold, as distinct from *double*. See the whimsical praise of 'double' things in Hood's Miss Kilmansegg, in the section entitled 'Her Honeymoon.'

XIV. A BALADE: WARNING MEN, ETC.

6. *see at y*, see by the outward appearance; cf. C. T., G 964, 1059. This Balade resembles no. XIII. Cf. l. 4 with XIII. 63, 81.

7. *et*, eateth, eats. This contracted form evidently best suits the scansion. The copy in MS. T. had originally *ette*, mis-spelt for *et*, with *ettyth* written above it, shewing that the old form *et* was obsolescent. *Et* (eateth) occurs in P. Plowman, C. vii. 431; and again, in the same, B. xv. 175, the MSS. have *eet, eteth, ette*, with the same sense. 'The blind eat many flies' is given in Hazlitt's Collection of Proverbs. Skelton has it, Works, ed. Dyce, i. 213; and Hazlitt gives four more references.

9. *geson*, scarce, rare, seldom found; see note to P. Plowman, B. xiii. 270.

19. Remember to pronounce *this is* (*this 's*) as *this*.

25. A common proverb; see note to C. T., G 962.

26. 'But ay fortune hath in hir hony galle'; C. T., B 3537.

29. The proverbial line quoted in T. is here referred to, viz. 'Fallere, flere, nere, tria sunt hec in muliere.' In the margin of the Corpus MS. of the C.T., opposite D 402, is written—'Fallere, flere, nere, dedit Deus in muliere.' See that passage in the Wife's Preamble.

33. *sleight*; pronounced (*sleit*), riming with *bait*; shewing that the *gh* was by this time a negligible quantity.

36. The reference is to the proverb quoted in the note to C. T., B 2297 (vol. v. p. 208) :—

> 'Vento quid leuius? fulgur; quid fulgure? flamma.
> Flamma quid? mulier.   Quid muliere? nichil.'

Hence *light* in l. 37 should be *leit*, as it means 'lightning'; which explains 'passeth in a throw,' i. e. passes away instantly. We also see that Lydgate's original varied, and must have run thus :—

> ' Aëre quid leuius? fulgur; quid fulgure? uentus.
> Vento quid? mulier.   Quid muliere? nichil.'

43. Curiously imitated in the modern song for children :—

> ' If all the world were paper, And all the sea were ink,
> And all the trees were bread and cheese, What *should* we do
>   for drink?'
>
>   The Baby's Bouquet, p. 26.

XV. THREE SAYINGS.

(A). 2. *Honour*, i.e. advancement. The Lat. proverb is—'Honores mutant mores'; on which Ray remarks—'As poverty depresseth and debaseth a man's mind, so great place and estate advance and enlarge it, but many times corrupt and puff it up.' *outrage*, extravagant self-importance.

XVI. LA BELLE DAME.

1–28. The first four stanzas are original; so also are the four at the end. These stanzas have seven lines; the rest have eight.

10. Read *called* as *call'd*; *Bell-e* and *Dam-e* are dissyllabic.

11. *Aleyn*; i.e. Alain Chartier, a French poet and prose writer, born in 1386, who died in 1458. He lived at the court of Charles VI and Charles VII, to whom he acted as secretary. Besides La Belle Dame sans Merci, he wrote several poems ; in one of these, called Le Livre de Quatre Dames, four ladies bewail the loss of their lovers in the battle of Agincourt. He also wrote some prose pieces, chiefly satirical; his *Curial*, directed against the vices of the court, was translated by Caxton. Caxton's translation was printed by him in 1484, and reprinted by the Early English Text Society in 1888. The best edition of Chartier's works is that by A. Duchesne (Paris, 1617); a new edition is much wanted.

45. I here quote the original of this stanza, as it settles the right reading of l. 47, where some MSS. have *eyen* or *eyn* for *pen*.

> 'Qui vouldroit mon vouloir contraindre
> A ioyeuses choses escrire,
> *Ma plume* n'y sçauroit attaindre,
> Non feroit ma langue à les dire.
> Ie n'ay bouche qui puisse rire
> Que les yeulx ne la desmentissent :
> Car le cueur l'en vouldroit desdire
> Par les lermes qui des yeulx issent.'

53. The original French is clearer :—

> 'Je laisse aux amoureulx malades,
> Qui ont espoir d'allegement,
> Faire chansons, ditz, et ballades.'

65, 66. *forcer*, casket; *unshet*, opened ; *sperd*, fastened, locked up.

103 (footnote). *deedly*, inanimate, dull, sleepy ; an unusual use of the word. Only in Thynne, who seems to be wrong.

105, 106. *som*, i.e. some male guests. *their juges*, (apparently) the ladies who ruled them, whom they wooed ; cf. l. 137. *demure*, serious, grave ; an early example of the word; cf. XX. 459, XXI. 82.

105. *most fresshest*, who had most newly arrived; 'Tels y ot qui à l'heure vinrent.'

137. *scole-maister*, i. e. his mistress who ruled him; cf. *her* in l. 139.

145. The right reading is *shot*, as in Thynne and MS. Ff., which are usually better authorities than MSS. F. and H.   The original has:—

> ' l'apperceu le *trait* de ses yeulx
> Tout empenné d'humbles requestes.'

154, 156. *mes*, dish or course of meats. *entremes*, ill-spelt *entre-mass* in Barbour's Bruce, xvi. 457; on which my note is : 'it is the O. F. *entremes*, now spelt *entremets*, [to mark its connection with F. *mettre*; but] *mets*, O. F. *mes*, is the Lat. *missum* [accusative of *missus*], a dish as *sent in* or served at table (Brachet). An *entremes* is a delicacy or side-dish (lit. a between-dish)'; and I added a reference to the present passage.   It is here used ironically.

166. *chase*, chose; apparently, a Northern form.

174. *apert*, as in MS. Ff., is obviously right; *pert*, as still in use, is due to the loss of the former syllable.   *prevy nor apert*, neither secretly nor openly, i. e. in no way; just as in Ch. C. T., F 531.

176. *frounter*; answering here, not to O. F. *frontier*, forehead, but to O. F. *frontiere*, front rank of an army, line of battle; whence the phrase *faire frontiere a*, to make an attack upon (Godefroy).   So here, the lady's beauty was exactly calculated to make an attack upon a lover's heart.   Sir R. Ros has 'a frounter *for*'; he should rather have written 'a frounter *on*.'   The original has :—' Pour faire au cueur d'amant *frontiere*'; also *garnison* in the preceding line.

182. 'Car ioye triste cueur traueille.'   Sir R. Ros actually takes *triste* with *ioye* instead of with *cueur*.   There are several other instances in which he does not seem to have understood his original.   See below.

184. *trayle*, trellis-work, or lattice-work, intertwined with pliant thick-leaved branches; Godefroy has O.F. '*treille, traille*, treillis, treillage'; cf. l. 195.   The original has :—' Si m'assis dessoubz une treille.'   A note explains *dessoubz* as *derriere*.

198. *neer*, nearer; as in l. 201.   *sought*, attacked (him).

230. 'Et se par honneur et sans blasme Ie suis vostre.'   That is, if I am yours, with honour *to myself*.   But the translator transfers the *worship*, i.e. the honour, to the lady.

259. 'Which promised utterly to deprive me of my trust.'

265. *Other or me*, me or some one else.   But the French is :—'Se moy ou autre vous regarde,' if I or some one else look at you; which is quite a different thing.

269–72. Obscure, and perhaps wrong; the original is :—

> ' S'aucun blesse autruy d'auenture
>   Par coulpe de celuy qui blesse,
> Quoi qu'il n'en peult mais par droicture,
>   Si en a il dueil et tristesse.'

282-3. 'Que peu de chose peult trop plaire
      Et vous vous voulez deceuoir.'

300. ' It were less harm for one to be sad than two.'

303. Read *sory* : ' D 'ung *dolent* faire deux joyeulx.'

324. *rechace*, chasing it back, which gives small sense ; and the reading *richesse* is worse, and will not rime. The French has *rachatz* = mod. F. *rachat*, redemption, ransom ; which has been misunderstood.

340. ' Preuue ses parolles par oeuure.'

348. *their* is an error for *his* (Love's), due to the translator. ' Lors il [Amour] descouure sa fierté.'

351. ' Tant plus aspre en est la poincture,
      Et plus. desplaisant le deffault.'

357. *oon*, one ; i. e. the same. MS. Ff. has *wone*, a very early example of the prefixed sound of *w*, as in modern English. See Zupitza's notes to Guy of Warwick.

393. Something is wrong. The French is :—' La mesure faulx semblant porte'; meaning (I suppose) moderation has a false appearance.

400. *As think*, i. e. pray think ; see *As* in the Gloss. in vol. vi.

443. ' A constrained reward, and a gift offered by way of thanks, cannot agree ' ; i. e. are quite different.

449. *wanteth*, is wanting, is lacking.

468. ' Qui soit donné à autre office.'

469. .' D'assez grant charge se cheuit,' he gets rid of a great responsibility. The translator gives the contrary sense.

506. ' D'en donner à qui les reffuse.'

509. That *He*, not *Who*, should begin the line, is certain by comparison with the French :—' *Il* ne doit pas cuider muser.'

514. *me mistook*, that I mistook myself, that I made a mistake.

519, 520. *prevayl you*, benefit you ; *after*, according to.

523-4. *after-game*, return-match, a second game played by one who has lost the first. I believe l. 524 to mean ' who cannot thoroughly afford to double his stakes.' To *set* often means to stake. The French is :—

      'Et celuy pert le ieu d'attente
      Qui ne scet faire son point double.'

531. *it ar*, they are. This use of *ar* with *it* is due to the pl. sb. *fantasyes* (i. e. vain fancies) immediately following ; *other counsayl* is equivalent to ' as for any other counsel,' which implies that there are more alternatives than one.

536. ' Who would like to conduct himself,' i. e. to regulate his conduct. ' Qui la veult conduire et ne peult.'

538. Read *sute* : ' Desespoir le met de sa *suite*.'

555. ' Ne de l'aprendre n'ay-ie cure.'

559. ' Et le deuoir d'amours payer Qui franc cueur a, prisé et droit.'

566. *That* is a mere conjunction ; the reading *Which* alters the sense, and gives a false meaning.

583. *let*, makes as though he knew not ; French, 'scet celler.'

594, 595. *Hath set* ; 'Mettroit en mes maulx fin et terme.' Line 595 should begin with *Then* rather than *Yet*, as there is no contrast.

605. ' De tous soit celuy deguerpiz.'

608. *or anything at al*, &c. ; 'et le bien fait De sa Dame qui l'a reffait Et ramené de mort a vie ' ; i.e. and the kindness of his Lady, who has new made him, and brought him back from death to life. The English follows some different reading, and is obscurely expressed.

614. ' A qui l'en puisse recourir ' ; to whom he could have recourse. But *recourir* has been read as *recovrir*, giving no good sense.

627. The reading *high* is right ; ' Que iamais *hault* honneur ne chiet.'

634. *reclaymed*, taught to come back ; a term in falconry ; French, ' bien reclamez.' Opposed to *hem to withholde*, i.e. to keep themselves from coming back.

635. ' Et si bien aprins qu'ils retiennent
     A changer dés qu'ils ont clamez.'

651. *fol*, foolish ; F. text, 'fol plaisir.'

667. *To have better*, to get a better lover. But the sense is wrongly given. In the French, this clause goes with what follows :—' D'auoir mieulx ne vous affiez,' i.e. expect to get nothing better.

667. *to have better*, to get a better lover.

668. ' Et prenez en gré le reffus.'

673. The original shews that *she* really refers to *Pity*, denoted by *it* in l. 671, not to the Lady herself.

680. ' Et iamais á bout n'en vendrez.'

706. *By* ; French, *De* ; hence *By* should be *Of.* Read *defame of cruëlty*, an ill name for cruelty. The mistake is the translator's.

741. *Male-bouche*, Slander ; a name probably taken from the Rom. de la Rose, 2847 ; called *Wikked-Tonge* in the English version, 3027.

750. *playn*, (all equally) flat. ' La terre n'est pas toute unie.'

757. *be nought*, are naughty, are wicked ; as in K. Lear, ii. 4. 136.

788. ' Que si tost mis en obli a.'

814. *avantours*, boasters ; see l. 735. F. text, ' venteus' ; cf. ' *Vanteux*, vaunting ' ; Cotgrave.

817. *Refus*, i.e. Denial ; personified. ' Reffuz a ses chasteaulx bastiz.'

829. The last four stanzas are original. Note the change from the 8-line to the 7-line stanza.

XVII. THE TESTAMENT OF CRESSEID.

This sequel to Chaucer's ' Troilus,' written by Robert Henryson of Dunfermline, is in the Northern dialect of the Scottish Lowlands. Thynne has not made any special attempt to alter the wording of this piece, but he frequently modifies the spelling ; printing *so* instead of *sa* (l. 3), *whan* for *quhen* (l. 3), *right* for *richt* (l. 4), and so on. I follow the Edinburgh edition of 1593. See further in the Introduction.

1. *Ane*, a ; altered by Thynne to *a*, throughout.

dooly (Th. *doly*), doleful, sad ; from the sb. *dool*, sorrow.

4-6. Here *fervent* seems to mean 'stormy' or 'severe,' as it obviously does not mean hot. *Discend* is used transitively; *can discend* means 'caused to descend.' This is an earlier example than that from Caxton in the New Eng. Dictionary. *Aries* clearly means the influence of Aries, and implies that the sun was in that sign, which it entered (at that date) about the 12th of March; see vol. iii. p. 188 (footnote). *Lent* is 'spring'; and the Old Germanic method is here followed, which divided each of the seasons into three months. In this view, the spring-months were March, April, and May, called, respectively, foreward Lent, midward Lent, and afterward Lent; see A Student's Pastime, p. 190. Hence the phrase *in middis of the Lent* does not mean precisely in the middle of the spring, but refers to the month of April; indeed, the sun passed out of Aries into Taurus on the 11th of the month. The date indicated is, accordingly, the *first week in April*, when the sun was still in Aries, and showers of hail, with a stormy north wind, were quite seasonable.

10. *sylit under cure*, covered up, (as if) under his care. The verb *to syle* is precisely the mod. E. *ceil*; which see in the New E. Dict.

12. *unto*, i.e. over against. The planet Venus, rising in the east, set her face over against the west, where the sun had set.

20. *shill*, shrill. *Shille* occurs as a variant of *schrille* in C. T., B 4585; see *schil* in Stratmann.

32. *douf* (spelt *doif* in the old edition) is the Northern form of 'deaf,' answering to the Icel. *daufr*; thus a nut without a kernel is called in the South 'a deaf nut,' but in Scotland 'a douf nit'; see Jamieson. For *deaf* in the senses of 'dull' and 'unproductive,' see the New E. Dict.

39. *cut*, curtail; illustrated from Lydgate in the New E. Dict.

42. Read *lusty*, to avoid the repetition of *worthy*; cf. l. 41. It should have been stated, in the footnotes, that the readings are: E. worthy; Th. lusty.

43. Referring to Troil. bk. v. In l. 92, we are told how Diomede led Criseyde away. Note particularly that, in l. 45, Henryson quotes Chaucer rather closely. Cf. 'For which wel neigh out of my wit I breyde'; Troil. v. 1262. And cf. ll. 47-9 with—'Betwixen hope and drede his herte lay'; Troil. v. 1207.

48. *Quhill*, till. The reading *Esperus* in E. is comic enough. Even Thynne has misread *esperans*, and has turned it into *esperous*. There can be little doubt that *esperans* here means 'hope,' as it is opposed to *wanhope* in the line above. The word was known to Henryson, as we find, in st. 8 of his Garment of Gude Ladyis : 'Hir slevis suld be of *esperance*, To keip hir *fra dispair.*' Cf. l. 49.

50. *behest*, promise; because she had promised to return to Troy within ten days; Troil. iv. 1595.

65. *this narratioun*, i.e. the sequel of the story, which he is about to tell. He does not tell us whence he derived it, but intimates that it is a fiction; I suppose he invented it himself.

74. *lybel of répudy*, Lat. 'libellum repudii,' as in Matt. xix. 7.

77. 'And, as some say, into the common court'; i. e. she became a courtesan.

78. *A-per-se*, i. e. the first letter of the alphabet, standing alone. A letter that was also a word in itself, as *A*, or *I*, or *O*, was called 'per se,' because it could stand alone. Of these, the *A-per-se* was a type of excellence. One of Dunbar's Poems (ed. Small, i. 276) begins :—' London, thou art of townes *A-per-se*.'

79. *fortunait*, the sport of fortune; oddly used, as it implies that she was 'an unfortunate.' Cf. l. 89.

94. *but*, without; and Thynne actually prints *without* in place of it.

97. *quhair*, where her father Chalcas (was). He was living among the Greeks; Troil. i. 80, 87.

106. In the medieval legend, Calchas was not a priest of Venus, but of Apollo, as Chaucer notes; see Troil. i. 66–70. So also in Lydgate, Siege of Troy, bk. ii. c. 17. Henryson probably altered this intentionally, because it enabled him to represent Criseyde as reproaching her father's god; see ll. 124, 134.

129. *outwaill*, outcast; one who is chosen out and rejected; from the verb *wail, wale*, to choose. There seems to be no other example of the word, though Jamieson gives '*outwailins*, leavings, things of little value.'

140. *forlane* can hardly mean 'left alone.' If so, it would be a word invented for the occasion, and improperly formed from *lane*, which is itself a docked form of *alane*. In all other passages, *forlane* or *forlain* is the pp. of *forliggen*; and the sense of 'defiled' is quite applicable. And further, it rimes with *slane*, which means 'slain.'

143. 'And, as it seemed, she heard, where she lay,' &c.

147. The seven planets; which, in the order of the magnitude of their orbits, are Saturn, Jupiter, Mars, the Sun, Venus, Mercury, and the Moon. And to this order the author carefully adheres throughout ll. 151–263.

155. *fronsit*, wrinkled; *frounse* is the mod. E. *flounce*, which formerly meant 'a pleat'; see *frounce, frouncen* in Stratmann, and the Gloss. to Chaucer. Misprinted *frosnit* in E.

'His complexion was like lead.' Lead was Saturn's metal; see C. T., G 828, and the note.

164. That *gyte* is the correct reading, is obvious from ll. 178, 260, where Thynne has preserved it. It is a Chaucerian word; see the Glossary in vol. vi. It seems to mean 'mantle.' The Edinburgh printer altered it to *gyis*, which is too general a term, at least in l. 260.

182. 'To ward off from us the wrath of his father (Saturn).'

198. Compare Ch. C. T., F 1031—'god and governour Of every plaunte, herbe, tree, and flour.'

205. Alluding to Phaethon's misguidance of the chariot of the sun;

'And that his faders cart amis he dryve'; Troil. v. 665. Laing prints *unricht*; but omits to say that E. has *upricht*.

211. *soyr*, sorrel-coloured, reddish-brown; see *Sorrel* in my Etym. Dict.

212-6. The names of the four horses are curiously corrupted from the names given in Ovid, Met. ii. 153, viz. Eöus, Æthon, Pyröeis, and Phlegon. As *Eous* means 'belonging to the dawn,' we may consider the words *into the Orient*, i. e. in the East, as explanatory of the name *Eoy*; 'called Eoy, (which signifies) in the East.' As to the name of the last horse, it was obviously meant to take the form *Philegoney*, in order to rime with *sey* (sea), and I have therefore restored this form. The two authorities, E. and Th., give it in the amazing form *Philologie* (*Philologee*), which can only mean 'philology'!

231. *lauch* and *weip* are infinitives, but appear to be meant for past tenses. If so, the former should be *leuch*; *weip* may answer to the strong pt. t. *weep* in Chaucer A. S. *wēop*).

246. He seems to be thinking of Chaucer's Doctor of Phisyk; cf. Ch. Prol. A 425-6, 439.

254. 'The last of all (in order), and swiftest in her orbit.'

256. Thynne has *tapere*=to appear; this passage is curiously cited, in Richardson's Dictionary, in illustration of the sb. *taper*!

261. *churl*, man; this is Chaucer's *cherl*, in Troil. i. 1024. See the note to that line.

263. *na nar*, no nearer; the moon's orbit, being the least, was the most remote from the outer heaven that enclosed the *primum mobile*.

273. *shew*, shewed; but it is false grammar, for the verb to *shew* (or *show*) was weak. Formed by analogy with *blew, grew, knew*; cf. *rew, mew, sew*, old strong preterites of *row, mow*, and *sow*.

290. As Henryson usually refrains from the addition of a syllable at the cæsura, we should probably read *injure*, not *injury*; see Troil. iii. 1018.

297, 298. *hyest*, i. e. Saturn; *lawest* (lowest), i. e. Cynthia.

299. *modify*, determine, specify; not here used in the modern sense.

318. Heat and moisture characterised the *sanguine* temperament (see vol. v. p. 33); coldness and dryness characterised the melancholy temperament (see P. Plowman, B-text, p. xix). Cf. l. 316.

343. 'With cup and clapper, like a leper.' It was usual for lepers to carry a cup (for their own use), and a clapper or clap-dish, which was used in order to give warning of their approach, and also as a receptacle for alms, to prevent actual contact; cf. l. 479 below. Compare the following :—

> 'Coppe and claper he bare ...
> As he a mesel [*leper*] were.'—Sir Tristrem, 3173.

'Than beg her bread with dish and clap' (referring to Criseyde).
Turbervile's Poems: The Lover in utter dispaire.

See further under *Clapper* in the New Eng. Dict.

lazarous is formed as an adj. in *-ous* from the sb. *lazar*, a leper; see l. 531.

350. *wa*, woful; 'God knows if she was woful enough.'

382. The accent on the second syllable of *hospital* was not uncommon; hence its frequent contraction to *spittal* or *spittel-house*; for which see l. 391 below.

386. Read *bevar* or *bever* (Th. has *beuer*); the reading *bawar* in E. gives no sense. I see no connection with Lowl. Sc. *bevar*, 'one who is worn out with age,' according to Jamieson, who merely guesses at the sense, as being perhaps allied to *bavard*, which he also explains as 'worn out'; although, if from the F. *bavard*, it rather means talkative, babbling, or idle. I believe that *bevar hat* simply means 'beaver hat,' formerly used by women as well as by men. Even Dickens alludes to 'farmer's wives in beaver bonnets,' in Martin Chuzzlewit, ch. 5. No doubt a beaver hat was, when new, an expensive luxury, as worn by Chaucer's 'Merchant' (Prol. l. 272); but they wore well and long, and were doubtless gladly used by beggars when cast off by their original owners.

407. The metre, in ll. 407-69, is borrowed from Chaucer's Anelida.

410. *blaiknit*, is not a derivative of M. E. *blak*, black, but of M. E. *blāk*, *bleik*, bleak, pallid, cheerless. It is here used in the sense of 'rendered cheerless'; and *bair* means 'bare' or 'barren.' See *blākien* in Stratmann.

413. 'Thy bale is in the growth,' or is sprouting. See *Braird*, the first shoots of corn or grass, in the New E. Dict., where two more examples of this phrase are cited from Henryson.

417. 'With goodly bed, and convenient embroidered bench-covers.' *Burelie* (mod. E. *burly*, prov. E. *bowerly*) answers to an A. S. form *būr-līc*, i. e. suitable for a lady's bower. This explains why it was appropriately used as an epithet for a bed. Cf. 'Quhair ane *burely* bed was wrocht in that wane'; Rauf Coilyear, 264. Hence 'a burly knight' was one suitable for a lady's bower, and therefore handsome, strong, well-grown, large; and by a degradation of meaning, huge, corpulent. The changes in sense are curious and instructive. In the New E. Dict., the etymology is not given. For *bene*, see *bain* in the New E. Dict.; and for *bankouris*, see *banker*.

421. *saipheroun sals*, saffron sauce. *Saffron* and *salt* were often used together in medieval cookery; see Two Fifteenth-Century Cookery Books, ed. Austin (E. E. T. S.). The Glossary to that book gives the spellings *safroun*, *saferon*, *saferoun*, and *sapheron*.

423. This is a very early mention of *lawn*. It is also mentioned in st. 10 of Lydgate's 'London Lickpeny.'

429. *walk*, wake. The history of this spelling is not quite clear; but the *l* was, in any case, mute; another spelling is *wauk*. I suspect that it originated in the misunderstanding of a symbol. The scribe, who wished to write *wakk*, used a symbol resembling *lk*, where the *l* was *really* the first *k*, indicated by its down-stroke only. For example,

the word *rokke* was (apparently) written *rolke*. See my article on Ghost-words; Phil. Soc. Trans. 1885, p. 369.

tak the dew, gather May-dew. The old custom of bathing the face with fresh dew on the 1st of May is referred to in Brand's Popular Antiquities. He gives an example as late as 1791. See Pepys' Diary, May 28, 1667, May 11, 1669; where we find that *any* day in May was then considered suitable for this health-giving operation.

433. I take *on every grane* to mean 'in every particular'; cf. 'a *grain* of sense.' We may also note the Fr. *teindre en graine*, to dye in grain, to dye of a fast colour; and we occasionally find *grain* in the sense of 'tint.' Godefroy cites 'ung couvertoer d'une *graigne* vermeille'; and 'une manche vermeille, ne sçay se c'est *graine* ou autre taincture.' *Grane* also means 'groan,' and 'groin,' and 'fork of a tree'; but none of these senses suit.

438. 'Take this leper-lodge in place of thy stately bower.'

450. In l. 407, we have *sop of sorrow*, i.e. sop, or sup, of sorrow. So here *sowpit in syte*, sopped, or drenched, in sorrow; an expression which Jamieson illustrates from Holland's Houlate, i. 4, and Douglas's Vergil, prologue to Book viii, l. 5.

463. This expression is imitated from Chaucer's Boethius, bk. iii. pr. 6. 3—'O glorie, glorie, thou art nothing elles but a greet sweller of eres!' See note to I. ii. 8. 68 (p. 472).

480. *leir* (Th. *lerne*); surely miscopied from l. 479. Read *live*.

490. *lipper* seems to be used collectively; so also in l. 494.

492. *shuik coppis*, shook their cups; it implies that they waved them aloft, to attract attention. They also used their clappers.

501. *ply*, plight. I know of no other example of *ply* in this sense; but *ply* (usually, a fold) and *plight* (incorrect spelling of M. E. *plyte*) are closely related; the former represents Lat. *plicitum*, the latter, Lat. *plicita*; from *plicare*, to fold (whence E. *ply*, verb, to bend).

541. 'With many a sorrowful cry and cold *or* sad (cry of) O hone!' Here *cald*=sad; and *Ochane* is the Irish and Scotch cry of *O hone*! or *Och hone*! See *O hone* in the Century Dict., s. v. *O*.

543. *will of wane*, lit. wild of weening, at a loss what to do. See Gloss. to Barbour's Bruce, s. v. *Will*.

550. 'And climbed so high upon the fickle wheel' (of Fortune). Cf. Troil. iv. 6, 11.

567. 'For they (women) are as constant as a weathercock in the wind.' Cf. '*unsad* . . and chaunging as a vane'; Ch. C. T., E 995.

588. *wellis*, streams, rills; as in Book Duch. 160.

589. *broche and belt*; Criseyde gave Diomede the brooch she had received from Troilus; see Troil. v. 1661, 1669, 1688. The *belt* is Henryson's addition.

600. 'His heart was ready to burst.'

XVIII. THE CUCKOO AND THE NIGHTINGALE.

In this piece, the final -*e* is much used as forming a distinct syllable; indeed, more freely than in Chaucer.

1, 2. Quoted from the Knightes Tale, A 1785-6.

4. The word *of* is inserted in Th., Ff. and S., and seems to be right; but as *hy-e* should be two syllables, perhaps the words *And of* were rapidly pronounced, in the time of a single syllable. Or omit *And*.

11-5. The lines of this stanza are wrongly arranged in Thynne, and in every printed edition except the present one; i.e. the lines 12 and 13 are transposed. But as the rime-formula is *aabba*, it is easy to see that *suffyse, devyse, agryse* rime together on the one hand, and *nyce, vyce*, on the other. The pronunciation *suffice* is comparatively modern; in Chaucer, the suffix -*yse* was pronounced with a voiced *s*, i.e. as *z*. Note the rimes *devyse, suffyse* in the Book of the Duch. 901-2; *suffyse, wyse, devyse*, in the C.T., B 3648-9; &c. The MSS. Ff., F., and B. all give the right arrangement.

18. *whom him lyketh*, him whom it pleases him (to gladden or sadden).

20, 23. *May*; cf. Troil. ii. 50-63; Rom. Rose, 51-2, 74-6, 85-6; Legend of Good Women, 108; C.T., A 1500-2.

36. *of feling*, from experience. *Spek-e* is dissyllabic.

39. *hoot*, hot, i.e. hopeful; *cold*, full of despair; *acces*, feverish attack, as in Troil. ii. 1315, 1543, 1578.

41. *fevers whyte*, feverish attacks (of love) that turn men pale; the same as *blaunche fevere* in Troil. i. 916; see note to that line.

48. *a comune tale*, a common saying. As a fact, one would expect to hear the cuckoo first. Prof. Newton, in his Dict. of Birds, says of the cuckoo, that it 'crosses the Mediterranean from its winter-quarters in Africa at the end of March or beginning of April. Its arrival is at once proclaimed by the peculiar ... cry of the cock.' Of the nightingale he says—'if the appearance of truth is to be regarded, it is dangerous to introduce a nightingale as singing in England before the 15th of April or after the 15th of June.'

As the change of style makes a difference of 12 days, this 15th of April corresponds to the 3rd of April in the time of Chaucer. It is remarkable that Hazlitt, in his Proverbs, p. 305, gives the following: —'On the third of April, comes in the cuckoo and the nightingale'; which may once have been correct as regards the latter. Hazlitt also says that, in Sussex, the 14th of April is supposed to be 'first cuckoo-day'; whereas it would better apply to the nightingale. And again, another proverb says (p. 380)—'The nightingale and the cuckoo sing both in one month.' It is clear that, whatever the facts may be, our ancestors had a notion that these birds arrived nearly at the same time, and attached some importance, by way of augury, to the possibility of hearing the nightingale first. They must frequently have been disappointed. See Milton's sonnet, as quoted in the Introduction.

54. *of*, during; exactly as in l. 42.

62. Read *inne*, the adverbial form; for the sake of the grammar and scansion. See *Inne* in the Gloss. in vol. vi. p. 135. *been* gives a false rime to *gren-e* and *sen-e*; shewing that *grene* and *sene* are here mono-syllabic (really *green* and *seen*), instead of being dissyllabic, as in Chaucer. *Sene* is the adj., meaning visible, not the pp., which then took the form *seyn*.

70. For *began*, which is singular, substitute the pl. form *begonne*. *to don hir houres*, to sing their matins, &c.; referring to the canoni-cal hours of church-service. Bell has the reading *to don honoures*, for which there is no early authority. Morris unluckily adopts the meaningless reading found in MSS. F. and B.

71. 'They knew that service all by rote,' i.e. by heart. Bell actually explains *rote* as a hurdy-gurdy; as to which see *Rote* (in senses 2 and 3) in the Gloss. in vol. vi. p. 218.

80. *Feverere* seems to have been pronounced *Fev'rer'*. Surely it must be right. Yet all the MSS. (except T.) actually have *Marche* (written *Mars* in Ff.), followed by *upon*, not *on*. Even Th. and T. have *upon*, not *on*; but it ruins the scansion, unless we adopt the reading *March*. It looks as if the author really *did* write *Marche*!

82, 85. *ron*, *mon*, for *ran*, *man*, are peculiar. As such forms occur in Myrc and Audelay (both Shropshire authors) and in Robert of Gloucester, they are perfectly consistent with the supposition that they are due to Clanvowe's connection with Herefordshire.

87. *swow*, swoon; cf. Book Duch. 215.

90. As *brid* is a monosyllable (cf. ll. 212, 260, 270, 271), it is neces-sary to make *lew-ed-e* a trisyllable; as also in l. 103. But it becomes *lew'de* in ll. 50, 94. Chaucer has *lew-ĕd*, P. F. 616, &c.

105. *him*; the cuckoo is male, but the nightingale, by way of con-trast, is supposed to be female.

118. *playn*, simple, having simple notes; cf. 'the plain-song cuckoo,' Mids. Nt. Dr. iii. 1. 134.

119. *crakel*, 'trill or quaver in singing; used in contempt'; New E. Dict.

124. *I* seems to be strongly accented. It is a pity that there is no authority for inserting *For* before it. Otherwise, read *I hav-ĕ*.

In Old French, *oci oci*, represented the cry of the nightingale; Gode-froy gives examples from Raoul de Houdenc, Froissart, and Des-champs. Moreover, *oci* was also the imperative of the O. F. verb *ccire*, to kill; with which it is here intentionally confused. Accordingly, the nightingale retorts that *oci* means 'kill! kill!' with reference to the enemies of love.

135. *grede*, exclaim, cry out. Not used by Chaucer, though found in most dialects of Middle-English. Clanvowe may have heard it in Herefordshire, as it occurs in Langland, Layamon, Robert of

Gloucester, and in the Coventry Mysteries, and must have been known in the west. But it was once a very common word. From A.S. *grǣdan*.

137. *to-drawe*, drawn asunder; cf. Havelok, 2001; Will. of Palerne, 1564.

140. *yok*, yoke; cf. Ch. C. T., E 113, 1285.

142. *unthryve*, become unsuccessful, meet with ill luck. A very rare word; but it also occurs in the Cursor Mundi (Fairfax MS.), l. 9450, where it is said of Adam that 'his wyf made him *to unthryve*.'

146. The first syllable of the line is deficient. Accent *What* strongly. Cf. 153–8 below.

151. The sentiment that love teaches all goodness, is common at this time; see Schick's note to Lydgate's Temple of Glas, l. 450.

152. The true reading is doubtful.

153–8. Here the author produces a considerable metrical effect, by beginning all of these lines with a strong accent. There are three such consecutive lines in the Wyf of Bathes Tale, D 869–71. Cf. ll. 161, 232, 242, 252, 261, 265, 268, 270, 278.

180. Bell and Morris read *haire*, without authority, and Bell explains it by 'he may full soon have the *hair* (!) which belongs to age, *scil.*, grey hair, said to be produced by anxiety.' But the M. E. form of 'hair' is *heer*, which will not give a true rime; and the word *heyr* represents the mod. E. *heir*. As the *h* was not sounded, it is also written *eir* (as in MS. T.) and *air* (as in MS. S.). The sense is—'For he who gets a little bliss of love may very soon find that his heir has come of age, unless he is always devoted to it.' This is a mild joke, signifying that he will soon find himself insecure, like one whose heir or successor has come of age, and whose inheritance is threatened. On the other hand, 'to have one's hair of age' is wholly without sense. Compare the next note.

185. 'And then you shall be called as *I* am.' I. e. your loved one will forsake you, and you will be called a cuckold. This remark is founded on the fact that the O. F. *coucou* or *cocu* had the double sense of cuckoo and cuckold. See *cocu* in Littré. This explains l. 186.

201–5. Bell, by an oversight, omits this stanza.

203. This reading (from the best MS., viz. Ff.) is much the best. The sense is—'And whom he hits he knows not, or whom he misses'; because he is blind.

216–25. All the early printed editions crush these two stanzas into one, by omitting ll. 217–9, and 224–5, and altering *thoughte me* (l. 223) to *me aloon*. This is much inferior to the text.

237. *leve*, believe; yet all the authorities but S. have the reading *loue*! Cf. l. 238.

243. *dayesye*, daisy. Cf. Legend of Good Women, 182–7, 201–2, 211.

266. *Ye witen* is the right reading; turned into *ye knowe* in F. and B. The old printed editions actually read *The cuckowe*!

267. A syllable seems lacking after *I*; such lines are common in

Lydgate. The reading *y-chid* would render the line complete; or we may read *hav-ë*, as perhaps in l. 124.

275. An obvious allusion to Chaucer's Parlement of Foules, in which he gives 'the royal egle' the first place (l. 330).

284. *The quene* ; queen Joan of Navarre, second wife of Henry IV, who received the manor of Woodstock as part of her dower.

285. *lay*, lea ; not a common word in M. E. poetry, though occurring in P. Plowman. The parliament of birds required a large open space.

389. *Terme* : during the whole term of my life ; cf. C. T., G 1479.

XIX. ENVOY TO ALISON.

1. *lewde book*, unlearned book. It is not known to what book this refers. It has nothing to do with the preceding poem. My guess, in vol. i. p. 40, that this piece might be Hoccleve's, is quite untenable. His pieces are all known, and the metrical form is of later date. See the next note.

11. Too long ; perhaps *servant* should be struck out. So in l. 13 we could spare the word *als*. But ll. 17, 18, 19, 20, are all of an unconscionable length.

22-7. I believe I was the first to detect the obvious acrostic on the name of Alison ; see vol. i. p. 40. The sense of ll. 25-6 (which are forced and poor) is—'I beseech (you) of your grace, let your writing (in reply) alleviate the sighs which I pour out in silence.'

XX. THE FLOWER AND THE LEAF.

I give numerous references below to ' A. L.', i. e. the Assembly of Ladies, printed at p. 380. The two poems have much in common.

1-2. Imitated from C. T., F 671 ; see note in vol. v. p. 386.

3. *Bole*, Bull, Taurus. The sun then entered Taurus about the middle of April ; hence the allusion to April showers in l. 4. Compare the opening lines of Chaucer's Prologue. But we learn, from l. 437, that it was already May. Hence the sun had really run half its course in Taurus. *certeinly* ; used at the end of the line, as in A. L. 85.

10. *very good* ; this adverbial use of *very* is noticeable ; cf. ll. 35, 315, 409, and A. L. 479. I believe Chaucer never uses *very* to qualify an adjective. It occurs, however, in Lydgate.

20. Cf. ' *more* at *hertes ese* ' ; A. L. 672.

25. Cf. ' at *springing of the day* ' ; A. L. 218.

26. Cf. ' That ye wold help me *on* with *myn aray* ' ; A. L. 241.

27-8. This rime of *passe* with *was* occurs again below (114-6) ; and in A. L. 436-8.

30. Chaucer has *hew-ë*, *new-ë* ; but here *hew*, *new* rime with the pt. t. *grew*. So, in A. L. 65-8, *hew*, *new* rime with the pt. t. *knew*.

* * *
* * * *   M m

31-2. Copied from the Book of the Duch. 419-20 :—

> 'And every tree stood by him-selve
> Fro other wel ten foot or twelve.'

35. ' The young leaves of the oak, when they first burst from the bud, are of a red, cinereous colour '; Bell.

37. Cf. 'this proces *for to here*'; A. L. 27. And again, 'pitous *for to here*'; A. L. 718.

39-42. This seems to be a direct allusion to the Cuckoo and the Nightingale, ll. 52-4 :—

> ' I wolde go som whider to assay
> If that I might *a nightingale here* ;
> For yet had I non *herd of al this yere.*'

43-5. From the Book of the Duch. 398-401 :—

> ' Doun by a floury grene wente
> *Ful thikke of gras,* ful softe and swete, . . .
> *And litel used,* it semed thus.'

Cf. A. L. 47 ; 'into a strait passage,' and the context.

47. *parde* ; a petty oath (being in French), such as a female writer might use ; so in A. L. 753.

49, 50. For the *herber* and *benches*, see A. L. 48-9; also L. G. W. 203-4. For the phrase *wel y-wrought*, see A. L. 165.

53. Bell and Morris read *wool*, which is obviously right ; but neither of them mention the fact that *both* Speght's editions have *wel*; and there is no other authority ! Clearly, Speght's MS. had *wol*, which he misread as *wel*.

56. *eglantere*, eglantine, sweet-briar. Entered under *eglatere* in the New E. Dict., though the earlier quotations, in 1387 and 1459, have *eglentere*. I find no authority for the form *eglatere* except Speght's misprint in this line, which he corrects in l. 80 below. Tennyson's *eglatere* (Dirge, 23) is clearly borrowed from this very line.

58. *by mesure* ; a tag which reappears in A. L. 81.

59. *by and by* ; another tag, for which see A. L. 87, 717.

60. *I you ensure* ; yet another tag ; see l. 457, and A. L. 52, 199, 495, 517.

62. The final *e* in *peyn-e* is suppressed ; so in A. L. 359, 416.

68. Cf. 'And as they sought hem-self thus *to and fro* '; A. L. 43.

75. Here *espyed* rimes with *syde, wyde* ; in A. L. 193, it rimes with *asyde* and *gyde*.

89. The *goldfinch* is afterwards opposed to the *nightingale*. Hence he replaces the *cuckoo* in the poem of the Cuckoo and Nightingale. Just as the Cuckoo and Nightingale represent the faithless and the constant, so the goldfinch and the nightingale are attached, respectively, to the bright Flower and the long-lasting Leaf. This is explicitly said below ; see ll. 439, 444.

98. *in this wyse*; appears also at the end of a line in A. L. 589; cf. *in her gyse*, A. L. 603; *in ful pitous wyse*, A. L. 584; *in no maner wyse*, A. L. 605.

99, 100. These lines correspond to the Cuckoo and Nightingale, 98-100.

113. *inly greet*, extremely great; cf. *inly fair*, A. L. 515.

115. ' Ye wold it *thinke* a very *paradyse* '; A. L. 168.

118. Better *I set me doun*, as in A. L. 77.

121. 'Withouten sleep, withouten mete or drinke'; L. G. W. 177 (note the context).

134. Here begins the description of the adherents of the Leaf, extending to l. 322, including the Nine Worthies, ll. 239-94. The reader must carefully bear in mind that the followers of the Leaf are clad in *white* (not in green, as we should now expect), though the nine Worthies are crowned with green laurel, and all the company gather under a huge Laurel-tree (l. 304). On the other hand the followers of the Flower, shortly described in ll. 323-50, are clad in *green*, though wearing chaplets of white and red flowers; for green was formerly an emblem of *inconstancy*.

137. Cf. ' *to* say you *very right* '; A. L. 750.

144. *oon and oon*, every one of them. This phrase is rare in Chaucer; it seems only to occur once, in C. T., A 679; but see A. L. 368, 543, 710.

146. *purfil* occurs in A. L. 87, in the same line with *by and by*; and in A. L. 522-4, we find *colour, sleves*, and *purfyl* close together.

148. Cf. ' With *grete perles*, ful fyne *and orient* '; A. L. 528. For *diamonds*, see A. L. 530.

150. Borrowed from Chaucer, Parl. Foules, 287 : ' of whiche the name I wante.' Hence *wante*, i. e. lack, is the right reading. The rime is imperfect.

155. The missing word is not *branches*, as suggested by Sir H. Nicolas, nor *floures*, as suggested by Morris, but *leves*; as the company of *the Leaf* is being described ; cf. l. 259. The epithets *fresh and grene* are very suitable. The leaves were of laurel, woodbine, and *agnus-castus*.

160. For *were* read *ware*; see ll. 267, 329, 335, 340 ; the sense is *wore*. Chaucer's form is *wered*, as the verb was originally weak; Gower and Lydgate also use the form *wered*. The present is perhaps one of the earliest examples of the strong form of this preterite.

agnus-castus ; 'from Gk. ἅγνος, the name of the tree, confused with ἁγνός, chaste, whence the second word Lat. *castus*, chaste. A tree, species of Vitex (*V. Agnus Castus*), once believed to be a preservative of chastity, called also Chaste-tree and Abraham's Balm '; New E. Dict. The same Dict. quotes from Trevisa: ' The herbe agnus-castus is alwaye grene, and the flowre therof is namly callyd Agnus Castus, for wyth smelle and vse it makyth men chaste as a lombe.'

163. For *But* Morris reads *And*, which is simpler.

164. *oon*, one. She was the goddess Diana (see l. 472), or the Lady of the Leaf.

171. Cf. 'That to beholde it was a greet plesaunce'; A. L. 59.

172. Cf. 'though it were *for a king*'; A. L. 158.

177-8. Speght has *Suse le foyle de vert moy* in l. 177, and *Seen et mon joly cuer en dormy* in l. 178. I see little good in guessing what it ought to be; so I leave it alone, merely correcting *Suse* and *foyle* to *Sus* and *foyl*; as the O. F. *foil* was masculine.

Bell alters *de vert* to *devers*, and for *Seen* puts *Son*; and supplies *est* after *cuer*; but it all gives no sense when it is done. We should have to read *Sus le foyl devers moy sied, et mon joli cuer est endormi*; sit down upon the foliage before me, and my merry heart has gone to sleep. Which can hardly be right. The Assembly of Ladies has the same peculiarity, of presenting unintelligible scraps of French to the bewildered reader.

180. *smal*, high, treble; chiefly valuable for explaining the same word in Chaucer's Balade to Rosemounde.

188-9. A parallel passage occurs in A. L. 384-5.

201. *the large wones*, the spacious dwellings; cf. Ch. C. T., D 2105.

202. Speght has *Pretir*, an obvious error for *Prester*. The authoress may easily have obtained her knowledge of Prester John from a MS. of Mandeville's Travels; see cap. 27 of that work. And see Yule's edition of Marco Polo. He was, according to Mandeville, one of the greatest potentates of Asia, next to the Great Khan.

209. *cereal*; borrowed from Chaucer:—'A *coroune* of a grene *ook cerial*'; C. T., A 2290. And Chaucer took it from Boccaccio; see note in vol. v. p. 87.

210. *trumpets*, i. e. trumpeters; as several times in Shakespeare. Cf. l. 213.

212. *tartarium*, thin silk from Tartary. Fully explained in my note to P. Plowman, C. xvii. 299 (B. xv. 163), and in the Glossary to the same. *bete*, lit. beaten; hence, adorned with beaten gold; see note to C. T., A 978 (vol. v. p. 64). *were*, (all of which) were; hence the plural.

213. Read *bere*, as in l. 223; A. S. *bǣron*, pt. t. pl.

220. *kinges of armes*, kings-at-arms; who presided over colleges of heralds. Sir David Lyndsay was Lord Lion king-at-arms.

224. Cf. 'Set with *saphyrs*'; A. L. 480.

233. *vel-u-et* is trisyllabic; as in The Black Knight, 80.

234. 'And certainly, they had nothing to learn as to how they should place the armour upon them.'

238. *in sute*, in their master's livery.

240. The celebrated Nine Worthies; see notes to IV. 281, XII. 86.

243. Cf. 'and *furred* wel *with gray*'; A. L. 305.

252. *henshmen*, youths mounted on horseback, who attended their lords. See numerous quotations for this word in A Student's Pastime, §§ 264, 272, 415-8. Each of them is called *a child*, l. 259.

253. For *every on*, it is absolutely necessary to read *the first upon*;

for the sense. Each of the nine worthies had three henchmen ; of these three, the first bore his helmet, the second his shield, and the third his spear.

257. Bell and Morris alter *nekke* to *bakke* ; but wrongly. The shields were carried by help of a strap which passed round the *neck* and over the shoulders ; called in Old French a *guige*. The convenience of this arrangement is obvious. See note to C. T., A 2504 (vol. v. p. 88).

272. In Lydgate's Temple of Glas, 508, we are told that hawthorn-leaves do not fade ; see ll. 551–3 below.

274. Read *hors*, not *horses* ; *hors* is the true plural ; see l. 293.

275. Cf. ' *trompes*, that . . . blowen *blody sounes* '; C. T., A 2511–2.

286–7. 'That *to beholde it was a greet plesaunce* ' ; A. L. 59. And again—' *I you ensure* '; A. L. 52.

289. I. e. the Nine Worthies ; see ll. 240, 249.

293. The reading *ninth* (as in Speght) is an absurd error for *nine* ; yet no one has hitherto corrected it. How could the ninth man alight from *their horses*? The ' remnant' were the twenty-seven henchmen and the other knights.

295. Cf. ' See how *they come togider, twain and twain* '; A. L. 350.

302. Cf. ' *Ful womanly* she gave me,' &c. ; A. L. 196.

305. ' Laden with leaves, with boughs of great breadth.'

323. Here begins the description of the company of the Flower. They were clad in *green*.

330. Cf. ' Her gown was *wel embrouded* '; A. L. 85.

348. *bargaret*, a pastoral ; a rustic song and dance ; O. F. *bergerete*, from *berger*, a shepherd. Godefroy notes that they were in special vogue at Easter.

350. We have here the refrain of a popular French pastoral. Warton suggests it may have been Froissart's ; but the refrain of Froissart's Ballade de la Marguerite happens to be different : ' Sur toutes flours j'aime la margherite '; see Spec. of O. French, ed. Toynbee, p. 302. In fact, Warton proceeds to remark, that ' it was common in France to give the title of Marguerites to studied panegyrics and flowery compositions of every kind.' It is quite impossible to say if a special compliment is intended ; most likely, the authoress thought of nothing of the kind. She again mentions *margarettes* in A. L. 57.

351. *in-fere*, together ; very common at the end of a line, as in ll. 384, 450; A. L. 407, 469, 546, 602, 719.

369. *withouten fail* ; this tag recurs in A. L. 567, 646, in the form *withouten any fail* ; and, unaltered, in A. L. 188, 537.

373. Those in white, the party of the Leaf.

379. *oon*, one of those in green ; this was queen Flora ; see l. 534.

403. Bell thinks this corrupt. I think it means, that, before engaging with them in jousts in a friendly manner, they procured some logs of wood and thoroughly dried them. Hence *To make hir justes*=in order to joust with them afterwards.

410. ' Quickly anointing the sick, wherever they went.'

417. *for any thing,* in any case, whatever might happen; cf. C. T., A 276, and the note (vol. v. p. 30).

427. 'For nothing was lacking that ought to belong to him.'

450. Here the story ends, and the telling of the moral begins.

457. The meeting with a 'fair lady' was convenient, as she wanted information. In the Assembly of Ladies, this simple device is resorted to repeatedly; see ll. 79, 191, 260, 400.

459. We find *ful demure* at the end of A. L. 82.

462, 467. *My doughter*; this assumes that the author was a female; so in ll. 500, 547; and in A. L. throughout.

475. Referring to l. 173; so l. 477 refers to l. 160; l. 479, to l. 158.

493. *some maner way,* some kind of way; cf. *what maner way,* A. L. 234.

502. Refers to ll. 240, 249. With l. 510, cf. C. T., A 1027.

512. Speght prints *bowes* for *boughes*; but the meaning is certain, as the reference is to ll. 270-1. Bows are not made of laurel; yet Dryden fell into the trap, and actually wrote as follows :—

> 'Who bear the bows were knights in Arthur's reign;
> Twelve they, and twelve the peers of Charlemagne;
> For bows the strength of brawny arms imply,
> Emblems of valour and of victory.'

This is probably the only instance, even in poetry, of knights being armed with bows and arrows.

515. For the knights of Arthur's round table, see Malory's Morte Arthure.

516. *Douseperes*; *les douze pers*, the twelve peers of Charlemagne, including Roland, Oliver, Ogier the Dane, Otuel, Ferumbras, the traitor Ganelon, and others. The names vary.

520. *in hir tyme,* formerly, in their day; shewing that the institution of the Knights of the Garter on April 23, 1349, by Edward III, was anything but a recent event.

530. I. e. 'Witness *him* of Rome, who was the founder of knighthood.' Alluding to Julius Cæsar, to whom was decreed by the senate the right of wearing a laurel-crown; Dryden mentions him by name.

550. Cf. '*De mieulx en mieulx*'; Temple of Glas, 310.

551-6. Apparently imitated from The Temple of Glas, 503-16.

567. Cf. 'We *thanked* her *in our most humble wyse*'; A. L. 729.

580. *Male-Bouche,* Slander; borrowed from the Rom. de la Rose. See note above, to VIII. 260.

589. Cf. 'to *put* it *in wryting*'; A. L. 664; 'she *put* it *in wryting*'; A. L. 629.

590. I. e. in the hope that it will be patronised.

591. Cf. 'As for this *book*'; A. L. (last stanza).

592. 'How darest thou thrust thyself among the throng?' i. e. enter into contest. Cf. 'In suych materys to *putte mysylff in prees*'; Lydgate, Secrees of Philosophers, ed. Steele, l. 555.

XXI. THE ASSEMBLY OF LADIES.

For numerous references to this poem, see Notes to the preceding poem.

Though apparently written by the authoress of the Flower and the Leaf, it is of later date, and much less use is made of the final *e*. That the author was a woman, is asserted in ll. 7, 18, 259, 284, 370, 379–85, 407, 450, 625.

17. *the mase*. They amused themselves by trying to find a way into a maze, similar to that at Hampton Court. Cf. l. 32.

29. Ll. 1–28 are introductory. The story of the dream now begins, but is likewise preceded by an introduction, down to l. 77.

34. The word *went* is repeated; the second time, it is an error for *wend*, weened. 'Some went (really) inwards, and imagined that they had gone outwards.' Which shews that the maze was well constructed. So, in l. 36, those who thought they were far behind, found themselves as far forward as the best of them.

42. That is, they cheated the deviser of the maze, by stepping over the rail put to strengthen the hedge. That was because they lost their temper.

44. The authoress got ahead of the rest; although sorely tired, she had gained a great advantage, and found the last narrow passage which led straight to the arbour in the centre. This was provided with benches (doubtless of turf, Flower and Leaf, l. 51) and well enclosed, having stone walls and a paved floor with a fountain in the middle of it.

54. There were stairs leading downwards, with a 'turning-wheel.' I do not think that turning-wheel here means a turn-stile, or what was formerly called a turn-pike. It simply means that the stair-case was of spiral form. Jamieson tells us that, in Lowland Scotch, the term *turn-pike* was applied (1) to the winding stair of a castle, and (2) to any set of stairs of spiral form; and quotes from Arnot to shew that a spiral stair-case was called a *turnpike stair*, whereas a straight one was called a *scale stair*. The pot of marjoram may have been placed on a support rising from the newel.

It may be noted that arbours, which varied greatly in size and construction, were often set upon a small 'mount' or mound; in which case it would be easy to make a small spiral stair-case in the centre. In the present case, it could hardly have been very large, as it occupied a space in the centre of a maze. For further illustration, see A History of Gardening in England, by the Hon. Alicia Amherst, pp. 33, 52, 78, 116, 118, 314.

60. 'And how they (the daisies) were accompanied with other flowers besides, viz. forget-me-nots and remember-mes; and the poor pansies were not ousted from the place.'

61. *Ne-m'oublie-mies*; from O. F. *ne m'oublie-mie*, a forget-me-not. Littré, s. v. *ne m'oubliez pas*, quotes, from Charles d'Orléans, 'Des

fleurs de *ne m'oubliez mie*'; and again, from a later source, 'Un diamant taillé en fleur de *ne m'oblie mie.*' · The recovery of this true reading (by the help of MS. A.) is very interesting ; as all the editions, who follow Thynne, are hopelessly wrong. Thynne, misreading the word, printed *Ne momblysnesse* ; whence arose the following extraordinary entry in Bailey's Dictionary :—'*Momblishness*, talk, muttering; Old Word.' This ghost-word is carefully preserved in the Century Dictionary in the form :—'*Momblishness*, muttering talk' ; Bailey (1731).

sovenez doubtless corresponds to the name *remember-me*, given in Yorkshire and Scotland to the *Veronica chamædrys*, more commonly called the germander speedwell, and in some counties forget-me-not. But we should rather, in this passage, take forget-me-not (above) to refer, as is most usual, to the *Myosotis*; as Littré also explains it. Here Thynne was once more at a loss, and printed the word as *souenesse*, which was 'improved' by Stowe into *sonenesse*. Hence another ghost-word, recorded by Bailey in the entry :—'*Sonenesse*, noise.' Cf. l. 86.

62. *pensees*, pansies ; alluding, of course, to the *Viola tricolor*. The spelling is correct, as it represents the O. F. *pensee*, thought ; and it seems to have been named, as Littré remarks, in a similar way to the forget-me-not, and (I may add) to the remember-me.

68. *stremes*, jets of water ; there was a little fountain in the middle.

73. The authoress had to wait till the other ladies also arrived in the centre of the maze. Cf. note to l. 736.

82. *sad*, settled, staid. *demure*, sober ; lit. mature.

83. *blewe*, blue ; which was the colour of constancy; see note to C. T., F 644 (vol. v. p. 386). For the lady's name was Perseverance. It is convenient to enumerate here the officers who are mentioned. They are : Perseveraunce, usher (91) ; Diligence (133, 198, 728); Countenance, porter (177, 277, 295) ; Discretion, purveyour (263); Acquaintance, herbergeour (269) ; Largesse, steward (318) ; Belchere, marshall (322) ; Remembrance, chamberlain (336) ; Avyseness, or Advisedness, secretary (343) ; and Attemperance, chancellor (508). The chief Lady is Loyalty (98), dwelling in the mansion of Pleasant Regard (170).

87. Here *word* means 'motto.' I here collect the French mottoes mentioned, viz. Bien et loyalement (88) ; Tant que je puis (208) ; A moi que je voy (308) ; Plus ne purroy (364) ; A endurer (489). Afterwards, four ladies are introduced, with the mottoes Sans que jamais (583) ; Une sanz chaungier (590) ; Oncques puis lever (598) ; and Entierment vostre (616). These ladies afterwards present petitions, on which were written, respectively, the phrases Cest sanz dire (627) ; En dieu est (645) ; Soyez en sure (666) ; and Bien moneste (675). The words, or mottoes, were embroidered on the sleeves of the ladies (119). See Lydgate's Temple of Glas, 308-10.

224. They said a pater-noster for the benefit of St. Julian, because

he was the patron-saint of wayfarers. ' Of this saynt Julyen somme saye that this is he that pylgryms and wey-faryng men calle and requyre for good herberowe, by-cause our lord was lodgyd in his hows'; Caxton's Golden Legend. The story occurs in the Gesta Romanorum, c. xviii., and in the Aurea Legenda. The following extract from an old translation of Boccaccio, Decam. Day 2. Nov. 2, explains the point of the allusion. ' Nevertheless, at all times, when I am thus in journey, in the morning before I depart my chamber, I say a *pater-noster* and an *Ave-Maria* for the souls of the father and mother of St. Julian ; and after that, I pray God and St. Julian to send me a good lodging at night'; &c. Dunlop, in his Hist. of Fiction, discussing this Novella, says : ' This saint was originally a knight, and, as was prophecied to him by a stag, he had the singular hap to kill his father and mother by mistake. As an atonement for his carelessness, he afterwards founded a sumptuous hospital for the accommodation of travellers, who, in return for their entertainment, were required to *repeat pater-nosters* for the souls of his unfortunate parents.'

241. Because she was to change her dress, and put on blue ; see ll. 258–9, 313–4, 413.

457. The reference is to the Legend of Good Women, which contains the story of Phyllis, Thisbe, and ' Cleopataras.' Cf. l. 465.

463. *Hawes*, probably the same name as *Havise*, which occurs in the old story of Fulke Fitzwarine. But it is remarkable that MS. A. has the reading :—' That other sydë was, how Enclusene '; and this looks like an error for *Melusene*, variant of *Melusine*. This would agree with the next line, which means ' was untruly deceived in her bath.' The story of Melusine is given in the Romance of Partenay. She was a fairy who married Raymound, son of the Earl of Forest, on the understanding that he was never to watch what she did on a Saturday. This he at last attempts to do, and discovers, through a hole in the door, that she was *in a bath*, and that her lower half was changed into a serpent. He tries to keep the knowledge of the secret, but one day, in a fit of anger, calls her a serpent. She reproaches him, and vanishes from his sight. See the Romans of Partenay, ed. Skeat (E.E.T.S.).

465. From Chaucer's poem of Anelida and the false Arcite ; vol. i. p. 365 ; for her Complaint, see the same, p. 373.

471. *umple* (MS. T. *vmpylle*), smooth gauze ; from O. F. *omple*, smooth, used as an epithet of cloth, satin, or other stuff (Godefroy). Here evidently applied to something of a very thin texture, as gauze ; see l. 473.

477. *stages*, steps. The chair or throne was set on a platform accessible by five steps, which were made of *cassidony*. Cotgrave explains O. F. *cassidonie* as meaning not only chaledony, but also a kind of marble ; and this latter sense may be here intended.

488. *Her word*, her motto ; *her* must refer to the great lady (l. 501) to whom the throne belonged.

499. *tapet*, a hanging cloth (Halliwell) ; here a portion of the hangings that could be lifted up, to give entrance.

526. *After a sort*, of one kind, alike.   *vent*, slit in front of a gown. ' *Vente*, the opening at the neck of the tunic or gown, as worn by both sexes during the Norman period, and which was closed by a brooch ' ; Gloss. to Fairholt's Costume in England. O. F. *fente*, a slit, cleft ; from Lat. *findere*. The collar and slit were alike bordered with ermine, covered with large pearls, and sprinkled with diamonds. Cf. also : 'Wyth armynes powdred bordred at the vent' ; Hawes, Pastime of Pleasure, ed. Wright, p. 80.

536. *balays*, a balas-ruby ; 'a delicate rose-red variety of the spinel ruby' ; New. E. Dict. *of entail*, lit. 'of cutting,' i. e. carefully cut ; the usual phrase ; see New E. Dict.

539. *a world*, worth a world ; cf. *a world* (great quantity) of ladies ; Flower and the Leaf, 137.

576–8. Alluding to the proverb : 'first come, first served' ; cf. C. T., D 389, and the note (vol. v. p. 301).

581. We find that the 'bills' are petitions made by the four ladies regarding their ill success in love-affairs.

592. I. e. yet not so much as she ought to have been, as she had all the trouble ; *she* refers to the lady herself.

598. *Oncques*, ever ; Lat. *unquam*. 'I can ever rise' seems at first sight to be meant ; but *ne* must be understood ; the true sense is, 'I can never rise' ; i. e. never succeed. See the context, ll. 605-9.

645. 'I trust in God' ; see l. 655.

675. 'Admonish well' ; from O. F. *monester*, to admonish, warn.

680. Here, and in l. 689, the speaker is the lady of the castle. In l. 682 (as in l. 690), the speaker appears to be the fourth lady ; it is none too clear.

689. *I hate you*, I command you. *Hate* should rather be written *hote* ; perhaps it was confused with the related pt. t. *hatte*, was called. The reference to Saint James of Compostella is noteworthy.

693. *it*, i. e. the bill, or petition ; it takes the form of a Complaint.

697–8. *And, if. ye wolde*, i. e. *ye wolde seme*, (see l. 696), ye would think so. *Seem* is still common in Devonshire in the sense of think or suppose ; usually pronounced *zim*.

699. *her* refers to the lady of the castle ; at least, it would appear so from l. 705. Else, it refers to Fortune.

736. *the water*, water thrown in her face by one of her companions, who had by this time entered the arbour.

752. A headless line ; accent the first syllable.

754–5. The Flower and the Leaf has a similar ending (ll. 582-3).

XXII. A GOODLY BALADE.

Obviously Lydgate's. See the Introduction.

1. *Moder of norture,* model of good breeding. The poem is evidently addressed to a lady named Margaret.

2. *flour,* daisy (for Margaret) ; see ll. 22, 23.

4. *Al be I,* although I am ; common in Lydgate.

9. *Thing,* i. e. anything, everything, whatever thing.

15. *Mieulx un,* one (is) better ; evidently cited from a motto or device. The meaning seems to be : it is better to have but *one* lover, and you have found one in a heart that will never shrink. In the Temple of Glas, 310, Lydgate uses the motto *de mieulx en mieulx.*

22-3. 'Daisy (born) of light; you are called the daughter of the sun.' Alluding to the name *day's eye,* which was also applied by Lydgate to the sun ; see note in vol. iii. p. 291 (l. 43). Imitated from Legend of Good Women, 60-4.

29. 'When the day dawns, (repairing) to its natural place (in the east), then your father Phœbus adorns the morrow.'

34. 'Were it not for the comfort in the day-time, when (the sun's) clear eyes make the daisy unclose.' Awkward and involved ; cf. Legend of Good Women, 48-50, 64-5.

43. *Je vouldray,* I should like ; purposely left incomplete.

44. *casuel,* uncertain ; see New E. Dict.

48-9. *god saith* ; implying that it is in the Bible. I do not find the words ; cf. Prov. xxi. 3 ; 1 Pet. ii. 20.

50. *Cautels,* artifices, deceits ; a word not used by Chaucer, but found in Lydgate ; see New E. Dict.

57. *Quaketh my penne,* my pen quakes; an expression used once by Chaucer, Troil. iv. 13, but pounced upon by Lydgate, who employs it repeatedly. See more than twenty examples in Schick's note to the Temple of Glas, 947. Cf. IX. 229.

59. Read *roseth,* grows rosy, grows red, as opposed to *welkeneth,* withers, fades. We find the pp. *rosed* twice in Shakespeare ; 'a maid yet *rosed over,*' Henry V, v. 2. 423 ; and 'thy *rosed* lips' ; Titus And. ii. 4. 24. The emendation seems a safe one, for it restores the sense as well as the rime.

welkeneth should probably be *welketh*; I find no other example of the verb *welkenen,* though *welwen* occurs in a like sense ; and *welketh* suits the rhythm.

60. *eft,* once again hot. These sudden transitions from cold to heat are common ; see Temple of Glas, 356 :—'For thoughe I brenne with *feruence* and with hete.'

64. Lydgate is always deploring his lack of eloquence ; cf. notes to Temple of Glas, ed. Schick, ll. 1393, 1400.

69. I can find no such word as *jouesse,* so I alter it to *jonesse,* i. e. youth. For the spelling *jonesce* in the 14th century, see Littré, s. v.

jeunesse. The expression *have more yet* implies that the phrase or motto *je serve jonesse* is added as a postscript, and that there was some special point in it; but the application of it is now lost to us. Cf. 'Princes *of youthe*, and flour of gentilesse,' Temple of Glas, 970.

XXIII. GO FORTH, KING.

This poem really consists of twelve precepts, intended to redress twelve abuses. The twelve abuses are given by the Latin lines above, which should be compared throughout. The whole poem is thus easily understood.

The accent is on the first syllable of the line in most of the lines. In l. 3, the word *Lord* stands alone in the first foot. The lines are somewhat unsteady, quite in Lydgate's usual manner. In l. 6, *jug -e* is probably dissyllabic. See further in the Introduction.

XXIV. THE COURT OF LOVE.

This late piece abounds with imitations of Lydgate, especially of his Temple of Glas; many of the resemblances are pointed out in Schick's edition of that poem, which I refer to by the contraction 'T. G.'

1. Cf. 'With quaking hert[e] of myn inward drede'; T. G. 978.

'Another feature characteristic of Lydgate is his self-deprec[i]atory vein'; T. G., Introd. p. cxl. We have here an instance of an imitation of it.

6. Cf. 'Save that he wol conveyen his matere'; C. T., E 55.

8. He refers to Cicero's flowers of rhetoric. He may have found the name in Chaucer, P. F. 31. But he probably took the whole idea from a line of Lydgate's:—'Of rethoriques *Tullius* fond the *floures*'; Minor Poems, p. 87.

9. *borne*, burnish, adorn; it rimes (as here) with *sojorne* in Troil. i. 327.

11. *Galfrid*, Geoffrey de Vinsauf; his 'craft' refers to his treatise on the art of poetry, entitled 'Nova Poetria'; see note to C. T., B 4537 (vol. v. p. 257). [I once thought (see vol. i. p. 43) that *Galfrid* here means Chaucer himself, as he also is twice called *Galfrid* in Lydgate's Troy-book. But I find that Dr. Schick thinks otherwise, and the use of the word *craft* is on his side. At the same time, this renders it impossible for Chaucer to have written 'The Court of Love'; *his* opinion of his namesake was the reverse of reverential.] With ll. 4-11 compare the opening lines of Benedict Burgh's Poem in Praise of Lydgate, pr. at p. xxxi of Steele's edition of Lydgate's Secrees of Philosophers.

19. *Calliope*; twice mentioned by Chaucer; also by Lydgate, T. G. 1303. Lydgate's Troy-book opens with an invocation to Mars, followed by one to Calliope:—'Helpe me also, o thou Callyope'; and only

four lines above there is a mention of 'Helicon the welle' (see l. 22 below).

22. *Elicon*, mount Helicon in Bœotia, sacred to Apollo and the Muses; confused by Chaucer and his followers with the fountain Hippocrene; see note in vol. i. p. 531. Hence Lydgate's expression 'Helicon the welle' in the last note and in T. G. 706, and the reference in the text to its *dropes*.

suger-dropes; Lydgate was fond of sugar; he has 'soote *sugred* armonye,' Minor Poems, p. 182; and '*sugrid* melody,' ib., p. 11. Also '*sugred* eloquence'; XII. 200 (p. 288); with which cf. l. 933 below. I have observed several other examples.

24. *Melpomene*; the muse who presided over tragedy.

28. Cf. 'This simpil tretis for to take *in gre*'; T. G. 1387. 'Taketh *at gre* the rudness of my style'; Lydgate, Secrees of Philosophers, 21.

30. *metriciens*, skilful in metre, poets; a word which has a remarkably late air about it. Richardson gives an example of it from Hall's Chronicle.

36. Compare the following, from T. G. 1379–81.

> 'I purpos here to maken and to write
> A litil tretise, and a processe make
> In pris of women, oonli for hir sake.'

40. *man*, servant, one who does her homage; cf. Chaucer, C. T., I 772; La Belle Dame, 244; T. G. 742.

42. Cf. 'So that here-after my ladi may it *loke*'; T. G. 1392.

45. Cf. 'Ther was enclosed *rype and sad corage*'; C. T., E 220.

49, 50. Here the mountain of Cithæron, in Bœotia, is confused with the island of Cythera, sacred to Venus, whence her name Cytherea was derived. The mistake arose, of course, from the similarity of the names, and occurs (as said in vol. v. p. 78, note to A 1936), in the Roman de la Rose, where we find :—

> 'Citeron est une montaigne ...
> Venus, qui les dames espire,
> Fist là son principal manoir'; ll. 15865–71.

Hence Chaucer makes the same confusion, but in a different way. Chaucer preserves the right name of the mountain, in the form *Citheroun*, which he rimes with *mencioun* (A 1936) and with *Adoun* (A 2223); but here we have the form *Citharee*, riming with *see*. For all this, the scribe corrects it to *Citheron* in l. 69, where he has no rime to deal with.

56. Cf. 'the *winged* god, Mercurie'; C. T., A 1385.

58. The MS. has *costes that it drewe*; Bell alters this to *had to it drew*, under the impression that *drew* is the pp. of *draw*! So again, in l. 78, he alters *saphir ind*, which is correct, to *saphir of Inde*; and

in general, alters the text at will without the least hint that he has done so.

78. *ind*, blue ; as in The Black Knight, 127.

80. *Baleis Turkeis* (MS. *Bales turkes*). *Baleis* is a better spelling, answering to F. *balais* in Littré. It also occurs as *balai* in O. F. ; and the word was probably suggested by the mention of it in Rom. de la Rose, 20125 :—'Que saphirs, rubis, ne *balai*.' Hence also the mention of it in the King's Quhair, st. 46, which see ; and in the Assembly of Ladies, 536. *Turkeis* is the A. F. equivalent of O. F. *Turkois*, i. e. Turkish, as in C. T., A 2895, on which see the note (vol. v. p. 93).

81. *shene*, a misspelling of *shine*, intimating that the author has confused the adj. *shene* with the verb ; or rather, that the poem was written at a time when the word *shine* could be used as riming to *been* ; since we find similar examples in lines 561, 768. So also we find *pretily* riming with *be* in The Flower and the Leaf, 89. The pt. t. *shoon* occurs in l. 83.

82. Cf. 'As doon the sterres in the frosty night' ; C. T., A 268. And again : '*bryght As sterrys in* the *wyntyr* nyght' ; Lydgate, Compleint following T. G., l. 548.

86. Cf. Compl. of Mars, 78–84, 104–5 ; C. T., A 2388 (and note) ; and T. G. 126–8.

88. Cf. 'Long as *a mast*,' &c. ; C. T., A 3264.

92. Cf. Troil. iii. 8–21 : '*In hevene and helle*,' &c. ; from Boccaccio ; see note (vol. ii. p. 475).

105. *Alceste*; evidently borrowed from Ch., Legend of Good Women, 224, 293–9, 432 ; cf. T. G. 70–4. *The quenes flour Alceste*=the flower of queen Alcestis ; a common idiom ; see note to C. T., F 209 (vol. v. p. 376).

107. *Admete*, Admetus ; see Troil. i. 664, and the note ; T. G. 72.

108. *ninetene*; copied from the Legend of Good Women, 283 ; just as the next line is from the same, 285–9. This is the more remarkable, because Chaucer never finished the poem, but mentions ten ladies only, in nine Legends. Cf. 'the book of *the nynetene Ladies*'; C. T., I 1086. Hawes also refers to Chaucer's 'tragidyes . . . of the xix. ladyes'; Pastime of Pleasure, ed. Wright, p. 53.

115. 'So fair was noon in alle Arras'; R. R. 1234.

116. *of esier availe*, of less value ; see *Avail* in the New E. Dict.

117. *saunz faile*; thrice in Ch. ; HF. 188, 429 ; C. T., B 501.

119. *Helisee*, Elysium ; '*the feld* . . . That hight *Elysos*'; Troil. iv. 789.

120. *saintes*, saints, martyrs for love ; cf. V. 316, above (p. 227), and the note. Cf. T. G. 414.

129. 'The king had Danger standing near him, and the queen had Disdain, who were chief of the council, to treat of affairs of state'; Bell.

138. Cf. T. G. 271, and the note, shewing how common gold hair is in Lydgate.

139, 140. 'Bihinde *her bak, a yerde long*'; C. T., A 1050.

148. *In mewet*, in an inaudible voice, to myself; like mod. F. *à la muette* (Littré).

167. *non erst*; false grammar for *non er*, no sooner; 'no soonest' is nonsense. We find, however, the phrases *not erst* and *never erst* elsewhere; see New E. Dict., s.v. *Erst*, § B. 4.

170. This is the earliest quotation given in the New E. Dict., s. v. *Assummon*; and the next is from the poet Daniel.

177. Chaucer has the compound *for-pampred*; Former Age, 5. I read *jolif*, joyful, to make sense; the MS. has the absurd word *ioylof* (*sic*); and Stowe has *ialous*, jealous, which is quite out of place here.

181. 'An allusion to the monkish story of the man who brought up a youth ignorant of women, and who, when he first saw them, told him they were geese. The story is in the *Promptuarium Exemplorum*. It was adopted by Boccaccio, from whom it was taken by Lafontaine, liv. iii. conte 1. See *Latin Stories*, edited by Mr. [T.] Wright.'—Bell.

194. From C. T., B 466: '*On many a* sory *meel* now *may she bayte.*'

202. Cf. '*Comfort is noon*'; Chaucer's A B C, 17.

207. *how*, however. Cf. 'that *boghten love* so *dere*'; Legend of Good Women, 258.

229. See the Book of the Duchess, 323–34, where the painted glass windows contain subjects from the Romance of the Rose and others. The story of Dido is common enough; but the reference to Chaucer's Anelida and the false Arcite, is remarkable, especially as it occurs also in XXI. 465 above (p. 395). 'The turtel trewe' is from the Parl. Foules, 577. See the parallel passage in T. G. 44–142, where Lydgate's *first* example is that of *Dido*, while at the same time he mentions Palamon, Emilie, and Canacee, all from Chaucer.

246. *blew*, blue, the colour of constancy; see l. 248.

250. 'And why that ye ben clothed thus *in blak*?' C. T., A 911.

255. *grene* only gives an assonance with *here*, not a rime. Green was the colour of inconstancy, and was sometimes used *for despyt*, to use Chaucer's phrase; see note to C. T., F 644 (vol. v. p. 386). White may refer to the White Friars or Carmelites, and russet to the hermits; cf. P. Plowman, C. prol. 3, C. xi. 1.

270. *an ho*, a proclamation commanding silence; see C. T., 2533. Quite distinct from *hue* (and cry), with which Bell confuses it. A hue and cry was only raised against fleeing criminals.

280. Clearly suggested by the God of Love's stern question in the Legend of Good Women, 315 :—'What dostow heer So nigh myn owne flour, so boldely?' At the same time the phrase *fer y-stope in yeres* is from Chaucer's *somdel stape in age*, C. T., B 4011, on which see the note (vol. v. p. 248). See the next note.

288. Similarly the God of Love pardoned Chaucer (L. G. W. 450), but upon a condition (ib. 548).

290. *serven*, false grammar for *serve*.

302. Here follow the twenty statutes; ll. 302-504. They are evidently expanded from the similar set of injunctions given by Venus to the Knight in The Temple of Glas, ll. 1152-213; as clearly shewn by Schick in his Introduction, p. cxxxi. The similarity extends to the first, second, third, fifth, sixth, seventh, ninth, tenth, twelfth, fourteenth and eighteenth statutes, which resemble passages found in the Temple of Glas, ll. 1152-213, or elsewhere in the same poem. It is also possible that the author, or Lydgate, or both of them, kept an eye upon Ovid's Art of Love. See also Rom. Rose (Eng. version), 2355-950, which is much to the point.

305. This is also the first injunction in T. G. 1152-3, and is immediately followed by the second, which enjoins *secrecy*. The reader should compare the passages for himself.

311. MS. *synk and flete*; which must of course be corrected to 'sink *or* flete,' as in Anelida, 182 ; C. T., A 2397.

317. '*Withoute chaunge* in parti or in al'; T. G. 1155.

319. The MS. has *brynde*, and Stowe has *brinde*; so I let the reading stand. Morris has *blynde*, and Bell *blind*; neither of them has a note as to the change made. Perhaps *brind*=*brend*=burnt, in the sense of 'inflamed by passion'; or it may be an error for *brim* =*breme*, furious, applied especially to the desire of the boar for the sow. The sense intended is clear enough; we should now write 'base.'

324-5. From C. T., A 2252-3 :—

> 'And on thyn [*Venus'*] *auter*, wher I ryde or go,
> I wol don sacrifice, and *fyres bete*.'

329. *passe forby*, to pass by, i. e. to get out of his way ; cf. C. T., B 1759, C 668. *an ese*, a relief, a way of escape. There is no difficulty, but all the editions have altered it to *passe, for thereby*, which will not scan.

330. *daungerous*, grudging, reluctant ; see C. T., D 514.

332. *of a sight*, of what one may see. *squeymous* (MS. *squymouse*, Stowe *squmous*), squeamish, particular ; see note to C. T., A 3337 (vol. v. p. 102). It is added that when the lady, on her part, was cruel, it was the lover's duty to toss about in bed and weep ; cf. T. G. 12 :—'The longe nyght *walowing* to and fro.' 'To *walwe and wepe*'; Troil. i. 699. And see Rom. Rose (Eng. version), 2553-62.

338. Cf. 'Him to complein, that he walk [*read* welk=walked] so sole'; T. G. 552. And cf. Book Duch. 449 ; Black Knight, 143 ; Rom. Rose, 2391-6, 2517-9.

340. Cf. 'as though he roughte nought Of life ne deth'; T. G. 939-40.

344. 'Abide awhile,' T. G. 1203 ; '*patiently* t'endure '; T. G. 1267.

347. *helden*, false grammar for *held*. The metre shews that it was intentional.

349. 'Fulli *to obeye*,' T. G. 1151 ; cf. 1145-50.

360-4. Cf. T. G. 1012-25; especially 'And when I trespas, goodli me correcte'; and 'neuyr yow offende.' And Ovid, Art. Amat. lib. ii. 199-202.

367. *yern*, earn; so *yearne* in Spenser, F. Q. vi. I. 40; A. S. *ge-earnian*.

368-9. 'Of *grace and pitè*, and nought of rightwisnes'; T. G. 979.

378. *a-croke* (MS. *a croke*), awry; see *Acrook* in the New E. Dict.

379-81. In l. 381, the MS. has *shon* (shun) distinctly; yet Morris prints *shoue*, and Stowe *showe*, destroying the sense. All have *knowe* in l. 379, but it should rather be *con*, which gives a perfect rime; for *con* represents A. S. *cunnan*, to know, and is frequently spelt *cun*; see *Con* in the New E. Dict. This statute refers to 'the comfort of Sweet-Looking'; see Rom. Rose, 2893-922; Gower, C. A., iii. 26-7.

390. See T. G. 170-1, 1014.

397. 'Yeve hir giftes, and get hir grace'; Rom. Rose, 2699. 'Auro conciliatur amor'; Ovid, Art. Amat. lib. ii. 278.

403. Cf. Rom. Rose, 2568-85.

412. 'And for no tales thin herte not remue'; T. G. 1182. Cf. C. T., A 3163-4; F 1483-5; and XII. 113-9 above (p. 289).

429. 'For love ne wol nat countrepleted be'; Legend of Good Women, 476. 'Quisquis erit cui favet illa, fave'; Ovid, Art. Amat. lib. i. 146.

431. '*Whyt* was this *crowe*'; C. T., H 133; cf. note to C. T., D 232.

456. Compare the Merchant's Tale; C.T., E 1245.

469. Cf. T. G. 1168-70: 'All trwe louers to relese of her payne,' &c.

475. 'Ai fressh and wel besein'; T. G. 1167. Cf. Rom. Rose, 2279-84. 'Munditiae placeant,' &c.; Ovid, Art. Amat. lib. i. 513.

484. 'Who loveth trewe hath no fatnesse'; Rom. Rose, 2686; 'Arguat et macies animum'; Ovid, Art. Amat. lib. i. 733.

491-504. Cf. Rom. Rose, 2419-39, 2817-20. In particular, ll. 496-7 seem to be actually copied from Rom. Rose, 2819-20: 'or of hir *chere That to thee made thy lady dere.*' This raises the suspicion that the Court of Love was written after 1532.

499. *thou seen* would be in Latin *tu videatis*; another example of false grammar.

523. *let been*, to let (them) be, to leave off.

526. *kepten been* (MS. *bene*); so in all the copies; but *kepten* is the pt. t. plural, as if we should say in Latin *seruauerunt sunt*. Unless, indeed, the *-en* is meant for the pp. suffix of a strong verb, as if we should make a Latin form *seruatiti*. The scansion shews that this false grammar came from the author.

529. 'Except God and the devil.'

536-7. Solomon and Samson; the usual stock examples. But probably in this case borrowed from Lydgate's Balade, XIV. 4 (p. 295), which is certainly quoted thrice again below.

542. This line is made up from Lydgate's Balade, XIV. 29-33, and 26; so again l. 544 resembles the same, l. 24. And Lydgate merely

* * *
* * * * N n

versifies the medieval proverb: 'Fallere,' &c.; see note to XIV.
29; p. 516.

547. *of kind,* by nature; as in XIV. 29 (p. 296).

550. 'An housbond shal *nat been inquisitif*'; C. T., A 3163.

556. *Citherea* is right; see l. 50; MS. and Stowe have *Cithera.*

560. 'You that are provided already with a lady.'—Bell. Cf. l. 561.

561-3. *eke, lyke,* a permissible rime, at a time when *e* had gained
the mod. E. sound. See note to l. 81 above.

570. See T. G. 143-6. With l. 577, cf. T. G. 50.

580. The reading *blisful* is certain; it is from T. G. 328 :—'O *blisful*
sterre, persant and ful of light.' The author uses *persant* below, in
l. 849.

582. See the second of the interpolated stanzas in T. G., p. 21,
ll. 6, 7 :—

> 'Withoute desert; wherefore that ye vouche
> To *ponysshe* hem dewely for here male-bouche.'

586. *loves daunce*; see references in the Glossary to vol. vi., s. v.
Daunce.

589. In T. G. 144, the lovers are only many a thousand; in the
Kingis Quair, st. 78, they are 'mony a' million; here they are
a thousand million. Such is evolution.

591. '*redresse* is elegantly put for *redresser*';—Bell. Then let the
credit of it be Lydgate's; cf. '*Redresse* of sorow, O Citheria';
T. G. 701.

592. Bell prints *yheried,* which is obviously right; but he does not
say that both the MS. and Stowe have *I hired*; see Troil. ii. 973,
iii. 7, 1804.

593. *loves bond*; founded on Boethius, lib. ii. met. 8, but doubtless
taken from Troil. iii. 1766; see note in vol. ii. p. 483.

598, 603. 'Make him teschwe euere synne and vice'; T. G. 450.

611-3. *Celsitude* and *pulcritude* are words that savour of the revival
of learning. Such words are common in Dunbar, who uses both of
them. For *celsitude,* see Dunbar, ed. Small, p. 271, 76, and p. 325, 25;
for *pulcritude,* see the same, p. 271, 74; p. 274, 2; p. 279, 5. He even
rimes them together; p. 271. Hawes also uses *pulchritude*; Pastime
of Pleasure, ed. Wright, pp. 5, 18.

614. Cf. '*Comparisoun may noon y-maked be*'; Legend of Good
Women, 122.

623. *fere,* fire (not fear); as in Troil. iii. 978.

628. *Beseech,* to beseech; note the anachronism in using the French
infin. *void-en* with a suffix, and the Eng. *beseech* with none at all.

634. *ure,* destiny; from O. F. *eur,* Lat. *augurium.* A word that
first appeared in Northern English; it occurs at least eight times in
Barbour's Bruce. And in the Kingis Quair, st. 10, we have the whole
phrase—'my fortúne and ure.' It is also used by Lydgate; see VIII.
151, 302, 482 (pp. 250, 254, 260).

641. An exact repetition of l. 633 above.

642. Here, for a wonder, is an example of the final *e*; the author took the whole phrase 'In thilk-ë place' from some previous author; cf. 'In thilke places' (*sic*); Rom. Rose, 660 (Thynne). *sign*, assign.

648. 'Bi god and be my trouthe'; T. G. 1011.

683. '*And holden werre* alwey with chastitee'; C. T., A 2236.

684. *I kepen*; false grammar; equivalent to Lat. *ego curamus.*

688. *yove*, gave; but in l. 690 the form is *gave*. I suspect that in l. 690, *gave* should be *gan*, and that *image* (for *images*) is to be taken as a genitive case; then the sense is—'And I began anon to ponder and weigh in my heart her image's fresh beauty.'

701. The idea is due to Chaucer's Compleynt to Pity; cf. l. 1324.

702. Cf. 'Him deyneth nat to *wreke him on a flye*'; Legend of Good Women, 381.

703. *eke him*, him also; but perhaps read *ete him.*

704. Cf. 'and tendre herte'; C. T., A 150.

725. *springen*; false grammar, as it is a plural form.

727. *endry*, suffer, endure; so again in l. 941. This ridiculous hybrid is rightly excluded from the New E. Dict., which gives, however, several similar formations. It was coined by prefixing the F. prefix *en-*, with an intensive force, to M. E. *drien*, variant of *dreogen*, to endure (A. S. *drēogan*), Lowl. Sc. *dree*. No other author uses it.

732. *spede*, succeed; Stowe's alteration to *speke* is unnecessary.

749. 'How are you the nearer for loving,' &c.

751. *fayn*, put for *feyn*, i. e. feign, tell an untruth.

755. *heth*, heath. Here, and in l. 757, the author refers to two occasions when he was in great danger of falling in love; but he does not go into details.

768. Here we must read *ee* (eye) for the rime; in other cases it appears as *eye, ye, y,* riming with words in *-y*. This points to a somewhat late date; see note to l. 81 above. As for *stremes*, it is Lydgate's word for glances of the eye; see T. G. 263, 582. And Lydgate had it from Chaucer, who mostly uses it of sunbeams, but twice applies it to the beams from the eyes of Criseyde; Troil. i. 305, iii. 129.

782. *flawe*, generally explained as representing Lat. *flauus*, yellowish, or the O. F. *flave*, with the same sense. Her hair was gold, so her eyebrows may have been of a similar colour. I suspect that *flawe* was a Northern form; cf. *braw*, as a Northern variant of *brave*.

783. *mene disseverance*, a moderate distance; evidently meant with reference to Criseyde, whose one demerit was that her eye-brows joined each other; Troil. v. 813.

787. *milk-whyt path*, the galaxy, or milky way; but surely this is quite a unique application of it, viz. to the prominent ridge of Rosial's nose.

789. *smaragde*, emerald. The eyes of Beatrice are called *smeraldi*; Dante, Purg. xxxi. 116. Juliet's nurse said that an eagle's eye was not so green as that of Paris; Romeo, iii. 5. 222. Eyes in Chaucer are

usually 'as gray as glas'; the O. F. *vair*, an epithet for eyes, meant grayish-blue.

797. *basse*, kiss, buss ; see *Bass* in the New E. Dict. *ben* is yet another instance of a false concord ; read *be*, as *basse* is singular. See next note.

798. Cornelius Maximianus Gallus, a poet of the sixth century, wrote six elegies which have come down to us. The quotation referred to occurs in the first Elegy (ll. 97-8), which is also quoted by Chaucer ; see note to C. T., C 727 (vol. v. p. 287). The lines are :—

> 'Flammea dilexi, modicumque tumentia labra,
>   Quae mihi gustanti basia plena darent.'

Hence the epithet *Flaming* in l. 793.

810. *bend*, a band, sash ; see New E. Dict., s. v. *Bend* (2), sb., 1. a.

811. 'With hair in tresses'; like Criseyde's ; see Troil. v. 810.

813. Cf. the Assembly of Ladies, 533-4 (p. 397) :—

> '*Aboute her nekke* a sort of faire *rubyes*
>   In whyte *floures* of right fyne enamayl.'

See also the Kingis Quair, st. 48.

815-6. See my note to Ch. Minor Poems, XXI. 20 (vol. i. p. 566).

821. *Calixto*, Callisto ; called *Calixte* in Parl. Foules, 286. The story is in Ovid, Met. ii. 409. *Alcmenia*, Alcmene, mother of Hercules ; see Ovid, Met. ix. 281 ; cf. Troil. iii. 1428 ; T. G. 123.

823. *Europa*, the story is in Ovid, Met. ii. 858. See Legend of Good Women, 113, and the note ; T. G. 118.

824. *Dane*, Danae, mother of Perseus ; see Ovid, Met. iv. 610. In Chaucer, C. T., A 2062, *Dane* means Daphne. *Antiopa*, mother of Amphion and Zethus ; it may be noted that Jupiter's intrigues with Europa, Antiopa, Alcmene, and Danae, are all mentioned together in Ovid, Met. vi. 103-13. It follows that our author had read Ovid.

831. '*There is no lak, saue* onli of pitè'; T. G. 749.

841. The word *the* was probably written like *ye*, giving, apparently, the reading *ye ye* ; then one of these was dropped. The long passage in ll. 841-903 may be compared with the pleadings of the lover in La Belle Dame sans Merci (p. 307, above) ; with T. G. 970-1039 ; and with the Kingis Quair, st. 99. Note the expression 'of beaute rote,' T. G. 972 ; and '*Princes* of youthe,' T. G. 970 (two lines above) ; see l. 843.

849. *persant*, piercing ; common in Lydgate ; T. G. 328, 756, 1341 ; Black Knight, 28, 358, 591, 613. Cf. 'And *with* the *stremes of your percyng* light'; Kingis Quair, 103.

852-3. Cf. T. G. 1038-9 ; Kingis Quair, st. 103, l. 7.

858. 'Of verrey routhe upon my peynes rewe'; T. G. 1001.

865. 'To love him best ne shal I *never repente*'; The Compleynt of Venus, 56, 64, 72. See note to l. 875.

872-3. Referring to Ch. Troilus, and Legend of Good Women, 580. 'To ben as trewe as was Antonyus To Cleopatre'; T. G. 778.

874. *thinkes*; observe this Northern form.

875. 'And therfore, certes, *to myn ending-day*'; The Compleynt of Venus, 55. See note to l. 865.

882. *expert*, experienced ; 'expert in love,' Troil. ii. 1367.

891. 'With al my hert I thanke yow *of youre profre*'; T. G. 1060.

897. Read *I*; this the scribe must have mistaken for the contraction for 'and.'

901. 'And I beseech you not to be disdainful.'

902. *seen my wil*, to see what I wish; but surely *wil* is an error for *bill*, petition ; see l. 916. Then *rede* means 'read it.'

906. *com of*, be quick ; see Troil. ii. 1738, 1742, 1750; and the numerous examples in Schick's note to T. G. 1272.

911. Stowe, like the MS., ends the line with *why*. Bell supplied *makes thou straunge*.

913. *Cambrige* ; this form is not found till after 1400. Chaucer has *Cant-e-brigg-e* (C. T., A 3921) in four syllables, which appears as *Cambrugge* in the late Lansdowne MS., after 1420. See Skeat, A Student's Pastime, pp. 397-8.

922. *and have*, i. e. and have loved. On this construction, see Schick's note to T. G. 1275.

925-7. *I . . doon*; more false grammar ; equivalent to Lat. *ego faciamus*.

929. 'And, whan I trespace, goodli *me correcte*' ; T. G. 1018.

931-52. Compare the answers of the lady in La Belle Dame sans Merci (p. 309, &c.).

988-9. Cf. Parl. Foules, 90-1 ; Compl. to his Lady, 47-9.

998. *dwale*, an opiate, a sleeping-draught ; made from the *dwale* or 'deadly nightshade' (*Atropa belladonna*). It occurs once in Chaucer ; C. T., A 4161. See my note to P. Plowman, C. xxiii. 379.

1000. *y-wis afrayed*, (being) certainly frightened. The use of *y-wis* in such a position is most unusual.

1016-7. 'Right as the fressh[e] rodi rose nwe Of hir coloure to wexin she bigan' ; T. G. 1042-3.

1023. Something is lost here. There is no gap in the MS.; but there was probably one in the MS. from which it was copied. I think six stanzas are lost ; see the Introduction.

1032-3. 'And their fellow-furtherer,' i. e. fellow-helper.

1034. *Dred* is one of the personifications from the Roman de la Rose ; see Rom. Rose, 3958; so in T. G. 631.

1040. 'Gall under honey' ; see l. 542 above. Cf. T. G. 192.

1042. 'Lay aside your confidence (courage), for all her white (flattering) words' ; cf. Troil. iii. 901.

1045. *thow wot*, false grammar for *thou wost*.

1049. *The ton = thet on*, the one ; *the toder = thet oder*, the other.

Oder is a remarkable form ; see Halliwell. So also *brodur*, in Le Bon Florence of Rome, ed. Ritson, 931.

1053-4. 'Hir kind is fret with doublenesse'; XIII. 80 (p. 293).

1055. 'So I cast about to get rid of Despair's company'; hence *taken*, in l. 1056, is in the infin. mood.

1058. *bay-window*; cf. Assembly of Ladies, 163. The earliest known quotation for *bay-window* is dated 1428, in a prosaic document.

1060. 'As any ravenes *fether* it shoon *for-blak*'; spoken of hair; C. T., A 2144.

1065. 'Ther needeth non *auctoritee allegge*'; C. T., A 3000.

1072. Cf. Troil. ii. 855-61.

1083. *were*, wear; altered by Bell to *ware*, which is a form of the past tense.

1087. *she* seems to be spoken casually of some woman in the company; and *prety man*, in l. 1088, is used in a similar way.

goth on patens, walks in pattens. A very early example of the word *paten*. It occurs in Palsgrave (1530). *fete*, neat, smart ; used by Lydgate; see *Feat* in the New E. Dict.

1095. Here the author comes back again to the Temple of Glas, 143-246, which see ; and cf. The Kingis Quair, stanzas 79-93.

1096. *black*, Dominican friars ; *white*, Carmelites ; *gray*, Franciscans.

1100. From T. G. 196-206 ; for the nuns, see T. G. 207-8.

1104. '*In wide* copis *perfeccion to feine*'; T. G. 204. See l. 1116.

1106. 'That *on hir freendis al the* wite they leide'; T. G. 208.

1116. '*In wide copis* perfeccion to feine'; T. G. 204.

1134. '*Ther thou were weel*, fro thennes artow weyved'; C. T., B 308.

1136. Cf. 'With sobbing teris, and with ful pitous soune'; T. G. 197.

1139. Cf. 'And other eke, that for *pouertè*'; T. G. 159.

1150. *prang*, pang (MS. *prange* ; and so in Stowe) ; altered to *pang* by Bell and Morris. '*Pronge*, Erumpna' [aerumna]; Prompt. Parv. '*Throwe* [throe], *womannys pronge*, Erumpna'; the same. '*Prange*, oppression, or constraint'; Hexham's Dutch Dict. Cf. Gothic : 'in allamma *ana-pragganai*,' we were troubled on every side, 2 Cor. vii. 5 ; where *gg* is written for *ng*, as in Greek. The mod. E. *pang* seems to have been made out of it, perhaps by confusion with *pank*, to pant.

1160, 1164. 'And pitousli *on god and kynde pleyne*'; T. G. 224. But the context requires the reading *god of kind*, i.e. God of nature. In l. 1166, *leften* must be meant for a pp. ; if so, it is erroneously formed, just like *kepten* above ; see note to l. 526.

1173. *werdes*, Fates ; obviously the right reading ; yet the MS., Stowe, and Morris have *wordes*, and Bell alters the line. The confusion between *e* and *o* at this time is endless. See *Werdes*, *Wierdes* in the Gloss. to Chaucer.

1177. *he*, another of the company ; cf. *she* in l. 1087. Both Morris and Bell alter the text. Bell reminds us that the character here described is that of Shakespeare's Benedict. But it is obviously copied from Troilus! see Troil. i. 904-38.

1189. The word *post* is from Troil. i. 1000 : ' That thou shalt be the beste *post*, I leve, Of al his lay.'

1198. *Shamefastness*, Bashfulness; borrowed from *Honte* in the Rom. de la Rose, 2821 ; called *Shame* in the E. version, 3034. Hence the reference to *roses* in l. 1203, though it comes in naturally enough.

1211. *were not she*, if it had not been for her.

1213. *returnith*, turns them back again ; used transitively.

1218. ' When Bashfulness is dead, Despair will be heir ' (will succeed in her place). Too bold lovers would be dismissed.

1219. *Avaunter*, Boaster ; as in Troil. iii. 308-14. The line sounds like an echo of ' Have at thee, Jason ! now thyn horn is blowe ! ' Legend of Good Women, 1383.

1222. *wowe*, woo ; evidently the right reading; so in Morris. Cf. The Letter of Cupid, V. 274-80 (p. 226).

1238. *statut*, i. e. the sixteenth statute (l. 435).

1242. ' *Avauntour* and *a lyere*, al is on'; Troil. iii. 309.

1253. *sojoure*, sojourn, dwell, used quite wrongly; for O. F. *sojur* (originally *sojorn*) is a sb. only, like mod. F. *séjour*. The O. F. verb was *sojorner*, *sojourner*, whence M. E. *sojornen*, *sojournen*, correctly used by Chaucer. The sb. *sojour* occurs in Rom. Rose, 4282, 5150. The mistake is so bad that even the scribe has here written *soiorne* ; but, unluckily, this destroys the rime.

1255. ' Envy is admirably represented as rocking himself to and fro with vexation, as he sits, dark, in a corner.'—Bell. For all this, I suspect the right word is *rouketh*, i. e. cowers, as in C. T., A 1308. *Rokken* is properly transitive, as in C. T., A 4157.

1257. For the description of Envy, see Rom. Rose, 247. But the author (in l. 1259) refers us to Ovid, Met. ii. 775-82, q. v.

1259. *Methamorphosose*; this terrible word is meant for *Metamorphoseos*, the form used by Chaucer, C. T., B 93. But the true ending is *-eōn*, gen. pl. The scribe has altered the suffix to *-ees*, thus carelessly destroying the rime.

1268. *Prevy Thought* is taken from *Doux-Pensers* in the Rom. de la Rose, 2633, called *Swete-Thought* in the E. Version, 2799 ; see the passage.

1288. Cf. ' Hir person he shal afore him sette ' ; R. R. 2808.

1290. Cf. ' This comfort wol I that thou take ' ; R. R. 2821.

1295. Cf. ' Awey his anger for to dryve' ; R. R. 2800.

1315. Schick refers us, for this fiction, to the Rom. Rose, 939-82, where Cupid has two sets of arrows, one set of *gold*, and the other set *black*. Gower, Conf. Amantis (ed. Pauli, i. 336), says that Cupid shot Phœbus with a dart of *gold*, but Daphne with a dart of *lead*. In the Kingis Quair, stanzas 94-5, Cupid has *three* arrows, one of *gold*, one of *silver*, and one of *steel*. But the fact is, that our author, like Gower, simply followed Ovid, Met. i. 470-1. Let Dryden explain it :—

'One shaft is pointed with refulgent gold
 To bribe the love, and make the lover bold;
 One blunt, and tipped with lead, whose base allay
 Provokes disdain, and drives desire away.'

1817. There is here a gap in the story. The speaker is Rosial, and she is addressing Philogenet, expressing herself favourably.

1319-20. *hight*, promised.   *had*, would have.

1324. *she*, i. e. Pity, as in l. 701.

1328. MS. *tender reich*; Stowe, *tenderiche*; which must be wrong; read *tender reuth*. Confusion between *ch* and *th* is common. *where I found*, where I (formerly) found much lack.

1332. For Pity's golden shrine, see l. 694.

1353. This notion of making the birds sing matins and lauds is hinted at in the Cuckoo and Nightingale—'That they begonne of May *to don hir houres*'; l. 70. It is obviously varied from Chaucer's Parl. Foules, where all the birds sing a roundel before departing.   Next, we find the idea expanded by Lydgate, in the poem called Devotions of the Fowls; Minor Poems, ed. Halliwell, p. 78; the singers are the popinjay, the pelican, the nightingale, the lark, and the dove.   All these reappear here, except the pelican.   A chorus of birds, including the mavis, merle, lark, and nightingale, is introduced at the close of Dunbar's Thistle and Rose.   The present passage was probably suggested by Lydgate's poem, but is conceived in a lighter vein.

The Latin quotations are easily followed by comparing them with The Prymer, or Lay Folks' Prayer-Book, ed. Littlehales (E. E. T. S.). They all appear in this 'common medieval Prayer-book'; and, in particular, in the Matins and Lauds of the Hours of the Blessed Virgin Mary.   The Matins end at l. 1407.   The Matins contain:—the opening, the *Venite*, a Hymn, three Psalms, an Antiphon, Versicles and Responses, three Lessons (each with Versicles and Responses), and the *Te Deum*. The Lauds contain:—the opening, eight Psalms (the *Benedicite* considered as one), Antiphon, Chapter, Hymn, the *Benedictus*; &c.   I point out the correspondences below.

1354. Observe that the nightingale sings *in a hawthorn* in the Cuckoo and Nightingale, 287 (p. 358).

1356. *Domine, labia mea aperies*, Lord, open thou my lips; 'the opening' of Matins.

1358. *bewrye*, a variant of *bewreye*, to bewray; used by Dunbar.

1359. *Venite, exultemus*, Ps. xcv (Vulgate, xciv); still in use.

1362. 'The unhappy chorister who comes late skulks in behind the desks and stalls.'—Bell.

1364. *Domine, Dominus noster*, Ps. viii. The 'first psalm.'

1366. *Celi enarrant*, Ps. xix (Vulgate, xviii). The 'second psalm.'

1370. *Domini est terra*, Ps. xxiv (Vulgate, xxiii). The 'third psalm.' *this Laten intent*, this Latin signifies; *intent* is the contracted form of *intendeth*; by analogy with *went* for *wendeth*.

1372. A queer reminiscence of Troil. iii. 690 :—'There was no more to *skippen nor to* traunce.'

1373. *Jube, Domine, benedicere*, 'Lord, comaunde us to blesse'; versicle preceding the first lesson; which explains l. 1374.

1375. Cf. 'Legende of Martres'; Letter of Cupid, 316 (p. 227); and the note.

1380. Here follows the second lesson. The *lectorn* is the mod. E. lectern, which supports the book from which the lessons are read.

1384. 'The glad month of us who sing.' Cf. 'lepten *on the spray*'; Cuckoo and Nightingale, 77 (p. 350).

1387. Here follows the third lesson, read by the dove.

1390. This looks like an allusion to the endless joke upon cuckolds, who are said, in our dramatists, to 'wear the horn'; which the offender is said 'to give.' If so, it is surely a very early allusion. Here *give an horn*=to scorn, mock.

1400. *Tu autem, domine, miserere nobis*, 'thou, lord, have merci of us,' said at the conclusion of each lesson; to which all responded *Deo gratias*, 'thanke we god!' See The Prymer, p. 5.

1401. *Te deum amoris*; substituted for *Te deum laudamus*, which is still in use; which concludes the matins.

1402. *Tuball*, who was supposed to have been 'the first musician.' As to this error, see note in vol. i. p. 492 (l. 1162).

1408. *Dominus regnavit*, Ps. xciii (Vulgate, xcii); the 'first psalm' at Lauds.

1411. *Jubilate deo*, Ps. c (Vulgate, xcix); the 'second psalm.' The third and fourth psalms are not mentioned.

1413. *Benedicite, omnia opera*; still in use in our morning service; counted as the 'fifth psalm.'

1415. *Laudate dominum*, Ps. cxlviii; the 'sixth psalm.' The seventh and eighth are passed over.

1416. *O admirabile*; the anthem. The E. version is :—'O thou wonderful chaunge! the makere of mankynde, takynge a bodi with a soule of a maide vouchide sauf be bore [*born*]; and so, forth-goynge man, with-outen seed, yaf to us his godhede'; Prymer, p. 12. The 'chapter' and hymn are omitted.

1422. *Benedictus Dominus Deus Israel*; still in use in our morning service. This is the last extract from 'the hours.'

1434. 'She gadereth floures, *party* whyte and rede To make a sotil *garland*'; C.T., A 1053.

1436. This is exactly like 'the battle of the flowers,' as seen in Italy.

1437. *the gold*, the marigold; see C. T., A 1929.

1440. *trew-love*; a name for herb paris (*Paris quadrifolia*). But as the 'true-love' is described as being *plited*, i. e. folded, it must rather be supposed to mean a true lover's knot or love-knot, which was simply a bow of ribbon given as a token of affection, and frequently worn by the lover afterwards. The bestowal of this token nearly made an end of him.

XXV. VIRELAI.

Not a true virelay, as the ending *-ing* does not reappear in the second stanza; for a correct example, see note to Anelida and Arcite, 256 (vol. i. p. 536). But it is of the nature of a virelai, inasmuch as the rime *-ate*, which concludes the first stanza, reappears in the second; and similarly, the ending *-ure*, which concludes the second stanza, reappears in the third; and so on, with the rime-endings *-ain* and *-aunce*. Compare the poem by Lord Rivers, in the same metre, alluded to in vol. i. p. 42.

11. *ure*, destiny; as above, sect. XXIV. 634 (and note, p. 546).

20. The pronunciation of *ende* as *ind* is not uncommon in East Anglia, and may have been intended.

XXVI. PROSPERITY.

From John Walton's translation of Boethius, A.D. 1410. See the Introduction.

XXVII. LEAULTE VAULT RICHESSE.

From the same MS. as the last.

7. *don but lent*, lit. 'done but lent,' i.e. merely lent (you). For this idiom, see note to Ch. C. T., B 171 (vol. v. p. 145).

XXVIII. SAYINGS.

5. Cf. Shak. King Lear, iii. 2. 91; see the Introduction.

XXIX. BALADE.

This Balade, printed by Stowe, seems like a poor imitation of the style of Lydgate.

GLOSSARIAL INDEX.

References to I. (The Testament of Love) are to the Book, Chapter, and Line; thus 'I. ii. 1. 7'=Testament of Love, bk. ii. ch. 1. l. 7. References containing '*pr.*' refer to the prologue to the same. In all other cases, the references are to the piece and to the line: thus 'V. 50'=Letter of Cupid, l. 50.

A, *v.* have, I. i. 2. 173; *ger.* I. i. 5. 93.
A deblys, (*perhaps*) to the devil, as if devoted to the devil, I. ii. 13. 99. See the note.
A dewe, (*perhaps for* à dieu), I. ii. 13. 99. See the note.
A this halfe, on this side, below, I. i. 9. 39.
A. b. c., *s.* alphabet, I. ii. 1. 113.
Abacke, *adv.* backward, III. 300; Abakke, VIII. 326.
Abbeys, *s. pl.* abbeys, XXIV. 1115.
Abeisen, *v.* (*for* Abasen), abase, put down, reprove, XXIV. 738.
Abit, *pr. s.* abides, IV. 284; XIII. 30.
Able, *imp. s.* enable, VII. 32; Abled, *pp.* l. ii. 9. 95; fitted, I. ii. 6. 4.
Abode, 2 *pt. s.* didst abide, I. ii. 4. 101; Abood, *pt. s.* remained, I. i. 5. 31.
Abouten, *adv.* all about, all round, I. ii. 8. 37.
Abregge, *ger.* to abridge, shorten, XIX. 18.
Abreyde, *ger.* to start up, awake, VIII. 15; Abraid, *pt. s.* started, went suddenly, XVII. 45; Abrayde, awoke, VIII. 154.
Abydinge, *s.* waiting, delay, I. i. 3. 38.
Abye, *v.* pay for (it), II. 1233; pay for, II. 1199.
Abyme, *s.* the abyss, X. 136.
A-cale, *pp. as adj.* frozen, afflicted with the cold, II. 71.
Accept, *pp.* accepted (as), I. ii. 13. 36; Accepte, *as adj. pl.* accepted, VIII. 427.

Acces, *s.* feverish attack, VIII. 229; XVIII. 39; Accesse, VIII. 136.
Accident, *s.* accidental quality, I. ii. 7. 144; accident, II. 1222.
Accompte, I *pr. s.* account, I. ii. 13. 91; *pp.* I. ii. 9. 48.
Accomptes, *s. pl.* accounts, II. 778.
Accord, *s.* agreement, XVIII. 280.
Accordaunce, *s.* agreement, I. ii. 5. 27.
Accordaunt, *adj.* agreeing, XVIII. 83.
Accorde, *ger.* to agree, to rime, II. 477; *pr. s.* suits, VIII. 183; 2 *pr. pl.* agree, III. 212; *pr. pl.* I. ii. 5. 26; *pres. pt.* XX. 112. See **Acorde.**
Acertained, *pp.* made sure, informed, XX. 568.
Achates, *s. pl.* purchases, I. ii. 2. 48.
Acomered, *pp.* encumbered, I. iii. 5. 57; troubled, I. ii. 7. 41.
Acompt, *v.* reckon, I. ii. 10. 88.
Acordaunces, *s. pl.* agreements, I. ii. 8. 54.
Acorde, *ger.* to agree, I. ii. 8. 47; *pr. s.* I. ii. 2. 52; *pr. pl.* IX. 210. *a. nothing,* in no wise agree, I. ii. 2. 74.
Acorn, *s.* acorn. VIII. 73.
A-croke, *adv.* amiss, XXIV. 378.
A-dayes, *adv.* by day-time, XXII. 34.
Adherand, *pres. pt.* cleaving, I. i. 9. 103.
Admirall, *s.* prince, chief, II. 194.
Adnulled, *pp.* annulled, I. iii. 3. 49.
Adnullinge, *s.* annulling, I. i. 4. 22.
Ado, to do, VIII. 161.
A-down, *adv.* down here, II. 1319.
A-drad, *pp.* afraid, I. ii 7. 61; IV. 89; filled with fear, I. i. 2. 12, 182.

Adulacioun, *s.* flattery, XII. 61.
Adversair, *s.* adversary, XXIV. 1035.
Advertence, *s.* attention, XI. 61.
Adverteth, *imp. pl.* heed, note, XIII. 45.
A-ferd, *pp.* afraid, II. 433; Aferde, I. i. 2. 10.
A-fere, on fire, X. 129.
A-ferre, *adv.* afar, VIII. 610.
Affect, *s.* desire, I. iii. 9. 43.
Affectuously, *adv.* with desire, I. iii. 6. 64.
Affermed, *pp.* affirmed, IV. 13.
Affiched, *pp.* fixed, set, I. ii. 9. 28.
Affirmatif, *s.* the affirmative, I. iii. 8. 40.
Affray, *s.* conflict, trouble, XX. 374.
Affrayed, *pp.* frightened away, XVIII. 235; frightened, XXIV. 1000.
Affy, *v.* trust, XXVII. 3; Affye, *pr. pl.* X. 63.
Aforn, *adv.* previously, VIII. 451; X. 107.
Afray, *ger.* to frighten, II. 859.
After, *adv.* afterwards, XVI. 380; After as, according as, I. i. *pr.* 44.
After, *prep.* for, I. ii. 3. 35; i. e. to get, I. ii. 14. 94; After oon, i. e. always alike, XVI. 161.
After-game, *s.* second game, return-match, XVI. 523.
After-reward, *s.* following reward, I. iii. 2. 123.
Agadred, *pp.* gathered together, II. 1335.
Agasteth, *pr. s.* frightens greatly, I. ii. 7. 77.
Agilted, *pt. s.* sinned against, II. 1308.
Agnelet, *s.* little lamb, X. 123.
Agnus-castus (see the note, p. 531), XX. 160.
Agoon, *pp.* gone away, VIII. 24; Ago, XVII. 238.
Agramed, *pp.* angered, II. 343.
Agryse, *v.* feel terror, II. 360, 841, 1216; XVIII. 15; *pr. pl. subj.* let them fear, II. 961.
Ague, *s.* feverish attack, IX. 37.
Air, *adv.* early, XVII. 82.
Akele, *v.* cool, XXIV. 1076.
Aken, *pr. pl.* ache, IV. 260; Ake, VIII. 524.
A-knowe, *pp.* perceived, recognised, XXIV. 1199.
Al, *conj.* although, I. i. 7. 61.
Alay, *s.* alloy, I. ii. 4. 131; Alayes, *pl.* VII. 136.
Alaye, *v.* allay, VIII. 109.

Alday, *adv.* continually, I. i. 2. 162; IV. 270.
Alder-last, *adv.* last of all, VIII. 561.
Aldernext, *adj.* next of all, XV. *a.* 3.
Ale, *s.* ale, II. 432.
Alegeaunce, *s.* alleviation, XVI. 54.
Aleged, *pp.* alleged, adduced, I. ii. 9. 143.
Alegement, *s.* alleviation, XII. 32.
Alegge, *v.* alleviate (me), VIII. 26.
Algate, *adv.* in any case, IV. 249; VIII. 519; always, IV. 271.
Algates, *adv.* in all ways, I. iii. 6. 14; at any rate, I. ii. 5. 71.
A-lighte, *v.* be glad, be cheerful, I. i. 3. 71.
Allegeaunce, *s.* alleviation, relief, XVI. 725; XXIV. 886; XXV. 17.
All-holyest, *adj.* holiest of all, II. 201.
Almesse, *s.* alms, II. 301; XXIII. 7; Almous, (his) pittance, XVII. 392.
Almoigner, *s.* almoner, I. i. *pr.* 108.
Aloes, *s.* aloes, I. i. 1. 100.
Al-only, *adv.* only, I. iii. 3. 44.
A-loughter, a-laughing, XXIV. 1426.
Al-out, *adv.* altogether outside, XVI. 575.
Alowe, *pr. s. subj.* may (He) approve, II. 1379; Alowed, *pp.* approved of, I. i. 8. 7.
Als, *adv.* as, XVII. 161, 571; Al-so, as, XII. 85.
Alterait, *pp.* altered, XVII. 227.
Alther-grettest, *adj.* greatest of all, very great, XVI. 298.
Alther-last, *adv.* last of all, VIII. 503.
A-maistry, *v.* conquer, I. ii. 11. 63; rule, I. i. 2. 105; Amaistrien, *v.* subdue, I. ii. 11. 32; *pr. s.* masters, overpowers, I. ii. 9. 60; compels, I. iii. 6. 157; *pp.* conquered, got by mastery, I. ii. 11. 59; overcome, I. i. 4. 28.
Amat, *pp.* cast down, VIII. 168.
Amayed, *pp.* dismayed, XVIII. 232.
Ambes as, double aces, XIII. 78. See note, p. 515.
Amendes, *s. pl.* amends, retribution, II. 1090.
Amerced, *pp.* fined, II. 1023.
Amisse-going, *s.* trespass, I. ii. 14. 94.
Amonesteth, *pr. s.* admonishes, I. i. 6. 109.
Among, *adv.* meanwhile, VIII. 154; X. 86; XXI. 300.
And, *conj.* if, I. i. 8. 13.
Ane, a, XVII. 1.
Aneuch, *adj.* enough, XVII. 110, 350.

Anguis, *adj.* distressful, I. ii. 8. 120; I. ii. 10. 94. See N. E. D.

A-night, by night, XIX. 23.

Anis, *adv.* once, XVII. 127.

Ankers, *s. pl.* anchors, I. ii. 10. 117.

Anon-right, *adv.* immediately, XX. 397, 402.

Anoy, *s.* vexation, I. ii. 1. 34; Annoy, discomfort, XX. 389.

Anoynt, *pp.* anointed, IV. 274.

Antecedent, *s.* antecedent statement, premiss, I. ii. 5. 12.

Anulled, *pp.* annulled, I. iii. 2. 81.

A-pace, *adv.* quickly, VIII. 120.

Apal, *v.* be appalled, faint, XXII. 15.

Apart, *adv.* apart, XXIV. 1400.

Apayed, *pp.* pleased, satisfied, III. 133, 248; Apayd, XXI. 208; *wel a.,* well pleased, XVIII. 231; *evel a.,* ill pleased, XVIII. 92.

Apayred, *pp.* depreciated, I. ii. 1. 66.

Apeche, *pr. pl.* impeach, XIII. 88; Apeched, *pp.* I. i. 9. 138.

Apend, *v.* belong, II. 666.

A-per-se, A by itself, the chief letter, prime thing, XVII. 78.

Apert, *adj.* open; *prevy nor apert,* secret nor open, in no respect, XVI. 174.

Apertly, *adv.* openly, I. iii. 8. 108; without concealment, I. i. 8. 29; Apertely, I. iii. 2. 28.

Apeted, *pp.* sought after, I. ii. 13. 53. See the note, p. 476.

Apeyre, *v.* suffer evil, be harmed, XVIII. 170; Apeyred, *pp.* injured, I. iii. 5. 24; defamed, I. i. 6. 11.

Apeyse, *v.* appease, XVI. 391.

A-place, into its right place, IV. 50.

Apostata, *s.* apostate, III. 37, 312; Apostatas, *pl.* III. 43.

Appair, *v.* blame, harm, XXIV. 416.

Appalle, *pr. s. subj.* fade, VI. 8.

Apparaile, *s.* ornamentation, XXIV. 114.

Apparaylen, *pr. pl.* attempt, I. i. 6. 171.

Appeired, *pp.* impaired, XX. 553; harmed (i. e. much harm is done), I. ii. 6. 161.

Apperceyved, *pp.* perceived, I. i. 2. 34.

Appertly, *adv.* openly, evidently, I. ii. 9. 178.

Appropred, *pp.* appropriated, reserved, I. ii. 6. 63; assigned, VI. 34.

Aptes, *s. pl.* natural tendencies, I. iii. 6. 60. (Unique.)

Aquytest, *pr. s.* payest, I. iii. 7. 152.

Ar, *pr. pl.* are; It ar, they are, XVI. 531.

Arayse, *ger.* to raise, I. ii. 14. 45.

Arbitrement, *s.* choice, I. iii. 2. 128; I. iii. 3. 76.

Areir, *adv.* behindhand, XVII. 423.

Arered, *pp.* set up, I. i. 5. 124.

Arest, *s.* spear-rest, XX. 282. ' With spere in thyn *arest* alway'; Rom. Rose, 7561.

Arest, *s.* stopping, arresting, I. ii. 6. 83; arrest, I. ii. 10. 98.

Areysed, *pp.* raised up, I. ii. 5. 113; raised, V. 144.

Ark, *s.* arc, course, VIII. 590.

Arke, *s.* ark, X. 134.

Armony, *s.* harmony, I. ii. 9. 9; I. ii. 13. 75; XXIV. 1403.

Armure, *s.* armour, XIII. 101.

Arn, *pr. pl.* are, VI. 43; IX. 153.

Arras, *s.* cloth of Arras, XXIV. 115.

Arsmetrike, *s.* arithmetic, I. iii. 1. 68.

Arted, *pl. s.* provoked, XXIV. 46.

Artyk, *adj.* northern, XVII. 20.

As, *with imp.,* pray, V. 30; As than, at that time, just then, XVII. 27.

As, *s. pl.* aces, XIII. 78.

Ash, *s.* ash-tree, VIII. 73.

Askaunce, *adv.* askance, aside, XVI. 604.

Asker, *s.* one who asks, I. ii. 3. 30.

Askes, *s. pl.* ashes (i. e. penance), II. 943.

Asketh, *pr. s.* requires, I. i. *pr.* 124; I. ii. 5. 28.

Aslaken, *v.* assuage, XXIV. 710.

Asotted, *pp.* besotted, XVI. 682.

Assay, *s.* trial, I. i. 5. 53; V. 147; attempt, XVI. 572; Assayes, *pl.* trials, I. ii. 3. 72.

Assembled, *pt. s.* brought (them) together, XVI. 691.

Assentaunt, *pres. pt.* assenting, I. i. 6. 53, 87; I. iii. 6. 150.

Asshen, *s. pl.* ashes, I. iii. 7. 38.

Assomoned, *pp.* summoned, XXIV. 170.

Assoyle, *ger.* to explain, I. iii. 4. 18; Asoile, *v.* answer, XXIV. 1283; *pp.* explained, I. iii. 4. 255; absolved, III. 312.

Assyse, *s.* way, fashion, II. 843; size, XXIV. 1313; *of a.,* of a like size, suitable to each other, XXI. 531.

Assysed, *pp.* fixed, set; *or perhaps,* assessed, rated, IV. 332; regulated, IV. 236.

Astarte, *pt. s.* escaped, II. 1350.

Astate, *s.* estate, rank, XXIV. 47.

Asterte, *v.* escape, I. i. 7. 87; V. 38;

Badde, *adj.* bad, evil, I. ii. 13. 11.

Badde-meninge, *adj.* ill-intentioned, I. ii. 1. 94 ; I. ii. 13. 16.

Baid, *pt. s.* abode, XVII. 490.

Baill, *s.* bale, sorrow, XVII. 110 ; harm, XVII. 413.

Bair, *s.* boar, XVII. 193.

Bair, *adj.* bare, XVII. 180, 206.

Bait, *s.* food (for horses), XVII. 210.

Bait, *v.* feed, XXIV. 194 (see note, p. 543) ; Baited, *pp.* baited, II. 648.

Bakbyte, *ger.* to backbite, XII. 124.

Bakker-more, *adv.* further back, XVI. 85.

Bal, *s.* ball, IV. 296 ; eye-ball, I. i. 4. 2.

Balaunce, *s.* balance, IV. 263 ; the balance, XIII. 91 ; *in b.*, in His sway, XVI. 851.

Balays, *s.* balas-ruby, XXI. 536 ; Baleis, XXIV. 80.

Bale, *s.* evil, I. ii. 9. 143.

Balefull, *adj.* evil, II. 120, 1234.

Balke, *s.* balk, check, difficulty, II. 488.

Ball, *s.* a horse's name, II. 402.

Ballet, *s.* ballad, poem, XVII. 610.

Bandon, *s.* disposal, I. ii. 5. 107.

Banere, *s.* banner, XX. 211.

Bankes, *s. pl.* banks, I. ii. 14. 44. See note to l. 40, p. 478.

Bankouris, *s. pl.* benches, soft seats, XVII. 417.

Banne, *pr. pl.* swear, XXIV. 1143.

Baptyme, *s.* baptism, III. 93.

Bar, *pt. s.* bore, carried, XX. 254, 257.

Bareyne, *adj.* barren, void, V. 298.

Bargaret, *s.* a pastoral song, XX. 348. See note, p. 533.

Barge, *s.* boat, XXIV. 187 ; ship, IV. 231.

Baselardes, *s. pl.* short swords, II. 918.

Basse, *s.* base, I. ii. 7. 90.

Basse, *s.* kiss, buss, XXIV. 797.

Batayled, *pp.* assaulted, IV. 194.

Baudriks, *s. pl.* belts, II. 918.

Baume, *s.* balm, VIII. 27.

Bawme-blossom, *s.* balm-blossom, X. 47.

Bay, *s.* bay ; *at bay*, II. 139.

Bayn, *s.* bath, XXI. 464.

Bay-window, *s.* window with a bay or recess, XXIV. 1058 ; *pl.* XXI. 163.

Be, *adv.* by the time that, when, XVII. 358.

Beau, *adj.* fair, XXIV. 1085.

Bede, *pt. s.* bade, II. 1229.

Bedred, *adj.* bedridden, III. 119.

Bedreint, *pp.* drenched, wetted, XXIV. 577.

Beestly, *adj.* animal, I. ii. 2. 79.

Beet, *pt. s.* beat, II. 1353.

Before-weting, *s.* foreknowledge, I. iii. 4. 63 ; Beforn-, I. iii. 4. 49.

Before-wist, *pp.* foreknown, I. iii. 4. 154.

Begeten, *pp.* begotten, I. iii. 4. 123 ; Begete, II. 1030.

Beggair, *s.* beggar, XVII. 483.

Begonne, *pt. pl.* began, XVIII. 70 ; *pp.* IV. 22.

Behave, *v.* behave (himself), I. i. 10. 16.

Behest, *s.* promise, I. i. 2. 93 ; *pl.* I. ii. 3. 38.

Behesten, *pr. pl.* promise, III. 334.

Behight, 1 *pr. s.* promise, assure, XX. 396 ; *pt. s.* promised, IV. 41 ; (apparently) commanded, XVI. 259.

Behold, *pp.* beheld, XXIV. 279.

Behoten, *pp.* promised, I. iii. 8. 76.

Behove, *s.* behoof, I. ii. 3. 86.

Behovely, *adj.* fit, suitable, IV. 304.

Beikit, 1 *pt. s.* warmed, XVII. 36.

Beildit, *pp.* built, XVII. 97.

Being, *s.* existence, I. ii. 5. 29.

Beinge-place, *s.* home, I. iii. 5. 77.

Be-knowe, *ger.* to acknowledge, I. ii. 1. 127.

Belchere, *s.* Good Cheer, XXI. 322.

Beleve, *s.* belief, XVI. 426 ; XVIII. 162.

Beleved, *pp.* left, I. ii. 10. 109.

Belive, *adv.* at once, XVII. 331.

Belle, *s.* bell, VIII. 262 ; *gen.* II. 40.

Benched, *pp.* provided with benches, VIII. 126 ; XX. 50.

Benches, *s. pl.* benches, or banks of turf, XXI. 49.

Bend, *s.* band, girdle, XXIV. 810 ; Bendes, *pl.* bonds, II. 537.

Bene, *adv.* excellently, XVII. 417.

Bene, *s.* bean, XXIV. 796.

Bene-breed, *s.* bean-bread, I. ii. 2. 56.

Benimen, *v.* take away, I. i. 9. 77.

Bequath, *pt. s.* bequeathed, IV. 178.

Beraft, *pp.* bereft, I. i. 10. 53 ; V. 362.

Berayned, *pp.* rained upon, X. 128.

Bere, *s.* bear, II. 139, 648.

Bere him in honde, make him believe, III. 323 ; *pt. pl.* bore, carried, XX. 213, 223 ; Berest in honde, 2 *pr. s.* accusest, III. 153 ; Beren on honde, accuse falsely, V. 274.

Berel, *s.* beryl, VIII. 37 ; XXI. 455.

Bernes, *s. pl.* barns, I. i. 3. 31.

Beseen, *pp.* adorned, XX. 169 ; Besene, arrayed, XVII. 416.

Besette, *v.* bestow, place, I. i. 9. 72 ;
XI. 15 ; *pp.* bestowed, XXIV. 391 ;
used, II. 1040 ; set up, VIII. 352.

Be-seyn, *pp.* adorned, XII. 9 ; XXIV.
121.

Beshet, *pp.* shut up, I. i. 3. 99.

Besmyteth, *pr. s.* defiles, I. ii. 6.
127. See the note, p. 469.

Besprad, *pt. pl.* spread over, XXIV.
266.

Bestad, *pp.* hardly beset, IV. 88 ;
Be-sted, *pp.* bestead, circumstanced,
II. 403.

Bestial, *adj.* bestial, I. ii. 4. 4 ; I.
ii. 10. 12.

Bestiallich, *adj.* bestial, I. ii. 4. 45.

Bestialtè, *s.* fleshliness, I. iii. 9. 48.

Beswinke, *ger.* to toil for, I. i. 1. 40.

Bet, *adv.* better, VIII. 337 ; XXII.
54.

Betake, *pp.* committed (to), I. ii. 6.
42.

Bete, *pp.* adorned with beaten gold,
XX. 212.

Beteich, I *pr. s.* bequeath, XVII.
577.

Beten, *v.* kindle, XXIV. 324.

Betiden (=betidden), *pt. pl.* happened (to), I. i. *pr.* 122.

Betokeneth, *pr. s.* means, III. 50.

Betrapped, *pp.* entrapped, V. 252.

Betrayden, *pt. pl.* betrayed, V. 198.

Betraysshed, *pt. s.* betrayed, I. ii. 7.
118.

Betterer, *adj.* better, I. ii. 13. 71.

Bevar, *adj.* made of beaver, XVII.
386.

Bewent, *pp.* turned aside, I. i. 1. 21.

Bewrye, *v.* disclose, utter, XXIV.
1358.

Bicche, *s.* bitch, II. 889.

Bigge, *ger.* to build, II. 473.

Bigon, *pp.* beset ; *wel b.*, well placed,
well situate, in a good position or
case, XX. 186. See *Bego* in the
New E. Dict.

Bil, *s.* petition, XXI. 325 ; Billes, *pl.*
XXI. 352.

Bileved, *pp.* believed, I. ii. 6. 20.

Bilowen, *pp.* lied against, belied, V.
196.

Biquath, *pt. s.* bequeathed, VII. 68.

Bit, *pr. s.* bids, XXIV. 469.

Bitte, *s.* bit, I. ii. 6. 83.

Bla, *adj.* livid, XVII. 159. Icel. *bldr.*

Blabbing, *pres. pt.* prattling, V. 116.

Blaiknit, *pp.* lit. made bleak, deprived, XVII. 410.

Blasours, *s.* proclaimers, trumpeters,
I. i. 10. 10.

Blemisshed, *pp.* injured, I. ii. 12. 93.

Blend, *pp.* blinded, II. 852.

Blenk, *s.* glance, look, XVII. 499.

Blenking, *s.* look, XVII. 503.

Blent, *pp.* blinded, II. 771 ; VIII.
461 (see note, p. 508).

Blere, *adj.* blear, dim, I. ii. 1. 123.

Blered, *pp.* bleared, dimmed, V. 105.

Bliss, I *pr. s.* bless, XXIV. 862.

Blobere, *v.* to blubber, to sob, I. ii.
3. 59.

Blustringe (*probably for* bluschinge),
s. brightness, I. i. 2. 10. See note,
p. 454.

Blyfe ; *as bl.*, as quickly as possible,
XXIV. 161 ; heartily, XXIV. 404 ;
as soon as possible, IX. 111 ; XXIV.
1441.

Blyvely, *adv.* soon, I. iii. 4. 19.

Bochour, *s.* butcher, II. 584.

Bode, I *pt. s.* remained, XXIV. 1351.

Boden, *pp.* bidden, III. 134.

Boistously, *adv.* rudely, XX. 595.

Boket, *s.* bucket, I. iii. 1. 145.

Bolded, *pp.* emboldened, XVI. 26.

Bole, *s.* bull, I. i. 5. 127 ; XX. 3 ;
Taurus, VIII. 4.

Bollen, *pp.* swollen, overcharged,
VIII. 101.

Bolne, *ger.* to swell, I. ii. 14. 42.

Bond, *s.* bond, II. 681.

Bond, *pt. s.* bound, VIII. 623.

Bondmen, *s. pl.* serfs, II. 1009.

Bood, I *pt. s.* abode, XVI. 99.

Boon, *s.* boon, petition, XXI. 621.

Boot, *s.* boat, XIII. 56.

Bordes, *s. pl.* tables, XVI. 101.

Bordure, *s.* border, rim, VIII. 594.

Bore, *s.* boar, VIII. 386.

Boren, *v.* bore, I. i. 4. 2.

Borne, *ger.* to burnish, ornament,
adorn, XXIV. 9.

Borowe, *s.* pledge ; *to b.*, as a security,
VIII. 12.

Bosardes, *s. pl.* buzzards, II. 1337.

Bosse, *s.* stud, boss, XX. 246.

Bost, *s.* boast, V. 234.

Bosteous, *adj.* noisy, XVII. 195.

Boster, *s.* boaster, II. 401.

Bote, *s.* good, benefit, VII. 56 ; help,
XX. 83.

Both, *s.* booth, tabernacle, I. ii. 10.
95.

Bouk, *s.* body ; *bouk and boon*, body
and bone, X. 122. See New E. D.

Boun, *adj.* ready, IV. 17 ; XVII. 600.

Bour, *s.* bower, II. 120.

Bowe, *v.* bend, give way, XVI. 491,
492.

Bowes, *s. pl.* boughs, VIII. 53, 583.

Boystous, *adj.* rough, boisterous, I. i. *pr.* 7 ; II. 139 ; rough, poor, lowly, II. 1052 ; rude, XXII. 26.

Brak, *pt. s.* brake, V. 378.

Brast, *pt. s.* burst, XVIII. 210 ; 1 *pt. s.* I. i. 4. 1 ; *pt. pl.* XX. 490 ; penetrated, XVII. 15.

Braunchelet, *s.* small branch, X. 44.

Braunches, *s. pl.* branches, I. iii. 7. 4.

Bravie, *s.* prize of running, X. 65. See note.

Brayd, *s.* moment, XXIV. 1173.

Braying, *pres. pt.* clanging, II. 166.

Brede, *s.* breadth, VIII. 162 ; XX. 43.

Breird, *s.* lit. blade (of grass, &c.) ; *on br.*, in growth, on the increase, XVII. 413.

Breist, *s.* breast, XVII. 110.

Brenne, *pr. s. subj.* burn, XVIII. 105 ; *pr. pl.* XVIII. 35 ; Brende, 1 *pt. s.* burnt, XI. 6 ; *pt. s. subj.* should burn, I. ii. 6. 29 ; Brent, *pt. s.* burnt, XXIV. 232 ; Brent, *pp.* II. 1234 ; Brend, *pp.* II. 674 ; *pres. pt.* burning, I. i. 3. 101 ; Brennende, I. i. 1. 21 ; Brennande, I. i. 1. 104.

Brenningly, *adv.* hotly, V. 239.

Brent, *adj.* high, smooth, XVII. 173.

Bretherhedes, *s. pl.* brotherhoods, III. 88.

Brid, *s.* bird, XVIII. 260, 270 ; Briddes, *pl.* VIII. 43 ; XVIII. 262.

Brige, *s.* contention, trouble, I. i. 7. 104. See note, p. 460.

Brind, *adj.* hot (lit. burnt), XXIV. 319. See note, p. 544.

Brinke, *s.* brink, edge, margin, I. ii. 14. 41 ; VIII. 90.

Broched, *pt. s.* violated, XXIV. 1234.

Broches, *s.* brooches, II. 904.

Broke, *s. dat.* brook, XVIII. 217 ; -syde, brook-side, XVIII. 60.

Broken, *pp.* torn, I. ii. 2. 65.

Broste, *pp.* burst, XI. 99. See Brast.

Brotel, *adj.* brittle, frail, I. i. 10. 110.

Brotelnesse, *s.* frailty, XIII. 22.

Brouk, 2 *pr. pl.* use, make use of, enjoy, XXI. 259.

Browdered, *pp.* braided, XXIV. 811 ; ornamented, XVII. 417.

Brukilnes, *s.* frailty, XVII. 86.

Brukkil, *adj.* brittle, XVII. 569.

Brydel, *ger.* to restrain, I. ii. 6. 83.

Buckelers, *s. pl.* bucklers, II. 917.

Bucket, *s.* bucket, II. 298. See note.

Buit, *s.* advantage, profit, help, XVII. 481. See Bote.

Bullar, *s.* bubble, XVII. 192.

Bulle, *s.* bull, IV. 208.

Burely, *adj.* fit for a lady's bower, XVII. 417 ; handsome, XVII. 173 ; large, XVII. 180. See p. 524.

Burjonen, *v.* bud, I. iii. 7. 51.

Burjoning, *s.* budding, bud, I. ii. 11. 105 ; I. iii. 7. 45.

Burjoning-tyme, *s.* time of budding, I. iii. 7. 70.

Burjons, *s. pl.* buds, I. iii. 7. 49.

Buskit, *pp.* adorned, XVII. 255.

Busteous, *adj.* boisterous, rough, XVII. 153 ; huge, XVII. 166. See Boystous.

But, *prep.* without, I. iii. 4. 135 ; XVII. 94, 194 ; except, I. iii. 6. 40.

But-if, *conj.* unless, I. i. 1. 124 ; I. ii. 7. 86.

Buxom, *adj.* obedient, hence, subject, I. i. 9. 40.

Buxumnesse, *s.* obedience, VI. 11.

By, *prep.* with reference to, XVII. 278 ; By that, for the reason that, I. i. 7. 57.

By and by, in due order, IX. 226 ; XX. 59, 145.

Bye, *v.* buy, I. i. 3. 123 ; 1 *pr. s.* VIII. 435.

Bylis, *s. pl.* boils, tumours, XVII. 395.

By-pathes, *s. pl.* by-ways, I. i. 4. 42.

Byte, *v.* bite, devour, II. 576 ; Bytande, *pres. pt.* biting, bitter, I. i. 10. 90.

Cables, *s. pl.* cables, I. ii. 10. 117.

Cacchende, *pres. pt.* catching, comprehensive, I. ii. 1. 57.

Cacching, *s.* getting money, II. 1017.

Cace, *s.* case ; *in. c.*, perchance, XVII. 507.

Cairful, *adj.* full of care, mournful, XVII. 1, 310.

Caitif, *adj.* wretched, XXIV. 205.

Caitived, Caytifved, *pp.* imprisoned, kept as a captive, I. i. 1. 16.

Cald, *adj.* cold, XVII. 541.

Call, *s.* caul, head-dress, II. 338.

Call, *adj.* (*prob. error for* Tall), II. 466. *See* Untall.

Calm, *s.* calm, VII. 140.

Can, 1 *pr. s.* know, possess, XVI. 733 ; *can pas*, did pass, went, XVII. 28 ; *can discend*, caused to descend, XVII. 6 ; Canst, *pr. s.* knowest, II. 1073.

Captyves, *s. pl.* wretches, captives, II. 291.

Cardiacle, *s.* a disease of the heart, pain in the heart, I. ii. 11. 125.

Cardinall, *s.* cardinal, II. 314, 456.

Care, *s.* misery, I. i. 3. 118.

Careckes, *s. pl.* characters, marks, II. 542.

Carkě, *v.* be anxious, II. 250, 1123.

Carpen, 1 *pr. pl.* talk about, discuss, I. ii. 8. 30.

Cassidony, *s.* chalcedony, XXI. 478. See note.

Cast me, 1 *pt. s.* designed, intended, XVI. 80.

Casuel, *adj.* subject to chance, XXII. 44.

Catel, *s.* wealth, I. ii. 5. 56 ; Catell, II. 385 ; Cattal, II. 250.

Cathedrals. *s. pl.* cathedrals, II. 313.

Cattel-cacching, *s.* getting money, II. 856.

Cauld, *s.* cold, XVII. 7.

Causeful, *adj.* circumstantial, weighty, I. iii. 5. 54.

Cautel, *s.* trick, III. 303 : Cautele, V. 286 ; *pl.* deceits, XXII. 50.

Cawdell, *s.* a warm gruel, mixed with wine or ale, and sweetened or spiced, given chiefly to sick people, XXIV. 438. See *Caudle* in the N. E. D.

Caytif, *s.* captive, wretch, I. i. 1. 122 ; *pl.* II. 71.

Caytifnesse, *s.* captivity, wretchedness, I. i. 2. 31.

Caytive, *adj.* wretched, XVII. 408.

Cedre, *s.* cedar, X. 39 ; *pl.* VIII. 67.

Cedule, *s.* schedule, writing, XXI. 345.

Celler, *s.* cellar, I. ii. 2. 27.

Celsitude, *s.* highness, XXIV. 611.

Celured, *pp.* ceiled, canopied, VIII. 52.

Cercle, *s.* circle, XXI. 536.

Cereal, *adj.* ; *c. okes,* holm-oaks, XX. 209. See note.

Cesse, *ger.* to cease, XVI. 37 ; Cessing that, when that ceases, V. 415.

Chace, *s.* chase (at tennis), IV. 295. See note.

Chafed, *pp.* heated, warmed, I. ii. 12. 8 : Chafinge, *pr. pt.* I. ii. 12. 8.

Chaffren, *pr. pl.* bargain for, II. 146.

Chair, *s.* chariot, car, XVII. 204 ; XX. 1.

Chalenge, *v.* claim, I. i. 10. 66 ; 1 *pr. s.* claim, XVI. 233 ; *pr. pl.* III. 22.

Chalmer, *s.* chamber, XVII. 28, 416.

Chamberer, *s.* lady of the chamber, XXIV. 158.

Chanons, *s. pl.* canons, II. 717, 1c62 ; III. 280.

Chapelayns, *s. pl.* chaplains, III. 348.

Chapelet, *s.* chaplet, XX. 154, 236 ; Chapelets, *pl.* XX. 159, 161, 209, 222.

Chapitre, *s.* chapter, I. iii. 9. 21.

Chapman, *s.* trader, III. 147 ; Chapmen, *p'.* III. 128.

Chapter-house, *s.* chapter-house, III. 75.

Char. *s.* chariot, VII. 177 ; VIII. 595.

Charge, *s.* responsibility, VIII. 328 ; XVI. 469 ; burden, I. i. 3. 15 ; blame, XXIV. 186 ; *pl.* burdens, I. ii. 7. 69.

Chase, *pr. pl.* chase, persecute, II. 1322.

Chase, *pt. s.* chose, XVI. 166.

Chauncellere, *s.* chancellor, XXI. 507.

Chaunsel, *s.* chancel, I. ii. 2. 63.

Chauntements, *s. pl.* enchantments, I. i. 9. 28.

Chauntours, *s.* singers, II. 870.

Chayre, *s.* throne, XXI. 476.

Chees ; see Chese.

Chere, *s.* demeanour, XXIV. 575 ; good cheer, XVI. 95 ; *pl.* looks, XIV. 8.

Cherelich, *adj.* prodigal, II. 1050. Read *not cherelich* ; see note, p. 491.

Cheryce, *v.* cherish, VII. 16 ; Cheryse, XXIV. 893.

Chese, *ger.* to choose, I. ii. 10. 21 ; Chesen, *ger.* VII. 185 ; 1 *pr. s.* IX. 249 ; *imp. s.* 3 *p.* let him choose, XVI. 313 ; Chees, *pt. s.* chose, IV. 31 ; VIII. 395 : Cheisit, *pt. pl.* chose, XVII. 265.

Chesing, *s.* choice, IX. 15.

Cheste, *s.* chest, VIII. 227.

Cheverit, *pt. pl.* shivered, shook, XVII. 156. See **Chiver.**

Chevisaunce, *s.* usury, dealing for profit, XII. 53.

Chevyce, *v.* preserve, V. 325.

Chid, *pp.* chid (pp. of *chide*), XVIII. 267.

Childing, *pres. pt.* bearing a child, X. 139.

Chippes, *s. pl.* chips, I. i. 9. 20.

Chiver, 1 *pr. s.* shiver, VIII. 230.

Chorl, *s.* churl, VIII. 390.

Chose, *pp.* chosen, IV. 4.

Choweth, *pr. s.* chews, II. 258.

Christned, *pp.* christened (person), II. 101.

Churlich, *adj.* churlish, poor, II. 1051.

Conne, v. know how (to), I. i. 1. 96 ;
I. iii. 3. 120 ; be able, I. ii. 4. 37 ;
pr. pl. know, II. 413, 842 ; IV. 24 ;
can, V. 18 ; may, I. iii. 7. 160.

Conneccion, s. connexion, I. ii. 8. 56.

Conning, s. skill, I. i. pr. 99.

Conservatrice, s. preserver. X. 117.

Consigned, pp. dedicated, X. 37.

Consistory, s. consistory-court, II.
880.

Constaunce, s. constancy, XIII. 3.

Constrewe, v. construe, translate, I.
ii. 2. 7 ; imp. s. I. iii. 6. 148.

Contenence, s. continence, XXVI. 2.

Contingence, s. contingence, conditional state, I. ii. 9. 181.

Contingent, adj. contingent, I. i. 4.
56 ; conditional, I. ii. 9. 147.

Contradiccion, s. a contradiction, I.
ii. 11. 116.

Contradictorie, s. opposite, I. ii. 13.
129.

Contrariaunt, adj. opposing, I. iii.
2. 96 ; Contrariant, I. ii. 9. 65 ;
Contrariauntes, pl. contravening, I.
i. 5. 64.

Contrarien, pr. pl. contradict (it), II.
936 ; pt. s. subj. should contradict,
I. ii. 4. 117 ; would oppose, I. iii.
2. 152.

Contraries, s. pl. contrary things, I.
ii. 6. 11.

Contrarious, adj. contrary, I. ii. 6. 95.

Contrariousteè, s. contrariety, I. ii. 8.
50 ; contradiction, I. iii. 4. 229 ;
opposition, I. iii. 1. 125.

Contrary-doers, s. pl. trespassers, I.
iii. 2. 8.

Convenient, adj. fitting, suitable, XI.
1 ; XX. 119 ; XXIV. 786.

Cop, s. cup, XVII. 343, 387.

Cop, s. top, I. iii. 1. 151.

Cope, s. cope, cape, III. 51 ; I. i. 3.
149 ; pl. XXIV. 116.

Cornes, s. pl. grains of corn, I. i. 5.
85.

Corowned, pp. crowned, I. iii. 2. 12.

Cosinage, s. relationship, I. ii. 2. 101 ;
relatives, I. ii. 2. 99.

Cost, s. side, XX. 76 ; pl. coasts,
regions, XXIV. 58.

Costages, s. pl. expenses, I. i. 2. 139.

Costey, v. coast along, VIII. 36.

Cote, s. coat, I. iii. 7. 132.

Couched, pp. set, XXI. 529.

Coude, pt. pl. knew, XVIII. 71.

Counten, pr. pl. (they) count, expect,
II. 927.

Countenaunce, s. sign, I. ii. 7. 122 ;
semblance, XVI. 50.

Counterfaytours, s. pl. counterfeit
dealers, II. 1061.

Counterpaysing, s. an equivalent, I.
i. 2. 128.

Counterplete, v. plead against, contradict, I. i. 8. 30 ; v. plead against
me, I. ii. 12. 101 ; pp. pleaded
against, XXIV. 429.

Countervayle, ger. to equal, I. i. 3.
132 ; pp. balanced, I. iii. 5. 131.

Countours, s. accquntants, II. 802.

Coupable, adj. culpable, V. 152.

Coure, v. cower, cringe, II. 207.

Courser, s. horse, II. 1004.

Courteours, s. courtiers, XXIV. 1313.

Courtes, s. pl. court-houses, III. 81.

Court-holding, s. holding of courts,
II. 790.

Couth, pt. s. knew how, XVI. 134.

Covenable, adj. suitable, I. iii. 8.
116.

Cover, v. recover (themselves), I. ii.
7. 97 ; obtain, I. ii. 5. 121.

Covert, adj. secretive, sly, very prudent, XVI. 177.

Covertours, s. coverings, II. 105.

Covins, s. pl. complots, I. i. 6. 167.

Cowpis, s. pl. cups, flagons, XVII.
419.

Crabbed, adj. crabbed, perverse, V.
324 ; Crabbit, cross, XVII. 353.

Crabbitly, adv. crabbedly, morosely,
XVII. 154.

Crake, pr. pl. boast, V. 328.

Crakel, v. quaver, XVIII. 119. See
note.

Crallit, pp. curled, twisted, II. 186.

Crampisshed, pt. s. oppressed, constrained, pained, IX. 49.

Crave, ger. to ask for again, XXVII.
8.

Crede, s. Creed, II. 413, 1066.

Crepè, v. creep, II. 942.

Cresse, s. blade of a cress, I. i. 5.
133 ; I. ii. 7. 109 ; I. iii. 5. 45.

Croke, pr. pl. go crooked, bend in, I.
ii. 7. 69.

Croked, adj. crooked, indirect, I. ii.
6. 163 ; curved, XIII. 17.

Croken, adj. crooked, I. ii. 7. 91.

Crokets, s. pl. rolls of hair, II. 306.
See note.

Crommes, s. pl. crumbs, I. i. pr.
105.

Cronique, s. chronicle, story, IV. 338,
369.

Crope, pp. crept, I. i. 4. 54.

Croppe, s. shoot, sprout, top, V. 17.

Crosse, s. cross, the cross marked on
a piece of money, III. 225.

Crosse-aleys, *s. pl.* cross-alleys, XXI. 10.

Crouche, *s.* cross, II. 942.

Crowes, *s. pl.* crows, II. 1334.

Croysery, *s.* crusade, II. 445.

Cukkow, *s.* cuckoo, XVIII. 50.

Culleth, *pr. s.* kills, II. 593, 1314; *pr. pl.* II. 267.

Cultre, *s.* coulter, II. 7.

Cure, *s.* care, XVI. 494; XXIV. 986; guard, XVII. 10; diligence, VIII. 311; attention, I. iii. 8. 52; cure (of souls), II. 1173; responsibility, XX. 61.

Curious, *adj.* curious, anxious, II. 384; nice, II. 1013; choice, VII. 66.

Currant, *s.* current, *or adj.* running, X. 51.

Curreyden, *pt. pl.* curried favour, I. i. 10. 11.

Currish, *adj.* like a cur, XVI. 389.

Curteys, *adj.* gentle, II. 482.

Custome, *s.* custom, I. iii. 1. 106.

Cut, *ger.* curtail, XVII. 39; *pp.* cut short, II. 929.

Dame, *s.* mother, I. ii. 2. 117; II. 1361; Dames tonge, mother-tongue, I. i. *pr.* 37.

Damoselles, *s. pl.* damsels, I. ii. 2. 42; girls, II. 928.

Dampnáble, *adj.* damnable, VI. 60.

Dampne, *v.* condemn, II. 630; *pr. s.* II. 224; *pp.* damned, I. i. 7. 55; condemned, VIII. 276.

Dased, *pp.* dazed, II. 1326.

Daunger, *s.* control, V. 257.

Daungerous, *adj.* disdainful, XXIV. 901; cross, XXIV. 330; difficult to please, XXIV. 761; forbidding, I. i. 2. 102.

Daunten, *v.* subdue, I. ii. 2. 131.

Dawe, *s. pl. dat.* days; *by elder dawe,* in olden times, II.643. A.S. *dagum.*

Daweninge, *s.* dawning, IX. 251.

Dawing, *pres. pt.* dawning, XXII. 29.

Dayesye, *s.* daisy, XVIII. 243.

Dayneth, *pr. s.* deigns, I. ii. 9. 122.

Deaurat, *pp.* gilded, made of a golden colour, VIII. 597.

Debat, *s.* strife, VII. 59; uneasiness, XVI. 698; *pl.* I. ii. 2. 48; combats, I. i. 4. 44.

Debated, *pp.* striven about, IV. 363. But read *delated,* i. e. deferred; the Trentham MS. has *deleated,* meant for *delated.*

Debonair, *adj.* courteous, XX. 501; gentle, V. 347.

Deed, *adj.* dead, II. 198.

Deedly, *adj.* mortal, I. ii. 12. 121; Deedliche, I. iii. 3. 65; Dedly, I. iii. 3. 68.

Deeth, *s.* death, VIII. 140.

Defame, *ger.* to accuse falsely, III. 305.

Defased, *pp.* defaced, I. i. 8. 115; made cheerless, I. i. 1. 66.

Defaut, *s.* default, trespass, I. i. 3. 95; XVI. 270 (obscure); XVI. 611; Defaute, fault, I. ii. 2. 17; III. 398; *pl.* IV. 267.

Defence, *s.* power to defend, X. 124.

Defend, *v.* forbid, II. 570; *pt. s.* forbade, I. iii. 8. 122; II. 1115; *pp.* forbidden, I. iii. 3. 57.

Defendinge, *s.* forbidding, I. iii. 3. 55.

Deformait, *adj.* deformed, ugly, XVII. 349.

Defoule, *ger.* to defile, V. 186; 1 *pt. s.* defiled, I. i. 8. 83; *pp.* I. ii. 13. 74.

Degest, *pp.* digested, considered, XVII. 303.

Deid, *s.* death, XVII. 70, 585.

Deid, *s.* deed, doing, XVII. 328.

Deificait, *pp.* accounted as gods, XVII. 288.

Del, *s.* portion; *every del,* every bit, XXI. 227.

Delated; see Debated.

Délectable, *adj.* delightful, XXI. 72.

Délitable, *adj.* delightful, VIII. 122.

Deliver, *adj.* nimble, VIII. 164.

Deliveraunce, *s.* deliverance, I. i. 7. 102.

Delytable, *adj.* delightful, I. ii. 4. 47.

Delyte, *v.* delight, VIII. 61, 381.

Deme, *v.* judge, XII. 7; 2 *pr. s. subj.* VII. 32; *pr. s.* condemns, I. ii. 7. 117; *pp.* judged, adjudged to be true, approved, II. 67; condemned, II. 198.

Demene, *s.* demeanour, XXIV. 734.

Demeyne, *s.* control, IX. 216; XVI. 132.

Demin, *v.* deem, suppose, I. iii. 3. 111; *pr. pl.* (?), II. 510. See Deme.

Deming, *s.* suspicion, XVII. 118.

Demure, *adj.* sedate, IX. 156; XVI. 106; XX. 459; XXI. 82; XXIV. 653.

Demurely, *adv.* sedately, XVI. 246.

Denarie, *s.* pay, wages, X. 66.

Denominacion, *s.* naming, I. ii. 9. 162.

Dent, *s.* stroke, blow, dint, I. iii. 7. 92, 100; XXIV. 836.

Denwere, *s.* doubt, I. i. 6. 193. A false form; see note, p. 459.

Departe, *v.* separate, XVI. 317;
sever, I. i. 1. 90; part, XXIV. 1399;
impart, XVI. 440; *pr. s. subj.* part,
I. i. 9. 86; *pp.* divided, I. ii. 10. 9;
parted, XI. 51; rent, XX. 193.

Departicion, *s.* divorce, I. iii. 2. 14.

Departing, *s.* separation, I. iii. 6. 158;
XVI. 659; distributing, I. ii. 5. 44.

Depeynt, *pp.* painted, VIII. 425;
Depeynted, XXIV. 100.

Dequace, *v.* suppress, I. i. 5. 77; put
down, I. i. 7. 26; *ger.* to repress, I.
ii. 1. 74.

Dere, *v.* do harm, I. i. 5. 72.

Dereworthinesse, *s.* fondness (for),
I. ii. 5. 99.

Dereworthly, *adv.* preciously, X. 39.

Dere-worthy, *adj.* precious, I. i. 10.
117.

Descry, *ger.* to describe, XXIV. 97.

Desesperaunce, *s.* despair, despera-
tion, XVI. 538, 652.

Deslavee, *adj.* unchaste, inordinate
in conduct, XII. 40.

Destenyed, *pp.* predestined, I. iii. 9.
13.

Desyrously, *adv.* eagerly, I. iii. 6. 70.

Determinacions, *s. pl.* ordinances,
settlements, I. i. 5. 52.

Determine, *adj.* fixed, XXIV. 647.

Determine, *ger.* to end, I. iii. 3. 129;
pp. settled, fixed, I. ii. 6. 20.

Determinison, *s.* determination, definition, I. ii. 13. 30.

Dettour, *s.* debtor, VI. 31.

Deviacion, *s.* deviation, going astray,
I. iii. 1. 6.

Devoir, *s.* duty, XVI. 559. (F. text,
devoir.)

Devoit, *adj.* devout, XVII. 115.

Devyn, *adj.* divine, XVII. 127.

Devynly, *adj.* divine-like, I. iii. 1. 55.

Devyse, *s.* device, XXI. 207.

Devyse, *v.* relate, XX. 97; XXI. 525.

Dew, *adj.* due, XXI. 51.

Dew-dropys, *s. pl.* dewdrops, XXIX.
6.

Dewe, *s.* due; *of dewe*, duly, XXIV.
1397.

Dewetè, *s.* duty, due course, IV. 232.

Deydest, *2 pt. s.* didst die, were to die,
I. i. 9. 65; *pt. s.* died, VII. 102.

Deyne, *v. refl.* deign, I. ii. 3. 3.

Deynous, *adj.* disdainful, I. i. 1. 130;
I. i. 2. 143 (see note); I. i. 3. 70;
Deynouse, *fem.* V. 150.

Deyntees, *s.* dainties, II. 1008.

Diamant, *s.* diamond, XXIV. 696.

Diffame, *pr. pl.* defame, I. i. 3. 7.

Diffyne, *v.* define, V. 463.

Dighteth, *pr. s.* gets ready, II. 978;
pr. s. subj. may (He) arrange *or*
place, X. 84; *pp.* ornamented, II.
894; XX. 254.

Digne, *adj.* worthy, V. 457; XIX.
11.

Digned. *pp.* honoured, X. 39.

Dinne, *s.* din, noise, I. ii. 9. 31.

Diourn, *adj.* daily, X. 66.

Diriges, *s. pl.* dirges, burials, III.
125.

Dirk, *adv.* in the dark, XXIV. 1256.

Disalowe, *v.* disapprove of, dispraise,
IV. 242.

Disaventure, *s.* ill fortune, IX. 72.

Disceyvable, *adj.* deceitful, I. ii. 4.
89.

Disciplyning, *s.* correction, I. ii. 11.
137.

Disclaunder, *v.* slander, II. 333;
pr. pl. II. 1053; *pr. s.* speaks slander, I. ii. 8. 74.

Disclaundring, *s.* slandering, I. ii.
3. 112.

Discomfit, *adj.* discomfited, sad,
XVI. 35.

Discomfiteth, *pr. s.* discomforts
himself, grieves, I. ii. 11. 55; *pp.*
discomforted, I. ii. 11. 57.

Discordaunce, *s.* disagreement, I. ii.
8. 47.

Discordaunt, *adj.* discordant, I. i. 9.
106; Discordantes, *s. pl.* things discordant, I. ii. 8. 54.

Discovert, *pp.* discovered, made
known, XVI. 403.

Discrete, *adj.* separate, I. iii. 1. 2.

Discryve, *v.* describe, VIII. 156;
IX. 112; XXIV. 778; *ger.* XXI.
512.

Disencrees, *s.* decrease, VIII. 202.

Disese, *s.* misery, woe, XVIII. 265;
XX. 377; annoyance, I. i. 1. 20, 28;
anger, II. 1260.

Disesed, *pp.* made wretched, I. i. 1.
31.

Disesely, *adj.* uncomfortable, I. iii. 1.
172.

Dishevel, *adj.* dishevelled, XXIV.
139.

Dishonest, *adj.* shameful, V. 184.

Disloged, *pp.* banished, XXI. 62.

Dismaye, *v.* feel dismay, I. ii. 9.
144.

Dispence, *s.* expence, II. 523; *pl.* I.
i. 7. 107.

Dispende, *ger.* to spend, VII. 40;
XXII. 16; *pr. pl.* II. 762; Dispent, *pp.* spent, I. i. 10. 53.

Dispense, *ger.* to dispense, III. 367.

Dispitous, *adj.* contemptuous, I. i. 10. 90 ; spiteful, XII. 26.

Displesaunce, *s.* displeasure, XVI. 544 ; XXI. 661 ; XXV. 19.

Disport, *s.* amusement, XVI. 98 ; *pl.* XVI. 410.

Disporte, *ger.* to amuse, interest, VIII. 602 ; *v. refl.* be merry, VIII. 10 ; 1 *pr. s. refl.* throw myself about, tumble and toss, I. i. 3. 102.

Dispreyse, *v.* blame, I. ii. 6. 91.

Dispyt, *s.* contempt, II. 712 ; VIII. 240.

Dissever, *v.* part, depart, IX. 175 ; *pp.* separated, II. 1242.

Disseveraunce, *s.* separation, XI. 13 ; XXIV. 783.

Dissimulacion, *s.* (*ill used for* simulation), imitation, I. ii. 14. 10.

Dissimulait, *adj.* full of dissimulation, XVII. 225.

Dissimulen, *v.* dissimulate, V. 18.

Dissolucioun, *s.* dissolute conduct, XII. 60.

Distaunce, *s.* strife, VI. 58 ; VII. 161 ; disagreement, II. 1166.

Distempreth, *pr. s.* intoxicates, XV. *a.* 7.

Distourbour, *s.* disturbance, I. iii. 5. 30.

Distraineth, *pr. s.* constrains, XXIV. 660 ; *pp.* afflicted, VIII. 134.

Distruccioun, *s.* destruction, IX. 88.

Distrye, *v.* destroy, II. 1235. (In II. 1144, perhaps *distry* should be *discry*, i. e. describe.)

Diurnal, *adj.* daily, VIII. 590.

Do, *imp. s.* cause, I. i. 1. 83 ; *pp.* done, IV. 97 ; come to an end, XIV. 18 ; Do way, do (it) away, put (it) aside, abandon (the idea), I. i. 9. 89.

Docke, *s.* dock (plant), I. i. 2. 167 ; I. iii. 6. 7.

Doctrine, *s.* learning, I. ii. 11. 136.

Dole, *s.* sorrow, woe, X. 10 ; XXIV. 1098.

Doleful, *adj.* sad (ones), X. 55.

Dolven, *pp.* buried, I. ii. 2. 69 ; wrought, I. i. *pr.* 11.

Dombe, *adj.* dumb, I. ii. 5. 98.

Dome, *s.* judgement, XX. 306 ; *gen.* II. 331.

Domesday, *s.* doom's-day, X. 84.

Don, *pp.* done ; *d. but lent,* only lent, XXVII. 7.

Donatyf, *s.* gift, reward, X. 72.

Donet, *s.* primer, I. ii. 12. 17. See note, p. 475.

Donne, *adj. pl.* dun, dark, IX. 115.

Dooly, *adj.* mournful, XVII. 1, 344.

Doon, *error for* Do, 1 *pr. s. subj.* do, act, XXIV. 927.

Dotage, *s.* folly, XV. *a.* 5, XV. *b.* 4.

Dote, *ger.* to be a fool, I. i. 2. 71 ; *v.* XXIV. 1047.

Doth, *imp. pl.* cause, make, XXIV. 1326.

Doublenesse, *s.* duplicity, XIII. 8.

Douceperes, *s. pl.* the twelve peers (of Charlemagne), XX. 516.

Douf (*old text* doif), benumbed (lit. deaf), XVII. 32. See note.

Doule, *s.* down-feather, II. 1272. See note.

Dour, *adj.* stern, severe, oppressive, XVII. 437.

Dout, *s.* fear, II. 697.

Doute, *ger.* to be feared, IV. 138 ; 1 *pr. s. refl.* fear, XXI. 246.

Dradde, 1 *pt. s.* dreaded ; feared, I. i. 3. 74 ; Drad, *pp.* frightened, II. 561 ; afraid, II. 1088.

Draught, *s.* draught, drawing, I. iii. 7. 102.

Drede, *s.* dread ; *withoute d.,* without doubt, XX. 152.

Drede, *ger.* to fear, V. 330.

Dredful, *adj.* timid, V. 348 ; XVI. 218 ; fearful, IX. 157 ; fearful (to offend), XXIII. 10.

Drenche, 1 *pr. s.* am drowned, I. i. 3. 162.

Dreriheed, *s.* dreariness, VIII. 9.

Dresse, *v. refl.* advance, XXIV. 113 ; address myself, VIII. 203 ; *ger.* to direct, XXIV. 179 ; Dresse, XIII. 62 ; *pr. pl. refl.* direct themselves, II. 379 ; 1 *pr. pl. subj.* direct our way, go forward, XXI. 215 ; Dress you, *imp. pl.* (*as s.*), direct yourself, go, XXIV. 554 ; Drest, 1 *pt. s. refl.* advanced, XX. 456 ; Dressed, *pt. s. refl.* advanced, I. iii. 3. 2.

Drive, *pp.* driven, I. i. 1. 2.

Dropping, *pres. pt.* dripping, XX. 371.

Drow, *pt. s.* withdrew, XVI. 806.

Drowpit, *pt. pl.* drooped, XVII. 157.

Drowry, *s.* love-token, XVII. 583.

Dualitè, *s.* duality, doubleness, I. ii. 13. 30.

Duchees, *s. pl.* duchies, V. 333.

Duëtee, *s.* duty, VI. 38 : IX. 5, 106.

Duleful, *adj.* grievous, XVII. 309.

Dullen, *v.* render dull, I. iii. 3. 196.

Duracioun, *s.* duration, endurance, X. 87.

Duresse, *s.* hardness, XVI. 703; force, I. iii. 7. 71; constraint, I. i. 6. 157; stress, I. i. 1. 87; cruelty, XVI. 784.

Dureth, *pr. s.* lasts, I. i. 3. 20.

During, *adj.* enduring, X. 131.

Dwale, *s.* a sleeping draught made from the deadly nightshade, XXIV. 998.

Dyamaunt, *s.* diamond, X. 87.

Dyking, *pres. pt.* ditching, II. 1043.

Dys, *s. pl.* dice, XIII. 74.

Dytè, *s.* ditty, song, poem, VIII. 606; IX. 268; XVII. 1.

Ebbe, *s.* ebb, VII. 143; XIII. 36.

Eche, *ger.* to increase, I. iii. 1. 147; Eched, *pp.* I. ii. 8. 79.

Edefye, *ger.* to build, I. i. 5. 110; *v.* VII. 77.

Edwyte, *v.* accuse, reproach, XII. 18.

Ee, *s.* eye, XXIV. 768. See **Eye**.

Eet, *pt. s.* ate, I. i. 8. 55; XX. 90; Eten, *pp.* eaten, XX. 95.

Effunde, 1 *pr. s.* pour out, XIX. 25.

Efter, *conj.* according as, XVII. 106.

Egall, *adj.* equal, XXIV. 1041.

Egally, *adv.* equally, impartially, XXIV. 365.

Eglantere, *s.* sweet-briar, XX. 56, 80. See the note, p. 520.

Eighteth, *adj.* eighth, I. i. 5. 103.

Eird, *s.* earth. XVII. 384.

Eirdly, *adj.* earthly, XVII. 52, 355.

Eke-names, *s. pl.* nicknames, I. ii. 1. 96.

Elde, *s.* old age, I. i. 6. 94; I. i. 8. 115.

Elde-faders, *s. pl.* ancestors, I. ii. 2. 125.

Eleccioun, *s.* choice, V. 236.

Electuairis, *s. pl.* electuaries, XVII. 246.

Elementes, *s. pl.* elements, I. ii. 9. 41.

Elenge, *adj.* mournful, miserable, XVIII. 115.

Embelisshed, *pp.* honoured, dignified, X. 104.

Embrouded, *pp.* embroidered, XXI. 85.

Emeraud, *adj.* emerald, XXIV. 79; *s. pl.* XX. 144.

Emispere, *s.* hemisphere, XXII. 27.

Empryse, *s.* enterprise, II. 960; design, V. 119; *pl.* VIII. 416.

Enamayl, *s.* enamel, XXI. 534.

Enbolded, *pp.* emboldened, I. i. 2. 23.

Enchace, *v.* chase, XVI. 416.

Enchesoun, *s.* reason, V. 429.

Encheynen, *ger.* to link together, *or*, to be linked together, I. ii. 6. 4.

Encomberaunce, *s.* encumbrance, trouble, XVI. 284, 775; XXI. 746.

Encombred, *pp.* encumbered, hindered, defeated, X. 103.

Encrees, *s.* increase, II. 72.

Endry, *v.* suffer, endure, XXIV. 727, 941. See note, p. 547.

Enduced, *pp.* induced, I. ii. 1. 60.

Endyte, *v.* indite, VIII. 196; IX. 231; *pr. pl.* indict, II. 1026.

Endyting, *s.* composition, inditing, XXII. 65.

Ene, *s. pl.* eyes, XVII. 157.

Enfame, *s.* disgrace, I. i. 8. 51; reproach, I. i. 6. 6.

Enfect, *pp.* infected, stained, XXIV. 217.

Enfeffed, *pp.* invested (with), possessed (of), XVI. 364.

Enforme, *ger.* to inform, I. ii. 11. 127; to give information, I. ii. 1. 51; *pr. pl.* instruct, I. ii. 2. 79.

Enfourmer, *s.* instructor, I. ii. 2. 87.

Engendrure, *s.* conception, I. ii. 6. 80; nativity, I. i. 6. 101; *pl.* I. ii. 9. 174.

Engyn, *s.* device, XXIV. 535; ingenuity, V. 296.

Enhaunce, *ger.* to exalt, V. 455; *pr. pl.* increase, I. ii. 8. 85; *pp.* advanced, II. 448.

Enlumineth, *pr. s.* illumines, I. ii. 1. 127; *pp.* I. i. 1. 23.

Enmoysed, *pp.* cheered, comforted, I. i. 3. 105. See note, p. 456.

Enpeche, *v.* impeach, accuse, I. i. 6. 86.

Enpeyred, *pp.* injured, I. i. 6. 8.

Enpight, *pp.* infixed, I. i. 2. 48.

Enpited, *pp.* filled with pity, I. ii. 4. 111. (The sole known example of the word.)

Enplede, *v.* plead against, II. 734.

Enpoysonen, *ger.* to poison, I. iii. 5. 115.

Enprent, *imp. s.* imprint, XXIV. 876.

Enprisoned, *pp.* imprisoned, I. ii. 4. 104.

Ensample, *s.* example, I. i. 5. 1.

Enseled, *pp.* sealed, I. i. 9. 94.

Ensure, 1 *pr. s.* assure, XX. 60, 287; XXI. 52.

Ensyse, *s.* kind, sort, II. 625.

Entalented, *pp.* excited, V. 338. See N.E.D.

Entayl, *s.* cutting; *of e.,* with excellent cutting, XXI. 536.

Entencion, *s.* intention, design, I. ii. 4. 42 ; V. 553; XXIV. 908; signification, I. iii. 2. 140; VIII. 431.

Entendaunce, *s.* service, VII. 173.

Entende, *v.* intend, XXII. 12.

Entent, *s.* intent, desire, XVI. 768; XXIV. 206 ; *pl.* II. 1159.

Ententyf, *adj.* attentive, V. 439.

Enterchaunged, *pp.* interchanged, I. ii. 9. 156.

Entere, *adj.* entire, XXIV. 354 ; true, IX. 163.

Entermeting, *pres. pt.* intermeddling, I. iii. 7. 163.

Entrechangen, *v.* interchange, I. ii. 9. 176.

Entrecomuned, *pp.* had communication, I. i. 5. 7.

Entremellen, *pr. pl.* intermingle, I. i. 5. 14.

Entremes, *s.* course between two more substantial ones, XVI. 156. See note.

Entreprise, *s.* enterprise, XVI. 515.

Entune, *s.* tune, tone, XI. 27.

Entuned, *pp.* kept in tune, XX. 180.

Enviroun, *adv.* all round, XXI. 53; Environ, XXIV. 1031.

Envolved, *pp.* enwrapped, I. i. 1. 111.

Envyroned, *pp.* surrounded, I. ii. 7. 94; Envyroning, *pres. pt.* encircling, VIII. 79.

Equipolent, *adj.* equal in power, XII. 15.

Equivocas, *s. pl.* words of like meaning, I. iii. 6. 64. See note, p. 482.

Er, *adv.* sooner, XVIII. 233.

Erber, *s.* arbour, XXIV. 757.

Erdly, *adj.* earthly, XXVII. 2.

Ermyne, *s.* ermine, XX. 243.

Ernest-silver, *s.* earnest money, I. i. 3. 151.

Erst, *adv.* soonest ; *non erst* (error for *non er*), no sooner, XXIV. 167.

Eschaunge, *s.* change, XIII. 96.

Eschetour, *s.* an escheator, I. ii. 2. 49.

Eschewing, *s.* avoidance, avoiding, XVI. 291, 307.

Esclaundre, *s.* scandal, V. 70.

Esperaunce, *s.* Hope, XXIV. 1033; Esperans, XVII. 48 ; *on e.,* in hope, XI. 26.

Esperus, Hesperus, the evening-star, VIII. 612.

Esploit, *s.* result, success, XI. 57; Esployte, I. i. 5. 20.

Espoire, *s.* hope, I. ii. 8. 23.

Estate, *s.* state, XXI. 486 ; *pl.* VII. 6.

Et, *pr. s.* (*short for* eteth), eats, XIV. 7, 14.

Eterne, *adj.* eternal, I. iii. 4. 205.

Evangely, *s.* gospel, II. 97 ; IV. 217.

Even, *adv.* close ; *e. by,* close by, XX. 134.

Even-Christen, *s.* fellow-Christian, III. 430.

Evenforth, *adv.* continually, I. ii. 11. 21 ; forwards, I. i. 1. 110.

Evenhed, *s.* equality, I. iii. 1. 89 ; I. iii. 5. 150.

Evenlich, *adv.* equally, I. iii. 4. 62 ; similarly, I. iii. 3. 95.

Evenliche, *adj.* equal, I. ii. 2. 122 ; I. iii. 5. 152.

Even-lyk, *adv.* exactly so, VIII. 201 ; exactly, VIII. 194.

Ever, *adv. as s.* eternity, I. i. 8. 117.

Ever in oon, *adv.* continually, VIII. 528.

Everich, *adj.* each one, XX. 151.

Everichon, *pron.* every one, XX. 168.

Eve-sterre, *s.* evening-star, I. ii. 13. 96.

Ewage, *s.* a precious stone having the colour of sea-water, X. 92, 93. See note.

Excitation, *s.* instigation, I. i. 3. 37.

Excitours, *s. pl.* exhorters, instigators, I. i. 6. 56.

Excusacion, *s.* excuse, I. i. 7. 33 ; V. 471.

Exemplair, *s.* exemplar, XX. 502.

Exempt, *pp.* exempted, III. 232.

Expert, *adj.* experienced, XXIV. 882.

Exploytes, *s. pl.* successes, successful results, I. i. 5. 69.

Expone, *v.* recount, XVII. 369; Expowne, *imp. s.* expound, I. iii. 5. 10.

Expuls, *s.* expulsion, repulse, XVII. 119.

Extend, *s.* extent, II. 658.

Eye, *s.* eye ; *at e.,* visibly, I. ii. 6. 16; Eyen, *pl.* XVI. 266. See Ee.

Eylen, *v.* ail, XVIII. 116.

Eyre, *s.* air, I. ii. 8. 48 ; VIII. 14; Eyr, XIV. 36.

Fachioun, *s.* falchion, curved sword, XVII. 187.

Facound, *adj.* eloquent, XVII. 268.

Facultees, *s. pl.* facilities, opportunities, I. i. 2. 29.

Fade, *adj.* dull, sombre, IV. 102.

Fade, *ger.* to cause to wither, I. i. 1. 27; Faidit, *pp.* XVII. 24.

Fain, *adj.* glad, XX. 378.

Fair, *s.* fare, XVII. 403.

Fallas, *s.* deceit, I. ii. 14. 52, 54.

Falle, *v.* happen, I. i. 1. 77; XVI. 539; *pr. s.* is suitable, III. 78.

Falowen, *pr. pl.* fade, I. ii. 8. 114.

Falsen, *ger.* to deceive, V. 307; *pt. s.* gave way, failed, I. ii. 8. 127; was false to, I. i. 2. 92.

Falsetè, *s.* falsehood, I. ii. 3. 57; *pl.* I. ii. 1. 73.

Falsheed, *s.* falsehood, I. iii. 6. 127.

Famed, *pp.* defamed, II. 341.

Familier, *adj* familiar, (once) friendly, I. ii. 7. 108.

Famulers, *s. pl.* familiar friends, I. ii. 7. 81.

Fand, 1 *pt. s.* found, XVII. 43.

Fanes, *s. pl.* vanes, weather-cocks, XXI. 161.

Fantasy, *s.* fancy, XXI. 597; XXVII. 1; folly, XIV. 20; pleasure, I. i. *pr.* 26; *pl.* XXI. 11.

Farced, *pp.* stuffed, filled, XXIV. 655.

Fare, *pr. pl.* go, XX. 341; fare, II. 1134; Farn, *pp.* fared, I. ii. 10. 58.

Fasoun, *s.* make, XXI. 305, 522; Fassioun, habit, XII. 46.

Faucon, *s.* falcon, XVI. 413.

Faute, *s.* lack, VIII. 443; Faut, fault, XXIV. 608.

Fay, *s.* faith, XVII. 571; XVIII. 115.

Fayn, 2 *pr. pl.* feign, make a pretence, XXIV. 751.

Fayrhede, *s.* beauty, I. ii. 3. 124.

Faytours, *s.* deceivers, II. 148, 327.

Fecht, *ger.* to fight, XVII. 185.

Federed, *pp.* feathered, XVI. 146; Fedderit, XVII. 168.

Feffe, *ger.* to endow, XXIV. 932; *pr. s.* XVI. 472.

Feill, *s.* experience, knowledge, XVII. 533.

Feird, *adj.* fourth, XVII. 216.

Fel, *adj.* cruel, wicked, XVI. 505; evil, XIII. 77.

Felauship, *s.* company, XXI. 730.

Felawes, *s. pl.* companions, XXI. 247.

Feld, *pp.* overthrown (lit. felled), I. i. 3. 148.

Fele, *adj.* many, XX. 5; XXIV. 110, 191.

Feled, *pp.* felt, perceived, I. ii. 1. 86.

Fell, *adj.* cruel, II. 859; terrible, XVII. 187; Fellest, worst, III. 6.

Felle, *v.* overturn, V. 234.

Felloun, *adj.* destructive, XVII. 167.

Felly, *adv.* cruelly, IX. 76.

Felonous, *adj.* evil, I. i. 6. 167; wicked, I. ii. 6. 56.

Felterit, *pp.* entangled, XVII. 163.

Femininitee, *s.* womanhood, IX. 148.

Feminitee (*for* Femininitee), *s.* womanliness, XVII. 80.

Fend, *s.* the fiend, XXIV. 529; *pl.* II. 1165.

Fenyeit, *pp.* feigned, XVII. 66.

Feorthe, *adj.* fourth, VII. (*title*).

Fer, *adv.* far, XXI. 141.

Ferd, 1. *pt. s.* fared, was, XXIV. 152.

Ferde, *s.* fear, I. i. 2. 15.

Ferde, *adj. pl.* afraid, I. ii. 9. 138.

Ferdeth, *pr. s.* feels fear, I. ii. 7. 42.

Ferdful, *adj.* timid, I. ii. 7. 43.

Ferdnesse, *s.* fear, terror, I. i. 1. 9; I. i. 1. 59; I. i. 2. 13; I. ii. 4. 102; I. iii. 1. 123; I. iii. 6. 126.

Fere, *s.* companion, comrade, I. i. 2. 123; I. i. 5. 128; Feres, *pl.* X. 88.

Fere, *s.* fire, VIII. 55; *on f.*, on fire, X. 4.

Ferforth, *adv.* far onward, I. ii. 10. 66; XXI. 37; far, XXI. 273.

Ferme, to, to farm, on hire, II. 325, 725; III. 83.

Fervence, *s.* ardour, VIII. 205; X. 130; XXII. 60.

Fervent, *adj.* severe, XVII. 4.

Fete, *adj.* neat, XXIV. 473.

Fettes, *pr. pl.* fetch, II. 471; Fet, *pp.* I. ii. 13. 40.

Fevers whyte, *s. pl.* attacks of lovelonging, XVIII. 41. See note.

Feyntyse, *s.* feigning, deceit, XVI. 385.

Fig; *a fig for,* XXIV. 685.

Figurait, *pp.* figured, imaged, XVII. 511.

Fikilnesse, *s.* fickleness, VI. 19.

Fil, *pt. s.* came to pass, IV. 43.

Filthes, *s. pl.* low women, V. 262.

Firre, *s.* fir, VIII. 73.

Fit, *s.* bout, XXIV. 984.

Flambing, *pres. pt.* flaming, X. 130.

Flaming, *adj.* flame-coloured, XXIV. 793. See note to l. 798.

Flanis, *s. pl.* arrows, XVII. 167.

Flash, *s.* sheaf, quiver (?), XVII. 167.

Flawe, *adj.* yellowish (?), XXIV. 782. See note.

Flebring, *s.* gossip (?), I. ii. 9. 54. Or is it an error for *fabling*?

Flees, *s.* fleece, V. 303 ; X. 132.

Flete, *v.* float, XXIV. 311.

Fley, *pt. s.* flew, XVIII. 219, 221.

Flickering, *adj.* wavering, I. ii. 5. 104.

Flitte, *v.* stir, I. i. 1. 79 ; move, I. i. 9. 69 ; change, XVI. 639 ; remove, XX. 489 ; *pr. pl.* go away, I. i. 7. 95 ; Flittinge, *pres. pt.* volatile, fading, I. ii. 8. 102.

Floon, *s. pl.* arrows, VIII. 468. See **Flanis.**

Florished, *pp.* garnished, III. 26.

Florisshinge, *s.* adornment, florid use, I. ii. 14. 33.

Flour, *s.* flower, chief, XXIV. 3 ; chastity, IV. 108.

Floured, *pp.* full of flower, VII. 48.

Flowe, *pp.* flown, II. 1306, 1311, 1344; come, I. i. 1. 128 ; gone, I. ii. 3. 69.

Flyte, *pr. pl.* chide, scold, II. 1022.

Foir-speikar, *s.* first speaker, XVII. 266.

Fol, *adj.* foolish, XVI. 651.

Folde, *pp.* enfolded, I. iii. 9. 76.

Fole, *s.* fool, II. 373 ; *voc.* XVIII. 126.

Fon, *v.* to be foolish, act foolishly, dote, XXIV. 458.

Fond, *pt. s.* found, VIII. 622.

Fongeth, *pr. pl.* take, II. 967.

Foole, *adj.* foolish, XIX. 1.

Foon, *s. pl.* foes, V. 466 ; VIII. 280.

For, *prep.* on account of, I. i. 3. 156; for fear of, II. 880; XVII. 118, 207.

For, *conj.* because, I. iii. 8. 22 ; III. 161.

Forayne, *adj.* foreign, alien, I. i. 2. 56 ; I. ii. 8. 97.

For-barre, *v.* bar up, repress, XVI. 259.

Forbed ; see **Forbit.**

Forbere, *v.* forbear, XXIV. 1341.

Forbit, *pr. s.* forbids, I. iii. 3. 71 ; Forbood, *pt. s.* forbade, II. 701 ; Forbed, II. 200 ; Forbode, *pp.* forbidden, I. ii. 2. 78 ; Forboden, *pp.* I. i. 7. 57.

Forbode, *s.* prohibition, II. 1315.

Forby, *adv.* by ; *passe forby,* to pass by, to take no notice, XXIV. 329.

Forcast, *pp.* cast away, VIII. 236.

Force ; *off.,* of necessity, XVII. 202 ; *no f.,* it is no matter, I. i. 1. 53.

Forcer, *s.* casket, shrine, XVI. 65.

Fordo, *v.* annul, III. 218 ; For-don, *pp.* destroyed, III. 431.

Fordoinge, *s.* annulling, I. iii. 8. 63 ; destruction, I. iii. 1. 11.

Fore-nempned, *pp.* aforenamed, I. ii. 9. 2.

Forfayture, *s.* trespass, IV. 133.

For-ferde, *pp. pl.* extremely afraid, I. i. 6. 135.

Forfeyt, *s.* injury, XVI. 789.

Forfeytest, 2 *pr. s.* offendest, I. ii. 14. 75.

Forged, *pp.* made, XXIV. 1165.

For-gerd, *pp.* ruined, destroyed, II. 1340. See Stratmann.

Forgete, *pp.* forgotten, XVI. 662.

Forgo, *v.* forgo, II. 319.

Forgoing, *s.* giving up, I. i. 8. 44.

Forgrowen, *pp.* overgrown, XX. 45.

Forjuged, *pp.* condemned, I. i. 3. 118 ; VIII. 274.

Forlane, *pp.* lit. for-lain, deflowered, XVII. 140.

Forleten, *pp.* forsaken, I. ii. 11. 45.

Forlyth, *pr. s.* lies with, IV. 108.

Forncast, *pp.* forecast, I. i. 6. 73.

For-quhy, *adv.* because, XVII. 53.

Fors, *s.* matter, III. 327 ; V. 273.

Forsake, *pp.* refused, rejected, XVI. 502.

For-shronk, *pp.* shrunken up, XX. 358.

Forsoken, *pt. pl.* forsook, V. 441.

Forswat, *pp.* covered with sweat, II. 14.

Forswonke, *pp.* worn with toil, II. 14.

Forswore, *pp.* forsworn, V. 310.

Fort, *adj.* strong, XIV. 4.

Forth, *adv.* forward ; *do f.,* go on, V. 327.

For-than, *adv.* therefore, II. 603.

Fortherer, *s.* Advancer, Promoter, XXIV. 1033.

Fortheringe, *s.* helping forward, preparing, I. ii. 3. 105.

Forthren, *v.* further, II. 1080 ; *pr. s.* advances, VIII. 384 ; *pp.* I. i. 9. 8.

Forthright, *adv.* immediately, XX. 439.

For-thy, *adv.* therefore, V. 264 ; *nat for-thy,* all the same, nevertheless, XVI. 3.

Fortunait, *adj.* afflicted by fortune, XVII. 79.

Fortuned, *pp.* directed by fortune, XIII. 73.

Forward, *adv.* afterwards, I. iii. 8. 146.

Forward, *s.* covenant, agreement, I. i. 9. 96 ; -warde, I. i. 3. 152.

For-weried, *pp.* tired out, XXI. 45.

Forweting, *s.* foreknowledge, I. iii. 2. 159 ; I. iii. 3. 78.

Forwot, *pr. s.* foresees, I. iii. 2. 155.
Foryete, *v.* forget, V. 423; Foryet, *pr. s.* II. 465; *pr. pl.* I. ii. 11. 136; *pp.* I. i. 2. 52.
Foryeting, *s.* forgetfulness, I. iii. 9. 86.
Foten, *pr. pl.* foot, dance, XXIV. 586.
Foul, *s.* a foul or evil fate, II. 60.
Foule, *adj.* ugly, VIII. 390.
Foulers, *gen.* fowler's, I. ii. 3. 55.
Foules, *s. pl.* birds, II. 83.
Foundement, *s.* foundation, I. i. 5. 111; I. ii. 14. 64.
Foyles, *s. pl.* leaves, X. 38.
Fra, *adv.* from, XVII. 7; from the time that, as soon as, XVII. 101.
Fraternitè, *s.* fraternity, III. 246.
Fraunchyse, *s.* freedom, XVI. 236, 364; liberality, XVI. 422; privileged place, VIII. 273.
Fraward, *adj.* froward, XVII. 352.
Fray, *ger.* to quarrel, XXIV. 682.
Frayne, *imp. s.* ask, III. 424; 1 *pt. s.* XXIV. 1275.
Freel-witted, *adj.* thin-witted, I. iii. 7. 57.
Freesed, *adj.* very cold, I. ii. 6. 105.
Freisit, *pt. s.* froze, XVI. 19.
Frele, *adj.* frail, VII. 22; XXII. 45.
Frend, *for* Fremd, *adj.* strange, II. 626.
Frended, *pp.* befriended, I. iii. 9. 109.
Freres, *s. pl.* friars, II. 1065; XXIV. 1097.
Fresshe, *ger.* to refresh, X. 61.
Fret, *s.* ornament, XX. 152.
Fret, *pp.* lit. adorned, XXIV. 124; hence, furnished, XIII. 80.
Frete, *pr. pl.* fret, annoy, XXIV. 940; Fretes, *pr. pl.* eat, devour, II. 151; Frettith, *pr. pl. (or s.),* vex, XXIV. 579.
Frith, *s.* coppice, XVI. 124.
Frivoll, *adj.* frivolous, hence, poor, base, XVII. 454.
Fro, *prep.* after, VIII. 233.
Fronsit, *pp.* wrinkled, XVII. 155.
Frounter, *s.* first attack, XVI. 176. See note.
Fruotif, *adj.* fruitful, X. 38.
Fructifying, *pres. pt.* fruit-producing, X. 133.
Fulfilled, *pp.* filled full, I. ii. 9. 54; V. 301.
Futur, *adj.* future, I. iii. 3. 177.
Fyle, *ger.* to file, to whet, VIII. 253, 441.
Fynding, *s.* food, II. 794.

Fyne, *s.* end, VIII. 343, 400; XVI. 594.
Fyned, *pp.* refined, I. ii. 4. 130.
Fynesse, *s.* fineness, I. ii. 12. 44; Fynenesse, I. ii. 12. 48.
Fyrles, *s.* without fire, X. 1:9.

Ga, *v.* go; *ga dy,* go and die, XVII. 203.
Gabbest, 2 *pr. s.* talkest idly, I. iii. 4. 171; Gabbeth, *pr. s.* lies, V. 142.
Gabbing, *s.* boasting, XVI. 342.
Gader, *ger.* gather, III. 301; *pp.* I. i. *pr.* 98.
Gaincome, *s.* coming again, XVII. 55.
Gair, *s.* gore, strip, XVII. 179.
Galeryes, *s. pl.* galleries, XXI. 165.
Galle, *s.* gall, bitterness, XIV. 26.
Gan, 1 *pt. s.* did, XXIV. 274.
Garmound, *s.* garment, XVII. 164.
Garnement, *s.* garment, I. iii. 7. 132.
Garnishing, *s.* ornamentation, XX. 143.
Garnisoun, *s.* garrison, XVII. 484; complete array, XVI. 175.
Gasteth, *pr. s.* frightens, I. ii. 7. 76.
Gayneth, *pr. s.* serves, helps, XVI. 623.
Geder, 2 *pr. pl.* gather, III. 191; *pres. pt.* collecting, II. 733.
Gemetrye, *s.* geometry, I. i. 1. 79.
Generabill, *adj.* that can be produced, created, XVII. 148, 171.
Generaltee, *s.* generality, V. 402.
Gentillesse, *s.* nobility, I. ii. 8. 94.
Gentilwoman, *s.* gentlewoman, XXI. 133.
Gentyled, *pp.* ennobled, I. ii. 8. 100.
Gere, *s.* dress, XX. 26; array, II. 651.
Gernere, *s.* garner, I. ii. 2. 27.
Geson, *adj.* scarce, XIV. 9.
Gesse, *pr. pl.* guess, make guesses, II. 170.
Gest, *s.* guest, I. ii. 5. 51; *pl.* II. 531.
Get, *pr. s.* gets, II. 275; Gete, *pp.* gotten, obtained, IV. 306; XVI. 67.
Gif, *pr. s. subj.* grant, XVII. 414.
Gif, *conj.* if, XVII. 64.
Gigges, *s. pl.* concubines, II. 759.
Giglot-lyk, *adj.* like a giglot, like a common woman, XVII. 83.
Ginne, 1 *pr. s.* begin, XI. 26; *pr. pl.* I. i. 3. 48.
Ginning, *s.* beginning, I. i. 3. 61; IX. 88, 253.
Glad, *adj.* pleasant, XX. 35.
Gladde, *ger.* to gladden, please, I. ii. 12. 86; *pp.* X. 99.

Gladsom, *adj.* pleasant, X. 43.

Glasse, *s.* glass, i.e. mirror, I. ii. I. 83.

Gledes, *s. pl.* kites, II. 1337.

Gleed, *s.* glowing coal, VIII. 231; Gledes, *pl.* I. iii. 7. 37.

Gleyve, *s.* glaive, sword, XXIV. 544.

Gliterande, *pres. pt.* glittering, I. ii. 13. 75; Glitterand, II. 134.

Glose, *s.* explanation, comment, II. 842.

Glose, *v.* explain (it) away, XXIV. 1260; *imp. s.* XXIV. 420; *pr. s.* glosses over (things), dissembles, XXII. 50; *pt. pl.* flattered, I. ii. 7. 105; *pp.* commented upon, II. 312.

Glosing, *s.* explaining, II. 1140; flattery, I. i. 6. 14; deception, I. i. 10. 58.

Glosours, *s. pl.* flatterers, I. i. 10. 11.

Gloton, *adj.* gluttonous, devouring, I. iii. 9. 65.

Glotoun, *s.* glutton, XII. 44.

Glowrand, *pres. pl.* glowering, lowering, XVII. 191.

Gnat, *s.* gnat, II. 459.

Gnawen, *pp.* gnawed, I. ii. 9. 113.

Godliheed, *error for* Godheed, *s.* godhead, I. i. 9. 117.

Goer, *s.* walker (on foot), I. ii. 1. 63.

Goinge, *s.* departure, I. i. 10. 110.

Gold, *s.* marigold, XXIV. 1437.

Gold-burned, *pp.* burnished like gold, VIII. 34.

Goldfinch, *s.* XX. 89; XXIV. 1368.

Gold-mastling, *s.* latten, II. 187. See note.

Gong, *s.* privy, II. 152.

Gonnen, *pt. pl.* began, VIII. 61; Gonne, VIII. 32.

Goodlihede, *s.* excellence, IX. 244.

Goodly, *adj.* courteous, XXI. 367.

Goodly, *adj. as s.* goodness, I. iii. 2. 99, 104.

Goodly, *adv.* well, justly, I. iii. 2. 106.

Gospel, *s.* gospel, truth, I. ii. 3. 38.

Gospell-book, *s.* gospel, II. 595.

Gostly, *adj.* spiritual, II. 1118.

Governaunce, *s.* guidance, VII. 139.

Governayl, *s.* steersman, II. 1078.

Governed, *pp.* steered, I. i. 1. 36.

Governeresse, *s.* mistress, XXII. 71.

Graffen, *pr. pl.* graft, I. ii. 3. 19; *pp.* I. ii. 3. 92; *gr. in,* become grafted into, I. i. *pr.* 6.

Grame, *s.* anger, II. 961; XXIV. 320; harm, XI. 55.

Grame, *v.* make angry, VI. 57.

Gramercy, *s.* great thanks, XX. 462.

Grane, *s.* grain, minute particular, XVII. 433. See note.

Graunteth, *pr. s.* admits (a thing), I. i. 7. 32.

Grave, *ger.* to engrave, V. 280; *pp.* buried, VII. 67; XVI. 171; engraved, I. iii. 8. 14.

Gray, *adj.* gray (referring to the Franciscans), XXIV. 1096.

Grede, 1 *pr. s.* exclaim, cry out, XVIII. 135.

Gree, *s.* rank, grade, I. iii. 1. 116; favour, II. 334; XXIV. 28; *to take in gr.,* to receive with favour, XVI. 842.

Greet-named, *adj.* renowned, I. i. 8. 112.

Greissis, *s. pl.* grasses, XVII. 425.

Grette, *pt. s.* greeted, X. 100; XXIV. 772.

Grevaunce, *s.* grievance, harm, XX. 311.

Greve, *v.* grieve, VI. 57; Greven, *error for* Greve, 1 *pr. s. subj.* grieve, XXIV. 928.

Greves, *s. pl.* groves, XX. 367.

Greyned, *pp.* formed like grain, I. ii. 2. 124.

Griffon, *s.* griffin, II. 86.

Gripe, *s.* grip, grasp, I. ii. 11. 71.

Grith, *s.* protection, II. 247.

Grobbed, *pp.* grubbed, dug round about, I. i. 5. 92.

Grome, *s.* groom, XXIV. 1433.

Grouf; *on gr.,* in a grovelling posture, XVII. 362. See Gruffe.

Grounde, *pp.* ground down, VIII. 225.

Grounded, *pp.* founded, I. ii. 5. 118.

Grucchen, *v.* murmur, XXIV. 960; grumble, II. 1164; *pr. s. subj.* may grumble (at), II. 886; murmur at, XXI. 47.

Gruffe, *adv.* grovelling, VIII. 167.

Grypen, *pr. pl.* grasp, II. 667.

Gubernatif, *adj.* governing, relating to government, political, I. i. 6. 120.

Guerdon, *s.* reward, I. i. 8. 136; VIII. 371; X. 6; XVI. 443.

Guerdoneth, *pr. s.* rewards, V. 97; *pp.* XXI. 591.

Guerdoning, *s.* reward, I. i. 8. 135.

Guerdonles, *adj.* without reward, VIII. 399.

Guyse, *s.* way, XXIV. 245.

Gydit, *pt. s.* guided, XVII. 205.

Gye, *v.* guide, VIII. 177; XIII. 55; preserve, VII. 79; direct, XXIV. 1250.

Gylour, *s.* traitor, XII. 74.

Gyse, *s.* manner, XXI. 9.

Gyte, *s.* mantle, XVII. 164, 178, 260. See note, p. 522.

Gyves, *s. pl.* fetters, II. 651.

Habirgeoun, *s.* coat of mail, XVII. 186.

Habit, *s.* friar's dress, III. 101 ; dress, I. ii. 11. 121.

Habounde, *adj.* abundant, X. 126.

Haboundeth, *pr. s.* abounds, I. i. 1. 75 ; I. ii. 2. 140.

Habundaunce, *s.* abundance, VI. 63.

Hace, *adj.* hoarse, XVII. 338, 445.

Haill, *adj.* whole, XVII. 73.

Hailsum, *adj.* wholesome, XVII. 249.

Hait, *adj.* hot, XVII. 29, 237.

Hale, *s.* the cry of 'haul,' II. 872.

Haleth, *pr s.* draws, I. i. 10. 104.

Halfe, *s.* side, direction, I. ii. 3. 47 ; *a goddes h.*, in God's name, I. ii. 4. 147.

Halke, *s.* nook, I. i. 3. 32 ; II. 489.

Halowe, *pr. pl.* consecrate, II. 277.

Halse, 1 *pr. s.* embrace, XXIV. 1289.

Halt, *pr. s.* holds, I. ii. 3. 12 ; VIII. 21 ; keeps, I. i. 1. 115.

Halte, *adj.* halt, VI. 43.

Halve, *s.* side, I. ii. 1. 7 ; part, I. iii. 7. 32 ; IV. 120 ; way, respect, I. ii. 12. 86.

Han, *pr. pl.* have, possess, I. ii. 5. 42 ; II. 601.

Hanche, *s.* haunch, hip, XVII. 187.

Handle, *ger.* to handle, feel, I. iii. 6. 52.

Hang, *pt. pl.* hung, XVII. 160.

Hap, *s.* chance, mere luck, I. i. 3. 121.

Happed, *pp.* chanced ; *was happed*, had such fortune, XX. 16.

Happy, *adj.* due to chance, casual, I. i. 3. 157 ; fortunate, V. 393.

Happyous, *adj.* chance, casual, I. i. 10. 29.

Harberowed, *pp.* harboured, lodged, I. ii. 2. 19.

Hard, *pt. s.* heard, XVII. 143.

Hardily, *adv.* certainly, XX. 234.

Hardyed, *pp.* emboldened, I. iii. 7. 30.

Hardyer, *adj.* more difficult, I. i. *pr.* 116.

Harlotry, *s.* evil conduct, II. 1100.

Harneys, *s.* defensive armour, I. i. 4. 45 ; XX. 242 ; Harnes, XVII. 186.

Harse, *s. perhaps an error for* harm, I. i. 3. 158.

Hart, *s.* hart, I. ii. 11. 43.

Hasel, *s.* hazel-bush, I. iii. 6. 5.

Hat, *pr. s.* is called, II. 454.

Hate, *v.* hate ; hence, put force upon, XVI. 729.

Hate, 1 *pr. s.* command, bid, XXI. 689. (Better, *hote.*)

Haunce, *pr. pl.* enhance, advance, VIII. 430.

Hautayn, *adj.* haughty, I. iii. 6. 89.

Havelesse, *adj.* indigent. as one that possesses nothing, XVI. 605.

Haw, *adj.* wan, dull of colour, XVII. 257 ; livid, XVII. 340.

Hawe, *s.* haw, II. 304 ; *setle nat an h.*, care not a haw, I. i. 7. 100.

Hayles, *s. pl.* hailstorms, I. iii. 5. 22.

Hayne, *s.* hatred, dislike, I. i. *pr.* 102 ; I. i. 7. 43.

Hecht, 1 *pt. s.* promised, XVII. 23 ; *pt. s.* was named, XVII. 213.

Hede-taking, *s.* taking heed, I. ii. 4. 67.

Heep, *s.* crowd, VI. 43.

Heer, *s.* hair, I. ii. 4. 22 (see note) ; XIII. 84.

Heerdes, *s. pl.* herds, I. iii. 3. 44.

Hegge, *s.* hedge, XX. 54, 66.

Heidit, *pp.* headed, XVII. 168.

Heil, *s.* health (E. *heit*), XVII. 334.

Heird, *prob. for* Heir it, hear it, XVII. 415. Cf. Lowl. Sc. *dude*, do it (Jamieson).

Heklit, *pp.* drawn forward over, XVII. 244. Cf. Icel. *hekla, hökull*.

Helde, *v.* hold, II. 704 ; Helden, 3 *pr. s. subj.* might hold, XXIV. 347 (ungrammatical).

Helded, *pp.* inclined, poured out, I. i. 4. 19.

Hele, *s.* health, XXIV. 193, 666 ; salvation, IV. 343 ; VII. 24.

Heledest, *pr. s.* didst conceal, I. i. 7. 117 ; *pp.* hidden, I. i. 8. 128 (obviously a false reading ; read *deled*, distributed).

Helen, *v.* (to) heal, I. ii. 11. 23 ; *pt. s.* healed ; *h. with his hele*, healed his heel with, I. i. 5. 45.

Heles, *s. pl.* heels, IV. 113.

Hell-yates, *s. pl.* hell-gates, II. 419.

Henne, *adv.* hence, XVIII. 102.

Hens-forward ; *from h.*, from henceforth, I. ii. 10. 144.

Henshmen, *s. pl.* henchmen, XX. 252.

Hente, *v.* catch, I. i. *pr.* 12 ; seize, I. i. 1. 12 ; *pr. s.* catches, I. iii. 4. 115 ; *pt. pl.* caught, seized, V. 257 ; *pp.* caught, II. 555 ; seized, XXIV. 1144 ; gained, I. i. 3. 121.

Heped, *pp.* heaped, i. e. great, V. 407.

Heraud, *s.* herald, XVI. 258 ; *pl.* XX. 233.

Herber, *s.* arbour, VIII. 125, 127 ; XVI. 191 ; XX. 48 ; XXI. 48.

Herbergere, *s.* harbinger, officer who provides apartments, XXI. 268, 389.

Herberowed, *pp.* lodged, I. ii. 2. 34.

Herberwe, *s.* harbour, X. 35 ; Herbery, shelter, XVII. 403.

Herdes, *s. pl.* shepherds, II. 339.

Here, *s.* hair, XX. 332.

Here, *pron.* her, V. 70, 71 ; IX 111.

Here-toforn, *adv.* formerly, I. i. 8. 6.

Hernes, *s. pl.* corners, II 489.

Herre, *s.* hinge ; *out of h.*, off the hinge, IV. 185. A.S. *heorr.*

Herted, *pp.* hardened, strengthened, I. iii. 7. 91.

Hertely, *adj.* dear to my heart, XI. 23 ; Hertly, severe, VIII. 139.

Hest, *s.* promise, VIII. 319 ; Heste, VIII. 571 ; command, III. 106 ; *pl.* commands, II. 209 ; V. 354.

Hete, *s.* heat, XXIV. 1379.

Hete, *v.* be called (*probably an error for* hote), I. ii. 6. 86. See Hote.

Heth, *s.* heath, XXIV. 755.

Hethenesse, *s.* pagan country, VI. 17.

Heve, *s.* the cry of 'heave,' II. 872. See note.

Heven-kay, *s.* the key of heaven, II. 865.

Hevye, *ger.* to be sorrowful, I. i. 4. 4.

Hewe, *ger.* to hew, IX. 158.

Hewmound, *s.* helmet, XVII. 186.

Hey, *interj.* hey ! II. 890.

Heyr, *s.* heir, successor, XVIII. 180 (see note) ; *pl.* III. 207.

Highnes, *s.* exaltation, II. 116.

Hight, *pr. s.* is named, XXI. 169 ; 2 *pr. pl.* XXII. 23 ; *do h.*, are called, XXIV. 145 ; 1 *pt. s.* promised, XXIV. 1319 ; *pp.* promised, VIII. 319 ; IX. 97.

Hildeth, *pr. s.* pours out, I. ii. 1. 13.

Hing, *pt. s.* hung, XXIV. 1201 ; Hingen, *pt. pl.* I. i. 4. 36 ; *pres. pt.* hanging, XXIV. 139. See Hong.

Hit, *pr. s.* hits, XVIII. 203.

Ho, *s.* proclamation, XXIV. 270. See note.

Hogges, *s. pl.* hogs, I. i. *pr.* 121.

Hoir, *adj.* lit. hoary, XVII. 163 ; old, feeble, XVII. 338, 445. See Hore.

Hold, *s.* fortress, II. 475.

Holden, *pp.* beholden, I. ii. 4. 122 ; compelled, I. iii. 7. 120 ; Holde, *pp.* bound, IV. 7.

Hole, *adj.* whole, IV. 226 ; XVIII. 7 ; entire, XXIV. 302 ; trustworthy, XIII. 39.

Hole, *adv.* wholly, II. 212 ; XXIV. 322.

Holownesse, *s.* hollow vault, concave, I. ii. 9. 109.

Holpen, *pp.* helped, I. ii. 12. 23.

Holtes, *s. pl.* woods, copses, VIII. 119 ; IX. 47.

Honde, *s.* hand, IV. 384.

Hong, *v.* hang, XX. 245 ; Hongen, *pr. pl.* IV. 263 ; Hong, *pt. s.* hung, II. 8 ; Honged, *pp.* hung on, II. 1042. See Hing.

Hony, *s.* honey, I. i. 2. 46 ; I. ii 9. 38 ; XXIV. 1040.

Honyed, *adj.* full of honey, I. ii. 14. 24.

Hony-soukels, *s. pl.* honeysuckles, I. iii. 6. 6.

Hookes, *s. pl.* hooks, I. i. 10. 105.

Hool. *adj. as adv.* wholly, XVI. 234 ; in full, XXI. 628.

Hoolly, *adv.* wholly, XXII. 14.

Hoolsom, *adj.* wholesome, VIII. 14 ; X. 36 ; XX. 6.

Hoomlinesse, *s.* plainness of speech, V. 132.

Hoot, *adj.* hot, VIII. 136.

Hoppen, *pr. pl.* dance, II. 872.

Hore, *adj. pl.* hoary, old, hence bare (as trees in winter), VIII. 119 ; IX. 47. See Hoir.

Horisons, *s. pl.* prayers, I. iii. 9. 92.

Horn, *s.* horn ; *give us an horn*, scoff at us, XXIV. 1390.

Horowe, *adj.* dirty, II. 1097.

Hors, *s. pl.* horses, XX. 201, 274.

Hors-harneys, *s.* horse-trappings, XX. 218, 226, 237.

Hospitall, *s.* hospital, XVII. 382.

Hostel, *s.* lodging, I. i. 2. 57

Hote, *v.* be called, I. ii. 4. 139 ; Hoten, have a name, XVIII. 185 ; Hote, *pt. s.* was named, XXIV. 159 ; *pp.* called, XXIV. 741.

Houge, *adj.* huge, great, II. 1109.

Houres, *s. pl.* services, as matins, &c., XVIII. 70. See note.

Houselin, *ger.* to receive the eucharist, II. 1211.

Houten, *pr. pl.* hoot, shout, II. 872.

How, *adv.* however, XXIV. 207.

How, *adj.* hollow, XVII. 157.

Howsinge, *s.* building of houses, III. 296.

Hude, *s.* hood, XVII. 244.

Huisht, *adj.* silent, I. ii. 7. 122.
See below.

Huissht, *interj.* whist! peace! I. i. 5.
90.

Hulfere, *s.* holly, VIII. 129.

Hy, *s.* haste; *in hy*, XVII. 361;
XXIV. 268, 698.

Hye, *v. refl.* hasten, I. iii. 5. 71; IX.
· 33; *imp. pl. refl.* XXI. 244; *pr. s.*
I. iii. 4. 98.

Hyly, *adv.* highly, IX. 185.

Hynd, *s.* hind, I. ii. 11. 43.

Hyne, *s.* hind, farm-labourer, II. 26.

I-cleped, *pp.* called, II. 73.

Ideot, *s.* idiot, I. i. 9. 87; *pl.* I. ii.
1. 94.

Idole, *s.* image, XVII. 507.

Ilke, *adj.* same, I. i. 3. 80; I. i. 9. 62.

Impedimentes, *s. pl.* hindrances, I.
ii. 6. 96.

Imperciable, *adj.* impervious, not to
be pierced, I. i. 4. 45.

Imperfite, *adj.* imperfect, III. 186,
199.

Importáble, *adj.* unbearable, I. i. 1.
108; V. 26.

Impossible, *s.* a thing impossible, I.
ii. 4. 152; Impossible, VII. 12.

Imprentit, *pp.* imprinted, XVII. 508.

Impression, *s.* impression, I. ii. 9. 32.

In principió, first verse of St. John's
gospel, III. 136.

Inchaungeable, *adj.* unchangeable,
I. i. *pr.* 52.

Inclose, *pp.* included, I. iii. 4. 164.

Incommoditè, *s.* inconvenience, I. iii.
8. 141.

Inconvenience, *s.* unfitness, I. iii. 4.
139; mistake, I. ii. 4. 153.

Inconvenient, *adj.* unfitting, I. iii.
9. 12.

Ind, *adj.* blue, XXIV. 78; Inde, *pl.*
VIII. 127.

Indifferent, *adj.* impartial, I. i. 7. 34.

Inductatife, *adj.* capable of being
reduced, I. ii. 13. 48.

Infame, *s.* ill fame, disgrace, I. i. 8.
49; ill report, I. i. 6. 70.

Infected, *pp.* impaired, XXIV. 1053.

In-fere, *adv.* together, II. 1212; V.
458; XVIII. 78, 263, 273; XXI.
407; fully, XXI. 602.

Inflat, *pp.* inflated, blown, XVII. 463.

Infortune, *s.* misfortune, IV. 49.

Inhaunsing, *s.* enhancing, II. 112.

Inke, *s.* ink, I. i. *pr.* 15.

Inly, *adv.* inwardly, extremely, XX.
113; very, XXI. 515, 747.

In-middes, *prep.* amid, XXI. 55.

Inne, *s.* inn, lodging, II. 977.

Inne, *adv.* within, in, XVIII. 62.

Innominable, *adj.* unnameable, I. i.
9. 55; I. ii. 4. 53.

Inobedience, *s.* disobedience, XXIII.
12.

Inpossession, *s.* an error for 'imposition,' i.e. the imposing of a
name, I. ii. 4. 141. See the note.

Input, *pp.* placed in, implanted, I. ii.
2. 120.

Inseër, *s.* investigator, looker into, I.
iii. 1. 141; I. iii. 9. 91; reader,
I. iii. 1. 25; *pl.* I. ii. 1. 103.

Insight, *s.* perception, I. ii. 6. 96.

Inspiracion, *s.* inspiration, I. ii. 1.
13.

Insuffisance, *s.* insufficiency, I. i. 9.
13.

Insuffysaunt, *adj.* insufficient, I. i.
4. 63.

Intent, *pr. s.* means, XXIV. 1370.

Intere, *adj.* entire, sincere, XIII. 31.

In-to, *prep.* in, XVII. 212.

Intrucioun, *s.* intrusion, I. i. 1. 17.

Inwit, *s.* conscience, I. i. 4. 17.

I-paynted, *pp.* painted, II. 135.

I-perled, *pp.* adorned with pearls, II.
158.

Ipocryte, *s.* hypocrite, XII. 65.

Irrecuperable, *adj.* irrecoverable, I.
ii. 1. 34.

Is, *pron.* them, II. 941.

Issewe, *s.* issue, flow, XVI. 52.

Itinerarie, *s.* road-book, guide, X.
64.

Ivorie, *s.* ivory, XI. 3.

Jangeling, *adj.* prattling, vain, I. iii.
6. 89.

Jangle, *ger.* to prattle, XVI. 744;
pr. s. prates, II. 791; XVI. 333.

Janglers, *s. pl.* praters, I. i. 4. 64.

Jangles, *s. pl.* idle words, I. ii. 9. 93.

Janglinge, *s.* discord, I. ii. 9. 52;
gossip, I. i. 5. 19; *pl.* babblings, I.
ii. 14. 10.

Jape, *s.* jest, I. i. 10. 87; XXI. 348;
pl. XXII. 53.

Jay, *s.* jay, I. i. *pr.* 30; II. 791.

Jeuse, *s.* juice, I. iii. 5. 115.

Jocounde, *adj.* jocund, pleasant, V.
475.

Joleyvinge, *pres. pt.* cheering, I. i.
1. 126.

Jolif, *adj.* happy, XXIV. 177; spruce,
XXIV. 473.

Jonesse, *s.* Youth, XXII. 69.

Jorned, 1 *pt. s.* journeyed, XXIV. 72.

Journey, *s.* day's work, I. i. 5. 31.

Jowall, s jewel, XVII. 521.

Joynt, pp. as s. a thing closed, II. 220.

Jumpere, v. jumble together; conne j., know how to mix, I. i. pr. 30.

Jupardye, s. risk, peril, VIII. 475.

Juparting, s. jeoparding, risking, VIII. 419.

Jurisdiccioun, s. jurisdiction, VIII. 271.

Justes, s. pl. jousts, tournaments, XX. 282.

Justificacion, s. justification, I. ii. 13. 88.

Juventè, s. youth, VII. 11.

Juyse, s. penalty, XVI. 622.

Kalends, s. the beginning, VII. 146.

Kele, ger to cool, XXIV. 775.

Kembe, pr. pl. comb, II. 306; Kemmit, pp. XVII. 222.

Kend, pp. known, XVII. 380.

Kendillis, pr. s. kindles, takes fire, XVII. 30.

Kepe, s. heed, XVIII. 207; I take no kepe, I take no heed, XVI. 267.

Kepen, 1 pr. s. (for Kepe), take care, XXIV. 684.

Kepten, pp. (false form, for Kept), kept, XXIV. 526.

Kerve, v. cut, XII. 121; pr. pl. V. 245.

Kidde, pt. s. shewed, V. 314; Kid, pp. made known, I. iii. 5. 70.

Kind, s. nature, XIII. 80.

Kinde, adj. natural, XXII. 29.

Kinges of armes, s. pl. kings-at-arms, XX. 220.

Kinrede, s. kindred, I. ii. 2. 113; V. 2; pl. III. 8.

Kinrest, s. rest for the people, time of rest, I. i. 5. 103. See the note.

Kirk, s. church, XVII. 117.

Kite, s. kite, XXIV. 1416.

Kith, s. native country, I. i. pr. 123.

Knette, v. knit, weave, suggest, I. i. 7. 39; Knitten, pr. pl. accept, lit. knit together, I. ii. 5. 34; imp. s. knit, fasten, XI. 17; pp. knit, IX. 171; Knit, pp. chosen, I. ii. 8. 62.

Knitting, s. choosing friends, I. ii. 8. 19.

Knot, s. knot, a fanciful term for the bliss for which a man strives, the summum bonum, I. ii. 4. 140.

Knowers, s. pl. men who know (it), I. ii. 8. 28.

Knowing, s. knowledge, I. ii. 9. 17.

Knowlegeden, pt. pl. acknowledged, I. i. 6. 157.

Knowleginge, s. knowledge, I. i. 8. 99; meaning, I. i. pr. 29.

Knyf, s. knife, II. 241.

Kyme, s. wretch, II. 695. See note.

Kynde, adj. kindred, I. i. 6. 49.

Kyndely, adj. natural, I. i. pr. 36; I. ii. 3. 52.

Kythen, v. (to) manifest, V. 224; imp. pl. shew, VI. 42.

Laborious, adj. full of endeavour, VII. 69.

Lacche, ger. to seize, grasp, I. i. 3. 51.

Lace, s. tie, bond, XI. 17.

Laced, pp. bound, I. i. 3. 144.

Lache, 2 pr. s. subj. loosen (it), let go, or perhaps, turn coward, relax, I. ii. 14. 83. F. lâcher.

Lacke, v. fail, III. 222.

Lacked, pp. dispraised, I. i. 8. 104; I. i. 10. 83.

Lacking, s. blaming, I. ii. 8. 33; dispraise, I. iii. 2. 112.

Ladde, 2 pt. pl. led, I. i. 3. 76; pp. IX. 219.

Lade, pp. laden, XX. 305.

Ladels, s. pl. cross-paths, by-paths, I. i. 3. 42. (See note, p. 456.)

Laft, pt. s. remained, XX. 364.

Lak, s. reproof, blame, reproach, XVII. 276.

Lake, s. linen cloth, X. 70.

Lakken, pr. pl. blame, V. 192.

Lamentacious, adj. mournful, I. i. 1. 128.

Lanes, s. pl. pathways, tracks, I. i. 3. 41.

Langoring, adj. full of langour, swooning, I. ii. 14. 59.

Lapwinges, s. pl. lapwings, II. 1339.

Larder, s. larder (i.e. slaughter), I. ii. 14. 13.

Large, adj. loose, too free, IX. 157; liberal, XVI. 455.

Large, s.; at hir l., at freedom, free, VIII. 329; at your l., IX. 15.

Largesse, s. bounty, II. 511; XVIII. 157; XXI. 318.

Larson, s. larceny, II. 323.

Las, adj. pl. less, XXI. 439.

Lasse, adj. less, I. ii. 9. 77; IV. 109.

Lasshed, pt. pl. burst, ran forth, flowed, I. i. 6. 71.

Last, pt. pl. lasted, XX. 288.

Lat, adj. late, behindhand, II. 457.

Lattit, pp. hindered, XVII. 27.

Lauch (for Leuch ?), pt. s. laughed, XVII. 231 (or infin. to laugh).

Laudest, 2 pr. s. praisest, I. i. 10. 76.

Laughande, *pres. pt.* laughing, I. i. 1. 47.

Laundě, *s.* glade, VIII. 120; XVIII. 61.

Laureat, *adj.* made of laurel, X. 68.

Laurer, *s.* laurel, VIII. 65; IX. 238; XX. 158; -tree, XX. 109.

Lauriole, *s.* laurel crown, X. 73.

Laverok, *s.* lark, X. 82.

Lawde, *s.* praise, XXIV. 1332.

Lawest, *adj.* lowest, XVII. 298.

Lawfully, *adv.* in a low tone, XVII. 312.

Lawn, *s.* lawn covering, lawn kerchief, XVII. 423.

Lay, *s.* lea, XVIII. 285.

Lay, *s.* lay, song, I. iii. 7. 53.

Lay, *s.* law, faith, belief, V. 433.

Lay-fee, *s.* fee belonging to laymen, II. 686, 741.

Layser, *s.* leisure, XI. 41.

Lazarous, *s.* leprous person, leper, XVII. 343, 531.

Leche, *s.* physician, I. iii. 7. 79; X. 42.

Lechecraft, *s.* healing, I. iii. 9. 69.

Lectorn, *s.* lectern, XXIV. 1382.

Leed, *s.* lead, II. 160.

Leef, *adj.* lief, dear, longed for, XXI. 694.

Leefful, *adj.* permissible, VII. 75.

Leefly, *adj.* permissible, I. ii. 14. 8.

Leel, *adj.* loyal, II. 755.

Lees, *s.* lie, V. 444.

Leet, *pt. s.* caused; *leet do crye*, caused to be cried or proclaimed, IV. 174.

Leffer, *adj.* liefer, XXIV. 1130.

Lefful, *adj.* permissible, I. iii. 2. 51; Leful, I. i. 3. 129.

Lefte, 1 *pt. s.* remained, V. 443; XXI. 190; abandoned, IV. 342; Leften, *error for* Left, *pp.* left, XXIV. 1166.

Lege, *adj.* liege, III. 10.

Legeaunce, *s.* allegiance, VIII. 551.

Legende, Legend, V. 316. See note.

Legge, *v.* allege, XXIV. 1065; Legen, *pr. pl.* allege, I. i. 7. 73; Leged, *pp.* alleged (to be), I. ii. 2. 103.

Legistres, *s. pl.* lawyers, I. ii. 2. 69.

Leid, *s.* lead, XVII. 155.

Leid, *s.* person, man, XVII. 449.

Leif, *ger.* to live, XVII. 384.

Leir, *ger.* to learn, XVII. 479.

Lemes, *s. pl.* rays, X. 116.

Lemman, *s.* leman, II. 883; *gen.* II. 338.

Lene, *pr. s. subj.* may lend, I. iii. 9. 78.

Lene, *adj.* lean, weak, V. 408.

Leneth, *pr. s.* leans, inclines, I. ii. 6. 53.

Lenger, *adv.* the longer, XVI. 678.

Lengest, *adv.* longest, I. ii. 9. 86.

Lent, *s.* spring, XVII. 5.

Lepre, *s.* leprosy, IV. 349.

Lere, *ger.* to learn, XX. 229; *pp.* learned, II. 754.

Lerne, *ger.* to learn, to be taught, XVI. 535; 2 *pr. pl.* teach, I. i. 4. 41; *pp.* instructed, XVI. 635.

Lese, *ger.* to lose, II. 591; IV. 295; 2 *pr. s.* I. i. 8. 131; *pr. s.* XVI. 388; *pr. pl.* XVI. 588; *imp. pl.* VII. 87.

Lesers, *s. pl.* losers, I. i. 10. 62.

Lesing, *s.* losing, loss, I. ii. 7. 65; I. ii. 10. 120.

Lesing, *s.* falsehood, lie, XVIII. 238; XXI. 263; XXIV. 422; *pl.* I. i. 6. 159; VIII. 421.

Leste, *pt. s.* lasted (*or*, might last), I. i. 5. 32.

Let, *pr. s.* letteth, lets, VIII. 464.

Let, *pr. s.* hinders, I. i. 1. 119.

Let, *pr. s.* leads, I. iii. 9. 11.

Lete, *v.* let go, spare, let alone, XX. 215; Let, *v.* pretend, XVI. 583; Lete, 2 *pr. pl.* allow to be, III. 362; Let commaunde, caused men to command, XXIV. 296.

Let-games, *s. pl.* hinderers of sport, I. i. 3. 124; I. i. 4. 61.

Lethy, *adj.* weak, I. iii. 7. 101.

Lette, *v.* hinder, III. 289; VIII. 251; *ger.* to prevent, II. 1189; *pp.* hindered, I. i. 8. 100.

Letting, *s.* hindrance, I. i. 9. 114.

Lettours, *s. pl.* hinderers, I. i. 3. 126.

Lettred, *pp.* learned, XXIV. 302.

Leude, *adj.* ignorant, I. i. *pr.* 16.

Leudnesse, *s.* ignorance, want of skill, I. i. *pr.* 19.

Leve, *s.* belief, II. 1135.

Leve, *adj. pl.* dear ones, IV. 354.

Leve, *v.* leave, abandon, XVI. 534; *pr. s.* leaves off, ceases, I. ii. 5. 46; remains, I. ii. 4. 7; is left, XVI. 668; *pp.* left, I. i. 7. 22; neglected, I. ii. 9. 191.

Leven, *ger.* to believe, II. 895; V. 56; *v.* I. ii. 13. 130; 1 *pr. s.* XVI. 710; *imp. s.* XVIII. 237; *pp.* I. i. 4. 69.

Lever, *adv.* sooner, rather, I. ii. 10. 71; VIII. 535.

Leves, *s. pl.* leaves, XXIV. 519.

Lewed, *adj.* ignorant, II. 146, 970; Lewde, unskilful, XIX. 1; ill-omened, XVIII. 50.

Leyser, *s.* leisure, V. 129; XIX. 13; Leysar, I. i. 2. 43.

Lich, *adj.* like, similar, I. i. 5. 42; II. 303; XXIV. 696; Liche, *pl.* alike, I. i. 5. 46.

Liche, *adv.* alike, XXI. 117.

Liere, *s.* Liar, XXIV. 1242.

Lift, *adj.* left, I. i. 1. 111; I. ii. 1. 6.

Lige, *adj.* liege, VI. 9.

Ligeaunce, *s.* allegiance, I. i. 6. 165; VI. 37.

Ligge, *ger.* to lie, I. ii. 6. 90; Lig, *v.* II. 4; 2 *pr. pl.* lodge, III. 81; *pr. pl.* lie still, III. 181.

Liggen, 2 *pr. pl.* lay, III. 46. (Incorrectly used.)

Light, *adj.* easy, IV. 218; Lighter, *comp.* I. ii. 12. 202.

Light, *s.* lightning, XIV. 37. See note. As 'lightning' is certainly meant, a better reading would be *leyt.*

Lighte, *pr. s. subj.* may alight, alight, X. 83; *pt. s.* I. i. 2. 5.

Lightinge, *pres. pt.* shining; *suche lightinge,* giving such a kind of light, I. ii. 6. 101.

Lightles, *adj.* deprived of light, I. i. 1. 20.

Lightly, *adv.* easily, I. ii. 5. 121; XVI. 426.

Lightsom, *adj.* light, XVI. 405; pleasant, X. 30.

Lignes (?), I. ii. 3. 10; see note, p. 467.

Limitacion, *s.* boundary, limit, III. 85.

Limitors, *s. pl.* friars begging within a fixed limit, III. 83.

Limmes, *s. pl.* limbs, IV. 260; XXIV. 228.

Linet, *s.* linnet, XXIV. 1408.

Lipper, *adj.* belonging to lepers, XVII. 438; leprous, XVII. 372.

Lipper-leid, *s.* leper-folk, XVII. 451.

Lisse, *s.* comfort, alleviation, I. ii. 14. 3.

Lissen, *v.* ease, relieve, XVIII. 245; *pp.* I. iii. 6. 13.

List, *pr. s.* is pleased, I. i. 3. 35; XVI. 455; *pr. s.* prefers, likes, XVII. 256; List, 2 *pr. pl.* are (you) pleased, XVI. 276; *pr. s. subj.* may please, IX. 63; *pt. s. subj.* (it) should please, IX. 255.

Listed, *pp.* listened, IX. 29.

Listis, *s. pl.* borders, XVII. 179.

Living, *pres. pt.* living, existing, (*but perhaps an error for* leming, i.e. shining), X. 24. See note.

Livinges, *s. pl.* modes of life (?), I. ii. 1. 119 (*perhaps an error for* livinge).

Lodemanage, *s.* pilotage, steering, XIII. 61.

Lodesterre, *s.* l<de-star, guiding star, XVI. 257.

Loënge, *s.* praise, IV. 371.

Logge, *s.* lodge, VIII. 585.

Logged, *pp.* lodged, I. i. 2. 18.

Logging, *s.* lodging, abode, XVI. 82.

Loke, *ger.* to look, I. iii. 6. 97; *pr. s. subj.* let (him) see, II. 834; Lokeden, *pt. pl.* looked, I. i. 7. 105.

Lokers, *s. pl.* onlookers, I. i. 5. 71.

Lollers, *s.* Lollards, II. 73, 88.

Londe, *s.* country, II. 1138.

Londlees, *adj.* landless, II. 73.

Lond-tillers, *s. pl.* farmers, I. i. 3. 32.

Longeth, *pr. s.* belongs, I. ii. 9. 78; II. 965; XVI. 53; is suitable, XXIV. 408; *pt. s.* XXI. 518.

Loos, *s.* praise, I. i. 7. 26; fame, VI. 8; *badde l.,* ill fame, I. i. 6. 179.

Lordlych, *adj.* lordly, II. 1052.

Lore, *s.* teaching, I. i. 4. 48; IX. 220.

Lore, *pp.* lost, II. 731, 986.

Lorell, *s.* abandoned wretch, II. 374, 1138.

Lorn, *pp.* lost, I. i. 4. 28; I. ii. 3. 77.

Lose, *s.* praise; *out of lose,* to my dispraise, IX. 234.

Losed, *pp.* praised, I. i. 8. 113, 126.

Losel, *s.* abandoned wretch, I. ii. 2. 49.

Losengeour, *s.* flatterer, I. ii. 2. 52.

Losengery, *s.* flattery, II. 635; III. 202.

Lothe, *adj.* hated, I. i. 3. 37; *pl.* hostile ones, IV. 354.

Lother, *adj.* more loath, XVIII. 160.

Lough, *pt. s.* laughed, XXI. 279.

Loupe, *s.* a hard knot in a gem, X. 92, 93. See note.

Loute, *v.* bow down, II. 181; *pt. pl.* I. i. 10. 10.

Loutinges, *s.* salutations, respects, I. i. 5. 116.

Loveday, *s.* day of reconciliation, I. i. 2. 95.

Lowe, *s.* blaze; *on a l.,* in a blaze, V. 61.

Lowed, *pp.* set low, put down, I. iii. 6. 11.

Lucerne, *s.* lantern, XIX. 23; XXIV. 632.

Lucifer, the morning-star, IX. 115.

Luifferis, *s. pl.* lovers, XVII. 140.

Luifis, *gen. sing.* love's, of love, XVII. 22.

Medlest, *pr. s.* takest part, interferest, I. i. 7. 111; *pp.* mingled, I. ii. 13. 76; I. iii. 7. 33; XVI. 657.

Medle-tree, *s.* medlar, XX. 86, 442.

Medlinge, *pres. pt.* meddling, I. ii. 10. 51; mixture, I. ii. 1. 92; interference, I. i. 6. 77.

Meedful, *adj.* meritorious, III. 178.

Mees, *s. pl.* dwellings, houses, V. 334. O. F. *mes, meis, meix,* 'ferme . . . habitation, démeure'; Godefroy.

Meid, *s.* reward, recompense, XVII. 277.

Melancolious, *adj.* melancholy, XX. 314.

Meldrop, *s.* hanging drop of mucus, XVII. 158.

Meles, *s. pl.* meals, II. 1036.

Mell, *v.* meddle, II. 857.

Memorial, *s.* memory, XXIV. 876.

Memour, *s.* memory, XVII. 465.

Mene, *adj.* intermediate, I. ii. 12. 56; middle, XXIV. 652.

Mene, *s.* mean, intermediate, III. 162; mean, I. iii. 5. 53; middle course, III. 170; mediator, I. ii. 2. 100; method, way, I. i. *pr.* 54; moderation (?), I. ii. 10. 43.

Mening, *s.* intention, XVI. 393; *pl.* I. i. 8. 30.

Merchande, *s.* (*perhaps*) merchants' meeting. VII. (*title*).

Merciable, *adj.* merciful, II. 96; XXII. 62; XXIV. 645.

Merciably, *adv.* mercifully, I. iii. 9. 73.

Merle, *s.* blackbird, XVII. 430.

Mervayl, *s.* marvel, XXI. 648.

Mery, *adj.* pleasant, I. ii. 9. 131.

Mes, *s.* dish, course of meats, XVI. 154.

Meschaunce, *s.* misfortune, VII. 179.

Mescreaunce, *s.* unbelief, VI. 50.

Mesurabelly, *adv.* with moderation, XVI. 248.

Mesurable, *adj.* moderate, V. 350.

Mesure, *imp. s.* moderate, X. 119.

Mete-borde, *s.* dining-table, I. ii. 2. 61.

Metely, *adj.* moderate, i. e. of middle height, XXI. 79.

Metricians, *s. pl.* men skilled in metre, XXIV. 30.

Mevable, *adj.* moveable; i. e. (more) moveable, XIV. 36.

Meve, *ger.* to move, I. i. 1. 109; *pr. s.* moves, V. 432; 2 *pt. pl.* discussed, I. iii. 5. 158.

Mevinges, *s. pl.* motions, I. ii. 9. 45.

Meward; *to m.,* towards me, i. ii. 9. 123.

Mewe, *s.* mew, coop; *in mewe,* under restraint, XVI. 338.

Mewet, *adj.* mute; *in m.,* in a tone unheard, to myself, XXIV. 148.

Meynall, *adj.* belonging to their household, domestic, II. 322. See note. p. 487.

Meynt, *pp.* mingled, VIII. 229.

Meyny, *s.* household, I. ii. 5. 52; crowd, I. i. 7. 104; followers, I. i. 6. 145.

Michel, *adv.* much, V. 142.

Middis, *s.* midst, XVII. 5.

Midle-erth, *s.* the earth, I. iii. 1. 65.

Milk-whyt, *adj.* milk-white, XXIV. 787.

Minde, *s.* remembrance, XI. 42.

Ming, *imp. s.* mix, XVII. 613; *pp.* 236.

Mirour, *s.* mirror, V. 179.

Mirthed, *pp.* cheered, I. ii. 3. 98.

Mis, *adj.* wrong, I. ii. 5. 111; II. 1197; VIII. 603; XXII. 61; *pl.* things that are wrong, I. ii. 9. 84.

Miscary, *v.* go astray, fail, I. ii. 14. 98; *pp.* gone astray, I. ii. 4. 106.

Mischaunce, *s.* a curse, ill luck, II. 1168; III. 423.

Mischese, 2 *pr. pl.* choose amiss, VII. 187.

Mischeves, *s.* diseases, X. 54.

Misclepinge, *s.* misnaming, I. i. 10. 46.

Miscorden, *pr. pl.* disagree, I. ii. 14. 27.

Miscreants, *s. pl.* unbelievers, IV. 268.

Misese, *s.* lack of ease, misery, I. ii. 5. 21.

Misesy, *adj.* uneasy, I. i. 3. 150.

Misglosed, *pp.* misinterpreted, I. ii. 1. 59.

Misgo, *pp.* gone astray, II. 756.

Misgoing, *s.* error, I. ii. 8. 129.

Mishapped, *pp.* come to misfortune, V. 217.

Mispend, *v.* misspend, II. 618.

Misplesaunce, *s.* displeasure, grief, I. i. 3. 22.

Misqueme, *pr. s. subj.* displease, II. 647.

Mis-seching, *s.* seeking amiss, I. ii. 11. 48.

Misse-mening, *adj.* ill-intentioned, I. ii. 9. 88.

Mister, *s.* occupation, handicraft; *m. folk,* craftsmen, XXIV. 227.

Mistihede, *s.* mistiness, darkness, XXII. 33.

Misturnen, *v.* overturn, change the fortunes of, I. i. 10. 31; *pp.* altered amiss, I. ii. 5. 88; misdirected, I. ii. 4. 11.

Misty, *adj.* mystic, mysterious, X. 134.

Misusing, *s.* misuse, VII. 95.

Miswent, *pp.* gone astray, I. ii. 10. 143.

Mo, *adv.* besides, X. 1; XVI. 713; *adj.* others, I. i. 5. 11; others besides, XVI. 329, 480; XXI. 60.

Moche-folde, *adj.* manifold, I. i. 8. 43.

Mochel, *adj.* much, XVIII. 240.

Moder, *s.* mother, I. iii. 8. 86.

Modify, *ger.* to adjudge, appoint, specify, XVII. 299.

Moeble, *s.* (moveable) property, wealth, I. i. 3. 231; I. i. 4. 62; *pl.* I. i. 9. 15.

Mokel, *adv.* much, I. ii. 6. 161.

Mokken, *ger.* to mock, XXIV. 1186.

Molles, *s. pl.* birds of the kite or buzzard family (see the context); II. 1338. (The exact sense is not known.)

Mone, *s.* moon, II. 2.

Mone, *s.* moan, lament, I. iii. 7. 23; X. 77; XI. 104.

Moned, *pp.* bemoaned, I. i. 2. 124.

Moneth, *s.* month, I. ii. 8. 113; XIII. 20.

Moo, *adj.* more numerous, III. 421.

Moon, *s.* moan, lament, XVI. 783.

Moot, *pr. s.* must, V. 35.

More, *adj.* greater, I. i. 1. 69; I. ii. 9. 73; I. iii. 1. 63; Mores, *adj. gen.*; *that mores,* of that greater thing, I. ii. 9. 74.

Morning, *s.* mourning, XXIV. 250.

Morow-day, *s.* morn, XXIV. 437.

Morowning, *s.* morning, VIII. 25.

Mote, *pr. s. subj.* may, II. 60; V. 111.

Motlé, *s.* motley, VIII. 72.

Mouche, *pr. pl.* sneak about, II. 947.

Moule, *v.* go mouldy, be putrid, II. 1275; *pp.* gone mouldy, I. ii. 2. 29.

Moun, 2 *pr. pl.* can, are able to, I. i. 5. 22.

Mountenance, *s.* amount, period, I. i. 9. 49.

Moustre, *s.* example, pattern, I. ii. 6. 86.

Mow, *pr. pl.* may, V. 381; Mowe, 2 *pr. pl.* can, III. 94; *pr. pl.* I. ii. 6. 155.

Mowlit, *adj.* mouldy, XVII. 441.

Mufe, *ger.* to move, provoke, XVII. 352.

Murthed, *pt. s.* cheered, I. i. 1. 11.

Muse, *v.* study, meditate, V. 238; *pt. s.* considered, II. 89.

Muskle, *s.* mussel (shell-fish), I. ii. 12. 32; *pl.* I. i. iii. 1. 45.

Mynd, *s.* memory, II. 1076; remembrance, I. i. 1. 20.

Myrre, *s.* myrrh, VIII. 66.

Mystere, *s.* ministry, II. 216.

Mystry, *s.* mystery, II. 1219.

Myte, *s.* mite, I. ii. 3. 68.

Nad, *pt. s.* had not, V. 357.

Naked, *pt. s.* deprived, V. 353.

Nale, *s.*; *at the nale = at then ale,* at the ale-house, II. 870.

Name-cleping, *s.* naming, I. iii. 1. 42.

Nameliche, *adv.* especially, I. iii. 6. 100; Namely, I. i. 2. 27; III. 264; V. 322; VIII. 480.

Namore, no more, V. 357.

Nar, *adv.* nearer, XVII. 263.

Nat-for-than, *adv.* nevertheless, I. iii. 5. 52.

Naught, *adj.* wicked, XVIII. 190; Naughty, I. ii. 5. 7.

Nay, *s.* denial, XVIII. 281; denying, XXI. 351, 521.

Nayed, *pp.* said no, I. i. 7. 7.

Nebule, *s.* mist, X. 53.

Nede, *s.* need, V. 77.

Nedes, *adv.* of necessity, I. iii. 2. 83.

Nedest, 2 *pr. s.* art needy, I. ii. 5. 16.

Nedy, *adj.* needy, II. 1086.

Needly, *adv.* needs, XXIV. 644.

Neer, *adv.* nearer, XVI. 198, 201.

Neet, *s. pl.* neat cattle, I. ii. 2. 31.

Neighe, *v.* approach, I. i. 2. 32; *pr. s.* approaches, I. ii. 12. 14; I. iii. 4. 100; Neigh, *pr. s. imp.* may it come near to, I. iii. 3. 131.

Neist, *adj.* nearest, XVII. 109.

Neld, *s.* needle, II. 780; XIII. 62.

Ne-moublie-mies, *s. pl.* forget-me-nots, XXI. 61. See note, p. 535.

Nempne, *v.* name, mention, I. i. 6. 172; I. iii. 8. 14; 2 *pr. s.* I. iii. 5. 143; 2 *pt. s.* didst name, I. ii. 4. 30; *pp.* I. i. 7. 48.

Ner, *adv.* nearer, XXIV. 113; Nere, XXIV. 749, 1274; nearly (i. e. it touched her very nearly), XXI. 663.

Nere, *adv.* never, I. i. 6. 89; XXIV. 1197.

Nere, *for* Ne were, were it not (for), XXII. 34; *n. it,* were it not, I. i. 3. 119.

Nessh, *adj.* soft, XXIV. 1092.

Nettil, *s.* nettle, I. i. 2. 167.

Never-the-latter (-later), nevertheless, I. i. 1. 19; I. i. 6. 137; I. ii. 1. 94.

Newe, *adj.*; *for the n.,* in the new guise, II. 926.

Newefangelnesse, *s.* newfangledness, IX. 173; XIII. 54.

Next, *adj.* nearest, most intimate, I. i. 4. 17.

Neyghed, 1 *pt. s.* drew near, I. i. 3. 45.

Nigard, *s.* niggard, XII. 47; Nigges, *pl.* II. 757.

Nightertale, *s.* night-time, XXIV. 999, 1355.

Nil, *pr. pl.* will not, I. i. 1. 102; II. 950; Nilt, wilt not, XI. 38.

Nist, 2 *pr. s.* knowest not, II. 1172.

Noblerer, *adj.* more noble, I. ii. 1. 106.

Nobles, *s. pl.* coins so called, I. iii. 5. 120. A *noble* was worth 6s. 8d.

Nobley, *s.* nobility, I. iii. 1. 142; VII. 73; nobleness, I. i. 1. 62; XVI. 473; excellence, I. ii. 9. 62.

Noght, *adj.* evil, V. 321.

No-kins wyse, lit. 'a way of no kind,' no kind of way, XVI. 384.

Nombre, *s.* number, proportion, I. i. 8. 119.

Nombred, *pp.* numbered, estimated, X. 100.

Nompere, *s.* umpire, I. i. 2. 96.

Non, none, i.e. not, I. i. 2. 62.

Non-certayn, *s.* uncertainty, I. iii. 1. 61.

Nones; *for the n.,* for the occasion, XX. 198.

Nonnes, *s. pl.* nuns, XXIV. 1102.

Nonpower, *s.* weakness, I. ii. 7. 36.

Noot, 1 *pr. s.* know not, XXIV. 909.

Norice, *s.* nurse, VI. 58.

Noriture, *s.* nutriment, I. i. 1. 34.

Norture, *s.* good breeding, XXII. 1.

Nory, *s.* pupil, I. i. 2. 37; *pl.* I. i. 2. 121.

Not, 1 *pr. s.* know not, I. i. 1. 119; I. iii. 1. 158; *pr. s.* knows not, XVIII. 203.

Nothing, *adv.* not at all, in no respect, I. i. 2. 139; XVI. 132.

Noughty, *adj.* needy, II. 1097.

Novelleries, *s. pl.* novelties, I. ii. 14. 42.

Now-a-dayes, *adv.* now-a-days, VII. 134.

Noy, 2 *pr. pl.* annoy, XVI. 795.

Nuisaunce, *s.* annoyance, VI. 47.

Nuncupacion, *s.* naming, I. i. 9. 119.

Nureis, *s.* nurse, nourisher, XVII. 171, 199.

Nutte, *s.* nut, I. i. 3. 32.

Nyce, *adj.* foolish, V. 148; VII. 14; XVIII. 13; Nyse, I. i. 4. 55.

Nycetè, *s.* folly, I. iii. 4. 257.

Nye-bore, *s.* neighbour, I. ii. 9. 144.

O, *adj.* one and the same, XI. 44.

Obediencer, *adj.* under obedience, I. iii. 1. 131.

Obeysaunce, *s.* obedience, XXIV. 47.

Obeysaunt, *adj.* obedient, II. 182.

Obumbred, *pp.* overshadowed, X. 102. See note, p. 512.

Occian, *s.* ocean, XIV. 45.

Occupacioun, *s.* occupation, employment, XX. 565.

Occupyer, *s.* owner, user, I. ii. 5. 75; I. ii. 6. 30.

Ochane, *s.* och hone! cry of woe, XVII. 541.

Ocy, *s.* French *oci,* an exclamation imitating the cry of a nightingale, XVIII. 124, 127, 135. See note.

Of, *prep.* for (with *biseche*), XIX. 26; during, XVIII. 42, 54; XX. 40.

Of-drow, *pt. s.* drew off, II. 7.

Offend, *pp.* offended, II. 538.

Office, *s.* duty, XVI. 468.

Offrend, *s.* offering, II. 490.

Of-new, *adv.* anew, XX. 319.

Oftsiss, *adv.* oftentimes, XXVI. 6; -syis, XVII. 525.

Okes, *s. pl.* oaks, I. iii. 6. 6.

On, *prep.* against, I. ii. 3. 101.

Onbelde, *ger.* to build on, X. 111.

On-brede, *adv.* abroad, VIII. 33.

Onbyde, *ger.* to abide, I. iii. 5. 68; *v.* I. iii. 6. 147; remain, I. iii. 7. 161; 1 *pr. s.* await, I. iii. 3. 128.

One, *pr. pl.* unite, I. iii. 4. 165; *pp.* joined together, I. ii. 8. 50.

Onheed, *s.* unity, I. iii. 3. 9; Onhed, I. ii. 13. 21.

On-loft, *adv.* aloft, upwards, XXIV. 1293.

On-lyve, *adv.* alive, II. 1223; IV. 71; VIII. 158; XIV. 22; XVIII. 141; XXIV. 780.

Ony, *pron.* any, III. 30; XVII. 118.

Oo, one, V. 165, 258.

Oo-fold, *adj.* simple, lit. one-fold, XIII. 90. Cf. Lat. *sim-plex.*

Ook, *s.* oak, VIII. 73.

Oon, one, any one, XX. 74; Oon and oon, severally, XX. 144.

Oonhed, *s.* unity, I. iii. 2. 34.

Ope, *adj.* open, XXIV. 262; Open, displayed, I. ii. 6. 79; *as s.* a thing open, II. 220.

Or, *conj.* ere, IV. 176; VII. 32; Or that, before, XVI. 802.

Orature, *s.* oratory, XVII. 8.

Ordenaunce, *s.* arrangement, XXI. 235. See **Ordinaunce.**

Orders, *s. pl.* orders (of friars), III. 28.

Ordinable, *adj.* adjustable, brought into relation with, I. ii. 13. 29.

Ordinaunce, *s.* order, XXI. 575; (apparently) self-control, decision, XVI. 153; warlike array, XVI. 818; orderly disposition, I. ii. 5. 43; a row, XXI. 57.

Orient, *adj.* (*as applied to gems*), of prime excellence, XX. 148 (see note); XXI. 528; XXIV. 788.

Orizont, *s.* horizon, VIII. 6.

Ornat, *adj.* ornate, XXIV. 34.

Otherwhile, *adv.* sometimes, I. i. 7. 56; I. ii. 13. 96; V. 49.

Otherwysed, *pp.* changed, altered, I. ii. 1. 9.

Ouches, *s.* settings for jewels, II. 904, 1006.

Ourfret, *pp.* covered over, XVII. 163.

Ourquhelmit, *pt. pl.* overwhelmed, covered, XVII. 401.

Ourspred, *pp.* overspread, marked all over, XVII. 339.

Out-bringe, *v.* educe, I. ii. 6. 88.

Outforth, *adv.* externally, I. ii. 5. 85; I. ii. 10. 145.

Out-helpes, *s. pl.* external aids, I. ii. 5. 46.

Outher, *conj.* either, V. 171.

Outherwhile, *adv.* sometimes, I. iii. 3. 107.

Outrage, *s.* violent act, IX. 213; extravagance of conduct, XV *a.* 2.

Outrage, *ger.* to banish, drive out, VII. 85.

Outragiousnesse, *s.* extravagance, II. 507.

Outrance, *s.* excessive injury, defeat, VI. 36.

Out-throwe, *pp.* thrown out, I. ii. 5. 116.

Outwaill, *s.* outcast, XVII. 129. See note.

Out-waye, out of the way, I. i. 8. 15. (But read *out-waye-going* as one

word, meaning deviation; see note to bk. iii. 1. 6; p. 479.)

Out-waye-going, *s.* deviation, error, I. ii. 8. 126.

Out-wreste, *v.* force out, VIII. 48.

Over, *prep.* besides, I. i. *pr.* 88.

Over-al, *adv.* everywhere, I. i. 3. 136; XII. 18.

Overcharge, *ger.* to overburden, III. 265.

Overchaunginges, *s.* changes, I. iii. 2. 49.

Overcoom, 2 *pt. s.* didst overcome, V. 425.

Overlede, *pr. pl.* oppress, treat cruelly, V. 332; overwhelm, XXII. 32.

Overleyn, *pp.* covered, I. iii. 7. 39.

Overloke, *ger.* to oversee, I. i. 3. 125.

Overlokers, *s. pl.* overseers, I. i. 3. 128; I. i. 4. 62.

Over-rede, *adj.* too red, XXIV. 793.

Oversee, *pr. pl.* are overseers of, II. 1021.

Overshake, *v.* pass away, XVI. 726.

Oversprad, *pp.* overspread, VIII. 51.

Overthrowe, *v.* tumble over, I. ii. 7. 70.

Overthwartly, *adv.* contrarily, adversely, I. i. 3. 56; perversely, I. iii. 7. 155.

Overtourning, *pres. pt.* overwhelming, I. i. 9. 83.

Over-whelmed, *pt. s.* overturned, I. ii. 2. 13.

Overwhelminges, *s. pl.* circuits overhead, I. iii. 4. 145.

Ow, *pr. s.* ought, II. 545; Oweth, *pr. s.* I. iii. 5. 54; ought (to be), I. ii. 8. 64; Owe, *pr. pl.* I. iii. 4. 251; Owande, *pres. pt.* due, I. ii. 1. 104.

Oyntmentes, *s. pl.* ointments, I. iii. 9. 78.

Paas, *s.* pace, XVI. 29.

Packe, *s.* pack, bundle of garments, I. ii. 3. 65; Pak, V. 110.

Padde, *s.* frog, toad, I. iii. 5. 37.

Palasy-yuel, *s.* paralysis, I. iii. 7. 40.

Palestre, *s.* wrestling match, struggle, X. 69.

Paleys, *s.* palace, V. 473.

Palfray, *s.* horse (for a lady), XX. 425.

Pall, *s.* fine cloth, II. 106, 299.

Palled, *pp.* rendered vapid, as stale liquor, X. 46; enfeebled, VII. 145.

Palme, *s.* palm-branch, XXIX. 4.

Pamflet, *s.* pamphlet, I. iii. 9. 54.

Pampired, *pp.* pampered, XXIV. 177.

Pane, *s.* pain, XVII. 291; Panis, *pl.* 277.

Pane, *s.* plot of ground, bed for flowers, XVII. 427; Pannes, *s. pl.* clothes, I. ii. 2. 29. See the note. (A better spelling is *panes.*)

Papinjay, *s.* parrot, used merely in scorn, XVIII. 222.

Parcel, *s.* part, portion, I. i. 10. 32; *as adv.* in part, VIII. 224.

Pardè, pardieu, XX. 47; XXI. 753.

Pardurable, *adj.* everlasting, I. ii. 8. 87.

Parfytë, *adj. fem.* perfect, IV. 316.

Parishens, *s. pl.* parishioners, II. 767; III. 114.

Partable, *adj.* divisible, I. ii. 10. 76.

Parted, *pt. s.* departed, XVI. 798.

Party, *s.* part, I. ii. 9. 95; XXIV. 1192; *pl. On some p.,* in some respects, XVI. 746; Partie, *adv.* partly, XXIV. 1434.

Passe, *ger.* to surpass, excel, I. ii. 2. 12; *v.* II. 972; XX. 63; Pas, *v.* pass beyond, XVI. 76; *pr. s.* IX. 114; *pr. pl.* III. 298; *pp.* past away, long ago dead, I. i. *pr.* 77.

Passif, *adj.* passive (man), I. i. 6. 122; (thing), I. ii. 9. 102.

Passing, *adj.* surpassing, great, severe, I. i. *pr.* 118.

Passinge, *prep.* surpassing, beyond, I. i. *pr.* 90.

Passingly, *adv.* surpassingly, XX. 352.

Passive, *s.* subject, I. ii. 12. 6.

Pastour, *s.* shepherd, pastor, II. 582.

Patens, *s. pl.* pattens, XXIV. 1087.

Patron, *s.* patron, founder, III. 33.

Pausacioun, *s.* waiting, repose, X. 61.

Pavilioun, *s.* tent, X. 60.

Pay, *s.* satisfaction; *her to pay,* for a satisfaction to her, VIII. 536.

Payën, *adj.* pagan, IV. 45; *s. pl.* IV. 183.

Paynims, *pl. adj.* pagan, I. ii. 1. 49; *s. pl.* I. ii. 1. 46.

Paynture, *s.* painting, I. ii. 13. 78.

Pecok, *s.* peacock, XXIV. 1408.

Pees, *s.* peace, IV. 62.

Pees, *s.* pea, I. i. 8. 118; Peese, I. ii. 9. 126.

Peirry, *s.* perry, XVII. 441.

Peise, *ger.* to weigh, consider, XXIV. 689; *pp.* XIII. 91.

Peitrel, *s.* poitrel, breast-strap (of a horse), XX. 246.

Pele, 1 *pr. s.* appeal, XVI. 783.

Pelure, *s.* fur, I. ii. 2. 30; II. 106.

Pend, *pp.* penned, II. 650.

Penny, *s.* money, fee, II. 309.

Pensees, *s. pl.* pansies, XXI. 62.

Pensifheed, *s.* pensiveness, VIII. 102.

Pensivenes, *s.* sadness, XVII. 317.

Penuritie, *s.* penury, XVII. 321.

Peny, *s.* money, III. 142.

Peragall, *s.* equal, II. 130.

Peraunter, *adv.* perhaps. I. ii. 13. 44.

Percas, *adv.* perchance, XXIV. 794.

Perce, *v.* pierce, X. 3.

Perdoned, *pp.* pardoned, XXIV. 288.

Perdurable, *adj.* everlasting, I. ii. 9. 40; IV. 371.

Pere, *s.* peer, II. 219; *pl.* XVIII. 277.

Peregal, *adj.* fully equal, XII. 16.

Pereles, *adj.* peerless, VIII. 346.

Perfiter, *adj.* more perfect, III. 387.

Perfitest, *adj.* most perfect, III. 29.

Perrey, *s.* jewellery, II. 159.

Persaunt, *adj.* piercing, VIII. 28, 358; XXIV. 849.

Perse, *pr. pl.* pierce, XXIV. 940.

Perséver, *v.* persevere, IX. 174.

Personage, *s.* dignity, title, II. 269, 723; titles, II. 953. See note to II. 723, p. 465.

Personer, *s.* a participant, I. ii. 2. 49. See the note.

Perte, *adj.* open, evident, I. iii. 7. 70.

Pertinacie, *s.* obstinacy, I. ii. 1. 46.

Perturbaunce, *s.* distress, VIII. 214.

Pese, *s.* pea, II. 1163.

Peynture, *s.* painting, description, I. i. 10. 42.

Peyreth, *pr. s.* impairs, XVI. 228. (Short for *apeyreth.*)

Peyse, *v.* weigh, ponder, IV. 143; *pr. pl.* I. ii. 9. 125.

Phane, *s.* vane, weathercock, I. ii. 1. 23.

Phenix, *s.* phœnix, II. 1343.

Philbert, *s.* filbert, VIII. 68.

Piler, *s.* pillar, VI. 13; *pl.* VIII. 358.

Pilgrimaged, 1 *pt. s.* made a pilgrimage, I. i. *pr.* 122.

Pill, *ger.* to pillage, rob, II. 355; III. 338; *pp.* III. 317.

Pinche at, *ger.* to find fault with, XIII. 68.

Piscyne, *s.* fish-pool, X. 134.

Pitous, *adj.* merciful, IV. 345; Pitousë, *fem.* piteous, V. 23.

Professed, *pp.* professed as members, III. 70; devoted, VIII. 296.

Proper, *adj.* own, I. i. 10. 112; Propre, peculiar, I. ii. 6. 135.

Proper, *s.* personal property, III. 190.

Propinquitè, *s.* nearness of kin, I. ii. 2. 101.

Proporcions, *s. pl.* suppositions, I. iii. 3. 19. (*Probably for* propositions.)

Propyne, *imp. s.* give to drink, afford, X. 52.

Protectrice, *s.* protectrix, X. 57.

Prove, *s.* proof, I. iii. 4. 73.

Proved, *pp.* approved, VIII. 161.

Provendre, *s.* prebend, I. ii. 2. 50.

Proyned, *pt. pl.* preened, trimmed, XVIII. 76.

Prunith, *pr. s. refl.* preens himself, trims himself, XXIV. 607.

Pryded, *pp.* made proud, IV. 257.

Pryen, *v.* pry (about), XX. 68.

Prymerose, *s.* primrose, XXIV. 1437.

Pryse, *s.* value, X. 11; Prys, glory, V. 308.

Psauter, *s.* psalter, I. ii. 14. 85.

Pucelle, *s.* maiden, X. 54.

Puissance, *s.* power, XII. 3.

Pulcritude, *s.* beauty, XXIV. 613.

Pull, *ger.* to pluck, tear, II. 1329.

Pungitive, *adj.* pungent, i. e. ready to sting, XVII. 229.

Punical, *adj.* Punic, X. 121. See Pome.

Punisshèment, *s.* punishment, V. 467; *pl.* II. 520.

Purchace, *s.* earning (it), obtaining (it), XVI. 322; Purchas, bargain, XVI. 74; purchase, XXVIII. 3.

Purchace, *imp. s.* purchase, procure, obtain, IV. 124; 1 *pr. s. subj.* XVI. 371.

Purfeling, *s.* edging, ornamenting an edge, XXI. 527.

Purfyl, *s.* edge (of her sleeve), XXI. 87, 524; *pl.* XX. 146.

Purfyled, *pp.* ornamented at the edge, XX. 328.

Purgacioun, *s.* purgation, a clearing of a false charge, II. 342.

Purpose, *pr. s. subj.* intend, V. 372.

Purse, *ger.* to put in their purse, II. 178.

Pursevauntes, *s. pl.* pursuivants, XX. 232.

Purtreyture, *s.* drawing, I. i. *pr.* 17; *pl.* I. ii. 13. 76.

Purvey, *ger.* to provide, XX. 429; *v.* XXIV. 1396; *pp.* I. ii. 14. 9; XVI. 219; destined, I. i. 1. 46.

Purveyaunce, *s.* providence, disposal,

I. i. 3. 130; IV. 21; VIII. 303; IX. 68; provision, XVI. 165.

Purveyour, *s.* purveyor, XXI. 266.

Putrye, *s.* whoredom, II. 287.

Puttockes, *s. pl.* kites, II. 1338. (Lit. poult(ry)-hawks.)

Pye, *s.* magpie, II. 1334; XXIV. 1421.

Pykes, *s. pl.* peaks, II. 930.

Pyles, *s. pl.* piles, strong stakes, I. ii. 5. 116.

Pyment, *s.* piment, wine mixed with honey and spices, II. 432.

Pynande, *pres. pt.* wearisome, I. i. 6. 77; Pynd, *pp.* pined, tortured, II. 481.

Pyne, *s.* pain, XVIII. 245; punishment, V. 399.

Pyne, *s.* pine, VIII. 65; -tree, X. 44.

Pype, *v.* pipe, whistle, I. iii. 7. 50.

Quair, *s.* book (lit. quire), XVII. 40; Quayre, VIII. 674.

Quake, *v.* quake, VIII. 181.

Quarele, *s.* complaint, IV. 242.

Quarters, *s. pl.* quarters (measures so called), I. iii. 5. 120.

Quayntly, *adv.* curiously, II. 186.

Queme, *s.*; *to qu.*, to your pleasure, VII. 30.

Queme, *v.* please, V. 39.

Quere, *s.* choir, XXIV. 1417.

Queynt, *pp.* quenched, I. ii. 2. 33; II. 40; Queint, XXIV. 457.

Queynte, *adj.* curious, XVIII. 182; particular, II. 1013; Queinte, pretty, XIII. 8.

Queyntyse, *s.* finery, ornaments, II. 627; Queyntyses, contrivances, I. i. 7. 40.

Quhair, *adv.* where, XVII. 34.

Quhais, *pron.* whose, of which, XVII. 146.

Quhen, *adv.* when, XVII. 5.

Quhetting, *pres. pt.* whetting, XVII. 193.

Quhilk, *pron.* which, XVII. 33.

Quhill, *adv.* until, XVII. 48, 482.

Quhisling, *pres. pt.* whistling, XVII. 20.

Quhyl, *adv.* sometimes, XVII. 49.

Quhytly, *adj.* whitish, XVII. 214.

Quik, *adj.* alive, IX. 256; Quicke, living, III. 71.

Quyte, *v.* requite, VIII. 401; repay, IV. 279; *ger.* to requite, XV *c.* 3; to redeem, IX. 230; Quitte, *pt. s.* requited, V. 304; *pt. pl.* V. 263.

Quytinge, *s.* requital, I. iii. 7. 125, 142.

Rote, *s.* rote, XVIII. 71. See note.

Rought, *pt. s. refl.* recked, I. i. 5. 61.

Roum, *s.* room, space, XXI. 552.

Rounde, *ger.* to cut all round, XIII. 84.

Roundel, *s.* roundel, XI. 40; XX. 176.

Rousty, *adj.* rusty, XVII. 187.

Rout, *s.* great company, XX. 196.

Rowe by rowe, in rows, I. i. 9. 70.

Rowes, *s. pl.* beams, VIII. 596.

Rowne, *ger.* to whisper, XIII. 67.

Rowning, *s.* whispering, I. i. 5. 89.

Rowte, *s.* company, XXIV. 70.

Rubifyed, *pp.* reddened, X. 85.

Ruik, *s.* rook (bird), VII. 445.

Ruse, *v.* praise, XVII. 573.

Russet, *adj.* russet-brown, XXIV. 255.

Ryall, *adj.* royal, XXIV. 306.

Ryally, *adv.* royally, XXIV. 71, 1350.

Ryaltee, *s.* royalty, XXIV. 126.

Ryatours, *s. pl.* rioters, riotous persons, II. 281.

Ryder, *s.* rider (on horseback), I. ii. 1. 62.

Ryme, *v.* rime, I. ii. 2. 74 (see the note, p. 466); write verses, IX. 101.

Ryping, *adj.* ripening, VII. 153.

Ryve, *v.* be rent, VIII. 576.

Ryve, *ger.* to arrive (at), X. 27.

Sa, *adv.* so, XVII. 3.

Sacrament, *s.* oath, I. i. 6. 165.

Sad, *adj.* settled, constant, steadfast, firm, XI. 107; XVII. 567; XXIV. 45.

Sadly, *adv.* staidly, in a staid manner, XX. 159; firmly, I. i. 1. 79; permanently, XXIV. 877.

Safe-conducte, *s.* safe conduct, I. iii. 1. 122.

Saipheron, *adj.* made with saffron, XVII. 421.

Sait, *s.* seat, XVII. 331.

Sals, *s.* sauce, XVII. 421.

Salued, 1 *pt. s.* saluted, I. i. 2. 25; XX. 460; 1 *pt. pl.* XXI. 442.

Salve, *s.* salve, healing, medicament, IV. 122.

Samin, *adv.* same, XVII. 58, 484.

Sans ose ieo dyre, without saying 'may I dare to mention it,' II. 955.

Saphyre, *s.* sapphire, X. 92; XX. 224; *pl.* XXI. 480.

Sapience, *s.* wisdom, VII. 50; XIX. 19; XXII. 66; XXIII. 1.

Sarazins, *s. pl.* Saracens, I. ii. 3. 100; IV. 250.

Sat, *pt. s.* affected, pressed upon, XXI. 663.

Sauf, *prep.* save, except, XXI. 507.

Sauf, *adj.* safe, IV. 158; Save, *pl.* IV. 291.

Saunz, *prep.* without, XXIV. 117.

Sautes, *s. pl.* assaults, VIII. 418.

Sautry, *s.* psaltery, XX. 337.

Savour, *s.* understanding, I. iii. 4. 79.

Sawe, *s.* saying, command, II. 359; teaching, II. 641; sayings, XXVIII. 1.

Sawin, *pp.* sown, XVII. 137.

Scaplerye, *s.* scapulary, III. 50.

Schrewis, *s. pl.* wicked persons, XXVI. 8.

Sclaunder, *pr. pl.* slander, III. 198; 2 *pr. s.* III. 153.

Scochones, *s. pl.* escutcheons, XX. 216, 223, 237.

Scole-maister, *s.* schoolmaster, oddly used to mean mistress, XVI. 137.

Scolers, *s. pl.* scholars, schoolboys, V. 211.

Scoles, *s. pl.* schools, XVI. 329.

Scorges, *s. pl.* scourges, I. iii. 9. 69.

Scourge, *ger.* to scourge, I. ii. 11. 94; Scorged, *pp.* I. iii. 9. 74.

Scribable, *adj.* fit to write on, XIV. 44.

Scrippe, *s.* scrip, II. 13.

Scripture, *s.* writing, I. i. 6. 195.

Scriveyn, *s.* scrivener, scribe, XIV. 47.

Sechers, *s. pl.* seekers, I. i. *pr.* 117.

Secheth, *imp. pl.* seek, XVI. 518.

Secree, *adj.* secret, IX. 195.

Secte, *s.* order, III. 38, 58, 106; sex, I. ii. 2. 139. II. 11. 138

See, *s.* seat, II. 113.

Seemely, *adj.* handsome, XX. 240.

Seemliheed, *s.* seemly behaviour, XVIII. 157.

Seer, *adj.* sere, withered, I. ii. 11. 105; I. iii. 7. 22.

See-sydes, *s. pl.* coasts, I. iii. 1. 45.

Seet, *pt. s.* sat, II. 464.

Seeth, *imp. pl.* see, VII. 158.

See-ward, sea-ward, I. iii. 5. 78.

Seid, *s.* seed, XVII. 137, 139.

Seint, *s.* girdle, XXIV. 817.

Seke, *adj. pl.* sick, XVI. 53; XVIII. 7; XXIV. 948.

Seke, *ger.* to seek, to learn, XX. 234 (cf. 229).

Seker, *adv.* surely, II. 625.

Sele, *s.* seal, III. 260; *pl.* II. 328.

Self, *adj.* same, XVII. 552.

Seliness, *s.* happiness, I. i. 10. 79; I. ii. 4. 6.

Sely, *adj.* happy, I. ii. 10. 108; simple, IX. 57; innocent, II. 695, 1312.

Semblable, *adj.* like, I. i. 9. 37; similar, V. 390.

Semblaunt, *s.* notice, appearance of taking notice, XVI. 107; glance, I. ii. 12. 3; mien, XVI. 293; method, I. i. 4. 13.

Semelich, *adj.* seemly, pleasing, I. i. *pr.* 11.

Semes, *s. pl.* seams, XX. 142.

Sen, *conj.* since, XVII. 288.

Send, *pp.* sent, II. 546.

Sene, *adj.* visible, VIII. 437; XVII. 353; XVIII. 65; obvious, I. ii. 6. 156.

Sene, *ger.* to behold, XX. 157.

Senged, *pp.* singed, II. 19.

Sengle, *adj.* single, XIII. 89.

Sentement, *s.* feeling, VIII. 197.

Sentence, *s.* meaning, I. i. *pr.* 9, 12.

Sepulture, *s.* sepulchre, XXIV. 699.

Sequele, *s.* following, X. 59.

Sere, *adj.* sear, withered, dead (?), I. i. 4. 23. Cf. '*derke* opinions.' Or *sere* may mean 'several, particular.'

Serment, *s.* oath, I. i. 7. 52.

Serpentynes, *adj. pl.* winding, tortuous, I. i. 7. 40.

Servaunt, *s.* lover, XVI. 321.

Serven, *error for* Serve, 2 *pr. s. subj.* serve, XXIV. 290.

Sessoun, *s.* seasoning, XVII. 421.

Set by, *pp.* esteemed, XVI. 420.

Sete, *s.* seat, I. ii. 10. 126.

Sete, *pp.* sat, XX. 436.

Setling, *s.* sapling, shoot, I. iii. 5. 23; I. iii. 6. 12.

Sette, *v.* (*perhaps*) lay down (a stake), XVI. 524 (see note); 1 *pr. s.* suppose, I. i. 9. 64; *pr. pl.* lay stakes (upon), run risk (upon), XIII. 77.

Sew, Sewe, *ger.* to follow up, pursue, XXI. 117; to sue, XXI. 420; *v.* sue, XXI. 594; pursue, XVI. 541; 1 *pr. s.* follow, pursue, XVI. 227; *pr. pl.* follow, II. 608, 776; go, II. 928; sue, XXIV. 265; *imp. s.* sue, XXI. 332.

Sewe, *pp.* sown, II. 55.

Sewe, *error for* Shewe, *ger.* to shew, II. 929.

Sey, *s* sea, XVII. 217.

Sey, 1 *pt. s.* saw, XXIV. 693; Seye, *pp.* seen, I. ii. 12. 13.

Shad, *pp.* shed, IV. 105.

Shaddow, *s.* reflexion, image, XVII. 347.

Shadowe, *v.* shelter, II. 587.

Shake, *ger.* to be shaken down, VIII. 63.

Shall, 1 *pr. s.* owe, XXIV. 131.

Shapen, *pp.* shaped, XX. 64; Shape, II. 926; *imp. pl.* endeavour, VII. 40.

Share, *s.* plough-share, II. 7.

Shede, *v.* part, II. 275.

Shede, *ger.* to shed, VIII. 3; *v.* part, II. 275; *pp.* dispersed, XVII. 18; poured out, I. ii. 2. 27.

Shedinge, *s.* that which is shed or dropped, I. i. *pr.* 112.

Sheef, *s.* sheaf, XXI. 3.

Shel, *s.* shell, I. i. 3. 78.

Shende, *ger.* to disgrace, I. i. 2. 122; I. iii. 9. 56; to harm, I. ii. 9. 57; to reprove, II. 485; *v.* disgrace, IX. 90; destroy, I. ii. 1. 19; *pr. s.* disgraces, I. ii. 2. 47; *pr. s. subj.* spoil, V. 132; *pr. pl. subj.* may (they) disgrace, XVI. 370; Shent, *pp.* reproached, II. 24; scolded, XVI. 766; exhausted, XX. 360; illtreated, II. 259; disgraced, I. ii. 3. 77.

Shene, *adj.* showy, fair, XVII. 419; bright, VIII. 3; XX. 34.

Shene, *ger.* to shine, XXIV. 81. Misused for *shine*.

Shepy, *adj.* sheepish, I. i. 6. 161.

Sheres, *s. pl.* shears, XIII. 84; XIV. 24.

Sherte, *s.* shirt, VIII. 489.

Sheteth, *pr. s.* shoots, VIII. 462.

Sheth, *s.* sheath, II. 571.

Shetinge, *s.* shooting, VIII. 466.

Shew, 1 *pr. s.* shew, XVII. 287.

Shilde, *pr. s. subj.* shield, XVIII. 259.

Shill, *adv.* shrilly, XVII. 20.

Shipcraft, *s.* use of a ship, I. i. 3. 46.

Shir, *s.* sir, XVII. 296.

Shit, *pp.* shut, XVI. 671; XXIV. 792.

Shiver, *v.* break, be shattered, VIII. 46.

Sho, *pron.* she, XVII. 142.

Shockes, *s. pl.* shocks of corn, I. i. *pr.* 105.

Shon, *ger.* to shun, XXIV. 381; *pp.* avoided, I. iii. 4. 38.

Shoon, *s. pl.* shoes, II. 930.

Shoop, *pt s.* endeavoured, I. i. 6. 148; Shopen, *pt. pl.* appointed, made, I. i. 6. 77; decreed, VIII. 489.

Shorers, *s.* posts to shore a thing up, props, I. ii. 7. 87.

Shot, *s.* glance, XVI. 145. (F. *trait.*)

Shove, *imp. pl.* push, VI. 36.

Shreudnes, *s.* wickedness, I. ii. 6. 14.

Shrewe, 1 *pr. s.* curse, XVIII. 250.

Shrifte-fathers, *s. pl.* confessors, III. 118.

Sote, *s.* soot, I. ii. 14. 60.

Sote, *adj.* sweet, I. ii. 14. 57 ; XX. 84.

Sotell-persing, *adj.* subtly piercing, XXIV. 768.

Soteltè, *s.* subtlety, XVI. 619.

Soth, *s.* truth, II. 171.

Sothed, *pp.* verified, I. i. 5. 110.

Sotilly, *adv.* subtly, V. 255.

Sotiltee, *s.* subtilty, V. 78.

Sotted, *pp.* besotted, I. i. 10. 18 ; XVI. 326.

Sottes, *s. pl.* dolts, I. iii. 7. 89.

Souded, *pp.* fixed, I. i. 1. 80.

Souke, *v.* suck, I. ii. 14. 53 ; I. iii. 1. 141.

Soukinges, *s. pl.* food for infants, I. i. 4. 27.

Souled, *pp.* conferred on the soul, I. iii. 1. 15.

Soulè-hele, *s.* health of the soul, salvation, II. 1193.

Soun, *s.* sound, VIII. 200.

Sounde, *s.* swoon, XXIV. 995.

Sounde, *ger.* to heal, VIII. 292.

Soupè, *v.* sup, II. 1096 ; *ger.* XX. 417.

Souple, *adj.* supple, weak, II. 58.

Souverain, *s.* mistress, XXIV. 1288.

Sovenez, *s. pl.* remember-me's, plants of germander, XXI. 61, 86. See note, p. 536.

Soverainnesse, *s.* sovereignty, I. ii. 2. 85.

Soverayne, *adj.* supreme, IX. 217.

Soverayntee, *s.* supremacy, I. ii. 6. 47 ; IX. 219.

Sowe, *pp.* sown, I. iii. 5. 32 ; V. 10.

Sowe, *ger.* to sew together, I. i. 8. 41.

Sown, *v.* sound, be heard, XXIV. 312 ; *pr. pl.* tend, XXIV. 527 ; *pres. pt.* tending, XVI. 530.

Sowne, *s.* sound, voice, I. i. 1. 127 ; XVI. 123 ; *pl.* XX. 275.

Sowpit, *pp.* drenched, XVII. 450. See note.

Soyle, *ger.* to absolve, II. 986.

Soyr, *adj.* sorrel (in colour), reddish brown, XVII. 211.

Span, *s.* span (in length), XXIV. 182.

Speces, *s. pl.* kinds, sorts, I. iii. 1. 52.

Spede, *v.* prosper, XXI. 226 ; expedite, II. 395 ; *pr. pl.* succeed, XXIV. 945 ; Sped, *pp.* provided with a mate, XXIV. 560.

Speid, *s.* speed ; *good sp.*, quickly, eagerly, XVII. 492.

Speir, *s.* spear, XVII. 161.

Speiris, *pr. s.* asks, XVII. 272.

Sperd, *pp.* fastened, shut up, XVI. 66.

Spere, *s.* sphere, VIII. 34 ; X. 53.

Sperkelande, *pres. pt.* wandering in different directions, I. i. 2. 75.

Spille, *ger.* to destroy, I. i. *pr.* 127 ; I. ii. 14. 43 ; to perish, to pine, I. i. 1. 7 ; *v.* perish, XVIII. 200 ; *pr. s.* spoils, XXIV. 385 ; Spilte, *pp.* destroyed, I. i. 2. 86.

Spinne, *ger.* to spin, XIV. 31.

Spire, *s.* blade, young shoot, I. iii. 5. 4, 9.

Spittail-hous, *s.* hospital, XVII. 391.

Splaye, *ger.* to display, VIII. 33.

Splene, *s.* spleen, ill temper, XVI. 327.

Sponne, *pp.* spun, IV. 299 ; VIII. 487.

Spontanye, *adj.* spontaneous, I. iii. 4. 33.

Spousayle, *s.* espousal, I. i. 9. 96 ; I. ii. 12. 27.

Sprad, *pp.* spread, I. i. *pr.* 1 ; I. i. 3. 55.

Spreit, *s.* spirit, XVII. 587 ; *pl.* XVII. 37.

Springen, *pr. s. subj. (for* Springe), may spring, should spring (abroad), XXIV. 725.

Springes, *s. pl.* growths, growing things, shoots, I. iii. 6. 4 ; sources, I. ii. 13. 59.

Springing, *s.* dawning, XX. 25 ; XXI. 218.

Spronge, *pp.* sprinkled, I. i. 1. 100. (The right form is *spreyned*.)

Spryt, *s.* spirit, II. 1182.

Spurnis, 2 *pr. s.* kickest, XVII. 475.

Spyces, *s. pl.* species, sorts of people, I. ii. 3. 86.

Spyne, *s.* thorn, X. 50.

Square, *v.* to square, make square by cutting, XX. 404.

Squeymous, *adj.* squeamish, XXIV. 332.

Stabelnesse, *s.* stability, XIII. 38.

Stablisshment, *s.* establishment, I. iii. 1. 132.

Stad, *pp.* bestead, beset, XI. 109 ; XVII. 542.

Stal, *pt. s.* stole, II. 618.

Stale, *adj.* late, II. 873.

Stalking, *pres. pt.* going stealthily, XXIV. 1030.

Stalle, *s.* stall, papal chair, IV. 483.

* * * *
* * * *

Q q

Stalle, *v.* install, VI. 32.
Stamped, *pp.* stamped, pressed, I. iii. 5. 114.
Stanche, *ger.* to quench, I. iii. 1. 152.
Stant, *pr. s.* stands, I. iii. 4. 15; IV. 6; is, XVI. 364.
Starkly, *adv.* strongly, severely, XVII. 280.
Starnis, *s. pl.* stars, XVII. 170.
Statly, *adj.* stately, costly, XX. 153.
Statut, *s.* statute, XXIV. 304.
Staunching, *s.* staying, I. iii. 1. 50.
Stayres, *s. pl.* stairs, XXI. 54.
Stedfastnesse, *s.* assurance, VIII. 425.
Stedship, *s.* security, safety (?), I. i. 4. 40. A coined word.
Steering, *s.* guidance, I. ii. 1. 9.
Steir, *ger.* to govern, XVII. 149.
Steir, *ger.* to stir, XVII. 352.
Stele, *s.* handle, V. 50.
Stelthe, *s.* stealth, subtle trick, V. 362.
Stent, *s.* rate; *at oo s.*, at one rate, valued equally, XVI. 769.
Stepmoder, *s.* stepmother, I. iii. 9. 86.
Stere, *s.* rudder, IV. 230; VII. 138.
Stere, *ger.* to stir, move men to, IV. 71; I. i. 8. 1; *pp.* I. ii. 1. 111; displaced, I. i. 9. 10; *pres. pt.* moving, XX. 199; active, I. ii. 11. 1.
Stering, *pres. pt.* guiding, XXIV. 603.
Stering, *s.* stirring, I. i. 4. 67; movement, I. i. *pr.* 82; provocation, XVIII. 23.
Steringe, *s.* management, I. ii. 3. 107.
Sterne, *s.* rudder, I. i. 1. 35.
Sterre, *s.* star, X. 22, 23, 68; (of Bethlehem), I. ii. 1. 50.
Sterry, *adj.* starry, XX. 2.
Sterte, *pt. s.* started, leapt, I. iii. 7. 160; darted, XVII. 537; 1 *pt. s.* started, XVIII. 216.
Sterve, *ger.* to die, XVIII. 134; *v.* I. i. 3. 120; 1 *pr. s.* IX. 97.
Stevin, *s.* voice, XVII. 491.
Steye, *ger.* to climb, I. i. 1. 45.
Steyers, *s. pl.* stairs, I. i. 1. 44.
Stigh, *pt. s.* ascended, IV. 177.
Stik, *v.* stick, remain, XXIV. 675.
Stinte, *v.* leave off, I. i. 3. 88; *pr. s.* ceases, I. iii. 5. 74; Stinten, *pr. pl.* (*error for* Stinteth, *pr. s.* ceases), I. ii. 9. 172; *pt. s.* ceased, I. ii. 3. 1; *pt. s. subj.* were to leave off, I. iii. 7. 104; *pp.* stopped, VIII. 256.

Stirpe, *s.* stock, race, XXIV. 16.
Stocke, *s.* trunk, stem, I. iii. 7. 12; idol, II. 893; *pl.* the stocks, I. i. 3. 144.
Stondmele, *adv.* at various times, I. ii. 9. 156.
Stoon, *s.* stone (but here used with reference to the magnet), XIII. 62.
Storied, *pp.* full of stories, representing various stories, I. ii. 13. 76.
Storiers, *s. pl. gen.* of story-tellers, I. iii. 4. 257. (Th. *starieres.*)
Stories, *s. pl.* histories, XIII. 87.
Stounde, *s.* time, IX. 64; XVIII. 6; meanwhile, XXIV. 769; sudden pain, XVII. 537; *pl.* times, hours, I. i. 1. 2; *pl.* acute pains, XVII. 542.
Stoundemele, *adv.* sometimes, now and then, I. ii. 13. 105; I. iii. 3. 108.
Stout, *adj.* proud, II. 699.
Strait, *adj.* strict, XVI. 28; narrow, XXI. 47.
Straunge, *adj.* distant in manner, XXIV. 834; *as s.* a stranger, I. i. 1. 17.
Strayne, *v.* constrain, I. ii. 14. 72.
Strayt, *adj.* strict, XVI. 550; close, XVI. 563; vexatious, I. ii. 5. 48.
Strecchen, *v.* extend, last, suffice, I. ii. 5. 22.
Stremes, *s. pl.* glances, beams, XXIV. 768; glances, XXIV. 849; rays, VIII. 3, 592; X. 22; XXII. 30.
Streming, *pres. pt.* beaming, X. 68.
Strene, *s.* race, kindred, strain, stock, XXIV. 370.
Strengtheth, *pr. s.* strengthens, I. iii. 8. 64.
Strengthinge, *s.* strengthening, I. ii. 4. 145.
Streyght, *pt. s.* stretched, I. ii. 14. 99.
Stro, *s.* straw, XVII. 439.
Stroy, *ger.* to destroy, XVI. 304.
Studient, *adj.* studious, I. iii. 6. 137.
Stulty, *adj.* foolish, I. ii. 3. 106.
Sturdily, *adv.* strongly, XX. 362.
Sturte, *pr. pl.* start up, II. 868.
Style, *s.* style, VIII. 177.
Styred, 1 *pt. s.* stirred, I. ii. 14. 79.
Styroppes, *s.* stirrups, II. 187.
Subget, *s.* subject, II. 1222.
Submit, *pp.* submitted, XVI. 234.
Substancial, *adj.* that which is substance, I. ii. 7. 144.
Suerly, *adv.* surely, verily, XXI. 318.

To-him-wardes, towards him, I. iii. 8. 148.

Tole, *s.* tool, instrument, II. 375, 575; *pl.* II. 919.

Tombestere, *s.* female dancer, I. ii. 2. 117.

To-morne, to-morrow, I. iii. 4. 214.

Tone; *the tone = thet one*, the one, XXIV. 1049, 1316.

To-pull, *pr. pl.* pull to pieces, II. 179.

To-race, *v.* tear to pieces, II. 1274.

Torcencious, *adj.* exacting, I. i. 9. 131. Apparently a false form; it should rather be *torcenous*, from O. F. *torconos*, *torcenous*, exacting; see Godefroy.

Torcious, *adj.* exacting, I. ii. 2. 73. Probably for *torcenous* (see above).

Tore, *pp.* torn, VIII. 220.

To-rent, *pp.* with garments much rent, XII. 17; much torn, II. 20.

Torned, *pp.* turned, XIV. 46.

Tort, *s.* wrong, I. ii. 2. 71.

To-tere, *v.* rend in pieces, II. 255; XX. 488; *pt. s.* tore to pieces, VII. 178.

Toteth, *pr. s.* looks, II. 74, 418.

Tother; *the tother = thet other*, that other, XX. 394.

To-torn, *pp.* with garments much torn, XII. 17.

Tour, *s.* tower, I. i. 5. 8.

Towayle, *s.* towel, I. ii. 2. 60; Towelles, *pl.* I. ii. 2. 62.

Town, *s.* farm, II. 1043.

To-yere, *adv.* this year, XVIII. 79. Cf. *to-day*.

Trace, *s.* a round (in a dance), XVI. 190.

Traistit, I *pt. s.* trusted, hoped, XVII. 22.

Traitory, *s.* treachery, III. 234; XIV. 48.

Transitorie, *adj.* transitory, I. iii. 1. 11; I. iii. 4. 148.

Transmew, *ger.* to move across, change, XIII. 44.

Transverse, *v.* gainsay, I. i. 2. 195.

Trapped, *pp.* adorned with trappings, XX. 262.

Trappures, *s. pl.* trappings, XX. 244.

Traunce, *s.* trance, dream, XVI. 407.

Travayle, *s.* toil, XVI. 471.

Traveyled, *pp.* worked for, I. iii. 5. 112; Travall, *pr. pl.* labour, II. 426.

Tray, *ger.* to betray, II. 808; *v.* II. 621.

Trayle, *s.* trellis, XVI. 184, 195. (F. text, *treille*.)

Traynes, *s. pl.* snares, IX. 90.

Trenchours, *s. pl.* trenchers, i.e. pieces of bread used as plates, I. i. *pr.* 109.

Trentall, *s.* trental, mass repeated for thirty days, III. 95.

Tresory, *s.* treasury, III. 302; XX. 202.

Treted, *pp.* treated, IV. 312.

Tretis, *s.* treatise, I. iii. 4. 253; Tretesse, XXIV. 28.

Trew-love, *s.* true-lover's knot, bow of ribbon, XXIV. 1440. See note.

Tristesse, *s.* sadness, XI. 55.

Troncheoun, *s.* thick and short staff (properly, a broken piece of a spear), XX. 253.

Trone, *s.* throne, IV. 378.

Troned, *pp.* enthroned, I. i. 2. 94.

Troublous, *adj.* troublesome, XX. 389.

Trumpe, *s.* trumpet, XX. 211; *pl.* XX. 192.

Trumpet, *s.* trumpeter, XX. 213; *pl.* XX. 210.

Trusse, *pr. pl.* pack up, II. 750.

Tucke, *s.* fold, I. i. 5. 132.

Tuilyour, *s.* quarreller; *t.-lyk*, quarrelsome, XVII. 194.

Turkeis (lit. Turkish), an epithet of Baleis, XXIV. 80.

Turtill-dove, *s.* turtle-dove, XXIV. 234, 1387.

Turtle, *s.* turtle-dove, X. 78.

Turved, *pp.* turfed, XX. 51.

Turves, *s. pl.* pieces of turf, XX. 50.

Tutele, *s.* guardian, X. 57.

Twey, *num.* two, I. iii. 1. 99; XXIV. 1313; Twa, XVII. 301.

Twinkling, *s.* small point, least matter, I. i. 1. 28. (Lit. glimmer, glimpse.)

Twinne, I *pr. s. subj.* may depart, IX. 256; 2 *pr. s.* V. 104.

Tythen, *ger.* to pay tithes, II. 1209.

Tything, *s.* tithe, II. 317, 861; *pl.* II. 1159.

Tytled, *pp.* entitled, I. ii. 1. 99.

Umple, fine stuff in a single fold, fine gauze or lawn, XXI. 471.

Unable, *adj.* weak, I. iii. 1. 171.

Unbodye, *ger.* to quit the body, I. i. 1. 88.

Unbrent, *pp.* unburnt, X. 129.

Unconning, *adj.* unskilful, I. i. 3. 164.

Unconning, *s.* ignorance, I. iii. 4. 224; VII. 7; Uncunning, III. 391.

Uncouth, *adj.* strange, unusual, XXIV. 451; unknown, I. ii. 11. 45.

Undefouled, *pp.* undefiled, X. 132.

Underfongen, *pp.* undertaken, IV. 264.

Underneminge, *s.* reproof, III. 110.

Undernime, 2 *pr. pl.* reprove, III. 109.

Underput, *pp.* shored up, supported, I. ii. 7. 72; subjected, I. i. 9. 38; subject, I. i. 9. 52.

Understonde, *pp.* understood, I. iii. 3. 77; II. 683; Understande, I. iii. 6. 65; Understont, *pr. s.* II. 792; Understondeth, *imp. pl.* V. 428.

Understonding, *adj.* intelligible, I. i. *pr.* 56.

Under-throwen, *pp.* made subject, I. iii. 8. 151.

Unfair, *adv.* horribly, XVII. 163.

Unfold, *pp.* unfolded, XX. 595.

Ungentil, *adj.* not of gentle birth, I. ii. 2. 129.

Ungoodly, *adj.* unkind, II. 387.

Ungoodly, *adv.* evilly, unfairly, VIII. 385.

Unhold, *adj.* faithless, II. 473.

Universal, *s.* the whole, I. ii. 13. 70.

Universitee, *s.* the universe, I. i. 9. 46.

Unkindly, *adj.* unnatural, XX. 413.

Unknit, *pp.* rejected, I. ii. 8. 36.

Unknowe, *pp.* unknown, I. ii. 10. 71.

Unkyndely, *adv.* unusually, I. i. *pr.* 126.

Unlefful, *adj.* not permissible, forbidden, I. ii. 14. 23.

Unlok, *v.* unlock, XXIV. 1403.

Unlust, *s.* listlessness, V. 227.

Unmete, *adj.* unsuitable, XX. 17.

Unmighty, *adj.* weak, feeble, I. ii. 7. 39; III. 394.

Unneth, *adv.* scarcely, I. i. *pr.* 28; II. 789; IV. 196; XX. 46; with difficulty, I. iii. 9. 76.

Unnethes, *adv.* scarcely, II. 311; V. 380.

Unpees, *s.* war, I. ii. 13. 86.

Unperfit, *adj.* imperfect, III. 66.

Unpower, *s.* weakness, III. 391.

Unpurveyed, *pp.* unprovided, XXI. 382; XXIV. 561.

Unreson, *s.* lack of reason, I. iii. 6. 133.

Unresty, *adj.* restless, X. 62.

Unricht, *adv.* wrongly, amiss, XVII. 205.

Unright, *s.* injustice, II. 1071; VIII. 334.

Unrightful, *adj.* unjust, I. iii. 3. 68.

Unsely, *adj.* unhappy, I. i. 10. 80.

Unsene, *adj.* invisible, I. i. *pr.* 57.

Unshitte, *v.* open, unfasten, I. iii. 1. 160; Unshit, disclose, XXIV. 1245; Unshet, 2 *pr. pl.* I. i. 4. 41; *pp.* opened, XVI. 65.

Unshrive, *pp.* unshriven, II. 751.

Untall, *adj.* not tall, weak, II. 74.

Unthrifty, *adj.* unprofitable, I. i. 4. 55.

Unthryve, *v.* prosper ill, have ill luck, XVIII. 142. See note.

Untrend, *pp.* not rolled up, II. 594. See note.

Unwar, *adv.* at unawares, XXIV. 848.

Unweldy, *adj.* unwieldy, hence, infirm, XV. *a.* 4; XV. *b.* 2; weak, VII. 145.

Unwetinge, *pres. pt.* unwitting, I. i. 7. 110; *but an error for* unwist, i. e. unknown.

Unworship, *s.* discredit, I. i. 5. 24.

Unworshipped, *pp.* treated with disrespect, I. ii. 6. 125.

Unwyse, *adj.* not wise, III. 155.

Uphap, *adv.* perhaps, I. i. 8. 132.

Uplande, i. e. living in the country, countryman, III. 1.

Upperest, *adj.* highest, I i. 10. 32.

Uprais, *pt. s.* rose, XVII. 12.

Ure, *s.* fortune, destiny, VIII. 151, 302, 482; XXIV. 634, 862; XXV. 11.

Us(e), *s.* use, I. iii. 6. 104; Use, 110.

Ussher, *s.* usher, XXI. 102.

Vailable, *adj.* useful, IV. 142.

Vaile, *s.* veil, XXIV. 1102.

Vailing, *pres. pt.* lowering, XVII. 271.

Vale, *s.* valley, VIII. 44.

Valewe, *s.* value, I. i. 7. 97.

Valey, *s.* valley, XVI. 24.

Valis, *pr. s.* avails, XXVII. 5. (Sing. after *what*.)

Varyaunt, *adj.* changeable, I. ii. 1. 24; variable, I. ii. 6. 148.

Vassalage, *s.* prowess, VII. 148.

Vaylance, *s.* benefit, profit, I. ii. 5. 85.

Vayleth, *pr. s.* availeth (it), XVI. 720; *pp.* I. i. 2. 163.

Veluët, *s.* velvet, VIII. 80; XX. 233; Veluet, XX. 141, 261.

Vengeable, *adj.* revengeful, I. ii. 11. 92; II. 805.

Vent, *s.* slit of a gown at the neck, XXI. 526. F. *fente.*

Venym, *s.* venom, V. 258.

Verament, *adv.* truly, II. 1224.

Vere, *s.* spring-time, I. ii. 9. 133.

Vermayle, *adj.* crimson, X. 45.

Vermelet, *adj.* red, XXIV. 142.

Vertules, *adj.* without virtue, VII. 133, 157.

Vertuous, *adj.* endowed with virtue or power, I. iii. 1. 45.

Very, *adv.* extremely, XX. 10, 35; very, XX. 409; XXI. 479.

Vestèment, *s.* vestment, II. 278, 934.

Viage, *s.* voyage, journey, I. i. 5. 84; IV. 57; XXI. 46.

Vibrat, *pp.* vibrated, X. 115.

Vicaire, *s.* vicar, II. 830; *pl.* III. 279.

Vinolent, *adj.* drunken, XII. 45.

Violet, *s.* violet, II. 96; XXIV. 1437.

Virelay, *s.* lay with recurring rimes, XI. 40. (Such as *aabaab . bbabba.*)

Virginal, *adj.* virgin-like, XII. 110.

Vocacioun, *s.* calling of an assembly together, XVII. 272.

Voiden, *v.* (to) take away, XXIV. 628; escape, XIII. 52; *pr. s.* retreats, I. i. 5. 34.

Voluntarious, *adj.* voluntary, free, I. ii. 8. 116.

Voluntè, *s.* free will, VIII. 299.

Voluptuously, *adv.* luxuriously, I ii. 10. 18.

Vouche, *pr. pl.* avouch, II. 945.

Voyde, *ger.* to banish, IX. 116; *v.* escape, I. i. 3. 140; set aside, I. iii. 6. 15; *pr. s.* dispels, I. ii. 10. 34; departs, I. i. 10. 95.

Vyntre, Vintry, VII. (*title*).

Vyole, *s.* vial, X. 113.

Vyse, *s.* advice, intention, I. i. 2. 60.

Vytre, *s.* glass, X. 113.

Wa, *adj.* sad, XVII. 350.

Wageours, *s. pl.* wagers, XXI. 383.

Wagge, *v.* move, stir, I. i. *pr.* 90; *ger.* XVII. 196.

Waillit, *pp.* chosen, choice, XVII. 440.

Wait, *pr. s.* knows, XVII. 64.

Waited, 1 *pt. s.* watched, XX. 106.

Wake, *s.* fair, II. 869.

Wake, *v.* keep a revel, I. ii. 2. 54.

Wald, *pt. s.* would (have), desired, XVII. 102.

Walet, *s.* wallet, bag, I. i. *pr.* 106.

Wall, *s.* well, II. 298. See note.

Walled, *pp.* walled, VIII. 42.

Walowe, *ger.* to toss about, XXIV. 334; 1 *pr. s.* I. i. 3. 102.

Wan, *adj.* pale, dim of colour, XIV. 43.

Wan, *pt. pl.* won, XX. 480. (A guess; the old ed. has *manly*!)

Wandred, *pp.* men who have wandered, X. 60.

Wane, *s.* weening, thought, XVII. 543. See Will.

Wang-tooth, *s.* molar tooth, II. 16.

Wanhope, *s.* despair, I. i. 1. 112; I. i. 4. 54; XVII. 47.

Want, 1 *pr. s.* lack, do not possess, do not know, XX. 150; *pr. s.* is lacking, XVI. 449.

Wantinge, *s.* lacking, I. i. *pr.* 83.

Wantrust, *s.* distrust, I. i. 8. 19; I. ii. 9. 50.

War, *adj.* aware, I. i. 3. 76; *be w.,* beware, VII. 180.

War, *adj.* worse, XVII. 460.

Warantyse, *s.* surety; *on w.,* on my surety, XXI. 406.

Warderobe, *s.* wardrobe, I. ii. 9. 140.

Waren, *pt. pl.* wore, XX. 267.

Waried, *pp.* cursed, XXIV. 1171.

Warldly, *adj.* worldly, XXVII. 1.

Warne, *v.* refuse, I. ii. 3. 31.

Warnisshe, *s.* protection, I. ii. 7. 78.

Warnisshed, *pp.* defended, I. ii. 7. 78.

Wastour, *s.* waster, XII. 72.

Waved, *pp.* wavered, I. i. 2. 167.

Wawes, *s. pl.* waves, I. i. *pr.* 125; I. i. 3. 57; VII. 80; XIII. 33.

Waxe, *v.* grow to be, II. 128; *pp.* become, II. 371.

Wayted, *pp.* watched, IV. 204.

Wayters, *s. pl.* spies, I. iii. 6. 88; guards, sentinels, I. i. 3. 124.

Waytinge, *s.* watching, lying in wait, I. ii. 9. 59.

Webbes, *s. pl.* dimness of vision, I. i. 2. 180. See note, p. 455.

Wede, *s.* covering, XIV. 26.

Weden, *pr. pl.* weed, III. 11.

Weder, *s.* weather, I. i. *pr.* 123; Wedder, XVII. 4; *pl.* storms, I. i. 3. 63; I. ii. 9. 130; I. iii. 5. 25.

Wedes, *s. pl.* weeds, X. 36.

Wedring, *s.* tempest, I. iii. 7. 74.

Weed, *s.* (*as. pl.*) garments, apparel, XX. 371; Weid, XVII. 165.

Weght, *s.* weight, XIII. 92.

Weip, *pt. s.* wept, XVII. 231 (or *infin.* to weep).

Weir, *s.* war, XVII. 196, 486.

Weir, *ger.* to guard, ward off, XVII. 182.

Weird, *s.* destiny, XVII. 384, 412.

Weiris, *pr. s.* wears, wastes away, XVII. 467.

Weked, *pp.* rendered weak (but read *wikked*), I. i. 6. 25.

Wel-condicioned, *adj.* of good condition, XX. 581.

Welde, *v.* possess, II. 118, 416, 702; manage, XXIV. 227; 1 *pr. s.* I. ii. 12. 91.

Weldoing, *s.* well-doing, I. ii. 10. 120.

Wele, *s.* wealth, II. 812; VII. 165.

Welfulnesse, *s.* wealth, I. i. 6. 24.

Welke, 1 *pr. s.* wither, I. ii. 11. 105; **Welked,** *pp.* withered, old, I. iii. 5. 33; withered, wrinkled, I. iii. 5. 37.

Welken, *s.* sky, I. i. 3. 57.

Welkeneth, *pr. s.* withers, fades, XXII. 59.

Welle, *s.* well, source, IX. 139; *pl.* streams, rills, XVII. 588.

Wellen, *pr. pl.* rise up, have their source, I. i. 2. 151; *pres. pt.* flowing, I. i. 1. 86.

Wel-meninge, *adj.* well-intentioned, I. ii. 5. 117.

Welterit, *pp.* overturned, XVII. 436.

Welth, *s.* happiness, I. i. 39.

Welwilly, *adj.* benignant, favourable, VIII. 627.

Wem, *s.* stain, I. i. 1. 74.

Wemlees, *adj.* spotless, X. 104.

Wende, *v.* go, XVIII. 252; *pt. s.* went, XVII. 474; *pp.* gone, II. 498.

Wene, *s. withoute w.,* without doubt, IX. 237; XIII. 12.

Wenen, *pr. pl.* imagine, I. ii. 3. 38; 1 *pt. s.* expected, I. i. 3. 65; 2 *pt. s.* didst expect, I. ii. 14. 80; **Wenden,** *pt. pl.* imagined, I. ii. 11. 9; **Wend** (*old text,* went), imagined, XXI. 34; **Went,** *pr. s.* weens, imagines, guesses, VIII. 462. See note.

Wening, *s.* fancy, XVI. 286.

Went, *pp.* gone, departed, I. ii. 1. 34.

Wepen, *s.* weapon, II. 1092.

Werbles, *s. pl.* warblings, notes, I. ii. 2. 6; I. iii. 1. 157.

Werche, *pr. s. subj.* operate, I. ii. 13. 127; *pres. pt.* working, active, I. ii. 5. 43.

Wercher, *s.* agent, I. iii. 2. 63.

Werchinge, *s.* operation, I. ii. 13. 118.

Werdes, *s. pl.* fates, XXIV. 1173.

Were, *s.* doubt, IX. 223; X. 5.

Were, *pt. pl. subj.* should be, XI. 64; **Wern,** *pt. pl.* were, I. iii. 8. 91.

Wereth, *pr. s* wears away, III. 45; *pr. pl.* wear, XXIV. 247.

Werien, *v.* grow weary, II. 1068.

Werne, 2 *pr. pl.* refuse, I. i. 4. 47; *pp.* IV. 26.

Werninges, *s. pl.* refusals, I. i. 2. 58.

Werre, *s.* war, VIII. 256.

Werrey, 1 *pr. s.* war, V. 431; *pp.* warred against, VIII. 665.

Werreyour, *s.* warrior, IV. 130; VI. 13.

Westreth, *pr. s.* sets in the west, XXII. 24.

Wete, *adj.* wet, I. iii. 3. 126; XX. 406.

Wete, *ger.* to know, I. i. 3. 18; **Weten,** 2 *pr. pl.* I. i. 8. 80; II. 1206; *pr. pl.* I. iii. 8. 128.

Wethercooke, *s.* weathercock, I. i. 2. 167.

Weting, *s.* knowledge, I. iii. 4. 62, 243.

Wexeth, *pr. s.* grows, XX. 14; *pres. pt.* I. iii. 1. 30; **Wexte,** *pt. s.* became, I. i. 2. 24.

Wexing, *s.* growth, I. i. 9. 42.

Weye, *ger.* to weigh, IV. 91; *pp.* 320.

Weymenting, *s.* lamenting, XXIV. 233.

Weyve, *ger.* to put away, I. ii. 10. 40; *v.* put aside, I. ii. 7. 100; *pr. s. subj.* I. iii. 1. 136; 2 *pr. s.* rejectest, I. iii. 6. 154; *pr. s.* rejects, I. ii. 13. 95; *pp.* I. i. 1. 63; I. ii. 14. 36; I. iii. 8. 154.

Wheder, *conj.* whether (or no), I. iii. 3. 30; XVI. 401.

Wheel, *s. turning wheel,* winding staircase, XXI. 55 (see note); orbit, I. ii. 1. 124.

Wherof, *adv.* to what purpose, XVI. 431.

Wherthrough, *adv.* whereby, I. i. 4. 53; X. 103; wherefore, I. ii. 13. 109.

Wherto, *adv.* why? I. i. 3. 87.

Whicche, *s.* hutch, chest, I. ii. 2. 29.

Whirled, *pp.* whirled, driven, XX. 2.

Whistel, *s.* whistle, I. ii. 3. 55.

Whyle, *s.* time, VIII. 244.

Whyt, *adj.* white, II. 1338; plausible, XXIV. 1042.

Wicche, *s.* witch, II. 891.

Wicht, *s.* wight, man, XXVII. 2.

Widdercock, *s.* weathercock, XVII. 567.

Widderit, *pp.* withered, XVII. 238; soiled by weather, XVII. 165.

Wight, *s.* person, XX. 38, 46.
Wikke, *adj.* noxious, X. 36.
Wikkit, *adj.* evil, XVII. 412.
Wilde, *adj.* wild (i.e. unquenchable), I. ii. 6. 29.
Wilde, *ger.* to become wild, I. i. 3. 45.
Will of wane, lit. wild of weening, at a loss as to what to do, XVII. 543.
Willers, *s. pl.* wishers, II. 228; *gen. such w.,* of men who so desire, II. 780.
Willingly, *adv.* wilfully, V. 391.
Wilne, *ger.* to desire, I. i. 6. 101; *v.* I. iii. 4. 11; 2 *pr. pl.* II. 1250; *pr. pl.* II. 118; *pp.* I. iii. 6. 111.
Wimpeln, *pr. pl.* cover as with a wimple, I. ii. 14. 25; *pp.* covered up, I. iii. 9. 76.
Wimple, *s.* chin-cloth, XXIV. 1102.
Winne, *v.* make a gain, II. 979.
Wisse, *pr. s. subj.* may (He) guide, keep away, II. 235.
Wite, *v.* know, XXI. 749; Witen, 2 *pr. pl.* know, XVIII. 266; Wistest, 2 *pt. s.* I. i. 8. 31; Wist, *pp.* known, II. 1092.
Withdrawe, *ger.* to draw back, hold in, I. ii. 6. 84; *pr. s.* draws away, I. ii. 5. 129.
With-holde, *pp.* retained, I. ii. 8. 121; XVIII. 289; kept back, I. iii. 3. 114.
Withies, *s. pl.* withies, twigs of willow, XVI. 186. (F. text, Entrelacee de *saulx vers.*)
Within-borde, on board, I. i. 3. 54.
Without, *conj.* unless, XXI. 299.
Withsaye, *ger.* to contradict, I. i. 2. 184; I. i. 8. 65; *v.* gainsay, II. 599.
Withsetten, *pp.* opposed, I. iii. 1. 133; Withset, I. ii. 7. 66.
Withsitte, *v.* resist, I. ii. 7. 133; *ger.* I. iii. 8. 64.
Withsittinge, *s.* opposition, I. ii. 7. 142.
Witles, *adj.* ignorant, II. 528.
Wittes, *s. pl.* wits, senses, I. iii. 5. 51.
Wivers, *s. pl.* vipers, serpents, snakes, I. iii. 5. 34.
Wlate, *v.* loathe, II. 1098.
Wo-bestad, *pp.* beset with woe, XXIV. 845.
Wode, *adj.* mad, I. iii. 7. 53.
Wodebinde, *s.* woodbine, VIII. 129; IX. 261.
Woir, *pt. s.* carried, wafted away, XVII. 165. (It seems to be merely a peculiar use of E. *wore,* pt. t. of *wear;* cf. *boir,* bore, in l. 166.)

Wol, *s.* wool, XX. 53. See **Wolle.**
Wolde, *pt. s. subj.* would wish, XVI. 272; Wold, *pp.* desired, V. 305.
Wolle, *s.* wool, I. ii. 2. 28 (see the note, p. 465); IV. 299; Woll, II. 177, 594.
Womanly, *adj.* woman-like, I. ii. 12. 114.
Won, *pr. s. subj.* dwell, XXIV. 500.
Wonder, *adj.* wonderful, III. 7; XX. 434.
Wonderly, *adv.* wondrously, XXIV. 100, 697.
Wonders, *adv.* wondrously, I. ii. 3. 45.
Wone, *s.* custom, XXI. 5.
Wones, *s. pl.* dwellings, XX. 201.
Woneth, *pr. s.* dwells, XXIV. 143; Wonneth, II. 1140.
Wonne, *pp.* won, XVI. 356.
Wonning, *s.* abode, VII. 86.
Wood, *adj.* mad, II. 299, 764, 1075, 1269; XVIII. 188.
Woodbind, *s.* woodbine, XX. 159.
Woode, *s. an error for* Weede, weed, III. 11. See note.
Woodnesse, *s.* madness, VI. 50; XVIII. 175.
Wook, 1 *pt. s.* awoke, XXI. 737.
Worch, *pr. pl.* work, II. 411.
Word, *s.* motto, XXI. 87, 310, 312; Wordes, *pl.* XXI. 119.
World, *s.* great quantity, XX. 137; a thing worth the world, XXI. 539.
Worship, *s.* honour, XIV. 382.
Worsted, *s.* worsted, II. 1002.
Worthyed, *pp.* honoured, I. i. 2. 109.
Wost, 2 *pr. s.* knowest, XVIII. 126; Wottest, I. i. 2. 74.
Wowe, *v.* woo, XXIV. 1222.
Woweth, *pr. pl.* move, I. ii. 1. 21. *Put for* waweth; and properly singular.
Wox, 1 *pt. s.* became, I. i. 4. 30; grew, XVII. 102; Woxen, *pp.* I. iii. 5. 24.
Wraikful, *adj.* vengeful, XVII. 329.
Wrait, *pt. s.* wrote, XVII. 64.
Wraith, *s.* wroth, XVII. 182.
Wrak, *s.* vengeance, XVII. 370.
Wrall, *pr. pl.* pervert, II. 370. Cf. M.E. *wrawe,* perverse.
Wranglen, *pr. pl.* wrangle, II. 426.
Wrapped, *pp.* involved; *in be w.,* been mixed up with, V. 216.
Wreche, *s.* misery, I. i. 1. 60; vengeance, VIII. 471.

INDEX OF NAMES.

INDEX

TO SOME

SUBJECTS EXPLAINED IN THE NOTES.

——◆——

A large number of the Notes refer to explanations of peculiar words and to proper names; the references to these will be found in the Glossarial Index and in the Index of Names. A few other subjects of more general interest are also discussed; the chief of these are indexed below. The references are to the pages.

Arbours described, 535.

Bell, Book, and Candle, cursing by, 485.
Birds singing the 'hours,' 552.
burly, etymology of, 524.
Burning of heretics, 489, 490, 494.

Cardinal Virtues, 479.
Chaucer's death alluded to, 510.
Chaucer's Boëthius, alluded to, 451, 453-4, 457-8, 461-3, 466-76, 481-3.
— Anelida, 537, 543.
— Book of the Duchess, 473, 530.
— Canterbury Tales, 456, 503, &c.
— Compleynt of Venus, 548-9.
— House of Fame, imitated, 467-8.
— Legend of Good Women, 452, 467, 483, 500-1, 537, 542-3, 547.
— Merciless Beautè, 513.
— Rom. of the Rose, 456-7, 504-6, 545, 549, 551.
— Troilus, 452, 455, 457, 459, 472, 481-3, 521-3, 525, 551.
Christine de Pisan, 499.
Creeping to the cross, 490.
Cupid's arrows, 531-2.

determission (a false form), 476.

Elements, the four, 462, 472.

Final cause, 464.
Forget-me-not, 536.
Friars, the, 493-6.

Geoffrey de Vinsauf, 540.
Gower's blindness, 498.
Griffin, the, 485.

Hengist, perhaps alluded to, 471.
Hercules, pillars of, 507.
'Hours,' Canonical, 552-3.

Knot, the, defined, 468.

Lent, three divisions of, 521.
Lepers, 523, 525.
Lollards, the, 464, 485, 489.
London, election of the mayor, 459.
Lydgate's Temple of Glass, imitated, 540, &c.

Margaret, meaning of, 475-6, 484; derivation of, 479.
Maze described, 535.
me, for *men* = *man*, 452.
Mottoes worn on sleeves, 536.

Pearl, virtues of the, 453, 475.
Pelican, the, 485.
Piers Plowman, imitated, 456-8, 464-6, 477, 482-4.

THE END.

COSIMO is a specialty publisher of books and publications that inspire, inform, and engage readers. Our mission is to offer unique books to niche audiences around the world.

COSIMO BOOKS publishes books and publications for innovative authors, nonprofit organizations, and businesses. **COSIMO BOOKS** specializes in bringing books back into print, publishing new books quickly and effectively, and making these publications available to readers around the world.

COSIMO CLASSICS offers a collection of distinctive titles by the great authors and thinkers throughout the ages. At **COSIMO CLASSICS** timeless works find new life as affordable books, covering a variety of subjects including: Business, Economics, History, Personal Development, Philosophy, Religion & Spirituality, and much more!

COSIMO REPORTS publishes public reports that affect your world, from global trends to the economy, and from health to geopolitics.

FOR MORE INFORMATION CONTACT US AT
INFO@COSIMOBOOKS.COM

❋ if you are a book lover interested in our current catalog of books

❋ if you represent a bookstore, book club, or anyone else interested in special discounts for bulk purchases

❋ if you are an author who wants to get published

❋ if you represent an organization or business seeking to publish books and other publications for your members, donors, or customers.

COSIMO BOOKS ARE ALWAYS
AVAILABLE AT ONLINE BOOKSTORES

_____ VISIT COSIMOBOOKS.COM _____
BE INSPIRED, BE INFORMED